I0760396

THE ORDER OF MERLIN

BOOKS 1-3 OMNIBUS HARDBACK

THOMAS K. CARPENTER

The Order of Merlin Omnibus

The Order of Merlin
Infernal Alliances
Tower of Horn and Blood

Hardcover Version

by Thomas K. Carpenter

Published by Black Moon Books

Cover design by Ravven
www.ravven.com

Other Images
@ 9george

Discover other titles by this author on:
www.thomaskcarpenter.com

ISBN-13: 978-1-958498-05-7

The Hundred Halls Universe

SEASON ONE

THE HUNDRED HALLS
Trials of Magic
Web of Lies
Alchemy of Souls
Gathering of Shadows
City of Sorcery

THE RELUCTANT ASSASSIN
The Reluctant Assassin
The Sorcerous Spy
The Veiled Diplomat
Agent Unraveled
The Webs That Bind

GAMEMAKERS ONLINE
The Warped Forest
Gladiators of Warsong
Citadel of Broken Dreams
Enter the Daemonpits
Plane of Twilight

ANIMALIANS HALL
Wild Magic
Bane of the Hunter
Mark of the Phoenix
Arcane Mutations
Untamed Destiny

STONE SINGERS HALL
Song of Siren and Blood
House of Snake and Tome
Storm of Dragon and Stone
Sonata of Shadow and Thorn
Well of Demon and Bone

THE ORDER OF MERLIN
The Order of Merlin
Infernal Alliances
Tower of Horn and Blood

THE ORDER OF MERLIN

Dedicated to my excellent beta team:

Tina Rak
Andie Alessandra Cáomhanach
Lana Turner
Alicia Manolas
Phyllis Simpson
Melanie Coupland

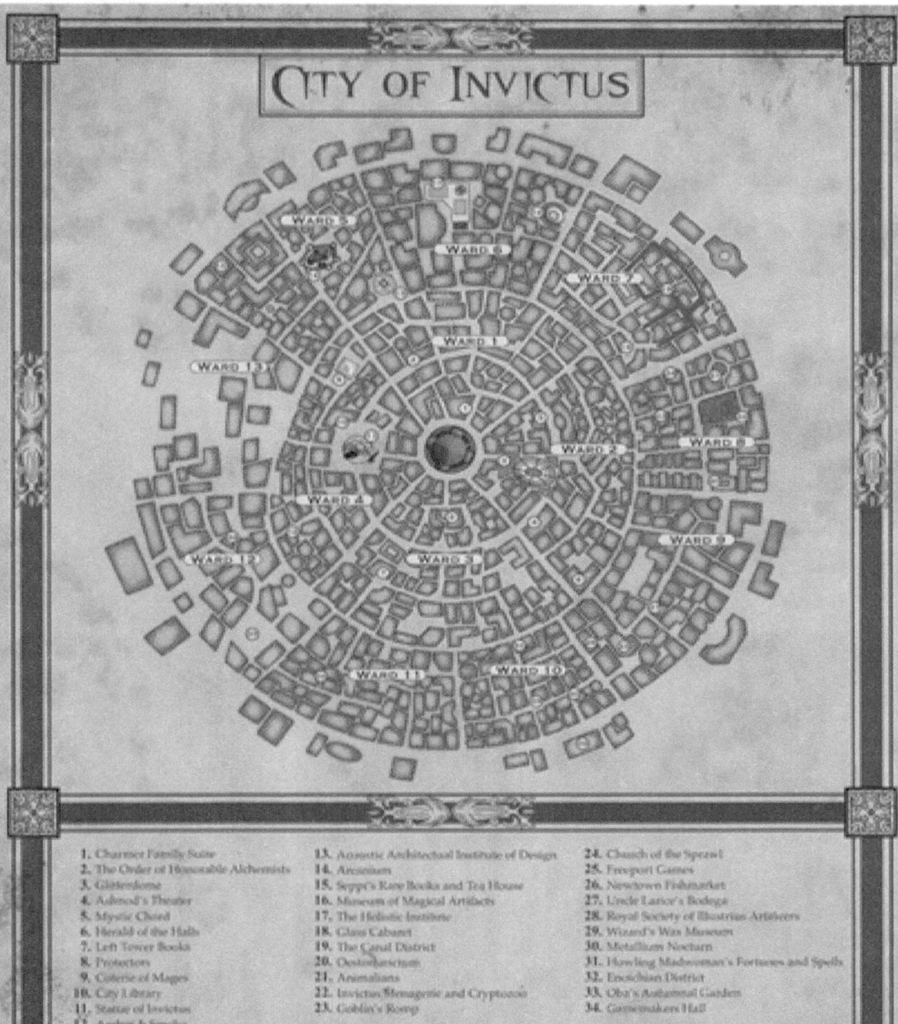
CITY OF INVICTUS
WARD 1
WARD 2
WARD 4
WARD 5
WARD 6
WARD 7
WARD 8
WARD 10
WARD 11
WARD 12
WARD 13
1. Charmer Family Suite
2. The Order of Honorable Alchemists
3. Glitterdome
4. Ashrod's Theater
5. Mystic Chord
6. Herald of the Halls
7. Left Tower Books
8. Protectors
9. Coterie of Mages
10. City Library
11. Statue of Invictus
12. Amber & Smoke
13. Acoustic Architectural Institute of Design
14. Arcanium
15. Seppi's Rare Books and Tea House
16. Museum of Magical Artifacts
17. The Holistic Institute
18. Glass Cabaret
19. The Canal District
21. Animalians
22. Invictus Menagerie and Cryptozoo
23. Goblin's Romp
24. Church of the Sprawl
25. Freeport Games
26. Newtown Fishmarket
27. Uncle Larice's Bodega
28. Royal Society of Illustrian Artificers
29. Wizard's Wax Museum
30. Metallium Nocturn
31. Howling Madwoman's Fortunes and Spells
33. Oba's Autumnal Garden
34. Gamemakers Hall

Arcanium loves books
Coterie adores power
Assassins will kill you
Stone Singers has a stone flower

Animalians is a zoo
Alchemists, you'll devour
Tinkers loves gadgets
Protectors makes you cower

Aura Healers wants to fix you
Blue Flame has a tower
Dramatics loves the spectacle
Oculus has grown sour

One Hundred Halls
Each with their own magic
The Patrons protect
Because faez madness is tragic

In the city of sorcery
Invictus is the Head
His students are many
But the foolish end up dead

- A Children's Rhyme

THE ORDER OF MERLIN

One

The ambush was going to be a strategic masterpiece or a complete train wreck. Beckett Dreadmarsh didn't know which. As stated by the eternally wise Professor Kingsley at Coterie of Mages, using magic in the heat of battle was like a frog trying to balance on a razor blade; sometimes the little green amphibian managed the dangerous feat like a tightrope walker, and other times the poor frog slipped and had his balls sliced right off.

Becks checked his watch. Another twenty minutes. He clicked the walkie-talkie.

"Everything in place?"

Two replies crackled through the plastic speaker in quick succession.

"Good as gold."

"Finger on the trigger, here." Then a moment later, "Signs?"

"I'll let you know when I see them. Becks out."

He let the walkie-talkie drop to his side. The cheap plastic communicators made him feel like he was playing a game and not planning a deadly ambush, but he hadn't wanted to use more magic than necessary. Hiding the enchantments for the trap had been his biggest worry. The targets might be some of the best mages to graduate from the Hundred Halls in the last fifty years, and as far as he understood, they'd survived some pretty heinous stuff during their time in school. Caution was warranted.

The roof of the refurbished warehouse in the eleventh ward had a good sight line of the two cross streets. The area had seen something of a revival in the last five years. Becks could see a silver-and-black Rolls Royce Archmage and a cherry red Maserati Fireball sitting in front of Lilith's, a trendy restaurant that served delicacies from other realms. Becks had heard the speckled locanath was a culinary delight. There were a few other restaurants, high-end shops, and late-night dance clubs that wouldn't open until after midnight. He would have preferred to set the ambush in an area that was completely uninhabited, but none of the buildings he'd scouted had the reinforced walls or mage-hardened floors necessary. The warehouse was normally a logistical transfer point for alchemical elixirs with dangerous natures: exothermic, pathogen carrying, or organically transformational. The features of the warehouse that helped protect the surrounding area from leaks would also mute the noise from the ambush.

Becks turned his head to the west. The sun was due to set soon. A low bank of clouds had been blocking it, but the orange-red glow burst through the gap, reflecting off the windows in the area, making them look like burning embers or demon eyes.

A strange light at the center of the city had Becks looking to the northeast. The city of Invictus was a huge metropolis of three million people living in thirteen wards. At the center was an enormous tower called the Spire that was twice as tall as any other building in the world. It was the administrative center for the Hundred Halls, as well as the home of the school's head patron, Invictus, for whom the city was named. The lower two-thirds of the windows on the Spire reflected the setting sun, while the upper third, was jet-black. Moments before, the upper section had been pulsing with an eldritch light that his mind thought was a deep blue, but he'd read that everyone saw the colors differently. The strange lights had been going on for the last year, a couple times a week, sometimes twice in the same day. No one knew why the lights were happening, or for what purpose. The head patron had always been an enigmatic figure, even more so after his long absence, and those unknowable lights reflected his personality.

Most thought he was performing experiments based on what he'd learned while he was "missing." Becks thought Invictus was purely a showman who liked to keep people guessing, reminding them why he was the most famous person in the world, making them believe he was important. The whole thing smacked of bullshit. Invictus had probably been in one of the other realms, drinking their version of mai tais and having sex with the locals, while the various halls of his school had turned on each other, making them more vulnerable to outside threats. Some in Becks' circle even thought Invictus might be behind the infernal warnings they'd been receiving, but even he wasn't so sure of that level of corruption. The more likely explanation was that Invictus was an old man who'd grown tired of running his school and had only come back when the complaints of the patrons had grown too loud.

Becks pulled a tiny stone no bigger than a diamond from his pocket. The angled milky surface looked like condensed smoke. No one knew what it was or why it'd come out of Byron's mouth during the ritual, only that the words that had followed had struck fear in everyone at the ceremony. He squeezed his fist around the stone. If they were successful in the ambush, the threat that had been revealed during the Convergence might be safely squelched before it could grow from embers to flame.

The sun slipped behind the clouds, and the blinding orange-red reflections on the windows turned black like obsidian. A dark blue Toyota Charmer turned the corner with its lights on. Becks' heart jumped in his chest. They were here.

"Target acquired," he said into the walkie-talkie before jogging away from the edge. He threw the device onto the roof before heading to the stairs that would take him to the main floor of the warehouse. Becks rubbed his sweaty hands on his pants, reminding himself that the two women about to enter the warehouse were going to cause—whether knowingly or unknowingly—the destruction of the city and possibly their entire world from an infernal invasion. As head of Chroma and Key, and in a way all the secret societies, it was his charge to protect the Hundred Halls from this threat. If he didn't stand up, then no one would. Becks just wished it hadn't happened on his watch.

The smooth floor of the empty warehouse echoed his footsteps. Becks found his mark at the halfway point and checked to make sure the bracelet was clasped around his wrist. If everything went as planned, he'd be safe as long as he stayed on that mark, then once the initial barrage was over, the bracelet would allow him to retreat to the back rooms, where they could be finished off from a safe location. Assuming they weren't dead already, but given their reputations, Becks wasn't going to take them lightly.

He inhaled deeply through his nose. It smelled like cleaning chemicals. No sign of faez—the raw stuff of magic—that would give away the ambush. Nothing that suggested the entire area was blanketed in wards and enchantments, ready to trigger at the right moment.

He knocked his dark brown hair out of his face and prepared the kind of smile that had always charmed his professors and dates, letting them know that he was just a regular guy. Not a member of the famous Dreadmarsh family. Nor the mage that had scored highest on the Merlins in the last thirty years, earning him a spot in Coterie of Mages, the only school that mattered in the Hundred Halls.

Smile, dammit, he told himself. *You're only here to kill them and save the world.*

Two

Aurelia "Aurie" Silverthorne turned the corner in her Toyota Charmer, heading into the eleventh ward at the moment her sister, Pythia, let out a chainsaw snore. She glanced over to see her curled in her seat, mouth open and tongue hanging out, hair shorn except for a pointed ridge in front. The position reminded Aurie of when they were kids, traveling with their parents, usually to take their mother to the airport for a research trip. Back when she was alive. When they both were.

There'd been a time when she wanted the pain of missing her parents to go away. She'd thought that grief was something to be choked down like a bitter drink, washed away into the rivers of the past, but now she wore it as a mantle of legacy. As long as she carried on their name, and their positions within the Order, they were never truly dead.

"Pi," she said, pushing her sister's shoulder. "Wake up. We're almost here."

"*The ten marks the eye of the hurricane*," said Pi in a voice that was not her own.

Aurie punched her sister in the shoulder as they passed the Enochian district. She could see the huge dragon statue at the center of the square. If they'd had more time, she might have stopped for a trip down memory lane, but she didn't want to make them late for their meeting with the head of Chroma and Key.

"Pi, wake up." Seeing that her sister was deep in slumber, she added, "Invictus wants you in the Eternal City, pronto."

"What?" asked Pi, startling awake, hands in fists as if she were going to throw punches. "Tell that bastard I'm all out of shits to give." Her sister wrinkled her forehead as she checked her surroundings. "Oh, that was cruel. I thought I was back at his place."

Aurie turned the wheel, heading into the newer area of the eleventh ward.

"You were talking in your sleep again."

Pi knuckled away the sleep in the corner of her eyes, yawning as she said, "Which one?"

"Don't know," said Aurie, lifting a single shoulder, "sounded like mumbo jumbo. The ten marks the eye of the hurricane."

Pi slapped her own cheeks lightly. "Doesn't ring a bell." She pressed her face to the window. "Where in the realms are we? None of this looks familiar."

"Eleventh ward. It's seen some changes, I guess."

"A Juju Juice? You've got to be kidding me. There's no soul left here. This place has clearly gone to shit. Look at that Maserati over there, probably a bunch of stick-up-the-butt Coterie bought up the cheap real estate and drove up the prices." Pi threw herself back into her seat. "This is all your fault, you know."

"You were a member of Coterie," said Aurie as she pulled into an empty spot further up the street, across from a restaurant called Lilith's. A waiter with a white towel over his arm was pouring wine for a couple by the window.

Pi tapped on her temple. "Still am."

"You know what I mean."

They climbed out of the sedan. A chill wind breezed through the area, leaving Aurie rubbing her arms. It'd been a warm February day, but now that the sun had gone down, it was cold.

Halfway up the block, almost to the warehouse, Pi paused. "Do you see that?"

"An empty street that hasn't yet been gentrified?"

"No," said Pi, hands on her hips. Her sister wore a Garbage Kings T-shirt with the sleeves cut off and shredded black jeans. She looked like she was headed to a punk show. "We're near the twelfth. I can see the old warehouse from here."

Aurie stretched her neck. An abandoned building covered in ivy with the upper windows knocked out stood at the end of the street. Six years ago her sister had summoned a demon to earn a sponsorship into Coterie of Mages, a task they'd later learned had been given under false pretenses. The demon Pazuzu had nearly escaped and would have caused havoc in the city.

"Any regrets?"

"You're kidding, right?" asked Pi as she rolled her eyes. "Come on, let's get this over with. Old Iron Balls needs me to renew the realm barrier when we get back."

Aurie let a smile get caught in her teeth. "You know he hates when you call him that."

"If I don't, then he reverts to that pompous know-it-all that no one can stand. It's hard enough to take when he barks at us like children and expects us to scurry off, scraping and bowing along the way."

"He has a dozen centuries on us," said Aurie. "Or more. But I understand what you mean. Sometimes I regret freeing him from his stasis."

Pi paused in the middle of the street as a car approached with its lights on. She slapped both hands on her cheeks in faux surprise. "The great and eminently perfect Aurelia Maximus

Silverthorne regrets being a hero? You're crumbling my fabric of reality over here."

The vehicle stopped a few feet from Pi and honked. She turned and gave them double fingers before slapping the hood and continuing on to the sidewalk.

"*Dooset daram.*"

Pi stuck her tongue out playfully. "Now who is this we're meeting again and why? I know, I know. I fell asleep when you were explaining earlier, but I haven't slept in three days."

"You hardly ever sleep."

"I know, but three days is a bit much even for me. The gang in my head wouldn't shut up about the trip to Caer Corsydd. You'd think they'd never been to a fae realm, even a backwater one like that."

Aurie smiled. In the nearly two years since they'd freed Invictus from his failed trip into the demonic realm, the head patron had been sending them to the other realms for information that might help them prevent an invasion. He told them he was too busy with his research to take the trip himself, but Aurie suspected it was because he'd alienated a lot of people over the centuries. Appearing as his representative often came with a lot of baggage, and more than once being greeted with weapons drawn.

"Beckett Dreadmarsh. Fifth year Coterie of Mages, and head of Chroma and Key, the secret society charged with protecting the realms from demons. We're talking to him because the societies do some ceremony every so often, but something happened and they did one early, resulting in some weird shit. Old Iron Balls thinks it might be important."

"Secret societies? Why weren't we invited to join one?" asked Pi.

Aurie didn't bother answering. Their time had been rife with intrigue between the original Halls. Those battles for control of the school were over now that Invictus had returned, but lingering suspicions remained. Aurie opened the door for her sister.

"Weird place for a meeting," muttered Pi as she eyed their surroundings.

"Didn't want anyone to know we were here," said Aurie.

"Still..."

"Yeah, stay on your toes."

The interior of the warehouse was entirely empty except for the occasional steel girder holding up the high roof. Faint runes could be seen on the smooth concrete slab walls. The enchantments appeared to be for a loss of containment of the dangerous chemicals and elixirs normally stored in the warehouse, but given the lack of materials, the runes weren't a current danger.

Aurie spotted Beckett near the center with his hands behind his back. He looked like every member of Coterie she'd met in the past, like he should have been lounging on a yacht with a drink in his hand, musing about the ups and downs of the stock market.

"Do you ever wonder if they give you that perfect hair when you get into Coterie or you can't be invited without it?" asked Pi.

Aurie shushed her sister, chuckling, before smoothing away her mirth and putting on a more formal expression as they neared Beckett.

"Aurie, Pi, it's nice to finally meet you," said Beckett, stepping forward and offering his hand.

"Finally?" asked Pi.

"Come on, now, you're both legends," he said.

"It's nice to meet you, Beckett," said Aurie.

"Please, call me Becks."

He was handsome and had a nice smile. She detected a hint of nervousness in the way he held his shoulders, but it was to be expected, since he might be giving them information that he was supposed to protect.

"A Dreadmarsh, huh?" asked Pi after shaking his hand. "Shouldn't you have a butler here or something?"

Becks cleared his throat. "I'm a second cousin off the main branch. Not to say that we aren't wealthy, but there are levels."

He clearly didn't know what to make of Pi, screwing up his face as he studied her clothing and her youthful expression. He glanced between them. More than one person had underestimated her based on looks, or hadn't realized they were sisters. Aurie was darker complected like their Iranian mother, Nahid, while Pi tended more towards their father, Kieran, and his pale Irish roots.

"Yeah, sure," said Pi, seemingly distracted by something on the floor.

"Thank you for meeting with us," said Aurie, getting Becks' attention.

"Of course," he said, smiling. "Anything for the sisters that brought back Invictus. Though I have to admit that I'm disappointed that you never revealed how that came about."

"We weren't interested in glory," said Aurie, trying not to be distracted by her sister's ambivalence. "And there were a lot of others that made it happen. We didn't want to take credit for something that required a team." She cleared her throat. "I'm sure you're busy, just like we are, so can we get right to the point? We heard there was an interesting development at the Convergence ceremony. We weren't in the societies, but we understand that it's used to gauge the danger that the demonic realm poses to ours, and this time, the warning was both severe and immediate."

"Yeah," said Becks, swallowing while staring at Pi. His boyish smile had disappeared beneath a pale exterior. A bead of sweat had formed on his forehead, which seemed strange to Aurie, given how chilly the empty warehouse was. "The Shaytan'asrar brought grave news..."

Pi was muttering to herself as she stared at Becks' feet. Aurie couldn't tell what she was saying until she looked over. "The ten marks the eye of the hurricane?"

Aurie looked to where Pi had been staring. There was a tiny "X" in paint marker on the floor between Becks' feet. The answer hit her like a smack to the forehead.

"Ten. An X."

They were both lifting their hands for spells when Beckett yelled, "*Dimittis*!"

Aurie managed to place a shield over them, expecting her sister to go after Beckett, only to hear the same spell repeated. A double shimmering dome formed over their heads at the moment an explosion of fiery pellets rained down.

At the same time the flaming projectiles ricocheted off their shield, she heard the overwhelming hiss of a thousand steam vents, and the air filled with a faint webbing of mist. Aurie had been in the middle of forming a new spell, one that would knock Beckett off his feet as he fled, but her movements were slowed by the enchantment field and she lost the rhythm of her magic.

"Fu...!" cried Pi, the curse coming out at half speed. The slow field was interfering with their spell casting, which required precise movements, sounds, and the proper application of faez—the raw stuff of magic—to achieve the desired effect.

The runes on the walls were glowing with ever more intensity. She sensed they were not unlike the protections of a kill room where dangerous magics could be practiced because the runes would annihilate anything in the space should something go terribly wrong. But given the more commercial nature of the warehouse, the runes were set to go off after a delay, giving them a chance to escape, which was why Beckett had created the slow field to keep them from moving too fast.

A secondary explosion blew a greenish gas into the warehouse from the southern wall. The billowing cloud crackled with electricity as it moved towards them like an oncoming storm. Three more explosions followed, each from the other three walls, trapping them at the center of the warehouse. Another complication to keep them occupied so they couldn't escape before the runes went off, destroying everything in the room, including them.

Three

The soul fragments in Pi's head shouted ideas on how to escape in a cacophony of information, the messages coming through in a garbled mess as four dark clouds striated with electricity roiled towards their location at the center of the warehouse.

"Shut up!"

Pi hadn't meant to say it out loud. Aurie gave her a strange look, but they were in too great a danger to stop and talk about her personal problems. When Pi had to ingest the soul fragments many years ago, she'd done so to save them, only to find out they'd given her the knowledge that those students had acquired during their time in the Hundred Halls.

She'd thought she'd absorb them, but they existed in her head like tiny soap bubbles of knowledge. There were nine soul fragments remaining in her mind, and each one had a competing idea. Most of them were focused on the shocking clouds. Disperse or counter them, but time wasn't on their side. The runes on the walls were intensifying. Any moment they were going to trigger and annihilate everything in the warehouse.

The problem was the slow field made escape nearly impossible as it acted on their bodies. Even if they had the supernatural speed of the Assassins' Hall, it wouldn't matter as the field created a maximum speed that couldn't be exceeded by self-propulsion.

But maybe they could escape by being pulled out of the path of the shock clouds.

A steel girder was a few feet from their location. Pi placed her hand on the quarter-inch-thick steel and drew faez from the base of her skull at the same time she spoke the spell that came from Metallum Nocturne—the Hall that had tasked itself with the magic of modern blacksmithing. The steel beneath her fingers glowed dull orange, then turned brighter until it was red hot. Pi squeezed, ripping the chunk of hot metal from the girder. A piece the size of an envelope quickly cooled in her hands.

"Hold onto me," said Pi, in her slow-motion voice.

Aurie had finished a wind spell that had barely dented the closest cloud. The roiling green and black gases were within a dozen feet. The hair on Pi's arms and the back of her neck stood at attention. A crackle of electricity jumped from cloud to cloud, snapping and popping as it crisped the air.

Her sister wrapped her arms around Pi, who was in the middle of chanting a second spell, this one to create an unnaturally strong magnetic attraction between the piece of steel in her hand and the girder near the door that led to the interior offices of the warehouse.

The spell completed as the danger closed in on their location. They were propelled across the warehouse, right through the gap in the clouds, the excitement of electrons leaving their hair standing tall.

Pi released the chunk of metal before slamming into the steel girder and tumbling to the ground. Aurie released her arms and slammed into the office wall. The runes in the warehouse were at peak intensity. Pi could feel them about to trigger.

The door resisted Pi's attempt to enter, and there was no time for a spell, but Aurie shouted, "Unlocked!"—a trick of mendancy, lying magic that convinced the door that it wasn't really locked—and the barrier no longer blocked their way.

They threw themselves inside at the moment a high-pitched keening formed in the warehouse. After the door slammed shut, they heard the sound reach a peak frequency and then dissipate like a train whistle after it'd passed.

"Too close," said Pi, enjoying the normal pace of speaking now that they were out of the slow field.

The room had a pair of desks with computers and a row of filing cabinets. Another door led deeper into the offices, where their attacker had fled.

"Where is that shit-weasel, Becks?" said Pi, heading towards the door.

"Careful, might be more traps ahead," said Aurie, always the cautious one.

"Doubtful," said Pi. "He probably thought his ambush was going to do the job."

She threw the door wide at the same time a wave of flame rushed down the hallway. Suddenly she was flung across the room to slam into a desk as the mass of searing energy slammed into the opposite wall, igniting the nearby papers.

Aurie was lying on top of her. The reason she wasn't in front of the door became clear. Her sister had tackled her.

"Don't be so smug about being right," said Pi as she climbed to her feet, helping her sister along the way.

"Out," Aurie told the fire as if she were reprimanding an unruly canine. The spreading flames reduced until they winked out, leaving charred bits of black paper floating through the room.

"I don't think I want to go down that hallway," said Pi, knocking the crisped edges of her burnt hair. "Can we get to the second floor?"

Aurie hopped onto a desk, kicking the computer off. She knocked away the ceiling tiles to reveal a steel-and-concrete floor blocking their path.

"Ideas?"

"Besides bringing this whole structure down on his head?"

"Without us in it," said Aurie, frowning. "I wish I knew what he was doing. I feel exposed down here."

"If I had some copper wire," said Pi, opening the drawers, "or maybe a paper clip." She nodded towards her sister. "Keep an eye on the door."

Pi found a paper clip in the desk and uncurled it as she knelt by an electrical socket. After a quick charm to insulate the wire, she shoved it into the prong holes. A tiny shock shot out, but the charm kept the paper clip from conducting the electricity.

Pi pulled a piece of gum from her pocket, quickly chewed it, then used it to hold the clip in the socket. She pulled her earbuds out, and after stripping the connecting wire, wrapped it around the clip. A brief spell later, Pi placed the buds in her ears, hearing faint static. She wiggled the clip until voices came into focus.

"...trapped in the entry room...yeah, I don't know how they got out in time, but it happened, and now we have to deal with it..."

"There are more than one. Becks is talking to someone else, but I don't think they're in the same room," she told Aurie.

"...the warehouse is a no go for another few minutes. Once the death field has gone away, then you can hit them from that side when I distract them..."

A snap, followed by the hiss of melting plastic, had Pi yanking the buds out of her ears. The gum she'd used was too wet and had created a connection, melting the cover.

"We have a few minutes before they're going to hit us from both sides." Pi kicked the wall, putting out the small fire. "We have to get to Becks. I can't wait to kill that sonofabitch."

"Pi," said Aurie in a way that was three parts their parents, two parts sisterly admonishment, and one part moral guidance, "we need his information, and even if we didn't, we shouldn't kill him."

Pi grumbled. "He tried to kill us first."

"Even so..."

"Fine," said Pi, feeling like every time she made the wrong decision she had to be reminded of all her past transgressions. "Can we focus on surviving this shit show?"

Aurie nodded. "He has a defensible position at the end of the hall." Her ponytail had come partially undone, leaving wisps of black hair around her forehead, some stuck with sweat.

"I can blow through the ceiling, but then he'll know we're coming," said Pi.

"I wish I could jump through the Veil like Zayn," said Aurie with her arms crossed.

"Hell, if he was here, that asswipe down the hall would already be dead." Pi rolled her eyes when Aurie frowned. "You miss him, don't you?"

"We don't have time for this...and yes, but he has his responsibilities, just like we have ours."

Under different circumstances, Pi would have called her sister on her bullshit. Aurie was still mad at Zayn for leaving with only a note as a goodbye.

"We need to get down that hallway," said Aurie.

"Yeah, yeah, I'm thinking."

The soul fragments had been quiet, but that wasn't unusual. Once things started to go sideways, they got pushed to the back in the frenzy of magic and action, and Pi had to reach out to get them to cooperate.

"I have an idea, or I should say Lydia does."

"Daring Maids?"

"Yeah," said Pi. "I'm going to form a one-woman shield wall and march down that hall while douche-nugget throws everything he can at me, and then when I get us there, you're going to take care of him."

"Are you sure that will hold? He's fifth-year Coterie and one of the top mages in the Halls right now," said Aurie.

"Just be ready when we get there," said Pi.

Pi formed the ghostly shield before she stepped into the hallway. The translucent barrier protected her from head to toe, but it wouldn't be enough against a powerful Coterie mage. She tapped into the soul fragments, repeating the shield spell, but tying the anchor to each one of them, rather than herself. The Daring Maids tasked themselves with protecting the innocent, which meant heading into war-torn areas. Their spell worked best in concert with others, forming a shield wall like the Viking shield maidens of old. Pi was only one person, but using the soul fragments she could make a facsimile of the shield wall.

When the overlapping shimmering ovals were complete, Pi stepped into the doorway. A wave of flame roiled down at her like fire from the throat of a dragon. She girded herself for the impact, which hit the shield wall, energy exploding outward.

She'd survived the first impact, but Becks would double his efforts. The next spell wouldn't be as easy.

At its core, all magic was made up of the five elements: fire, water, earth, wind, and force. Her force shields were a good counter for fire, but she knew he'd likely switch to air, which would make her shields less effective.

As expected, a hurricane whipped down the hallway, but Pi infused the shields with a twist of earth. The ghostly overlapping ovals intensified with grit and rocks. The impact slammed into the shields, increasing the air pressure and making her ears pop, but the barrier held.

Pi smirked to herself as she hurried down the hallway. Becks might be a powerful mage in his own right, but she'd survived countless dangers and learned new tricks along the way. Two more blasts—water and earth—followed, but Pi was ready for both. When the Coterie mage went for a last strike, full-on force, Pi tuned her shields to deflect the impact.

Like two speeding trains slamming into each other, the force waves exploded outward, ripping through the walls and shattering the glass of the nearby offices. Pi was knocked off her feet and the wind blasted from her lungs.

As she struggled to sit up, Aurie leapt over to stop Becks from further spellcasting, but she slowed to a walk, her footsteps crunching on broken glass. Pi found she could breathe again, and she saw why her sister no longer moved with urgency.

The blowback had exploded the surrounding windows. Becks' body was littered with shards, blood leaking from countless wounds. He was gasping for air like a fish out of water, his breath coming slower.

"Why did you try to kill us?" asked Aurie.

His gaze darted between them. "You...you'll be the death of us all."

It hurt to speak, but Pi managed. "Bullshit. We've done more for the city than anyone else. Why? Why did you try?"

Becks reached out his hand, which was shaking like a leaf. "Please..."

"Can you do anything for him?" asked Aurie.

Pi shook her head. "I know a few Aura Healer tricks, but nothing that would fix this."

"Come on."

She threw her hands up. "I'm serious. He's way beyond my knowledge. I'm not trying to get my revenge. Really." Pi looked to Becks, whose breath was coming both rapidly and shallowly. "You need to make him talk before he passes."

It was hard to look at him. The fear was in his eyes. Naked, raw fear. The reflection of death went right through Pi.

"Pi, you know it'll make it go quicker."

"Aurie, now."

Her sister nodded, understanding the need. As a member of Arcanium, the hall that dedicated itself to the pursuit of knowledge and truth, Aurie could perform minor miracles with only a few words.

"Beckett Dreadmarsh. Tell us why you tried to kill us and what was said at the Convergence."

Aurie's words were imbued with a singular force. Even standing next to her, Pi felt the reverberation, as if a divine being had spoken, not her older sister.

"It was a warning"—his breath was getting slower and his eyes were fluttering—"to stop you before you could bring about the invasion...the newest of the connected eight, fallen now... must end them before they ensure his return...or the city will die..." His voice trailed off and his eyes unfocused.

"Merlin's tits, he thought he was doing something good by coming after us," said Pi.

Becks' body shuddered quietly and then a nimbus formed around him like a cocoon of light before condensing into a bead and whooshing out of the room.

"What was that?" asked Pi, following the light with her eyes until it was gone.

Aurie made a few gestures, faez detection spells. "It was a tattletale charm. It'll tell whoever it's linked to that we killed him."

"But we didn't," said Pi. "The fool did it to himself trying to break through my shield."

"Doesn't matter," said Aurie with lips bunched. "They'll blame us, whoever they are."

"We have to leave."

They found a staircase leading to the roof. Pi worried they'd have to jump to get off, but there was emergency scaffolding that led down to the street. As they made their way to their car, a host of sirens grew louder, probably drawn by the triggering of the runes in the warehouse.

Four

Aurie entered the Spire with her sister through the hidden entrance in the lowest levels. An elevator took them three-quarters the height of the building. The ride lasted four minutes, nearly all of it in silence.

She didn't know what her sister had been thinking about, but Aurie had been trying to figure out how the encounter in the warehouse might have gone different. Even though Beckett had tried to kill them, he'd thought he was performing a good deed. Or at least it seemed that way to her.

"Do you have any idea of what—"

"No," said Pi, who'd been frowning with her arms crossed the entire way up. "I'll worry about what it means after I reapply the barrier."

"You could let me try. I might be able to—"

"No," said Pi, cutting her off, voice threaded with frustration. "As much as I wish you could, you can't help. I can barely manage the stupid spell. It's like trying to hold up a mountain. I'm just hoping Old Iron Balls isn't around so I don't have to listen to his crap."

"He'll want an explanation of what we learned."

Pi kicked the silvery interior of the elevator. "No he won't. You know how he gets, that arrogant ass—he'll want to know what Beckett meant. Connected eight, what does that even mean?"

Aurie had halfway mustered a word of encouragement when the doors opened and Pi stormed out, heading through the entrance area and through the portal that led to Invictus' quarters. Aurie followed but at a slower pace. They'd spent the last six months bouncing around dozens of realms chasing leads and support, but had come back virtually empty-handed. The worst part was that Invictus had barely cared that they hadn't been successful, which had only infuriated her sister.

Invictus' personal quarters at least reminded her of Arcanium with its long shelves filled with books and historical curiosities like the fearsome crimson Tengu mask or the worn bronze beads from the third millennium BCE. An enormous crystalline ball hovered over the central area, its interior quivering with the energy that powered his rooms.

Aurie knew she should be trying to figure out what Beckett had said before he died, but she was relishing the idea of not traveling or being in danger for a brief moment in time. They'd barely gotten back from their trip when Invictus had sent them right back out. Her duffle bag was near the elevator, still unpacked and covered in mud from their trip to Caer Corsydd.

The windows drew her like a magnet. She pressed her forehead against the glass. It wasn't cool as she would have normally expected, because it wasn't a true window, but rather a looking glass that let her think she was viewing the city, when really Invictus' quarters were a pocket realm built into the Spire.

Seeing the lights of the city spread out beneath her helped soothe the pain of regret. Aurie wished she'd been able to save Beckett, and not just to further question him. His misguided reasons for trying to kill them didn't sit well with her.

The view was of the northwest. A little to her left in the first ward was the obsidian structure called the Obelisk that was the home to Coterie of Mages. The glistening black stone warped the lights in the surrounding blocks, making it a giant alien thumb sticking out of the ground. The news of Beckett's death had probably reached the other students of that hall, confusion and anger spreading like wildfire. Though there was a chance it was welcomed, as Coterie was known for its cutthroat attitudes about interhall rivalry. Aurie was glad that her sister had been able to leave Coterie after a single year. That hall would have further tempted Pi's moral ambivalence, already compromised by her association with Radoslav.

Near the edge of the fifth ward was a medieval castle. Her home for five wonderful years at Arcanium. She hadn't been back since she'd graduated two years ago. With Invictus returned, he'd kept them constantly busy chasing down leads.

The red and blue flashing lights of an emergency helicopter descended onto the helipad on top of Golden Willow, the hospital in the sixth ward to her north that was the premiere specialist for supernatural afflictions. Aurie had worked on the Children's Floor as an orderly before she joined the magical university.

Her eyes darted about the nighttime city, picking out the larger Halls she could see from her perch in the sky: the stone flower of Stone Singers, the glass building that housed the Order of Honorable Alchemists, and the Holistic Institute building near Golden Willow. She knew there were dozens of smaller halls scattered throughout the city blocks specializing in obscure magics, but she didn't know where they were located. The name of the school, the Hundred Halls, was something of a misnomer because the true number fluctuated constantly, and during

Invictus' seventeen-year absence when no new Halls could be added, the figure had declined precipitously.

The city was the most important place in the world and not only because it was the home of the Hundred Halls, the only magical university in the world, but because unbeknownst to most outside its storied halls, it was a nexus point for interrealm travel. Most of the other realms were underdeveloped backwaters that would have no connection to the others if it weren't for the city's portals. And except for a few like the Eternal City, home of the maetrie commonly called the city elves, and the demonic realm, most posed no threat to their world.

Beckett's last words floated up from the depths of her mind. *The newest of the connected eight, fallen now.* Aurie had no idea what it meant. Who were the connected eight? And why were they fallen? Was it a secret organization?

The problem was they lacked the resources to learn anything important. The Order of Merlin had once been a larger organization, but now it was only four of them, which included Invictus and Sam Arlington. Requests to expand their numbers had been met with indifference from the head patron, and they were never in the city, so they couldn't create contacts or keep abreast of what was happening. In the last two years, Aurie figured they'd been in the city for a total of forty days, and even when they were members of the Halls, they'd spent their time as outcasts due to the conflicts between Arcanium and the other original halls: Coterie of Mages, the Order of Honorable Alchemists, Protectors, and the Society for the Subtle Arts—also known as Assassins.

The muted echoes of shouting reached Aurie. Unless Sam was back from his trip, which she seriously doubted, there were only two other people in the space. Invictus and Pi were like oil and water, or maybe fire and gasoline was a more appropriate analogy. Aurie briefly thought about trying to calm them down, but both of them were hotheaded. It was best to let them burn it out. Besides, she had an idea of who might be able to figure out the "connected eight" reference. An old friend from Arcanium, who had once been her rival. Aurie headed towards the exit portal as something made of glass crashed, relief following as muted shouts disappeared behind.

Five

"You're nothing but a bully," shouted Pi, hating the way the rage filled her mind with bright lights. "No wonder the original patrons were happy when you disappeared."

The head patron of the Hundred Halls was not as tall as most people expected, yet he took up space as if he were a giant. Long, wavy black hair threaded with gray framed his deeply tanned face. His eyes, which could be as mercurial as a summer storm, burned bright with anger.

"Insults won't cover up for your failures, Pythia," said the head patron, glowering at her in his gray robes.

Pi could never get over how the wrinkles in his face creased with emotion. A man who was over a thousand years old should be wielding expressions with the inflexibility of a petrified tree, or smoothed with sorcery like the patrons of the halls.

"I don't know why you have me renew the realm barrier charm every time I come back. We don't need it here, and the damn spell gives me a migraine for days."

"I ask because it's important someone else knows," said Invictus in his deep baritone voice. "I don't think I need to remind you that *my* foolishness nearly brought down the Halls and endangered the entire realm."

"The spell is too hard, even for me," said Pi.

"Your mother, Nahid, managed the spell and without all this whining."

Pi's hands clenched into fists. "My mother is dead, and as I recall you explaining on more than one occasion, you spent decades training them, while you've done nothing more than send us on errands that feel more like you're trying to get us out of your hair while you play with your toys after being absent for so long," said Pi.

Invictus growled under his breath and turned away. "I've had more cordial conversations with a pack of demons than you, girl. You argue too much and listen too little." He picked up the brass cylinder that he'd been fussing with before she entered his room, and ran his fingertips across the smooth surface as he muttered an incantation that woke hidden runes. With the spell finished, he turned back to her. "Why are you still here? You have work to do."

Arguing with him was like running into a brick wall. She knew she wasn't going to get anywhere new, but she kept doing it just the same.

Pi headed into the portal room. A blank stone wall beneath an archway was directly across from a panel of gears and knobs with a giant lever on the side. The Helmsman of the Planes provided their easy and private travel through the realms rather than having to use the regular portal system.

She faced the wall, tracing her fingers across the smooth surface. The soul fragments in her head were quiet at least. The events at the warehouse had worn everyone out, including her. She knew she should take a break, eat something, or rest her eyes for a moment before attempting the spell, but if Invictus found her lounging around, he'd never let her hear the end of it.

The finger mechanics of the barrier spell weren't difficult, nor were the few phrases required, but the faez load on her mind was staggering. Every time she cast the spell, she thought she was ready to carry the weight, but it was like having a car dropped on her shoulders from a second-story window.

Her right knee buckled slightly even though the impact wasn't physical. Recharging the barrier was like diving deep underwater and holding one's breath. The longer she held it, the more the strain on her mind. Sometimes she smelled burning, as if her mind was crisping under the pressure like overloaded circuits.

The urge to give up and let the spell release and wash over her like a flood was strong, but she could hear Invictus' earlier comment like a ball of constricting barbwire around her heart. *Your mother, Nahid, managed the spell and without all this whining.* Her parents had died when she was just ten, leaving her and Aurie to the mercy of the orphanage system. Pi knew part of the reason she always clashed with Invictus was because she was mad at him for not being around. Nahid and Kieran would be alive if Invictus hadn't gotten caught in emergency stasis trying to escape the demonic realm.

A bolt of pain shot through her mind, leaving dark spots across her vision. Pi leaned against the wall as the spell's blowback crushed her thoughts. A whimper slipped out her lips as first darkness then a bright vision flashed into her mind. The image of Invictus standing on a high rock, the air sparkling with golden light, a creature the size of a commercial aircraft winging through sky while he spoke to a man that looked like a thousand living swords, was as clear as if she were standing right there. They stood in a place ringed with jagged, impossible mountains, too steep and angled, like crystals growing from the earth. The place seemed important, though she didn't know why. Other features caught her eye, something high in the mountains, a connection between two places, but she felt like she was seeing something she wasn't meant to. As soon as that thought intruded, vertigo ripped her from her spot, throwing her back into the void.

The vision ended and Pi found herself lying on her back covered in a patina of sweat. The barrier spell that she'd labored so hard to maintain had evaporated like mist on a desert highway.

Pi worked her way into a sitting position. Every muscle in her body felt like she'd been through a ten-round fight and her temples throbbed with the threat of an oncoming migraine. She didn't know what to make of the vision, except that it might have been something left over from when Invictus had been trapped between this realm and the demonic one, locked in a protective stasis of his own making. Being stuck in one place for seventeen years might have left psychic imprints...or, she reminded herself, the strain of casting the spell might have knocked her out and the vision had merely been an anxiety filled nightmare. After all, they'd heard Invictus' story about entering the demonic realm a dozen times and at no point had he been conversing with the locals.

"Why are you sitting on your ass and not refreshing the barrier?" asked Invictus from the edge of the room.

Pi almost told him about her vision, but decided he'd only deride it as the delusions of someone trying to get out of work.

"I, uhm, thought I'd take a break first. You know, on account of nearly getting killed at the warehouse. Great tip by the way. Were you trying to get rid of us, or are you that incompetent?"

Invictus had been about to head to wherever he was going, but paused and wrinkled his forehead. For a brief moment, he looked like a concerned grandfather.

"You were attacked?"

"Yeah, that asshole Beckett set up an ambush, nearly got us both, but got himself killed in the back blow. We escaped before anyone else could arrive, but he had a tattletale charm and a couple of coconspirators we never saw."

"Why didn't you say this when you arrived?"

"Because we're alive, and we thought that you would only want to hear about it once we figured out what Beckett meant," said Pi.

"Where's your sister? I don't sense her anywhere in my quarters," said Invictus, turning his head.

"I don't know, probably went out for a walk. Or she's asleep trying to get some rest, since you know, we just walked in when you sent us right back out the door."

His worried expression smoothed away, and for a moment, Pi thought he might apologize, but then he disappeared from the doorway. She hung her head between her bent knees.

"Screw this. I'm getting something to eat and a shower before I do this again."

Six

The *Herald of the Halls* headquarters was in the second ward, near the edge of the ninth. Nightfall had brought a chill wind whipping through the streets, but Aurie strode down the sidewalk oblivious to the temperatures due to her warmth charm. A few passersby gave her a long, second look as if they suspected she was a mage.

Aurie was never sure if it was jealousy or just normal human curiosity. From the earliest days of her life, she'd known she had magical ability, but had to resist the urge to use her magic frequently, or risk faez madness because her young mind couldn't handle the raw energies coursing through it. Like most kids her age, she still played Five Elements with her sister in their rooms late at night when their parents were asleep. Then when she was protected by her patron, Semyon Grey, the head of Arcanium, those restraints were ripped away. Magic was a comfortable cloak that hugged her like an old friend, but it also came with a target on the back.

She paused outside the building, looking up to see only a few lights, mostly in the upper levels. While the rest of the employees had left, Aurie was certain her friend Violet Cardwell would still be working.

The security guard at the front desk hesitated to let her into the building until she told the man her name, and then he was hurrying to the elevator and typing in his code so she could ascend. On the way up, regrets crept into Aurie's mind. What if Violet had changed? What if she wasn't her friend anymore?

Those thoughts were obliterated when Violet Cardwell greeted her at the top of the elevator. Her fellow Arcanium alumni looked nothing like the privileged rich girl that had made her first few years in the Hall a living hell.

"Aurie!"

They embraced in a long hug. A little wetness formed at the corner of her eyes at the renewal of their friendship. Violet held her at arm's length.

"Broken hells, you've been through some shit," said Violet, giving her a once-over. "Is that blood on your sleeve? And you know you have mud caked on your shoes?"

"Invictus keeps us busy," said Aurie, reaching out to touch the side of Violet's head, "but not as much as you. Aren't you a little young for gray hair?"

Violet's bottle-blonde hair had been allowed to turn a darker shade.

"I think I'd rather fight a battle to the death than deal with the board of the *Herald*," said Violet, hooking her arm and leading her towards the back of the floor. A half dozen employees were still at their desks. A few looked up from their computers and smiled before returning to their work. "Not only do they hate working for someone half their age, but you'd think they'd been born in the 1800s based on their ideas. I'm trying to drag the paper into this new age, but all they want the paper to cover are fluff pieces on how the patrons are making the world a better place. I wouldn't be surprised if half of them are getting kickbacks from Celesse, the way our paper fawns over her alchemical corporation."

The office at the end of the floor wasn't much bigger than the others Aurie had seen. She plopped into a chair across from Violet, who dug into a drawer for a bottle of amber liquid.

"Care to share?"

"Drinking on the job?"

"Benefits of working late," said Violet with a heavy sigh. "We had to make a late update to a big expose we were writing about your boss on how he's barely been seen since his return. Care to add anything? Off the record, since we're already printing in the basement."

"If I knew what the old bastard was doing, I'd be happy to tell you, but he keeps us running around the realms on errands." Aurie plucked a piece of mud from her boot and flicked it into the wastebasket. "Last one was a swamp, a beautiful one, as swamps go, but still a swamp."

Two glasses were poured. Aurie grabbed hers and clinked it against Violet's when offered. The amber liquid burned going down, making her screw up her face.

"Augh, I forgot I don't like whiskey," said Aurie, sticking out her tongue.

Violet swirled her glass and threw the rest down her throat as if this was a regular occurrence. "It grows on you." She leaned forward. "Any truth to the rumblings about a problem with the demonic realm? I've got reports from all over the city about increased activity from supernatural creatures, strange spikes of faez, other weird events like an ice cream maker in the fifth who found his bin of rocky road had turned to blood."

"I'd have to be in the city to know these things," said Aurie, tapping on the glass with a fingernail. "But I can tell you that it's what Invictus was investigating when he disappeared. He keeps things close to the vest, even from us, but it would be hard not to be worried."

Violet leaned back, nodding. "We're running a front-page story next month about it. We've got copies of faez readings in the Undercity that show something's going on down there, plus sightings of creatures that could only come from the demonic realm. If you have information that would help clarify, I would really appreciate it. We have a duty to the city to let them know they'll be safe. Or if not, how best to protect themselves."

"I'll see what I can come up with," said Aurie.

As much as she wanted to help her friend, the things she knew would only make people more afraid, or get them killed if they went looking in the Undercity. Most people thought of the caverns and passages beneath the city as a curiosity, not realizing how extensive and dangerous they were. The barrier between their world and the demonic one was thinnest below, and especially around the wells of power. And those weren't the only dangers. There were whole communities that lived below because they weren't welcome in the light, non-humans or those who had been changed by magic, as well as dangerous gangs who used the place to hide their illicit activities.

"You didn't come to visit because you wanted to provide background for my paper," said Violet, reaching towards the bottle of whiskey before staying her hand. "What did you need?"

"I'm looking for someone," said Aurie.

"I'm hardly the missing persons department," said Violet.

"No," said Aurie, "but you know everyone and everything about this city."

"What's the name?"

"That's the problem—I don't have a name," said Aurie. "Any idea who the 'connected eight' is?"

"The connected eight? That's vague," said Violet, biting her lower lip. "But not out of character for you. Anything else that might help me narrow down who that might be?"

"Technically, I'm looking for the newest of the connected eight, and they're fallen now, whatever that means," said Aurie, gesturing randomly.

Violet drummed her fingers on the desk as she looked out the side window. "Sounds familiar for some reason, but I can't place it. Connected...connected. Like an influencer?"

"Maybe?"

She opened up her laptop and started typing furiously, occasionally muttering, "No" or "Not them."

"Do you think they're specific to the city?" asked Violet.

"Probably."

After a few more rounds of furious typing, the focus on Violet's face smoothed away to recognition. She spun the laptop around and leaned back in her chair.

Aurie was looking at a newspaper article that looked a decade old. It showed a well-dressed family of eight standing before a mantle. The parents both had dark hair, though the father looked considerably older than the mother. There was something in the man's eyes that bothered Aurie, but she couldn't place it. She expanded the picture to get a better look at the kids. The six children were arrayed before the parents as if they were show horses. The headline read "Charming the World: How the Charmer family conquered the business of connection."

"Charmers? Never heard of them," said Aurie.

"Not surprised. They're the elite of the elite. Or were. Then a bunch of tragedies befell them. All the kids are members of the Halls and the societies too. Not just the run-of-the-mill ones, but top tier. Coterie of Mages. Alchemists. Assassins. Chroma and Key. Snake and Tome, and so on," said Violet, making a rotating motion with her hand.

"Then? You said tragedy."

"The eldest, Solstice, died under suspicious circumstances, maybe about ten years ago. I remember reading about it at the time. Later it turned into an interfamily combat over control of the company. The father won out initially, but there was a lot of stuff that came up. Really nasty things about his kids that had opposed him. Murder. Blackmail. Drugs. A disaster at the plant they acquired in some far-off realm. Montanhas, I think. Then the father disappeared and the company dissolved. Fallen would be a good label for the Charmer family. They used to be top dogs, and now no one has heard from them since."

Aurie tapped on the screen. The smallest girl didn't wear the same smile as the others as if she hadn't been happy to be included. "The youngest is named Andromeda. That must be who the newest connected eight is. Any idea where she's at?"

Another round of typing and Violet said, "She joined a traveling festival. She was in the Weird Circus."

"Oestomancers? I thought you said the kids were all in the top Halls?"

"All of them except Andromeda. I guess she was the rebel of the group."

"Traveling festival," said Aurie, grumbling.

"You're in luck," said Violet. "The Mystique is returning to Invictus next week. I only know because they bought a lot of ads from the paper. They sent me some tickets, but I had no plan to attend." She reached into a drawer and produced an envelope. "Four VIP tickets. All yours."

"Thanks. There's four. Wanna join us?"

Violet chuckled. "I would, Aurie. It would be fun to catch up, it really would. I'd love to hear more about your adventures in the other realms. Truth be told, I'm a little jealous of you and your sister. It was one of those things I always wanted to do, see the many worlds, though I thought I'd be a world-famous alchemist like Celesse, and do it under more luxurious circumstances." She chuckled, smoothing the front of her desk with a flat hand. "But I have a paper to run, and as much I would like to catch up, you and your sister attract problems like a Coterie mage attracts venereal diseases. I only have to look at the blood on your sleeve to know that hasn't changed. You're welcome to come back here anytime, especially if you can illuminate those earlier topics, but I'm afraid you're too dangerous to spend time with outside these guarded walls." She paused, bunching up her mouth. "I hope you understand."

The rest of the conversation moved to safer topics: reminiscing about their favorite professors in Arcanium, the new little Halls that were popping up with Invictus back, and news about old friends. When Aurie sensed that Violet wanted to get back to work, she excused herself and headed back to the elevator after a long hug and a promise to keep in touch.

Aurie examined the tickets for the Mystique on the way down. When she pulled them out of the envelope, a miniature illusionary tightrope walker carrying a hellhound on their shoulders appeared above the surface of the thick, colorful paper. The image morphed into a group of Renaissance clowns doing backflips and sending tiny fireballs into the air, where they exploded like fireworks. The final example was a young woman with a rainbow Mohawk with short blades stuck through her limbs. She pulled a dagger from her forearm, licked the blood off, then threw the weapon high in the air. The illusion winked out the moment before the blade was going to land on her upturned face, leaving Aurie to jump in anticipation of the impact.

The miniature version of the Mystique was quite realistic, and after spending a fair amount of time staring at the newspaper article in Violet's office, Aurie was certain that the final performer, the one with the blades sticking out of their body, was the youngest Charmer, Andromeda.

"What did your family do to you that you joined the circus?" she asked aloud, shoving the tickets into her shoulder bag. "And more importantly, why does Beckett Dreadmarsh think you're a danger to the city of Invictus and the entire world?"

Seven

The lines outside the Glitterdome snaked around the building. Pi climbed out of their vehicle as Aurie tossed the keys to the valet attendant. Cars honked their horns at the busy crowds crossing the street, which stank of exhaust. Kids rode on their parents' shoulders, faces artfully painted with bright colors, some wearing cheap versions of the Mystique performers' costumes. A young girl no older than ten ran in front of Pi wearing black-and-white-striped leggings with an aquamarine top covered in sequins. A floppy witches hat nearly fell off her head as she hurried to get in line while her parents pushed a stroller and struggled to keep up.

"That's her," said Pi as they headed to the VIP lines, which were much shorter. "A cheap kid version."

Aurie turned her head and screwed up her face. "Huh? Who?"

"Andromeda. Or Bonnie Bedlam, her stage name. It's a clever play on words."

"It is?"

Pi punched her sister in the arm. "What's the deal? You seem distracted. Word play should be easy for you."

"Sorry. I still can't get over Beckett. I know we spent our years in school fighting with the other major Halls, but I thought that was over with Invictus back. The ambush was way worse than a little intra-Hall conflict. I researched him. He wasn't a bad guy. Well thought of by his classmates and the societies. Despite being a Dreadmarsh, he was known for his work in the charities. Things like that."

"Not a bad guy except for the fact he tried to kill us," said Pi with an eye roll.

"My point is, what drove him to think we were a danger? I wish we could have heard the rest of what he learned at the Convergence ceremony. I feel like whatever he had to say wasn't the whole picture."

The VIP line moved quickly. Black-clad bouncers waved enchantment detection wands over the people entering the Glitterdome. The information about the show said that personal magics were not allowed as they might interfere with the performances.

"What makes you say that? Other than he died before getting it all out," said Pi, catching a horrified look from an older woman wearing a shimmering gold dress in front of them. They'd been traveling in strange places for the last few years, and Pi'd forgotten to be circumspect in public.

"This," said Aurie, gesturing around them. "What would a performer in the Mystique traveling circus have to do with anything related to what Old Iron Balls has us chasing? This is the second ward, a place of frivolous entertainment where you can see giant illusionary robots battle dragons over the buildings, or buy worthless, overpriced trinkets that only work for a single night from sketchy street vendors. It's hardly a den of intrigue."

Pi glanced back as they passed the security check, catching sight of a flock of illusionary harpies circling down upon the crowd gathered to cross the street, bringing cries of delight and horror.

"Not everything has to be so serious," said Pi as she handed over her ticket.

An attendant pointed them in the direction of the VIP section. The back third of the arena had been cordoned off with black sheeting, and an elongated stage, surrounded by seats, filled the floor. Their spots were near the stage. An attendant brought them drinks and gave them a menu for food, all complementary.

"I think we're the youngest in the VIP section by about thirty years," Pi muttered to Aurie as she glanced around.

A short while after they arrived, the lights turned down and a woman in a top hat and makeup that made her look like she was being moved by invisible strings ambled onto the stage. The show had been advertised as Final Night at the Marionette Shop.

Pi leaned over and whispered to her sister, "It would have been cool to see something like this with Mom and Dad."

Aurie nodded and reached out to squeeze her hand.

As the Mistress of Marionettes spoke, the entire stage transformed from black sheets and flat stages to a workshop where the wooden puppets were being manufactured. Pi had come to the event to meet Andromeda after the show, but quickly found herself immersed in the tale presented on the stage.

The story followed the Maker of Marionettes, a gentle looking old tinkerer with wavy gray hair who loved his wooden puppets and imbued them with his special magic to make them more lifelike, but the Cutter of Strings whispered lies to the wooden creatures and convinced them to rebel against their master. The defiance, unbeknownst to the marionettes, came at great cost as the Cutter took the Maker's place once he'd been murdered by his favorite puppet, Laughing

Leesa.

All this played out with much pomp and theatrics. Tightrope walkers scurried across lines set at strange angles that no regular human performer should be able to stay on, but they moved across them like spiders on a web. The marionettes, some not completely finished by the Maker when they were turned, put on amusing little side stories—like Mul-T, who'd been built from parts of old broken puppets. Her limbs took on the personalities of their original owners to great comic effect.

At the beginning of the performances, Pi found herself picking out which Halls might have lent their expertise to the show. The basilisk handler was clearly from Animalians, though she had no idea how they were going to return the puppet that was turned to stone back to flesh afterwards. The bullet catcher was most likely the Daring Maids, or possibly Protectors. Any one of the acrobats could have learned their craft in the Assassin's Guild or in Explorers, but there were other ways to learn such impressive physical arts.

As she became immersed in the story, she forgot why she was inside the Glitterdome. The performance took her back to when she was trying to get into the Hundred Halls. Back to when they lived in a shitty twelfth ward apartment and only had each other for practicing the skills necessary to pass the Merlin Trials—the dangerous tests that allowed entrance into the magical university. Pi felt like those puppets who never really knew who was in charge, or what their motives were. Even after two years of working for Invictus, and knowing that she was distantly related to him, she never really trusted the head patron.

These thoughts were obliterated the moment Bonnie Bedlam, aka Andromeda Charmer, came flying into the stadium, standing on a levitating carpet, hollering like an Old West cowboy. Her character was an agent of chaos, a voice from outside the marionette shop that convinced the puppets to question their new master, the Cutter of Strings.

Her performance elicited the largest reactions from the crowd, especially when an old box that had once housed Jacqueline the Casketmaker exploded, sending shards of wood into Bonnie Bedlam. The long shards stuck through Bonnie's body, piercing her like a pincushion. A few of the older viewers in the VIP section hurried out of the arena, disgusted by the display, while Pi found herself amused by the body horror.

To the delight of the crowd, Bonnie Bedlam, a favorite of the younger audience members, helped Mul-T, Laughing Leesa, and the other marionettes overthrow the Cutter of Strings. When the lights came up and the show was over, the crowd applauded for ten minutes straight.

Pi followed her sister backstage. They'd put in a request to "interview" Andromeda as representatives of the *Herald of the Halls*. The security around the performers wasn't as tight as getting into the Glitterdome, though they were scanned for enchantments and magical trinkets again.

After a knock on the door from a backstage production assistant in black clothing, a muted "come in" had them stepping inside a dressing room. Bonnie Bedlam sat before a lighted mirror, removing the makeup from her face with an alcohol pad while two women that were some of the background marionettes spoke with her in French.

"Reporters from the *Herald*," said the production assistant before disappearing into the flow of people moving around backstage.

Andromeda glanced at them through the mirror. The meeting of their gazes brought Pi a little shock in her midsection.

"You don't look like reporters."

The two performers on the couch stared ambivalently. Aurie stepped into the room.

"Might we speak with you in private?" asked her sister.

"You don't work for the *Herald*," said Andromeda as she cleaned her jutted chin with the wipe. "I've already told those other assholes I'm not interested in your conspiracy theories. Please remove yourselves from my dressing room."

The ladies on the couch smirked. Pi felt like she should say something but there was something magnetic that drew her to Andromeda and made her mouth go dry. It was only when her sister started speaking that Pi was able to shake off the feeling and recognize the message that Andromeda had just delivered.

"Violet Caldwell, owner of the *Herald*, gave us these tickets herself, and while we may not be regular reporters, we are here on her behalf," said Aurie, her tone growing harsher as she spoke. Pi elbowed her in the side, and her sister took a deep breath and continued in a calmer voice. "As for those other assholes, we don't know what you're talking about. We're not with anyone else."

"Except the *Herald*," said Andromeda dryly.

The two ladies on the couch chuckled and then spoke in French, bringing laughter from Andromeda and making Pi wish she spoke that language.

"I'm not interested in whatever you're selling," said Andromeda.

Aurie was about to launch into an angry retort when Pi grabbed her arm.

"Our parents were similar," said Pi, stepping into the room and hating the way her voice cracked.

"What? I doubt it," said Andromeda as she took out a new pad and started cleaning off her forehead. As she lifted her arm, Pi caught the crusted blood on her shoulder where the wood shard had gone through. During the performance, Pi had thought the injuries an illusion, but no longer.

"Maybe not in most things, but they liked weird names. I'm Pythia, or Pi, and this is Aurelia, or Aurie. I know your brothers' and sisters' names. Ares, Ivan, Catherine, Moriganne, and Solstice. My condolences about your eldest sister."

It'd seemed like a good idea when she started speaking, but the way Andromeda was looking at her made Pi feel like she wanted to crawl into a hole.

"Aurelia and Pythia," said Andromeda as if she were tasting their names. She turned her head towards the performers on the couch and tilted her head towards the door as she spoke in French.

The ladies seemed surprised, but stood up and headed out. The taller girl, who had short auburn hair, leaned in and gave Andromeda a kiss on the corner of her mouth before brushing past them, which made Pi unexpectedly jealous. When it was just the three of them, she closed the door.

"You were the ones that brought back Invictus," said Andromeda. "I read about that. Amongst other things. Where you two go, trouble follows."

"Or maybe we go where trouble is," said Aurie, crossing her arms.

Andromeda turned her chair towards them and Pi caught a flash of letters streaming across her knuckles as if they were a theater marquee. Oestomancers were skilled at body modification, including using the flesh as a living canvas. Pi only saw the CK, but had a pretty good idea what the message was.

"Which suggests you think that *I'm* going to be trouble," Andromeda said, hooking her arm over the back of the chair.

"Someone thinks you'll be," said Aurie. "Someone tried to kill us last week, and one of the last things they said pointed us to you. The fact that others have already talked to you suggests that we were right to come here. What did they want?"

"None of your business," said Andromeda, leaning down and opening a small refrigerator below the counter. She pulled out a stout milk bottle, but the liquid inside looked chalky green. With a preemptive grimace, Andromeda choked the liquid back, shivering with distaste when it was gone. "Speeds the healing."

"You're in danger," said Aurie.

"From who?"

"We don't know yet, but if they were willing to kill us, then who knows what they'll do to you. We can protect you," said Aurie.

"I can protect myself," said Andromeda, oozing confidence. The arrogance was familiar. Mages and hubris went together like magic and mayhem. Pi knew because she had oodles of it herself. So did her sister, but Aurie also had a blind spot for her own faults. Young, arrogant mages thought themselves immune to problems because they could solve so many of them with the wave of a few fingers. The comic books and movies were filled with the exploits of heroic mages defying odds and saving the world. The reality was more gruesome and tragic.

Heading into the meeting, Pi would have been surprised to see the mantle of conceit on Andromeda's shoulders. Sure, she was a world-famous performer in a traveling troupe that drew rave reviews wherever she went, but she was just an oestomancer—a bone mage. There was something deeper in Andromeda's eyes, experience with the darker aspects of their world. Pi was both worried and excited by the prospect, because she'd had those experiences herself. Andromeda had layers. Depths which would require time to peel back. Histories to uncover. Over a cup of coffee, or a long weekend, was preferred.

Aurie, however, was still looking at Andromeda like the performer she was, rather than the hidden talent of resolve that Pi suspected. A chuckle, the recognition of mismatched expectations, brought a searing look from her sister.

"Do you know why you might be in danger?" asked Pi, containing her grin.

She noticed that when Andromeda looked from her sister to her that her expression softened, which brought a warmth to her midsection. Maybe the French marionette was just a friend, the kiss lacking the depths that Pi desired.

The question sat on Andromeda's brow until she started quivering with laughter. "You really don't know much about my family, do you?" She picked up a new alcohol pad but left it sitting in her palm. "Why do you care about my safety? From what I know about you two, you're a couple of busybodies that probably cheated to win the Second Year Contest, caused more strife in the Halls than would have been there otherwise, and lucked into finding Invictus."

Aurie took a step towards Andromeda. "We didn't cheat."

"Then how did two members of Arcanium end up on the same team?"

Before Aurie could respond, Pi said, "Without a long weekend to explain, I couldn't begin to give you even the beginning of it. But we work for Invictus. Do you think he'd entrust us with his tasks if we were out for ourselves?"

Andromeda lifted a shoulder. "You can't believe *everything* you read on the internet. But some of it *is* true."

"We don't believe the stuff we read about you," said Pi, hoping to engender sympathy.

Andromeda's lips squeezed white as she stared back at Pi. "Maybe you should."

There was a lot of pain and history in those eyes. Pi wanted desperately to hear about those things over a series of long dinners and longer overnight stays.

"Can you tell us any reason why these people think you're a danger?" asked Aurie.

"I don't trust you." She blinked and looked away. "I'd like to. I really would, but some secrets are better left unsaid."

"I understand that," said Pi, catching the shared smile.

"Pi," said Aurie, "you're supposed to be helping."

When her sister looked away, Pi gave Andromeda a little lift of the shoulders along with a sly grin, which brought a little chuckle.

"The city is in danger," said Aurie, glancing suspiciously at Pi.

"The city is *always* in danger," said Andromeda, rolling her eyes.

"The threat is real and immediate," said Aurie. "From the demonic realm. That's why Invictus was gone for so long and why he hasn't been seen in the last two years."

Pi caught the flinch of recognition when her sister said "demonic realm." The Oculus soul fragment woke slightly as well, attuning Pi to the conversation more keenly.

"I don't have anything to do with that," said Andromeda, looking away. "I'm sorry. You'll have to find your answers somewhere else. Besides, after we leave here, we're headed to Canada for a six-week tour. I don't have the time or luxury of hiding from danger, and I love what I do." She inhaled slowly. "And as earnest as your arguments are, I have a lot of trust issues. There's nothing you can say that will make me believe you have my best interests in mind."

"What if I gave you a truth bond?" asked Aurie.

The comment was like a slap across Pi's cheek. She turned on her sister. "No, Aurie, that's too dangerous."

"You would?" asked Andromeda, taken aback, eyes rounded with shock and worry.

"That's how important this is," said Aurie. "I know you think the Mystique is important, but in the larger scheme of things, it's meaningless."

"You really have a way with words, don't you?" asked Andromeda.

"What my very steadfast sister is trying to say," said Pi, "is that if the people that came after us tried to kill us, and they think you're a danger somehow, then why would being in the Mystique protect you from that? Also, I've been wanting to add that I loved your performance. You were the star of the show. I couldn't take my eyes off you."

Andromeda perked up, tilting her head curiously at the last line. "Thank you."

She glanced suspiciously at Aurie. "A truth bond? That's how serious you are?"

"She's annoying that way," said Pi, catching another elbow to the ribs.

Andromeda turned towards the mirror and leaned her head back as she pinched her nose between her forefinger and thumb. "I really wish I was done with all this. I'm happy here. For the first time, I found my people. Don't get me wrong, I love my family, well, most of it, but they're more fucked up than a clown car heading off a cliff. The Mystique is my home. I don't want to lose that."

Pi had only just met Andromeda, but she wanted to pull her into her arms for the longest hug. Tell her everything was going to be okay, even when it wasn't. She knew exactly how that felt. Pi had gone to the Hundred Halls thinking that becoming a great and powerful mage would protect her from the kinds of danger that had killed her parents, only to learn that having that power only invited more peril.

"That's why I'm offering the truth bond," said Aurie.

"Fuck," said Andromeda to the air, shaking her head. "I suppose it won't hurt to hear what you have to say, and I plan on asking you some personal questions, so if you don't want me probing your history to see if I can trust you, you'd better retract the offer."

"I have nothing to be ashamed of," said Aurie.

"Well," started Pi, "there was that time you called that old woman Mister. That was pretty embarrassing."

Andromeda chuckled lightly. "Fine. Let's do this. I have to get to the buses in an hour."

"Wait," said Pi, "you have to promise to release it after you've had a chance to confirm what my sister has to say."

The pause was filled with a slow smile forming on Andromeda's lips. "Sure, I promise."

Pi took a step back as her sister approached Andromeda, who had stayed seated in the chair. They clasped hands and Pi was a little regretful that it wasn't her doing the truth bond. The spell was common knowledge in the Halls, one of those charms that people discussed over late-night drinks or at the coffee shop. Who would you be willing to give a truth bond? Could you tell the truth, no matter the question, when your life was on the line?

"Bind my heart and hope not to die," said Aurie as a light tingle of spent magic filled the air, "I offer my life if I chance to lie."

A flash of bluish light formed around their clasped hands. When they released, Aurie said, "It is done. Ask your questions."

Andromeda opened her mouth at the same time the phone on the desk rattled to life, followed by a barking dog noise that sounded recorded rather than downloaded. She held up a finger.

"Sorry. It's the troupe manager. I have to take this."

The short phone call was punctuated with Andromeda saying, "Yes" and "I understand," eyelids fluttering with annoyance, before she clicked the phone off. Her squeezed expression and apologetic cast told Pi what was going to be said, even before she heard it.

"I am terribly, terribly sorry. But I have to step out. The troupe manager says I have an important visitor to meet. It'll only take a few minutes and then I'll come right back."

"You can't leave with that spell still connecting you," said Pi, holding out her hand as Andromeda rose to her feet and tossed the phone on the desk. "Make the visitor wait."

"I have to go. The visitor is a big backer of the company. Touring doesn't cover all costs. It requires a lot of donations." She inhaled. "I can end the spell and we can reform it when I get back if you want."

"No," said Aurie, looking tired. "I trust you, and making the truth bond takes a lot out of a person. I'd like to get it over with and take a nap."

"I'm sorry," said Andromeda as she stepped around Pi's outstretched hand. "I'll be quick."

The door closed behind her, leaving Pi alone in the room with her sister.

"You shouldn't have made the truth bond," said Pi. "It's too dangerous."

"I did what had to be done," said Aurie. "Besides, it would take too long for you to ask her out and then try to get the information that way."

"Was I that obvious?"

Aurie tilted her head. "I'm just glad to see you thinking about dating again."

"Not that it matters. It looks like she has a French girlfriend," said Pi as she fussed with her short spiked hair.

Aurie checked her watch. "Hopefully it's not too long." Her eyes widened as she looked at a poster of Andromeda's show personality on the wall. "Oh! Bedlam and beldam. I should have gotten that earlier."

"Not like you to take so long," said Pi.

Aurie climbed into the chair in front of the lighted mirrors and checked the bags under her eyes by pulling down with her forefinger.

"Someday I'd like to get some rest. No more running around, spend some time figuring out who I am anymore," said Aurie.

The moment of self-doubt from her sister brought a host of questions to Pi's lips, but they never made it out as the ground rumbled as if there'd been an explosion somewhere in the arena. A distant scream followed. She met her sister's worried gaze.

"Oh no."

Eight

The truth bond was like having a cold hand wrap around her heart, threatening to squeeze with all its might and crush the life from her chest. It'd made sense to offer it. Aurie was certain that was the only way forward.

Until the explosion.

Aurie raced out of the dressing room on her sister's heels. Black-clothed men and women with lanyards around their necks raced in every direction as if an ant farm had been upended. People were shouting into radios. A security guard tried to grab Pi's elbow and lead her away from the backstage area, but she merely condensed a ball of icy flame in her palm and he went searching for other maidens to rescue.

"Where the fuck did she go?" asked Pi when they came to a standstill. No one seemed to know what was going on.

The truth bond wasn't meant to be a long-term connection. Nor should it have allowed information to flow back to her, but something on Andromeda's end must have caused a lot of anguish, because Aurie knew exactly where she was.

"They're taking her below." Aurie grabbed a production assistant who had been yelling into a radio. "What's beneath the stage area? Is there a parking garage there?"

The woman looked like she wasn't going to answer, but thought better of it when she glanced up. "Uhm, not a garage, but a loading dock for the equipment. It heads onto Allanon street."

"How do I get there? Quickly."

Another moment of indecision followed by an arm outstretched towards a glowing red exit sign.

"Tell anyone you can that someone's kidnapped Andromeda. They need to close the loading docks, or whatever they can do to stop them."

Pi had burst towards the door before Aurie was moving. They hit the stairs like a stampede, knocking the few people using them out of their way. A sign detoured them into the loading area, where they found two security guards in runed Kevlar armor lying unconscious on the concrete floor, enchanted automatic weapons beside them.

The sounds of squealing tires came from deeper in the loading area along with the smell of burnt hair and, inexplicably, coal smoke. The *rat-a-tat-tat* of gunfire had Aurie ducking, even though it'd come from deeper in the docks.

Her sister was sprinting ahead without an ounce of caution. Normally reckless, and now smitten, Pi was a danger to herself.

Aurie called out as her sister curled around the corner and then threw herself back as the roar of black, superheated smoke came rolling past. Pi cried out, the flesh on her arm blistering from the intensity. Aurie reversed a flame spell and *twisted* it with water, sending out a spray of white mist that sent fat snowflakes spiraling away. The winter blast hit the superheated smoke, driving it back and protecting her sister from further harm.

Eyes hazy from pain, Pi rose to her feet, standing well away from the corner. A woman screamed from around the corner. Aurie chanced a glance to see Andromeda struggling against a broad-shouldered guy with a sleeve of tattoos shoving her into the back of a large van. Her gaze was drawn to the creature standing guard near the white vehicle. Aurie didn't know what to make of it. As big as a lion, covered in feathers that glistened with sharp edges, it had the silvery head of a cobra.

When the creature trained its black eyes on her, Aurie felt her mind go hazy as if she'd had too much to drink. The cobra head reared back and she found herself transfixed by the scintillating scales. Its mouth filled with a swirling black cloud, seething with embers, which hastened towards her in a coal-fired breath.

Aurie found herself yanked backwards, tumbling onto her sister as the wall of heat rushed past, crisping the paint of a blue SUV and melting the plastic light fixtures on the ceiling, sending down a cascade of sparks.

"Owww, fuck, get off me," said Pi as they struggled to regain their feet.

A sliding door slammed shut, followed by the roar of an engine. The white van headed the opposite way. Aurie risked a glance to see the strange cobra-headed creature trotting behind it while a woman wearing a tight-fitting black hood hiding her face ran beside it. They leapt into a second van. Aurie thought to pursue, but a man in the passenger side tossed a small box out the window. It tumbled across the concrete and then exploded into a shimmering field that blocked the passage. He extended his middle finger as they followed the van that had Andromeda.

"Is there another way—"

The words died on her lips when she saw her sister's arm, angry red with welts and boils across the length.

"I think I'm going to be sick," said Pi, leaning over, holding her arm away from her body.

A group of security personnel came rushing around the corner in Kevlar armor, runes across the front glowing from the attunement to danger. A half dozen automatic weapons were trained on them.

"Hands up! On your knees!" screamed the woman in the lead.

Hearing the urgency and anger in her voice, Aurie threw herself onto the concrete while shouting and nodding her head towards the shimmering barrier. "They took her in a van that way!"

Four guards tackled them. Someone grabbed her arms and curled them behind her back. An eye-watering scream from her sister as they grabbed her burned arm echoed in the underground garage.

"She's hurt!" Aurie screamed, but someone kicked her in the back and shoved her face against the cold concrete.

Pi continued to scream as they wrangled her arms into the bindings. The restraints lasted a single second, then her sister flexed and the two guards flew away, landing on their backs. Pi looked like a caged animal, eyes wide and terror-filled, as a host of automatic weapons were trained on her. The intent to fire was clear in the guards' eyes.

With half her mouth getting smashed into the concrete, Aurie focused her entire being into a single word of mendancy.

"Jammed!"

Two of the guards pulled their triggers. The weapons clicked impotently.

As someone put their hand over Aurie's mouth, the woman who had led the security team into the loading dock screamed at the others.

"Hold your fire! Hold your fire! These aren't the kidnappers."

There was a moment of standoff, then the pressure from the side of her head was released. Aurie was allowed to sit up, though the restraints weren't removed from her wrists.

"You okay?" Aurie asked her sister, who was shivering, but nodded rapidly. In the tussle, her burnt arm had gotten mangled and it was a bloody and black mess. "Can you get my sister some medical help? Whatever creature they had nearly roasted her alive."

The woman in charge of the security team leaned into Aurie's face. "What were you doing down here?"

"Trying to get Andromeda back. They shoved her in a white van and the creature hopped in another." Aurie wanted to scream. "Can you please call for medical attention? She's going into shock over there."

"Five of the security team are lying dead in this loading dock." The woman squinted. "What did you do to their weapons?"

"Can we not do this right now? My sister's hurt and I don't know what happened except we got here just as they were taking Andromeda," said Aurie.

The woman blinked and stood up, talking into a radio. "You said two white vans?" Aurie nodded. "Send out an alert. Be on the lookout for two white vans. One of them has the victim, the other has a powerful supernatural creature."

"They're not going to catch them," said Pi, holding her wounded arm to her chest as her teeth chattered. "Those were all academy trained mages. They probably have obfuscation enchantments, or have transformed the vans into something else already."

"I know." Aurie swallowed as she saw how bloodshot and hazy her sister's eyes were. She was barely staying conscious. The pain had to be horrific.

A short time later, an older gentleman in a white coat that had the swirling galaxy badge of the Mystique on the front appeared with a bag. He immediately started tending Pi, giving her an elixir for the pain and then muttering incantations over her arm as he gestured. When Pi slumped against the wall, unconscious, he said to Aurie, "She'll need better medical attention at Golden Willow, but I made sure that she wasn't in pain anymore and that the wound won't get infected." He glanced back. "I honestly can't believe she was conscious when I arrived. Those were third-degree burns. She should have been screaming."

The restraints were eventually removed from Aurie's wrists, but only after another round of questioning from the head of the security team. An emergency vehicle was brought round for Pi, and together they rode to the hospital, where they spent a long and uncomfortable night.

Aurie sat in a chair, watching her sister sleep, asking herself a million questions, none of which she could answer. The worst part wasn't even her sister's injuries, or the rough treatment they'd endured at the hands of the security team. It was that she'd given Andromeda a truth bond, and now she was in the hands of people who had probably been working with Beckett Dreadmarsh. If they found that enchantment on her, or if Andromeda disclosed it, then there were a lot of awful ways they could manipulate it to hurt Aurie.

Nine

The healing flesh beneath the hardened case around her forearm itched as if she'd run it through a field of nettles. Pi banged on the black casing, flexing her hand to relieve the pressure. The flesh injured by the strange creature they'd encountered beneath the Glitterdome had resisted normal methods of healing.

"Is there a coat hanger in this place? If I don't scratch my arm soon, I'm going to start killing people," she said to Aurie, who was near the open refrigerator.

After two days at Golden Willow, they'd returned to Invictus' living space. Technically, there were areas where they ate and slept when they weren't traveling around the various realms, but it never felt like home to Pi. Especially when they were living with the most ill-mannered roommate in all of creation.

"You okay up there? Normally that kind of outburst gets a motherly response from you," said Pi as she struggled to eat a bowl of yogurt and granola with her off-hand.

"Huh? Oh, yeah, sorry," said Aurie, frowning and closing the refrigerator that she'd been standing in front of for the last three minutes.

"The bond?"

"Yeah," said Aurie, "it's like the Sword of Damocles above my head. I keep waiting for it to fall. If they figure out that I linked myself to her, there's nothing I can do."

"We'll find her," said Pi.

Her sister looked up, more pained and worried than she'd ever seen her. "Thanks for not saying 'I told you so.'"

"I still might," said Pi with a mouth full of yogurt, "but for now, let's concentrate on getting her back. Any chance we can trace her with the bond? You said you felt her in the loading dock." A wave of itching rose up from her arm. Pi slammed the case onto the marble counter repeatedly until it lessened in severeness.

"What in the thirteen hells is going on?" asked Invictus as he marched into the kitchen with a serrated knife in one hand and blood dripping from his forearm. "I'm in the middle of an important ritual. I can't have distractions."

Pi held up her encased arm. "Have any anti-itch cream around here? The only thing I found in the hall closet was a mummified rat-thing and a jar of petrified eyeballs."

Invictus started to answer, until he realized she was messing with him. He growled under his breath. "Pythia Silverthorne, you are a pest beyond all pests."

"And you're a cantankerous old know-it-all that has had us running around like hydras with our heads cut off." Pi threw the spoon in the bowl. "We need help. The two of us can't keep up with everything you want us to do. And now with the truth bond, Aurie's compromised. We need help. Can you at least bring Sam back from wherever he's been? Or let us bring in more members for your so-called Order?"

Invictus glanced at the bleeding wound on his arm. He grunted, and the cut closed of its own volition.

"She shouldn't have offered the truth bond. That's a dangerous magic that can't be bandied about lightly. The two of you are all the help I need. Speaking of which, I have an errand for you both. Something that needs to be accomplished with due haste."

"Yes, we might be all the help *you* need," said Pi, "but *we* need the help. Neither of us have had a chance to catch our breath in two years. Sometimes I forget when I've had a bath or shower or a good night's sleep."

"You shouldn't have become mages if you didn't want a challenge," said Invictus, waving his ritual knife around. "I don't want more members in the Order. It would be too difficult to vet them during this critical time. Trust me when I say that we do not need them either, or to be running around chasing lost circus performers. The Charmer girl is of no concern. She has no bearing on the greater issues."

"No bearing?" exclaimed Pi. "The asshole who tried to kill us thought she was important. And so did those people that kidnapped her! Aurie's in danger because of that bond. We have to find and rescue her. Not only for the sake of my sister's life, but Andromeda's clearly a key to this whole thing."

"I seriously doubt it," Invictus said dismissively. "Like I said, a circus performer, a bone-witch. Talented, sure, but ultimately useless to our cause. Let them have her. They've made a terrible mistake."

At the rear of the counter, Aurie cautioned Pi, but the white-hot rage that she'd wanted to unleash on the kidnappers came out in its own fiery breath of words.

"You mean old goat. You don't care a lick about anyone. Not even us, who you say you're related to. But I guess it's just like you did with our parents, used them up and then let them die while you were playing your little games. This is serious."

Invictus had been standing in the entryway of the kitchen holding his serrated knife and talking with them as if they were having a Sunday morning conversation. But when Pi finished barking at him, he seemed to double in size, towering above her in both height and fury. If the casual way he'd fixed the slice in his arm wasn't proof enough of his power, the way the entire kitchen shook when he yelled left Pi regretting her words.

"You ungrateful, arrogant mouthy peasant. Yes, I called you a peasant. You think because the two of you have survived so many trials in your short time alive, half of which were created by your own hubris, rushing from one make-believe problem to the next, that you understand how things work. You don't yet understand this world, this realm, or even an inkling of any of the others. You know nothing, Pythia Silverthorne. You are an ant trying to understand the mechanics of portal translocation. And while I would like to teach you, for one, time is of the essence, and for two, you'd never shut your cursed mouth long enough for me to explain!"

The reprimand left Pi numb. The will to bark back had been sucked dry, and even the itching on her arm had disappeared. Invictus seemed to sense her reduction and reduced his tenor, speaking softer on his follow-up.

"I know the two of you are quite exhausted. I understand your pain, but I must ask you to trust me. I need your services once again. As soon as you are capable of leaving."

"What do you need?" asked Aurie.

"There is a realm called Montanhas. Five years ago it was overrun by demons when the Lifestone company delved too deep and shattered the barrier between the realms." Invictus frowned, which was like saying a catastrophic earthquake was only the ground shaking. Pi understood his reluctance as he continued speaking. "The Charmer family bought Lifestone right before the Montanhas plant's unfortunate end. Your performer friend had no part in it. Nor is this coincidence consequential."

"You can't seriously expect us not to make those links? Was there something that happened in Montanhas that made them suspect Andromeda?" asked Pi.

His weighty gaze fell upon her and the urge to speak was squashed.

"A coincidence. Leave it," said Invictus, his tone making her bristle.

"I'm not a dog," she muttered quietly.

"No, but you're impulsive and prone to act without thinking. Might I remind you that you summoned a dangerous demon before you'd even joined the Halls because you were manipulated by Professor Trebleton, and only escaped with your life because of your sister's intervention."

Pi hung her head as the itching returned beneath her casing. She drummed her fingers on the hard plastic.

Invictus sighed and spoke in a calmer voice. "Pythia Silverthorne. I cannot do this without you. I know you don't understand my methods, but I assure you that I am doing what I can to stop this invasion. Please respect my experience on this matter. We don't need anyone else, we don't need to find Andromeda Charmer, and we need to scout Montanhas to understand how the barrier collapsed."

The ancient mage reached out and touched her arm. The maddening desire to scrub her healing flesh with sandpaper evaporated.

"What about the bond?" asked Aurie. "Is there any way to get rid of it without Andromeda's consent?"

"Not that I'm aware of," said Invictus, "which is the point of a truth bond. If there's a way, Priyanka would know, but even then, I have my strong doubts. I'll leave my instructions in the portal room along with the coordinates for the Helm." He turned away, but leaned back for one last comment. "I'll brew up an elixir for the itching."

Pi faced her sister after Invictus left. Aurie touched her ear and tilted her head, then after a nod, created a bubble of privacy around them. It looked like a shimmering dome had appeared above the kitchen counter.

"We're not going to Montanhas, are we?" asked Aurie.

"You heard him. Priyanka might know how to get rid of the bond. We should find her first and then we can head to Montanhas."

"First off, we don't know where Priyanka is. As the head of the Assassin's guild, she could be anywhere. Second, Invictus said Montanhas was important. We should listen to him."

"My dear sister, aren't you at all interested in seeing Zayn again? You know that he'll be with Priyanka."

"I am," said Aurie, grimacing, "but not to defy Invictus for no reason."

"I have a reason. More than one, in fact. I hadn't told you, but when I was doing the barrier spell, I had a vision. It felt like a memory left over from when Invictus was stuck in stasis there. It was of the old goat talking with the demons beyond the barrier. It was as real as anything I've experienced."

"But he never talked to them. Said he was chased down from the moment he stepped into that place," said Aurie skeptically.

"That's the story he told us, but what if he's been keeping things from us? It's not like he's been forthcoming about anything. He keeps sending us from one mission to the next without giving us the larger context, just saying *trust me*," she said, with the last two words in finger air quotes.

"What are you trying to say? That he's not really on our side? That's a little far-fetched and conspiracy laden, even for you."

"I'm not saying that. I'm just saying that he's older than the trees in the city, or in most cities. He has the tact of a sledgehammer, the arrogance of a young mage, and keeps things so close to the vest that he should get them tattooed on his skin. He's said himself many times that his foray into the demonic realm was a mistake. He's not perfect, and I know, I know, neither are we. I'm not saying we disobey him, but that we make a short detour to find out if the truth bond can be removed, and then head to Montanhas." She raised her encased arm. "I'm not fully healed anyway. The last thing I want to do is get into a scrap and not be able to fight."

Aurie put her fingertips against her temples and started massaging them. "I don't know, Pi. Why do you get me into these situations? This sounds like a mistake."

"Come on, sis. Think about it. Zayn. More healing. Removing the sword from your neck. It's a win-win-win. There's practically no downside."

"Even if I said yes, which I haven't yet, you don't even know where Zayn, I mean Priyanka, is at," said Aurie, her cheeks growing rosy with embarrassment.

"How about this. You go study the information Old Iron Balls left us about Montanhas. Prepare us for the journey. If I can't find out where Priyanka"—Pi winked—"is at by the time we're ready to leave, then we'll go to Montanhas as requested. But if I do find the answer, and it's in a place we can reach and return from quickly, then we're going. Think how much easier it will be to get his work done without the truth bond on your soul."

"This is why I keep finding gray hairs," said Aurie. "Fine. I'll agree. But you'd better be back here by midnight. Any later, even if you have her location, and we're sticking to Montanhas."

"Great," said Pi, jumping to her feet. "I'll be back long before midnight."

The realization of where she was headed slowly dawned on Aurie. "Wait. No more deals. It took you five years to work off your last one!"

Pi smirked as she left the kitchen. Her sister, outstanding citizen of the city, had a friendship with the owner of the *Herald of the Halls*. A great place to find information about the reputable denizens of their fair town. But not everything important that happened was in the light.

The Academy of the Subtle Arts, or Assassin's Guild as it was commonly called, had tasked itself with protecting the city from the dangers of the other realms (minus the demonic one). But most other places weren't as civilized as their world with legal protections and a general code of conduct expected of its citizens. Criminal elements, or at least rampant corruption, ruled many of the other realms, which meant to understand the threats one had to be deep within their circles.

To find out where Priyanka Sai was located, Pi would have to visit an old friend. A purveyor of information and fixer of unusual problems. But these favors didn't come cheap, as she knew quite well. During her time in the Hundred Halls, Pi had worked for this gentleman. He was mercurial and secretive, a former war criminal from his realm, and as sour as rancid milk laced with arsenic. On more than one occasion, the tasks he'd set her upon had nearly cost her life.

Pi couldn't wait to see him again.

Interlude One

Running the vacuum made hearing the music playing on her headphones difficult, but Laila sang along at the top of her lungs.

"...just pretending until I've ascended..."

She wanted to cut corners and forget the back room since she had three more jobs to complete before the day was over, but the owner of the third-ward flat had complained about dust bunnies under the couch last time she'd been there. Under the couch? Who even looked there? She'd be afraid to look under the ratty lime green couch she had at home. Probably more leftover cereal and plastic toys than dust bunnies.

Laila eyed the expensive paintings on the wall. One of them was a portrait of an old man from the 1800s in a silk robe. The first time she'd come in she'd thought it was Invictus, but the face was all wrong. Arrogant. Rich, for sure. There were other trappings of wealth and arcana: the cappuccino maker, a shelf of weird jars filled with white powder that looked like salt, a black horn on the wall.

She couldn't remember the owner's name, but could likely guess it if she tried. Lockwood. Kingsley. Charmer. It wasn't one of those, but something similar. Older. Would have been nice to have been born in one of their families.

She finished vacuuming and was able to turn her music down. After dumping the dust bucket, Laila took a drink from the sink, careful not to smudge the stainless steel or she'd get complaints.

She wiped her forehead with the back of her hand. It was cold in the flat, but she'd worked up a good sweat while cleaning. She took a step towards the vacuum, but a stabbing migraine stopped her in her tracks. Laila wavered on her feet, holding her fingertips up to her temple. As the pain receded, a sweet fragrance filled her nostrils until she was choking on the smell.

A clarity filled her mind, followed by a chill down her spine. It reminded her of when she was in high school and she had a sudden overwhelming urge to pull the fire alarm on a late April day. Two things she remembered about the aftermath of that event: Cindy Appleton got caught in the janitorial closet having sex with a teacher, and after she was kicked off the cheerleading squad, Laila took her place. The sweet overwhelming scent had foreshadowed the fire alarm pull, so when it happened again, she waited for the compulsion to follow, knowing that it would result in good things for her.

Laila approached the desk in the little office off the main room. She opened the right-hand drawer, finding a single key on a chain and architectural drawings of an unfamiliar place. There was a large central room with a sunken center and what appeared to be four bars surrounding the space. The rest of the map confused her. It looked like caverns or passages. Must be the Undercity. She folded up the map and the key, placed them in an envelope, and wrote "OR" on the front. She had no idea why she did it, but didn't really care when she knew good tidings were headed her way.

After cleaning up her supplies, Laila left the flat half-finished. Something in her gut told her it wouldn't matter, that whoever lived there wasn't coming back. She threw her gear in the back of her little hatchback and drove to a seedy area in the eighth ward. A bar called the Goblin's Romp thumped with speed metal. The bartender eyed her work clothes while he cleaned the bar top with a rag.

Without saying a word, she tossed the envelope next to his hand. He frowned at it, but when he read the front, his forehead smoothed flat. Laila started to leave, but the big man held up a hand. After a quick visit to the cash register, he handed over a stack of bills. More than she'd made in a day's work. With the money clutched to her chest, Laila left the Goblin's Romp and returned to her hatchback, filled with the warmth of purpose.

Ten

Invictus had once explained to Pi that most of the realms were like stars in a galaxy, spinning inexorably on a relatively flat plane, but shifting in relation to each other based on some multiverse-wide gravity that few understood. The ability to move between them was impacted by these movements and distances. The only exception was the demonic realm. It touched all the others because it was an underrealm, a primitive version that was so awash in faez that it warped everything that lived there, and some speculated the others sprung from it in the distant past.

One of the closest realms was the Eternal City, the home of the maetrie, commonly called the city elves. That realm had been moving closer during the last century, while the more pastoral fey, the Courts of Summer and Winter, had been moving away. The Eternal City was an endless realm where buildings moved and the streets were filled with dangerous critters made of concrete, glass, or smoke. The Courts were criminal gangs rather than monarchies, ruling through deceit and intimidation.

Most maetrie in the city of Invictus kept to the shadows, preferring to do their business with the criminal elements that lived in the Undercity. One of their kind had chosen to open up a jazz bar in the seventh ward for reasons that Pi only partially understood, even after working for him for five years.

A line snaked down the sidewalk leading into the Glass Cabaret. Well-dressed prospective customers fidgeted with their expensive clothes, hoping to be let into the exclusive establishment and experience its otherworldly delights.

Pi had chosen a silvery flapper dress with starburst patterns and a simple headband that matched her short black hair. She strolled past the other customers, ducked under the rope barrier—which elicited many complaints—and threw her arms around the rhino-sized bouncer at the door.

"Dagon!"

"Miss Pythia," said the enormous man. He was exactly as she remembered—shaved head and arms as big as her waist. He picked her up and spun her around like a child. "It's been far too long."

Pi leaned up on her tippy-toes and gave the bouncer a peck on the cheek. "My new boss keeps me as busy as the old one."

Dagon's eyes glistened with memories as his mouth shifted to the side. "I'm very sorry. You never get a break, do you?" His gaze fell upon the hardened plastic case around her forearm. "Are you injured? Do I need to hurt someone for you?"

"I'll take care of 'em eventually. But thanks." She held up the black case. "Nothing a few spells and elixirs won't fix."

He didn't believe her but nodded her inside. The other customers protested, but their voices fell away as she stepped inside the bar, finding her heart welling up with memories. The first time she'd strolled into this place, she'd only been seventeen, a waif of a girl and barely a mage, desperate for the tools she needed to acquire an invite to Coterie of Mages. Nearly seven years later, she felt like that nervous young woman and a hardened veteran of many wars at the same time.

Hearing the music tinkling on the speakers, she had a revelation of why Radoslav had opened a jazz bar rather than a different establishment. The complex chords, deconstructed and often improvised, had a wild, unstructured feel. Jazz was both high civilization and low chaos, a perfect metaphor for the maetrie and their home, the Eternal City.

The tall chalky-gray figure haunted the space behind the bar, wiping down the perfectly clean bar for the thousandth time that day. A couple of older ladies seated at the end were speaking in high voices, almost nonsensical chatter as they played with their drinks like nervous schoolgirls. Radoslav acted like he was listening to them, but his gaze had flitted to her as soon as she'd entered.

Pi wasn't attracted to the owner of the Glass Cabaret. The maetrie were far too aloof, even if they were so attractive it hurt to look at them too long, or without special protection. Almost like an eclipse. Most had high cheekbones and deep-set eyes that were pooled with eternal sadness. Their race had consigned itself to continuous battle, not knowing how to break the cycle and live in relative harmony as humans had. It was one of the few areas where humans were superior to the maetrie, who had more raw power in the tip of their pinky than the average mage. As evidenced by the two women who could barely keep their thoughts straight sitting in his presence.

"You're drunk on his aura," she told the women, nodding towards the two empty seats at a table full of similarly aged women. It was the one thing that had annoyed her when she was in his bar, how the tourists dared themselves to speak to him, knowing they'd turn to babbling idiots the moment they neared.

The women blinked and with slow understanding returned to their table, where they'd be interrogated by their friends about the experience.

Pi wasn't immune to the maetrie aura, though having spent time around him and others of his race, she wasn't as susceptible. It felt akin to walking in a stiff wind. She could make progress, but it took a lot of effort.

"You don't work here anymore," said Radoslav, a tiny twitch at the corner of his lips betraying his emotions.

"Miss me that much?"

"My life was easier after you left," he said. "I should have released you from my service long before Invictus came back."

"Ouch, you really know how to hurt a girl."

Radoslav pulled a dark bottle of a silvery liquid from the top shelf. From behind, he looked quite dashing in his dark gray waistcoat over a patterned shirt and black pants. He was slender and fit as a mountain climber.

The drink was poured into two shot glasses. It looked like mercury.

"To Invictus."

"To Invictus," she repeated, not knowing if he meant the city or the person.

They clinked and threw them back. The liquid was as cold as a winter storm at first, then warmed to a high dry desert, finishing with a sour kick that left her jaw aching. The glasses disappeared beneath the bar faster than her eyes could follow.

"Where's Nells?"

"On her honeymoon."

"Honeymoon? I didn't know you allowed your employees to have personal lives."

She grinned. He didn't. Pi liked to think of their relationship as complicated, but coming back to the bar, she was reminded that he'd had no problem putting her life in danger when it suited his needs. Radoslav was a living accounting book, trying to balance the sins of his past while not allowing anyone else the courtesy. Even when he'd released her debts, it'd only been to protect himself from Invictus, a man even the maetrie feared.

"I need a favor."

"Here I thought you came for the chitchat."

It was the closest thing to a joke she'd ever heard from Radoslav. In shock, she almost forgot what she was going to say. He wasn't the same as when she'd first met him, but she didn't want to delude herself into thinking their relationship was altruistic.

"Priyanka. I need to find her."

"That's an unusual request. You can contact her Hall and they might tell you, or set up an appointment."

"I'm on a tight schedule and would prefer not to let anyone know I'm looking for her."

"You're telling me."

"You're not anyone," said Pi. "Look, I know you can find out. If I'd asked for what the president of Moldova ate for breakfast this morning, you'd probably already have that information in your little book."

"She likes prunes I hear."

"Can you get the information?"

Radoslav blinked. His eyes were as black as the veils of night. He left the bar, heading into his office. He wasn't there long. Barely enough for a phone call. When he returned, he slid a folded piece of paper across the table.

"What'll this cost?"

He held out a fist, then slowly turned it over, revealing a black beetle the size of a coin. The insect reminded her of the scarabs in the Egyptian tomb from her first year. She'd acquired a powerful curse from one that had required an ancient artifact to fix.

"Keep this with you at all times."

She inhaled slowly. Volunteering to carry a beetle, even if it wouldn't give her a curse, made her hesitate. This wasn't the kind of favor she was imagining, but there was no negotiating. Take it or leave it. That was how he operated.

"What does it do?"

"It won't hurt you, or compromise what you and your new boss are working on. Nor will it spy on you." He kept his palm out. The little insect cooled its yellowish-brown hind wings.

"Wonderful."

She held out her hand, bumping her fingertips against his, which brought his eyes up. It took every effort not to flinch. She wanted to show him that she was a force to be reckoned with, not the young woman who'd come into his bar so many years ago. The beetle strolled across the bridge of hands. Its tiny legs marched up her forearm, crawling under the sleeve of her dress. She felt it move across her shoulder and settle against a spot near her heart, then she could feel its presence no longer. She held her hand above the fabric of her silver dress near the beetle's last location.

"Going to be quite a surprise if I bring a date back to my room for a little horizontal fun."

Radoslav stared back ambivalently. "The beetle will stay camouflaged until the appropriate time. Do not worry. You cannot hurt it."

Pi risked a peek down the neck of her dress to see the soft swell of her chest, no glistening black beetle in sight.

"Not creepy at all." She met his gaze. "Thanks, Raddie."

The nickname brought a creasing of the eyes as he reached into an interior pocket, producing a gemstone the size of a marble. The opaque stone had swirls of gold, crimson, jade, and black.

"You'll need this to get where you need to go."

She accepted the item. It was cold to the touch and made her stomach twist because she knew where it'd come from. The Eternal City. Pi knew there was a good chance that Priyanka was there, which explained how quickly Radoslav was able to find the information.

"What is it?"

"A vyklyk. You'll need it at the appropriate time," he said sourly.

The beetle against her heart brought back memories of her previous visit to the Eternal City when she was used in an assassination attempt against Lady Kikala, the queen of the Jade Court.

"Wait a second," she said. "I'm not another Trojan horse, am I?"

"You wanted to find Priyanka. Quickly. This is the method by which it might happen if you are clever."

"You're making me regret coming here."

"You knew what you were asking," he said.

She had no further comment because he was right. Radoslav traded in favors. The kinds of people that came to him were either unsavory, compromised, or desperate. Sometimes all three.

"Try not to die," he said.

There was nothing she could say that seemed appropriate, so she lifted the folded paper as a sign of thanks and left the Glass Cabaret, knowing Radoslav's eyes would be upon her. Dagon was busy with an annoying bachelorette party that was demanding entry, so she didn't have to say goodbye.

Leaving Radoslav's bar brought a mix of emotions. Part of her missed working for him. His sigil could get her into a lot of places that she wasn't welcome now, and despite never truly knowing his motives, she had a pretty good idea that he cared about her in his own strange, maetrie way. Radoslav was her adopted father, she realized. She wondered if he saw their relationship in the same way. And if he did, what did that make her, given his role as the Black Butcher? On the other hand, he'd sent her into the Eternal City with an agenda she wasn't completely aware of, nor was sure she wanted to participate in. Conflict and deceit were like breathing air to the city elves. Maybe she was right that Radoslav saw her as a pseudo daughter, but that didn't mean he wouldn't use her to get his way.

Away from the long lines and honking cars, Pi flipped the paper open. A symbol had been meticulously drawn in neat lines, which made her want to immediately crumple it up in disgust.

Eleven

Aurie had finished packing their equipment for the journey when her sister came storming into the portal room with a piece of half-crumpled paper in her fist. The silvery starburst flapper dress and headband looked quite fashionable on her sister, but also completely out of place in Invictus' quarters.

A good part of her had hoped that her sister would fail in her quest to find Priyanka's location. Better not to antagonize Invictus, whose temper was prone to fits, especially as he worked endless sleepless nights on projects that he kept to himself. But the unresolved truth bond was like a cold hand around her heart. She could never quite rest.

"Read it," said Pi, shaking the paper as she squeezed her lips white.

"There's nothing to read," said Aurie, turning over the paper, "just a drawing of a diamond. I don't understand."

"The Diamond Court," said Pi.

"Oh," said Aurie, understanding her sister's apprehension. "We don't have to go, or did you make a deal with Radoslav?"

"The deal stands whether or not we use his information," said Pi.

The Eternal City. Her sister's stories from her brief trip in her second year combined with the few things that Zayn had let slip during their time together did not tickle her desire to visit the home of the maetrie.

"Why couldn't Priyanka be on Bora Bora or someplace a little more inviting? I don't know, the center of the Earth, or something." She leaned on her fingertips. "We don't have to do this. Maybe they won't find the truth bond on Andromeda."

Pi turned her head towards the entrance to the portal room and raised an eyebrow.

"Don't worry, he went through the portal an hour ago on some errand that he didn't want to explain. The coordinates are unfamiliar. He could be anywhere."

"We need Priyanka and we need Andromeda, despite what Old Iron Balls says."

"Is it really worth going into the Eternal City? Even after everything we've been through, I don't feel comfortable on a trip like that, especially to the Diamond Court. Well, any of the courts. We don't know their rules or where Priyanka might be. We don't even know if we'd be allowed to come back."

Pi touched a spot above her heart. A strange, muted smile formed on her lips. Her relationship with the maetrie bar owner had always mystified Aurie. He was a dangerous criminal. But her sister was always looking for new father figures.

"I'm willing to take the risk," said Pi. "Come on. We've access to some of Invictus' toys, and we've survived worse."

"What did Radoslav ask you to do? Is that why you want to go? Or have to go?"

Pi lifted a single shoulder. "His request was a bit cryptic, even for him. I'd tell you but it wouldn't help. I want to go because I think it's important. I have a good feeling about it."

"Like you did when you summoned a major demon and almost brought ruin upon the city?"

"Aurie. We should grab our things and go before he returns."

Aurie knew her sister wasn't telling the whole truth about her meeting with Radoslav and the request, but interrogating her wouldn't reveal it. She sighed. The cold fist around her heart gave a light squeeze. It could have been her imagination, or the connection between her and Andromeda. Either way, it was a reminder that her life was not in her own hands anymore.

"Okay," said Aurie, "we'll go, but only because it provides an opportunity to track down Andromeda. As much as I hate to agree with you, I think you're right about her importance. Invictus is still stuck in his old thinking, the thought patterns that got him trapped in stasis for seventeen years with a hundred blades through his body."

Pi drummed her hands on the table as her face lit up. "I'll get changed and grab a few things."

"I'll find the coordinates, assuming there are some," said Aurie, shaking her head and already regretting the choice.

The Tome of Planes wasn't an artifact like the Helmsman of the Planes, but without it, the portal maker was as useless as a mage from Gamemaker's Hall. Aurie paged through the thick book. The outer bindings were made of brass and the thick sheets between them something that definitely wasn't paper.

In the ledger for the Eternal City, there were only a half dozen entries. Sometimes, Invictus had left notes that explained the exact details of the landing location, including dangers that might be lurking near. There were two problems with these notes in regards to the maetrie realm. The first was that Invictus himself hadn't been using the portal device for most of the last two decades. Since he'd been back, he'd taken few trips and had never updated the tome. Secondly, the Eternal City changed more than an Assassins' mage transformed their face. The place moved and shifted like a piece of dough being stretched and elongated. The coordinates listed next to the notation of the Golden Ossuary, which was Lady Zaire's place, the home of the Diamond Court, could place them in a completely different place than originally intended. This portal jump would be more fraught with danger than anything they'd done before.

Aurie set the coordinates into the Helmsman of the Planes and went to gather her things, changing into something more appropriate for the Eternal City and the Diamond Court. When she returned to the portal room, Pi was waiting for her. She wore a crimson-and-gold chest plate made of overlapping metal scales and padded cloth. A lion was stamped into the front. The armor fit surprisingly well and with her sister's black ensemble beneath, she looked like an ancient warrior come back to life.

"Where did you get that?" asked Aurie.

"It was on a statue in one of the back areas. I've been eyeing it for a while, thought it might be appropriate. It has some interesting enchantments on it."

Aurie fit the return bracelet on her wrist. The item would allow a return trip to the portal realm when they were finished.

"Ready?"

"No," said Pi with a heavy exhale, "but let's go anyway."

A thrown lever brought a hum into the chamber. The regular portals that the patrons used to move around the city were made from obsidian, and except for a few exceptions, only allowed travel from one specific location to another. The Helmsman could open a portal to almost any point in the realms, though there were no guarantees of safety.

The flat stone wall beneath the archway turned to a hazy gray, then silver run through with lines, which eventually formed into gritty streets with a city landscape in the background. A few bits of trash swirled near a stone wall, but otherwise, there was no sign of anything living or dead beyond the portal.

"This doesn't look like Invictus' notes, but it doesn't look terrible either," said Pi, tilting her head as she stared through the archway.

"Do we know where we're going?"

"No, but that's not a problem in the Eternal City."

They clasped hands and walked through. Contact wasn't necessary for traversing the realms, but if something went wrong during the transition, they didn't want to lose each other. A tingle traveled over Aurie's body as if she'd been dipped in mint, but without the vertigo of the stationary obsidian portals.

The archway leading into Invictus' quarters remained for two heartbeats after they stepped through and then winked out of existence, leaving them in the middle of the Eternal City. The smell of industry was pervasive. An oily puddle reflected the muted gray skies, and the buildings and streets looked like they'd been sucked dry of color. Aurie shivered even though she wasn't cold.

"Where to?"

Her sister shrugged and started walking forward.

"Try to think about finding Priyanka."

"And that's supposed to help?"

"There are no directions in the Eternal City. You get from one place to another through intention. I'm surprised Zayn didn't tell you that."

"We didn't spend a lot of our time talking about that," said Aurie.

The truth was both of them were deep in their own problems and the few times they got to spend together, using their mouths for speaking really hadn't come up. Aurie hadn't thought much about seeing Zayn, as there was no guarantee he was with Priyanka, but her cheeks and midsection warmed at the thought of reunion.

For someone who was a member of the Academy of the Subtle Arts, a trained assassin and skilled practitioner of magic, Zayn had a kind heart and kinder eyes. His rich brown skin was cool with jewel undertones as if he was blushing constantly. But she reminded herself that as strong as their attraction had been, she knew little about him, except that he performed an important role for Priyanka and had become her assistant in the ways of her Hall.

At first the Eternal City made Aurie miss the bright colors of her world, but as her eyes adjusted, she realized its colors were more subtle, like looking at the oil glistening in a puddle and seeing the kaleidoscope of colors swirling like faraway galaxies. In the distance, neon signs with strange pictographs buzzed their message into the world. A few times, dark things moved high in the sky, but never came lower for a look even though she knew they'd been spotted.

About fifteen minutes after they walked through the portal, Pi clucked her tongue and nodded behind them. The message was clear: they were being followed.

Aurie risked a glance backwards to see a group of bulky humanoids with powerful bodies, olive green skin, and ridged foreheads. They wore dark clothing smudged with grease and dirt and marched with the intent of violence. Dolgants. The worker class of the Eternal City.

"We should deal with this," she told her sister.

They faced off as the five dolgants approached, talking amongst themselves in a language that sounded like growling dogs. Two of them wore what looked like brass knuckles dipped in broken glass.

Before they could close the distance, Aurie said, "Watch your step, your shoes are coated with industrial-grade grease."

The mendancy, liar magic, made the dolgants bristle, raising fists and weapons as a threat, as the spell took hold of their footwear. A lunge from the lead dolgant ended ungracefully as his foot went out from under, spilling him onto his back and nearly toppling the one next to him. Further movements were hampered by the slick shoes, but if the hulking creatures grabbed ahold, then a little wobbling wouldn't keep them from getting their heads smashed in.

A dolgant with a truncheon took mincing, comical steps forward, raising his weapon high.

Pi countered his approach with a force blast that knocked them over like bowling pins. The five dolgants interfered with each other as they struggled to regain their feet.

"Aren't you worried we'll attract attention?" asked Aurie, who had used the minimum faez she thought necessary for the mendancy.

"I'm counting on it."

They continued their stroll, finding the dolgants had lost interest in assaulting them. Shortly after, the character of the streets changed from run-down noir to gangster chic. Neon signs, which were distant before, dotted the street they'd entered. There were more dolgants as well as gray-skinned maetrie milling about like disaffected teenagers.

Aurie's experience with the maetrie was mostly limited to the owner of the Glass Cabaret. She'd thought them all slender and elegant, but with a persuasive darkness that haunted their souls. The city elves on the street looked like common criminals: faces marred with scars, the ambivalent gazes turned mean. A body that looked like a maetrie lay prone near an alleyway, glittering bugs that looked like broken glass crawling over his flesh, while other maetrie played games only a few feet away.

At first Aurie thought the sudden reaction that rippled down the street was meant for them, but as the maetrie disappeared into the buildings or faded deeper into the alleyways, she realized they were afraid of someone or something approaching from the opposite direction.

"We should get off the street," said Aurie, but her sister was already moving towards the alley where the dead body lay. She stepped over the corpse, noting the little glass bugs taking tiny bites out of the gray-skinned maetrie's body.

She heard the hoofbeats first. They sounded like a hammer driving a nail into someone's palm, and her heart reacted appropriately. Aurie was going to slide deeper into the alleyway, but Pi grabbed her upper arm.

"I want to see who this is. We might not be far."

"Far from where?"

"I don't know, that's why I want to see," said Pi.

Aurie trusted her sister's judgement normally, but her experience with the maetrie was limited. When a carriage turned onto the street, Aurie didn't know what she was looking at. The carriage looked like an ebony skull, and it moved on its own without horses or other draft animals—that she could see, anyway—pulling it. As it grew closer, she saw a black cloud hovering around the yoke and sensed hunger in it.

The carriage slowed as it passed their location. They hadn't bothered to hide. Dark green curtains in the skull's eyes rustled slightly, but never opened. The vehicle returned to its previous pace, leaving them behind.

"What was that?"

"Dunno, but I'm pretty sure we're headed the right direction," said Pi.

The skyscrapers that had been in the distance seemed much closer after the carriage had passed, as if the streets had adjusted themselves for its passenger, and they were getting to follow in the wake.

A few blocks later, a knot of maetrie near a glowing neon sign brought Aurie's heart rate up. Unlike the last area, these maetrie reacted to their appearance immediately. Whatever had been going on a moment before wasn't as important as their arrival.

"Oh, balls," said Pi, "I guess we're not avoiding a fight."

It looked that way to Aurie too. The maetrie were pulling up their sleeves and producing weapons in their fists. As they approached, their collective auras hit her like a wave of disorientation. One maetrie didn't bother her, but a dozen was overwhelming.

"You okay?" asked Pi, forehead hunched with concern.

"I'll be fine." She paused. "But you do the talking."

The maetrie surrounded them, violence in their eyes.

"We're headed to the Golden Ossuary," said Pi, turning slowly in a circle. Aurie was having trouble concentrating. Being around so many of them was like sucking up a big hit of nitrous at the dentist. Her head throbbed and the world was distant. Vision narrowed.

A few of them spoke, but Aurie didn't understand a word. Pi repeated her comment, eliciting no more reaction than if she'd told them their grocery list.

"I think we're going to have to fight," Pi said under her breath. "Can you manage?"

"I will."

Aurie prepared to use her true name to knock a path through the circle. But the maetrie aura was making it hard to think. She'd mustered the will to act when Pi touched her shoulder. The maetrie were no longer focused on them. Aurie expected to see another carriage, but instead a group of riders sauntered down the street.

Pi leaned over and shoved the vyklyk into her hand, which seemed to dispel the lingering effects that the maetrie aura had on her. Aurie was able to concentrate on the approaching group.

The maetrie riding the mounts seemed like performers of some kind. They wore little. A few scraps of colorful clothing that covered up their chests and groins. Some wore half-masks, homages to creatures that Aurie didn't have the shared history to understand.

The maetrie weren't the strangest part.

Their horse-like mounts were nothing like the fleshy creatures from her realm. They seemed to have more in common with the glass insects that had been feasting on the dead body a ways back. They looked like stained glass windows that had been ground up and reformed into a horse shape. Not all their surface was angled and sharp—a few places were bulbous and round, glowing with an inner light as if they carried lava lamps in their bellies. Aurie could imagine them haunting misty swamps, their glows looking like forgotten apparitions at a distance.

The maetrie that rode the beasts sat on dark mats, which seemed sensible, because Aurie was certain if she tried to pet one, she'd come away with a bloody hand from the shards of glass. There were six mounts and about a dozen of the strangely attired maetrie. The ones that had surrounded them stepped back and the flood of headiness receded, leaving Aurie in control of her thoughts again. The passing maetrie glanced their way, but otherwise kept moving, except for a smallish rider with a mask that trailed shadowy fog behind, who approached in an arrogant saunter.

"This isn't a place for mages," said the maetrie sourly.

The others that had surrounded them previously faded back to the buildings.

"We're headed to the Golden Ossuary," said Aurie, finding herself more in control of her thoughts than before.

"Why? No one is there."

Before she could answer, the other riders spoke to the maetrie woman, who responded with a nod. They seemed to accept her answer and continued on without her.

"We have business with the Diamond Court," said Pi.

"You are fools," said the maetrie. "They see humans as playthings. You won't be allowed to leave."

Pi produced the multicolored gemstone, which brought an inbreath of surprise from the rider.

"How did you come by a *vyklyk*?"

"Where is the court if not at the Ossuary?" asked Pi. "Is that where you're headed?"

"The Rasakupol. It is not far. There you will find your court, and many others."

"What is that place?" asked Aurie.

The maetrie flattened her lips. "Go back to your realm. Forget whatever it is you think you're doing. It is not for the likes of you."

"Tell us what it is," said Pi. "So we might be prepared."

"It is not the what that matters, but the why," said the maetrie as she slowly gained speed, forcing them to catch up.

"Why?" asked Aurie.

"Do you know the maetrie word *oxyvain*? No? It means to win by all means necessary. That is what you will find in that cursed place."

"Then why are you going?" asked Aurie, yelling as she was falling behind.

The flat look of disappointment was unmistakable. The rider kicked her mount and sped forward, catching up to the others, who were hazy in the distance. Black smoke trailed behind her mask, and the quick-moving mount sounded like broken glass being ground to sand in a barrel.

"Oxyvain," said her sister as if she were tasting the word. "If you're not cheating, you're not trying."

If they'd been in a normal realm, reaching the end of the block should have brought more worn stone streets as they could see nothing taller than a five-story building for a long ways. But as they reached the spot where they'd last seen the riders and their strange mounts, an enormous building was found blocking their way.

The structure reminded Aurie of the Glitterdome with its dome-like shape, but only if it'd been made of the bones of giants and the rib cages of dragons. Golden light trickled through the gaps in the building as if a hoard of treasure lay within. Further along the curve, carriages deposited well-dressed maetrie to stroll into the building. The vehicles varied in outlandishness, the ebony skull that had passed them earlier serving as the midpoint of strange, with one made of pulsating hearts stretching the willingness to believe, and the ironness of her stomach.

"I guess this is the Rasakupol," said Aurie. "Do you really think we'll find Priyanka?"

"I trust Radoslav, but on the other hand, I don't think we should tell anyone what we're doing. Be as vague as possible," said Pi.

"Shouldn't be a problem since *I* barely know what we're doing," said Aurie.

The entrance where the carriages stopped to let their passengers out looked like the golden throat of a dead dragon. A hulking maetrie the size of a small mountain with golden lines running down the side of his neck stood guard at the entrance. He held out his hand as they approached, bristling with menace, until Pi produced the *vyklyk*.

The long bony throat led them deeper into the structure. Pressure built up in Aurie's ears then popped as the golden light at the end faded, leaving the interior visible as they stepped out.

"Oh, shit," said Pi, "it's a racetrack."

Twelve

The interior of the Rasakupol looked like a cross between a horse racing and motocross track, except the surfaces were made of slick and curved bone. The oval depression at the center of the dome was ringed with seats holding the kinds of maetrie that'd nearly assaulted them, but Pi knew that wasn't where they needed to be.

High above the seats and track, because height meant status no matter the race, there was a platform where the well-dressed maetrie that had been seen getting out of the carriages were headed. Pi found her legs didn't want to move at first. Whatever purpose the beetle over her heart had, it would probably come to fruition up there with the nobility of the courts, and leave her with a new round of complications.

A glance to her sister's upturned face, lips squeezed with apprehension, was the salve she needed to continue. Without Priyanka's help, they were unlikely to be able to free Aurie from the truth bond or track down Andromeda.

"I'm feeling underdressed," said Aurie as a couple of maetrie in glittering gold gowns sauntered up the ramp to the exclusive area.

"I think they're the version of wearing the band T-shirt at the concert," said Pi. "Besides, I like that outfit."

Her sister was wearing a dark brown ensemble with voluminous sleeves and an overlapping front that looked like a martial arts Gi. Aurie tended more towards their mother, with almond-shaped eyes, strong cheekbones, and a prominent nose. She had a regal manner even when she wasn't trying to act condescending, which she could wield like a hammer if necessary, but her arrogance was nothing like the maetrie's.

As they ascended the ramp, the vyklyk stone provided their introduction, and Pi realized that she did not like the maetrie, even though she'd worked for Radoslav for many years. They were a harsh race, keen on endless conflict. Radoslav had been born for that purpose, a matchless warrior who had escaped to the city of sorcery to keep from being used further. And that was all the difference. Choice. He had made his choice, choosing exile over further genocide. It was why Pi trusted Radoslav enough to carry the beetle into the depths of the maetrie world for him.

The others, high-born maetrie who ruled over each other in the Eternal City, they had made their choice too. Pi saw them for that decision.

When they reached the platform, many eyes turned their direction. Pi felt like the country bumpkin who'd mistakenly wandered into Buckingham Palace. She saw members of the three courts: Ruby, Jade, and of course Diamond, since it was their party.

"Pythia Silverthorne," said a maetrie off to her right in a jet-black three-piece suit with a black tie. "Here I was, thinking this event would be a dull affair, and here we have the fucking traitor's mageling in our midst."

When she first saw who was speaking, she had a brief worry that the beetle was meant for him, but remembered Radoslav's feelings for his family.

"Slyvan. I'm surprised they let you show your face here after what happened," said Pi, "but I guess they need something to scare the younglings into behaving."

The last time Pi had seen Slyvan it had been at the Jade Court, after an attempted assassination of Lady Kikala to draw Radoslav back to the maetrie realm. Lady Amethyte, the Ruby Queen, failed in her attempt to eliminate a rival, and former lover, but clearly that kind of intrigue was expected. Pi thought his appearance normal as if this were the Great Houses of the Old Empires of Earth.

Slyvan stood before Aurie in a wide stance, his gaze flitting between them. He was all angles. Cheekbones like daggers, hips narrow as the center of an hourglass. The only thing he was missing in her eyes was a lit cigarette dangling from his lower lip.

"Why'd Raddie send a babysitter with his mageling?"

"I don't work for him."

Aurie shot her a covert glance. She sensed the animosity. Pi made a "hold" gesture.

A light of understanding filled Slyvan's black eyes. "Oh, that's right. Your little headmaster came back, not that it'll do the lot of you any good. You're a doomed race. I'm just sorry ol' Raddie ain't gonna survive much longer."

Drawn by the bait, Aurie spoke before Pi could motion for silence. "Why do you say that? What do you know?"

Slyvan chuckled and left them to speak to a heavyset maetrie wearing a pinstriped suit and a top hat made of black glass that was holding court across the platform. Pi was surprised by Slyvan's comment even though she knew she shouldn't be. If their realm was due to be overrun by a demonic horde, the realm closest would want to know about the danger so they could close any passages between.

"Who was that?" asked Aurie after Slyvan was out of earshot.

"Radoslav's brother."

"Really?"

"Half-brother, I guess."

An attendant circled past, offering a tray of golden drinks, but Pi waved them off. They would have to subsist on the sustenance they'd brought with them. To partake of the maetrie food or drink was to commit to never leaving their realm again.

"Any sign of Priyanka or Zayn?" asked Pi.

"Not a one, and I would think that there would have been mention of other humans if they were here. Are you sure he sent us to the right place?"

"Absolutely," said Pi, even as her gut said otherwise. "We just need to find out where they're hiding."

A bright chime brought everyone's head up. The platform shifted towards the rail, bringing the horde of maetrie and two small humans. The increased chatter suggested bets were being made, or at least speculation about what was about to transpire. At the edge of the race oval, Pi spied six riders perched atop the strange glass beasts they'd seen on the streets. She didn't see the diminutive maetrie who had warned them away.

"Care to wager?" asked a maetrie with slicked-back hair and a pinstriped suit.

He leaned on the railing to her right, penetrating eyes shooting right through her. There was something feral in his gaze, covered by a thin veneer of civility.

"I don't have anything to wager," said Pi.

The corner of his mouth twitched into the semblance of a smile. "The stone in your pocket. The answer to a question. Time in service. All these can be coin."

The way he addressed her, not like a child looking down upon an insect and deciding whether or not to crush it with a rock, but rather like a potential business partner, had Pi intrigued. He wasn't like the other maetrie she'd met. Not that she trusted him anymore.

"Hurry now, the race is about to start."

"I'm outmatched by your knowledge," she said.

"Then we'll start small. The answer to a question. I'm sure you're not here for your health. I promise it won't be too probing, should I win," he said with a sour grin.

Aurie elbowed her in the ribs, the warning not to engage, but he was right. They needed answers, and what better way to start?

"The answer to a question," she said, nodding, "but you have to explain the contest that I'm betting on as part of the deal."

"A deal."

To her surprise, he extended a hand as if they were back in the city of Invictus rather than in the Eternal City. Handshakes were a human custom. He'd been in their realm before, or at least was familiar enough with humans.

"Pi."

"Dominion." He leaned against the railing and she matched him. "Which stelynka do you choose? The horse-like creatures," he added, another confirmation that he'd been in her realm.

Pi eyed the line of riders. Unlike human jockeys, they weren't equally sized. The maetrie on the backs of the stelynka varied as much as the others of their race, which suggested that lightness wasn't the most important feature. The other thing she noticed was the lack of the mats that the rider they'd met in the streets had been riding on. Did that mean they were exposing themselves to the sharp edges of the mount? Her previous observation made less sense, as she would want to be light so she wouldn't get thrown around and injure herself.

"The first race is about to start," said Dominion.

"You choose," she said. "I'll make my selection afterwards."

His black eyes glittered with amusement. "I'll take the rider wearing the Onyx mask."

The rider that Dominion had chosen rested on his stelynka as if it were a bench in a park on a Sunday afternoon. Pi searched the others for one equally relaxed.

"Hurry," he prodded.

"The Sapphire mask," she said, right as the chime rang.

The stelynka with their riders burst from the line, racing up the slope towards a ridge that would require leaping to get over.

"The race," she said, "how far do they go?"

"The first gonka, or brutal race in your language, is the shortest, a single lap," said Dominion, not taking his eyes off the riders. "There are eleven races, the last including all available riders for eleven trips around the oval."

Her next question caught in her throat as the riders approached the bone barrier, which was below her location along the rail. As the stelynka with the Onyx rider leapt, she saw how his chest slapped against the sharp edges of the creature's neck, slicing ribbons of crimson. But he kept moving forward, staying in the lead and pushing his mount towards the next set of obstacles.

The riders behind, including her Sapphire, did not make the leap as smoothly. A rider with a mask that reminded her of the dolgant workers that had tried to assault them landed hard, sliding partially off the mount before climbing back on, arm dripping with blood. The others fared better, but not a single rider escaped the leap without a wound.

"You're beginning to see the challenge of the race," said Dominion. "In the gonka, like maetrie society, pain cannot be avoided. Skill and craft will reduce the amount one endures, but no one escapes without blood dripping down their limbs."

"That's awful," said Aurie, eliciting a smirk from Dominion.

The obstacles grew more difficult as the riders circled the track. The slick bone surface made for treacherous maneuvers, and more than once, riders were thrown hard and had to wrangle the mounts to return to their backs, causing more pain. The track, which Pi guessed was about two miles, brought the riders around for the final stretch, directly opposite their location.

To her surprise, the Sapphire mount was right behind Onyx. The obstacles remaining were a quad set of deep humps. The first rider leapt from the first to land nimbly on the second, rather than traverse the valley between. The maneuver was not without its price, as she could see him grimace as he held on tight to keep from being thrown.

Sapphire made the same leap, catching up with his stelynka's longer stride. By the third hump, they were neck and neck. Pi thought she had a good chance to win. As they both made the final jump, the Onyx rider stuck out his foot and kicked the back end of Sapphire's mount.

Onyx landed awkwardly, due to the unusual maneuver, but recovered quickly for the final length. Sapphire, however, fared much worse. The impact to the stelynka's haunches created a difficult landing. The stelynka hit the final hump off-kilter. The rider could have leapt from its back, saving himself, but he tried to keep his mount on course. The snap of the front leg was like a gunshot. No one except Pi and her sister flinched.

Stelynka and rider tumbled over. The quick, violent rotations ended with the mount atop. In a human race, Pi would have expected a hushed silence to fall upon the crowd, solidarity with the injured. But the maetrie, cruel and capricious as they were, applauded. She wasn't sure if it was the kick or the landing that brought their agreement, but either made Pi sick to her stomach.

Dominion added his applause as the Onyx rider passed the finish line. The other four riders, minus Sapphire, followed him over.

Attendants with the same gold lines streaking down their neck as the bouncer at the front walked to the fallen rider as if they already knew the result. After a brief check, the attendant held his thumb down, which brought rapturous cheering.

"A fortuitous event," said Dominion with an in-breath that sounded like a hiss.

"He's dead?"

"The stelynka too," said Dominion, eyes alight with excitement. "That means there are only eleven competitors." He turned on her. "And you have lost."

Pi wanted to rage at the events that had transpired, but knew that her human emotions would only be ridiculed in the Eternal City. She steeled her reaction.

"Eleven competitors? How do they endure each race? Would they not be ribbons by the end?"

Dominion nodded towards the end of the oval, where the five riders accepted golden chalices and then promptly threw them back.

"That is udovol. It heals the flesh and provides pleasure equal to the pain endured. The more brutal the ride, the higher the ecstasy at the end."

The construction of the event shouldn't have surprised Pi. It was a microcosm of maetrie society.

"I lost," said Pi, facing Dominion. "What's your question?"

He hesitated, which confused her. Dominion glanced to the racetrack, where a couple of hulking maetrie were dragging away the fallen pair with long hooks.

"I cede my victory," said Dominion, who looked like he was trying to smile, but it came out like a grimace. "Out of respect to the fallen. You may ask me questions of your desire. Nothing personal, but I can pull away the veil of your ignorance."

Pi could hear the mocking of her human customs in his voice, but didn't want to give up the opportunity to learn more. She didn't know why he'd decided not to hold her to the bet, but something about the first race had changed it. Her first desire was to ask questions that would lead them to Priyanka, but she didn't want to give away the purpose of their visit.

"Tell me why representatives of the courts gather here, even as they conspire against each other."

Dominion made tsking noises. "Come now, you can do better than that. What is combat without a field of battle? They come here for the game and to ensure their advantages are not ceded in their absence."

"Which court is ascended?"

He creased his eyes. "A difficult calculation as much occurs beneath the surface. Ruby was diminished by its failed attempt on Jade some years ago." His lips curled at the corners, suggesting he knew her role in those events. "While Diamond failed its attempt to infiltrate your city of sorcery, losing its favored son, Prince Aethalstar, in the process. One could say that Jade is rising, but that would be false too. The battle is stagnant, possibly because the combatants have grown too cautious in recent years." His gaze flitted to the bone racetrack, where Sapphire had fallen. "But to overreach is to invite disaster."

"Tell me about the Diamond Court. If Queen Zaire lost her favored son, then who is her favorite now?" asked Pi.

Dominion licked his lips. "Under normal circumstances, Prince Orráine would have taken his brother's place, but he has a soft heart and consorts with outsiders." He nodded towards the section of the platform where the nobility were clustered tightly. A smallish maetrie wearing the regal clothing of the Diamond Court stood alone. "To allow him to ascend the throne would be the end of the court."

"There is another?"

"Princess Ylassa," said Dominion with a sigh. "She is young, not yet a century old, and while she is as cunning as her mother, she is often absent, refusing to participate in the machinations of the court. Do not look for her. She is not here. Some say she is on her Liebereisen, which is a Journey of Discovery."

"You seem quite different than the other maetrie," said Pi. "Have you spent time in our realm? Or are there other humans here that have previously made your acquaintance?"

"To come here would be foolish," he said. "No one else would dare, but I suppose you have the protection of your head patron, though even he has limits."

A warning chime had her looking to the racetrack, where six new riders including the maetrie who had spoken to them in the streets had lined up.

"Care to bet again?" she asked, hoping to learn more.

Dominion clucked his tongue. "Better to leave our conversation on a good note." He inclined his head. "I have business with Duke Charon. May we speak again in the future when it would be profitable to both."

Her companion at the rail headed towards a knot of maetrie, including the heavyset one with the glass top hat. Their affiliations were unknown, but Pi quickly lost interest as the chime sounded for the start of the race.

Aurie tugged on her arm. "We should check out the Diamond Court area. Maybe someone can clue us to where Priyanka is."

"Wait," said Pi, staying her sister's hand, "I want to watch."

"We need to find her." Aurie glanced to the track. "This race is an abomination."

"It is, but if we're going to find them, we need to understand the maetrie better."

Her sister but took her position at the rail right as the riders approached the first obstacle. Pi watched in earnest, her gut tightening as the maetrie with the smoky mask made the leap, a few steps behind the others. Her passage was graceful, but the other riders were pushing their limits, risking pain and being rewarded by gaining distance.

Before this visit, Pi had thought herself an expert on the maetrie. Working for Radoslav had taught her much, but now that she was seeing them in their element, she recognized that there were many facets of behavior she didn't understand. Oxyvain. The rider had warned them. It wasn't a what but a why. The same was true for the maetrie.

Pi checked back to the nobles, who were chatting as if they were at a Sunday brunch, while the riders fought for position in a race that had claimed one of their own already. The riders did not hold back. She saw more kicks when stelynka drew too close. To win by all means necessary. Oxyvain made the capitalism of her world into a child's game. They came here to compete, whether it was on the track or on the platform.

The second race wasn't as exciting as the first, as the lead rider crossed well before the others, and the rider she was rooting for came in last by a good margin. Pi didn't know if she was holding back, since they'd be racing many times this day, or if it was her caution that was to blame.

While the riders drank from their golden chalices, a diminutive maetrie, Prince Orráine, approached. He was everything the other maetrie were not: short, cherub-faced, sickly. Yet, he carried a strength in his gaze that was unlike the others—not a challenge but a sense of self-knowledge.

"We rarely receive visitors in our realm," said Prince Orráine, clasping his hands in front.

"Rarely, but not never?" asked Pi as the beetle made a tiny flutter against her heart. She resisted the urge to put her hand there, fearful that the insect was meant for the prince.

"It's lovely to meet you, Prince Orráine," said Aurie, stepping to her side.

"Your kind words are strange to hear," said Prince Orráine. "Like climbing into an active volcano to find a field of spring flowers."

"You have been to our realm," said Pi.

"I have," he said wistfully. "I enjoyed it. But you should not be here. This is not a place for humans, even the prodigies of Invictus."

"Thank you for your warning," said Aurie.

"How do you like the gonka?" he asked sourly.

"It is unusual and frightening," said Aurie, frowning. "I can't say I like it."

"What is the mask of that rider? The one who came in last?" asked Pi.

Prince Orráine stared down to the track, near the finish line. "That is the Wraithhawk. A fearsome predator that lives in the more uninhabited regions of the Eternal City. They suck the victims dry of energy, leaving them defenseless while they're eaten alive." He shifted his mouth to the side. "A poor choice of mask for that rider, who is too timid for the gonkas."

"The Sapphire was too bold and lost his life," said Pi.

"The riders reap no rewards unless they are victorious," said Prince Orráine. "For the lower classes, the only way to climb out of their station is through violence and pain. If Wraithhawk cannot win a single race, then she will not be allowed to return, and there are always more clamoring to join the gonkas." His gaze was filled with unusual sadness. "Why did you come to the Eternal City?"

Aurie started to speak, but Pi placed her hand on her sister's arm to stop her.

"We have our reasons."

Prince Orráine frowned. Not at them, but for them, she realized.

"Before the gonka is over, you must present yourself to my mother, Queen Zaire. She will wish to interrogate you. Be warned she does not suffer fools and is in a foul mood because she misses her daughter, who has been absent for too long. My mother wonders why you are here and assumes the worst. If you are careful, you might yet still survive this day. The blessings of elevens may yet presage your success."

"Why do you help us?" she asked.

He smiled, a twinkle in his eyes relaying an unspoken history, before he inclined his head and left them for other parties.

"Shall we?" asked Pi.

"I have a strong feeling that Priyanka is not here," said Aurie. "Radoslav sent us here for his own purposes."

The ashy feeling rotted her insides. She didn't muster a disagreement, because she was beginning to worry that her sister was right. If Priyanka or Zayn were present, they would have shown their faces to them, or given a signal. Their appearance at the Diamond Court was much too unusual not to draw notice.

As she headed up the ramp towards the upper platform, Pi's gut tightened further, like a great machine was cinching it until she would bend in half from the tension. In her time in the Halls, she'd met both the other queens, each as different from each other as they were to the one before her. When she'd met Lady Kikala, she'd been nervous but the Jade Queen had been disarming in her conversation. Of course, Pi had attended the Reaping Ceremony as a representative of the Jade Queen's son, which had made their introduction easier. The Ruby Queen,

Lady Amethyte, had been playing an instrument as large as a cavern when they met, wearing simple padded leather armor to protect herself from the concussive sounds emanating from the instrument. She seemed a practical woman, more mobster boss than nobility.

The Diamond Queen bore her regality like the sun. She rested on a bone divan, speaking softly to a pair of ladies sitting with her. Lady Zaire was like a knife unsheathed. She wore a pale gown, edged with golden glitter, that hung on her thin frame. Black hair, wrapped into a braided crown, rested across her brow. Her piercing gaze swept across the crowd of nobles, derision in every glance.

Pi hovered near the divan as the third race finished to the whistles of the crowd. The queen's sharp gaze sliced through Pi's armor before a single word was spoken.

"Don't lurk in the presence of a queen," said Lady Zaire with chin lifted. "I'm already annoyed by the stench of your flesh and now you flit about the edges of my vision like a disoriented faeila."

Pi hurried forward, keeping her head bowed. Words of greeting stuck in her throat, but Aurie filled in the silence.

"Greetings, Queen Zaire, we are—"

"I know who you are," spat the queen. "Meddlers and nuisance-makers. I should send you both to mines where you won't last but a few days and rid the realms of your middling influence, just like I should have done to your master, before he grew in power."

Lady Zaire had a hawkish nose and her chalky gray skin seemed powdered. Pi could see her ribs protruding along her side through the slices in her gown.

"We mean no trouble," said Aurie.

"Yet, trouble you are, stirring up questions on why you are here. The bold Silverthorne sisters gracing the Rasakupol. Maybe we should have you join the gonka, and if you win you get to leave with your lives." Her smile curdled upon itself. "Of course, your weak flesh wouldn't make it past the first rise, and the udovol would burn you alive from the inside." Lady Zaire spoke quietly to a maetrie woman next to her, who then spirited away on an errand. The other maetrie woman to the queen's left stared without remorse. "Why have you chosen to taint my event? Spite? Arrogance? Or are you too stupid to understand why you should not have come here?"

The queen's words left Pi shaken. Having Old Iron Balls dress her down over minor mistakes was nothing compared to Lady Zaire's fiery invectives, which came with the real threat of immediate death.

"We apologize, but—"

Lady Zaire cut Aurie off with an angled swipe of her hand, like a sword strike, slicing the words off in midair.

"I refuse your apology. Tell me why you are here this instant before I call my guards."

The tension on the platform had grown tenfold. The other maetrie watched the races with feigned interest while their true focus was on the queen's visitors. Out of the corner of Pi's eyes, she spotted guards in golden breastplates approaching.

"Invictus extends his invitation to Lady Zaire for a visit to the city of sorcery," said Pi, hating the way her voice wavered as she spoke.

Lady Zaire's expression erupted in revulsion. "Why would I want to subject myself to the disgusting airs of your realm? Would you crawl into a pen with a pig and root around in the mud with them? No. I think not. Invictus would never offer such an invite, which means you are lying about your reasons for being here."

The circle tightened further around them. Both the nobles and the guards came closer. Pi felt the beetle above her heart flutter with interest, which only increased her anxiety. She felt like she'd been shoved on stage and asked to speak her lines, but she didn't know what play it was.

Aurie took a half-step forward. "You might be aware that our realm is under threat from the demonic one."

"A problem of your own making," said Lady Zaire dismissively. "Magic is not a toy, yet your kind wield it like one, using it blindly and without regard to the consequences. It's your own fault that your barrier is breaking down, and I will not lend a single finger to help."

The queen was prepared to continue, but the other maetrie on the divan touched her wrist. They spoke quietly together. The guard nearest the divan stared through her with gold-flecked eyes and a sneer that felt like a slap. Somewhere behind them, a chime sounded, but most of the platform was paying attention to their conversation rather than the race.

Pi glanced to the portal bracelet on her sister's wrist, but they were too far from their point of entry to use it. Until they could leave the Rasakupol and journey back to within a few blocks of where they'd arrived, they were stuck in the maetrie realm.

The queen finished taking her counsel and turned to them. "Lady Sebella suggests that you are here on behalf of one of the other queens, and I should not allow you to be so near my royal personage. The events that transpired at the Reaping Ceremony with Lady Kikala would not have happened without you, Pythia Silverthorne, and your consorting with the Black Butcher is well known. The only thing staying my hand at this point is the vyklyk stone and the promise of elevens from the first gonka. Tell me again, Pythia, why are you here?"

The words that Pi summoned to use were quickly lost as the beetle fluttered against her heart again, making her breath catch in her throat. She glanced surreptitiously at those nearby, seeing Prince Orráine, Dominion, and the other maetrie that had been milling about the platform. The beetle was meant for one of them, but who?

"When a queen asks a question, she expects an answer, not a dumbfounded expression," said Lady Zaire menacingly.

As the beetle dislodged itself from her upper breast, Pi worried she was having a heart attack. She couldn't speak, and slipped to her knees, which caused an uproar amongst the nobility. Pi fell to her side as the beetle slipped from behind the breastplate, eliciting a gasp from the assembled, before it fluttered its hind wings. A rush of fear filled Pi as the horrified gazes of the sharp-eyed maetrie focused on her.

It's happening, was followed by, *Radoslav used me.*

Her worst fears were confirmed when splayed on her back, limbs stiff with pain, Pi watched the glistening black insect rise into the air and shoot towards Prince Orráine.

Thirteen

Aurie didn't know what to do when her sister collapsed onto her side. Had she been poisoned? Had someone shot her with a needle or used another covert method of assassination? She glanced to the guards, but saw their shock and confusion matching the nobility's. The world dialed in around them.

High above, Aurie heard the sound of a chime, but no one was watching the race. The only contest that mattered was the one on the platform, and it would end in death, that much Aurie knew.

When the black beetle crawled from her sister's crimson-and-gold breastplate, the nobles erupted in fervor as if a wasp had entered a crowded limousine. Aurie reached to grab her sister as if she might drag her away in the heat of confusion, when the golden-eyed guard grabbed her upper arm with the strength of a vise.

Lady Zaire rose from the bone divan, shouting for someone to stop the beetle when it unfurled its hind wings and shot towards Prince Orráine as fast as an arrow. Fell energies rose. Aurie sensed the chaos that was about to ensue.

The yellowish wings of the insect beat so fast she couldn't see it. The beetle flew directly at the prince. The diminutive maetrie made no effort to escape.

Then, the beetle veered upward and over Prince Orráine, towards Duke Charon, who gaped open-mouthed at the incoming insect. To the shock and horror of the assembled, the beetle went directly into the duke's orifice, the tiny legs wriggling as they forced their way into his throat.

The top hat tipped off the duke's head and crashed to the ground, exploding into shards of glass as he struggled against the insect that had disappeared into his mouth. His face grew deeper shades of gray, like a storm cloud gathering rain.

There was a moment that Aurie was certain that their lives were forfeit. When the duke fell to his knees, hands around his throat and eyes pleading for help, she knew they would be killed for providing the means of his assassination.

Until his face started to change.

As black lines of corruption snaked away from his double chins, the generous flesh on his face started melting away as if he were made of wax. The reveal brought a collective moving away, except for the maetrie house guards of the Diamond Court who had surrounded the duke, or what had passed itself off as him.

In the span of a half dozen heartbeats, the heavyset Duke Charon in his top hat and long-tailed jacket dissolved away until something smaller and more alien with wide, expressive eyes and rounded shoulders was revealed. The creature burst away, discarding the husk of the duke to slop upon the platform, evading the guards, who moved like flashes of golden light, proving to a stunned Aurie that she would have had no chance to escape.

The chase quickly disappeared over the edge of the platform, the creature leaping into the lower-class areas, scattering the maetrie, and then bounding onto the track. A race had just finished. The guards, while quick, made those leaps with less alacrity, falling further behind.

Aurie managed to twist her arm out of the guard's grasp and attended to her sister, who was sitting up with a worried expression. The outer casing of the duke was dissolving into a pile of goo that hissed with rapid thermal decomposition.

"Are you okay?" she managed to ask, but never got an answer because the guards grabbed her and her sister, pulling them into standing positions.

Facing Lady Zaire, Aurie didn't know how to judge her expression. Anger. Fear. Confusion. All of it underpinned with fury. A thousand painful deaths filled Aurie's mind. Her sister's trust of Radoslav had been their undoing.

"Precept," said the queen to the guard holding her arm. "Take them by the railing while I consider their punishment. Kill them if they resist."

Aurie made no effort to escape as the maetrie guard led them away. Her sister was held by another guard, and more surrounded them as if they were dangerous criminals. Not wanting to watch the debate that would end her life, Aurie focused on the race, which had continued even after the strange creature had bounded across the track and disappeared into the guts of the structure.

The maetrie with the Wraithhawk mask was in the middle of the pack, jostling with the other riders as they leapt over the swells and curves of the track. As they came around the bend, a fist knocked Wraithhawk from her stelynka, and she tumbled hard and slid beneath the thundering hooves of the other riders, narrowly escaping being trampled through an impressive number of rapid contortions. The rider returned to her mount, well behind the others, with little chance to catch up.

Aurie felt like the Wraithhawk rider, thinking she was progressing but having just been knocked in the head by a fist. The shock still reverberated through her mind.

The gonka continued for two more laps, the riders slowly stretching out with the Onyx rider taking a comfortable lead. By the time Wraithhawk finished the race in dead last, the Diamond Queen called for their return.

The naked fury had been contained, but barely. The queen looked like she could explode at any moment. Aurie kept her head down as if the meek display might help avoid her wrath.

"I should have known that you weren't here on behalf of Invictus. I gather he's unaware of your existence in this realm." Lady Zaire drummed her fingers on the armrest of the bone divan. "Speak. Explain yourself."

Aurie checked to her sister, who looked stunned by the events, so she reached for her own words, which stumbled from her lips as she formed her thoughts.

"The creature that was hiding as Duke Charon was meant to assassinate you."

"The creature," said Lady Zaire mockingly. "You don't even know what it's called."

"Pokyksh," muttered Pi as she averted her eyes. "A changeling."

"Why would you care about my safety? I know your master, he's not a kind man. He would prefer to see me in the grave, especially after what my son tried to do in his city," said Lady Zaire keenly.

"He would prefer to see the balance of power remain in the Eternal City," said Aurie, not knowing if it were true or not.

"How did he discover this plot?"

"We would prefer not to reveal," said Aurie.

The queen leaned back, seeming to accept their story as fact. She continued to drum her fingers, staring into the distance.

"I thought these kinds of plots were the purview of Priyanka. Has Invictus lost faith in her?" asked the queen.

"Priyanka is a busy woman with many responsibilities," said Aurie, "and we do as Invictus instructs."

"I seriously doubt that," said Lady Zaire. "The pair of you look far too enamored with yourselves to follow blindly, and now I am presented with a problem. Had you informed me of the imposter I would have dealt with him on my terms, but you took it upon yourself to attack him, and despite the benefits to my court, you have overstepped your bounds. A slight that cannot go unpunished if I am to remain in control." She'd been staring into the distance but brought the full weight of her royal gaze upon them. "To merely strike a royal person is to lose one's hand. Do you know what the punishment for an attempted killing at one of our gatherings is? No matter that he was an imposter. If we let anyone act with impunity then our gatherings will turn to chaos. Even one as justified as what happened? The punishment is death."

Aurie glanced at her sister, who hung her head in shame for trusting Radoslav. She didn't blame Pi, but wished she'd done a better job of figuring out his motives before entering the

Eternal City.

"There is the matter of the elevens," said Lady Zaire, her expression softening. "A good omen that cannot be ignored."

In her studies at Arcanium, the concept of truth was a major source of power. She was a skilled user of vermancy and mendancy, truth and liar magic, because she had a good grasp on those realities for herself. As magic was an instruction for the mind, that unvarnished belief made her magics more powerful. But faith was a tricky concept that included culture and the expectations of society.

Lady Zaire was caught in a conflict of cultural truths. On one hand, they'd defied her edict and attacked a guest, even one there under false pretenses and with possible intent to cause their own havoc. To allow a pair of outsiders to act with impunity would undermine her. A queen was not an individual, but the embodiment of the state. Letting it go would be worse than if the duke had actually attempted an assassination.

But the truth of her power was in conflict with a societal norm. Aurie had heard the mention of elevens from the other guests enough to piece together the superstitious number. When the Sapphire rider had died during the first race, it had changed their number from twelve to eleven, which made the final and eleventh race a contest between that perfect number. The maetrie saw this as a good sign, and given the outcome of the duke's reveal, to punish them would be seen as an affront to the expectations of luck in maetrie society.

Aurie saw a narrow path that might allow the queen to save face while letting them leave the Eternal City with their lives. Though her sister was more of an expert on the maetrie, the time spent watching the gonkas and meeting the various characters attending the gathering had instructed Aurie in ways that her sister was blind. There were truths hidden within the court and contest that even the queen had not seen.

"May I offer a suggestion?" asked Aurie.

The only others near the queen's divan were her guards and Lady Sebella, who stood off to the side, watching with muted interest.

"You may," said Lady Zaire, "carefully."

"Today is a day of fortune, announced on the backs of the elevens," said Aurie.

The corners of Lady Zaire's eyes creased. "Continue."

"The eleventh and final race is almost upon us," said Aurie, "during which eleven riders will compete. Shouldn't that be the race that decides our fate?"

The queen reacted with a slow, spreading smile, while Lady Sebella strangely frowned. Was there something she was missing about the queen's consort? Aurie pushed the thought out of her mind as she concentrated on the head of the court.

"It would," said Lady Zaire with a keen smile. "What do you suggest?"

"My sister and I choose a rider, while you choose another. If our rider wins, we walk free. If yours wins, then your punishment should be as severe as you deem necessary."

"What if another rider wins?" asked the queen.

"If you would like, have each noble choose their champion. If theirs wins, then they can judge us however they'd like," said Aurie.

The queen sucked in her breath in pleasure, eyes alighting with the prospect of solving the problem and entertaining the nobles with a grand spectacle. This would be an event that would be talked about for ages.

While the queen was considering the idea, Pi put her hand on Aurie's arm, but she shook it off. Her sister was worried about the contest, but Aurie couldn't explain her reasoning in front of the others. She had no intention of playing fairly. The prospect of oxyvain meant that anything was on the table when it came to winning in maetrie society.

"I accept this proposal," said Lady Zaire. She looked to a set of lights above the racetrack. "The eleventh race is upon us. Gather the riders on the platform for the choosing."

Pi leaned into her ear while they waited for the riders to be brought and the nobles to return.

"What are you doing? One in eleven chance? Are you crazy? Even if we pick the best one, the others are going to try to take them down for the sake of cruelty. Whoever we choose, it'll be a death sentence for them. And us." The anguish in her sister's eyes made the event more fraught.

"Trust me," whispered Aurie, then under her breath and mostly to herself, she added, "I hope."

While they waited, Aurie caught a strange look from the guard, Precept. His stoic expression was replaced by a pinched frown. She sensed disappointment, even though she didn't understand why, but there was no further time to consider as the riders were set in a line opposite the queen's divan.

After a brief explanation by the queen about the events that would transpire around the eleventh and final race, which brought a giddy excitement from the nobles, she added, "The Silverthorne sisters may choose first."

Pi leaned into her ear. "We're choosing Onyx, right? He's won most of the races he's been in."

"No," said Aurie, frowning as she realized a problem. "Do the common maetrie speak our language?"

"Some, but not all," said Pi.

Aurie approached the first rider. Emerald mask. She didn't particularly remember how well he'd fared in the gonkas, but it didn't matter. She stood before him as if she were evaluating him, and if she were going on human terms, he would be a likely candidate, as he was lithe and fit with a hungry cast to eyes that peeked from beneath his jewel-encrusted mask.

She leaned on her tippy-toes and spoke quietly in his ear. He reacted as if he'd received a small shock, but to his credit, kept facing forward towards the queen rather than looking down the line at his fellow competitors. After the first, the nobles tittered with questions, chattering amongst themselves about what she might be telling the riders.

"You cannot bribe them," said the queen, "not that you have anything of value that they would accept."

"I offer no bribes, only truth."

The queen seemed suspicious, but allowed it to continue. Aurie guessed that her royalness couldn't fathom how she might taint the race when so much was on the line.

Aurie continued to address each rider in turn, giving the same message to all but one. The ones that heard the common message reacted similarly, except for the few that couldn't understand her speech, but she assumed the others would explain once they hit the starting line.

"Have you made your decision?" asked Lady Zaire with chin raised.

Aurie returned to her sister's side, squeezed her hand, and spoke in a loud voice so all could hear.

"We choose Wraithhawk."

Gasps were quickly swallowed by laughter. The nobles had been watching the same races, so they knew that Wraithhawk was the worst of the riders. A timid racer who was outmatched in physicality and willingness to accept pain.

Pi turned towards her. "Wraithhawk? I was rooting for her, but not with our lives on the line."

Lady Zaire smirked. "Then I choose Onyx."

The other nine selections were given to nobles of prominent stations, but Aurie wasn't listening anymore. Hers was the only choice that mattered, and she was reviewing her decision to make sure she hadn't missed anything that would upset her strategy.

Before the riders were released for the final race, the queen spoke to them in both the maetrie language and English.

"To encourage a spirited gonka and to pay homage to elevens, the winner will be provided with a generous prize far beyond the usual reward."

As Lady Zaire turned away, she smiled knowingly at Aurie. The additional gift would push the riders to compete more brutally than normal. Unless what she'd said to them was enough to counter their normal ways.

As the riders left for the starting line, Wraithhawk glanced back suspiciously. When she had leaned into that rider's ear, Aurie had said nothing, and then pulled back with a smile. Wraithhawk continued her observation, checking the other riders, trying to decide why she'd been chosen over the others.

The attention that was given the races increased tenfold for the final and eleventh gonka. Aurie took position along the rail with her sister, to her surprise, finding Lady Sebella on her left.

"You play a dangerous and foolish game," said Lady Sebella.

"I play to win."

The older dark-haired maetrie looked down upon Aurie as if she were a peasant. "Should one of the nobles win, they will delight in torturing you for your hubris, while our queen will end your life as an example for those who tempt fate. Why would you risk so much to keep the balance in the Eternal City?"

The noble's plain speech took Aurie off guard. "Some things are important enough to risk all."

"Eventually time and chance catch up with everyone," said Lady Sebella. "Better to risk little and play for the next game."

The response that Aurie had ready was lost the moment the chime sounded, announcing the start of the race. She had no idea if her ploy would come to fruition, and with a long race of eleven laps, she might not know until the end.

The previous gonkas had included six riders, which left room for maneuvering and jockeying as they navigated the obstacles on the bone track. With eleven that space was nearly non-existent. Wraithhawk was third from the left, and when the chime sounded, she tried to get out ahead of the others, but her stelynka wasn't as quick as the two next to her.

On the opposite side, Onyx confidently took the lead as the riders nearest allowed him the space to surge to the front. This was the part of her strategy that was suspect, as having various personages attached to each rider meant it was not a contest of skill and speed, but one of prestige.

The first lap was a tight affair with only one thrown rider, the Amber mask, who nearly slid off the track when he was kicked by Emerald. The other riders kept their machinations to a minimum, sensing the long race would give ample opportunity for oxyvain without jeopardizing their own positions.

During the second lap, Onyx stayed in the lead, followed by Dolgant and Pearl. Wraithhawk was stuck in a pack that always seemed to stay around her. She kicked out at Amber, who had caught up during their slow pace, but he avoided it rather than engage back.

During the third lap, Wraithhawk rammed another rider to break free of the pack that had been keeping her hemmed in. The others tried to catch up and limit her room to run, but she made a few skillful leaps over the swales and moved out ahead. Lady Sebella sucked in a breath and turned to stare at Aurie.

Wraithhawk was still half a length behind the group of four at the front where Onyx kept his lead. The riders in front had mostly kept to themselves, focusing on speed and navigating the obstacles rather than interfering with each other, leaving them less bloodied than in some of the previous races.

Aurie supposed this made sense. In a short race, there was little time to affect your opponents. A longer gonka allowed for strategies to play out over time. She hoped that would be the case for hers.

"Come on, Wraithhawk," said her sister, leaning against the railing as if she could will the rider faster.

Laps three through eight were almost like a horse race from their realm, as the riders pushed their mounts. Wraithhawk managed to catch up as they came around for the ninth lap, leaving five competitors in front with a chance to win.

The coordination from the other riders that had hemmed in Wraithhawk at the beginning was absent down the stretch. Wraithhawk proved she was an able rider, navigating the obstacles with grace. At first the crowd reacted to each jump and swerve as if it might be her last, because they expected her opponents to veer into her or kick out with a leg to throw her from the stelynka as they had in previous races. But as the blows did not come, the crowd began to jeer and whistle. If it were a human race, Aurie would have expected bottles and cans to be thrown onto the track. The commoners were the first to sense something was amiss, but the nobles saw the difference in the race slightly after.

Lady Sebella chuckled softly with understanding as the riders came around for the last lap. "A bold ploy. You might just win."

The realization of why the others weren't attacking Wraithhawk rippled through the nobility. They were seeing what Aurie had recognized earlier in the races. The rider that had spoken to them on the street was none other than Princess Ylassa. The queen's daughter was on her Liebereisen, which was a journey of self-discovery, and had chosen to disguise herself as a common rider for reasons only she understood.

The law that prevented commoners from striking nobility was keeping the other riders from interfering with Princess Ylassa. In the earlier races, she'd been knocked from her stelynka numerous times, not because she was unskilled at riding, but because she seemed to lack the brutality of the commoners, who had everything to lose. After meeting Prince Orráine and watching the races, Aurie had realized that his sister was similar, an unusual maetrie who was looking for a different path.

This did not ensure victory, as Wraithhawk still had to be the fastest and most skilled rider, but at least it kept the others from interfering with her during the race.

Her sister noticed a few moments later with a muttered curse as the pack rounded the last curve towards the finish line. Aurie's heart was in her throat. She looked to the queen, who for a brief second had an expression of relief, but it quickly disappeared beneath the mask of authority.

But the result was not assured. Onyx and Wraithhawk were striving together, having outpaced the other competitors in the upper pack. Aurie had hoped that Onyx was merely a brute whose success came from his cutthroat tactics, but his skill on the stelynka matched the princess'. The two riders were covered in a patina of blood from the long race as even their relatively calm efforts came with pain. They hit the quad swales on the final stretch, leaping from peak to peak to keep up their speed.

At the last obstacle, Wraithhawk took the lead. She looked like a vision of horror, arms kissed with crimson streaks, little droplets of blood rising behind her at each stride. Her stelynka arced through the air gracefully, and given the pace that had allowed her to catch up, Aurie was confident Wraithhawk could cross the line first. Aurie's entire body was covered in goosebumps. Beside her, Pi sucked in a breath of anticipation. The excitement of victory.

"We're going to win," said her sister as she reached out and squeezed her hand in solidarity.

As the two stelynka landed, Wraithhawk slightly ahead of Onyx, the queen's rider shot out his leg in an awkward maneuver that would have sliced the inside of his thigh. His foot caught the hind leg of Princess Ylassa's mount. In the span of a single heartbeat, she went from thundering down the final stretch for victory, to the agony of betrayal. Her mount hit the bone track clumsily, barely keeping its hooves. Princess Ylassa was knocked from its back, but not so far that she fell, and she clung to the stelynka's broken glass neck as it thundered towards the finish line.

"No," said Pi, emptily.

Onyx fared little better on the landing. His kickout had caused him to hit hard, but he recovered faster as he'd been expecting the interference, unlike Princess Ylassa. Onyx quickly righted himself and strode towards the finish line, and Wraithhawk, clinging to the neck of her stelynka, passed half a second afterwards.

She'd lost.

They'd lost.

"Fools," said Lady Sebella, marching away, shaking her head inexplicably.

The brief taste of victory was bitter on her tongue, having turned to ash by Onyx's last maneuver. The nobles, having been enraptured by the thrilling race, turned to Aurie and her sister, hunger in their black eyes for the punishment that would come.

"We lost," said Pi. "I can't believe we lost."

Aurie was numb.

I lost.

Fourteen

The crash of emotions left Pi empty and confused. For a brief moment, she'd thought they'd won. Her sister's stratagem had been nearly perfect, except that it failed to anticipate the greed that would overcome the rule against striking a princess.

Golden-armored guards hauled them towards the queen. It wasn't supposed to end like this. Pi thought briefly of trying to make a run for it. The many souls in her head would provide the lubrication that might help them escape, but she knew it was an ill-considered thought. The maetrie guards alone were formidable enough to make escape impossible, let alone the opportunistic nobles who might want to earn favor with the queen through their capture.

But their failure wasn't at the top of Lady Zaire's interest. As they were presented to the head of the Diamond Court, her daughter, Princess Ylassa, appeared at their side without the wraithhawk mask.

The resemblance to both the queen and her brother, Prince Orráine, was unmistakable, though each in different ways. The princess had the hawkish nose of her mother, lithe and sharp, like a folded knife, but they differed in the eyes. Where her mother's were hard, a polished obsidian regarding the world with suspicion, Princess Ylassa reminded Pi of her brother the prince. There was much left undecided in those eyes, as if she were open to new experiences—and new ideas.

This was contrasted by the wash of pink blood covering her flesh and miniscule clothing. Princess Ylassa had forsaken the chalice of healing as she was brought before her mother. The grimace of pain and the blood freely flowing from her flesh as she waited for the admonishment that lurked so clearly on her mother's brow, made Pi wonder which was worse.

"Ylassa."

Lady Zaire spoke with both authority and longing. Pi had no idea how long her daughter had been on her Liebereisen, but it was clear that it'd been long enough to create a fissure between them.

"Why do you debase yourself with them?" asked Lady Zaire.

Princess Ylassa glanced over, forehead knitted with thought.

"Not all lessons can be learned in a palace," she said, examining her flayed hands idly as they dripped blood on the slick bone platform.

Their conversation halted when the Onyx rider was brought before them, surrounded by the queen's guards. His encrusted mask hung idly in his hand, arrogance on his brow as he stood amongst the nobles. The ecstasy of the chalice haunted his eyes as he smirked at nothing in particular. He was covered in the same patina of blood as Princess Ylassa, but his wounds were closing as they watched. The Onyx rider looked formidable, a specimen of brutality cruelly honed by the maetrie systems.

Lady Zaire looked annoyed by the appearance of the rider as if she'd forgotten her previous choice. His actions at the final stretch created new conflicts.

"Congratulations on your victory," said Lady Zaire flatly. "You will receive all the rewards that you deserve. Bury his body with a fortune of gold, and if he has any descendants, provide for their rise in station."

The Onyx rider's expression fell, even as the pleasurable effects of the chalice roiled through his body. His smile was both blissful and perverse.

"No, Mother," said Princess Ylassa. "He fought by the rules of the gonka. Had the outsiders not interfered, his victory would be untainted by knowledge."

"Oxyvain," said Lady Zaire emphatically. "The Silverthorne sisters played well, even if they failed in the end." She gestured towards them. "And if he is dead, then one might be able to say that you were the true winner."

Hope bloomed in Pi's chest. A narrow avenue for escape was opening.

"We cannot continue this way, Mother," said Princess Ylassa. "We are the most powerful race in all the realms, yet we squander our skills on eternal combat that has no end. We are consumed by competition. Our city falls to ruin at the edges and only in the beating heart does the blood flow...and spill." She gestured towards them. "Better we learn from the humans, who have set aside their conflicts to grow together."

The choice hit Pi in the breastbone. Their lives were balanced against the Onyx rider, a commoner maetrie, who had fought by the rules of the gonka and lost. If they were judged by the standards of the maetrie, they would escape with their lives, but if it were by their own human ideals, they would lose.

The queen turned, spearing them in her sights. "What say you? Are you the idealist humans that my starry-eyed daughter thinks exist? Or are you willing to do what it takes to survive? Should Onyx be killed for his transgression and give my daughter the victory? Or should you accept the punishment for your failure?" Lady Zaire licked her lips as she looked between the two of them. "Pythia Silverthorne. You've worked for the Black Butcher. Show my daughter how the humans are not so different than us. That they thrive not because they are strong but because they are weak, because who cares what the insects do beneath our boots. Tell me, Pythia. Who lives and who dies? Will it be you and your sister? Or Onyx?"

Pi took a long look at the winning rider. The effects of the chalice still coursed through his veins. He staggered on his feet, drunk by the ecstasy of his wounds. She knew his struggle. After their parents had died, they'd had to do what was necessary to survive. Would she have made a different decision in his shoes? She wasn't so sure.

"See how the human twists on the knife, Ylassa? Even she desires the death of Onyx. Human flesh is weak."

Pi looked to her sister, whose face was pinched with concern. She knew what her sister would choose. That was the difference between them and why the queen had chosen her to decide. They could live, but only if another would die. In absence of her sister, the choice would have been simple. A calculation of survival. But that was the way of the maetrie. It was too easy. Place everything on the balance and if it tilted one way, that was the choice. The queen was proving a point to her long-absent daughter.

"Make your decision," said Lady Zaire. "Or all lives will be forfeit."

The words seemed to come from someone else, even though she knew they were her lips.

"Onyx should be spared. He did not create this system." Pi hung her head. "We accept our fate."

A hissing laughter reverberated through the nobles. They couldn't believe themselves. For them, the choice would have been easy, and most of them would have been happy to slit Onyx's throat themselves.

Aurie gave her hand a second squeeze, a measure of support. The Onyx rider stared suspiciously at them, clearly trying to piece together how they would profit from the decision, not understanding it'd been a moral choice, not a calculation of survival. And now it was up to the queen to decide their fate. Pi had to hope that the maetrie might know mercy.

Lady Zaire stared at the floor as if stunned by the choice. After a few seconds of inner conflict, she lifted her chin, lips squeezed tight. "Sequester them in my chambers while I decide their punishment."

As they were led away, the blood-soaked Princess Ylassa watched. The maetrie were a difficult race to read.

A contingent of guards brought them into the queen's quarters, a resplendent gilded palace that would have made the pharaohs of their world jealous. Under other circumstances, the tinkling of fountains would have provided a relaxing backdrop.

"I'm sorry," said Pi, shaking her head. "I shouldn't have accepted the beetle. I thought I could trust Radoslav. And I'm sorry I chose Onyx."

"I'm proud of you, sis," said Aurie. "It was the right decision."

"I feel sick about having to make it. Shouldn't making the right decision give me some feel-good chemicals or something? I could throw up," said Pi, sitting on the edge of a bone column and leaning forward on her knees.

A ripple of surprise passed through the guards. A trio of maetrie appeared in the entryway: Princess Ylassa, Lady Sebella, and the head of the guards, Precept. The latter spoke to his charges and they slipped back out to the main platform. The reason for the three visitors didn't make sense to Pi, unless this was the beginning of their sentencing.

"I should let my mother have you killed for outing me," said Princess Ylassa, who had taken the time to clean the blood from her flesh. The wounds were closing, but she didn't have the same hazy gaze as Onyx had after the chalice, suggesting her healing had come by other means.

"My apologies," said Aurie, "It was the only way I saw to win the race."

Princess Ylassa wiped a spot of blood from her jaw and looked at it momentarily before flicking it against a bone wall. "I heard about the changeling. My mother should be thanking you for taking care of the imposter Duke Charon, but the rules of the maetrie are as much a collar to her as they are to the commoners."

"Is that why you disguised yourself as a rider?" asked Pi.

"Among other things," said the princess. "My brother's Liebereisen brought him much wisdom...and doubt." She glanced to Precept with a frown. "The last few decades have begotten nothing but death. If we continue down this path, we will exterminate ourselves, which makes it more fitting that you pardoned Onyx."

"What will Lady Zaire decide?" asked Aurie.

Lady Sebella sighed. "She will have no choice but to have you killed. The nobles will delight in the spectacle, momentarily distracted until the meaning of the imposter Duke Charon is discovered, which will lead to a new round of warring between the courts. It could have been worse."

"Do you know who was behind it?" asked Pi.

"Only suspect," said Lady Sebella, frowning. "Had he been successful in assassinating the queen, there would have been even more chaos and bloodshed. I assume that beetle was given to you by Radoslav?"

Pi hesitated, feeling like there was much she was missing.

"You need not worry," said Lady Sebella. "You and I have met before. I know the trouble that the Silverthorne sisters can create firsthand."

"You should show them," said Princess Ylassa. "I am blocking all methods of scrying. We are safe here."

Lady Sebella waved her hand across her face, dissolving the image away as if she were washing away a watercolor. The angled cheekbones of the maetrie noble were replaced with the rich brown skin of Priyanka Sai, the head of the Academy of the Subtle Arts.

"Now you understand," said Priyanka grimly. "I hope you have a good reason for this disturbance. You're causing me to risk much on your behalf. I should let the queen have you to keep the peace."

Neither the princess or the guard, Precept, seemed surprised by the reveal. When Pi looked to her sister, who was staring at the maetrie guard as if she knew him, she understood. Priyanka nodded, then gestured to Precept.

The head of the guard waved his hand before his face. Beneath the maetrie exterior was Zayn Carter, who only had eyes for her sister. He was slim, with a handsome russet brown face that always looked on the verge of a smile. Zayn and her sister had a brief relationship during the year that their time in the Halls overlapped, before Zayn disappeared on tasks for his Hall.

"Zayn."

"Aurie."

The longing in their voices made Pi ache for them. Priyanka cleared her throat, bringing the attention back to her. She appeared annoyed by their reunion. "Quickly, explain why you foolishly came to the Diamond Court."

Her sister gave a brief explanation of what had transpired with Beckett and then Andromeda and the truth bond. She ended with the question, "Is there a way to get rid of it?"

"No," said Priyanka, gaze searching, "not really. But you might be able to track her down using the bond." She looked to Pi. "Radoslav sent you here with the beetle?"

"He did. I thought I could trust him. He said it wouldn't put me in harm's way."

Priyanka raised an exquisite eyebrow. "After all the time working for him, you trusted that explanation?"

She saw it now for what it was: a cold calculation. He'd traded on their friendship for a chance to save his race from their own destruction. It was the same reason that she'd chosen Onyx, but she didn't know if she could forgive him, since it was her life on the line.

"Will you come back to Invictus with us?" asked Aurie. "The head patron grows worried about the fate of our realm. The demonic invasion nears."

"A fate he has claimed was imminent for much longer than you've been alive," said Priyanka, frowning. "Not that I don't believe he will be right eventually, but we each have our own tasks. I must stay here. The Eternal City is its own threat, both to itself and our realm."

"Are we to be sacrificed then for your silence?" asked Pi.

"So quick with wit, but never stopping to think before you open your mouth, girl," said Priyanka. "The reason you see the three of us is because we're getting you out of here. There will be many questions, but the queen will overlook them. She does not wish your demise either, even as she would be forced to take your heads. The choice you made was not the one she expected." The head of Assassins smirked. "Maybe someday she might yet change her mind."

Relief that they wouldn't be sent back to the queen for punishment flooded up from Pi's gut. The whirlwind day left her exhausted.

"We should go if we're taking them out of here, Pri," said Zayn.

"Not we. But you. We will return to the platform, during which they will overcome Precept and escape. The punishment for losing them will be severe, but not as final as Lady Zaire has no real interest in your deaths. The nobles will suspect they've been played, but no one will understand the real story beneath the action. They trade in conspiracies like children. This will provide them entertainment, not answers," said Priyanka.

Zayn glanced to Aurie and back to Priyanka. The pain was evident on his brow. Not the potential punishment, but the ending of their brief reunion.

"I owe you a debt," said Princess Ylassa. "Had you encouraged Onyx's death, it would have undermined all that I hope to change about our race. Your sacrifice gives me hope, which is why I wanted to ensure that you were not punished for it." She inclined her head. "Go. Zayn will take you through the hidden passages where you can return to your portal."

The false face returned to Priyanka and then it was two maetrie and three humans. The other two loitered while Zayn took them to a hidden passage behind a statue of Lady Zaire. They traveled through the center of a huge bone, which brought them onto the streets outside the Rasakupol.

"Thank you, Zayn," said Aurie, reaching her hand towards him, but pulling back as if she were afraid what that touch might mean for them. "I'm sorry you're having to take the punishment for us."

"There's no need to apologize," said Zayn, glancing up the empty street. "I'm coming with you."

"What?" Aurie and Pi exclaimed at the same time.

"Priyanka is blind to the problems of our realm. She's been so worried about the maetrie that she can't see the danger that's already there." He paused. "This isn't the first time I've been warned about the invasion. I tried to pass it along to Pri, but she refused to listen, stating we're the only ones that could deal with the threats from the Eternal City."

"Are you sure? Won't she be furious?" asked Pi.

"Absolutely, but it's a sacrifice I'm willing to make, just like you were back there. Besides, we have to find Andromeda so you can get rid of the truth bond. I'd hate myself if I didn't help you." He checked behind him. "Come on, we should hurry before they realize we're gone."

Switching back to the guise of Precept, Zayn led them through the streets. The journey back to their portal took less than the other way around. The whole time, Aurie stared at Zayn's back, so Pi had to smack her in the shoulder to remind her that they were still in danger.

When they reached the area, Aurie held up her arm. The bracelet pulsed softly, signaling they were in range of a return trip.

Aurie held out her hands and the three of them formed a triangle. Zayn's hands were softer than she would have expected. Her sister's cheeks blushed at the touch, which Pi hoped wouldn't become a problem.

"Hey Zayn," said Pi, forcing him to look away from her sister.

"Yeah."

"Glad to have you with us. It's been getting pretty annoying just hanging out with my sister all the time."

Aurie had barely registered what she'd said because she was too busy triggering the bracelet, opening up the archway that led to Invictus' private demi-realm. As the three of them walked through the shimmering field that separated the two worlds, her sister's exclamation was cut off during the transfer.

"Hey you—"

Interlude Two

Mary Seder sat at her beige kitchen table surrounded by a sea of bills and receipts. The little pieces of paper were curled and crumpled in piles that wouldn't stay neat no matter how many times she fixed them. The urge to sweep them into the trash bin was constant, but it wouldn't make the problem go away.

The television was playing in the other room. Her husband, Jack, had been watching *Deadly Deceptions*, a show about the crimes that students of the Halls had committed that had been covered up by the patrons. He loved the series, watched it religiously, and then complained to everyone who would listen about how these mages couldn't be trusted, that power like that shouldn't be given a free pass.

While Mary knew that mistakes had been made, she worked with a few mages at the alchemical research facility in the ninth ward and didn't want to think they might not be good people. They were from the smaller halls, the ones rarely in the paper, but mages were mages. She was jealous of the little charms they used to make everyday life easier, and once a month she visited an Oculus mage who had a fortune-reading shop in the tenth. He promised them they were about to come into a lot of money, but he wouldn't say where. Mary was beginning to worry that he was scamming her, but the first two tips he'd given her had panned out.

Pinching her nose between forefinger and thumb, she inhaled deeply, trying not to let the frustration of tax season get to her. To pay for Jack's medical bills from when he got hurt during a freak windstorm that had blown up on his construction job, they'd adjusted her weekly pay to take less taxes out, but now that the end of the year had come, they were woefully behind. She didn't know how she was going to cover the difference without resorting to shady payday loan businesses or asking her father for assistance, a request that would come with a ton of baggage.

Mary opened her eyes only to grow strangely and intensely dizzy, slapping her hands flat on the table for stability. A stabbing migraine hit right between the eyes. The pain was followed by nausea and then there was that smell. Sweet and cloying. She knew it instantly. Lilacs. Her neighbors had lilac bushes and she inhaled deeply every time she passed the fragrant flowers.

When she could open her eyes again, the lime green refrigerator was too bright. She squinted until her eyes adjusted. The migraine was fading. She used to have terrible bouts of them when she was younger, but hadn't had one in years. Mary stared at the bills, knowing they were likely the trigger.

There was something else. A thought that lingered along with the lilacs. She pinched her nose, trying to rid herself of the smell, but it was stuck in her head along with the idea. A mad idea that at first didn't make sense, but the more she thought about it, the more the pieces fit.

It'd never sat right with her that she hadn't a speck of magical ability while so many others—awful people even—had more than they could handle. Her Merlin score had been nearly nonexistent. The test had been flawed. She was sure of it, because sometimes she'd had these compulsions that when she'd followed through had brought her a bit of luck. It was one of the reasons she liked going to the fortune-teller. The interaction might one day awaken her inner eye, help her harness the faez she knew she had.

She snapped her fingers. That's what the lilac smell was, the synapses in her brain firing from the faez. It was like stroke victims smelling burnt toast, except this was a good thing.

Mary's concerns about the compulsion disappeared as she realized this was her ability awakening. A chance to prove that she could wield magic, a boon that would help drag them out of their debts, get them out of the eleventh-ward apartment.

She threw on a bright blue jumpsuit with the D'Agastine symbol on the front and grabbed the largest purse she had in the closet. After kissing her snoring husband on the forehead, she headed to the green line station near their house that would take her to the facility.

The guards gave her side-eye at the strange hour of her arrival, since she wouldn't be expected at work until morning, but she was a team lead and it wasn't unusual for them to be called in during emergencies. Mary went straight for the supply closets. Her team mixed the larger alchemical test batches for the researchers once the formulas were narrowed down.

The materials had to be recorded, but she marked down another project from the lab on the fourth floor and put that team lead's name down on the sheet. It was unlikely that the theft would be followed up on. The two cannisters went into her oversized purse. She buried them beneath her spare underwear and sanitary napkins.

After lingering in the lab to give the impression she'd been actually working, but really playing games on her phone, Mary headed out of the facility. The guards gave her purse a cursory inspection, but never dug past the upper layer.

At this hour of the night, the green line was filled with people heading to or returning from the bars, red-eyed and staring vacantly at the reflections in the windows as the train rumbled down the track. Her heart was in her throat and every time she wondered if she was acting crazy, the lilacs returned.

When she got off at her station, she didn't head home, but into the twelfth ward. The dim streetlights of the eleventh were never bright enough in her opinion, but at least they existed. Mary hurried down the darkened streets, convinced that someone might be following, checking over her shoulder every ten steps.

A few times she saw clusters of men hanging out on street corners. Drug dealers. Gang members. They could have been an acapella group for all she knew, but she never got close enough to find out, cutting through back alleys towards a place she'd never been but was a beacon in her mind.

She slipped through the cut fence at the back of an industrial factory that had long been claimed by rust and vines. There were people living in the buildings, fires in old barrels, but she kept to the shadows and made it through without being seen.

Halfway through, the insanity of what she was doing crept into her mind, stilling her feet and making her check her surroundings. Mary felt like a drug addict waking up from a long bender, wondering how they'd ended up where they were. The promise of magic seemed so far away. An illusion. Or delusion.

Tears pooled at the corner of her eyes but before she could wipe them away the migraine returned like a tsunami, dropping her to her knees. A cry slipped out, and if someone was nearby, she didn't care.

When she could open her eyes again, the scent of lilacs was choking her. *Am I going crazy?*

A voice in the back of her mind assured her that she wasn't, but could she believe it? *A little bit further*, it coaxed. *It's almost over.* To gain power one had to do odd things. The mages of the Halls were proof of that.

Wiping her cheeks with the back of her hand, she hoisted the heavy purse and continued through the darkness. On the other side, the vision in her head came to fruition, leaving her breathless. The brick three-story building looked like a solitary tower as it was the only structure within a block. The rest of the old neighborhood had been knocked down. It was a sure sign that she wasn't hallucinating, that the compulsion was proof of her magical ability. It'd worked when she was younger, like the time she'd mixed tin into a batch of warding salt and gotten promoted a week later to team lead even though she was the newest member of the group. The tension around her chest released, allowing her to breathe normally again.

A third-floor light was on in the building, but the blinds were closed, so she couldn't see who the owner was. She crept to the back of the fence line where a metal shed was located. Something inside rattled against the wall like nails scratching steel, making the hair on the back of her neck stand tall. Whoever the owner was, they were keeping something dangerous on the property. Fear brought a metallic taste into her mouth, but she persisted, taking out the two containers and using the screwdriver she'd liberated from the lab to pop the lids.

The first one contained a silvery liquid that moved with lazy grace as she shifted it. Mercury. Labels warning not to touch weren't necessary. She tipped the liquid out to spill into a crack at the back of the fence by the shed. The silvery fluid ran under the barrier and the creature in the shed, which had been banging against the metal walls, grew silent.

The second container had a pungent smell. Turpentine. She wrinkled her nose and held it away from her. Lobbing it over the fence without getting any on her wasn't going to be easy. Mary measured the arc, then tossed the liquid, being careful not to lose the container. The corrosive fluid splashed against the side of the shed. A direct hit. There was a little left in the container, so she threw the rest, but this time mostly hit the fence.

Mary left the way she came, tossing the two containers against a rusty dumpster that smelled of old garbage. She made it home after one in the morning, changing out of her work clothes, even though she'd have to put them back on in a few hours. The piles of bills on the table seemed less imposing than they were before.

She found Jack still asleep on the couch. Turned off the television and kissed his forehead. Bleary-eyed, he followed her to the bedroom and collapsed on his side of the bed. Naked and beneath the covers, she tried to sleep but the excitement of the night kept her wide-eyed for another few hours as she wondered how her reward would come. Magic was strange and mystical. The arcane worked in unfathomable ways. She held her hand above the covers and imagined burning flame rippling off her fingertips.

"I can do magic," she whispered to herself in the dark of the night. "I'm a secret mage."

Fifteen

Zayn was relieved to be back in the human world. His eyes adjusted to the bright lights of the new room—a place of great magics—after a long time in the Eternal City. The maetrie realm had a muted, washed-out feeling as if the true colors had been sucked away by constant conflict. Some saw the streets as a dangerous haven for gang wars between the lesser maetrie, but Zayn saw them for what they were: the leftover scraps of survival in a city torn apart by constant, cold war.

He unhooked the clasps that held the armor to his chest, stretching his lungs, which had been confined by the tight chest plate, and rubbed the spot under his arm where the buckles bit into his ribs. The false-face charms didn't adjust for the minor differences in body shape, and while Precept was similarly sized, his personally made armor rubbed in a few awkward places.

With the chest plate clattering to the floor, he looked up to see Aurie taking a long drink from a bottle, water spilling around her generous lips. A heat formed in his belly, quickly spreading to his cheeks. He'd spent the last few years purposely not thinking about her, and now that she was only a few steps away, his mind was making up for the lost time, sending a barrage of images to his hungry libido.

His thoughts only made him blush deeper. What was he thinking? They'd only been together a few times. Two trains passing at great speeds on their journeys through the Halls. The truth was they barely knew each other, and how could he think that in the middle of the great threat to the city that she would have time for rekindling the relationship—no, it hadn't even been that much—the brief fling they'd had? As strong as the feeling in his gut was, they'd been two puzzle pieces not quite matching. But that was the way of things for mages. Worse for them. At least the majority graduated and went on to relatively normal lives in academia or corporate life. Some abandoned their studies altogether and branched out into mundane careers, having found that the world of the arcane brought too much drama. Not so for the three of them, who had only gone deeper into this world.

A sharp pinch on his arm had him spinning around to find Pi frowning at him. She'd seen the longing on his brow and knew it for what it was: trouble.

The younger Silverthorne had much in common with her older sister, but she tended towards shorter, spikier hairstyles while Aurie went for softer, longer locks. Aurie had a welcoming smile while Pi looked like she was always on the verge of a biting comment.

"Could you help me undo this?" asked Pi with an eyebrow raised as she was reaching back to unhook the buckle on her crimson-and-gold scale armor. She turned her back, giving him access to the buckle, which he unhooked. She slid out of the armor while his eyes fell upon a strange brass and gemstone panel with levers and dials.

"What is that?" he asked, reaching towards a brass knob that looked like it'd been made in a far-off realm.

Pi slapped his hand. "A dangerous artifact. No touching, unless you want to find yourself flinging through space in some empty realm that long ago blew itself up."

"The Helmsman of the Planes," said Aurie with a hungry light in her eyes as she wiped the wetness from her lips with the back of her hand. Staring straight at her was like gazing at the sun. He had to look away or find himself blinded. An enormous open tome filled with numbers and symbols was by the Helmsman, while a painting of an alien landscape of reddish rock with three moons hanging over the horizon adorned the far wall.

"Where are we?"

When they'd stepped through the portal, he'd assumed it was part of the Garden Network, which was how the patrons moved around the city.

"Invictus' private demi-realm," said Aurie. "Technically, everyone thinks we're in the top of the Spire, but that's not really where we're at. He made this private little bubble of reality."

"He will be very disappointed to find we've brought a visitor," said Pi. "We should grab our gear and get moving before he gets back."

"Wait," said Zayn. "If this isn't in the top of the Spire, then what is? I haven't been back in the city very often these last few years, but even I'm aware of the strange lights that have been coming from it since he's been back."

Aurie lifted a single shoulder. "Wish we knew, but Invictus is pretty tight-lipped about everything except what he wants us to know. Which isn't much."

A cold realization crept into his bones. "So...he didn't send you to the Eternal City?"

Aurie bit her lower lip and looked away, while Pi said, "Yeah, about that. We're supposed to be in Montanhas taking faez samples. Old Iron Balls told us not to worry about Andromeda or the truth bond."

"Old Iron Balls? You're calling the most famous, and probably oldest, mage in the world

Old Iron Balls?" asked Zayn incredulously.

"Spend a little time around him and you'd understand. He can be a bit of a prima donna," said Pi with a smirk.

Zayn leaned against the table. "I thought when I was coming with you that I'd at least have Old...Invictus' support." He leaned his head back. "Augh, Pri's gonna kill me."

Aurie met his gaze, which sent a little shock through him. "Want us to open up the portal? You could be back in the Eternal City in no time."

"I, uhm, no. The truth bond is too important. And I meant what I said back there. Priyanka's too focused on the Eternal City, which while dangerous, isn't the immediate problem."

"You say that like you already know something," said Pi as she took sips from her water bottle.

"Nothing specific, but the rumblings in the Undercity aren't new. I've seen the wells. The patrons have done everything they can to prevent them from deteriorating further, but there's only so much they can do. Faez is corrosive. The more we use magic, the more the barrier breaks down. This problem is inevitable." He rubbed the back of his neck. "Wait. You mentioned going to Montanhas. You know the Charmer family was there before it went to shit, right?"

"We do," said Aurie. "Do you think that's why they took Andromeda?"

"She wasn't there," said Zayn.

"Seems suspicious," said Pi.

"Not really," said Zayn. "She was the least involved with the family business."

"You say that like you know her."

"Not Andromeda, but Kitty was in my Hall. We worked together once," said Zayn.

"Maybe she might know where her sister is, or would want to help us get her back," said Pi.

"As far as I know, she hasn't been seen in years, but I haven't been around much, so my information might be dated," said Zayn. "Now what's this about Montanhas?"

Aurie pulled a runed cylinder out of a carryall that had been hanging on the wall. "We have to take this and get readings from the place that the barrier was breached. Invictus left us a set of coordinates. A supposedly safe place where we can land and scout from. I found some maps of the Lifestone plant and the nearby town from some old company websites."

"That's it? That's all he gave you?"

The Silverthorne sisters shared flat glances.

"He's been sending us throughout the realms with little more than a few comments, or notes on a scrap of paper. This feels like a formal invitation in comparison," said Aurie.

"It's not like there's much else. The town was wiped out years ago," said Pi. "This should be a pretty simple scouting trip. Your imbuements should make this easier, but we'll be overprepared in case. I need to grab a few things before we go."

"Is there any food I can grab? And a bathroom? The maetrie have famously large bladders. It was always hard to get away as Precept."

Aurie grinned and looked at her shoes. "The kitchen's through here. There are a couple of bathrooms down the hall. Invictus didn't hire an interior decorator, so it can be a little confusing."

Before he left for the kitchen, Zayn paused briefly to study the Helmsman of the Planes. He wasn't really interested in the artifact, but it kept him from thinking too deeply about how furious Priyanka was going to be about his betrayal. He worried most that she would think it cowardice about the potential punishment as Precept, but it wasn't that. They'd spent the last few years in the Eternal City with little more to show for it than a few unhappy nobles about the way things were going in the maetrie realm. He didn't feel like they were protecting anything, not even themselves, let alone the human realms.

The kitchen looked like something out of the 1970s with lime green countertops and gas stoves. A butcher knife that looked like it'd been used in ancient Rome hung on the wall. A cast iron pot with a dark red liquid sat on the central island. The smell reminded him of cranberries.

Zayn dug into the refrigerator, grabbing a handful of carrots and ripping off a hunk from a baguette. The bread was stale, nothing like his sister Neveah could make. He got excited when he found a box of mint cookies, but a big red "I" had been scrawled onto the side in handwriting that looked like an ancient rune.

"You've got to be kidding me," he said, chuckling at the idea that the most famous mage in the world had to mark his favorite cookies, or they'd be eaten. He found a bag of salted chips and worked on that, chugging water he got from the sink. The mundane aspects of the kitchen had him longing to see his family.

The last he heard, and it was probably outdated, his parents were in Alaska with the twins and Imani, his sister Neveah had made sous-chef at a top Parisian restaurant, and Roy was working construction. It was the only downside to fixing his hometown of Varna. When no one could leave, he at least knew where they were. That, and his cousin Keelan would still be alive.

An ache in his breastbone had him wanting to abandon helping the Silverthorne sisters and catch a plane to Paris. Priyanka had promised him that working for her, he'd get to see the world, many worlds, but sometimes he just wanted to see his family.

Lost in thought with half a hunk of bread in his hand, he wasn't really thinking when he pushed through the bathroom door to find Aurie washing her hands in the sink.

"Oh, crap, sorry," said Zayn, feeling heat rise to his cheeks.

"It's a little confusing around here," said Aurie. "Nothing like moving in with the world's oldest bachelor. Be careful touching anything. That oblong stone in the corner has a minor curse on it. Nothing bad but you'll have the worst itching for a few hours."

He let her pass, feeling the warmth from her body, inhaling her sweet scent. She grinned and closed the door behind him, leaving him alone.

The red-and-black stone in the corner looked like a giant paint-splattered bean. He resisted the urge to touch it just to see if Aurie was messing with him. He used the facilities and then after washing up, splashed water on his face and used a towel to rub his pits and freshen up.

Pulling up his shirt he was reminded of the spiderweb of tattoos across his chest, the imbuements from his Hall that gave him his strength, speed, and a few other useful abilities. Having to transform his body in the Eternal City meant he hadn't seen his real flesh in ages. He lifted the shirt up higher; his brown skin was more washed out around his chest since it hadn't seen the sun since he couldn't remember when. Zayn rubbed the scar over his right breast, where the blade had gone in. A tattoo of "KW" was etched beneath the knotted flesh.

Zayn could never forget the sacrifice his cousin made. None of them would be free from Varna if it weren't for him. He finished in the bathroom, tucking in his shirt and giving his pits one last sniff before returning to the portal room.

When Aurie and Pi returned, they had stuffed packs around their shoulders filled with items and materials that might help them against infernal creatures. They had a third one for him. If the rumors were true, and the Montanhas realm had been breached by the demonic one, then they would need every advantage they could get.

Aurie adjusted the Helmsman, turning dials and knobs to the set of coordinates that Invictus had left them. When she threw the lever, a hum filled the air and reverberated in his breastbone as the space beneath the archway shimmered into existence.

Dim, grainy light made seeing much further than a dozen feet beyond the portal difficult. They each applied darkvision enchantments on their eyes and approached the archway. The landing location looked like it came out behind an abandoned building. He couldn't see the surrounding landscape, but knew the realm had mostly impassable mountains with a few inhabitable valleys between.

"Ready?" asked Aurie, holding out her hands.

Zayn took hers, feeling the warmth of her palm against his, wrapping his fingers tightly around hers. When he'd accepted Priyanka's offer to work directly for her, she'd warned him that he wouldn't get a personal life, that protecting their realm from threats outside of it was more important. She'd promised that as mages who had the potential of living a long life, once the threat was past, there'd be time for reconnecting with old friends. But the moment he'd seen Aurie at Rasakupol, he knew that he couldn't stand being apart for a moment longer.

As they stepped through the archway, the barrier tickled his flesh, bringing goosebumps across his body. Zayn immediately inhaled the cool mountain air, catching the distant scent of burning and rotting trash. His vision adjusted to the strange light of the new realm in time to see a figure dart out of a gap in a wall and head directly towards them.

Sixteen

The crush of palms. Zayn's musky scent. The sudden sharp tickle of burning air. Preoccupied by sudden change, Aurie barely had time to register the shape darting into a large crack in the crumbling building, let alone the much larger one ambling after.

The shout to her left, followed by the shimmering wave of force throwing up a cloud of dust, barely left her time to register their travel through the portal. Dim, shadow-filled corners in the street swallowed the pursuing creature. The burning grit in the air made seeing difficult.

"What was that?" she asked.

Zayn surged ahead, but she grabbed his arm. "Not until we know what's going on."

He started to pull away, but she said, "Zayn." He frowned but made no motion to move.

Pi leapt onto a piece of concrete that had broken free from a wall sometime in the past. Swirling black smoke drifted over the buildings, making her eyes ache. Someone was burning tires, or trash. They stood behind a cluster of buildings. Through the smoke, the outlines of mountains soared overhead. A gap in the fumes revealed the glittering starry sky.

"I hear something," whispered Zayn, who'd fallen into a crouch and slipped out of her grasp. A moment later, they were surrounded by figures on either end of the street wielding rifles and crossbows.

Aurie hadn't expected this development. As far as she knew, the entire settlement had been wiped out when the barrier between realms broke down. The figures, humans by their shapes, stepped into view, but kept their weapons trained on them. They spoke angrily in a vaguely familiar language. Aurie had the sense that something was wrong and they were being blamed for it.

"Hello," said Aurie, holding her hands up. "We're from Invictus."

A few of the figures spoke to each other until one of them shifted into English.

"Invictus?"

"Yes," said Aurie, relieved that they shared a common language, but before she could continue, a thunderous roar filled the air, bouncing off the mountains and sending a spike of unrelenting primal fear through her gut. The people ducked away, hurrying towards the rocky slope behind the buildings. A woman paused at the back of the group and waved them on while glancing nervously at the sky.

The enormity of the sound, as if a piece of the mountain had broken free, had Aurie scurrying after them. They scrambled over rocks and bushes. She cut her hand on a rocky protrusion. After a two-hundred-meter dash up the rocky hill, dodging around gnarled trees and upthrust rocks, the group stopped in a natural hollow at the center of a protrusion along the cliff.

Their appearance seemed less important than watching the skies. The group of three men, two women, and a final figure that seemed larger than the others crouched in the sandy soil, scanning the sky for danger.

Aurie knelt by the woman who had waved them on. Her soot-covered face was haunted and emaciated. Filthy clothes hung loosely on her frame. As far as Aurie could remember, the disaster in Montanhas had happened around five years ago. It'd been assumed that all lives had been lost, but clearly that had been incorrect.

When she opened her mouth to speak, the woman shook her head, eyes searching the night sky nervously. Aurie followed the woman's gaze. They were near the base of foothills that led higher into the snow-kissed mountains. She couldn't see a moon, but the peaks glowed, suggesting it hadn't risen yet.

Scattered across the valley beneath them was a settlement, but no lights flickered. The town was empty. Dead. Swirling black smoke rose from an unknown source at the center of a large building. Even in the hills, the acrid smoke burned her nostrils and made her eyes water.

Whatever had made the awful noise in the sky was nowhere to be seen. She checked to Zayn, who shook his head. If his superior senses couldn't detect the airborne creature then it wasn't there.

"What—"

She'd barely whispered the word when she was shushed. The larger figure in a heavy coat motioned for them to follow. They traveled along a hidden trail through the rocks and trees for an hour, slowly gaining in altitude until the path brought them into a narrow canyon. The awareness of the sky never left the group as someone was always glancing back into the valley, but whatever danger had been present was gone.

They were led into a hidden cave that wasn't visible from the canyon as it was protected by the gnarled trees that seemed common for the region. After a heavy tarp was pulled over the entrance, a weak lantern was lit, sending out a faint glow that turned their already haunted eyes into caverns. The standoff lasted until Pi brought a mage light into existence, the brightness of the white light making their hosts flinch. Aurie would have expected thanks, but their expressions hardened at the display of magic. She couldn't help but notice the dried blood on their clothes, the old wounds, and the fact that the largest amongst them did not quite look human and had kept his hood pulled around his enormous head. The only thing well cared for were their weapons. They looked like survivors of an apocalypse.

"Is this all of you?" she asked.

The survivors glanced nervously amongst themselves. The woman who had urged them to follow stepped forward, wearing the weary countenance of a leader who had never expected to be in the position. Her lips were cracked, while her right eye was bloodshot from a recent wound.

"There are a few more, mostly children, the elderly, or those that cannot fight anymore." She patted her chest. "I am Benedita." She paused, heavy with emotion. "Why now? Why have you returned to save us now? After all these years, after all this loss. Why now?"

A great hollowness filled Aurie's chest as she looked to the survivors. There was a mix of pain and anger pulsing in their jaws.

"We didn't know anyone was left," said Aurie, finding her words seemed empty as she spoke. "We're not here to rescue you."

She regretted her words instantly as they traveled through the small group like wildfire. Gun barrels that had been pointed at the ground lifted towards them.

"You fucking parasites," screamed a tall man with a white beard and a craggy face. "You ruined our lives! Our town! Everything we built for nothing but greed!"

His outburst spurred the others and before Aurie could calm things, the cave echoed with anger and sorrow. She tried to explain, but they were no longer listening. Pi stood to the side with her arms crossed, frowning at the survivors as if they were children in the middle of a tantrum, while Zayn tried to help her calm them.

The eruption ended the moment a horrific sky-ripping sound reached them through the tarp covering up the cave. Everyone went dead silent, staring at the entrance as if it were about to burst open. Whatever danger the noise indicated was a familiar one to the survivors. She could see the fear and the lingering pain on their knotted brows.

"We're not with Lifestone, or any company," said Aurie in a low voice.

The survivors kept their gazes on the dirty tarp as the words worked through their heads, turning them eventually back to her.

"Then why are you here?"

Sensing they were frail and on edge, Aurie said, "We were sent here to figure out what happened."

"After all these years?" asked Benedita. "Why?"

"Because—" began Pi, but Aurie held out her hand. Her sister wanted to get straight to the point, lay it all out like she always did, but that wouldn't help these people. They needed hope, or at least not further pain.

"It's complicated," said Aurie.

"Fucking liar," said the angry bearded man as he shook his rifle. "Those are a politician's words. You don't want to tell us because you're afraid to. Admit it. You left us here to die." His voice cracked. He looked ready to collapse, and his companions patted him on his back.

"Aurie," said Pi emphatically. "We should level with them. They deserve that much."

Benedita had been rubbing the bearded man's back and speaking softly to him. She had real strength. Probably one of the only things holding the group together.

"We're all going to die soon," said Benedita. "We're out of food, any crops we were able to maintain are long dead, and it's getting too hard to sneak into town anymore for scavenging. Last week we lost three of our members to a gigante. We can't sustain many more losses."

The woman to Benedita's left shuddered from raw pain. She'd clearly lost someone in that group. A lover. A friend. It didn't matter. They were dwindling to nothing, the survivors being left to carry the burden of being alive.

"Please tell us you can get us out of here," said Benedita.

Aurie touched the bracelet on her wrist as she met her sister's gaze. Pi nodded towards the survivors. The message in her eyes was clear: *if you don't tell them, I will.*

"We can't," said Aurie, hating the way they flinched as if she'd just shot one of them. "The method of travel we're using requires the travelers to be faez-users."

Desolation filled their eyes. Benedita nodded grimly, the brief ember of hope squashed before it could become a fire in her heart.

Aurie was searching for something to say that might help the situation when the sobbing bearded man exploded from their group, his rifle coming up along with a scream of rage. She was surprised. Everyone was, even the survivors. There was nothing she could do to stop him from firing his weapon at point-blank range. Bullets were faster than the Five Elements.

She sucked in a breath, expecting to feel pain ripping through her chest, when a blur to her right ended with gunfire sent into the rocky ceiling bringing dust upon their heads. When Aurie opened her eyes again, she saw Zayn holding down the bearded man, who was still trying to fire, sobbing openly the whole time.

He was blubbering, "My Angelina, my Angelina..."

Zayn easily wrenched the rifle from the bearded man's hands and stepped away before handing over the weapon to one of their number. Wide-eyed stares at the display of speed were not lost on Aurie. Benedita in particular seemed to harden her expression at Zayn, a warning of future problems. The bearded man broke free of the hands trying to help him and rushed out of the cave.

"Let him go," Benedita told the others, then turned to them. "Tomás is still grieving. He lost his daughter a few months ago. His heart can't take much more."

The nods from the others in the group suggested it was the same for all of them. They were at their ragged ends.

"I'm sorry," said Aurie, finding she didn't know what else to say and maybe there was nothing she could. "I know this might be difficult, but can you tell us what happened? After, you know, the disaster?"

Benedita stared straight ahead, but nodded. "We shouldn't be traveling now anyway. Not with the...we shouldn't be traveling. Daytime is soon. Besides, we need to wait for Tomás."

"What was that noise in the sky?" asked Zayn.

Benedita closed her eyes briefly. "Let us not speak of it. An ill omen." She gestured to others. "Set up camp. We're staying here until daylight."

"We have food," said Pi, digging into her satchel. This brought the creasing of eyes. Small pleasures. It was all they had left.

A small fire was built in the center of the cave. Aurie was worried about smoke, but Benedita assured them the ground would swallow it up long before it reached the air. During the setup, they exchanged names. Benedita and Tomás, they'd heard already. The other woman was Callie, and the two other men were Lucas and Duarte. The final member of the group who kept apart during this time was Nurn, a member of the native population known as Montas. Aurie found it unusual that none of them were asked which Halls they were from. The reaction to their displays of magic suggested animosity or, at the very least, distrust.

Settled around the weak fire with the survivors on one side and the three mages on the other, Benedita started the tale with the facts that Aurie and her companions were aware of from the many newspaper articles and TV programs that went over the details in the aftermath of the disaster.

The company Lifestone had come to Montanhas many decades ago to manufacture their flagship life-extending elixir, Aevita, in the mountainous realm for reasons that were never really understood. In the final year of the plant's existence, the Charmer family bought Lifestone, and four of the Hall-aged kids came to Montanhas. During their few months at the Lifestone plant, the barrier between realms was breaking down, and there was unrest between the workers, the plant management, and the town—which had been settled long before Lifestone came by a group of Portuguese. As it became clear that a disaster was in the making, the Charmer family promised to evacuate all those that wished to return to their own realm, but then during the tumultuous final days, escaped home without bringing a single person with them, and the portal that connected the plant to the city of Invictus was destroyed irrevocably.

This first part, Aurie knew. The Charmer family was eventually cleared of financial responsibility, and the legal battles were partially to blame for the company's collapse. Since travel to other realms was extremely challenging without the Helmsman of the Planes—which at that time was locked in Invictus' private realm—no attempt to reestablish the portal to Montanhas was made.

The aftermath of the disaster was considered a done deal by the papers. All lives were assumed to be lost. The tragedy spawned a half dozen TV shows that traded on rampant speculation for their stories.

The next part of Benedita's explanation proved that was too simple. The first few days and weeks after the portal was destroyed, the town lost half its population as the gigantes—which was the enormous humanoid creature they'd briefly seen in town—and other horrific demonic creatures overran them. During this time, there was a larger population of Montas, and resistance allowed for people to escape to the hidden places in the surrounding mountains.

Once that initial battle was over, there was slow, painful deterioration of their situation. The mountainous region had little natural food, which meant they had to make forays into town to harvest the untended gardens or the old supplies that had been brought through the portal before the disaster.

Eventually mistakes claimed the lives of their friends and families. The gigantes could be killed, but usually at great cost, so they learned to avoid them. The gigantes mostly kept to the old plant and showed little interest in tracking them down. The few scouting missions of that area proved that the gigantes had set up their homes in the old buildings, attempting to make a settlement out of the plant.

The real danger came from other creatures, namely scorpics, which were bony scorpion-like demons the size of a lion that prowled the mountains and attacked without remorse. The thing in the sky that had made the noise like the collapsing of a mountain was mentioned only as a thing that lived amongst the peaks and made leaving the valley impossible. The pass that traveled along the Road of the Spine was visible from long distances, and past attempts at leaving had ended in tragedy.

Once they'd accepted they could never leave the valley, the survivors had spent their time scraping together a meager existence with dwindling numbers, which over time became less and less tenable. When they asked about the other Montas, Nurn explained that his people pulled away from the area once the disaster happened, but he'd stayed, for reasons he declined to explain.

In the aftermath of the explanation, no one spoke. Benedita had given them the overview of the situation, but condensing five years into an hour left out a lot of sorrow and pain.

Eventually, Benedita asked, "Why are you here?"

"The thing that happened to you," said Aurie, "it's happening in Invictus. The barrier is breaking down. We're here to take samples from the plant and understand what happened."

"You can't go to the plant," said Nurn. "It's too dangerous and you don't know your way around."

Benedita nodded. "He's right. You wouldn't make it back."

"I know we look young," said Aurie, "but we've survived worse. The samples we need to take are important. If we can understand the conditions that led to the collapse here, we might be able to predict it back home."

"Is there something we could do to help you?" asked Zayn. "It's not much, but we can leave our food. Or could we help you escape the valley?"

"Not possible," said Benedita, shaking her head. "Nothing in the open survives long."

"We might surprise you," said Zayn. "Wouldn't you want to try, rather than starve to death eventually?"

Benedita and Nurn shared a glance. The Monta spoke when she nodded towards him.

"We have to talk to our elders first. When night falls again, come with us to our hidden place. We can decide there."

"That's good," said Zayn, smiling.

After a meal of lean rations, Tomás returned as daylight was breaking. The bright light had everyone squinting until the tarp returned over the cave entrance.

"Is this going to be a problem?" asked Pi, nodding towards the older man.

"We'll keep an eye on him," said Benedita.

The two groups split up in the cave with the Hall mages taking a spot in the corner and the locals taking a spot near the entrance.

"I don't trust them," said Pi, glancing covertly as she threw pebbles against the wall.

"They're traumatized," said Aurie. "We should give them room to grieve."

"Scared people do stupid things," said Pi.

"I have to agree with your sister," said Zayn. "Sorry. We should take turns keeping watch during the night. Tomás might not be finished."

As much as she hated the idea of having to keep an eye on their fellow humans, people that had been subjected to the horrors of civilization collapse and the murders of their friends and family, the idea was prudent. She agreed to take the first watch as she wasn't yet tired. Sleep probably wouldn't come regardless.

Seventeen

Zayn had honed the art of sleeping with his eyes open in the Eternal City when he was on guard duty as Precept for the queen. He sat against the rocky wall, facing the survivors, but trying not to look like he was watching them. It was bad enough there was distrust amongst the two groups, but he could understand how that might be, given the way they'd been abandoned. Benedita in particular observed him whenever she thought he wouldn't notice. He suspected it had to do with the Hall powers he'd displayed when he'd moved faster than they could see to subdue Tomás before he could fire his weapon. Had she interacted with Kitty Charmer while she was here in Montanhas? He could think of no other reason for the distrust, which would only make their task harder.

When they'd come to Montanhas, getting into the plant had been assumed to be a simple job. Learning that the gigantes—the word the locals used for the demonic humanoids that had come through the barrier—had taken residence there complicated things. If they could get more recent information about the condition, it would go a long way towards completing the task.

After night fell, the locals gathered their equipment for the journey to their hidden place. The rifle that Tomás had been using was given back before they left the cave, but Zayn wasn't worried about a reprisal.

It took a couple hours to reach their destination, which was higher along the slope. They moved slowly, constantly checking the sight lines for danger. The greenery was sparser at the higher elevations, but the rockfalls more frequent, providing ample places to twist an ankle.

Zayn didn't know what to expect when they reached the hidden place. They came up a path along rail lines, which eventually led to what appeared to be an old mine shaft. The entrance wasn't in the deteriorated wood building, but in what looked like a dead end around a rocky outcropping. He smelled their human waste—it appeared they buried it in the sandy soil outside the mine, but his imbuement-aided senses picked it up. He hoped the creatures that stalked the valley weren't as sensitive.

A crack in the earth led to a lighted chamber about a hundred feet across. Around two dozen people milled about or sat upon pallets of old blankets, staring blankly at the wall or mending clothes with needle and thread. Many of them had bandaged wounds. An old woman had a bloody covering over her right eye and a chest-rattling cough. A few children ran around a big rock playing tag, but even their cries of delight were muted by the grim circumstances.

Their appearance brought most of the adults and a few curious children. Zayn's heart broke as he heard the whispers, saw the hope in their eyes, which was quickly dashed as Benedita gave the explanation of who they were and why they'd come.

They were led to an offshoot of the main chamber. Zayn could see by the folds in the walls that there was more than one. Two figures sat on a bed of dirty blankets, like beggars beneath a bridge, next to a lumpy table with a sheet thrown over it. The first was a woman with wispy gray hair and wrinkles as deep as valleys. Her ice-blue eyes were so sharp they looked like they could see through time. The second figure was twice the size as the woman, female as far as Zayn could tell, but it was difficult given the differences. A Monta. But unlike Nurn, who'd kept his hood up to hide the small protrusions on his forehead, the elder Monta before them had two larger curls that stuck out from her cranial plate. Horns. The meaning was not lost on him.

"Madre. Mais Velho," said Benedita as she inclined her head towards the two figures on the blankets. "These are mages from the Halls. They are not here to rescue us."

Benedita didn't say their names, but their titles. Mother and Eldest. These were the leaders of their small hidden settlement. The old woman rubbed her bony hands in her lap. She didn't seem surprised by their appearance or that they weren't there to rescue them. Using his imbuements, he sensed that she was neither angry nor disappointed by the news. The Monta was harder to read, assuming that the physical clues—the tightening of lips, creasing of eyes, and other micro-emotions were similar to human ones. Zayn had never been to Montanhas. He was aware of the Portuguese roots of its settlers, but not much about the locals.

"What do you bring?" asked the old woman in a thick accent.

Zayn stepped forward before the Silverthorne sisters could speak. He bent down to one knee so he was eye level with the two elder women.

"Olá, bom dia."

Madre was delighted by his greeting, eyes alighting as she clapped her bony hands. Mais Velho was less so.

"Falas português?"

Zayn held out his hand, waffling it back and forth. "A little. I'm rusty."

His Hall was known by most as Assassins, but that was the least of what they did. Spying and diplomacy were their common trades, and the ones he enjoyed most, but the general populous couldn't shake that they might be hired killers.

Madre reached out and squeezed his hand, adding a wink for good measure. "Thank you for trying and for kneeling. Looking up gives an old woman a neck ache, and I have enough of them already without adding new ones. We can speak English. For them," she said, nodding to the Silverthornes.

"Thank you," he said, inclining his head.

"It's wonderful to have visitors, even under these terrible circumstances. Don't you agree, Lala?"

The enormous Monta frowned. "It was the visitors that brought this danger."

"Ah, yes," said Madre, "but not these. I like this one." She winked playfully. "I would like to make you my special arroz de pato and introduce you to a granddaughter, but alas, I have neither duck nor any living relatives." The corner of her eyes twitched. "You have family? Brothers and sisters?"

"I do. Neveah, Imani, Izzy, and Max. My parents are Sela and Maceo."

"Lovely names, I would like to meet them," said Madre as if they were greeting at a picnic rather than inside an old cave, hiding from demons in a realm she couldn't escape.

Zayn smiled. He knew what she was doing. The old woman was a skilled manipulator. There would be a request.

"They would like you."

She sighed. "Why do you come?"

He gave a brief explanation after which the two elders asked a number of clarifying questions.

"We could use any information you have about the plant and the gigantes that live there. After we take the samples, we can come back and help you escape the valley," he said, anticipating what he thought she might request. "I wish we could take you back directly, but if there are other places you can survive outside of the valley, that's the best we can do."

"The offer is generous. The Eater in the Sky is like nothing else you've likely encountered," said Madre, and her expression went hard for a moment before she forced a smile. The old woman reached out to Mais Velho and squeezed her hand. "Let us discuss your offer. I want Benedita's opinion too. Give us time. We will let you know."

The three mages returned to the main cavern.

"I'm going to see if I can help some of them," said Pi, shifting the backpack off her shoulder as she nodded towards the scattered infirm.

"Good idea."

While they weren't Aura Healers, every mage could perform minor wound closings or purification charms to cleanse infected flesh. Zayn found a little boy that couldn't be older than six sitting next to the old woman with a bandaged eye. His left arm ended in a stump around his wrist and he had an angry looking scar on his cheek.

"May I take a look?" he asked the old woman. She squinted, but nodded with understanding, speaking to the boy in his language.

As Zayn performed the simple charms he knew, he realized that the boy must have been born right around the time of the disaster. The child knew nothing of a normal life. His vitality had been sapped. At the boy's age, the twins, Izzy and Max, were delightful terrors, creating chaos in their wake.

When he was finished, the old woman thanked him, but the boy sat on the blanket, staring straight ahead. This is what would happen if the barrier was allowed to be breached in Invictus. Except worse. Much, much worse. The break here had been the equivalent of a gas expulsion from a sometimes dormant volcano. If it happened in their world, it would be like all the volcanos of the world erupting at once.

Summoned back to the elder's room, Zayn found Benedita along with three others, including the grieving old man, Tomás, standing by the blanket.

"We have decided," said Madre, looking up to them. "You may go to the plant with our blessing. But. You must take Benedita and the others with you. Before you decline, know that any information you have is old. They can get you into the plant for your sample and back here."

"Forgive me for saying this, Madre, but we're three experienced Hall mages. We work better alone. It would be better if you kept your people here until we returned. Prepare for the trip over the pass," he said.

"This is not a negotiation, this is the price for our information. Otherwise, you will fail and we will remain stuck here until we die." She smiled grimly. "While death is an end that I am looking forward to, I would like the younger ones to have a chance at life."

Aurie and Pi clearly didn't like it either. Pi was chewing on the inside of her lip and had her arms crossed so tight she looked like she was hugging herself. Aurie had the presence of mind to not be so visibly disagreeable, holding her hands behind her.

He motioned them out of the cavern.

"No, no way," said Pi, glancing behind them. "I don't trust Tomás, and Benedita looks at you funny sometimes. They have an agenda."

"We have to," said Aurie. "Madre is not backing down and the others take their lead from her. Montanhas isn't what we thought it was going to be. The disaster was supposed to be long over, the demons scattered to the mountains, not contained to the exact place we want to go."

"I agree with both of you," said Zayn, nodding. "I think they have an agenda, but we should take them anyway. They're not going to jeopardize their friends' and families' lives. We're all on the same side here. Sure, they're not happy with the people that came before—"

"Especially the mages," said Pi.

"Especially the mages," repeated Zayn, "but they want us to succeed as much as we do."

"I don't like it," said Pi.

"Neither do I," said Zayn, "but I can lead the team back to the plant just the same."

Aurie frowned. "I thought I would be lead. This is our mission."

Zayn exhaled slowly. "I understand that, but this is the kind of thing my Hall excels at. I'm not usurping your authority here, but I think I'm best suited for this task."

"Aurie..." said Pi, tilting her head

A world of emotions passed across Aurie's face. Zayn hated disappointing her, but he knew he was right.

With lips pinched, Aurie said, "Fine. You can lead. But if there's a mission critical decision that has to be made, check back with me."

This was the part he hadn't expected. Should have expected. Here he was, getting his emotions tied into a knot about being around her, when she was focused on the mission. He was being stupid. Their entire realm was at stake and he was mooning over an old fling with a person who clearly didn't have the same feelings. He nodded as they went back into the cavern.

"We'll accept your help," said Aurie to Madre, who glanced between them. "But we lead the mission. You take direction from us."

Madre's heavy-lidded gaze was less friendly than before. "It is agreed. You should leave within the half-hour."

"Half-hour?" asked Aurie. "The other side of the valley is hours away, we'll be pushing towards daylight if we leave then. Better to wait for tomorrow for a full night of movement."

Benedita lifted her chin. "A storm is moving in. The clouds usually get trapped on the peaks and drop their snow there, but this one looks bigger than normal. If it breaks over, and we think it will, then it'll provide a better opportunity to get into the plant."

"I assume the Eater doesn't care about visibility," said Pi.

"No," said Benedita. "That was one of first things we tried, to move during a storm, but it saw us. We lost a lot of people that first attempt over the pass." She gestured towards her group. "Tomás. Callie. Nurn. Gather your things. We leave soon. Be ready to move quickly."

The three of them gathered near the exit of the cavern system. Pi pulled out a container of elixirs, but Zayn waved them off.

"Save them for when we're closer. The others won't be able to keep up if we take them."

"I thought we might need them earlier, in case things go wrong." Pi covertly watched Tomás picking up his weapon and a bag of ammo.

"We're in this together," said Aurie.

"Is this gonna be worth it?" asked Zayn.

Aurie's head snapped around. "Huh? Worth it?"

"The faez samples," said Zayn, lifting his shoulders. "Seems a lot of trouble for a small thing. I don't know. Bothers me, I guess, but you would know Invictus better."

The look the sisters gave each other suggested they hadn't considered it, but then again, they'd been running around the realms on tasks for the head patron. Eventually, they'd gotten tired and forgotten to ask why.

He hoped it wasn't a question that would prove to be important. He really did.

Eighteen

Aurie ducked behind the rocky outcropping, next to a cliff striated with darker shades of ochre. A few snowflakes swirled past her face. Zayn stood at the front of the line, fist held by his head, signaling to hold. The team held position while he disappeared onto the path.

It shouldn't have bothered Aurie to let Zayn take the lead of the small group. They'd been bouncing around the realms for two years, just her and Pi. It was nice to have others to help. After all, it'd been what they'd been complaining about to Invictus, the old goat. But now that they had the help, Aurie found herself weighing the pros and cons of the team lead, when it'd already been decided. It was stupid, wasted mental energy.

Pi punched her in the shoulder, leaned into her ear. "What's going on? You're barely paying attention. Do I need to get you an elixir?"

"No," said Aurie a little too loudly, getting angry looks from the others. They hugged their rifles to their chests, keeping their heads on a swivel. They'd survived because they hadn't let their guards down. Like she was.

She lowered her voice. "I'll get it together. Not used to, you know, others."

Before Pi could answer, Zayn appeared at the head of the group, motioning to resume their march across the hills. They'd split into two halves, mages in front, people with guns in back. Mostly to keep the two groups from accidently shooting or torching someone should the need for combat arise.

That was what she should be focused on. She'd wanted a team and now she had one. How the hell did one keep seven people organized should things go wrong? She and Pi had worked together for so long, they tended to anticipate each other's moves, like in the warehouse when Beckett had ambushed them.

The hand signals were good. Zayn had taught them before they'd moved out. The locals already knew them, but with slight variations.

They'd traveled the length of the valley in a short amount of time due to the darkvision enchantments that allowed them to move without worrying about tripping over tree roots or chunks of fallen rock. Massive bone-white clouds had pushed over the other mountain chain, blotting out that side of the valley. It hadn't quite moved into the shallow pass that separated the old Portuguese settlement from the Lifestone plant, but it swirled nearby.

Benedita had them detour into a shattered house on the ridge to wait for the clouds to finish their slow advance across the valley. The snow was coming down in thicker swirls and the trees were kissed with white. As they ducked into the destroyed building, half of it having collapsed sometime in the recent past, plumes of breath shot from their lips. The temperature had dropped again.

"I will check ahead to see if the hidden path that goes over the pass is open," said Benedita. "If I don't come back, you know why."

"I'll come with you," said Zayn.

Benedita stared back, before nodding. "Okay, we go."

The pair of them left, leaving Aurie to feel a little useless. Pi had taken off her pack and was readjusting the load inside, pulling out runed bars and a jar of high-quality salt. The other three clustered together in the corner. Tomás still bristled "stay-away," but Aurie wanted to connect with the team and understand them better, or at least what to expect. As she neared, Tomás flared his nostrils and said, "I have to piss."

He disappeared outside. Callie went to keep watch for him. Nearer the plant, the scorpics were more active. Aurie hadn't seen one yet, but the brief description sounded like something out of a nightmare.

"How are the darkvision enchantments?" she asked Nurn, touching her eye.

The Monta had a larger head with tiny nubs on the front of his forehead. "Good, thank you. Little things make this better."

"Why are you here?" she asked, hating her words as soon as they came out, then shaking her head. "I mean, why were you with the humans? My understanding is the Montas live deep in the mountains and there wasn't a lot of mixing."

His inky black eyes were more ambiguous in the dim light of her enchantment-aided vision. He sucked on his teeth before answering.

"Debts must be paid."

Further inquiries were left unsaid, as Zayn and Benedita reappeared, motioning to leave right away. The clouds had shifted and the pass was covered. After a quick reshouldering of gear, they hurried back into the night.

Wind gusts battered them as they scooted along the ridge. The bite of cold was distant for Aurie as her weather enchantment kept her warm. A wall of white had pushed across the valley. The settlement had been swallowed, and by the time they were heading up towards the low pass, they moved through the thick cloud, which didn't allow vision past ten meters and muted the scuff of their boots.

The path brought them high on the ridge, traveling across a cliff edge that gave little protection from the increasing winds. At the top of the pass, the cloud cover brought visibility down to a few meters, making Aurie feel like she was one step from falling through an infinite universe.

But eventually they came out the other side of the pass. Burning eyes peeked through the white cloud, glowing brighter. A brief swirl gave them a glimpse of a huge figure sitting by a fire near the bottom of the cliff, holding its hands over the heat, before he was obscured by the surging, dense cloud.

The path grew narrower, requiring hugging the rocky wall at times, but there were thick vines to grab at intervals, making it less terrifying than it would have been otherwise. A ledge gave the group a chance to surveil the old Lifestone plant, which had become more visible as they'd come down into the smaller connected valley.

Aurie was slightly familiar with the look of an industrial park. After their parents' death, they'd lived in the outer wards of Invictus, where the old plants that had been active in the 70s and 80s had fallen into disrepair. Half the facility looked like those, with grimy HVAC units hunkered down on the roof.

Fires were more common across the front half of the facility. The gigantes had built their homes in the old buildings, picking the ones still standing after the disaster. The back half of the facility looked like a giant fist had demolished it. Mangled girders and broken concrete stuck up at odd angles. From the shattered buildings, it appeared it'd first collapsed on itself and then exploded back outward.

As they sat on their haunches, reviewing the condition of the old Lifestone plant, a strange creature ambled out of the gloom along the shredded fence line that had once protected the plant. It was the color of faded bone, which made it harder to see in the swirling snow, with pointed legs and a scorpion tail that was held in curled anticipation. The creature looked bigger than a horse. The scorpic ducked through a hole in the fence and then wandered deeper into the destroyed section of the plant, leaving Aurie with a sense of dread. Pi caught her attention, frowning towards the disappeared scorpic.

"Do you really need to take the sample there?" asked Benedita, gesturing towards the shattered buildings. "It looks like that scorpic is making its home inside."

Aurie nodded, wishing Invictus' instructions had said different. He said he needed the faez samples from the source of the break, otherwise the contamination from the air of Montanhas would make it unrecognizable. *It's important*, he'd said. Aurie was beginning to wonder if it was important enough. That if he was in Montanhas, he might say that it was too risky.

"The good thing is the gigantes are scattered amongst the outbuildings," whispered Benedita, motioning towards the flickering fires near the front of the plant. Tomás grunted in what sounded like disagreement as he glared into the mist. The older man looked paler than before as he chewed on the inside of his cheek.

"How do you kill one?" asked Pi, nodding after the scorpic.

No one answered. Tomás scowled, looking away.

Eventually Benedita said, "We've never killed one. Even the small ones, like a dog, nearly killed the old mages. The ones before."

The Charmers.

Benedita held up a small plastic bottle filled with silvery liquid. "Mercury. The scorpics are drawn to it. Drink it down as if it were melted ice cream. Sometimes we can use it to distract them."

"What happened back here?" asked Zayn, nodding towards the mangled section of the plant.

"Someone set off a lot of explosives," Nurn said grimly. "It didn't do what they expected it to do."

Zayn checked over the edge of the cliff. "I'll set a drop line so everyone can climb down."

Aurie handed him a climbing rope and a piton. He found a crack in the wall, and using his imbuement-aided strength, he shoved the metal hook into the cliff. After testing it a few times, he tied the rope and threw it over the edge. Aurie found herself a little jealous of his physical talents. Arcanium's purpose was the study of arcane truth. She could have convinced the piton to hold fast in the stone with a bit of mendancy, but it would only be temporary, and if she didn't do a good enough job of it, they would risk falling. Truth was subjective. A piece of iron in a cliff wall was not.

Her sister went down first. She held the rope steady at the bottom of the cliff. The mix of soul fragments in her head made Pi the most versatile of mages, probably in the entire Halls. Tomás and Callie went next. When it was Aurie's turn, she nodded to Zayn as she descended the rope. Her lips briefly curled to a smile, but he was too busy checking their surroundings for danger to pay attention to her.

As she gripped the thick nylon rope, she saw Benedita pull a walkie-talkie from a pocket and toggle the receiver rapidly a few times, before shoving it away. Aurie averted her eyes when Benedita checked back so she wouldn't know that she'd seen, but the covert communication confused her, unless it was merely to let the others know that they were still alive. Aurie pushed it out of her mind to focus on the descent, but promised herself to keep an eye out.

Once everyone was at the cliff base, Pi sidled up next to her and shoved an elixir into her hands. Thumbing off the lid, Aurie threw it back. This batch tasted like week-old milky mint. Worse than the others, but not as bad as some. Neither of them was a skilled alchemist, so the potions they made varied in taste and intensity. The last batch had triggered her gag reflex, so she was relieved this one only caused a slight grimace.

Zayn led them through the fence, following the path that the scorpic had taken about fifteen minutes before. When they'd been at the top of the cliff, the cloud layer had been thinner, allowing sight that reached across the facility, but now down in it, she could see no further than five meters. The world grew claustrophobic. Aurie found herself constantly checking her surroundings because it felt like everything was pushing in.

Then the elixir kicked in and the small circle of perception, hemmed in by the cloud and the cold weather, expanded along with her senses. Old oils soaked into the soil caught in her nostrils. The grunting language of two gigantes speaking to each other in another part of the facility echoed in her hearing. The mist kissed her skin pleasantly, but a tiny rock that had snuck into her shoe rubbed against the back of her heel. It wasn't a problem now but would form a blister if she let it stay.

Aurie paused, shoving her finger into the back of her shoe to dislodge the grit, and she caught the scent of faez rising up through the shattered building. It wasn't exactly as she expected. Like taking a drink of a favorite soda but finding out that the formula had been changed.

The meaning of the difference was lost when she heard a distant gunshot. Or was it a gunshot? It could have been something breaking. The snap of a two-by-four.

Aurie looked up in time to see Tomás lifting his automatic rifle into a chest-forward position. He met her gaze, and it sent cold fear into her belly.

Nineteen

Pi should have known they were going to be betrayed the moment they stepped into the smaller valley where the Lifestone plant was located. The signs were there. The soul fragments in her head were usually like energetic pool balls, bouncing around with scattered thoughts. They could be annoying at times, but she'd never once regretted ingesting the twelve vials, saving them from certain annihilation. Her only regret was that she'd used up three of the soul fragments to save herself, back when she was still in the Halls. A mistake she would never make again.

As they'd neared the valley, the fragments had aligned in their thinking, like schooling fish all turning the same way at once. Nothing specifically pointed to betrayal. Usually there weren't concrete thoughts, only nudges in certain directions. The Daring Maids fragment noticed that Tomás wasn't carrying a heavy pack like the others, but had a Kevlar vest with a Lifestone security badge on the label. Metallum Nocturn picked out the way Nurn and Benedita stared at the old diesel tanks near the front of the plant that were reinforced with enchanted steel, protecting them from the harsh Montanhas elements. There were other things. The way Benedita kept touching the walkie-talkie in her pocket when she wasn't thinking about it. Tomás occasionally pulling out a necklace from beneath his shirt and kissing the emblem. Even the brief pinched head nod between Nurn and Tomás before the latter descended the rope.

The problem was that Pi had assumed they all had the same agenda.

As they headed through the fence line, she was focused on the shadows beneath the bent girders and rusty fallen sections of corrugated sheet metal, looking for lurking scorpics, not the traitorous members of her own team.

When Tomás reached into a pocket and pulled out a compact object the size of his fist, she thought it was something to eat. Especially when he lifted it to his mouth, grabbing the circular end of the pin with his teeth.

"Grenade," said Zayn, a moment before the word came to her lips.

Pi froze, unsure of what was about to happen. A wild-eyed Tomás had his rifle tucked under one arm, his finger on the trigger, and the grenade in his other fist squeezed tight to hold the lever.

"Forgive me, Angelina."

Rather than throw the grenade into their midst as Pi expected, Tomás burst past a surprised Zayn, heading deeper into the shadows. He was quickly out of sight, then the echoing rattle of automatic gunfire shocked Pi out of her stupor.

"Sonofa—he's going to bring everything down on our heads," said Aurie, heading after. "Hurry, or we'll never be able to take the sample."

Pi wasn't sure when the other three peeled off. The next few minutes were a wild scramble after Tomás. She thought he'd lost his mind from grief and was committing suicide by scorpic, attempting to take them down at the same time. She quickly dismissed that idea when she checked behind them, fifty meters deep into the narrow passages that formed the collapsed building, finding Benedita, Callie, and Nurn no longer there.

"Aurie. Zayn," she said, repeating it when they didn't slow. "They're gone."

Their blank expressions slowly changed to knitted foreheads and squeezed lips as the meaning of her words sank in.

"Merlin's balls, what's going on?" said Aurie, listing about, looking for someone to be angry with.

A burst of gunfire from deep inside the facility made Pi flinch. Tomás was alive, but he would draw everything with even shitty hearing down upon his head.

"It's a distraction," said Zayn, furiously working through the problem.

"For what?"

"I don't know."

"The sample," said Aurie, shaking her head. "We have to get the sample. It's what Invictus sent us here to do. Whatever they're doing doesn't matter."

"Except for the scorpics," said Pi. "That old fool is going to get us all killed."

Zayn moved out first with Aurie behind. Pi took up the rear. The pace was faster than she would have liked, especially as they went deeper into the shattered plant. The fallen steel, bent and overlapping, provided pathways and hidden cubbies. Too many places for an ambush. Pi hoped that Tomás' distraction would keep the scorpics from lying in wait.

In the upper portion of the collapsed section, the pathways were more natural, winding and varied. The scorpics followed the torturous tracks, the only sign of their passage deep grooves along the crossbeams where their razor-sharp tails scraped past. Lower in the plant, the compacted metal and concrete required the scorpics to dig their way through. They traveled through tunnels hewn out of a wreck. The reason why the enormous critters would take the time when there were ample places to nest elsewhere in the valley worried Pi. She didn't think she'd like the answer.

The muffled thump of an explosion, followed by the vibration traveling through the interlocked steel, left dust steaming onto their heads. Some got in her mouth, which she spit out. Tomás. She didn't know how to feel about his death. The old man was clearly grieving, but he'd put their lives in danger for whatever distraction he was providing.

Zayn slowed. "No more distraction. How close do we have to be for the sample?"

"Invictus wants it taken at the source of the breach," said Aurie.

"Does the air smell different here?" asked Pi, wrinkling her nose.

"It smells like death," said Zayn grimly. "Wish we had some mercury."

The pace slowed. They came to a crossway. The scorpics clearly thought they needed more than one passage through the collapsed plant, but she didn't understand why until a minute later.

They came to a bubble beneath the steel, a place that had naturally formed during the explosion. Old, rusty tanks connected by pipes were bisected by a mangled wall. Pi was drawn to the faded writings across the bent surface.

"These are wards," she whispered. "But I don't recognize these. Different symbols, but I'm no expert."

"Would explain why they're not hanging out in here," said Aurie. "Otherwise this looks like a nice spot."

Zayn was peeking through a hole that led deeper when Aurie cleared her throat, gesturing towards two sets of bones that had been picked clean. One set, still wearing a Kevlar vest, looked human, while the other much larger bones could only be a gigante.

"Tomás went through here," whispered Zayn, tapping near a droplet of blood where he'd cut his arm sliding through the gap.

The pressure on her shoulders as she followed Zayn through the narrow passage made Pi sick to her stomach. The elixir ramped up her senses, but that worked double for the emotions that were keyed to them. Her mind was screaming for her to get out, that it was too dangerous, but the task Invictus had set them on required her to keep her feet moving forward.

Zayn paused at the bend, holding his hand beside his head in a fist, then motioned to move up slowly. Pi felt cooler air on her skin. The mountain weather was reaching this place somehow.

The scene below their vantage point made her skin crawl. A natural cavern lay beneath a dome of interlocking steel and old concrete. In the old explosion, the structure had fallen in and then been pushed outward, leaving a livable space beneath. At least for the scorpics. Nests were scattered throughout the region. Pi saw at least a half dozen of the horse-sized creatures lying in huge depressions they'd made in the stone.

"Are we close enough?" mouthed Zayn.

Aurie pulled the runed cylinder out of her backpack. The runes glowed faintly. She shook her head and gestured toward the back of the cavern, which their darkvision didn't reveal. Zayn took the runed cylinder and pointed to the ground, then to himself. Before either of them could say anything, he stepped into the cavern full of scorpics.

And disappeared.

Twenty

The Academy of the Subtle Arts, Zayn's home for five years, had given him the abilities that he'd come to rely on to survive. During his time there, he was given magical imbuements, tattoos etched into his skin that provided powers he could access whenever he wanted. The first two provided strength and speed, along with a hardening of the body to handle the impact of those abilities. These were the most commonly used imbuements, as being able to move faster than anyone else solved a lot of sticky problems.

The third imbuement, the ability to move through the Veil, which was the region between life and death, was both a help and a hindrance. As Zayn flooded his third imbuement with faez, triggering the passage into the nether realm, the world took on a greenish cast, like the sky before a Midwestern storm. It wouldn't allow him to move through physical objects, but the creatures of this realm wouldn't be able to see him.

Entering the Veil came with danger.

As a member of the living, he was not welcome in the Veil, even though he'd made friends with some of the beings that made it their home. As soon as he stepped into this world, the hair on the back of his neck stood up. Traveling through the Veil had to be done sparingly, or one wouldn't come back at all.

Zayn leapt from the top of the mangled stairs, landing a few feet from a nesting scorpic that lifted its bony, grotesque head as if it sensed him. He ran as if his hair were on fire, a count-down in his head. Already he sensed things moving towards him. Like the demonic realm, the Veil was connected to all realms, which meant it housed a lot of dead. None of them wanted him in their home.

When he reached the back of the cavern, he almost dropped out of the Veil in surprise. It looked like a crystalline garden. The ground had buckled in places, white stones sticking to the sides like tiny teeth ready to bite into his limbs. Even in the Veil he sensed the difference. It was much worse when he dropped out, shoving himself into a corner.

The scorpic nests were nowhere near the back of the cavern as if even they didn't want to be too close. He felt like he was standing at the spot of a nuclear disaster. The runed cylinder glowed bright when he pulled it out, making him turn his body to shield the light.

Zayn triggered the cylinder, which gave off an even brighter, bluish light and a high-pitched whine that made his teeth itch. The scrape of claws on stone sent a quiver of fear through him. The scorpics were alerted to his presence. He tried to block the increasing illumination but it was like trying to hold back the sun.

Mercifully, the bright, bluish light went out and the runes faded to cold, dark. A scorpic stood at the opposite end of the cracked stone, tilting its alien head towards the space he was hiding in. Zayn shifted into the Veil before the scorpic came to investigate.

He shifted right back out when he found something waiting for him.

The Veil was a place of brief refuge, but there was no way to survive against even the most minor of beings there. That one had found him so quickly was bad luck. He wouldn't be able to return through the Veil and now the scorpics were alerted. Four of them had left their nests and ambled toward the back of the cavern where he was hidden behind a fold in the wall. Their mandibles clacked as they tapped on the stone in what he hoped wasn't communication. It was bad enough they were so big, and reportedly extremely dangerous, but if they were intelligent too, that was not going to work out for him.

The only thing keeping them away was the strange shattered stone filled with crystals. The air smelled different where he was standing. A quick inhale through the nose provided a sharp stab of faez, but it was mellower where he was, as if it'd been watered down.

When the first scorpic started climbing across the broken stone, he knew he couldn't stay in his location much longer. His first three imbuements weren't the only tools he had available. Zayn reached for his fourth.

The imbuement had been specially designed for him. It allowed him to influence non-humans through their pheromones. He hoped it worked on creatures from the demonic realm.

Using the tattoos on his right ribs, Zayn sucked in the air. The intake slammed into him like a drug overdose. He fell to his knees as the world wavered around him. It felt like taking a hit of pure faez. He was drunk on power, yet staggered by its overwhelming nature. With the right spell, he could blow a hole through the moon, he thought.

That narcissistic sense of power was tempered by the approach of the scorpic, picking its way across the shattered stone. Using the left side of the imbuement, he pushed back on the scorpic. *Go somewhere else, there's nothing here*, he told it.

Using his fourth imbuement made him feel like he had invisible hands to push on the world, but as he tried to convince the scorpic to return to its nest, he felt like he was pushing on a greased ice cube. Zayn *shoved.* The impact went right past the scorpic, which was only about fifteen feet from his location. If he didn't do something soon, he was going to be trapped, and there wasn't enough time to access his fifth imbuement.

The moment the scorpic caught sight of him, he had to act. Zayn darted from the cubby, only to find his equilibrium off. He ran right into the bony midsection of the scorpic. The creature was as surprised as him. It stabbed a foot into a crack in the ground as he vaulted over it, avoiding the stinger that flew by his head.

Two more scorpics blocked his path.

Zayn leapt between them, but he misjudged the height, catching himself on a low-hanging beam, spinning into an empty nest filled with small bones that crunched when he landed. His arm was covered in wet.

Sucking in the pheromones had left him disoriented. He moved toward the entrance of the cavern as a scorpic moved to intercept. The tap-tap-tap of its many legs as it skittered across the stone echoed through the cavern like a drum line.

He dodged past the critter, his ugly gait bringing him right into the strike of the stinger. The bony protrusion sent him tumbling into the rusty, split-open tanks that lined the entrance to the cavern. A bright line of pain shot through his arm. He knew he was injured but there was no time. Staggering to his feet, he found the scorpic barreling towards him.

"Aurelia!"

The older Silverthorne stepped in the creature's path. Her shout was a thundercrack. Two front pincers snapped off with the fury of an axe blow. The creature punted forward on its narrow head, the others running into its tilted-up rear.

As the scorpics maneuvered around their injured brethren, Pi's hands moved in a circular motion, as if she were turning a great wheel. A dim star-shaped blacklight formed in the air, sending off crackles of energy, snapping at the scorpics, creating a miniature gravitational pull that left them disoriented.

Aurie grabbed his hand and yanked him towards the tunnel.

"It won't hold them long," said Pi, following behind.

Aurie halted, examining his arm, which had been flayed from forearm to wrist. Dangerous amounts of blood flowed from the wound. She held her hand over the chasm and said, "Close."

The two edges of the wound collapsed together, forming a long, crimson-beaded line on his arm.

"It won't hold long, but maybe enough for us to get out of here."

A screech, followed by the sounds of electricity popping and crackling from the cavern, spurred them on. Pi led them, as he could barely move in a straight line. They ran through the twisted labyrinth of old steel that had been tunneled out by the scorpics over the years. Four or five turns later, they stumbled upon a dead scorpic, half its bony body ripped open, green goo oozing on the ground. They were about to move on, when he heard something from deep in the wreckage.

"Wait."

Their expressions said there was no time, but he heard sobbing. The quiet moans of a dying man. A mage light revealed Tomás curled into a cubby; his chest was soaked, black with blood. The automatic rifle lay at his feet.

"Merlin's tits," exclaimed Pi.

"Can you do something for him?" Zayn asked Aurie, who shook her head.

"Even what I did for you is only temporary."

Tomás' gaze came up. He was seeing them, but he looked like a man half in consciousness and trying to flee for good. The old man mumbled in Portuguese.

"What's he saying?" asked Pi, checking back to him.

Zayn listened with his imbuement.

"No estrando? No estradno?" He filtered the word until it came clear. "No boom!"

"Looks like a boom," said Aurie, checking the dead scorpic that had clearly been killed by his grenade.

Tomás grew more lucid. Looked directly at them. "No estrando. No escapar."

"No boom, no escape," repeated Zayn. "That's it. That's where the others went. They're going to blow something up. Cause a distraction for the Eater so the others can escape. That's why they wanted to come with us. Tomás was providing a distraction for them."

Aurie tilted her head. "I haven't heard an explosion."

"Which means it hasn't worked," said Zayn.

"We have to get out of here," said Pi. "The other scorpics can't be far."

"What about him?" he asked.

"There's nothing we can do for him," said Aurie, hesitating at the passage.

The poor sod had sacrificed himself for his family. Zayn knew that pain dearly. He touched the old wound above his heart.

Aurie led them out of the mangled part of the plant. The valley was still in the clouds, but it was less dense. Snowflakes came down in waves. Half an inch was already on the ground.

An ache in his arm had him looking down. The pressed-together slice started peeling apart, blood gushing out in gulps. Aurie slipped out of her backpack and pulled a box of first aid supplies out.

Pi took a good look at the crimson snow beneath his arm. "I'll set some warding lines, keep the scorpics from finding us."

The younger Silverthorne disappeared back into the collapsed plant with a jar of salt while Aurie wrapped the bandage tightly to stop the bleeding. Zayn drank an elixir that would help the healing while she worked. Closing up the wound from his wrist to his upper arm took the entire roll. The whole thing throbbed with the beat of his heart. He was lucky it wasn't worse.

"Let's get back to the portal location and get the hell out of here," said Aurie as she shoved the leftover medical supplies back into the bag.

"Do you hear that?" he asked, looking towards the front part of the plant.

Aurie squinted. "No. Your hearing is better than mine."

"Silence. No estrando. No escapar," he repeated in a perfect imitation of Tomás' speech pattern.

"Not our problem," said Aurie. "Not after they betrayed us."

"We promised to help them over the pass."

She checked over her shoulder. "If we don't hear anything, they're probably dead."

Pi returned from the tunnels, the jar of salt half empty. She shouldered back into her pack, snowflakes caught in her spikey black hair.

As they trotted towards the cliff where the rope waited for their ascent, Zayn couldn't help but think of his family. The twins, Izzy and Max, always causing mischief, while Imani in her lion costume harried them as if she were the real predator. Neveah, with her sharp tongue and even sharper intellect, which she poured into her culinary skills. Keelan, his cousin, who had sacrificed himself for them, just like Tomás had for his family.

As Aurie grabbed the nylon rope heading up the cliff, Zayn said, "We have to help them. We can't let Tomás die for nothing."

"No boom. They failed. They're already dead," said Aurie.

Pi hadn't been there for the conversation. She glanced between them and then at their surroundings. Visibility was improving. The time for stealth was coming to an end.

"Then we finish it for them. They must have had explosives. This old plant should have some leftover gas tanks or something," said Zayn.

"We have to go," said Aurie.

"I agree with my sister. Tomás could have gotten us killed. Maybe if they would have asked..."

"Sometimes you can't ask," said Zayn. "I'm going. I'll meet you at the portal location."

Aurie growled under her breath in frustration. "That's not how this works. You're here with us, you take our direction."

"I'm not compromising the mission." He handed over the inert cylinder. The runes were black. "If I'm wrong, then you go on without me."

"Zayn," implored Aurie.

Pi cracked her neck. "Maybe we should just go help. The gigantes can't be any worse than the scorpics."

"You'd go if Pi were in trouble."

Aurie stared back, flat-lipped. He could see the disappointment on her brow. If there'd been a chance they might rekindle their relationship, he'd just killed it. Nothing like inviting a new member into your team, only to have them disobey your orders.

"Fine," said Aurie, annoyed, "we'll go."

They hugged the fence line as they headed into the plant proper, ducking under towers that fed old waste material into rusted barrels. Zayn sensed the creatures ahead in the gloom. He held up his fist, trusting the sisters would stop.

Four gigantes. He wasn't sure how formidable they were. His only clue was they were twice his size. Given how wrong his attempt to influence the scorpics had gone, he had to assume the gigantes would cause equally unique problems. They stood talking like a group of teenagers loitering on a busy street corner.

A door into the main plant provided a way around the four gigantes that didn't seem like were planning on moving anytime soon. Zayn motioned for the sisters to follow. The doors had been ripped off the hinges in the distant past, the metal pieces lying connected to the concrete wall on the cracked tiles. The peach-colored hallways had faded with time. Trash lay along the sides, the gigantes having picked through the room, leaving their refuse everywhere. A poster hung on the wall still in its frame, the interior bubbled from condensation, showing a group of workers with their hands held high. Work is Family! Their fake, actor smiles were nothing short of insulting. At least growing up in Varna and attending the Halls had protected him from inane corporate life.

The old cafeteria was empty. Most of the windows had been smashed or blown out. The cloud layer was thinning and glowed with the approach of dawn. If they didn't leave soon, they would be trapped. Aurie's expression said as much as she frowned at the light.

"If we can't find them, we're leaving," said Aurie.

Using the Veil was out of the question. Zayn stepped through a broken window, creeping out to get a better view of the front part of the facility. Fires flickered in the mist, thick shapes moving around them. He counted at least a half dozen gigantes, more than he cared to tangle with.

Eventually he found what he was looking for. Two enormous diesel tanks with ladders heading up the sides of each. Reaching them would mean traversing the open area and risking being spotted. A gigantes' fire was set between the two tanks, probably to block the winds that came from that side of the valley.

It was interesting that the gigantes, after coming from the demonic realm, had hunkered down to survive rather than head into the valley on some murderous rampage. Made him wonder what it was like beyond the barrier. Maybe they were just happy to have a place to call home.

"There are two big diesel tanks around the corner. That has to be where they were planning to go. A few charges set on them would pack a hefty punch."

"Did you see them?"

"No, but there's nowhere else to go that's going to cause the kind of distraction they need. There's a camp of gigantes near them, but I think if we're careful we can avoid them," said Zayn.

"I hope you're right," said Aurie.

He led them outside the cafeteria and along the building line. The camp near the tanks looked like it'd been made with old wooden shipping pallets. If he ignored the ten-foot-tall humanoids lingering about, the camps could have been a shantytown in any third-world country.

They made it to the far side of the tanks. That was where Zayn saw the problem. Callie was lying behind a pallet, a few feet away from a pair of gigantes. A black bag was sitting on the top of the pallets, where she'd dropped it. It appeared Callie had been climbing the metal ladder when a rung had snapped. He could see the broken metal about halfway up. She'd taken a tumble and couldn't move to reclaim the bag, which probably held the explosives, without being spotted. Zayn didn't remember the black bag, which meant it'd been hidden in the area. This was a plan long in the making.

Now that he had identified her, he spotted the other two, crouched on the roof of the tank, peering over. Benedita gave them a curt wave.

"The clouds are breaking up and it's going to be morning soon," said Aurie.

"Three gigantes. Rather not fight them," said Zayn.

"I'll lure them away," said Pi.

"Careful," said Zayn. "My imbuement didn't work on the scorpics as expected."

Pi winked, heading back towards the cafeteria.

"She's cocky."

Aurie rolled her eyes. "At least she didn't run directly into a scorpic."

"You saw that?"

"You looked like a drunk trying to weave to the bar for another round," said Aurie, mirth on her lips.

"I did it to confuse them," said Zayn, "which I might add, worked, because I didn't get stung."

Aurie gestured towards his arm.

"Tis but a scratch."

A haunting song brought both their heads around. The gigantes near the tanks noticed too. After a few back-and-forth grunts, two of them headed in the direction of the noise.

Zayn motioned for Aurie to follow. They curled around to the backside of the pallets where Callie was lying. She looked both embarrassed and apologetic.

Aurie helped Callie to her feet, but it was clear she'd injured her ankle. She couldn't put weight on it. The single gigante was on the other side of the makeshift pallet house. Zayn wasn't sure he could take it out in one blow, and they had to act soon, before they might be discovered.

The cloud layer was dissipating fast. Other buildings were appearing out of the gloom. Zayn pulled a dagger from a hidden pocket. The gigante was too tall for him to hit the neck or other potentially vital locations without taking a different approach than he normally would. He picked up a pebble and threw it to a spot away from the tanks. When the gigante turned its head towards the noise, Zayn sped past the humanoid, leaping towards the tank and then pushing off to arc back towards the lone guard. Zayn landed on the gigante's shoulders. The blade found the flesh at the front of its neck. He had to keep the gigante from crying out. The blade went in four times before the creature realized it. Zayn backflipped from its shoulders, landing on his feet, then sliced the lower section of its calves in one blow. The gigante fell onto its knees, holding its spurting neck. Using the force of his imbuement, he severed the gigante's spine near the neck by shoving the dagger in deep. The creature collapsed on its stomach, quivering in final death throes.

Zayn leapt onto the ladder, grabbing the black bag as he scurried up to the top of the tank. Benedita and Nurn hovered near the edge.

"I'm sorry—"

Before Benedita could finish, he said, "Task first. Bullshit later."

Nurn pulled a few sticks of explosives from the bag along with an electronic timer that was cracked in half from the fall. Benedita and Nurn looked at each other for a long moment, both of them speaking at once.

"I'll do it."

Nurn followed up. "No. I should be the one. You know that."

"Isn't there another way?"

Nurn gestured at the air, growing brighter by the moment. The sun was climbing the blocking mountain range. When it ascended into the sky, the cloud layer would burn off completely, exposing them.

"Right."

He'd only just met the Monta and wished he'd had time to get to know him, especially the reason for his sacrifice, which seemed like a penance for something he'd done in the past.

"Go," said Nurn. "I'll trigger it when you're safely away."

Zayn quickly climbed back down, followed by Benedita. Aurie was holding up Callie, who looked pained by her injury.

"I'll carry you—"

The words were barely out of his mouth when an eight-legged bony scorpic came skittering out of the mist. The stinger punctured Callie, the tip sticking through her gut, surprise on her face lasting until she was flung away by the enormous critter.

Twenty-One

Any hope of escaping from the old Lifestone plant without getting into a pitched battle ended the moment Callie's body was flung into the dirt by the scorpic. There'd been no time to react. Aurie had checked back to where Pi had lured the other gigantes, and right when Zayn returned from the top of the tank, it'd appeared.

She ducked when gunfire exploded next to her. Benedita unleashed her rifle on the scorpic, bullets chewing through the bony outer casing. Her barrel rose from the kickback, curling towards the exposed steel tank. An errant bullet could pierce the outer shell, and with a spark, annihilate them.

But Benedita released the trigger before such disaster. The staggered scorpic wavered on its many legs. Aurie heard shouts of alarm from other parts of the plant, and hulking figures ran towards their location.

The scorpic surged forward. A second burst of gunfire, this time from Nurn on the top of the tank, kept the critter from reaching them.

"Go! Run!"

Benedita ran towards a building behind the cafeteria. Aurie followed, but shouted to her left where Pi had disappeared.

"This way!"

The fading mist crackled with energy, turning the pale cloud to bruise purple. Her sister burst from the center of the thunderhead, a maniacal grin on her lips.

The outbuilding was about a hundred meters from the tanks. Aurie checked over her shoulder at the pursuing gigantes. Two of them were only a dozen feet behind. She was considering hitting them with a force wave when a hand shoved her in the back hard. She tumbled head over heels, landing in a heap as a concussive wave roiled out from the exploded tank.

Lying on her back, ears ringing from the blast, she watched the second tank blow. The bright light made her close her eyes, but she could still see the outlines of the buildings through her lids. The ground rumbled.

When she could open her eyes again, she found that one of the pursuing gigantes was lying next to her. The resemblance to Nurn wasn't lost on her. The big demon grabbed her by the neck before she could use magic. As flames erupted from the tank husks, hair-crisping heat making breathing difficult, the gigante squeezed her neck, crushing her windpipe. Aurie beat at the enormous arm, but she may as well have been trying to bend a titanium rod.

As the dots in her eyes began to connect, she saw something move next to the gigante. The next thing she knew, Pi was shaking her arm and she was flat on her back.

Aurie tried to speak but it hurt. Without her voice she was useless as a mage. Most of her Arcanium-given magics relied on the ability to speak. Her sister yanked her to her feet. A gigante with a dagger in its skull lay in the dirt, eyes unfocused.

Benedita led them into the building and they entered a shaft leading into the maintenance tunnels. Aurie had trouble keeping up. She was dizzy from being strangled. Pi leaned into her face and tried speaking to her, but the blast had left bells in her ears. She was happy enough to put one foot in front of the other, as the ringing interfered with her sense of balance.

After a long traverse through tunnels filled with old pipes, they came out in a different part of the facility. Benedita led them up a ladder into a building that wasn't too far from the fence line.

The sun was behind the mountains, but it was daylight and the mist had burned away, revealing rolling black smoke from the double tank detonation. The ground rattled again from a secondary explosion as they made their way to the rope on the cliff.

"Hurry," said Benedita, "we need to get up there before the Eater arrives."

Aurie didn't really hear the words, but she read Benedita's lips enough to get the idea. Sliding down the rope had been easy, but hand-over-hand climbing took time and Aurie wasn't feeling great after getting thrown and choked by a creature that outweighed her by three or four times.

She made it up the rope, even though she barely remembered. Pi was already there, hugging the cliff wall. Her sister touched the side of her head, gesturing towards Aurie. When she copied the gesture, she came away with fingers wet with blood.

Zayn made it up the rope last. They moved along the path as thick black diesel smoke burned their eyes. When they reached the wider section of the trail, a horrific noise reverberated through the valley. Aurie found herself cowering against the rocks. Naked fear had pinned her to the spot. She wasn't the only one. The four of them were kneeling on the path. It wasn't until she saw the shadow in the sky that she understood. The Eater.

The terror in her heart made it impossible to look directly at it, but she had the impression of something dark and big with wings the size of a field. It carried shadows with it, defying the rising sun. A screech sounded like a thousand nails on a thousand chalkboards.

The urge to lie down and let whatever it was come and dine on her soul was strong. The others felt it too. Staggering to her feet, she grabbed her sister by the shoulder and hauled her forward. They had to keep moving.

Aurie hardly remembered stumbling from the smaller valley, climbing over the pass on the rocky trail surrounded by gnarled bushes. The only thing that probably saved them was the cloud of black smoke from the diesel fires. The Eater circled the facility, but never caught sight of them.

When they reached the valley where the old settlement was, the pressure on their minds melted away. Aurie could think again. She was relieved to find that the four of them made it. Not Nurn. Not Callie. Not Tomás. But at least someone had gotten out.

The journey back to the portal location took a half hour. It wasn't until they were looking down at the old buildings that Aurie realized what Benedita had done. Without any magical ability, they couldn't bring her back using the tether.

"You can't go over," she said, the ringing in her ears down to a dull buzz. "You're trapped in the valley."

Benedita leaned against a rock. There was smeared blood and diesel soot on her face. The ache of the day haunted her gaze. She had her arms crossed, lips squeezed white.

"Maybe." She leaned her head back and glanced at the high mountains behind them. The peaks rose like daggers against the sky. "I will wait for a snowy day, climb through those, hope for no avalanches. It is enough."

The weight of Benedita's sacrifice pushed down Aurie's shoulders, erasing the betrayal.

"The four of you joined us, knowing you probably wouldn't come back," said Aurie.

Benedita nodded. "Thank you for helping, even when you did not have to. The others should be over the pass by now. They will live." She closed her eyes. "You should go. Before the Eater returns. Being out here in the day is bad. I'm going to hide until night."

No one knew what to say. They each reached out, gripped her hand. Not so much a greeting, or farewell, but the acknowledgement of pain. Before, the idea that they couldn't take anyone back with them was an immutable fact. Now, after Benedita had given up her chance at freedom, nearly dying in the process, Aurie wanted more than ever to be able to take her with them.

It couldn't be.

They picked their way down to the settlement. Benedita watched them for a while. When Aurie looked up a last time, she wasn't there. Headed to a safe place for the day.

A screech echoed across the valley. The Eater was restless. Hunting.

It was good they were leaving, but Aurie hated that they couldn't help the woman reach her friends. For all they knew, she would die in the snow trying to summit the treacherous mountains. Sometimes there was nothing she could do.

Aurie gathered together with Pi and Zayn. No one spoke. There was nothing to say. She activated the tether, yanking them back into the Spire, feeling heartsick and empty, even though they'd been successful.

They appeared in the portal room. The relief that flooded into her veins at escaping Montanhas lasted about two seconds until she heard the grumbling baritone of the head patron.

"What in the broken hells is he doing here?"

Twenty-Two

The grim reality facing Benedita was the only thing on Pi's mind when she stepped through the portal. Benedita was a survivor, fighting a war she'd never wanted a part of, and she would keep on battling, long after they'd left her in Montanhas.

So when the gruff tone of Invictus intruded into her solemn meditation on Benedita's sacrifice, Pi couldn't help the ball of flame that climbed out of her throat and formed itself as a collection of fiery words, directed at the head patron.

"You ancient, wrinkly ball sack," said Pi.

She took a step forward, but felt a little dizziness from the portal travel and getting her head knocked around by twin explosions.

"We wouldn't have survived that shit show without Zayn. Might I add that your notes were complete bullshit. There were survivors on Montanhas, demons too. We barely got out with our lives. Look at my sister."

The old man glowered from across the table. Fury condensed itself in his black eyes, and if he opened his mouth and hot gasses blew out, turning them to ashes, Pi wouldn't have been surprised.

"You don't know what you're messing with," said Invictus. "You're children with great powers. Nothing more."

"If we don't know, then tell us!" exclaimed Pi. "You're asking us to trust you, yet you've done nothing but ship us around the realms with little more than a few phrases to keep us on the right path."

Invictus lifted his chin. "If I told you, then you'd want to know more, and that knowledge would drag you deeper and deeper into ruination."

"People died in Montanhas," said Pi. "It was awful. They sacrificed themselves."

The ancient mage snarled. "Then you understand what might become of you. I make no apologies for my actions. This realm is at great risk. I will spare no effort to save it from the demonic one, and that includes sacrificing the lot of you. Especially when you're being foolish and bringing others into the Order without my permission."

Aurie took a step forward, stumbled, and grabbed the table for balance. Everyone in the room stared at her. A twitch of sympathy passed across Invictus' expression. Only a twitch.

"Why? Why do you keep us in the dark as if ignorance is a virtue?"

"In this case it is," said Invictus. "The beings that we're dealing with have power over thought itself. To know is to risk!"

Aurie pinched the bridge of her nose between forefinger and thumb. She wavered, and Pi went to hold her up, but she waved her off. They shared a brief smile.

"I just watched a group of people head into a place they knew they would probably never return from. They didn't do it because they were ordered, they did it because they were family," said Aurie.

"I'm your family," said Invictus with booming gravitas.

"It sure doesn't feel like it," said Aurie.

Up to this point, Zayn had been standing to the side, trying to look as small as possible. The mention of family brought his eyebrows up. Outside the room, no one else besides Sam Arlington knew they were distantly related to the Head Patron of Invictus. That's how he'd populated the Order of Merlin before, with those of his family.

The ancient mage looked prepared to fire another invective, but he closed his mouth and grumbled under his breath.

"You're more troublesome than your parents," he said haughtily.

"Maybe it's because they were dead when we needed them," said Pi.

The comment made Invictus flinch. The man with immense powers who had lived an impossibly long time and survived against a horde of murderous demons went from the tallest person in the room to a shrunken version of himself. He curled his arms against his chest, contemplating what she'd said.

"We're not asking a lot," said Aurie. "We need more members in the Order. We can't do this alone, just Pi and I. We wouldn't have survived Montanhas without his help." She reached into the backpack, pulled out the cylinder, and set it on the table. "We got your sample. I hope it was worth it." She took a step forward and almost fell again before righting herself. "I need to lie down."

For the first time, Invictus saw their injuries—the diesel smoke coating their flesh and clothes, the dried blood, the bandages.

"Dear me," said Invictus, leaning against the table, the centuries weighing on his body. "I am a terrible person. You're not a soldier, yet I treat you like one."

"We're not even getting paid," said Pi.

"No, Pythia Silverthorne, you're not even getting paid," he said, a tiny curl of amusement at the corner of his lips. Invictus looked around the room as if he were seeing things for the first time. "Go. Shower. Eat. Rest. We can talk later. Discuss your proposal. I'll leave some elixirs by your door to help with the injuries. Proper healing draughts, not those disgusting potions that you mess up my lab with, and probably don't do a damn thing."

Zayn stepped forward, holding out his hand awkwardly. "I'm Zayn Carter."

Invictus frowned, the wrinkles in his face as deep as valleys. "I know who you are, boy. Like I wouldn't know Priyanka's prodigy and the one who saved Varna from the Lady. I know all my students, especially the ones who have sacrificed much. Like you two." He shook his head. "I'm an old man. Forgive me for forgetting how to be a human. It's something I forget from time to time. If we don't have family, then what do we have?"

He shuffled out of the room, leaving the three of them to stare at each other.

"That was Invictus?" asked Zayn. "I mean, I know that was Invictus, but he was nothing like I expected."

"He's like an old rash that you've grown fond of," said Pi.

"Or a mangy dog that bites your hand to remind you it can still be mean," said Aurie, chuckling, then her face went rigid. "Oh, I need to lie down. I feel like I could throw up. Shower first."

She disappeared, leaving Pi with Zayn.

"What should I do?"

"Follow me," she told him. "There are more rooms than necessary around here. Multiple bathrooms. Quite lovely actually. The décor is a little old. This one has weird seashell critters some might call ugly, but the showerheads work, and that's really all that matters."

The shower wasn't hot or hard enough to remove the stain from her heart. Alone, covered in the steaming spray, Pi let the horrors of the day consume her. It was easiest to sob in the privacy of the little space. Then she scrubbed her flesh pink with a loofa until the tiles were covered in pink and black.

By the time she returned to the living area, the others were sitting around the kitchen counter, clean and in new clothes. Zayn hadn't brought anything with him, but he was wearing a patterned sweater and jeans that looked like something from Sam's closet.

To her surprise, Invictus was standing in front of the stove in an apron, working multiple pots and pans, whistling cheerfully. She didn't know what to think. She'd never seen Invictus in the kitchen except to grab a handful of sliced meats and one of his weird green drinks that he existed on, before disappearing into his workshop. She wasn't aware that he could even cook.

"Ahh, Pythia, looking much better with a nice hot shower," said Invictus, glancing over his shoulder. "There's an elixir on the table for you."

As she grabbed the vial and popped the stopper out, she looked to her sister, who shrugged her shoulders and mouthed, "I have no idea."

The potion went down creamy smooth, like a shot of melted vanilla ice cream. Warmth flooded through her system, along with localized tingles around her injuries. The worst was inside her ears, which she wanted to poke with a Q-tip until the irritation subsided.

"Is that bacon?" she asked. Until she'd drank the elixir, her senses, especially hearing and smell, had been muted from the diesel explosion. The cleansing tingles had reawakened her senses.

A skillet of sizzling greasy bacon sat on the right side of the stove. Pi circled around, looking to snag a piece that was drying on a pile of paper towels, but Invictus slapped her hand.

"It'll be ready in a moment. Take a seat with the others."

True to his word, a minute after she took a seat at the counter, Invictus was sliding plates of eggs Benedict, bacon, hash browns, and a strange looking jelly toast across the table. The crisp bacon was exploding on her tongue before she'd even grabbed a fork. Ravenous hunger gave her eyes only for the meal.

"What is this jelly?" asked Zayn with a quarter of the toast already in his mouth. "It's delicious."

"Cthulhu jelly," said Invictus with a wink, "stripped of toxins of course. It has a delightful tingle on the tongue."

Zayn stared at his toast as if it'd come alive, but hunger overcame whatever history he had with the creatures, and he continued inhaling his breakfast.

Pi took a tentative bite of the pale, almost translucent jelly toast to find it, as Invictus said, covered her mouth in a pleasing tingle. It was a non-hot version of a ghost pepper. By the end of the meal, she was soaking up the egg juice with the crusts of her toast, picking off the tiny shards of bacon that had escaped her earlier scouring.

Invictus let loose an earth-shattering belch as he pushed his plate away. Zayn got up to clear his plate, but the ancient mage held out his hand.

"I'll clean up later. We have much to discuss."

The conversation started with how Zayn came to join them and then moved to the events in Montanhas. Interactions with Invictus had always been a bit strange for Pi. He was the most famous person in the world, a wizard whose longevity spawned a thousand conspiracy theories about who he might really be and things he might have done in the past. When he was being grouchy, a real asshole, she could forget those things, but having him quietly ask questions like a wrinkly, wavy-haired reporter was almost too much for Pi.

Somewhere during Aurie's explanation of the scorpics beneath the plant, Pi blurted out.

"Who are you?"

Invictus straightened, fixing the gray robes he liked to wear around the space. They weren't the formal ones he was most known for, with patterns suggesting runes along the hems and a light sheen to the fabric that made one think that it was otherworldly, but they gave him an unknowable cast.

"What do you mean, Pythia?"

His penchant for saying her full name was grating on her and she didn't know why.

"Why being all nicey-nice? You've been a complete ass to us for the past two years, and now you're suddenly being a sweetheart? Making us breakfast and elixirs, something you've never bothered to do before, no matter how beat up we came back. You fixed Zayn's arm without a fuss when before you'd send us to Golden Willow because you didn't have time for *trivialities*"—she made air quotes—"while you were deep in your work. It makes me wonder if the real Invictus came back from your last trip. Do we have an imposter, or have you finally lost your mind after all these centuries?"

He raised an eyebrow. "I can be a terrible old man if you'd prefer."

"I don't prefer that at all. I just want to know why the change."

"Oh, Pythia, always having to know." He shook his head. "Sometimes knowledge isn't a good thing. The wrong kind of knowledge, anyway. That's what I've been trying to shield you from, but it appears I cannot do so any longer and possibly the burden grows too great for even my shoulders. It's why I created the Order in the first place, because I was going mad with too many problems."

Invictus picked a curl of bacon fat from his nearly empty plate and popped it in his mouth.

"You know the one thing that has always been delicious, no matter the century, has been bacon. It might be the world's most perfect food."

"You're dissembling, old man," said Pi with a smile in her teeth.

"Caught again," he said with a wry grin that turned sour as he prepared to speak. "Have you heard the name Elosian? Lord of Spies?"

Zayn and Aurie shook their heads, but when he'd asked the question, he'd stared directly at her, and she knew why.

"I do."

"Yes, you do. Pythia Silverthorne. Nearly summoned a major demon before she was even a member of the Halls. I would say that such a thing had never been done before, but prior to the Halls, wanna-be sorcerers accomplished all sorts of things on pure moxie. Few survived. You summoned Pazuzu, but that wasn't who you initially considered, was it?"

The memories were old. Seven years ago. A lot of events from that time were lost to the trials that came after. But not that.

"No," said Pi, "how do you know this?" When he lifted his chin, a smirk forming on his lips, she understood. "Patron Malden."

"You spent a year in his Hall, invited at the time by a mysterious party that you eventually learned was Professor Trebleton. What you didn't know was that the professor had not learned about the Rod or the tome that provided the summoning spell on his own. It took time to track down the real source of his information, but what Malden and I learned was that it wasn't an idea of his own making, but a suggestion, skillfully placed by Elosian, the Prince of Whispers."

A shiver of concern ripped through them. The name was a boogeyman. The other two didn't know enough to understand why they should be worried, while she knew far too well.

"This demon lord has had designs on our realm for as long as he's been aware of it. Over the years, he's made countless attempts to cross over, but each time, he's been thwarted by chance or the efforts of mages like yourselves. I know of some, but I'm sure there are other events that are hidden by time and circumstances.

"But now, I'm afraid that his schemes are coming to a head. Too many snowballs are rolling down the hill, creating an avalanche that we cannot stop. The signs are there. The divinations from Oculus have been converging on this eventuality for some time. Even I cannot stop it."

"You're saying that a demon lord is manipulating people into doing what he wants through the barrier?" asked Zayn.

"Exactly. To hear him is to be deceived. He is patient and cunning, willing to keep a thousand small plots in the air in hopes that one of them will blossom into victory."

Pi snapped her fingers. "Beckett Dreadmarsh. That's why he came after us. Elosian got to him."

"Possibly," said Invictus. "That's the problem with his schemes, it's hard to track down the source. But given the time and what you learned, I would not be surprised to find that Elosian was behind the attack."

"But why would they listen to him?" asked Aurie.

"Because it is not Elosian they are hearing, but their friends and family. He cannot enter our realm on his own, but he has found ways to whisper into people's ears, letting them think it was their idea. Our modern world has made his task easier. Conspiracy theories bloom from thousands of seeds that he placed in unusual places. In our fantastic world, how hard is it not to believe them, especially when the world is out of your control."

"So we're at the mercy of the idiots of the world," groused Pi.

"Do not think yourself immune to his machinations. Greater mages than yourselves have been deceived. His cleverness is unmatched because he knows how to speak the words that people want to hear, tug on the desires of their heart, trigger the fears that drive them."

"This is why you've been keeping us in the dark," said Pi. "You're afraid that we're being manipulated. But how do you know you're not the one that's getting nudged in the wrong direction? Maybe Elosian doesn't want us to find help. Maybe he knows that if it's just a few of us, we cannot stop him."

Invictus raised an eyebrow. "An astute observation that I have had myself many times."

"Then why a change of heart?" asked Aurie.

A smile formed, mostly in his eyes. The dark edges of his lids made it look like he wore eyeliner.

"In all the trials and tribulations that you have experienced, Aurelia and Pythia Silverthorne, what was it that carried you through?"

Pi didn't have to think. She looked right to her sister, who was looking back at her.

"Family. We wouldn't have survived without each other," said Pi, reaching out and squeezing her sister's hand.

Invictus nodded. Turned to Zayn. "What about you, Zayn Carter?"

He touched a spot over his heart, eyes wistful and wet with memories.

"I wouldn't be here today without family. My cousin, Keelan, my sister Neveah, they each played their part. Broken hells, I wouldn't have even gone through with all of it if it weren't for my family. They got me through the dark times when it seemed the entire world was against me."

"Exactly," said Invictus. "Elosian has his lies, his schemes, his cunning. But he doesn't have family."

"Family can be manipulated," said Pi. "You just said so."

"True, but it's harder. He might be able to co-opt your desires, but in the end, family will see through the lies. I've been so bent on protecting you from Elosian I forgot the most important thing. Your foulmouthed outburst reminded me of that. All three of you survived horrific events because of family. If we're going to get through this, I need to stop thinking about what the enemy is going to do, and focus on what makes us stronger."

"So we can recruit more members of the Order?" asked Aurie hopefully.

"A few," said Invictus, rapping his knuckles on the counter, "with my permission."

Elosian's methods were a burr in Pi's mind. It kept her thoughts on a Ferris wheel.

"But how do we avoid falling into his traps?" asked Pi. "Beckett believed he was doing a good thing in trying to kill us. How do we know that we're not the ones being manipulated?"

"That's always been the struggle with Elosian, and part of his methods. Once you're worried about motives, expecting a hidden knife in every fist, it's hard to trust, it's hard to bond. That's how he wins, by creating strife and division."

"Great," said Pi, "you're saying we can't know."

Invictus shook his head. "No, you can't. He's clever. But it's like debating free will. You just have to examine all the information and trust yourself in the end. Sometimes it's the questioning, the thoughtful introspection that's enough. Or it isn't."

"So...when they snatched Andromeda, that might be part of a larger plan? That's why you didn't want us to go after her?" asked Pi.

"My fears," said Invictus, eyes creasing with thought, "but that's the danger. My fears of being manipulated were driving a wedge between us. Your defiance taught me that no matter how hard I squeeze the controls, I cannot make others do what I want. A lesson it seems I am cursed to learn over and over, especially in the Halls."

"So you'll tell us what the cylinder was for?" asked Aurie.

Invictus leaned back, chuckling. "No, there are some things I am keeping close to the vest. You'll have to trust me on that, just as I will learn to trust you on the needs of the Order."

"Should or should we not go after Andromeda?" said Aurie, looking directly at the head patron.

He took a long drink from his orange juice, slurping comically before setting down the glass.

"I'll leave it up to your judgement," said Invictus. "It's probable that it's a trap. I see no other reason for them abducting Andromeda, but that's for you to decide. I have my tasks. You have yours."

With that, he rose to his feet, reminded them to leave the dishes for him to clean, and left them to their discussion. The three of them stared at each other for a while.

Pi spoke first. "I hate myself for saying this but I think I liked it better when he was giving us directions. I could decide whether or not I was going to follow them. This is so open-ended I'm already questioning everything."

"Maybe that's the point," said Zayn with a shrug. "He's trying to keep Elosian guessing."

"What do we do?" asked Pi.

"Whether or not she's important to Elosian, we need to find Andromeda. The truth bond is like a sword over my head. I keep expecting to keel over, or find spiders crawling out of my skin from some remote curse," said Aurie.

"Two questions," said Zayn, "where is she, and do we have enough firepower to get her back? You said a team kidnapped her."

Pi searched her memory. Her haste had almost gotten her killed.

"Five or six, maybe? There was the big guy that shoved Andromeda into the van, the one that seemed to be handling the weird cobra-headed creature, and that asshole that threw the warding box out of the window and flipped me off. I didn't see the drivers, which is two more. Could have been others," said Pi.

"There were at least two more at the warehouse ambush," said Aurie. "Might be the same, could be different."

"We have an unknown number of mages, at least five, but probably more, acting without their knowledge on Elosian's behalf," said Pi, "and no way to find them."

"If we can figure out who they are, we might," said Zayn. "Anything you remember that might narrow it down? Defining physicality? Scars? Tattoos?"

"Tattoos," said Pi right away. "The guy that shoved her into the van had a sleeve of them. Too far away and too hectic for me to remember."

"I can help you there," said Aurie.

"Right." Arcanium were masters of memory and truth, all things that Pi distrusted, even though she'd been a member for a few years. "I guess we're making an alumni visit."

"I can ask around about the others. The creature you described is pretty distinct." Zayn narrowed his gaze. "Reminds me of something, but I can't place it. I'm sure it'll come to me."

"What about new members?" asked Pi.

"What about your old friends, the Misfits?" asked Aurie.

Pi shook her head. "Love 'em to death, but this is way beyond them. They were never in a Hall, remember."

"Had to ask," said Aurie, shoulders heavy with guilt. "No one from Arcanium springs to mind. Most of them were more research based, and after what happened a few years ago with Isabella, I hate to put them in danger. What about you, Zayn?"

"Possibly," he said. "I don't know where they are at this time, but I'll put out feelers. They might all be busy."

"Too busy for the end of the world?" asked Pi.

"You know what I mean."

"Meet back here when we're done," said Aurie, starting to carry her plate to the sink, then reluctantly setting it back down.

Zayn stepped away from the counter, confusion on his brow. "Uhm, how do I get out of here?"

Twenty-Three

The Animalians campus was in the eighth ward next to the Invictus Menagerie and Cryptozoo. It wasn't the first time Zayn had visited, but it hadn't been since he was training in his Hall.

He bypassed the zoo, headed towards the Animalians campus, which was a collection of buildings scattered across green grass. The unnaturally warm March day brought the students onto the lawns, seated on blankets, laughing and throwing frisbees like at any other campus. An enormous silverback gorilla stood near a glass building, speaking with a group of students using sign language and an interpreter.

Compared to the last few years, spent mostly in the Eternal City, infiltrating the Animalians campus was a cakewalk. If he'd wanted to bypass the subterfuge, he could head straight up to a professor and present himself as Priyanka's assistant, but he didn't want word of their search to get back to the people that had kidnapped Andromeda. A more subtle approach would be required.

After watching from a distance, using his imbuement-aided senses, Zayn picked out a student with a similar build heading off campus, probably to grab lunch or run errands. Zayn walked briskly towards the guy, who was barely paying attention, wearing a big set of bright orange headphones and nodding his head to the beat.

Zayn had brought an old backpack and stuffed it with random books to look like he was a current resident of the Halls. As he passed the Animalians student, Zayn drifted into the way, their shoulders colliding. The unzippered pack spilled papers into a cloud, which the other student hurried to collect.

"I am so sorry," said Zayn, receiving the mostly blank papers from the student. "I should have been paying attention. First nice day in weeks, I guess."

The guy had pale skin, a peach fuzz beard, and a few pimples on his forehead. He pulled the headphones to his neck. An electronica beat thumped out of the orange speakers.

"It is quite alright," said the guy cheerfully in a thick accent that Zayn couldn't place. "Beautiful sky, hard not to enjoy. You have good day."

Shoving the papers into his backpack as the guy left, Zayn repeated his words to find the flavor of his accent.

"It is quite alright. Beautiful sky, hard not to enjoy. You have good day." He repeated the phrasing, feeling where the weight was placed on the words as he looked through the wallet that he'd lifted during the exchange. Emre Tekin. The ID was an Invictus city one, not a passport. He guessed Emre was from Jordan or Greece, or somewhere in the region. Turkey maybe.

Zayn preferred to practice an accent longer before having to put it into use, but he wanted to figure out something about the creature before the Silverthornes returned from their trip to Arcanium. He ran a hand over his face, modifying it to match Emre's, then changing his skin tone, adjusting it until he felt he had a close match. Zayn checked himself in his phone camera, coaxing pimples and peach fuzz onto his face to complete the mimicry.

With the disguise in place, Zayn hunched his shoulders and headed back to campus. The clothes weren't the same, but most people's memories convinced them they were incorrect. As long as he got the major things right, the minor details could be dismissed.

Zayn avoided the ongoing lecture from the silverback gorilla. Professors were more astute to the possibilities of magic, and were generally suspicious.

A lone guy was sitting on a blanket off to himself. He had a tome open in his lap and was mumbling softly as he read the text. There was a picture of a hulking, gray-skinned humanoid creature with its fist stuck into a cliff wall, ripping out a chunk as if it were butter.

"Hey," said Zayn.

The guy looked up. He was wearing glasses. His ambivalent expression was a mix of interruption and confusion. Zayn could see the pulse on his neck increase. Annoyance. He needed to get him on his side quickly.

"It never ends, huh," said Zayn in what he hoped was a faithful recreation of Emre's accent.

The guy squinted, then looked down at his book, frowning. "Yeah. Not sure I can keep up with the memorization. How do you do it? I thought the magic stuff would be the hardest part."

"A little bit every day," said Zayn.

"A little? Feels like too much."

Reading the words on his open page, Zayn gathered that he was studying supernatural creatures. He knew little about how Animalians worked, but since the critter kingdom was their charge, it was probably a lot like Assassins, which taught them how to understand and infiltrate various cultures of intelligent beings.

"Better to have that knowledge in a pinch than to make the wrong move in a bad spot."

"I thought when I came here, I wanted to be a Hunter, but no way. They have to learn too much. I think I'd rather be a Shifter and specialize in some lazy species in a nice place."

"It's tough being a first year," said Zayn, hoping he was correct about the student's placement in the school. "But it goes quickly."

An appreciative nod told him he had pegged him appropriately, but that meant he probably wouldn't be knowledgeable about what Zayn wanted to know.

"Here's one for you. Pop quiz."

The kid sat tall, hands on the open tome as he looked up. "Sure, why not?"

"What kind of creature is as big as a lion, has a cobra for a head that breathes coal smoke, and brass feathers?"

The kid blinked and shook his head with his mouth shifted to the side. "No idea. I think that's book four or something. Chimeratic kingdom. I'm only on book one."

"That's okay. It's a fun one, not trying to mess with you." Zayn nodded towards the big glass building nearby. "Gotta go. See you around."

The kid's expression brightened into a smile. He pushed his glasses back on his nose and returned to his memorization.

Keeping to what he'd just said, Zayn headed into the building with the big glass front. An enormous swimming-pool-sized saltwater tank was positioned on one side of the interior. It was filled with colorful fish and pink coral. He couldn't help but drift near it, drawn by the hundreds of species inside.

An octopus with deep brown coloring, accented with specks of ochre, floated out of the gloom, its many legs undulating. As it neared, the octopus made distinct motions with its limbs that suggested communication. It seemed to make a fist and nod towards him, then tapped on its ochre body. It finished with its attention on Zayn as if expecting a response. Delighted by the interaction, but also worried about being discovered, Zayn gave the octopus a little wave and headed deeper into the facility.

On the other side of the room, an open-air cage housed dozens of birds, including a few big ravens that squawked when he approached. A couple of students sat on a bench speaking quietly.

"Hey," said Zayn with a cocked smile, trying to appear both friendly and humble, "how's it going?"

The girl and guy both frowned at his interruption. The wave of animosity radiating from the couple on the bench made his smile falter. Every Hall had its rivalries. Zayn knew that Animalians was broken up into different disciplines: Tamers, Hunters, Keepers, and Shifters.

"Great view," he said, receiving no response.

The pair hadn't turned themselves to him. He detected heat in their cheeks, a mix of lingering warmth and a newer version that bristled with *Go Away*. He reinterpreted his earlier assumption that they were annoyed because he was a member of another discipline in Animalians—he realized he'd interrupted a date, an early one based on the distance between them. They'd been speaking quietly, getting to know each other when he'd waltzed up.

"Right. Sorry for the interruption."

Zayn backed away with his hands up. They resumed their conversation. He overheard their admonishment at his interruption, but didn't take offense. As Emre he probably wouldn't have known not to approach them.

Spinning around as he turned the corner, he nearly ran into a girl coming the other way. She had stone-white hair and a red blotch on her chin and was headed out of the building with a backpack slung over her shoulder. She had a button nose. Cute.

"Emre. Hey, I thought you were headed into town." Her forehead knitted. "Where are the cans?"

She held her hands near her head signifying the bright orange headphones Emre had been wearing when he saw him.

"Broken," he said with a disappointed shrug. "Skateboarder ran into me, ripped the wire. Ruined."

Her sympathetic expression warmed his heart even though the reason was a lie.

"I'm so sorry. You love those things." Her face went through a brief contortion. "Since you're not headed into town, you have time to help me with something? Nothing you can't handle."

"Yeah, sure," he said.

When she turned back towards the interior of the building, he scoured her backpack for a name tag, but there was nothing. She turned and smiled at him, sensing his examination, so he grinned back. Eager attention could hide a lot of awkwardness. He was just glad he wasn't in the Eternal City anymore with their micro expressions and willingness to read anything as an insult to further their battles. Just the way one held their hands when drinking from a goblet could be interpreted as a cultural slap akin to flipping someone off.

The way she kept glancing back to him with a slight smile suggested that she had a crush on Emre. The pulse on her neck had tripled in rate since he ran into her in the hallway.

"What's the job?" he asked as they approached a door with a security block.

She pulled a badge out of a pocket and tapped it on the black plastic casing, turning the red lights to green. He caught her name before the ID disappeared. Karina. Zayn fumbled out the stolen wallet, quickly tapped the block, and followed her into the inner area.

"Taking some samples for Professor Ansel."

Samples. That probably meant dealing with physical animals. His willingness to help got more complicated.

"Karina," he said, hoping that she didn't go by a nickname. Her smile and nod lessened his tension. "I was working on something interesting this morning. Research. I came across a creature that I was unfamiliar with. Nothing I've read before."

"Uh-huh," she said as she led them into a room filled with cages. It smelled like cedar chips. Dozens of containers with various lizards and serpents filled the room. He would have preferred spiders, but wasn't sure where they fit in the Animalians' repertoire.

"Let's get started and then we can talk about your problem," she said.

"Right. Good idea," he said, even though he hated it. He was hoping to get his answer and disappear before exposing himself as an imposter.

His heart climbed into his throat as she passed the cages with the snakes. Relief flooded in when she stopped at an enclosure with a trio of bright crimson iguanas sunning themselves on the hot rocks in the cage. He could feel the heat radiating through the glass.

"Gland work," she said, rolling her eyes as if it were a petty, simple job.

Karina had given every indication that she liked Emre, so he stood close to her. The nearness would be a distraction, hopefully hiding the little mistakes he was bound to make. There were thick leather gloves that went up to the elbow hanging on the front of the cage.

"What's the plan?" he asked, staring into her eyes until she blushed and glanced away.

"You grab 'em, I'll take the sample," said Karina as she dipped into a metal box next to the cage, producing an industrial-sized syringe.

The leather gloves went all the way to his elbows. Zayn searched the lid for a lock, but didn't find one. He lifted it up, found the stay that would hold it aloft, and clicked it into place.

Karina was smiling at him. He couldn't figure out if it was attraction or expectation of the work. When he reached into the cage and her expression crashed, he yanked his arms out.

"Aren't you going to?" she asked expectantly.

Zayn fluttered his eyes. "Sorry. After the headphones thing, and I've had a headache all day...would you mind?"

"No," she said, "totally understand. I had a favorite pen that I dropped into a sewer last week. Been bummed since."

Karina set the syringe down and made a few gestures as she said a few key words. The spell was easy, he was sure he could repeat it if necessary, but it didn't matter since the iguanas froze on the rocks.

Zayn grabbed an iguana around the midsection. Karina frowned, but said nothing about the placement of his hand. He held the critter towards her, but she made a twirling motion with her forefinger, and he reversed the iguana. A stick into the reproductive parts of the iguana made him glad he was only holding them, not trying to find the gland with the syringe. She pulled the stopper, filling the syringe with a few milliliters of a brownish-green liquid. This was repeated two more times with the other two iguanas, after which she took the vial on the end to a centrifuge machine along the wall.

"What's the critter query?" she asked as she placed the vial into the centrifuge and started the machine. It quickly spun to a gently rattling hum. Karina leaned against the table.

While Zayn took off the leather gloves and placed them on the hook, he said, "Ever heard of a creature as big as a lion but with a cobra head that can breathe coal smoke, and has feathers made of brass?" He remembered what the kid on the blanket said outside. "Chimeratic kingdom, of course."

Her eyes darted around the room as if the walls contained the information.

"What's it for? Extra credit? Special project?"

"Professional curiosity." He scratched his nose to covertly change the tone of his cheeks, making them slightly pink as if he were blushing. "Found some random stuff on the Internet. Probably not real, but you know, wondered if it was."

Karina exhaled heavily, bunching up her cheeks before blowing out. "Chimeratic. Wow. Could be anything. People breed some really weird stuff. Have the link to show me?"

Zayn patted his jeans and then said, "Oh. Not on me. Laptop."

She wandered across the space between the two tables, leaned against the one next to him.

"It's nice having help. You're usually much quieter. It's nice to see you coming out of your shell."

He met her smile, but groaned inside. He could feel her desire, radiating towards him. He certainly did not want to initiate a relationship that would be very complicated when the real Emre showed up.

Karina leaned over, lips parted slightly, tongue resting on her bottom teeth. She'd moved faster than he could consider how to avoid the kiss. Using his elbow, he nudged the cage hard, which loosened the latch, slamming the lid down between them. Both of them startled away, the kiss interrupted. She blushed and looked at her shoes, while he searched for a way to extricate himself before she made a second attempt.

"Karina. I have to run out."

"Oh," she said, crestfallen. "I understand."

"It has been nice working beside you," he said. "I'd like to do it again sometime." Her lips curled up. "But. I feel like I've made a total ass of myself. When we meet again, please act like this didn't happen."

"Sure, totally. You know I don't care. Right?"

"I do, but it's a mental thing." He tapped on the side of his head. "I should go. I swear this isn't because I'm not enjoying this, but let's do it another time."

Leaving Karina a little shocked and confused, Zayn slipped out of the room. He decided that he wasn't going to find the information he needed quickly, and probably needed to leave before Emre returned, realizing that he didn't have his wallet anymore.

On the way out of the building, he checked back towards the zoo, spotting a set of orange headphones bobbing his direction. Zayn hurried past the glass building, and the kid on the blanket, whose head popped up as he was going by.

"Hey."

"Hey."

"About that creature. It's probably not what you're looking for, but it reminded me of what happened at the Portland Zoo a few years ago with that giant flying snake."

The mention was like a thunderbolt for Zayn. He'd been in another realm when it happened, but it was such big news for so long that he'd read a little about it when he'd returned. Must have missed the flying snake part. He'd read about the Animalians students that had put their lives on the line to save people trapped in the dangerous domes.

"Thanks."

The real Emre was approaching fast, head down, but if he looked up, he'd see his doppelganger. Zayn strode away from the blanket, checked around, and returned to his original self along the way.

"Hey, Emre," he said, pulling out the wallet as he approached. "You're Emre, right?"

"Yeah?" asked Emre, clearly confused.

"I was looking for you. Found your wallet on the sidewalk. Must have happened when I ran into you."

Emre snapped his fingers. "I was wondering. Thank you."

"No problem. Was my fault after all," he said. "By the way, while I was looking for you, I ran into some girl, cute, button nose. Anyway, sounded like she's totally into you by the way she talked about you when I said your name. But you know, don't say anything. Be casual, right?"

"Yeah, thanks again," he said, eyebrows moving up and down.

A veranda in the nearby park was a good place for him to stop. Zayn pulled out his phone and typed in "Portland Zoo Disaster." It wasn't hard to find the pictures of the flying snake. He hadn't seen what Pi saw, but the creature gave him the shivers. What was more interesting was the write-up on the students that had gone into the zoo during the height of the chaos, rescuing dozens of people from the horrific event.

"Liam Miller. Logan Lovelace. Janelle Morrison. Jae-Yong Kwan. Pax Nygard."

The final picture showing the curly redheaded girl included a four-legged creature that looked like a fox but was far too big to be one. Its name was Kali. There was something about the both of them. Two candles burning bright.

These five students had run into danger rather than away. Not only did they know something about the flying snake, but they knew something about bravery. Maybe one of them could join the Order. He dug back into his phone, typing in their names one at a time to learn more about them and where they might be. He had other more direct options for information, but this was the easiest place to start.

"What kind of creature are you, Kali?"

Twenty-Four

The drawbridge leading into the medieval-style castle at the center of the fifth ward had always been a bit of a mistake in Pi's opinion. If Arcanium was supposed to contain the guardians of truth, delvers into arcane magics and the explorers of great knowledge, then having a big door that flipped up to block entrance like a giant middle finger wasn't the best of images. Or maybe that was just her.

Next to her, Aurie was as giddy as a little kid with a pocket full of cash at a Scholastic book fair as they strode across the heavy wooden timbers towards the stone barbican. A tingle across her entire body announced their passing through the wards. It wasn't typical for alumni to have access to Arcanium, but they weren't normal alumni. Aurie had gotten permission to use the extensive libraries for pre-travel research.

Pi had yet to use her access, content to leave Aurie to the mind-numbing research. In truth, Arcanium had never really been a draw for Pi. The only reason she'd put that name down in the Tome of Record was as an appeasement to her sister. Coterie of Mages, the Hall that prided itself on pushing the limits of the arcane, had always been the place for her. If it hadn't been for Professor Trebleton, she probably would have stayed.

A woman with steel-gray hair bound into a thick braid greeted them from her wheelchair beyond the front hallway.

"Professor Mali," said Aurie, "it's lovely to see you again."

"Hey, Joanne," said Pi, catching a sour look from the professor. She wished it'd been Professor Longakers meeting them, but he was a popular teacher and probably had more classes than he could handle.

"Aurie. Pi. More research?" asked the professor, hands resting on the blanket in her lap.

When her sister opened her mouth, Pi knew there was going to be a long back-and-forth between her and the professor. The two had never really gotten along, and Pi wasn't in the mood for the social dancing that would slowly promenade them to the final answer.

"We need to use the Verum Locus," said Pi.

Professor Mali's lips squeezed together in disappointment. "Those aren't the facilities that Patron Semyon agreed you could use."

Aurie gave her a stern, motherly look, which Pi responded to with an eye roll.

"Not all research is in a book," said Pi with a wink.

"What my sister is trying to say is that we need access to a recent memory in her head and would very much appreciate using the facilities. We wouldn't ask if it weren't important."

The look from the professor pulled a sigh from Pi's lips. She could see the intractable nature in her eyes. If there wasn't a rule or law about it, the professor didn't know how to deal with it.

"Look," said Pi, "we could use some long and overly complicated spells to accomplish the same thing, but the Verum Locus is easy to access and doesn't require all the setup which we don't have time for. If you'd like, we can get our boss down here to smooth over the negotiations. You know how he loves interrupting his research for trivial points of order."

The narrowing of Professor Mali's gaze brought a warmth of pride from Pi. They both knew that Invictus was a grade-A asshole and that she'd just thrown the gauntlet in her lap. The professor checked her watch.

"There's a class down there at this moment, but you can use them when they're finished. Please try to stay out of the way, and avoid being seen as much as possible. We don't want our students to think this is a playground after they leave these hallowed walls."

"Thanks, Joanne," said Pi as they headed deeper into Arcanium.

Away from the professor, Aurie turned to her. "Why do you torment her like that? She's not bad. You remember she was there for us when things got tight."

"She needs to unclench those butt cheeks a little. It's not good for you to hold a stick up there. I'm providing a valuable health service," said Pi, skipping as she walked. "She should be thanking me."

A couple of students clutching their books on the way to a class hurried the other way. Pi made sure to wave and tell them hello, which only received horrified, incredulous glances from them.

"You love pushing buttons, don't you?"

"It's not so much that I love it, but that I see it as a necessary act," said Pi. "Laws, rules, these are all well and good, but they can become a straightjacket too. At least not all the professors were like Joanne. She's brilliant and all, but stifling as a lead blanket."

The room that contained the Verum Locus was along the outer wall of Arcanium. She could hear muted car noises beyond the thick stone. A group of students were sitting in the outer area, waiting patiently for the last of them to leave the inner space. Those waiting were talking quietly or playing games of Five Elements, and Professor Chopra was dozing in a chair along the wall with a book leaning against his chest.

Only a few years separated Pi and her sister from the students in the room, but it felt like a gulf of decades. In the arcane world, time was not a shortcut for experience. Pi looked to the napping professor and was pretty sure she had more real-world knowledge to offer the kids than him. Not that he was a bad professor. He was a little stuffy like Joanne, but his heart was in the right place.

Pi was watching from the entrance to the room when a girl with two black braids hanging over her shoulder stumbled out of the Verum Locus, a look of devastation in her gaze. Her eyeliner had smudged around the bottom of her eyes. She plopped into a chair away from the others, lost in the eddy of memories she'd experienced inside the room.

When another student went through the door into the Verum Locus, Pi leaned out and spoke to her sister, who was thumbing through her phone.

"Were we ever that young and naïve?"

"Naïve? No. Arrogant, yes," said Aurie, meticulous eyebrow arched playfully. "Especially you, dear sister."

"I'm not arrogant," said Pi.

"You're not...okay, this is a new one to me, what are you then?"

"Confident in my ability to survive and then learn from my mistakes," said Pi.

"Sounds like arrogance to me."

"They're different. Arrogance means you believe your own hype," said Pi. "I'm not above a fuckup, every now and then."

Aurie shoved the phone in her pocket. "I sometimes wonder if it's all those extra voices making your head so big, but then I remember you were like that well before that happened."

The sounds of class breaking up ended their conversation. The students filing out grew wide-eyed at seeing who was lurking outside their classroom. Pi heard their names whispered with awe and reverence. Professor Chopra, true to form, was busy reading his book when he left, completely missing them.

"Okay," said Pi, skipping into the room and holding up her forefinger and thumb a hair apart, "maybe a little arrogant."

Aurie approached the door leading to the Verum Locus. She placed her hands on the smooth stone surface.

"It never looked like much," said Pi, arms crossed.

"Seeing Mom and Dad die over and over in here," said Aurie, "I've never been quite sure if I hate this place or not." She tapped her knuckles against the door. "No. I'm wrong. Definitely hate it."

Until she stepped into the room, Pi didn't realize how much she was dreading using the Verum Locus. They wouldn't be using it for its intended purpose, delving into the painful past of her life, but visiting the recent memory of when Andromeda was kidnapped.

Pi approached the door and ran her palm along the smooth surface. "You know, I don't know why I never came here and used this to relive some of my favorite memories. There's no reason this place has to be all doom and gloom. I could have spent some time with Jade again. Or Pepper."

"Or Mom and Dad?"

Pi inhaled through her nose. "Yeah, or Mom and Dad. Let's do this. We need to get some new members in the Order before Old Iron Balls changes his mind."

The room was simple enough—four walls and the single door, which Aurie closed behind her with a nod. Pi jumped a little when it clicked.

"It's just a room," she told herself as golden-speckled light trickled into existence, like a million stars awakening around her. It was the only place she'd ever seen so much faez in raw form.

"Focus on the memory," said Pi, closing her eyes and centering her thoughts on Andromeda's abduction. "Focus on the memory."

The stench of coal smoke came first, followed by the burning in her nose. The room dissolved around her, replaced by the concrete parking garage beneath the Glitterdome. Her heart rate climbed until she had to force her hands to unclench.

Shouts and the clacking of claws on stone echoed through the space. Andromeda was fighting against the guy, but she couldn't see it yet. She only had access to the memories she'd experienced, so trying to move around the line of cars to see what was happening wouldn't help. The two security guards were already lying by the door, face-first on the ground. Unconscious she'd thought at the time, but would later learn they had died from unknown causes.

The door burst open, startling Pi as the version of herself from that night went thundering across the concrete, oblivious to the danger. She threw herself around the corner as the black smoke came rolling past, prompting a fast retreat, but not fast enough to avoid getting burned by the superheated air.

Broken hells I was an idiot.

Pi touched her arm in response, the memory of that flash of pain recent enough to make her grimace. Now that she'd been around the corner, Pi positioned herself to examine the team of mages that had abducted Andromeda.

The first thing she noticed was the young performer. Fit and attractive in all the ways Pi enjoyed, but that wasn't why she'd come to the memory. She refocused her attention on the others, looking for details that might help them track them down.

The creature that had nearly burnt her to a crisp was hard not to stare at. The cobra head attached to a lion's body and covered in what looked like brass feathers was so oddly horrible it was like trying not to stare at a terrible car crash.

The young woman handling the chimeratic creature had her hood up, face hiding in shadows. Pi shifted to get a better look and caught the aquiline nose beneath the hood, but nothing more as she turned away.

The big guy manhandling Andromeda was easier. Wide head with a soldier's haircut, sleeve of tattoos including a granite fist that Pi was well acquainted with: Blackstone Security. She didn't let herself get too distracted by the symbol, looking for the others on their team. There were two drivers, neither of which she could see, except for a pair of gloved hands. But as the white van pulled away and the dirty-blond-haired guy in the passenger side threw out the little box that exploded into a shimmering ward, she spotted the temporary license tag hanging beneath the mirror.

"Gotcha."

As the vans squealed out of sight, Pi turned, placing the memory of the door into her mind so she could escape the re-creation. But rather than seeing the rest of the parking garage, where the cars had been burnt by the superheated coal breath, or the plain door inside the Verum Locus, she found herself in an unfamiliar landscape.

Fear crept in like a thief.

Jagged mountains angled in impossible directions like crystals in a cave surrounded her. At first she thought it was Montanhas, but these ranges were gravity-defying and made her sick to her stomach just looking at them. Pi stepped on something that crunched beneath her feet. The grass had shattered as if it were made of glass. A swirling black cloud formed in the sky directly above her, prompting her to wonder where the sun was. Nothing but diffuse light refracted off a million surfaces. The cloud disappeared as quickly as it'd formed, as if the atmosphere was unstable.

A cold trickle of fear climbed up her spine, leaving her to spin around, expecting to find danger but seeing nothing. *What am I doing here? This isn't my memory.* Pi closed her eyes and tried to focus on the Verum Locus, but found herself in a different place when she opened them again. The change gave her a spat of vertigo, but not as much as the realization that she stood on the side of a mountain, or maybe it wasn't a mountain at all. Gravity should have been pulling her down, but she was able to stand on the angled slope without fear of falling. A crystalline forest provided a tunnel away from her location, and at the far end, she saw a pathway that crossed a gap.

Heart in her throat, pulse pounding like a drum in her neck, Pi walked through the forest. The trees shifted and changed as she passed beneath their multitude of colors as if the artist that had created them was constantly changing their mind. As she neared the end of the tunnel beneath the trees, she saw what was ahead. A bridge.

"Pythia."

The voice had her spinning around. It sounded like honey poured over broken glass. She grabbed her gut as if a knife had been shoved there. But when she looked down, there was nothing. When she looked back through the tunnel beneath the crystalline trees, she saw a figure with backward facing legs watching her. Dread filled her like hot lead. She turned to run across the bridge—

"Pythia!"

Only to find herself in the white room of the Verum Locus with Aurie shaking her, eyes wide with fright, repeating her name over and over.

"I'm back. Stop shaking me."

Aurie was pale, eyes searching. "You wouldn't wake up. The spell ended but then you didn't come out. I gave it a minute and then came in, but you were staring at the wall as if you were seeing something and I couldn't get you to move, or wake. It was frightening."

"I was somewhere else, not my memory." She sucked in a breath. "It was the same place as when I had the vision. The demonic realm, or I assume it was. There was a place, a bridge, I was trying to go towards it. Then something called my name. I didn't like it. It was waiting for me in the trees. That was when you woke me."

"Who or what was it?"

A pit opened in her stomach. "Elosian."

"Are you sure?"

"No...but that's what it felt like."

"I don't understand. I thought he put thoughts into people's minds without them knowing. Why would he come to you directly? Or was that a memory?" said Aurie. "I'm confused."

"Me too."

Pi wanted to climb into a shower and blast her skin with hot water to get the feeling off. It felt like a hundred spiders had been walking across her flesh. She could still feel the way his voice crawled across her body.

"Did you get anything useful? You know, before the vision," said Aurie.

Pi exhaled. "I think so. Enough that I don't want to risk another try. The big guy is a member of Blackstone Security. I saw his dumb tattoo and the vans had temporary tags, which means they were newly rented, or bought. We should be able to track them down that way. I'll research the guy's name, and maybe between those two points of data, we can narrow down where these assholes are."

Her sister was nodding, but seemed distracted. "I'm fine, Aurie. Really."

She looked at her sideways, worry on her brow. "You didn't see the way you wouldn't wake up. I almost slapped you, or burnt your arm to break you out of it."

"I'm here," said Pi. "I never went anywhere."

"I can't lose you too," said Aurie.

"You won't. Then you wouldn't have anyone to keep you from getting too righteous."

"Righteous?" asked Aurie.

"Me arrogant, you righteous," she said, poking them each in the chest. "Come on, let's get out of here before Joanne comes back and busts our balls for something trivial."

Her sister went out of the Verum Locus first. Pi followed, checking behind as if she could still feel the eyes of Elosian watching her.

It wasn't the first time she'd seen the Prince of Whispers. She hoped it would be her last.

Twenty-Five

Aurie caught sight of Zayn, sitting at the kitchen counter eating a sandwich, humming quietly. He had a nice voice, better lips, and was a great kisser. Remembering how they'd climbed the Spire on a date only a couple of talented mages could manage brought warmth to her midsection.

"Find anything out?" she asked, circling the counter.

Zayn's cheeks were puffed out as he chewed, holding a hand over his mouth like the polite Southerner that he was.

"Sorry. Eating," he said.

"I can hear your accent," she said, grinning.

Zayn swallowed. Blushed. "It's harder to maintain with food in the mouth. Something Instructor Pennywhistle warned us about." He dabbed his mouth with a napkin, folded it, and set it in his lap before reaching for his phone. He thumbed it open, found a picture, and slid it over. A girl with bright red hair was staring back. A newspaper article picture.

"Who's this?"

"One of the survivors of the Portland Zoo massacre," said Zayn.

"I read a little about it."

"Where's Pi?" he asked, looking over her shoulder.

"Tracking down a couple of vans. I'll fill her in later."

Zayn squinted at mention of the vans, but continued with his explanation. "The zoo had a big celebration for their newest expansion, when all their safety systems broke down. There happened to be five Animalians students present." He tapped on the picture. "Pax Nygard worked at the zoo before she joined the Halls. Three of the others were her friends, the fifth, the son of the donor that made the expansion happen. They saved a lot of lives, killed the creature that supposedly caused the chaos."

He flipped the picture to a grainy one of an enormous snake with wings hovering over a field.

"That's what caused it?"

"Aepep. Supposedly it's been around for centuries, or millenniums. One of the students recommended I investigate Aepep when I brought up the chimeratic creature you tangled with beneath the Glitterdome. I'm not sure I understand the connection, but it led me to Pax. I think she might be who we need for the Order, especially if we're going after that creature. We're gonna need someone that knows how to deal with them."

"Why her? Why not one of the others?" she asked, hoping that the question didn't sound jealous.

"The donor's son died during the event, the only other girl was a double-major with Aura Healers and she's in the middle of her residency at Golden Willow, so she's not available. Of the other two guys, one of them is in Patagonia helping the locals deal with a kappa infestation, the other is a model in London."

Aurie cocked a grin and tried to lean on the counter playfully. "Afraid of bringing the model onto the team? Or do you have a thing for redheads?"

Deep undercurrents flowed through his eyes. Zayn cleared his throat as he looked away, grabbing his phone to swipe to a new picture.

"The others might be able to help, but I think Pax might be best suited for what we're trying to do."

The newest picture on the phone showed the redheaded girl standing next to a creature that looked like an enormous fox. Its head came up to the girl's midsection, but she didn't see multiple tails.

"Not a kitsune?"

"A thoratic fox," said Zayn with his head tilted, "but no thoratic foxes are known to grow that big. Maybe it's part kitsune. Or something else entirely. The name is Kali."

"Kali," said Aurie, tasting the name. "Pax and Kali. Why do you think they might help us, or join the Order?"

A sly grin formed on Zayn's lips. "Because everywhere they go, trouble follows. That sounds like someone else I know. A pair of someones to be exact."

"Promising," said Aurie. "Where do we find this troublesome pair?"

Zayn screwed up his face. "That's the difficult part."

Twenty-Six

The Cessna Skylane dropped through the cloud layer, sending Pi's stomach into her throat. She dug her fingernails into the old rubber handle near the door as the hum of the engine drowned out her moans of nausea.

The mustached pilot next to her smirked as he leveled the plane out beneath the clouds, giving them a view of the Kamchatka Peninsula. Far off to her left, a column of smoke lifted from a conic volcano covered in snow, a view that would have been lovely had it not been for the knot in her throat as she fought to keep from yakking in the little bag the pilot had given her an hour ago when the turbulence started.

Pi toggled the headset to talk to her sister and Zayn, who were sitting in the back of the little plane. The seats barely had enough room for their legs, but they seemed to be getting along fine.

"Being cramped into a flying sardine can is miserable," said Pi as she kept her gaze on the horizon to minimize the nausea. "I'm not going anywhere that Invictus doesn't have coordinates for again."

The headset crackled, providing a venue for communication in the noisy, bouncy plane. Pi would have preferred music, but she could barely look at her phone to pick a new song without feeling sick, and the earbuds she'd brought weren't tight enough to block out the bone-rattling engine noise.

"Landing soon," said the pilot in Russian-accented English.

The final descent was a nightmare. By the time it was over, Pi was covered in a cold sweat. She poured herself out the door, sliding down the wing ladder to lie on the frozen concrete, letting the warmth of the sun calm her agitated stomach as snowflakes drifted onto her prone body.

When she could move again, Zayn appeared in a Jeep knockoff that looked like it'd been through some battles. A gouge in the side could have been made by a sword. Aurie handed her an elixir, which helped diminish the worst of the cotton-headed feeling of thirty-something hours of nonstop travel.

"I'm driving," she said, yanking Zayn out of the seat. "Either that or you're going to have to knock me out for the rest of the trip."

Aurie took the passenger side, leaving Zayn to ride in back with their bags. The vehicle had extra cannisters of gas strapped to the ceiling for a long overland trip. The road out of Yelizovo was paved for the first four hours, then as they veered onto bumpy gravel, Zayn pulled out an old accordion map that was notated in Russian.

The roads had taken them deeper into the peninsula to avoid the string of snow-covered mountains, dotted with the occasional volcano, before heading towards the western coast, which wasn't covered in sea ice. The inner regions were thick with white, fields buried, but the roads were relatively clear. As they headed towards the coast, the warmer air meant less snow, but more mud and potholes, making Pi's shoulders sore after a few hours of bumpy travel.

It wasn't just the irritation of physical and exhausting travel that was bothering Pi. She'd grown used to portal jumping across the realms, using the Helmsman of the Planes or the network in the city. Life as a mage smoothed over the little annoying bumps of everyday existence. There were always elixirs or spells for just about any problem. So having to make the long journey using the travel methods of everyday citizens wore on her and gave her far too much time to think about her visions from the infernal realm. The experience had given a tacit realness to a problem that had begun to feel like an exercise rather than a dangerous threat.

"If they're not there when we finally arrive, I'm going to murder someone," said Pi, rubbing the back of her neck with her free hand.

"I made a formal request through his company, Tundra Awakening," said Zayn. "I was told they'd be there on the *Tundra Spear*, his yacht."

"I don't trust this billionaire philanthropist that she's out here with," said Pi.

"Seems charitable. Does a lot of great work on climate change and other ecological issues. Why?"

She shrugged. "Dunno. Don't have a reason."

"My sister has an aversion to authority and rich people," said Aurie from the back with her eyes closed and head jammed against a little pillow she'd bought at the New York airport.

"I have an aversion to spending two days traveling when a simple phone call would have sufficed. I might need to have my uterus reset after all this banging around," said Pi.

Eventually roads they needed to travel were unmarked and they had to use mountainous landmarks and a compass to navigate. They hadn't seen another vehicle in an hour, only sheep on bright green hillsides.

"I think we're walking from here," said Pi as she stopped the vehicle at the end of the gravel road. A boggy stretch dotted with trees was between them and the coastline.

They left most of their gear in the vehicle, opting for small daypacks and rubber boots. The ground was wet and sucked at their footwear.

"Now I remember why I hate the countryside. There's a criminal lack of sidewalks," said Pi.

"It's not as bad as Caer Corsydd," said Aurie.

"At least there were things trying to kill us there so I never really noticed the mud or insects or lack of public transportation."

Their travel required circumventing small ponds, some covered in thin ice, as summertime neared, until the ground sloped towards the ocean. Pi breathed a sigh of relief when she heard waves crashing against rocks.

"I see it," said Zayn, holding his hand against his forehead to block the sun, which had decided at that moment to break free of the heavy gray clouds.

Further down the coast, a white yacht rocked gently in a natural harbor protected from the heavier waves that crashed against the shore sending spray thirty feet into the air. After another forty minutes of picking their way through the rocks, small ponds, and clumps of trees, they made it to the bay.

The yacht, clearly marked *Tundra Spear* on the back, was anchored about twenty feet from the edge of the shore. The boat bristled with antennae. It looked like it could house twenty people comfortably.

Aurie cupped her hands around her mouth. "Hello! Anyone home?" She tried a few times before giving up. "Not here, I guess."

Zayn checked his watch. "We're half a day early. They might not be expecting us until morning."

"Where are they then? It's not like you can just waltz around out here," said Pi, crossing her arms and trying not to think about the Thai noodle shop near the Spire that she had been salivating over during the last leg of the drive.

"I'm pretty sure you could wander around naked all day and no one would notice," said Zayn.

"Be my guest," said Aurie, grinning suggestively as she gestured towards the scattered copses of trees and small sky-reflecting ponds that hugged the coast.

"I'm right here," said Pi, picking up a rock near her boot and tossing it into the water. "Anyone care for a swim across to lower the walkway? I'm sure they won't mind if we wait on their deck."

Zayn craned his neck towards the sky. "Under normal circumstances, I would say that would be rude, but given how late it's getting and how far we are from the wanna-be Jeep, I'll volunteer to go over and lower the drawbridge."

"Feel free to get as naked as you want," said Pi. "I promise I'll avert my eyes for a second or two."

Instead of moving towards the water's edge, Zayn moved back about thirty feet and then in a blur of movement, took a running leap over the gap, landing on the deck of the *Tundra Spear*. He laid out the landing plank for them to cross.

"The doors are locked," said Pi, rattling the handle. "Care to work your Hall magic?"

Zayn found a bench near the front and put his feet up on a white plastic table that was made to withstand the elements. "Rude enough us boarding the yacht without permission. I'm not going to poke around in their private things."

"I am," said Pi, strangely awake despite not having slept in a few days. Ever since the Verum Locus, the idea of closing her eyes was less appealing. Dreams and that method of memory exploration were totally different, but seeing the strange landscape of the demonic realm and having Elosian, Prince of Whispers, call her name had left her feeling brittle, afraid the demon would somehow sneak into her mind during the night.

She moved around the deck, looking into the storage bins where water rescue equipment, life jackets, and other things were stored. In a bin near the cabin, she found a fancy wooden box sitting in the bottom. She thought about leaving it for half a second, but decided that without cell phone coverage, or anything else to do, she needed a moment's distraction.

Carrying the box to the sitting area on the yacht brought raised eyebrows from Zayn and Aurie.

"You sure you should be digging around in their stuff?"

"If you don't want something picked through, then don't leave it out. Besides, it was in an outer bin, can't be that interesting. Probably a set of bocce balls, or lawn darts."

She flipped open the lid to find a pile of black leather straps and buckles coiled together like a sleeping snake. Pi lifted a section of the black leather out of the box. Two lengths dangled together into a "V." It wasn't until she heard Zayn's snort that she recognized it as a harness. She wasn't shy by any means, but digging through someone's BDSM gear wasn't what she had intended. Heat rising to her cheeks, Pi quickly stuffed the leather equipment back into the box while Zayn smirked from his bench.

"Maybe you should have *restrained* yourself from digging in their gear," said Zayn, eliciting a chuckle from Aurie, who was sitting on the railing, staring into the shifting ocean waves.

"That's probably why they're not here," said her sister. "All tied up."

"Enough. Curiosity sated," said Pi, climbing onto a bench with a view of both the mountains and the bay.

"I don't know," said Zayn, grinning towards Aurie, "you should check around some more. Might be they're getting ready for next year's holidays, you know, those joke gifts."

"Right, gag gifts," said Pi, rolling her eyes. "Got it. You're making me miss the nausea from the plane ride."

The sun started setting not long after they arrived on the yacht. They applied weather enchantments, sipped from their water bottles, and ate the food bars from their day packs. When it was dark, not an artificial light in sight, a wind whipping down from the north along the inner part of the peninsula brought chill winds, rocking the yacht. The only pleasant thing Pi could say about the wait was the bright swath of stars across the night sky.

"There wasn't a bathroom open anywhere was there?" asked Pi, feeling the pressure on her bladder after chugging her water all evening and wishing it was a vodka tonic.

"You can lean your ass off the back of the boat," said Aurie.

"I think I'll head to shore. With the boat rocking, the last thing I want to do is slip off the edge and fall into the water," said Pi.

Rubbing her forearms for warmth since they left their heavier gear in the Jeep, Pi jogged onto the shore. A line of thick trees looked like a good place for a bathroom break. She stepped through the other side near a nice flat clearing, unbuckled her jeans, and squatted near a bush.

Beneath the canopy, the bright line of stars in the sky was barely visible. Pi craned her neck, hoping for shooting stars, when something huge blocked out the sky for a second. Her gut clenched, but she wasn't ready to move. The sound of large wings beating was followed by the crunch of something heavy landing in the clearing behind her.

As she hiked up her jeans and underwear, Pi turned to see an enormous head leaning over the bushes. It was as big as a small car, with ridges over the wide eyes, a long sloped forehead, and dirty white scales. A dragon. Hunched wings rose up above the body.

Fear hijacked her mind, sending alarm bells throughout her body. None of her limbs seemed to work right.

"Oh fuck," said Pi, sprinting through the trees, falling into the spongy wet soil, and splashing through puddles as she made her way back to the yacht.

"Forget the toilet paper?" asked Zayn as he pulled the headphones from his ears. Aurie was curled onto the bench, using his thigh as a pillow. She looked up, bleary eyed.

Pi's mouth was full of marbles. She swallowed hard. "A dragon. I was in the trees and it landed right behind me."

"If you're trying to get back at us for our bondage puns, it's not a very good joke. There aren't any dragons known to live in this region," said Aurie, sitting up.

Curiously, Zayn was looking to the sky, frowning. He seemed to be taking her comment more seriously.

The sound of claws on the metal bridge that connected the yacht to the shore brought the three of them to their feet. Golden eyes peered out of the darkness at the edge of the yacht. They'd been sitting in the dark with only the stars and their enchantment-aided vision for seeing.

"Who's there?" called Zayn.

A confident male voice cut through the night. "I might ask the same. It's not polite to board someone's boat without permission."

The mention of ownership let Pi take a breath, even if the encounter with the dragon had her body ramped up and ready for action. Already she was wondering if she'd imagined it, or some sorcery had been at work.

Two figures crested the ramp onto the deck of the *Tundra Spear*. She recognized both of them from the newspaper articles. Okho was better looking than his pictures. Dark, messy hair and an intensity that had her connecting dots. He looked like the kind of guy that could fix an engine and do complex mathematics in his head.

The girl, Pax, wore her hair differently than in the pictures. It was pulled back in an unruly ponytail, curls exploding from the wrap as if they were medusa's snakes. She looked like she'd been caught in a windstorm, while he looked neat and pressed. Between them strode the foxlike creature named Kali. Pi glanced at her sister, who was seeing the similarities, and yet differences, from their friend, the kitsune Inari.

Pi had gone into the visit expecting a billionaire philanthropist and his girlfriend, a mage of the Animalians hall, which if she was being honest with herself, wasn't one that she really thought much about. But this Pax and Kali—they seemed connected in ways that she could only instinctively sense—carried themselves with supreme confidence even as they found three strangers on their boat. She wasn't a run-of-the-mill mage who'd spent her five years at the Hundred Halls passing the time. She could understand how they might have survived the horrific events at the Portland Zoo.

"It's my fault," said Aurie, extending a hand. "We arrived earlier than planned and when we found your yacht uninhabited, we thought it better to wait on deck than on the shore. We haven't gone inside."

Pi followed her sisters lead, stepping forward for a greeting. When she shook Okho's hand, she felt a spark of recognition. Their visit just got a lot more complicated. She checked back to Zayn, who seemed equally tense. While she could be completely off base about her experience, she was nearly certain that the dragon in the trees had been Okho. This was a development that she neither understood nor had expected.

Okho smiled, gesturing inside. "No worries. Given the remoteness of the location, I accept your reasoning. And as you said, you stayed to the deck"—he shot a glance at Pi—"but please, come in. We're both famished from our journey today."

The interior of the *Tundra Spear* was luxurious and large. Pax brought them drinks while Okho worked the stove in the kitchen, grilling up elk steaks while they chatted about mundane topics like their trip and the current state of the Hundred Halls. When they moved to the dinner table, the conversation shifted to the goals of Tundra Awakening and what they were doing all the way out on the peninsula. Both Pax and Okho were vague about their efforts, mostly talking about tracking ocean creatures and sampling the ecosystem, which all seemed plausible to Pi, as she'd seen an extensive eco-lab in the lower deck when she used the bathroom.

After dinner, they helped their hosts clean up and then Okho announced they were headed into the Sea of Oktosk. While he piloted the yacht out of the bay and into the choppy waves of the interior of the peninsula, Pax poured them shots of vodka while Kali lay on the bench, watching them interestedly with her golden eyes.

"What brings you all the way out here? Long way to travel for a question about cryptids," said Pax as she threw the shot back. "Even for the sisters who saved Invictus from some unknown fate." She glanced to Zayn. "I'm sorry I don't know much about your exploits, but I assume if you're with them, you're no slouch."

"I like to think I'm a terrific slouch if the conditions require it," said Zayn, leaning back on his bench with his arms hooked around the back, receiving a coy smile from Pax as she leaned against the bar.

Pi threw down her shot, trying not to grimace as the alcohol went down. She coughed as she said, "Zayn is Priyanka's right-hand man. Before he was with us, he was deep undercover in the Eternal City."

Pax smiled sheepishly. "I'm sorry. I'll admit I don't know much about the maetrie, but that sounds impressive."

Pi couldn't quite decide if she was being condescending or she was that narrowly focused.

"Our cryptid question is a bit unusual," said Aurie.

"Given who you all are, I wouldn't expect anything less," said Pax.

A set of intermittent beeping came from the front cabin where Okho was piloting the yacht. The noise had neither the steadiness of radar or the impatience of a warning, nor were the residents of the ship worried about it, so Pi put it out of her head.

"The reason that Invictus was missing for a long time was he was trying to stop an invasion from the infernal realm. He failed, and now we're helping him renew those efforts, but it appears there are those opposed to us. We were tracking down a lead when the girl we were talking to was kidnapped."

Pax crossed her arms. "I'm still not seeing where I come in."

Pi was playing with the empty shot glass between her hands. "My sister is dancing around the fact that I nearly got immolated by a creature that after investigation was suggested to be similar to the flying snake thingy that you killed at the zoo."

The redhead had been casually leaning against the bar, but as soon as Pi finished speaking, she shot erect. Kali immediately rose to her feet on the bench, making Zayn lean away. The foxlike creature had the aura of menace in its eyes.

"What was it?" asked Pax, lips squeezed white. It didn't take Zayn's senses to see how her heart rate had increased and she seemed extremely agitated by the mention. Okho leaned back from the helm, frowning at the change in mood. He seemed focused on Pax, rather than their information, which gave Pi the impression that the encounter had left a lingering trauma.

For the next hour, the three of them explained the events of the last few weeks—from the ambush in the warehouse to Andromeda's kidnapping to the mountains of Montanhas—but left out any mention of Elosian. Pax and Okho occasionally asked questions, but mostly listened intently. The description of the cobra-headed creature received frequent questions from Pax.

"Is it like your flying snake thing?" asked Pi.

Pax went from listening intensively to leaning forward, angrily retorting, "It's not a *flying snake thing*. It was a god. A terrible being from the ancient world that fed on chaos and death."

There was a lot more behind the outburst, but Pi wasn't going to press further since they barely knew the Animalians mage. Pax stared at the ground for a moment.

"But yes, it sounds like something that came from or was inspired by Aepep. A chimeratic beast bred for a specific purpose." Pax's expression hardened. "I assume you didn't come all this way to ask a few questions."

Aurie leaned forward. "No. We need your help. The threat from the demonic realm is real and immediate. We don't know how, or why, but Andromeda is a part of it. We need to get her back, but we were totally outclassed by that team of mages, especially with that creature. We each have our specialties, but the cryptid world is beyond us."

Pax stared out the darkened windows. "I have important work to do out here. The world of humans is entirely capable of fucking up their own spaces. Why should I step in to save them?"

When Kali growled lightly under her breath, Pi realized that the pair were not just companions, but probably psychically linked. Neither Aurie nor Zayn answered her. The angry retort had surprised them, but not Pi. The flying snake Aepep, the disaster at the zoo—these had impacted Pax in ways she probably hadn't resolved. That's why she'd come out to this far-flung place. A way to avoid the things that had hurt her most. Pi knew because she was aware that she'd been doing the same thing since her parents had died. If she ever had a chance to think too hard about what happened, she knew she'd probably be in trouble. It was one of reasons she'd allowed Invictus to send her all over the realms, because not being busy was a recipe for introspection, and she was afraid of the answers.

"Your friend Janelle works at Aura Healers," said Pi, sensing the need for a good push.

Pax screwed up her face, part question, part accusation. "So?"

"So," said Pi, taking on a casual tone, "when we say our realm is under threat of infernal invasion, that means that the city of Invictus is ground zero for the breach. The barrier between our world and theirs is rotten. The patrons have been doing what they can to shore up the wells, but the extent of their efforts is coming to an end. We're on the precipice of disaster. Possibly annihilation. That means Golden Willow, the Animalians campus, the zoo, anyone else you care for in the city is going to be on the front line sooner rather than later. What we told you about Montanhas? That was just a warm-up for the real thing. You can choose not to help, but the creatures that will come through the barrier won't care about humans or animals, they'll slaughter everything, starting with your friend at Golden Willow."

"She can handle herself."

"So can we, but I'll let you know right now that I'm terrified. The demon lord we're up against, Elosian, has only one goal and that's the subjugation of our entire world," said Pi.

The beeping from the front cabin had gone from passive to insistent. Even Pax couldn't completely pay attention to the conversation. She kept glancing towards Okho and the noisy equipment.

"Elosian?"

Pi checked with her sister, who gave a nod to continue.

"Elosian, Prince of Whispers, Lord of Lies. He's a demon lord intent on our realm. He feeds on chaos and lies. We think that other team is unknowingly working for him."

"Unknowingly?"

"When Beckett Dreadmarsh was dying after the blowback from his spell, he claimed he was trying to save the city from us," said Pi. "Said that we were going to be the cause of destruction. That's why they grabbed Andromeda, because they think she's part of it, but we're fairly certain that the information came from Elosian."

"How do you know you're not working for him?" asked Pax.

"We don't, honestly," said Pi, "but we figure if we're working with Invictus, we're probably doing better than most."

Pax inhaled deeply, a pained expression on her face as she looked out the windows.

"We're close," said Okho.

A wistful smile formed on her lips. "Come with me. I have something to show you."

Pax led them to the bow of the ship. Okho was faintly visible through the cabin window, the bluish lights of the monitors reflecting on his face. The sea was calmer further out from shore, with long, shallow swells. The engine had been cut and they drifted in the quiet, gently rocking.

"What are you tracking?" asked Zayn, who looked down to find Kali beneath his hand. He gave the creature a rub on the back of the neck, which had Kali leaning into him. Pi was a little jealous of the interaction.

Pax leaned on the front rail, peering into the darkness. Pi could sense something. She wasn't sure if it was the anticipation of exploration, or that her soul fragments were sensitive to something out in the water. The back of her neck prickled with warning.

Eventually they were all pressed against the rail, even Kali, who put her enormous paws on the smooth brown surface, straining forward. Pi felt the presence before she saw the swell. About two hundred feet out, something massive crested the water. It looked smooth like a submarine, but much larger, and not metal.

"Merlin's tits," breathed Aurie.

An irrational fear stole into Pi. She found herself gripping the railing as if she were holding on for dear life. The creature broke the surface again, this time closer. It dwarfed the yacht by a factor of a hundred to one, and they were only seeing a small part of the creature—whatever it was.

"Nothing is that big," said Zayn, jaw pulsing. "Nothing natural."

The creature passed beneath the *Tundra Spear*, swelling the waves to push them higher. Pi feared for a moment that they'd get sucked under but the boat slid down the wave without issue. They moved to the back of the yacht and watched the creature undulate out of sight during the next ten minutes. It felt like every time she thought the creature was gone, a new piece of it would surface briefly.

"What was that?" asked Aurie as Okho joined them at the stern.

"The Jörmungandr," said Pax.

"That's not a real creature. A myth," said Aurie breathlessly.

"You're right and wrong," said Okho. "It's not the world serpent of legend, but a creature recent to this world."

"Are you tracking it to kill it?" asked Pi.

"No," said Pax, forcefully. "It's not a danger except to those that wish to hurt it or use it for their own sick purposes."

"It came from the cult of Aepep, though I suppose it wasn't much of a cult at the end. More like a corporation," said Pax, staring into the dark waters.

"Same difference," said Zayn.

"In ancient times, Aepep fed on lies and chaos, driving its members to their own deaths as they attempted to prove their fealty. They believed they were going to gain great powers, but ended up dead on the creature's poison." Pax turned her head. "This Elosian sounds a lot like Aepep."

"Except, forgive me for saying this," said Pi, "but Elosian is more devious and cunning. We don't know how he whispers into our world, but his lies move many on his behalf."

"Maybe Aepep had some connection to Elosian," said Pax, "though it would be hard to know since the flying snake was trapped in a tomb in Caer Corsydd for a thousand years."

Pi shared a glance with her sister but said nothing.

"You're asking me to give up everything I have here to track down a missing girl, and you have no idea about how she fits into the larger scheme." Pax clasped hands with Okho, who gazed at her with solemnity. "And help you fight battles I care nothing about."

"If the barrier is breached there will be no bystanders. Your friends, the animals of this world, the kids at the Halls now, everyone will be on the front line," said Pi.

"I need a minute," said Pax, gazing into Okho's serene face.

She and Okho stayed outside, while the others returned to the interior of the yacht. No one spoke. Pi wasn't sure if it was the weight of the decision or the experience with the gargantuan worm keeping their lips shut. She hadn't been sure about coming all this way for a mage from Animalians, but after meeting Pax and Kali, and learning that she had a relationship with a dragon—a creature not known for their love of humans—Pi was hoping that they would be returning with the redhead.

After fifteen minutes, Pax and Kali entered to the interior. Okho stayed outside.

"Before I give you my answer, I have one question. This girl, Andromeda Charmer. How do you know that Beckett Dreadmarsh wasn't right about her? What if she's a danger to the city and the world? You seem determined to find her despite the threat. Why? It feels like there's something else going on."

Pi found herself looking at the golden-eyed Kali. A tickle in her mind could have been her imagination. Thoratic foxes were known to be psychic, but she didn't think they could read thoughts. The others looked to her. They'd agreed not to tell Pax about the truth bond, but Pi wondered if that was the correct choice. If they didn't lay it all out, why would Pax trust them to come back to Invictus?

"We met her after the show at the Glitterdome. I know dangerous people, she's not one."

"How can you be sure?"

Pi pictured the girl from the performance in her stage costume taking painful blows in the faux-quest to liberate the marionettes. There was something in her that was deeply wounded, an injury that drew Pi towards her. And maybe that was the thing. It wasn't that Andromeda was dangerous, but that she might cause others to act on her behalf. The things Pi would do for her sister, the things she *had* done. The danger could lie in other directions.

"We can't," said Pi, shaking her head.

"That's what I'm worried about," said Pax. "I've been keeping touch with Janelle, and reading about the goings-on in Invictus and the Halls. The Charmer name comes with a lot of baggage, rumors of ritual sacrifice—hell, they got funding from Magnus Dreadmarsh when their company was failing. Doesn't that worry you that Beckett is somehow connected?"

"We've thought about that," said Aurie. "That's why we hope to talk to Andromeda so we can understand what happened. Maybe we'll find the clues in what she knows. She was about to talk to us when she was kidnapped."

Pax crossed her arms. Pi could tell that she hadn't decided to come with them yet. Might not. There was something holding her back.

"There is one other thing," said Pi, checking back to her sister. Aurie looked like she was half out of her seat. "Another reason we have to find Andromeda."

"Pi—"

"We have to level with her, about everything."

The reaction from Pax suggested she'd already known. There was more to this pair than they were letting on.

"To convince Andromeda to tell us what she knew, Aurie gave her a truth bond. A bond that's still active and if the other mages figure out is there, they can use it to do just anything they want to my sister."

"Thank you for being honest with me, Pi. I'll consider coming with you on one condition. That before you go after Andromeda, we exhaust the other leads."

"What other leads?" asked Zayn.

"The other Charmers."

Twenty-Seven

Pax stepped out of the SUV, regretting her decision to come back to the city the moment the heat and the voices pressed against her mind. The years of solitude, traveling the world on the *Tundra Spear* with only Kali and Okho as her companions, had reduced her mental defenses. Kali leaned against her leg in solidarity, a brief whimper slipping out. A man with a bushy mustache passed them on the sidewalk, fear radiating from him as he gave Kali a wide berth.

"Are you okay?" asked Pi, touching her upper arm.

The contact made Pax feel like she was looking at the younger Silverthorne through a broken mirror. A dozen reflections looked back at her, creating an overwhelming sense of vertigo. She pulled her arm away from Pi's touch, creating a feedback loop of shame and distrust.

"Been a while since I've been around so many people," she said as Zayn and Aurie came around the back of the vehicle, hauling their travel bags. They gave her a worried look. "Wasn't as sensitive before."

"Sorry," said Pi. "We would have gone through the underground access, but we need to get you the badges for getting in and out of the Spire."

"It's okay. I'll manage."

Pax didn't bother craning her neck back to see the top of the Spire. They were too near the base to get a good look, and the sun's reflection would have only hurt her eyes.

<Many minds>

Yes, Kali, many minds. We have to put up our walls again.

A family of five passed them. The smallest child held out her chubby arms towards Kali. "Puppy!"

The parents pulled the girl away, picking her up before she stumbled into Kali.

"Sorry," they said in unison as they circled around.

No matter where they went, Kali elicited fear in adults. Even her new companions had eyed Kali suspiciously upon first seeing her on the yacht. Pax shouldered her bags, fighting to maintain the mental barrier that had been second nature when she was a member of the Halls.

They led her into the Spire. The Silverthornes navigated the interior while Zayn followed along, quietly observing. He'd spoken the least during the two-day journey, but she felt like she knew him best. He had a warm soul despite the nature of his Hall. That Kali liked him told her a lot about his personality.

The Silverthornes were a contradiction. Pax had read about them, and thought she knew what to expect from what had been in the *Herald.* The older sister took charge whenever there was a question of leadership, even when it seemed the other two might know better. Pax knew overcompensation when she saw it. They were orphans. Their parents had been killed in an explosion in the seventh ward when they were kids, and Aurie was trying to make sure nothing like that happened again.

Brushing up against the younger Silverthorne mind was like being in a crowded elevator with a group of unwashed strangers. Pax couldn't get over how overwhelming Pi was. Being near her was exhausting mentally, even if she enjoyed speaking with her more than the others because of her lack of a filter.

Acquiring the badge only took a few minutes. Pax had been sure there would be problems with Kali, but inside the Spire she was treated differently. After four years outside the city, she'd forgotten how familiar most residents were with flashy displays of magic and the presence of supernatural creatures. They passed a tall guy with a ring-tailed sniken hanging onto his neck, and then later on the way the elevators a woman carrying a glass box glowing with bluish light that looked like a small apparition. The last and only time she'd been in the Spire was for the Merlin Trials, the tests that allowed her access to the Halls once she'd passed. She didn't know which portion of the Spire they were held in, but even thinking about them got her heart rate up.

During the ride up, Pi said, "I sent a message to Old Iron Balls to let him know we were coming." She screwed up her face. "Fair warning, he can be kind of a prick at times. You never know which version you're gonna get, so be ready."

"Old Iron Balls?"

"Respect for elders is something my sister has never really bought into," said Aurie.

Pi rolled her eyes and ran a hand through her short spiky hair. "Congratulations, you managed to stay alive for an unusual length of time. Never been quite sure why that requires my kissing their ass. Some turtles live to be hundreds of years old but we're not worshiping them."

"Giant tortoise."

"Huh?" asked Pi.

"It can live to be two or three hundred years old."

"And they're probably not cantankerous."

Pax didn't quite understand, but said, "Probably not."

Pi smirked. "I need to tell Old Iron Balls about them so he can understand that it's not a requirement to be an asshole once you reach a certain age."

Pax was a little mortified at the way she was talking about the oldest and most famous mage in the world, but she figured there had to be a good reason.

There was a short introduction to the staff that worked outside the portal and then they approached the archway.

"Once you pass through here, you're not actually going higher in the Spire," explained Aurie. "It's a little demi-realm, a place he carved out for himself."

"Then what's in the upper portion of the Spire? I always thought that's where he lived," said Pax, craning her head as if she could see it.

Aurie lifted a shoulder. "No one knows, and it's one of those secrets he's not willing to divulge." She turned, then turned back. "Oh, and try not to touch anything until you understand what's dangerous and what's not. There's some rather unusual artifacts in his little domain. Some of them don't play nice with human flesh."

The proper signs awakened the runes on the portal. Until that point, Pax hadn't been nervous about meeting Invictus. The way the sisters talked about him made him seem normal. But then the images on the TV, the articles she'd read, and the documentaries about his life and disappearance all came back to her. Here was a man who'd lived over a thousand years and had founded not only the city, but the Hundred Halls, which had finally placed magical abilities in a place of reverence rather than suspicion.

Be respectful, she told Kali. *He's an old, old man.*

A wave of nervous emotion came back from her companion as she looked up with her kind golden eyes.

The portal transit was mercifully brief and with none of the nausea that plagued their training trips to Caer Corsydd. She'd barely reoriented herself in the enormous space that went in multiple directions before she was drawn to a man in silken robes standing a dozen paces from her with a welcoming smile.

Under normal circumstances, she would have been craning her neck at the wonders in his demi-realm: the floating ball of golden energy near the ceiling, the endless rows of shelves, a suit of crimson-and-gold armor that looked like it'd been knocked in its case, and so on. It was part Great Library and part mad scientist laboratory. But these weren't normal circumstances.

The man before her wasn't as tall as she'd expected, but his presence was like standing too close to a raging fire. Pax sucked in a breath. His wavy black hair hung around his shoulders as he clasped his hands in front, his serene smile both welcoming and wise.

"Pax Nygard and Kali," he said in a melodic tone, "it's wonderful to meet you."

He crouched down and to her and everyone else's surprise, Kali hurried to the old mage and curled against him as he dug his fingers into her thick fur, scratching furiously.

"Who the fuck are you?" spat out Pi, forehead hunched with confusion. "Do we need to make sure you haven't had your brains sucked out by a mind flayer and replaced with a bowl of pudding?"

The profanity and degradation left Pax's jaw open. She checked back to Invictus, expecting a verbal dressing down, but the ancient mage merely said, "Pythia, would you be a dear and renew the barrier for me?"

Pi rolled her eyes and strode from the entrance to a deeper location. Aurie and Zayn stood nearby, watching with wide eyes.

Invictus crossed the space between them, offering a hand which she shook while feeling like she was standing outside her body. Up close, he bore more wrinkles than she would have expected, but they seemed pulled tight, and not in the way the patrons, or other wealthy mages looked, as they had their skin modified with a sorcerous sheen. It was his face, but natural and bulwarked by centuries of magical use.

"It's nice to meet you, Pax." He grinned. "And Kali. I don't recall if I've ever met a callidus."

"You know what she is?" asked Pax.

"I met a few Descendants of Bastet many centuries ago and have been aware of their existence, but our paths have never crossed."

"You're not what I expected."

"Seldom am." Invictus raised an eyebrow in the direction that Pi had left. "I'm certain that she told you what to expect, and previous to recent times, she would have been correct. I've been distracted and inconsiderate. A real ass." He winked. "I, however, enjoyed her reaction."

As if they sensed the show was over, Aurie and Zayn disappeared, leaving her alone with the head patron of the Hundred Halls.

"What's the barrier that you sent her to renew?"

"Ahh, yes. When I traveled to the infernal realm, hoping in my foolishness to put things to right, I managed to damage the barrier that protects my demi-realm from intrusion. I've added a secondary layer but it requires frequent renewal, a task Pythia is uniquely suited to do."

"Why is that?"

Invictus placed his hands behind his back as they strolled. She wanted to enjoy the sights, but his presence required absolute attention.

"I'll let her explain that in good time. We each have our secrets, some more painful than others." He turned to face her. "You had quite an experience at the Portland Zoo a few years ago."

The mention brought a rush of adrenaline as if she was back in the zoo, facing down a park full of escaped supernatural animals.

"It was, yeah, we survived."

"Sometimes that's all you can do, survive."

She hadn't been paying attention to where they were walking, but found herself before a great window looking down upon the city. Sunlight reflected off glass gondolas floating through the sky. They were looking east. Further out in the ring-like city, she could see the green patches that made up the Animalians campus and the brick buildings holding the small zoo.

"Wait? I thought we were in your demi-realm."

Invictus winked. "A trick of sorcery. Would hate to have this great location and not enjoy the view."

He stared out the window. She followed his gaze, wondering if there was something she was supposed to be doing. Kali was sitting between them.

What do you think? she asked her companion.

<Like Adele but brighter and more dangerous>

Brighter and more dangerous. That summed up her experience. Adele was the head of Animalians, a strange human warped by both sorcery and time spent transformed into various supernatural creatures, but a pale shadow in comparison to the head of the Halls.

Invictus leaned over conspiratorially. "Now is the time for you to ask questions."

"Oh, sorry," she said sheepishly, "it's been a long journey."

"You get used to it."

Standing close let her taste his aura: a marbled, layered thing tempered by time and magic. She sensed that he was allowing this inspection and could close off access in the blink of an eye. It made her wonder if he was truly like this, or if it was a carefully constructed psychic personality for her and Kali.

"Is the barrier really that close to failing? Looking at the city, it looks peaceful...in its own cluttered urban way, but not on the verge of invasion," said Pax, hating the question as she asked it. It felt like a child asking a parent if people really stopped existing when they died. "I guess I'm asking why we're allowing the city to go about like normal. Shouldn't we warn them?"

Invictus stared into the streets below as his aura took on shades of wavering blue and pulsing red as he oscillated between concern and admiration. "It's a good question. The city looks peaceful, so how can it be on the verge of destruction? It makes our task ever more fraught. This won't be a battle fought like the wars of this world, where the lines are drawn and defenses can be set ahead of time. No one here would believe that they are at risk. At times I've thought about organizing an evacuation, but over the centuries I've learned that people don't respond to danger until it's almost too late. And sometimes after it's too late."

"I don't know how much help I can be," said Pax. "Before I came to the Halls, I expected to spend my life working at the Portland Zoo, tending its inhabitants. I don't know anything about demons or barriers."

Invictus chuckled. His outward appearance didn't match his inner thoughts. She sensed the conflict and concern. He'd cleaned himself up for her arrival.

"We can blame religion for the misguided views of the infernal realm. It is not the fiery regions of hell made for lost souls, nor even a place that is altogether that hot. It is a realm like any other, though stranger and more malleable than most. It was one of the earliest realms that managed to stay in existence, but while it follows its own unique rules, it is not a monolith, and the creatures that live there, are that, creatures, which you are wholly suited to deal with, just as you did the calamity at the zoo." He patted her arm. "But hopefully we don't get that far. Better we stop the invasion before it begins."

"That reminds me," said Pax, searching for the right way to ask, "they told me about the one who is behind it. Elosian."

The moment she said the name, the access to his aura disappeared as if a huge sliding wall had come down. She could feel the vibration of the impact. Even Kali looked up, bushy eyebrows working furiously. But before he'd closed off access, she'd sensed a host of emotions that she didn't know how to parse: frustration, pain, worry, focus—but also, inexplicably, longing and a strange ache.

Invictus appeared embarrassed by the reveal. He looked on the verge of explanation when a shout brought their heads around. She followed the head patron through the maze of shelves and rooms to find a space with a great brass machine at the center and a blank archway on one wall.

Pi lay on the ground beneath the archway with Aurie holding her. The younger sibling was blinking furiously, fighting to open her eyes.

Aurie's expression was hardened with concern. "She won't wake up."

Twenty-Eight

"I'm fine," said Pi, trying to distract the concern from her sister. "Stop looking at me and pay attention to the road."

Zayn had been staring out the window at the city, musing if his past self could have guessed how strange his life would become after the Halls. Working for Priyanka was one thing, she was the highly competent head of an unusual supernatural intelligence agency, but Invictus was an entirely different level of odd.

"You were unconscious and wouldn't wake up," said Aurie, frowning. "I'm still not sure you should have come."

"We're still in the city," said Pi with a sigh, palming her forehead, "and from what I've read about this Ivan, we've nothing to worry about."

The collapse had been worrying, but Pi had woken up not long after everyone ran into the room, complaining of a weird smell and refusing to admit that she remembered anything. Invictus had absolved her of her duties with the barrier, and when they left, Zayn had the impression that something had happened that the younger Silverthorne wasn't willing to talk about.

But it wasn't just Pi holding back. His imbuement allowed him to see the micro-emotions that revealed mental states. Aurie was both worried about her sister and suspicious of her explanation. The same was true of Pax, who Zayn suspected had psychic abilities gained from her relationship with Kali. The hyperawareness of each member and their reticence to share wasn't helping the comradery in the group.

Zayn leaned back in the seat, finding Kali's head resting beside his. The foxlike creature sat in the back of Invictus' old Ford Momentum, which had been big enough for the five of them, unlike the Silverthornes' vehicle. Pax smiled from her side of the back seat. He could see the apprehension in her gaze. She was probably wondering why she'd agreed to come all this way when they clearly weren't much of a team.

"Rather than worry about me when I'm clearly fine, we should be wondering why the head patron has a bag of stale Good & Plenty in the glove box," said Pi, digging into the front compartment. "Not only are they the grossest candy, but they'll yank your teeth right out."

"I never imagined that he would actually drive around," said Pax with a pinched expression. "I always thought he just kind of, you know." She made open and close motions with her hand to simulate teleporting.

"Maybe he likes the wind in his hair," said Aurie as she turned onto a cross street.

"When did the eleventh get a Juju Juice?" asked Pax, pressing her face against the window.

"Augh, I know," said Pi. "This place has gone to shit."

"I like Juju Juice," said Pax with a little hurt in her tone. "Their Triple Berry Blast with an extra shot of caffeine got me through all the nomenclature memorization required. I practically lived on the stuff. There was one right off campus in the seventh."

"We grew up here," said Pi. "It was one of the few places non-humans had a chance to have a normal life outside of the Undercity, but now it's all Coterie mages and the rest of their society friends."

"Speaking of," said Aurie, "any hits on the kidnappers?"

Pi rolled down the window, which was an actual handle she had to turn, and yelled at a trio of guys in pastel button-downs with frosted hair and yacht tans. "Take Daddy's guilt money and ruin somewhere else, you spray-tanned douche bonnets!"

A trio of middle fingers were shot back at Pi as she pulled back into the passenger seat, sulking in her spot.

"Any hits? Oh, a few nibbles on the ghost traps, but nothing substantial."

"Ghost traps?" asked Pax.

"A program that waits for the right information to crawl across its path, then snatches up a ghost version of the data so no one knows it's been grabbed."

Pax leaned forward. "Wait, you're a hacker too? I thought you were Arcanium."

There was no answer from the front seat, which brought tensed shoulders from Pax, and a reflective growl near his left ear. Sensing the need to change the subject, Zayn said, "Everyone know about Ivan Charmer?"

The front seat was a chorus of "Of course," while Pax shook her head.

"Ivan Charmer," began Zayn, "fourth slash fifth child of Victor and Monique Charmer, fraternal twin with his sister Catherine, or Kitty. Member of Well and Stone society and considered one of the most brilliant alchemists to come out of that hall in the last few decades. At one time, he was responsible for half the party drug trade in the Halls and hosted raves that were considered an art form unto themselves. Was brought up on charges during the feud with his father, but those were dismissed after Victor disappeared and the patrons put in a good word with the authorities."

"Where's his father?" asked Pax.

"No one knows," said Zayn, "which seems a little shady, and now the youngest Charmer has disappeared and no one seems to be looking for her but us."

There was no opportunity for further discussion as they pulled up to the small campus that made up Great & Terrible, the alchemy company founded by Ivan Charmer. An old squat brick house sat next to a repurposed warehouse. A pair of workers in lab coats were standing outside the larger building drinking coffee.

Aurie parked the Momentum next to a row of scooters at a charging station.

"Not that way," said Zayn when the others headed towards the laboratory. "All the research happens here."

The front door was painted bright purple. He could see through the window that Ivan had good taste, even if it were a little eclectic. Before anyone could touch the ringer, a young woman appeared in the doorway in a white lab coat. She had a cherubic face, wore a low-cut dress, and appeared a little flush. From Zayn's research, he believed she was Ivan's girlfriend and business partner, Audrey.

"Business inquiries should be taken to the main building," said Audrey as she started to close the door.

"We're here to see Ivan."

The woman kept her head stuck out the opening. "He's very busy and we're not interested in financial backers, despite what the papers said about G&T."

"It's about his sister," said Zayn, holding his hand out.

The door wavered. Audrey looked out with half her face hidden, frowning. "We have on-site security and a vicious guard dog." She glanced to Kali and her frown deepened.

"We were with her when she was kidnapped," said Aurie. "Nearly got killed trying to get her back."

The mention loosened the tightness around Audrey's mouth. She headed further inside, motioning for them to follow. As soon as they entered, a brown-and-white mutt came bounding down the stairs, saw them, then gave a single bark before skittering back to the second floor, bringing chuckles from the group.

The lower area was an open floor plan with a huge lounging area near the kitchen. A poster from the Mystique showcasing Andromeda on the front in her Bonnie Bedlam costume was above the mantle. A few others lined the walls including a Minnie & the Moves world tour poster and a Lifestone-branded ad that showed a trio of older people with their fists in the air as if they'd won a championship even though they were just riding bikes. He even saw a copy of the "Work is Family!" corporate poster near the stairs.

The upper area looked like a proper laboratory. The whirl of centrifuges provided a background hum as pulsing EDM played over hidden speakers. A guy in a purple lab coat that matched the front door was tossing powders into a wide-necked beaker with haphazard glee.

Audrey approached him and spoke quietly in his ear. Zayn could have eavesdropped on the conversation, but didn't need to.

"You were with my sister when she was abducted?" he asked, shoving his safety goggles onto his head, which pushed his hair into wild spikes.

"We were," said Aurie, gesturing between her and her sister.

"Are they your backup singers or something?" asked Ivan.

The beaker on the table was bubbling, froth threatening to push out of the glassware.

"Uhm," said Pax, "excuse me, but your thingy is about to boil over."

Ivan didn't turn his head. "It'll be fine." He frowned. "Who are you and why didn't the cops mention you when they informed me about the kidnapping?"

Aurie made introductions, which brought raised eyebrows from both Audrey and Ivan. While she was speaking, Kali crept over to a submissive Barkley, who was lying on his back, tail thumping for a gentle inspection.

"Don't know why they didn't tell you," said Aurie, "but I'm more curious why you're not more concerned about her kidnapping?"

"I have what you call a good poker face," said Ivan, leaning against the counter. He gestured towards his head. "All you see is this handsome exterior, calm and collected, but really inside I'm a raging case of anxiety."

He was right. Ivan had a good poker face, but Zayn could see past the smooth expression to the pounding of his pulse and smell the cloying body odor. He was also thoroughly annoyed by Aurie, whose aggressive question had put Ivan on his back foot.

"Do you know anything that the cops haven't told us?" asked Zayn.

"Why do you care?" asked Ivan. "Or are you short on busybody points and have to stick your nose into everyone else's business? No offense, but I've had my time in the limelight of the city and it's exhausting."

"What about Andromeda?" asked Aurie suspiciously. "Aren't you worried about her?"

"Of course I am, but contrary to what they've printed in the papers about me, I'm not really good at much besides being the mix master of munchies."

"Have you spoken with your siblings? Made any plans to find her?" asked Aurie.

Ivan screwed up his face. "You guys are worse than the cops. Why do you care?"

"Because someone thinks Andromeda will be the cause of an infernal calamity," said Pi. "We don't know how, or why, but we had a group of mages try to kill us thinking we're part of this plot."

"Andy?" asked Ivan incredulously. "She's the least likeliest person I know to cause trouble beyond a razor-sharp level of snark. You're crazy if you think she's involved with anything like that. She's been touring with Mystique since she graduated, for Merlin's sake. When would she have time?"

"It's not a matter of what she's up to, but what others think she's up to," said Zayn, sensing that Ivan knew more than he was saying. When he checked to Audrey, she had her arms held around her upper body in a defensive position.

"I don't know what to tell you," said Ivan, "but don't believe the rumors. A lot of crazy shit has been attached to my family name from Montanhas to that other bullshit. I'm not saying we're not more fucked up than a donkey on acid, but the truth only gets you so far."

"We've been to Montanhas," said Zayn right away, catching Ivan off guard. He pulled back, standing tall, the color draining from his face. Audrey took a step like she wanted to console him, but held back because of their presence.

"You can't have been there," he said grimly. "The portal was destroyed. We barely got out ourselves."

"We work for Invictus," said Aurie, "which brings a lot of resources not available to others."

Ivan grabbed a beaker and almost took a drink of the lime green liquid, before setting it down and finding his coffee cup, which he drained with a quivering hand. He leaned on the table, refusing to meet their gazes.

"What did you find?"

Aurie gave a description of the plant and the general plot to help the survivors out of the valley, leaving out the betrayals. Ivan leaned against the counter with his eyes closed when she was finished. Audrey clutched him to her side.

"Scorpics as big as horses, eh? As if I didn't have nightmares before," said Ivan, setting his cup down and staring at the floor while Audrey rubbed his back.

"Does Montanhas have anything to do with her abduction?" asked Pax, cautiously.

"Montanhas? No," said Ivan, "I can't imagine it did. She wasn't there and until our father purchased Lifestone, we didn't know a damn thing about it. Wrong place, spectacularly wrong time."

"Could it have anything to do with the disappearance of the head of Lifestone security, Mikhail Dresden? Revenge? Anything?" asked Aurie.

"No one liked that asshole, so I can't imagine they'd hold onto baggage for what, five, six years now," said Ivan.

"What about your other siblings? Or your mother?" asked Aurie. "Do they have any theories on what happened or why? Anyone planning on going after her?"

"I haven't spoken to them in years, and Monique lives at the bottom of a very expensive bottle of Chablis."

"Your father?" asked Aurie.

His pulsing jaw and flat expression told Zayn a lot about their relationship, not that it'd been hard to infer that from reading about the famously ruthless head of Charmer Inc. A lot of competing CEOs had breathed a sigh of relief when he disappeared.

"He's probably where he deserves to be, wherever that is," said Ivan in a low voice.

"Do you know where your twin is? Or Moriganne? We haven't been able to locate them," said Zayn.

Ivan looked away. "Like I said, I haven't seen my siblings, and I think you can understand that if even half the things that were said in the papers were true, we had a pretty rough go of it during our time in the Halls. We're all trying to heal in our own ways. I would leave well enough alone."

The tension in Ivan was ratcheted up to an eleven. He was focusing on his breathing as he stared at the floor.

"It's probably time for you all to leave now," said Audrey as Ivan dug into an interior pocket and threw back a couple of pills.

Sensing there was more to learn, Zayn said, "Have you heard the name Elosian before?"

The flinch was as clear cut as a verbal acknowledgement. Ivan looked up, sour smile on his lips, the earlier claims to a good poker face long gone.

"No."

Audrey ushered them out while Ivan stayed at the lab counter, staring into space. Pax had to coax Kali away from Barkley, who had curled up next to the big foxlike creature during the discussion.

"Please don't come back," said Audrey, ashen-faced at the door. "He's been doing good for a long time."

"You know the name and the significance," said Zayn before she could close the door. "Both of you. I saw it in your faces. Look, I know some of the shit that was going on back then. Kitty came to me for help with the assassin Kavano, and I've seen the family's old house manager back in the Eternal City. He was devoted to Victor Charmer, which means whatever happened to him was permanent, or he would have never left. Audrey, please, give us something. We can all see that Ivan isn't ready to be involved, but we can do something about it. Save his sister. Stop whatever is going on."

"Leave it alone," said Audrey. "You think you understand, but you don't. Better to walk away, act like it never happened."

"Can you explain why?" asked Zayn. "Give us something, anything."

"Talk to Ares."

She tried to close the door but Zayn stuck his foot in. "We'd like to but we can't find him. He's disappeared off the map."

Audrey stared back blankly before answering. "Twelfth ward. You'll know it when you see it."

The door slammed shut before anyone could ask any more questions.

"It's obvious they know something about Elosian," said Pi. "Right? I wasn't the only one that saw that."

"They're worried about his lies," said Aurie. "That's why Invictus didn't want us to be involved for a while. He's afraid that Elosian is leading us into a trap. Ivan and Audrey were too."

"Maybe we'll find answers with Ares," said Pi.

Zayn rubbed the back of his neck. "Or maybe it is a trap."

Twenty-Nine

Like the eleventh, the twelfth ward held a lot of old memories for Aurie from when they were in the Halls. But unlike the eleventh, it hadn't changed. There was no polite gentrification, or Juju Juices popping up in previously run-down corners. The ward held a lot of old industrial buildings, faded with rust and covered with graffiti.

Aurie drove the group through the streets. Everyone made their guesses as to Ares' new home. There was brief confusion when they drove by the colorful building that was Gamemakers Hall, but they quickly figured out that it wasn't where they were looking for by the two kids with pimpled foreheads who were heading through the fenced yard, backpacks slung over their shoulders.

There were other places that Aurie was aware of in the ward. Places that you couldn't find unless you knew they were there, but she avoided them. Not everyone in the city of sorcery wanted to, or should, be found.

Pi spotted the tower from two streets over, glancing through a couple of run-down industrial parks. It wasn't really a tower upon closer inspection, but a three-story brick house that had no other buildings nearby. Double chain-link fences with barbed wire at the top was a clear "Stay Out," but that's not what clued them in to the identity of the owner. Runes covered the walls in the density reserved for the graffiti on the warehouses.

"Those are wardings," said Pi as they climbed out of the Momentum. "Some of them I saw in Montanhas. I wonder if he was the author of them."

A camera at the sliding gate had a green light on. Her sister stared into the lens and waved.

"Kindly fuck off," said a voice over a speaker.

"Is this Ares Charmer?" asked Aurie, focusing her voice towards the camera.

"Do the words *fuck off* not mean anything anymore?"

"We want to talk to you about Andromeda," said Aurie.

They stared at the speaker, expecting it to crackle to life again. Nothing. She looked to Zayn, who lifted his shoulders and mouthed a single word. She nodded.

"We've been to Montanhas."

There was another long pause and Aurie was sure that he wasn't going to answer but then the gate lurched into motion, opening wide enough for them to pass and no more. They hurried inside, and the gate closed behind them.

"That's weird," said Pax, holding Kali to her side.

A pathway had been painted on the cracked concrete in a light blue paint, but it wasn't the straightest line between two points, but a torturous, meandering journey that took them around the space.

"This seems purposeful, and given the runes and other precautions I think it means we're to follow the light blue brick road," said Aurie.

"I think it's to protect against whatever's in there," said Pax, gesturing towards a heavily reinforced shed in the back corner of the concrete yard. The exterior of the small outbuilding had bulges outward and small holes in the steel, mostly in the lower third. Runes covered the building. "Kali can sense it, and it's angry."

"We should continue on the path he left us," said Aurie.

"I wasn't suggesting otherwise," said Pax, frowning.

Feeling like Dorothy and her companions, Aurie led them around the path to the door, which was open upon their arrival. Ares was waiting for them. His broad shoulders and handsome face were tempered by a deep concern as he clutched a coffee cup to his chest.

"I know you," he said, looking at Pax and her companion. "You're the girl from the zoo." His gaze shifted to Aurie. "And you're the sisters who brought back Invictus. But I don't know who you are."

"For good reason," said Zayn, "but I know who you are."

"Why are you lying about Montanhas?"

"We're not lying. We've been there, recently," said Aurie.

"Invictus?"

"In a way, yes," she said. "Do you want to hear about it?"

"Maybe," said Ares, "but not now. I want to hear why you came to my door talking about Andromeda."

Aurie examined the room for the first time since entering. The walls were covered in sketches, runes, and newspaper articles. The drawings were of various creatures, including the scorpics and gigantes, but included many others that she wasn't familiar with. A shotgun leaned on the wall near a tub of high-grade salt. The place had the air of a person who'd gone deep into conspiracy theories, or was a doomsday prepper, or both.

Pi spoke up, gesturing towards a set of runes written in beautiful penmanship. "We saw those in Montanhas. You wrote them. They're not like other warding runes I've studied. Why?"

Ares ignored her sister's comment and stared back at Aurie. "What have you learned about Andromeda? Do you know where she is?"

"We're working on it," said Aurie.

"Please don't misunderstand what I'm trying to say, but if you do figure it out, don't go after her."

"You're afraid of Elosian."

"Afraid?" A clipped laugh came out. "I wish it was just afraid. If you know that name, then you know why you can't go after her. It's like those stupid joke finger cuffs, the more you struggle, the more you find yourself caught."

"Is that why you're out here in the middle of the twelfth? Hiding from him?" asked Aurie.

"Does this look like hiding?" he asked, gesturing wildly.

She eyed him carefully. He looked like a man on the edge of madness, someone who carried a lot of guilt and the burden of knowledge.

"I'd rather not say what this looks like," she said, prompting a narrowing of his gaze.

"You want to know why I'm out here? I'll show you," he said, grabbing the shotgun on the way out of the door.

On the concrete steps, he made two short gestures and the entire concrete area outside of the pathway flashed pale green for a second before returning to dull gray. He marched towards the reinforced shed with the group of them on his heels. A sliding door on the front revealed a narrow set of bars. A moment after it was open, something screeched inside, pounding against the steel, creating new dents and making everyone take a step back. Ares moved to the side and clicked a button that bloomed light inside the shed.

"Take a look," said Ares, clutching his shotgun like an Appalachian miner on guard duty. "The tail barbs shouldn't have regrown yet, but don't linger too long in case they have."

The warning left her apprehensive, yet she found herself pulled towards the small window. Her heart was caught in her throat as her eyes fell upon a bony creature the size of a big dog hunched in the corner, a long, segmented tail ending in a ball covered in spikes.

"It looks like a manticore with the skin pulled off," said Pax, peering over her shoulder. "What is it?"

"A mantic. It's what I call it anyway."

Behind them, Kali stared at the shed growling, her hackles at full attention, but Aurie's attention was focused inside. The creature reminded her of the scorpic from Montanhas—what was it doing here? As she looked closer, she saw a silvery liquid around the mantic's stubby bone feet.

"What's that smell?" asked Zayn, stepping to the side of the shed. "Is that turpentine?"

"That thing is huge," said Pi, when she managed to get a look inside.

"Huge?" repeated Ares. "It's the size of a terrier."

"Not sure what kind of terriers you owned, but this looks like a mastiff or a Great Dane," said Pi.

Ares forced himself in front of the shed. "What the fuck? Why is there mercury on the concrete?"

"Mercury? I don't understand," said Pax.

"It's superfood for demons," said Ares, turning his head.

Kali jumped back a second before the mantic threw itself at the side of the shed, bending the steel bars outward. Ares curled around to the side.

"What happened to my runes?"

Upon the second impact, the steel split open and before anyone could move, the mantic burst out of the side of the shed and threw a volley of spikes.

Thirty

The moment the mantic exploded from the shed, Pi raised her hands, summoning a ghostly shield to protect them from the spikes flying into their midst. As the defensive measure shimmered into existence, the others were moving with equal fervor.

"Aurelia!"

The true name shout from her sister slammed into the shield Pi had just formed, catching the brunt of the impact that should have hit the mantic. The deflection of energy spun Zayn into the fence line as a pair of blades appeared in his hands.

As the confluence of magical energies scattered them like leaves, the mantic leapt between them, escaping the corner of the concrete yard.

§

The mantic flew through the gap as Pax shouted, "*Shayut*!"

The slam mark caught the demonic creature's hindquarters, shifting it off course, but due to the sudden change in everyone's location, it mostly hit the younger Silverthorne, knocking her to the ground.

The mantic headed towards the front gate. Pax wasn't sure if the creature could get past of the warded fencing, but she didn't want to risk the chance, and poured faez into the magesteel enchantments that were installed into her back. She leapt to her feet, speeding towards the mantic right as a shotgun blast ripped into her arm.

§

Zayn shook off the impact, retrieving his blades in the blink of an eye. As he blurred after the mantic, he saw Ares pull the trigger on his shotgun, right as Pax surged into its path, catching half the shot. Zayn managed to duck beneath the pellet spread and shoulder charged the mantic, throwing it off course before it could hit the gate.

Spinning around with surprising speed, the mantic faced him, flicking its tail, which made him throw himself to the side, not realizing that the bony ball at the end was devoid of spikes. As he curled back around he saw a condensed ball of dark energy forming above the mantic too late to avoid getting caught in its gravitational pull.

§

The dark star pulsed and stuttered, sending out sparks and warping gravity around it. Pi had conjured it into existence to keep the mantic from escaping, but she'd only managed to trap Zayn in the effects.

The mantic leapt forward, claws ready to rake him across the chest, forcing her to dismiss the spell to give Zayn a chance to avoid the hit. The demonic creature tackled him backwards, and for a moment, Pi thought he had taken a claw to the neck, but Zayn flipped the mantic backwards to crash against the fence.

§

Aurie ran towards Zayn, who she was sure had been mortally injured, only to get tangled with him as he rose to his feet, narrowly missing her arm with a blade.

"Out of my way."

She turned towards the mantic, who was busy righting itself, but the chaos made going after it directly difficult. The tight space and destructive magics had been a hindrance. She spotted Pax lying on the ground, clutching her bloody arm. The others had trapped the mantic against the fence, but it looked ready to leap again.

"No one move!" shouted Pi as she extended her arms as if she were about to give the mantic an enormous hug.

§

The mantic was in her sights. No one was in the way for once. Pi had rarely utilized the soul fragment from Metallum Nocturn, but an idea formed, and before the creature could escape she drew on deep reserves of faez.

A burning ball of molten energy formed before her. It was as if she'd conjured a scoop full of liquid iron from nothingness. The heat was excruciating. Before the mantic could leap again, she blasted it with the molten ball.

§

Her arm screaming in pain from the shotgun blast, Pax gritted her teeth, relying on her connection to Kali. She lumbered to standing as a bright ball of orange-red energy formed before Pi. The spell would annihilate the mantic, but as she threw her arms forward, Pax sensed the demonic creature's impending leap, which would bring it right back onto the younger Silverthorne, catching her in her own spell.

"*Skorost!*"

Between the speed mark and the magesteel enchantment, Pax moved almost as fast as

Zayn could, slamming into Pi with her shoulder and throwing them both out of the way as the molten ball impacted the leaping mantic.

§

A shout found its way out of Aurie's lips as she saw her sister's impending death. The destructive spell was about to get dragged back onto her as the mantic leapt. Before anyone could move, Pax tackled Pi out of the way.

The mantic screamed as the molten ball splattered over its body, turning the bony creature into smoking black char. It writhed around in the middle of the concrete, sending out splatters of iron as everyone backed up to watch it die. The creature lasted longer than Aurie thought possible, given the wicked heat from her sister's spell.

When the mantic was finally dead, no one spoke. They stared at the charred lump on the concrete, then at each other.

Pi untangled herself from Pax, who grimaced from her shotgun wounds. When her sister regained her feet, she looked at all of them.

"That could have gone better."

Thirty-One

Pax wished her injuries had been worse so she would have a reason to go to Golden Willow and see her friend Janelle. After picking out the shotgun pellets, an apologetic Ares had wrapped her arm before returning to examine the makeshift jail that had failed to keep the mantic trapped.

"Everything okay?" asked Zayn as the Silverthorne sisters argued about the battle on the opposite side of the concrete yard.

Pax held up her arm. "I've had worse."

"You took a shotgun blast to the arm." He screwed up his face. "I didn't know Animalians were built to withstand things like that."

"I'm a Hunter, which means they gave us extra treatments for surviving things like this, though usually it comes in the form of claws or teeth, not friendly fire."

"Yeah," he said, pumping his eyebrows, "this was a mess. We did more damage to each other than the mantic."

Kali whined at her feet, so she leaned down and rubbed her companion's ear.

"I'm wondering if we're cut out to work together," she said.

"Different Halls. It might take time."

"Which we don't have." She nodded to Ares, who was pacing around the shed. "What do you think of him? Do you believe that it was sabotage? Or Elosian?"

Zayn shifted his mouth to the side. "Sure seems like it, but first impressions can be deceiving. I can tell he's not lying to us. Not about this."

She nodded. Through Kali's psychic lens, she sensed Ares' pained honesty about the mantic and the suspected sabotage.

"He doesn't really hide things well," said Zayn. "He's an open book."

"How can you tell?" she asked.

Zayn tapped beneath his eye and then his ear. "I'd love to play poker against him." He glanced back. "But not you."

"Let's see if we can find more out while he's distracted," said Pax.

Zayn smirked. "I like the way you think."

Ares was mumbling under his breath when they arrived, pacing as he examined the damage to the shed and the silvery liquid that hid within the cracks.

"Someone must have poured the mercury behind the shed, and it ran inside. The same person had to have thrown turpentine on the runes."

"Don't you have cameras?" asked Zayn.

"Not back here. They point to the road and inside the fence, but I'll have to add some to the roofline, give me a three-sixty." Ares glanced towards the abandoned industrial buildings. "Whoever it was, they probably came from that direction."

"Do you have enemies?" asked Pax.

"Let's be real," said Ares, "we all know who it was."

"Elosian."

"Who else?" said Ares, frowning.

"Why did you even have it? And where did it come from?" asked Pax.

"The barrier in the Undercity is at its weakest. There's a canyon near the fire well that the gangs drop people in so they'll get eaten. I captured the mantic and brought it back here for study."

"It's like the scorpics," said Zayn.

"But different," said Ares, cupping his chin in his hand. "The ones in Montanhas required different runes. I had to experiment to find something that kept them from killing us. The one I captured responded to the normal wardings that I learned in Coterie."

"The demonic realm isn't a monolith," said Pax, and when the two guys looked at her curiously, she said, "That was something Invictus told me."

"She's right, though it's not something that was understood until recently," said Ares, furrowing his brow. "I wish I knew why. I feel like it's something important." He shook his head, sighing. "I really thought I'd protected myself from Elosian. I'm wondering if it's even possible."

"Maybe you can't," said Pax. "Maybe you have to do what you think is right. Elosian's been trying to get into this world for centuries, and he hasn't yet."

"Not without some very close calls," said Ares. "Not that I have personal experience with that. I learned that as part of my studies at Coterie."

She shared a glance with Zayn. They both knew he was lying, but clearly he wasn't going to explain himself.

"Why not go after your sister? Aren't you worried about her?"

"Terribly," said Ares "She's the least Charmer of us—that's a compliment if you didn't know."

Through Kali's link, Pax sensed a great deal of concern and deception from Ares. He'd nearly let something out.

"When they," said Pax, nodding back towards Aurie and Pi, who were still arguing, "talked with Beckett Dreadmarsh before he died, he said something about the newest of the connected eight. A prophecy or something he heard. Does that mean anything to you?"

The surge of emotion from Ares told her that it was significant, even as he shook his head. He paused for a moment in thought, the brief smoothing away of his knotted forehead suggesting a revelation.

"*Newest* of the connected eight? Huh. That's pretty vague. He was head of Chroma and Key, right?"

"Like you," said Zayn.

"It's not the right time for the Convergence," said Ares, looking away. "Where could he have heard that?"

"The Convergence?"

"Oh, yeah," he said, "none of you were society members. The four major societies were formed to protect the city from a potential invasion, though that purpose was lost a long time ago and it became a way to help each other get ahead in business and society. Yeah, I'm sure you're shocked." He rolled his eyes. "The Convergence ceremony was the one time all four societies came together for a reading. In my time, we were told that the invasion was nearing. Soon. But now is the wrong time for another Convergence ceremony. If a reading was done, it wasn't the usual one."

"Is that significant?" asked Pax.

"Maybe. But since I wasn't there, I don't know. Alumni aren't allowed, and I've lost contact with most of the others I knew back then."

"Will you try and find out?" asked Zayn.

"I'm not sure that would be a good idea." Ares held his hands to his temples. "No matter how hard I try to keep clear of his deceptions, they keep pulling me in."

"Maybe that's what this was," said Pax. "Elosian knows you're getting close to learning something, or doing something, and this attack was his attempt at keeping you from doing it. You can't back down, no matter what it looks like. We're going to need you. We're going to need everyone, possibly."

"Have you spoken with your other sisters?" asked Zayn.

Ares swallowed. Shook his head. "They're traveling. Haven't seen 'em in a few years, and before you ask, I don't know how to get ahold of them."

The answer was suspicious, but Pi waved them over urgently. They left Ares by the busted shed.

"Is it just me or is it really strange that the other sisters are nowhere to be found?"

"Extremely," said Zayn. "He's hiding something. It's not like Kitty to go underground. She was one of the most talented members of my Hall when she was there, someone I wouldn't want to go against if I didn't have to."

The younger Silverthorne was holding up her phone.

"I got a hit on the mages. We have to go."

Thirty-Two

"I was able to identify the Protector mage, Lennie Fane, from his tattoos. He used to work for Blackstone Security," said Pi as her sister sped through the streets towards the third ward. "Might still, but my inquires came back that he was no longer employed by them. The ghost trap was looking for online activity. I got a hit from a Wizard's Coffee in the fourth. If we hurry, we might be able to follow them to Andromeda's location."

Traffic was light and they managed to park near the Wizard's Coffee about two blocks from the statue of Invictus, a hundred-foot version of the head patron that Pi thought contributed to people thinking he was much taller than he actually was in person.

"Let me take a look," said Zayn. "Kali is a little suspicious, and you two have famous faces."

When Zayn strode away, he carried himself like he wasn't a powerful assassin's mage, shoulders pinched and head nodding to the beat on his headphones. If he'd changed his face, she couldn't see from her perspective.

Almost as soon as he neared the Wizard's Coffee, Lennie Fane exited with a large cup in one hand and a bagel sandwich in the other. The Animalians mage that had been tending the cobra-headed creature came out right behind. She wore a sleeveless black hoodie and had the sides of her head shaved into a faux-hawk.

"I know her," said Pax right away. "A few years younger. Sammi Parlov. Tamers. She looks different."

The two mages spoke to each other and then split apart, with Sammi headed the opposite direction and Lennie headed towards them.

"Shit," said Pi. "Back in the car."

They piled into the Momentum. The sidewalks were busy with tourists on the warm and sunny early April day, but if he looked over he might spot them. Pax made Kali lie down in the back and everyone kept their heads down as Lennie passed them without notice.

Ten seconds later, Zayn appeared at the window. "Which one do we follow?"

"Both," said Pi at the same time as her sister.

"I'll go with Zayn," said Aurie, "and follow Lennie. You two are better with the Animalians mage."

Pi didn't agree with the pairings, but there wasn't time to argue. They let Kali out of the back and hurried up the sidewalk in the direction Sammi had left. Pi had thought it'd be a struggle to move against the flow, but the people parted inexplicably and barely gave Kali a second look as they passed.

"Is she doing that?" asked Pi as she hurried to keep up with Pax and her companion. They moved with long strides and barely a breath as if they were ultra-marathoners on a warm-up jog.

Pax blinked, a little confused. "Oh yeah, I guess so."

"I don't see Sammi," said Pi after a block.

"She's still ahead," said Pax, then looked up at the street sign. "There's a station around the corner. I bet she's headed there."

Long lines piled into the busy train station. Pi worried about losing Sammi, but Pax seemed confident that Kali could monitor without getting too close. They purchased tickets at a kiosk, since Pax didn't have an IR card. The train arrived right as they crested the platform, giving them a good sight line to Sammi entering the car further up. They piled through a door three cars behind Sammi, finding a spot near the window.

"She's still there," said Pax, who looked like she'd eaten something sour, "but she also has some sort of block. I can't get much more than that she's existing."

"Probably blocks on scrying or mental intrusions. It's what I would do if I were her."

The other riders in their car gave them a wide berth, which meant Pi didn't have to jostle against other people during the rattling ride. She watched out the window, and checked back to the map frequently, trying to guess where Sammi might get off.

"Why are you holding back?" asked Pax.

"Huh? What do you mean?"

"I'm not blind. You and your sister aren't telling me everything, and you in particular... look, I'm not reading your mind, or anything, I can't do that, but brushing up against you is like getting thrown into a noisy restaurant where everyone's telling the same waitress their order."

"I have a complicated history," said Pi, checking around them. "One not suited for a conversation in a public place."

If Pi hadn't known that Pax was in a relationship with the billionaire philanthropist and shape-shifting dragon, Okho, she could have found her way to a crush on the redhead. But she was also pretty sure that Pax had no interest in her.

"You and your sister both know Zayn," said Pax, chewing on her lower lip. "I don't know any of you, outside of an exhausting two-day round the world trip. Let me in a little, please. I feel like an outsider."

Pi repressed a sigh. "What do you want to know?"

"Anything?"

"That's a pretty big topic."

Pax sighed. "I don't know, where you grew up? What your parents were like? Were they mages or are you the first of your family in the Halls?"

The earnestness in her gaze tempered the knot of anger that formed inexplicably in Pi's throat.

"We grew up here in the seventh ward. Our parents were mages, Aura Healers and Arcanium, but they died in a gas explosion when we were kids. After that we got shuttled around the orphanage system until we managed to scrape our way into the Halls."

"I'm sorry about your parents, that must have been tough."

Pi looked into her open palm, then closed it into a fist. "I am who I am because of them, even in death. I saw what happened to them and decided I never wanted to be powerless like that."

"They were killed?"

"We don't know for sure. Aurie did a lot of soul-searching about it. She blamed herself for what happened, delving into her memories in the Verum Locus, but I didn't want to do that. In a way it doesn't matter. They're dead, and we only had each other to rely on."

The knot in her throat tightened as she spoke. She'd told herself this a thousand times, but the way Pax looked at her suggested she didn't believe this explanation.

"Maybe you'll learn to rely on me eventually," said Pax, the corner of her lips curled up optimistically.

"I don't really know you."

Pax seemed neither shocked nor angry. As the train slowed towards the next station, she said, "Sammi's getting off."

They maneuvered their way to the door. The exit stairs gave them a chance to follow Sammi without being seen. Pi hoped two things were in their favor: Sammi wasn't expecting to be followed, and the other mages didn't know they'd recruited Pax and Kali. On the other hand, Pax knew Sammi, which meant it went the other way around, and if she saw either of them, the connections would be easy to make.

The station was in the northwest corner of the ward, but Sammi was heading out towards the thirteenth. While the eleventh was the poorest part of town and the twelfth's industry had long ago faded, the last ward of Invictus was neither used nor abandoned. A few buildings lined the edge near the other wards, but generally the construction didn't go much further in. Wide swaths of reclaimed fields with collapsed and rotted buildings in the foliage made the thirteenth a wild spot.

"Where is she going?" asked Pax. "There's nothing in the thirteenth."

"It feels like a trap," said Pi.

Kali turned her furry head towards them as if she agreed.

They stayed a block behind Sammi, who never made any attempt to check her surroundings, which seemed suspicious, as if she were luring them away from civilization. The line of brick houses ended at Talbot street. Sammi hurried into a field.

"It looks like there's a group of buildings back there through the trees," said Pi.

Spring growth brought green grass sticking up through the brown shoots of last year. Buds formed on the trees. The changing seasons and the empty spaces brought a rustling wind. Pi checked back to the center of the city to see the Spire reflect the sun like a beacon. An ache formed in her breastbone at the reminder of her weakness inside Invictus' realm. She hadn't had time to ponder the visions she'd had while the others thought her unconscious, but they left her uneasy about what they were trying to accomplish.

"Follow her into a trap, or go back and get the other two?" asked Pax, crouched at the corner of the building as they watched Sammi wade through the high grass.

"A little further," said Pi. "Enough to know if this is where they're keeping Andromeda, but first sign of trouble, we get the hell out."

"I'll follow your lead," said Pax as she rubbed the back of Kali's neck. "I trust you."

As they crossed the street, Pi wondered if she trusted herself after the collapse at the portal barrier.

Thirty-Three

A block after they started following Lennie, he paused at the corner, waiting to cross the street. Zayn sensed that he would turn his head, so he grabbed Aurie's hand and pulled her into a tight hug so their faces wouldn't be visible.

Aurie's breathy exclamation and flush cheeks told him she was confused until she shot a side-eye towards Lennie, understanding following.

"Has he crossed yet?" he asked, their foreheads nearly touching.

"Yeah, he is now."

In the turn to follow, Zayn's hand brushed hers and they held onto each other's fingers for half a second before racing to cross the street before the light changed. Now wasn't the time for thoughts about Aurie, but he couldn't help but parse their interaction. Was she following his lead, leaning into the deception, or was she still interested in him? Time and distance had loosened the bonds that had once drawn them together.

The fourth ward was filled with tourists, making their job of tailing Lennie both easy and difficult. It was easy to stay lost in the crowd but hard to push through the waves that came and went with the traffic lights. Lennie was a big man but had the long strides of a distance runner. His size made traversing the busy sidewalks easy, and most oncoming pedestrians moved out of his way instinctively. Not so for Zayn and Aurie, who had to dodge around families with strollers and businesspeople on their phones, ignorant of their surroundings.

Near the blue line station, Lennie checked his phone, then crossed the jammed street, dodging around honking cars, and headed down the ramp of a multilevel parking garage in the middle of construction. Orange fences blocked the way, but Lennie had hopped them easily. A banner as tall as three floors hung above the entrance with a happy family giving a thumbs-up and "Coming Soon: Sept 2024!" along the bottom.

"Wait," said Zayn, holding Aurie back when she made to follow. "He might have sensed we were on his tail. If we cross now, he could see us from the shadows."

"But if we don't, we'll lose him, and possibly Andromeda," said Aurie, intensity in her gaze. She was chomping to follow, even more than her normal headstrong self, and there was an ache in her eyes.

"The truth bond?"

"I keep feeling these stabs, right at the base of my skull, as if they're tracing it backwards, like running a tap on a phone line. I hate what it might mean. We need to find her, for many reasons."

The construction site looked empty, or the workers were in an area he couldn't see. The way Aurie looked at him overcame his reluctance.

"Fine. We'll go, but stay behind me, and if I say run, we run."

A few cars honked at them as they crossed the barely moving street. The flimsy orange fencing bent beneath their touch. The darkness of the ramp quickly turned to dim lights posted on the concrete pillars.

"Where'd he go?" whispered Aurie. "Down further or across to the other side?"

Zayn inhaled deeply, parsing the scents in the air. It was a trick that only worked if there weren't a lot of competing smells, and the empty parking garage was the perfect environment.

"Down."

He kept a light amount of faez in his first three imbuements to be ready for an ambush. Aurie was much less protected, so he kept himself in front of where he thought an attack might come.

Fewer lights existed the deeper they went. Every other plastic light fixture was dark, which made sense if they weren't working in the area. Zayn held his fist up and scanned the area, sensing he was missing something. There was a tickle in his mind, an incongruity that his subconscious awareness had picked up. He scanned the shadows, expecting to see a lump or slight discoloration.

"What is it?" Aurie whispered from behind him. He could smell her nervousness.

"I don't know..."

After convincing himself that he was just being overly cautious, he continued down the ramp. They reached the B3 level before he realized what he was missing. The plastic light fixtures that weren't working were different than the others. They were only placed on the pillars near the ramp. He'd halfway turned to tell Aurie to run back up when they exploded.

Thirty-Four

The tall grass made it difficult for Kali to see, so Pax had to be her eyes.

Sammi went through the trees.

<Pax like Sammi>

I like Sammi too, but she might be our enemy now. We have to be ready.

The buildings ended up to be a trio of cottages, set at three corners, facing each other with a circle of stones at the center where a campfire might be set. The buildings were new and brightly colored. A gravel road reached the cottages from the other direction and a sign halfway angled away from them said "Camp Lucky" in bold, bright letters.

Pi crouched behind a tree and Pax followed her lead. "Why else would they come out here except to hide Andromeda?"

"Or set up an ambush."

"Or that," conceded Pi.

Pax was right on Pi's shoulder. A tension went deep, more than even the circumstances allowed. The younger Silverthorne seemed distracted by her thoughts. A few times as they waded through the grass she'd thought Pi had been mumbling to herself.

"Do you see Sammi?" asked Pi, then looking at Kali, she added, "Or sense her?"

<Empty space>

"Empty?" Pax asked aloud for Pi's benefit.

<Empty...no tastee crunchy ones...no skitter longtails...nothing>

"They're blocking the area with some sort of psychic field. Kali's not even picking up insects or rats."

"Would make sense," said Pi, squinting. "Don't want us scrying their location. So there's a high likelihood that this is where they're keeping Andromeda."

"It could also be a trap."

"We should see if we can spot her before we call in the others." Pi checked her phone, frowning when it was blank. "If we can identify how many others are here, then we know what kind of prep we'll need to surprise them. I'll sneak up to that back window. See what I can see. It looks like there's a lamp on."

Pax didn't like it but she didn't have a good enough argument otherwise.

"Fine, but get out of there at the first sign of trouble. I'll tell you if there's something wrong." She nodded towards Kali. "Through her."

"Really?"

"Show her, Kali."

Pi's expression brightened, followed by a smile. "Hey there, Miss Kali. She has a warm voice."

Before she left, Pi made gestures, draping enchantments over her body. The purpose of the spells was unknown to Pax, but as Pi moved across the grass to the back of the blue cottage, she found it hard to track Pi with her eyes.

"Curious."

Pax knew that Pi had started in Coterie and then moved to Arcanium, which was highly unusual. She wasn't aware of any other student changing halls, but both the Silverthornes exuded an exceptionalism that went far beyond their association with Invictus. During the fight at Ares' place, Pi had thrown up a ghostly shield that seemed like a tool of the Daring Maids, then had blasted the mantic with a molten ball of liquid iron that had to be a spell from Metallum Nocturn. There was nothing keeping students from using the secrets of the other halls as long as they could acquire the knowledge. The source of Pi's power was a fascinating mystery, one that she was interested to know the truth of at another time.

<Run>

The warning was projected to both her and Pi. She saw the reaction in the younger Silverthorne, who halted in mid-crouch, arms out and head snapping to the side in search of danger. Pax caught the reflection a moment later, a crack in the façade of the idyllic cottages.

She saw Sammi first, coming around the corner, but then Pax only had eyes for the cobra-headed creature with her. It was as big as a lion with brass feathers, tips going past the tail suggesting wings, and the upright curved head of a cobra. The parallels to Aepep, the flying snake god that she'd destroyed at the Portland Zoo, were unmistakable. If it wasn't a direct descendent, it was at least an attempted copy. A chimeratic abomination which had only one purpose.

Kali sensed the person in the trees before Pax saw them. She only got a glimpse: dark goggles and dark gloves with lines of blue and purple lights scintillating through them. A spot on her right thigh grew painfully hot, until she could do nothing else but slap her leg. It was her cell phone. She yanked it out, burning her fingertips to throw it into the grass as it exploded into flame.

Off to her left, she saw the cobra-headed creature breathe coal smoke at Pi, but Pax was too focused on the girl with the gloves headed her way to see how her friend fared. Kali leapt out of the grass at the girl, but a crackle of lightning from her gloves blasted her away.

Rage filled Pax as she felt the blowback of pain from her companion. She flooded her magesteel enchantments, blurring forward before the girl with the gloves could react, punching her in the head. The glasses shattered from her fist, and the girl tipped backward into the grass like a stiff board.

Curling around towards a whimpering Kali, Pax checked to see her companion's injuries were superficial. The side of her haunch was crisped, burnt hair wafting in the air, but only a few lines of burn had reached flesh.

Pi, on the other hand, looked in dire straits. She'd managed to put up a shimmering force wall that was keeping the cobra-headed creature from immolating her. Its breath plumed upward from the impact, sending black smoke streaming in all directions.

But creeping up from the side unseen, a third member of their team was readying to hit Pi with a spell. Pax was too far away to intervene, so she did the only thing she could think to do.

"On your right!"

The younger Silverthorne was buttressing her shield. Pax didn't think there was anything she could do to stop the approaching mage, but Pi turned her head and spoke, freezing the girl in place with a few words.

Pax was at least fifty feet away and had only half heard Pi's voice, but the words burst like tendrils of confusion in her mind, leaving her momentarily stunned with indecision before Kali's mental fortitude helped her shake it off. Pax was beginning to understand how Pi had gained her dangerous reputation.

The cobra-headed creature was wearing down Pi's shield, so Pax sprinted to a spot perpendicular, using a speed mark as extra fuel.

"Khoplat!"

The slam mark should have crippled the creature. Pax had put everything she could into the spell, but it barely bent its knees. That was when she remembered Sammi was a Tamer, and was reinforcing the cobra-headed creature so it could resist her marks.

Instead of blasting the creature a second time, Pax sent a knife-like gust of air at Sammi, knocking her off her feet. She followed up with a second slam mark, this time staggering the cobra-headed creature so it stopped its coal breath.

Pi didn't need to be reminded to run. She changed direction, and Kali joined her. The three of them sprinted away from Camp Lucky, keeping up the pace until they were back in the safety of the fourth-ward streets.

"Thanks," said Pi, leaning on her knees and heaving with breath. "That other girl had me dead to rights." She reached into her pocket and pulled out her phone, which looked blackened along the back, but hadn't combusted like hers. "Can you call my sister?"

"She got mine somehow. Burned up in my pocket. Probably have some burns on my thigh," said Pax.

"Shit, that explains how they set up this trap. The other girl was from Cybermagics. I know a few tricks, but nothing like a real pro. She must have sniffed out my ghost trap."

"This probably isn't the time, but how?" asked Pax. "I've seen you use spells from at least six different Halls. My friend Janelle was a double major with Aura Healers, but no one learns six."

"Twelve," said Pi, tilting her head. "Or I guess, thirteen, counting Arcanium."

"That doesn't make any sense."

Pi looked down the street, deeper into the ward. "If they ambushed us, then they probably set up another for my sister and Zayn. It won't be easy to find them, but we should head that way." She paused. "I'll explain why so many halls another time. I promise."

"Fair enough. And if we get close, Kali should be able to pick them up."

"Let's go," said Pi. "I hope they're okay."

Thirty-Five

Zayn crept ahead of Aurie, head making small movements as he checked the shadows in the underground levels. She had neither his senses nor speed, which made their creeping advance more fraught in her mind. Something was off. They could both sense it.

"What is it?"

He paused. "I don't know..."

Aurie checked to her left. Zayn was a few steps ahead. Then something slammed into her side, throwing her across the space into a concrete barrier as the space she was just standing in exploded. A concussive wave of flame washed over them. Zayn was lying on top of her, having thrown them both out of the way a moment before the explosion went off.

A pop-pop-pop, followed by Zayn rolling behind a column holding his leg, had Aurie realizing they were in a terrible spot. He'd been shot, right in the calf. Blood leaked through his fingers. Aurie poked her head to the opposite side of the column to see Lennie striding confidently up the ramp holding an automatic rifle to his shoulder, the strap wrapped around his forearm as he looked down the sights.

She went to grab Zayn to haul him in the opposite direction when she saw the dirty-blond guy with skin so pale she could see the veins in his arms throw something into the path out of the garage. It exploded into a shimmering shield that blocked their exit.

"Can you run?"

Zayn nodded, grimacing. "We have to take out Lennie first. He'll chew us up if we try."

"Let me take care of that," she said, leaning around the column, finding that he had anticipated her move and was squeezing the trigger. "Jam!"

Nothing punched her in the chest. The bit of mendancy had convinced the rifle not to fire, but it wouldn't stop the man behind the weapon. Lennie threw it aside and started running up the ramp at the same time she saw a third mage coming from a perpendicular direction. She had lustrous black skin and an inner intensity that made Aurie want to flee as fast as possible, but they were trapped on the ramp. The only way out was through the mages or over the edge to a twenty-foot drop. Aurie pushed Zayn towards the barrier.

"Over."

"Are you sure?"

She didn't bother answering Zayn, but told her running shoes, "Cushion."

The impact went through her knees and made her teeth clack together. It could have been worse. Zayn landed beside her in a crouch. They headed away from the ramp as Lennie landed behind them. Zayn was limping but he could still run faster than her.

"I don't want to get tied up in a fight with him," said Zayn as he checked over his shoulder.

The underground garage grew dimmer away from the ramp. The empty concrete echoed their footsteps. She spied a red exit sign on the far wall.

"STOP!"

The shout came from behind. Her feet froze in place. Zayn was stilled too. Lennie came sauntering towards them, a lip-peeled grin mocking their immobility.

"You're not the only one who can use their voice," said Lennie, cracking his knuckles against his palms. Aurie had forgotten about the Protectors' voice of command. As police officers, it allowed them to control even riotous scenes with ease. It was also going to get them killed.

The other two weren't far behind. Aurie fired a force bolt, which he knocked away as if it were a light gust of wind. She was pretty sure he could break her neck with the twitch of his hand should he get ahold of her.

Aurie spoke towards her shoes. "You're free."

She managed to pick one foot up before Lennie shouted "Stop" again.

"I can do this all day," he said.

He was right. Spell and counter spell were too easy. Too simple. He could keep them distracted until the others arrived, making it three on two.

"Free my feet," said Zayn. "I'll be ready this time."

Aurie spoke the words. Before Lennie could use his voice of command, Zayn's entire body disappeared into a green mist as he shifted forward. The big Protector halted his progress, holding up his fists as if he were expecting to be attacked.

With Lennie distracted by Zayn's disappearance, Aurie hit him with a force bolt that staggered the big man. She was preparing a second volley when a trio of translucent balls rolled near her feet. Before she could leap away, they exploded into a sticky web that held her fast. The gooey material was stretchy, but rapidly hardening.

The third member of their group approached with a serene arrogance, decked out in fashionable clothes. Even before she began her spell, Aurie marked her as a member of Coterie of Mages. The quiet, intense muttering as she moved her arms in swirling motions had Aurie worried about what was to come.

"Brittle," she said to the thick webbing, and it turned from taffy to crystalline in a heartbeat, allowing her to shatter the constraints into dust. Then towards Lennie, "Aurelia!"

The true name shout blasted through his attempted shielding, knocking him to a knees. His black shirt had been split along the front, and blood leaked out of the slice.

The pale Tinker mage reached into his pouch to throw more projectiles but as the little ornate box tumbled through the air, she yelled, "Malfunction." It landed impotently at her feet, prompting a snarling disappointment from him.

The Coterie mage completed her spell, and suddenly Aurie couldn't see. It was like a blanket of night had fallen upon her. In a panic, Aurie sent force bolts in random directions to keep anyone from getting near.

"I can see," she told herself, but the spell held. Vermancy and mendancy, while flexible, lacked the power of more advanced spells. Until she could find a counter, she wouldn't be able to see.

As she backed up with her hands out, throwing force bolts in the direction she thought the other mages were located, she heard the woman in back cry out in pain. More noises followed, including what sounded like someone dumping a box of ball bearings onto the concrete, and then the air grew unnaturally warm. A fight broke out. Aurie heard grunts and the slap of flesh on flesh. After ten seconds of furious action, the parking garage went silent. Aurie didn't know how to interpret the quiet, so she held her hands out and backed away slowly, hoping to hit the wall and eventually find the exit.

A squeal slipped out when someone grabbed her arm. "It's me."

"I can't see," she told Zayn.

"Run with me."

It was disconcerting to run without sight, but she trusted him to lead her to safety. When they reached the exit, he gave her instructions so she wouldn't knock herself out on the wall or door frame. They headed up the stairs and after a few flights, exited onto the busy street filled with car noises.

"Hey!" cried a voice to her left, prompting her to lift her hands for a spell, but Zayn held his hands over hers. "You can't be there. This is a fucking construction zone, for Merlin's sake, you could be killed!"

"Sorry, mate," said Zayn, "we got lost trying to take a shortcut. Won't happen again."

She held Zayn's hand as he led her over obstacles and eventually the plastic fencing that bent beneath her touch. Aurie heard him groan slightly.

"You're still hurt," she said.

"I'm fine for now. I had a receipt in my pocket that I shoved into the hole. It's not bleeding too much."

"Where are we?" she asked, still clutching his hand and resisting the urge to lean into his shoulder for support.

"About four blocks from the Statue of Invictus, standing on a street corner. Where should we go?"

"If they ambushed us here, they probably did the same with the others. Let me try my phone," said Aurie, digging into her pocket.

It took some work but she managed to make the call with Zayn's help. The phone rang and eventually went to voice mail.

"Hi, this is Pi," said her recorded voice. "Messages will be responded to in the order of fucks given."

"Ideas?" asked Zayn.

"Back to the Spire. It's a big city. We have no way of knowing which way they went." She sighed. "Besides, I'm useless without sight and you need your leg fixed. Hail a cab."

The ride through the city without sight was disorienting to Aurie. She hoped Invictus was around to counter the enchantment. The only good thing about the spell was that she kept holding Zayn's hand during the ride, leaning against his shoulder and trying not to worry about her sister.

"They'll be fine. Your sister's a badass, and Pax and Kali seem like they can hold their own."

She squeezed his hand.

A half-hour later, they entered the portal to Invictus' demi-realm. Aurie heard her sister's exclamation upon their arrival.

"About time. We got ambushed, it was a close one...were you two on a date while those assholes were trying to murder us?"

Thirty-Six

Using the extensive library in Invictus' realm, Pi managed to fix her sister's blindness and the gunshot wound in Zayn's calf. They gathered in the kitchen while Zayn made them grilled cheese with sliced tomatoes and garlic salt to discuss the ambush.

"It looks like there are at least six mages that kidnapped Andromeda, maybe more if they left some behind to guard her," said Aurie.

"Doubtful," said Zayn from the grill. "You wouldn't leave anyone behind if you're going to try to kill someone. You want overwhelming odds. What they should have done is split us up, and have the other five gang up on the two of us. We wouldn't have stood a chance. They got greedy, tried to take us all out at once."

"Lucky for us," said Pi, then took a bite of the cheesy sandwich. "Mmmm...Zayn, these are delicious."

"The real chef is my sister, Neveah. She's working in Paris. Wish she was here," he said wistfully.

Aurie had a pad of paper and a pen poised in her hand like a proper gold star student.

"Do we know who the mages were? Lennie Fane was one. He's a Protector, graduated about five years ago, worked briefly for Blackstone Security. Dropped off the map a year ago," said Aurie as she scribbled on the paper in a neat handwriting that annoyed Pi with its perfectness.

"Sammi Parlov," said Pax as she shared her grilled cheese with Kali, who was smacking her lips as she devoured the hunk. "She's a Tamer. The girl that blew up our phones and nearly took me out was from Cybermagics. Had some weird glove things. And the third one at our ambush, I don't know anything about. The fight was too hectic. I was happy to get out of there with our lives."

"I'll just write third mage, female, on my list," said Aurie. "On our side, we had Lennie and two others. The one was clearly a Tinkerer, and the other I think was in Coterie."

"Nandi Musa," said Zayn. "I looked her up. You're right. She's Coterie. But how do they all know each other? Did Beckett recruit them? Or is it something else?"

"Do you think they were behind the sabotage at Ares' place?" asked Pax.

"Seems too primitive," said Pi. "That was something else, I think."

"Nandi is Chroma and Key. Any of the others in the societies?" asked Zayn.

"Beckett was," said Aurie, pulling out her phone. "Let me check online. I'm sure someone has a list of society members."

A few minutes later, Aurie said, "Got 'em. You're right, Zayn. They're all society. Lennie Fane is Well and Stone. Sammi Parlov is Snake and Tome. The Tinker mage is Gregor Niles, also Snake and Tome. The girl with the gloves is Daria Brown, Silence. The only one we don't know is that last girl, but we can probably assume she's in a society."

"I think they were radicalized by that reading they got," said Pax.

"Seems likely. It's what set Beckett off, and Ares said the societies' original purpose was to protect against the demonic realm," said Aurie, "but remember what else he said, about it being the wrong time for the Convergence ceremony? What if Elosian tricked them with a reading, pointing them in our direction?"

"Would make sense," said Pi, "but what I don't understand is why Andromeda. After talking to Ares, I'm even less convinced of her importance to whatever is going on. When we told him what Beckett had said, he seemed surprised, as if he thought they'd read it wrong."

"I had that impression, too," said Aurie. "He didn't lie but he held something back."

Zayn and Pax both nodded.

"So we're in agreement he was lying, or maybe not lying, but sensed something wrong," said Pi.

"Why Andromeda?" asked Pax. "She's a performing member of a traveling troupe and a mage from the Weird Circus, which is hardly a bastion of demonic knowledge. The only thing she has going for her is that she's a Charmer, a family associated with a lot of shady things."

As soon as Pax said it, everyone's head came around. The grilled cheese on Zayn's spatula slipped off and hit the floor, much to Kali's delight. She pounced and scarfed it before anyone could say otherwise.

"It's the wrong Charmer," said Pi. "Newest. Does anyone else think that's an unusual term? Why not youngest?" A few nods told her she was on the right track. "Let's assume that Andromeda was never the threat. Ivan seemed like a mess, and Ares has become a hermit dedicated to stopping the invasion. The other two sisters are nowhere to be found. I bet that's for a reason."

"If I had to guess I'd say it was Kitty," said Zayn, frowning. "She's formidable."

"That's great, but where are they?" asked Aurie.

"Ares was lying when he said he didn't know where they were," said Zayn. "He looked to his phone on the table, which meant he probably called them as soon as we left. Pi, can you, you know, do a thing?" He made typing motions with his fingers.

"Yeah," said Pi, "should be simple. He lives out by himself, so a quick hack to the cell tower should give me any recent calls he's made. Would never work if he lived in a busier section."

As Pi rose from the counter, Pax threw up her hands. "Does everyone know why you know so many Halls besides me?"

"Ahhh...why don't you guys explain while I find out if Ares called his sisters to warn them."

Aurie started explaining her complicated past as Pi went into her room and opened her laptop. The hack wasn't too difficult. It didn't even require magic, just a brute-force stack overflow attack on the servers. A half hour later she strolled back into the kitchen. The incredulous look she got from Pax was tinged with sadness.

"Twelve souls?"

"Fragments," said Pi. "I had to save them."

"Is that...thing, or person still out there?" asked Pax.

"With a little help from Inari, we managed to take care of him."

"That's good. Soul stealing sounds awful." Pax set her empty plate on the floor for Kali to lick. "Did he call them?"

"Yep. They went about as far away from this city as you can get without heading into another realm." Pi paused. "Chiang Mai, Thailand. I already checked the tome. There's a set of coordinates to Bangkok and then it's a short flight to their city."

"I wonder why they went all the way across the world to Chiang Mai," Pax said.

Pi took a spot at the counter. "I guess we're gonna find out."

Interlude Three

He wasn't mad. He didn't care what people thought of his appearance, but he damn sure wasn't crazy.

"I'm not mad," he told the old woman who'd been reading from her paperback on the train.

The car had been crowded before he spoke, but then it seemed like he had all the room he wanted. People stood far away. They eyed him carefully as if he might sprout a second head at any moment.

Ollie tapped his foot and wished the train would move faster. If all was right in the world, it would. Take him to his destination much faster. He'd be a hero. They'd make statues of him like they had Invictus. Everyone would know his name. He'd get the justice he deserved after getting knocked out of the Merlin Trials and never making it into the Halls.

He touched the key in his pocket for the fiftieth time. He knew it was a bad idea. It would only signal to thieves where his valuables were but he had to make sure it was still there. Providence had brought it to him. Proof that the world was making up for screwing him before.

When he stepped out of the car in the fourth, he heard their muttered relief and lunged back in, making a young girl in a pink shirt jump back.

"I'm going to save you all! A fucking invasion is coming and you're too blind to know it! Fucking sheeple, you don't deserve it!"

He chuckled to himself as he strolled down the stairs towards the street level. Gave 'em a show, he did. They'd be talking about it for days, or weeks. Then later on, they'd remember. Feel blessed they would.

Ollie entered the tunnel behind the old Chinese restaurant. The way into the Undercity was long, but he'd brought his water bottle and snacks. Never travel underground without something to munch on. And a gun. He patted his hip where the pistol lay hidden.

He preferred magic, but these days he knew he was pushing his luck. Wasn't mad yet, but could happen if he kept using it. Only for emergencies, he reminded himself. Like when that bitch, Moriganne Charmer, tried to kill him. If only he would have turned the tables on her. Might have ended the whole plot, right then and there.

Demon whore.

Ollie unfolded the map when he reached the caverns. Gave himself darkvision. Wasn't his first choice, but he needed to see. The map didn't show how to reach it, but he knew generally where it was. He'd watched those traitorous society members go into the old Korean grocery store. Wasn't hard to make the connection underground.

An hour later, he found the concrete wall blocking the tunnel. Based on the map, he knew where he was. Ollie would have liked to have blown it wide with a spell, but he didn't know any that worked that good. He made the journey back to the surface, found a hardware store, bought a pickaxe and then hit a bodega for food and drinks for a couple of days. Got some of that orange fizzy elixir he loved best, and a fistful of jerky.

Back in the tunnels, he got to work. Progress was slow, but he was patient. There'd been a time he thought surviving was the only course, but why not be a hero? Why not stop the thing cold in its tracks? He'd have a thousand mouths waiting to suck his cock when he saved them. Not the sneering he got whenever he was above ground.

Time passed without his knowledge. He didn't have a watch to know how long it took to get through the concrete. He slept once and took a couple of breaks. Most of the orange drink and jerky was gone. Then he snapped a large piece away from the tunnel, big enough for him to slip through, as slender as he was.

Ollie left the pickaxe and snacks in the tunnel. A hundred feet past the gap, he found a door. The key in his pocket felt like gold. He kissed it before putting it into the hole. The click of the handle brought a grin to his lips. The enemy's headquarters. It was probably empty, but he pulled out the pistol just in case. A reconnaissance trip and then he could start gathering supplies. He still had a few friends left from his days in the Razor clan. Knew where they kept the explosives they used to make their secret tunnels too. Everything he needed was within reach.

Ollie lifted the gun and slipped through the door. Destiny awaited.

Thirty-Seven

After portalling to Bangkok and catching a pond-hopper to Chiang Mai, Aurie climbed out of a taxi near a street café. They'd passed numerous Buddhist temples on the way through the city. A golden-and-crimson-roofed palace sat opposite the eating area. Tourists strolled up the manicured entryway to enter the temple.

"Where to?" asked Pax as she came around the back of the taxi with Kali at her side.

The enormous foxlike creature got second glances from the people on the sidewalk.

"Not a clue," said Aurie, craning her neck in all directions. "Pi didn't get anything more than this city."

"Wish they were here," said Pax.

"Someone has to figure out where Andromeda is being held."

As Aurie readjusted the pack on her back, a stab of pain from the base of her skull had her knees bending. A vision of a small auditorium came to her as if she were standing inside. There were symbols on the wall, but she only got a glimpse and was too focused on the people. Andromeda was sitting on a chair, ghostly chains wrapped around her arms and legs as she grimaced. Standing over her was Nandi, fingers working a spell, examining the youngest Charmer. Aurie couldn't hear what they were saying, but it appeared the examination was uncovering the truth bond.

When Aurie came to, Pax was holding her up, concern on her brow. "Are you okay? You nearly fell over."

"They found it. Or are finding it," she said breathlessly.

"The truth bond?"

Aurie nodded.

"That's not good."

"No," said Aurie. "We have less time than I thought."

"Should we return to Invictus?"

Aurie paused. "No. We need to talk to the last Charmers. They hold too many secrets."

"Let's stretch our legs then," said Pax. "We're stiff from the journey. We can figure out our next step when we get our brains back."

Aurie had gotten used to Pax speaking in plural terms. While they hadn't spent much time together, only a few days since they'd brought them back from Russia, there seemed to be a constant conversation happening between Pax and her companion. Aurie hadn't minded being left out during the long flight in first class. She'd tried to sleep most of the time, but now that they were out, she was missing the banter she had with her sister, especially now that they'd found the truth bond. At least if Pi was here, she'd have someone to distract her.

"Do many students at Animalians have companions?" asked Aurie as they strolled down a busy sidewalk, wanting to take her mind off the bomb in her head. Oncoming pedestrian traffic dodged around the enormous Kali.

"I was the only one that I was aware of. Patron Adele invited me to return as an instructor, but I haven't wanted to yet. I need more time away." Pax paused and turned her head. "I still can't get over your sister and the soul fragments. How do you know which part is her and which part is them?"

Aurie forced a smile. "I've spent most of my life with her on a regular basis. It's a lot like you and Kali. I can tell. Sometimes she has little habits that get stuck. The fragments aren't the whole people, so they don't have all their old thoughts, just a collection of memories and tics. Like there was a week a year ago that Pi couldn't stop eating oranges. Bags of them every day. She'd probably eaten a hundred of them before she traced it to the Oculus fragment. Laird. He'd been eating an orange when his soul got snatched. Pi visited the place where he'd been taken, and it calmed that fragment."

"Must be confusing with all those foreign thoughts in her head," said Pax.

A group of scooters zoomed past their location with music blaring from a speaker. Aurie waited before speaking again.

"Can't be that different from you and Kali," said Aurie.

"She's always been there," said Pax. "I hardly remember a time before Kali."

"Do you think the nature of our Halls defines us as people?" asked Aurie, craning her neck at the beautiful flowers in hanging baskets above a market entrance. Both locals and tourists engaged in bartering for fruits, vegetables, and handmade goods in the open air market around the same time she heard distant voices discussing the enchantment they'd found on Andromeda. They were narrowing in on the truth bond. It wouldn't be long now.

"Absolutely," said Pax. "I was in Hunters. When I see a creature—anything, even if it doesn't have supernatural abilities—my mind goes right to the nomenclature, assessing the potential threats and the best way to counter them. I can't turn it off."

"I analyze the levels of truth in every statement," said Aurie. "Even my own. I evaluate the shades of accuracy with an annoying level of snark. You really didn't mean to say blue, it was really a cobalt with a hint of aquamarine." She rolled her eyes.

Pax chuckled. "I can't open a plastic container without wanting to check for stowaway critters. Sometimes I'll open a box of cereal away from my face as if a ghost viper will come flying out of it."

"Do ghost vipers hide in cereal boxes?"

"Merlin's no, but I can't convince my mind otherwise," said Pax.

"When Pi enters her room, she's always checking for hidden magical traps," said Aurie.

"They put traps in rooms in Arcanium?"

"It's from her year in Coterie. Interhall battles between the students is encouraged there. Competition without limits."

"Gross," said Pax, then tilted her head. "You're thinking about Kitty and Moriganne, aren't you? Is there something that defines them as people that might help us find them."

"Did you read my mind?" asked Aurie, looking at Kali.

"No," said Pax, "but it's smart."

"I don't know a lot about Stone Singers except that they're musical and can shape stone with their voice. Assassins, on the other hand, see everything as a threat."

"I wonder if being a Charmer was more impactful than their halls," said Pax. "I read about them on the flight. If even a quarter of the rumors were true, they were a messed-up family. The missing father, Victor, sounds like a real asshole. Used his kids as pawns in his games. Would make one very paranoid."

"Which means they probably wouldn't want to stay in the city," said Aurie. "It'd be too exhausting to be evaluating everyone all the time."

"If we have to search the countryside too, it could take us weeks," said Pax.

"Unless they were content that being halfway across the world was protection enough."

"If you're willing to come this far..."

Aurie massaged her forehead. "I need caffeine to think. Let's find a café."

There was a small one around the corner near a busy street. Taxis and scooters zoomed by, the latter sometimes packed with more gear than she thought possible to fit on the small vehicles.

As they sipped from their cups, pleasant music played over the speakers. Kali lay at their feet, watching the pedestrians, her eyebrows going up and down.

"What was it like during the zoo disaster?" asked Aurie.

Pax tensed up instantly, sitting tall in her seat, jaw pulsing.

"I'm sorry," said Aurie, "I shouldn't have asked."

The slow inhale and exhale from her travel companion was followed by the rounding of eyes. Kali looked up and whined.

"Sometimes I have nightmares about it. That I'm back in one of the domes, trapped by, well, all of it. Except in this version, I don't get my friends out, and I watch them get slaughtered." Pax closed her eyes. "Sorry. A little dark."

"Not dark. Reality. Sometimes I think that I keep throwing myself at new problems so I never have to think about the old ones."

"Your parents?"

"Yeah. Pi tell you?"

Pax nodded.

"There's a chance that I might have been the reason they were killed. We were playing Five Elements and there was a gas leak. My parents were in the basement. They never got out."

"Broken hells, I'm sorry," said Pax, reaching out and covering her hand. "And you went back into the Verum Locus to re-experience that?"

"Yeah."

"And I thought my nightmares were bad. At least my friends actually got out."

Aurie drummed her fingers on the table. "What if that's why they came out here? To get away from old memories?"

"Possibly. But they've been here for a couple of years. Long time to just sit around. If they're like us, and they've been through some shit, they're not going to brood on their problems, but find something to keep them busy, make productive use of their time."

Aurie was staring into the street waiting for another vision when a change in the music had her turning her head to the side. Pax squinted, catching the motion, and looked up at the hanging speakers.

"Music."

"Yeah," said Pax, "I have no idea what an Assassins' Hall alumni would do, but Stone Singers would find a way to practice their craft, their music at the very least."

After finishing their coffee, they started asking the locals if they'd seen a couple of American women, giving the description, and adding the possibility of music or sculpture. It wasn't until they were at a knickknack shop near another temple that the owner mentioned a music school in the hills. He thought their description matched the women who ran it.

None of the taxis were willing to take them up the gravel roads to the school, so they rented bikes. Halfway up the hillside, it started raining. Rivulets of water careened down the gravel road, turning the tiny rivers into milky streams. Kali appeared to be enjoying the rain, while the only thing keeping Aurie from being completely miserable was the enchantments she'd placed on her gear to keep it from getting soaked.

They reached the school as the sun dipped towards the mountains. The building was an older style with hand-cut timbers and a wide sloping roof covered in thatched tiles that diverted the water into clever PVC pipes that zigzagged down the hill. The building was on stilts to keep it above the water flows. A chorus of young voices echoed from inside.

Aurie parked her bike by the others. They climbed onto the front porch and spent a few minutes drying themselves with spells. Halfway through the process, Pax made motions with her eyes that suggested they were being watched. It took all her resolve not to look around. If Kitty had decided they were a threat, there was little they could do about it.

No longer dripping with water, Aurie looked through the open front door. A group of kids, ages eight to fourteen or so, were standing in a line, taking turns singing. The blonde woman leading them bore the deep tan of someone who spent a lot of time outdoors. She had the confidence of someone much older. Despite the humidity, she wore a long-sleeve shirt. They were noticed right away, but Moriganne kept leading the class in their exercises.

"Alright everyone, that's enough for today," said Moriganne, clapping her hands. The kids gave her hugs and kisses on the cheek before heading outside to grab their bikes and disappear down the gravel road, oblivious to the rain.

"Can we come in?" asked Aurie.

Moriganne waved them inside. "You got here faster than I thought possible. Is there a portal in Bangkok?"

"Something like that," said Aurie.

"Is your sister around?" asked Pax with her hand on Kali's back.

"Worried about her?" asked Moriganne with an eyebrow raised.

"We don't want to have to explain everything twice," said Pax.

"I'm right here," said Kitty, causing them to startle.

A woman with spikey black hair stood near the wall. She was a knife unsheathed. Aurie had met other members of her Hall, but had never felt as exposed as she did in that moment. It was as if Kitty was identifying the places she would stab them with her knives.

"Ares warned you."

There was no need for acknowledgement. They all knew it was true.

"Are you with them?" asked Moriganne with her arms crossed. The joy that had been present during the music class was locked behind a stern expression.

"Them?"

"Magnus. The Coterie patron."

Aurie shared a glance with Pax. This was news. "No, but we're curious why you would think that."

"They're with Invictus," said Kitty from the side. "I recognize her. Aurelia Silverthorne." She turned towards Pax. "You survived the zoo massacre. Your friend is rather unique."

"Her name is Kali."

Kitty's mouth twitched as she crouched slightly. "Hi, Kali."

"How is Ares?" asked Moriganne.

"Paranoid," said Aurie.

"For good reason," said Moriganne. "You shouldn't have come. There's nothing we can do for you."

"Did your brother explain why we were looking for you?" asked Aurie.

"No," said Moriganne, "he just said that you were going to try and find us."

The dynamic in the room confused Aurie. It was mostly Moriganne speaking while Kitty stood to the side as if on guard. She'd thought they were looking for Ivan's twin, but now she wondered if it were Moriganne.

"He didn't tell you?"

"No," said Moriganne. "The message was brief."

"But you're still here," said Pax.

"We weren't expecting you for another day at least," said Kitty. "The plan was to head into the remote areas where we have friends. You would have never found us."

"And now?" asked Aurie.

Moriganne closed her eyes briefly. When she opened them again, there was lingering pain. "Why did you come?"

"Your sister, Andromeda," said Aurie. "She's been kidnapped."

The sisters tensed up, glancing between each other.

"Why?" asked Kitty.

Aurie wished the sisters were standing near each other so she could read their expressions. "They think she's a danger to the city. An infernal invasion."

"She's not a danger to anyone," said Moriganne.

"We've gathered that, which makes us wonder if they have the wrong Charmer," said Aurie.

The undercurrents between Moriganne and Kitty were thick. Aurie could tell they wanted to talk, but were afraid to in front of strangers.

"Why?" asked Moriganne. "Why do they think Andy's a threat?"

Aurie gave an explanation of events since Beckett Dreadmarsh ambushed them. Mention of the "newest of the connected eight" brought arched brows, and when they got to the tale about Montanhas, and especially the parts with Benedita and Nurn, Kitty had fists at her sides.

"You think she made it over the mountains?"

Kitty looked like she might break in half waiting for the answer.

"We have no way of knowing," said Aurie, shaking her head. "Maybe we can go back at a later date and help the survivors, set up a new portal, but for now we don't have the resources."

Kitty's gaze faltered. She stared at the wall. The events in Montanhas had done a lot of damage to the Charmers. When she'd been reading the newspaper accounts, they'd been made out to be the villains, but hearing the concern in Kitty's voice, the anguish in both their gazes, showed the truths not apparent in the articles.

The rest of their explanation received no questions. Moriganne and Kitty seemed numb by the news.

"Who are they really looking for?" asked Aurie in the silence afterwards.

Moriganne bunched up her lips.

"Aren't you worried about your sister?" asked Pax.

"Of course," said Moriganne. "But they have the wrong person."

"Will you tell us why?" asked Aurie.

"For the same reasons you came here, because you know that Andromeda isn't a threat. Whatever that reading said, it was wrong."

"Will you come back with us? Help us free her? Zayn and Pi are looking for where they're keeping her. The ambush left a lot of trails that we think will lead us to them."

"Zayn will find her," said Kitty, nodding.

"He thinks highly of you," said Aurie.

"We can't go back," said Kitty, shaking her head. "Too risky."

"Why? Why won't any of her siblings tell us why you won't go after her? Are you that afraid of Elosian?" The dual flinch was unmistakable. Aurie saw her opportunity. "What aren't you telling us? Why are you so afraid?"

"We're not afraid," said Kitty.

"Bullshit," said Aurie. "Why else would you be hiding all the way out here?"

"It's not fear, it's prudence," said Moriganne, holding onto her forearm as if it pained her.

"I don't know what's going on with your family," said Aurie. "Every time I mention Elosian I can see your muscles clench. Something happened. Something that terrified you. We're trying to stop the invasion, but we don't have all the pieces."

"You know how he operates, right? Knowing will only make it worse," said Moriganne. "That's why we left. It was safer to not be in the city."

"What about Ares and Ivan?"

"They chose differently."

"Is it something that happened with your father?" asked Pax.

Aurie didn't need Kali's psychic ability to see that the question had hit true.

"What happened?" asked Aurie.

"We're not going to talk about it," said Kitty abruptly as if she were afraid Moriganne might say something. They shared a cross look.

"Why can't you help? We're trying to unravel a web of lies while blindfolded. Tell us something, anything to get us on the right track."

"That's the point," said Kitty. "Elosian lets you know things that get you to act in a certain way. A web of lies is right. Once you get caught in it, you're like a fly, struggling to get out but making yourself more stuck the longer you fight. It's better to never fly into the web."

"Your sister's in the web," said Aurie.

"She's the bait," said Moriganne, receiving a scowl from Kitty

"Come back to Invictus, help us rescue her, and then you can disappear again. Take your secrets with you," said Aurie.

"We're outnumbered otherwise," said Pax.

"I want to, I really want to," said Moriganne, closing her eyes in pain.

"Mori. We can't."

"It's not we, it's you," said Pax to Moriganne. "You're the reason you don't want to go back. You're the newest of the connected eight, even if that doesn't make sense."

The glare proved that Pax was right.

"I can't. Won't."

"Even if it means your sister dies?" asked Aurie.

"Why haven't they killed her yet?" asked Kitty. "If they think she's that dangerous."

"Because they think we're dangerous too."

"Elosian is pulling your threads and you don't even see it," said Kitty, disgusted.

Aurie opened her mouth to disagree when a wallop of pain knocked her to her knees. It was as if she'd been hit in the back of the head with a two-by-four. Her mouth hung open as she was in two places at once: inside the Thai music school and in a strange auditorium surrounded by the other mages and a bound Andromeda.

Nandi stared at Aurie as if she could see her. A pointed finger was followed by a brief speech.

"I found your link, Aurelia Silverthorne. I can kill you whenever I want now. Tomorrow, I want to see you and your sister at Camp Lucky. No one else. We get even a hint that you've brought your new friends, we'll kill her, and then the rest of you."

Nandi jerked her hand as if she were tugging on the truth bond, and it was like someone had kicked her in the heart. Aurie fell onto the wooden floor, severed from the vision.

She woke with the others in Thailand standing around her. Aurie was curled on her side. Kali gave her a tentative lick to the cheek and whined in solidarity.

"The truth bond?" asked Pax.

Aurie nodded as they helped her to a sitting position. "They're going to kill her unless Pi and I meet them at Camp Lucky. No one else."

"Truth bond?"

Aurie was too exhausted from the forced vision, so Pax explained the link that had been given after the Mystique performance.

Moriganne crossed her arms. "Kitty. We have to. We'll get her back and then they can take us wherever we want. But we can't let them kill Andromeda." Her gaze flitted over. "Or them."

The anguish on Kitty's face was followed by pacing, chin cupped in a hand. After a round of frustrated cursing, she turned back.

"Yeah. I know. I wouldn't let anything bad hurt her." Kitty sighed and stared out the open door where the rain had slowed to a drizzle. "I just was hoping I would never have to kill again."

Thirty-Eight

The moment Moriganne stepped through the portal to return to the city of Invictus, she feared she'd made a terrible mistake. The wonderous nature of her new surroundings were lost beneath the weight of memories.

Aurie had barely given them time to post a notice that the music school would be closed. Return date unknown. Moriganne had wanted to put a date that was only a few days away, but there was something in her gut that told her that leaving again wouldn't be easy. Elosian had laid his traps well, and now it was her turn to stumble into them.

Kitty was scanning the room upon their arrival, examining the doorway and corners as if she was expecting a threat. Moriganne smiled at her younger sister. When they'd first arrived in Thailand, a few local gangs had tried to extort them, or force kids to pay a travel fee to get to the school, but Kitty made sure no one would mess with them and for once she hadn't had to kill anyone to make it happen.

The other two members of their team appeared in the doorway. Kitty's expression broke into a half-smile.

"Hey, Zayn."

"Kitty." He nodded. "Good to have you here."

"Wish it was under better circumstances," she said.

While they were talking, Moriganne couldn't help but stare at Pythia. Something about the other Silverthorne drew her gaze. The bridge tattoo on Moriganne's arm ached with recognition. A curious omen that made her wonder if they'd made the right choice in coming back. Moriganne tugged the sleeve of her shirt past her wrist to make sure the tattoo wasn't spotted.

Pi approached, holding out a silvery bag. "Phones in here. Don't want Cybermagics spying on us."

Everyone dumped their phones inside while Aurie led them through introductions, though it felt like they all knew each other by reputation.

"We can talk in the kitchen."

"Shouldn't there be some grand table that we sit around? Like the knights of the round table," said Moriganne, trying to counter her nervousness with banter.

"Sure, if we were based on the legends of King Arthur," said Pi. "Not Merlin the ageless asshole. If we were going for an appropriate meeting venue, it'd probably be an old cave filled with the bones of the people that got sacrificed for his schemes."

"Where *is* Invictus?" asked Aurie.

"There was a note," said Pi, rolling her eyes. "There's always a note. Something something vague, somewhere important, blah blah blah. He shouldn't try so hard to be obtuse. Just a simple *gone, be back later*, would suffice."

"Would be nice to have him help with the other mages," said Pax.

"Wouldn't have happened," said Pi. "He thinks we're stupid for getting mixed up with Andromeda. He warned us from talking to her."

"For good reason," said Kitty, grumbling.

Pi opened the refrigerator. "Anyone want BLTs?"

A round of nods as they sat at the table launched her into motion.

"What's the plan?" asked Kitty. "And how do we know they're not listening through the truth bond?"

Everyone looked at each other. Aurie looked embarrassed that she'd ensnared them with her problem. "I can tell. But it's a good question."

"Who are we up against?" asked Kitty, getting right to business. During the few years in Thailand, her sister had never truly relaxed except at odd times when she caught her sitting on the thatched roof staring across the valley at the temples shining in the sun.

Aurie grabbed a yellow notepad on the counter and read them the list of mages, their halls, and societies.

"If it wasn't for the truth bond, it'd be a pretty even match," said Kitty. "But they'll take you out the moment they realize you're not there to turn yourselves in."

"Which means we have to get Andromeda first," said Pi, nodding to her sister as she pulled a piece of bacon out of the package and laid it on the griddle. "They'll have someone posted by her, ready to swing the sword, but that means one less of them is worried about us."

"Is there a way to protect Aurie from the truth bond until we free Andromeda?" asked Zayn.

"Let's not forget about Andy," said Moriganne. "She's in danger too."

"I don't think there's anything we can do about the truth bond," said Aurie in a low voice.

"Then let me lead a sneak attack on them," said Zayn. "Hit them before they know it, free

Andromeda, and then you can unravel the bond at your leisure."

"No," said Aurie, shaking her head. "We need answers. I was planning on doing as they said. Let them take us in. I'm sure I can get them to talk. It's what I do. We need to understand what they know."

"That'd be stupid," said Zayn. "Sorry, but you know it's true. Once they have you, then we're outnumbered. Let me and Kitty sneak in. We can take care of them and then the rest of you can come in for cleanup."

"If we kill them we won't know what Elosian's planning," said Aurie.

"I'm not killing anyone unless it's the last resort," said Kitty. "Every time I did in the past, I ended up regretting it. You said it yourself, they *think* we're the enemy. But we're not. They're not either. If we start killing each other then we make it easier for Elosian later."

"They threatened your sister with death," said Pi incredulously.

"If they wanted her dead, they would have done it already," said Kitty. "As much as past me would be surprised to hear this, we can't kill our way out of this mess."

Aurie slapped her hand against the counter, getting everyone's attention.

"We're not going in guns a blazing." She shot Zayn a pained look threaded with regret. "I'm sorry, but we brought you in to help, not take over. Until recently, the Order of Merlin was just me and Pi. We're doing it my way. We're going in like we're handing ourselves over, then once we've learned what we need to know, we'll flip the tables on them."

"Why wouldn't they just kill you right away?" asked Zayn, lips bunched.

"For the same reason we don't want to. They have answers we need and vice versa."

Zayn looked away. "I think your plan is going to get you and your sister killed, but I'll do what you want."

The ache in Aurie's eyes as she stared across the counter at Zayn told Moriganne everything she needed to know about their relationship. They had a past, that much she was sure about, but it hadn't been rekindled as they'd both hoped. A truth she'd learned in her seventy-plus years was that events changed you irrevocably. When she'd first become Moriganne Charmer, she'd had illusions of returning to her music career, except with the wealth and backing of the family, but later realized she was a completely different person, both inside and out.

"This is going great," muttered Kitty with a scowl.

Moriganne kicked her in the leg, receiving a frowning glare for the effort.

"What's the plan, Aurie?" asked Moriganne, hoping to get everyone on the same page.

"Before we get to that, I have a question," said Aurie. "Why are you the *newest* of the connected eight? You never answered me in Thailand, and we need to put all our cards on the table. No secrets, or we're going to get each other killed."

Moriganne looked to Kitty, who offered a lifted shoulder.

"Because I'm not really Moriganne Charmer."

The reveal brought heads up and muttered gasps. Pi had been in the middle of flipping bacon and turned around with the spatula in her hand and surprise on her face.

"Then who are you?" asked Aurie.

"Minerva Sune. I was a pop singer."

Everyone looked to Kitty, who said, "I know. We all know. My family, anyway."

"After the original Moriganne got into Stone Singers," continued Moriganne, "she struggled to master the curriculum, so Victor brought in someone to steal my soul and put it in this body so his daughter would have access to my singing ability. I thought I was coming to the suite to give music lessons and ended up in a battle for control of this body. I won obviously and spent the next five years trying to survive."

Halfway through her explanation, Pi and Aurie looked like they were going to climb out of their skins. Looking like she'd seen a ghost, Pi said, "Can you describe the individual who took your soul?"

"I thought of him as the Ginger Man, but I recall Victor calling him Rütsch. He had freckles, an Irish brogue."

"Did he have a tattoo of a bunch of leaves on his arm?" asked Pi sternly. "Might have seen a bridge too."

Moriganne resisted the urge to touch her elbow where the tattoo now rested.

"He did. You know him?"

"He showed up about four years ago claiming to be our uncle. He spent that year stealing souls. Killing students from each hall."

"He's dead, I think," said Moriganne.

"He is," said Pi, stone-faced, the memory of that moment clear on her face. "I killed him."

"You can't have," said Moriganne, shaking her head. "He was like a god."

"I had help," said Pi. "But I didn't let him get away to cause more havoc. Just like we shouldn't let these mages get away." She looked to her sister. "You know I'm right. We can't let them continue to interfere with us. The whole city is at stake."

The idea that Pi had killed the ginger man furthered the mistrust she'd had when she first entered. Where did her power come from? Was it stable?

"That's what they think too, and look where we're at," said Aurie.

"You should listen to your sister," said Kitty. "She's wise."

Moriganne was still a little stunned from learning that the person before her had killed the ginger man. Maybe that was why she felt some connection between the bridge tattoo and Pythia—something in his death had grabbed onto the younger Silverthorne. That was the explanation she was willing to consider. The alternatives were less pleasing, given the tattoo's sensitivity to infernal creatures.

"We're not killing anyone unless we can't help it," said Aurie.

"I agree," said Moriganne in a show of solidarity.

Aurie narrowed her gaze at Moriganne, making her feel like she'd done something wrong. "Are you sure you should come with us? I didn't know Stone Singers could do much beyond civil engineering or sculpture. I don't want to have to protect you in the middle of all this."

"I can handle my own."

Kitty nodded, which brought reluctant agreement from Aurie.

"Fine. Pi and I go in, let them capture us. I'll need you two"—she gestured at the Assassins mages—"to take out whoever is guarding Andromeda so they don't kill me before this starts."

"We'll have to get close," said Kitty, shaking her head. "That won't be easy."

"We can go in the night before, set up in the trees near the camp," said Zayn. "But keeping five of us hidden will be a challenge."

"I have a solution," said Pax. "We use blinds when monitoring wild supernatural creatures. They sell them at outdoor stores. A few modifications make them work as well for people. I can run out and pick up a pack."

Aurie nodded. "Once we get the information we need, you can hit Andromeda's guard at the same time we break out of our bonds. We should be able to do some damage with our voices, at least slow them down until you can get us out. Then we can grab Andromeda and escape back here. Remember, no killing unless you absolutely can't help it."

"No killing except for that cobra-headed thing," added Pi. "It's an abomination. It needs to die."

"You don't know that," said Pax, pounding a fist on the counter. "Sammi is a Tamer. She's the one to blame."

"That thing nearly burned me alive," said Pi, holding up her arm where knotted flesh around her elbow had yet to heal.

"It's just a creature, brought into this world by magic through no fault of its own," said Pax.

The air in the room was thick with tension. No one spoke. They were fractured by their opinions on how to tackle the other mages and rescue Andromeda. If it weren't for the danger to her younger sister, Moriganne would have been asking to return to Thailand.

"Bacon's ready," said Pi. "We might not agree on how to do this thing, but we can all agree that bacon is delicious."

A reluctant sigh slipped from Pax's lips. "I'm a vegetarian."

Thirty-Nine

"I'm an idiot," said Aurie as they strolled down the gravel road towards Camp Lucky. "I'm going to get us killed. I should have listened to Zayn."

Pi tilted her head, trying not to smirk in this moment of high tension. "Is that because you still want to get into his pants, or you have actual doubts?"

Their desire was obvious to everyone but each other. Pi didn't know what it was about emotions that sometimes got in the way of the very thing they were trying to encourage. Though with all the soul fragments in her head, she'd lost track of where her desires ended and theirs began. The other day she'd found herself eating sardines in a sour cream sauce on crackers, and she hated those tiny hairy fishies.

"I wish it was the first."

"What's the deal with you two?" said Pi. "Sometimes you're both staring all moon-eyed at each other and then moments later bickering like disgruntled co-workers."

"Can we not," said Aurie, grimacing. "We might die soon."

"What better time to resolve the knots in your head? Want to die with an open heart, right?" asked Pi, trying to calm her sister.

Aurie elbowed Pi in the ribs, shaking her head. "Dooset daram."

"Dooset daram."

The cottages were quaint sitting in the middle of a field in the thirteenth ward. It almost felt like an entirely different place, until she glanced back to the Spire, which was only partially visible due to the heavy cloud layer. Gray bottoms threatened rain. A lone glass gondola floated through the air on invisible wires, barely noticeable without the sun's reflection.

Pi inhaled through her nose, long and slow, then exhaled to calm her beating heart. Nandi and Lennie waited on the road, out front near the Camp Lucky sign, which displayed cheerful adults sitting around a campfire with drinks and treats. She'd seen Sammi and the cobra-headed creature lurking near the center of the cottages, but none of the others. She had no idea where Andromeda was being kept, but that was a task for the others. Theirs was a bit more nuanced.

When they got within a hundred feet, Pi spoke without moving her lips. "It's a good plan. You'll get the truth out of them, just like you said."

The brief crease around her sister's eyes was weak, but there was no going back now.

"We're not going to hurt you," said Nandi in a husky voice as she held out her hands, palms up, in a gesture of peace. "We want answers."

"Then why'd you try to kill us a few days ago?" asked Pi.

"Who said we were trying to kill you?" Nandi responded.

Lennie stepped forward. He wore runed Kevlar armor and had an automatic rifle hanging from a strap on his back. The apprehension in his gaze at their approach made Pi pleased. They were clearly worried. Probably still expected a trap. It was the wise thing. After all, they'd avoided the ambush in the warehouse, and then again with their team split up. Pi hoped the addition of Moriganne and Kitty would help tip the scales. At the very least, their presence was unknown to the other team, or so she hoped.

"Hands together," he said with a friendly smile as if they were guests being asked to remove their shoes. "I'm going to put some magical restraints on you. Can't have any mischief while we're talking."

Pi did as requested. The ease with which Lennie threw the ghostly chains on them proved his excellence, not that his membership in the societies or Blackstone Security didn't suggest that already. Her earlier confidence drained away at seeing the high competence of their opposition.

They were led into the middle cottage. The interior included a big screen TV and a well-stocked bar, but no sign of Andromeda.

"Where is she?" asked Aurie.

"Alive and well, and will continue to be so while you cooperate," said Nandi.

Two chairs were set out. Pi took one while her sister took the other. Lennie pulled a leather strap out, woke an enchantment on it with his breath, which made it glow briefly, and then wrapped it around Aurie's mouth.

"Hey I can't—"

A pit opened in Pi's stomach. The plan had been for Aurie to talk, weaving in subtle truth magic to tug the answers out. Her sister was a skilled practitioner of the Arcanium arts, while Pi knew she was best at making people mad.

Nandi smirked. "I can't have you doing your mendancy tricks on us. You gave Lennie a fit when you jammed his weapon with a word. Your reputation is well deserved. I was almost glad you got away, because it allowed me to see you and your boyfriend in action." She tapped on her ear. "And don't think you're going to do anything, Pythia. You might not be as skilled as your sister, but we saw what you did to Lil during the ambush."

Aurie's devastated expression didn't help Pi's confidence. The plan was unraveling. Pi searched for ideas on how to get the answers they wanted but her mind was painfully blank. She felt like she was standing behind the curtains ready to go on stage for a play she'd never rehearsed.

"Before we start, I want to remind you that Lil is standing by Andromeda, and that if you cause any problems, or refuse to answer our questions, we'll turn the lights out permanently with that truth bond." Nandi frowned. "Which leads me to wonder what was so important with Andromeda that you were willing to offer that?" She jutted her chin at Pi. "Answer, Pythia."

Pi swallowed. Sifting through her thoughts was like trying to find a penny in a jar of mud.

"It's Pi," she began. "I, uhm, it was because of Beckett. Before he died, he told us part of the prophecy, or reading, whatever you call it. We determined the newest of the connected eight was Andromeda. Desperate for answers when she wouldn't talk to us, my sister offered the truth bond. Unfortunately for us, you nabbed her before we could talk."

Nandi looked to Lennie and he nodded. Pi stared the ghostly chains holding tight on her hands. She didn't know a lot about Protectors, but they usually worked in police stations, or special forces for the military. Discovering the truth in an interrogation was important for both roles.

"What is Invictus working on? When the Spire changes colors and when sparks can be seen jumping from the top into the clouds, what is it? Is that how he's going to make the invasion happen?"

"Make the invasion happen? You realize that he's trying to stop it. As for that jam band light show at the top of the Spire, I have no idea, because Old Iron Balls doesn't explain his secrets. He thinks we're all too daft to understand his brilliance."

If she'd been in their shoes, she would have worn the same shocked expressions. Everyone liked to think that the head patron was a kind and generous man, given that his life's work had been to improve the practicing of magic throughout the world. It was always a shock, as it'd been for her, to find out that he was a crotchety old bastard who played everyone as if they were keys on his piano.

Lennie nodded again, though he seemed to be reckoning with her explanation as well.

"We have reason to believe that Invictus isn't who he says he is. That he's working to bring about the invasion, rather than stop it," said Nandi.

Pi was pretty sure her face betrayed the partial agreement. While she believed he was working to stop the invasion, the visions she'd had about the demonic realm when she was casting the barrier spell told her that he was hiding something. She'd seen him talking to the bladed creature in the reflected memory, when Invictus claimed that he never spoke to a single being.

Lennie leaned over and whispered in Nandi's ear, prompting a wrinkling of her forehead.

"I can tell you most emphatically that he's working to stop the invasion. When we rescued him, we found the old bastard stuck in stasis between this realm and the other, stuck through with a thousand blades. He'd been trying to escape."

"What was he doing there?"

"Trying to stop it," said Pi. "Look, if he wanted to open up the barrier between realms, he would do it. He has that power on his own and the artifacts to support it. We'd be swimming in scorpics and mantics if he so chose."

When Nandi looked to Lennie, he said, "She believes she's telling the truth."

The Coterie mage frowned. "He could be mind-controlling them somehow."

"Trust me," said Pi, "that would never happen. He's all about free will and the brutality of consequences. Besides, he knows my sister is a goody-two-shoes girl scout who can't help but throw herself in the way of oncoming trains. He doesn't have to control her."

Aurie made muffled, angry noises behind the gag. Pi smiled and lifted a shoulder. "Sorry, sis. It's true." Then to the others she said, "We've been, well, I've been quite forthcoming with our information. What about you? I think it's time to share."

"Why would we do that?" asked Nandi.

Pi paused before she answered. She knew they were close but she needed to push them over the edge, and she couldn't use magic or they'd know they were being manipulated.

"I don't know. Hubris? Doubt? I mean, how do you know you're the good ones? We're working for Invictus, the most famous mage in the world, the one that made it okay for people like us to *be* mages. Unlike before, when we were hunted as freaks and monsters. But you? You've straight up tried to murder us in cold blood. Had we been a little slower in the warehouse, none of this would have happened."

"You killed Beckett."

"He killed himself. Reflected spells are a bitch. Would have saved him if we could but the damage was too great. I'm sorry if he was your friend."

The squeezed lips from Nandi suggested he was more than a friend. She looked away and then back to them.

"We know we're the good ones," said Nandi with the annoying confidence of just about every mage from her hall. Doubt was not a thing that Coterie of Mages encouraged. If you were going to push the limits of arcane studies, then doubt was an emotion that would get you killed. She knew since she'd spent a year in that hall.

"The prophecy? Or reading? I still don't know what it is you thought you heard. But you're wrong. You're being fed lies, a carefully constructed fiction that is helping you cause the very thing you're trying to prevent."

"How do you know it's not you that's creating it?" Nandi chewed on the inside of her cheek as her gaze shot between the two of them. "You don't know what we know."

Pi leaned her neck onto the back of the chair, staring at the wood-paneled ceiling. "We don't, really, but at least we weren't trying to kill you. For all you know, we're the only ones that can stop the invasion and if you kill us, then there will be no one standing in its way."

"You should tell her," said Lennie. "Maybe she can explain the parts we don't understand."

"We agreed not to."

Lennie checked over his shoulder. Sammi was visible through the window. "They're being paranoid and we need answers. Besides, we're in complete control."

The weight of the decision fell heavy upon Nandi's shoulders. She pinched the bridge of her nose between forefinger and thumb and sighed.

"If it makes you feel any better," said Pi, "we're not sure we're doing the right thing either. This whole thing is a mess. Why not work together? Think about it. The two groups combined would be unstoppable. Surely we could prevent the invasion."

"Fine. I will tell you, but only if you promise that you'll explain what you know." Nandi rubbed her upper arm. "And then you'll see why we don't trust you or Invictus."

"I promise," said Pi.

Nandi didn't seem like she believed her, but she went ahead anyway after taking a big breath. When she started speaking, it was the voice of memorization, of words so impactful that they'd imprinted themselves in her mind.

"In the time of joyous return
When all think right of the world
The celebrated sisters will ensure its doom
At the hand of the fallen father
When the newest of the connected eight
And those that call her friend
Ignore the seeds of the past
And make a triumphant return home
Thus ensuring that order will fall
And with it the city of sorcery."

The expectation of explanation was heavy on their captors' brows. Pi would have liked a consultation with her sister, because she seemed to have understood it more clearly, but since she was in charge, she went with her gut.

"That sounds like a metric ton of bullshit to me," said Pi. "I'm all for prophecies, I've tried to follow my fair share of them, but isn't it a *little* too convenient?"

"We followed the rituals, spoke to the Shaytan'asrar as required in the benehajar," said Nandi with the feverish gaze of a believer. "This was the answer we received."

"I'm telling you what it sounds like," said Pi. "Even if I didn't understand half those words."

"We're the last line of defense for the city. The societies, all four, were made like pieces of a puzzle to protect and serve the Hundred Halls. The ritual was handed down from class to class. The warnings have grown ever more dire, but now we know that the time is upon us. We'll do anything we can to stop it. Even if means killing you. I'm sorry. The lives of this city outweigh the few."

"You did the ritual at the wrong time," said Pi. "You don't know that was the Shaytan... whatever it was you said."

"How can you know that?"

"Ares Charmer told us."

"He's cursed," said Nandi. "That family, all of them, are known to consort with demons. That's why they'd linked themselves to the Dreadmarshs, the oldest of demon lovers."

"But Beckett?"

"He was trying to amend for the sins of his family. He saw his duty to the Halls was greater than his last name." Nandi took a step forward, fists at her side. She'd worked herself up and Pi feared the end was coming soon. "We know the rumors about you, Pythia Silverthorne. It has not gone unnoticed that you once tried to bring Pazuzu, Prince of Storms, into the city and then made yourself useful to the most criminal elements."

"Hey, Radoslav's not a bad guy. You just have to get to know him." She grinned, hoping to delay while she thought of a plan to escape. They were rapidly running out of time.

"What the fuck?"

Lennie was staring out the window. While they'd been speaking, the sky had grown dark, and winds were picking up at a furious pace. A section of clouds broke free and swirled towards the ground, kicking up plumes of dust. A crimson light shone through the fledgling tornado that was rapidly gaining speed. It was headed directly at the cottages. They both looked to Pi and her sister.

"I haven't the slightest clue," said Pi. "That is *not* us."

Forty

“What are they saying?” asked Pax in the hidden blind.

“Quiet,” said both Zayn and Kitty as they leaned forward.

The sisters had entered the cottage minutes ago and things had gone wrong right away. They’d bound Aurie’s mouth and Andromeda was nowhere to be found.

Pax dug her fingers into Kali’s thick fur. She really wanted to get up and walk around since they’d been in the cramped blind all night. It wasn’t made for five. The only consolations were that Kali made a great pillow during the night and that it hadn’t rained despite the thickening clouds that threatened a storm.

“Have you figured out where Andromeda is?” whispered Moriganne.

Zayn waved her off. They’d said she was in the cottage where Aurie and Pi had been brought, but no one sensed her presence. During the night, she’d somehow been whisked away. Zayn and Kitty had been taking turns watching with their superior senses, but they both claimed they’d seen and heard nothing.

“If we can’t get to her, then they’ll kill Aurie first thing,” said Moriganne.

“Quiet,” said Zayn, “they’re telling them the prophecy.”

Can you sense her, Kali? I know you tried before but we need to find Andromeda. Is there a blank spot like last time?

<No empty spots>

“We need to do something,” said Kitty. “They’re going to kill them soon. I can hear it in Nandi’s voice. She’s nervous.”

“But if we don’t know where Andromeda is, they’ll just kill Aurie and Andromeda too,” said Zayn.

"They have to be in one of the cottages," said Kitty.

"Is there a basement?" asked Moriganne.

"I'd check online but we left our phones back in the Spire," said Pax.

"We have to make a decision, quick," said Zayn.

"I'm getting out of the blind," said Moriganne. "I'll cause a distraction."

Zayn wrinkled his forehead. "What kind of—"

"Don't worry," said Kitty, putting her hand on his forearm. "We need to get into position." She looked back to Pax. "Make sure that creature doesn't cause any problems."

Moriganne climbed out. The blind was hidden in the trees about a hundred yards from the cottages. Thick foliage added an extra layer of reduced visibility. Pax went out the other side with Kali, preparing to creep towards the open field between the trees and the cottages whenever the distraction happened.

The blonde Charmer began singing in a soft, ethereal voice that made Pax think of wind whistling through the trees. The song was almost imperceptible. Pax couldn't see the other mages, but hoped it wasn't loud enough for them to notice.

As she watched Moriganne's chin rise, along with the volume and intensity of the song, Pax could see the decades of experience in the way she held herself. Tiny movements, the masterful control of the notes—all proof that she was the septuagenarian inside. Not that Pax needed proof. Kali had made cryptic comments about Moriganne when she first arrived, sensing that her interior age was much greater, even if her companion didn't understand why.

The song switched from effortless mood music to tempest levels in the matter of a few heartbeats. Gusts battered the trees and the sky above the ward grew black with hints of green. The air pressure pushed into her ears. Through the gap in the leaves, Pax saw Sammi and her companion glancing into the ominous sky.

<Scary circle winds>

Pax didn't know what Kali meant until she saw past the cottages into the grassy field beyond. Part of the cloud layer had broken free and was condensing into a swirling rotation. A cyclone. When Moriganne had said she could handle herself, Pax had no idea that it was this level of magic. She was both proud of her new friend and frightened.

"Come on, Kali, let's get into place."

Pax checked back to the two assassins to find them no longer present. They were likely moving towards the cottage to free Andromeda—if they could find her.

The cyclone touched down in the field, sending up plumes of grass and dirt. A crimson light infused the spinning winds, making it hard for Pax not to stare at it, rather than move towards Sammi and the cobra-headed creature.

When they broke free of the tree line, Sammi's head snapped towards them. Pax hated the idea that she was going against a former classmate of Animalians.

Blind the creature.

Pax didn't wait to find out if Kali had accomplished the task. She used the magesteel enchantments in her shoulder blades to cross the gap between her and Sammi. The cobra-headed creature turned towards her approach.

<Not blind>

The urgency in Kali's mental voice made Pax stumble to halt, halfway between the trees and the middle cottage. Cobra-head extended its shimmering brass wings and a twisting plume of superheated coal smoke came firing out in a column. Without the magesteel enchantments, she would have never avoided a fiery death. Pax shot perpendicular as the grass beneath the breath charred black. The heat was unbearable for a few seconds until she ran out of the corridor.

Thinking she had escaped the immediate danger, Pax slowed near a copse of trees, ready with a spell, but the dirty-blond Tinker mage popped his head through the leaves of the tree and tossed a small box towards her. It tumbled through the air faster than she could move, exploding into a sticky web that splattered across her body, pinning her to the grass.

"Gotcha."

Forty-One

Kitty had only stepped through the Veil a few times in the presence of another living human. She glanced to her right to see Zayn moving towards the middle cottage. A faint mist flowed from his skin and she wondered if the same was true for her. The greenish sky of the nether realm mimicked the stormy one of theirs. Lightning crackled above the cottages. In the distance, she heard a shrill cry, a warning they shouldn't be in the Veil long. Dark shapes winged through the air.

They'd agreed to split up. Kitty headed toward the cottage near the front of the camp while Zayn took the one with Aurie and Pi. Kitty didn't bother going through the front door. She dove through the window as she shifted out of the Veil, glass shattering around her, the wooden grills bending around her upper body, which she shook off as she rolled onto her feet inside the quaint cottage.

As the tornado swirled towards the camp—sending loose grass against the windows and making the hair on the back of her neck stand up—Kitty scanned the interior of the cottage. She could tell something was wrong. There was a visual annoyance like an itch she couldn't scratch. Kitty spun on her heels, looking for the disturbance, when a loud burst was followed by a punch in the stomach, knocking her backwards.

Kitty put her hands to her stomach, coming away with bright blood. There was a hole in her gut. She didn't understand until a shimmering field near the old timey themed bar evaporated, revealing the sixth member of the other team. It was the girl that nearly got Pi while she was distracted with the cobra-headed creature. She was thinner and mousier than expected, with a sour, disappointed gaze as she held a pistol between two shaky hands.

Behind the bar, Andromeda was bound with a series of rods and chains clearly designed to keep the oestomancer from escaping using her body modifications. But saving her younger sister had become the least of her worries. The gunshot wound was deep. Nearly point-blank range had meant maximum damage. It'd be fatal if she couldn't get to a hospital or healer soon.

"I'm sorry," said the girl as she appeared to be aiming for the final shot.

Kitty could have thrown her knife. She wasn't sure who would be faster. The whole arm motion versus the squeeze of a trigger finger, but the gun wasn't the larger concern as she spied the spinning wall of wind hitting the cottage. She threw herself behind the couch as the front of the building cracked in half.

Forty-Two

Through the window like Kitty would have been the most expedient manner to enter the cottage, but unlike hers, this cottage had two dangerous mages inside. If he wanted to save the Silverthorne sisters, he wasn't going to be able to do it with brute force.

Nandi and Lennie were distracted by the whirling tornado. Zayn found it hard to believe Moriganne had created the violent rotating column, but there it was, hurtling towards the cottages beneath a crimson-tinged sky. The sound was like the roar of a train going overhead. He used the distraction to slip inside the cottage behind the two mages.

Both Silverthorne sisters saw him, their eyes widening with relief, but they weren't the only ones to notice his entrance. Lennie spun around. He punched the air, which hit Zayn like a fist, throwing him into a side table and shattering the lamp. He put his elbow through the window as he dove out of the way of the massive mage.

Winds from the storm whipped into the cottage, throwing open the door and sending loose grass swirling into the room. Zayn rolled onto his feet. Nandi sent a force bolt at his head, but he jammed his foot into the ground, redirecting himself into a leap. A blade appeared in his fist, but it never made it from his fingertips, as Lennie tackled him into the wall.

The big man moved faster than expected. Zayn wasn't aware that Protectors could move that quick, but everyone had their secrets. Lennie tried to knock him out with a blow to the head, but Zayn exploded a force wave into the big man's gut, throwing him away. He looked like popcorn exploding from a pan as he hit the ceiling.

Pi was shouting from her chair, but between the tornado and the battle, he couldn't understand what she was saying. Ghostly chains swirled around their arms, keeping them from using magic. He'd thought Pi could use her voice, but she didn't seem to be trying.

A huge crack sounded from the cottage to their left as the tornado slammed into it, sending half the roof into the sky. Zayn hoped that Kitty had gotten out before the impact.

But he had more immediate problems. Nandi was behind Aurie, hands curled in readiness near her head.

"Move and I'll splatter her brains across the wall."

Aurie's wild-eyed plea made him freeze in his tracks.

"It's over," said Nandi, nostrils flaring as the tornado demolished the first cottage.

Forty-Three

Moriganne had never unleashed the full might of the tempest. There'd been times she'd let the winds kick up and create havoc, but she'd let them dissipate before they grew too wild. She'd never summoned them beneath the open sky, nor when the air seemed poised for a storm already.

In the years spent in Thailand, she'd thought that she'd become a different person. Teaching the kids in the idyllic mountain house had given her that illusion. Without her previous claustrophobic hidden life as a Charmer, the stress of school, and the demonic threats that had plagued her family and friends, Moriganne had begun to believe that the bad things that had happened before were gone. She was safe. A new life was possible.

But back in the city of Invictus, her youngest sister in danger, those old fears came back. She let her emotions flood into the music, letting the tempest winds rise. There was so much potential energy in the storm already. It'd been lingering around the city, waiting for a moment like this. It was like directing a firehose of gasoline into an electrical field.

She'd meant the winds as a distraction, but they coalesced into a tornado within seconds after she began singing. There was a part of her that was pleased by the development. Unleashing the magic in her soul, letting the pain flow into the swirling winds as both song and fury, was cathartic in a way that teaching the kids had never been. Six decades of pain weren't easily washed away by a few calm years.

The bridge tattoo added its power. Her elbow burned. The glow of embers could be seen through her long-sleeve shirt, smoldering against the fabric.

Within the span of half a minute, the distraction had become a problem. Moriganne fought against the tornado that had dropped from the storm, pushing it back with her voice, but it barreled ahead.

The girl with the weird gloves, who had been standing out front watching the sky, tried to outrun the winds, but it overtook her. The dust and grass covered her up, mute surprise the last emotion before she was lifted into the air.

Moriganne's shock turned to horror when she saw the tornado heading directly at the cottage Kitty had gone in.

No!

The funnel grabbed the roof of the cottage, ripped half of it free, and tossed it high into the sky.

That's when she knew what the bridge was: chaos. Unfettered, unbridled chaos. There was no menace to it. The bridge tattoo was like an unshielded nuclear reactor with excited dangerous particles going in all directions. The sigil had given her tempest powers the leash and she wasn't able to get control. Moriganne growled, the notes coming out with angry ferocity as she attempted to push the tornado the other direction.

Kitty hadn't come out.

The cyclone chewed through the building, sending splinters and planks out in an explosion of shattered wood. Nothing inside could be alive.

Forty-Four

The leather strap bit into the corners of Aurie's mouth as the roof of the first cottage was sent high into the sky. She was split between the battle and the oncoming tornado, either of which could end her life.

"Move and I'll splatter her brains across the wall," said Nandi with a hand near her head.

Zayn froze in place as Lennie climbed to his feet shakily, having been knocked away like a throw pillow.

Aurie bulged her eyes at Zayn to keep fighting, but fear for her had stilled him.

"It's over."

She could barely hear the words that Nandi spoke even as she stood behind her while the tornado was scattering the first cottage. The windows on that side shattered.

Before anyone could move, Pi threw herself into Nandi, chair and all. The two toppled backwards, freeing Aurie from certain death. To her surprise, Zayn lunged forward, slicing across her cheek with a blade. The leather strap fell away along with a bright line of pain on her cheek.

Aurie ignored the slice on her face. Before Lennie could stop either of them, she blasted him full force with her true name shout.

"Aurelia!"

The impact threw the Protector mage through the window. The ghostly chains around her wrists disappeared. She spun around to find Nandi with her hands up and Pi climbing free of her restraints with murderous intent.

"No," said Aurie, grabbing her sister before she could cast a spell.

Nandi dodged around them and hopped out the broken window on the opposite side of the tornado where Lennie had gone through. The swirling winds were growing closer. She could hardly hear herself think.

"We have to get out."

But they were already moving that way. Zayn knocked out a window for them to jump through. Aurie tripped climbing out, but Zayn helped her up, and they ran back towards their blind as debris flew past their heads. In the chaos of the escape, Aurie didn't know where her sister had gone. She turned to go back but Zayn grabbed her arm, pulling her towards the relative safety of the trees.

Forty-Five

The sticky webbing held Pax fast against the ground. The Tinker mage approached, half his attention on her and half on the tornado currently chewing through the first cottage. He pulled out a device that looked like a collar with runes.

The cobra-headed creature spread its wings as it approached, like a peacock showing dominance. Pax struggled against the webbing but it was like getting caught in a bucket of taffy. She sensed through Kali's link that the creature meant her harm, even if the Tinker mage didn't realize it.

"You'd better run," she told him.

He screwed up his face in confusion, looking to the tornado rather than the approaching creature.

The cobra-headed beast opened its mouth. They were both going to be cooked alive.

Kali!

With a free hand, she managed a slam mark that hit the Tinker mage in the chest, throwing him backwards as the beast unleashed its superheated breath.

Pax felt the psychic blast from her companion the moment the column of coal smoke came flowing out. Everyone within the range of the projection was suddenly struck blind—except Pax. She felt the fear and concern and rage radiating out from Kali.

The cobra-headed creature snapped its head to the right, reacting to the sudden blindness. The billowing black smoke shifted away from immolating her, but the burning air crisped the hair on her legs and melted the webbing. The hem of her sleeve caught fire as she scrambled away. It was as if she'd stood too close to a bonfire. Parts of her arm were burnt but there was no time for the pain.

Pax climbed to her feet and hit the cobra-headed creature with a stun mark, hoping to incapacitate it. Sammi stood a ways back, stumbling around blind. The mark knocked the creature to its front knees, the curved head flailing around.

The younger Silverthorne appeared between Sammi and the beast. Pax's heart soared at her escape, until Pi focused on the cobra-headed creature, a familiar spell forming, the one she'd used to annihilate the mantic.

Pax sped across the charred grass, oblivious to the approaching tornado and the other mages escaping the cottage, leveling her shoulder and hitting Pi at full speed. They tumbled head over heels, landing near the wall of the third cottage.

"What the fuck are you doing?" growled Pi as she climbed to her feet.

"No killing it," said Pax with fists at her sides.

Further conversation was impossible if they wanted to live. The tornado barreled down on them.

<Run!>

Pax hurried towards the trees as the second cottage disintegrated under the might of the swirling winds and the other mages fled north, away from the destruction.

Forty-Six

Kitty watched as the back half of the cottage exploded. A plank hit the girl in the back, puncturing her through the middle. The gun slipped out of her hands as she fell to the floor, mouth open with the final surprise. Ignoring the pain in her stomach, Kitty grabbed her sister, who was still bound, and threw her over her shoulder. She sprinted from the cottage as it collapsed behind them.

Glass and splintered debris filled the air. A piece sliced her neck, but her hands were too busy to check the damage. At one point, Kitty thought the winds would lift her into the air and send her high into the sky like the roof, but she managed to escape the suction and make it to the tree line where Moriganne stood like a statue, clearly fighting the tornado with her voice.

Kitty fell into the high grass when she grew dizzy from blood loss. Andromeda fell hard, and as dots formed in Kitty's eyes, she knew that if she didn't free her sister, then there'd be nobody to stop the bleeding. Using her bare hands and the power of her imbuements, Kitty snapped the metal bars, overloading her body, a price she'd have to pay later.

With her sister free, Kitty collapsed into the grass as the tornado chewed through the second cottage, sending pieces high into the air.

"I've got you," said Andromeda, placing her hands against the gut wound, forcing the flesh to close up.

"You're getting good at that," said Kitty deliriously as she stared up at her sister.

"I get a lot of practice," said Andromeda, heavy with thought.

Lying on her back, looking past her kneeling sister, Kitty watched the tornado lift into the sky, the swirling winds dissipating into gray wisps. In the span of a dozen heartbeats the chaotic storm disappeared and the sky above the demolished cottages revealed a deep blue.

Moriganne appeared by their side moments later. Eyes were wide with pain. "I did that, didn't I?"

"No," said Kitty, trying to smile but it came out a grimace. "That bitch shot me."

Moriganne glanced over her shoulder, but Kitty added, "Don't worry. Tornado got her before she could finish us off."

"Mori. Your tattoo," said Andromeda.

The sleeve of her shirt had burnt off, and the bridge glowed with embers.

The others appeared, each looking battered by the storm or the conflict, but they'd all made it out. Something had happened between Pax and Pi—they stood far from each other, giving angry side-eye.

"Is she okay?" Aurie asked Andromeda, who nodded.

"Good enough to move. She'll need real healing later."

"She's not the only one," said Zayn, who seemed to be limping, but he wasn't talking about himself, but nodding to Pax. The left side of her clothes were burnt and her arm was bright red.

"We should move," said Aurie. "The last thing we want is to get caught up by the authorities or splashed across the papers."

Moriganne helped Kitty to her feet and offered a shoulder, but she declined. As they stumbled away from Camp Lucky, Aurie spied the bridge tattoo on Moriganne's arm. Kitty's gut clenched as she saw the look in Aurie's eyes.

"What. Is. That?"

Before Moriganne could answer, Kitty grabbed Aurie by the arm.

"A conversation for later."

But the concerned glance between Aurie and Pi told Kitty that it wasn't going to be a pleasant one.

Forty-Seven

Ares watched the Invictus' prodigies leave from the relative safety of his concrete yard in the twelfth ward. The awful burnt smell of the scorched mantic tainted his nose. He'd been planning to eat before they'd arrived, but after the battle, he had no appetite.

The sabotage of his wardings left him rubbing the back of his neck. He went around to the back of the fence and looked around for signs of the perpetrator, but the concrete held few clues. He jogged to the abandoned industrial park where transients and drug addicts made their home and spent the next hour asking if they'd seen anyone pass through on the way to his home. Most wouldn't speak to him—they probably thought he was part of Invictus PD—and the few that did had nothing useful to say.

It had to have come from Elosian, but this was the most overt action that Ares had seen in some time. The big question was why? Did Elosian think he could take some of them out before they could...what? Get Andromeda back? He had a good idea that Andromeda's capture was meant to draw Moriganne back to the city. When he returned to his house, he called a number she'd left in case of emergencies and warned her about his visitors.

Then he returned to his research, refocusing his efforts on what Elosian was truly after. The part he didn't understand was how the invasion was going to happen. The barrier between realms was thin, but not as bad as it was in Montanhas. That mountainous place was known for its regular incursions of demons—little bubbles of invasions regularly interspersed between centuries.

Which meant for a full-scale invasion to happen, help from this side would be required. It was the only way. And it had to be something that would evade the patrons' watchful eyes. The wells of power were the most likely passage point. Fire was the weakest. That was where he'd captured the mantic. But the creatures that were passing through the barrier were small. The energy required to move between realms was large, and much bigger for creatures with power. For someone like Elosian, the passage cost was exponential. It couldn't be done without help from this side, and now that the Tome of Whispers was safely in control of the patrons, Ares didn't think that would be the method.

He pulled up his hand-drawn map of the Undercity. Most of the vast caverns beneath the city were unknown except to the most determined of explorers. Between excess faez creating unusual and dangerous creatures, the criminal gangs, and the unsavory types practicing their illicit magics beneath the surface, it wasn't a place to visit except under extreme circumstances. He knew that firsthand from when he was captured by the Drops.

The four wells were scattered about the Undercity: fire beneath the eleventh, air under the fifth, water at the ninth, and earth below the seventh. He'd managed to acquire the faez levels that the patrons tracked. They were high, but none of them in particularly dangerous levels. The protections they'd created for the wells, to keep them from breaking down, had been successful, even if few people above the surface were aware. It was like building four Hoover dams without anyone knowing it. After seeing the Well of Fire himself, he understood the undertaking the patrons had made to protect the city.

It wasn't possible to use conventional explosives against the wells. The runed shielding was too thick, too protected for that to work, and it would more likely destroy the caverns and bring them crashing down on the wells, making them less likely to be traversed from the demonic realm. Ares wasn't as knowledgeable about realm-travel, but he'd confirmed his theories with the professors at Coterie, so he knew that wasn't going to be the method.

To destroy the barrier, it had to be environmental faez damage, or something magical breaking it down. But bringing that to bear against a place rich in faez would more likely get the perpetrator immolated long before they reached the well. Besides, each one had a guardian that was significantly more powerful than even a team of skilled mages.

Ares was standing in his house, staring at the hand-drawn map, tapping his chin when he remembered he'd forgotten one. The fifth well, which was called the benehajar. The fifth had been capped a century ago by the patrons due to instability. Now it was the home of the societies, the place they performed the Convergence ceremony to wrest answers from the demonic realm. He was pretty sure that Beckett had been tricked by Elosian when he performed the ceremony not at the appointed time, but it was only a theory. Since Beckett was dead and his conspirators had been in hiding since they'd kidnapped Andromeda, he couldn't ask them.

It hurt not to go after his youngest sister. But since Elosian wanted to push them in that direction, he knew that resisting was best. Even if it pained him. A lot. Even then, he wasn't sure he'd made the right choice in not helping the Silverthorne sisters. As long as Moriganne didn't come back to Invictus, everything would be fine. Eventually, they'd give up or release Andromeda.

Ares spent the rest of that day calling around to his fellow alumni to see if he could learn about the so-called prophecy that Beckett had acquired. But none of them knew anything, or that Beckett had even attempted such a thing. He'd probably performed the ceremony with his small group of believers.

When he finished calling the alumni that had graduated around his time, Ares dialed Glen Davenport, whom he had sponsored for Coterie. He was four years younger. Glen had graduated last year and worked for his father's law firm. Most Coterie alumni had no intention of applying the arcane knowledge that they'd learned. Attending the most prestigious Hall at the university was more about connections than know-how. Ares was an exception to the rule, though that wouldn't have been the case if his father was still alive, or the family company still existed. But he bore no bitterness or regrets. Truth be told, he enjoyed his lonely scholarship more than the palm-pressing of high society. He'd never truly been a fit, even if he'd looked the part. Had his father recognized that at the Bastille charity event, maybe his life would have been much different. But they'd never been children to their father, but pawns on the chessboard that eventually turned on him and took him off the board.

"Ares?" Glen's voice cracked. "Wow. What a surprise. I thought you, I don't know, moved to another realm or something."

"Nope," said Ares, trying to project surety into his voice. "Been busy on some private initiatives in the city."

"In the city? Why don't you go to...oh, I'm sorry, I forgot. I'm such an ass," said Glen.

Ares smiled on his side of the phone. Glen was being genuine. He was about as ill-suited for the life as Ares was. Sometimes having the last name didn't mean you had the killer instinct that had put the family into that position.

"Hey, I'm sure you've heard about Beckett..."

"Oh, yeah, fucking tragic. The Dreadmarshs are in a tizzy, but Ares, it's weird. I thought they'd be going after whoever did it, but nothing. They closed up ranks and haven't said a peep. I wonder if that means they're sending private assassins after whoever did it, or something like that."

"Maybe," said Ares.

He knew why they hadn't tried to find the Silverthorne sisters. Leo and Jacqueline Dreadmarsh had probably made an ultimatum within the family that nothing would happen. Their family was in trouble already due to what Magnus had done for his father. It wouldn't help their family name to be associated with more unrest.

"You haven't by any chance heard anything about Beckett doing an unplanned Convergence ceremony?" asked Ares.

"I've heard rumors, but nothing substantiated. You know how it is. Everybody has a fucking theory. It's gross. The poor kid died. Had the world ahead of him. A tragedy."

"Do any of those rumors include details about the reading they received? Or anything else?"

A pause on the other side of the phone. Ares could imagine him wrinkling his forehead in thought or pushing his glasses back on his nose.

"What gives? Why the interest?"

"Scholarship," said Ares. "After everything that happened with the family business, I thought I'd devote a few years to continuing my studies. I work with Professor Sinclair still, though not at the Obelisk, obviously."

"Not planning on reviving Charmer Inc.?"

"Maybe after I've scratched the scholarship itch," said Ares, even though he had no intention of continuing his father's influencer work.

"Right, right. Makes sense," said Glen. "No, I haven't heard anything directly, but there was a break-in at Beckett's place in the third. No one knows what's missing, because it happened around the time he died and it appeared they had the keys. Not sure if it's related, but it sure is suspicious."

A chill went down Ares' spine. He knew it was important, even if he didn't know why.

"Thanks, Glen. I appreciate it."

"You should come out some time, Ares. Everyone would love to see you. People talk about you like you're dead. Past tense, and everything."

Ares grinned. They talked about him that way because as far as they were concerned, he *was* dead. No money. No influence. It amounted to the same thing. But Glen was a decent guy and didn't think of things in those terms. His offer was genuine.

"When all this is wrapped up, I'll look you up. It would be good to catch up."

"Great, great. I'll talk to you later. Bye, Ares."

Ares held the phone in his hands long after he hung up. Someone had stolen something from Beckett. Ares had an idea that Elosian was behind it, but he wasn't certain. Pieces were moving all over the board and Ares didn't know why. He needed more facts.

He made a few more calls. This time to his old society contacts until he tracked down Baron Niles, a member of Silence from Protectors, who was working at Invictus PD as a special investigator. Ares cashed in a favor with his old friend to learn what might have been taken from Beckett's flat. The list was speculative as the family wasn't cooperating, but Ares figured out that most of what was stolen had been in relation to the societies. After he hung up, he stared at his map, directly at the fifth well, ideas percolating.

The other thing Baron had mentioned in their conversation was that whoever had broken into Beckett's place had taken the food in the refrigerator, three big jars of high-quality summoning salt, and a family summoning focus. There might have been other materials missing, but he wasn't positive.

The missing salt made him think back to Ollie Rend. He'd been responsible for his sister failing the Merlin Trials and then had tried to kill her later on, thinking she was a demon. Ollie had been a former member of the Razors, an Undercity clan. Ares was surprised that Ollie was still alive after betraying a promise of safety from the clan leader.

Ollie was paranoid because he'd been using magic without the protection of a patron. Classic faez madness. That he hadn't blown himself up or gotten thrown into a psych ward by now was a miracle. Most didn't last this long, especially with how frequently he used magic. Ollie was convinced, and not without justification, that a demonic invasion would happen soon. He'd holed himself up in the Undercity, plastering infernal wards all over his cave, expecting that it was imminent.

If Ollie was aware of the Convergence ceremony, he might think that the societies were implicit in wanting the demonic invasion, not the other way around. Breaking into Beckett's place to gain information...or keys...would be the next step.

Ares dug into his old society gear to find a duplicate of the benehajar key that he'd squirrelled away. If Ollie had stolen a key, he would probably break into the society HQ. For what purpose? Ares had no idea, but it would be a good time to check as the facilities would probably be empty. They were only used a few times a year, or when horny members brought their dates to show off and encourage carnal activities. On more than one occasion, Ares had found a forgotten pair of panties in the middle of the summoning circle or in the back offices.

After locking up his place, Ares headed to the old Korean grocery store in the fourth ward. The old woman behind the counter nodded in recognition as he went into the back of her store. The secret passage opened to his touch. It'd been years since he'd passed through the water-stained concrete passage, and when he reached the elevator, those memories came back in full, including the horrific ones from his last year. He had a debt to pay. That was for sure. Maybe solving this problem could take the weight off his chest. Or maybe it'd be there until the end of his days.

On the long ride into the Undercity, Ares thought about the fifth well. It'd been capped a long time ago, but relative to the others, it was pretty much unguarded. If someone wanted to open a portal, it would be a damn good place.

The missing summoning focus could be used to wedge open a gap, assuming that the layers of rock and the capstone were removed. It would be a difficult job, but not impossible to pull off with a small crew. Especially if the facilities were left unguarded as they were. If Ollie wanted to get into the benehajar unseen, there were ways through the Undercity. Technically, they'd been blocked a long time ago, but he couldn't remember the last time those passages had been checked. At least not when he was head of Chroma and Key.

The rich smell of mahogany brought back memories of his time in school and the boardroom table of his father's suite. Ares wasn't sure what he was looking for. He moved around the rooms, looking for signs of trespassing. Few records were kept down there. It was a meeting place more than anything.

Ares headed into the ceremony room. The lower section held a permanent summoning circle, one specifically designed for the Ceremony. The rest of the room looked like a social club with four bars, each beneath the sigil of its society, on the four walls. In retrospect, the societies had lost their way, only giving a brief nod towards the underlining purpose with the

Convergence and then treating it like a social club during all other times. At least Beckett had rediscovered it, even if his attack on the Silverthornes was misguided.

He was so lost in his memories that he didn't hear the newcomer until they clicked their pistol off safety. Ares turned to find a disheveled Ollie Rend pointing a gun at him. He could smell him from across the room. He looked like he hadn't bathed in weeks.

"What a wonderful surprise," said Ollie. "To think I was just making an exploratory visit and here I find the enemy in his home."

Ares held up his hands trying to be as nonthreatening as possible while simultaneously looking for an opportunity to escape.

"We're on the same side, Ollie. We both want to stop the invasion."

"Liars gonna lie," said Ollie, sneering. "I know how your cursed family works. You know, some say the Dreadmarshs are the ones to watch out for, but I know the truth. It's been the Charmers all along. Everyone should see it, right? Montanhas. Your father's disappearance. The ritual killings. I bet your father figured out that you were all in league with the other side and so you whacked him."

"Couldn't be further from the truth," said Ares, taking a step backwards as Ollie came forward, closing the distance between them. "Why are you here, Ollie? Why did you break into Beckett's place and steal his summoning gear?"

Ollie placed his other hand on the gun to steady it. "I'm going to stop it, Ares Charmer. I'm going to be the hero. When everyone else has failed. Me, without a Hall, will be the savior of the city. Invictus will be forced to take me as his apprentice. Not those cursed sisters. Demons in disguise. Me. Ollie Rend."

"What are you doing to do?" Ares asked calmly.

Ollie opened his mouth and then smiled big. "Oh, you almost tricked me. You and your demon ways. I almost spilled the beans. Sure, it's not gonna matter for you much longer, but I'm not telling you how I'm going to do it."

His gaze flitted to the permanent summoning circle where they were standing.

"You're going to do something here at the fifth well," said Ares.

The light in Ollie's eyes betrayed the truth. "I'll stop it. I know where they want to come through and I'll make sure it never happens."

"Ollie. Please listen to me. Whatever you're planning, it'll only make it worse. You'll ensure the thing you want to stop."

"Quiet!" shouted Ollie. "No more lies! No! More! Lies!" His face was bright red. "I'm going to do it. I'm going to save the city. You can't tell me otherwise. Fuck you, Ares Charmer, and your demon-loving family. I don't have everything I need yet, but soon. And then I'll fix it. I'll be the one. You won't be able to stop me."

A noise came from the back room. A door closing. Both their heads came around. Someone was already here. Probably a couple of society members looking for a novel place for sex.

Before Ollie's head came back around, Ares went for a force bolt. He'd hit his hands with the impactful magic and then make a run for the other rooms.

The pistol went off before he finished his spell. Ares stepped backwards. Something had hit him in his chest. His shirt was a mess of blood, and how could there be a hole there? He slipped to a knee.

He heard footsteps and shouting, but he was already on his side, blood running onto the wooden floor, running over the summoning circle like a crimson flood.

Someone was leaning into his vision, but the darkness was converging, erasing the world. He knew it was the end. Wished he was surrounded by his family, not dying at the hands of a madman at the fifth well. His missed his siblings. All of them. Even Moriganne.

Ares fought against the darkness. He hated that all his investigations would be lost. There was so much he needed to tell them if they were going to stop the invasion, including that he loved them. Time felt infinite until it wasn't. His vision had become a tunnel. The warmth was leaving his body.

"You must—"

The darkness won.

Forty-Eight

Aurie rubbed the line on her cheek where Zayn had cut her getting the strap off her mouth. She knew she should say something, but the fight had drained them. Drained her. They sat around the living room in Moriganne's old flat in the fifth ward because it was the closest place to find refuge after the fight, and traveling across the city looking as beat up as they did wasn't a good idea. The refrigerator was empty since she hadn't been in the place in over two years, so they had glasses of barely cool water. Andromeda had suggested ordering delivery, but it'd fallen on deaf ears. Aurie was relieved that at least the truth bond had been severed.

"We all survived and we got Andromeda out—that's all that should matter," said Zayn.

Something had happened between her sister and Pax because the two sat on opposite sides of the room and they wouldn't make eye contact with each other. But that wasn't Aurie's biggest concern and the reason she hadn't spoken yet.

"Where did you get it?" asked Aurie.

She hadn't meant for it to come out accusatorially, but Moriganne flinched and held her hand over the tattoo, which had burnt through her shirt during the fight.

"After the Ginger Man shoved my soul in here, he threatened to reveal that I'd been the winner, and not the real Moriganne, unless I retrieved something for him. I broke into Victor's vault and this tattoo was imbedded in a painting. When I touched it, the tattoo transferred to me, and then I brought it to him outside the family suite. But it never completely left. As the years went on, it started coming in slowly, and then all at once, I think around the time you killed him. It's been mine ever since."

It was the truth, but not the whole truth. Aurie could see it the way she carefully told her story and in her sisters' reaction—their familiar glances and eyebrow twitches. Aurie wasn't sure why, but the bridge tattoo was important.

"I thought the tattoo was his." Aurie nodded towards her sister. "We both did."

"I did too. Until it came back."

"What is it then?"

Moriganne chewed on her lower lip and wouldn't make eye contact. No one would look at Aurie.

Pi spoke up, anger coloring her voice. "When the newest of the connected eight and those that call her friend ignore the seeds of the past and make a triumphant return home thus ensuring that order will fall and with it the city of sorcery." She sat tall, her gaze daring anyone to look at her. "Sounds pretty clear to me. Somehow I doubt that a simple Stone Singer is going to cause the fall of civilization. No, that tornado was a pretty clear sign that you're not who we think you are. I'm not even sure I buy this Minerva Sune story."

"I *am* Minerva, or was, anyway," said Moriganne.

"Then what's the prophecy about? We understand why you're the *newest* of the connected eight, but why are you going to ensure the destruction of Invictus?" asked Pi.

"This is important," said Aurie. "And it's not like we don't know your family is hiding something. Every one of you has been dancing around the topic, and if we wanted to believe the rumors, it wouldn't be hard to believe that Nandi and her team were right."

"You have no idea what she's been through," said Andromeda angrily, leaning forward and nearly knocking her glass off the table. "She didn't ask for this life. None of us did."

Kitty had been leaning her elbows on her knees, staring at the floor. The wound in her gut had been partially healed, but would still need more healing. She sat up, grimaced from pain, and said, "Let me tell them. They deserve to know."

Moriganne nodded.

Kitty sat up and adjusted how she was sitting because it clearly hurt just to exist.

"In the last few years of our father, Victor's life, he was dying. He had no intention of letting that happen, but without magical ability, there was little he could do. Looking back, I assume this is a plan he hatched in middle age. He married our mother, a wealthy mage with numerous connections in high society, and then we came along.

"He sent us each to different halls, and societies, better to spread the family around for connections, and to facilitate his eventual goal. Our father had a summoning tome stolen from the head of Coterie, and then with Magnus Dreadmarsh's help, tried to summon Elosian, Prince of Lies, to make a deal for immortality and magic."

The news made Aurie's limbs grow cold with fright.

"We tried to stop him. Even Ares, who had been his lackey for too long, but as Elosian does, he seeded the tools of his escape within my father's team, and he was able to get free of the wards. He went straight for Moriganne, calling the tattoo the lost prince's sigil. If he would have been able to take it, no one would have been able to stop him. No one. But Ares and

Magnus managed to reverse the ritual, using the connection to Victor, and send Elosian and our father into the demonic realm."

Aurie sucked in a breath through her teeth. "That's why you left the city. You went as far away as possible so he couldn't reach the tattoo again."

"Do you know who the lost prince is?" asked Pax.

The Charmers shook their heads.

"No. The Ginger Man had the tattoo for centuries, at least from the time of the druids and ritual sacrifices in the forests of Europe," said Moriganne. "But before that? I have no idea. I haven't looked."

"You're leaving soon," said Pi.

"When we recover," said Moriganne. "Staying in the city a moment longer than necessary is too dangerous."

"And I have to get back on tour," said Andromeda, swallowing.

Moriganne nodded. "But I'm afraid something will happen, making it hard to leave."

The desire to tell Moriganne that everything would be alright rose to Aurie's lips, but she never uttered the words because she knew that it wasn't true. It felt like their lives had been hurtling towards this moment since they first practiced magic. Learning about Elosian had been like figuring out how the chaotic pieces of their past had been meant to fit together, except she wasn't going to like the picture that it presented.

Zayn had been quiet for a while but he lifted his head. "Does anyone else understand the line in the prophecy, *and those that call her friend ignore the seeds of the past*?"

"It's all bullshit," said Pi, grumbling. "More of Elosian's lies. He fed them that so they'd come after us, nothing more."

"I agree, but also, there could be clues in how he plans on breaking into our realm contained within the prophecy," said Zayn.

"That's how he works," said Andromeda, eyes welling with emotion. "That's how he fooled my father, nearly killed us all. He offered lies and promises to them, leading them into the darkness."

"I get that," said Zayn, "but that's one of the principles of my Hall. Look, I know most call us the Assassins' hall, instead of our real name, the Academy of the Subtle Arts. One of those arts is divining the truth of our enemies so that we might unravel them. You can't run away, or appease them, and if you do, you give them an easy path to victory. No, you have to oppose them at every step of the way. That's how you came away with your lives when he broke the wardings. It's really quite remarkable. You stood up to a demon lord and sent him back to his realm. We fight. We always fight, even when it seems like we don't have a chance."

"How are we going to fight?" asked Aurie. "It feels like Elosian has the upper hand. He knows everything about us, but we know nothing about him, except his lies. We don't know his plan. How he intends to break down the barrier. Nothing."

Zayn squeezed his lips tight with thought. "He has a plan and for that plan to work, he needs us to do certain things, like Moriganne coming back to the city. There are other things, but we don't know what they are yet. But they're all cause and effect, like someone dumping the mercury into the mantic's cage. We just need to follow them back to the source, figure out what the final intention is, and then we stop it."

"You make it sound too simple," said Andromeda.

"It's not," said Zayn, "but all of us in this room have survived terrible events. And why? Because we never stopped fighting. Elosian wants people to be afraid of his reputation. It keeps people off balance."

"What about Victor?" asked Moriganne.

"It sounds like it didn't take any lies to convince him. That desire for immortality was entirely his own." Zayn sat up tall. "I don't know what it means, but I think the phrase *ignore the seeds of the past* is where we start."

"Whose past?" asked Aurie.

Zayn lifted his shoulders. "I don't know. All of ours?"

Moriganne shook her head. "I know my past and I know my future. It involves going back to Thailand. My students need me and it's safer for the sigil to be there, rather than here where Elosian can reach it."

"Shouldn't we be more curious about the lost prince?" asked Pax. "He sounds like a person that might be an ally."

"A demon?" asked Andromeda. "Are you crazy?"

"I wasn't in Montanhas with you all, but didn't you figure out that Montas were really descendants from demons that had come through the barriers in previous centuries? And Invictus said that the demonic realm isn't a monolith. Did he ever say how he was going to stop the invasion when he went there?"

"He's not exactly what you'd call a sharer," said Pi, exasperated.

"If we find the prince, maybe we find an ally who can help us with Elosian, someone to stop the invasion."

"Seems a little thin," said Pi. "This prince came over a long, long time ago, gave up his power, and disappeared. For all we know he's dead and the sigil is the only thing left. Just like the Ginger Man is dead, but Moriganne has the tattoo." She frowned. "For that matter, how do we know that it's not changing your intentions? Are you sure that your thoughts are your own?"

"I'm sure," said Moriganne abruptly.

"Then what happened with the tornado?"

Moriganne touched her elbow. "It had nothing to do with the sigil. I'm a tempest. It got out of control." She inhaled, then sighed heavily. "This is great and all, but you're going to have to do this without me and Kitty. As soon as possible, I'd like to get a ride back to Thailand, and if you're not willing to let me use the portal, then we'll do it the long way even if I'm not looking forward to a day on a plane. It's not safe for me to be here."

"We need you if we're going to unravel this," said Zayn.

"I've made up my mind. I'm leaving," said Moriganne. "As soon as we get Kitty's gut patched up."

Aurie nodded. "We'll take you back to Thailand. Whenever you need."

A wistful smile broke across Moriganne's face. "Thank you, and I'm sorry."

"I'd like to go back as well," said Pax. "The work we're doing is important. Probably not as important as what you're doing here, but I'm not sure how helpful I can be." The glance at Pi suggested she hadn't forgiven her for attempting to destroy the cobra-headed creature. "I'm probably not a good fit for the Order."

The unraveling of the team was an anchor on Aurie's heart. She looked to Zayn, but his pinched lips told her that he was considering leaving too.

"I'll stay and help...after I check in with Priyanka. Just a quick stop to make sure everything is good. She might have some resources for us."

Aurie smiled at him but it was weak. She believed he wanted to stay, but he was probably hoping Priyanka would make him remain in the Eternal City. She wanted to accuse him of being disingenuous before, but realized that it was her own insecurities that were leading her to think he was lying. He'd been arguing for more investigation earlier. Why would he bail now?

Pi leaned under the table and tossed the silvery bag on top. She'd hauled it in from the trunk of the car. "Might as well grab your phones. Moriganne saw the Cybermagics mage get sucked up into the tornado, so I think we're safe from being spied on."

The phones were distributed. No one spoke. Aurie looked at their faces. For a brief moment, they'd been a team. As chaotic and almost disastrous as it was, they'd come through with everyone intact, and Andromeda rescued. A victory even if it didn't feel that way.

"I wish this wasn't the end," said Aurie, trying not to get emotional. "We did good back there. It's just been me and Pi all this time in the Order, and having the rest of you by our side has been...nothing short of wonderful. The threat isn't going away."

"Probably," said Moriganne, "but the city will be safer without me in it. That much I know for sure."

Kitty's phone rattled to life on the table, startling everyone. She stared at it suspiciously before muttering, "It's Ivan."

Aurie wasn't sure why but as soon as the phone went to Kitty's ear, a cold stone formed in her gut and she could do nothing but stare. Kitty's curious expression paled within seconds of speaking with her twin. More than paled. Devastated.

"What?" asked Andromeda, eyes wide with alarm. "What's wrong?"

The phone drifted from Kitty's ear. She could barely make eye contact with her sisters.

"Ares. Ares is..."

Kitty closed her eyes and hung her head. Tears traced a path down her cheeks.

"Dead."

§§§

INFERNAL ALLIANCES

One

The air was thick with power and golden light. Invictus held out his aged hand as if he were catching snowflakes, not the infinitesimal particles of faez. A tiny glimmering dot descended onto—and then through—his palm, bringing a brief creasing of his eyes.

Invictus reached into his gray robes to make sure the package was still resting in the inner pocket. The clothes were a bit cliché, but he enjoyed the mystery that they presented. He'd thought about shifting his look to a nice, tailored suit, but feared that he wouldn't inspire the same fear and adoration that he did in the traditional robes of his craft.

A great *whooshing* sound echoed through the cavern. His chest tightened as he assessed the glowing runed wall. Flame the color of an oil slick danced across the surface of the outer shell. The well of earth had vented excess faez. Invictus could feel the pressure on his skin. It was familiar—refreshing, bringing old memories to the forefront, the labors of centuries. Yet, there was darkness too. He couldn't look at the well without feeling an ache in his heart. Not tired. He was that too, but this was the feeling of standing on the edge of an abyss, toes jutting over, the endless expanse tugging him forward.

"A marvel of magic and pure will," said a voice coming up from behind.

Invictus had heard him five minutes ago, traversing the tunnels, cursing at each stumble.

"Thank you for coming, Malden."

Invictus turned in time to see the shimmering field around the head of Coterie of Mages dissipate, either by the action of its owner or the instability of the faez-rich air. Gray hair tainted the edges of his usually dark hair. The mottled scaled flesh on his jaw looked cracked and painful, as did his right eye, blotched with crimson. Malden squeezed the bandage on his arm as if it was causing issues.

"Are you well, my friend?" asked Invictus.

Malden took a spot by his side and stared at the metal casing that kept the well from exploding from the constant buildup of faez. He touched the gray hair at his temple.

"I'm not Celesse. I don't have time for vanity, especially when I already look like this."

"Does it hurt?"

"Now more than ever," said Malden with a sigh. "It feels awake."

"If it causes you more discomfort, come see me, and I'll make a poultice."

"Thank you." Malden arched an eyebrow. "But we didn't come here to swap healing advice like a couple of old midwives."

"How is your Hall?"

More frowns. "I feel like I'm presiding over a yacht club. The unbound scholarship of the past is...well, that...a thing of the past. Half my students come with no intention of using what they learn, only to use that badge as a key to unlock the doors of wealth. The other half are too timid, or ill-prepared for the rigors of high arcana. I have half a mind to knock the whole thing down and start over."

"I'm sure you recall when half of Adele's students could be considered domestic terrorists, the way they went after the zoos and private collectors with a certain amount of intensity."

Malden chuckled, which brought a brief grimace of pain. "Intensity? They killed dozens, and then more died when the creatures they set loose went after unsuspecting humans."

"Adjustments were made and now her Hall is functioning as she intended," said Invictus.

"You didn't bring me down here for a lecture on running my Hall. You've never cared about that."

"No," said Invictus, staring into the prismatic lights exploding from the steel casing. "I haven't. It's been of secondary importance."

He didn't need to look over to feel the naked apprehension radiating from his companion.

"It's time, isn't it?"

Without looking over, Invictus nodded. "It's time."

"I fear what's to come."

"As do I."

"Is that why we're here?" asked Malden.

"No. Not yet. Not here, anyway. I don't believe."

Malden turned to face him. "You never have doubts."

"On the contrary, I'm filled with them," said Invictus. "But as a crotchety old man I've made more mistakes than all the patrons of the Halls combined, so I tend not to look so self-flagellating about them, even when some of them have been quite horrific."

Malden nodded as if he understood, and as one of the oldest patrons, he had more knowledge than most. Invictus assumed he'd probably researched his past, which meant he knew the extent of his crimes.

"I'm inspecting the wells," said Invictus.

Malden said nothing. There was no need to.

"I need a favor."

The head of Coterie nodded once. His eyes shifted to the well and then back.

"I need you to deliver a message."

"A message?" asked Malden apprehensively. "There's only one reason you would ask *me* to deliver a message."

"You are correct, my friend."

Invictus handed over the package. The thin metal box was covered in ancient runes, an intricate interlocking design that few human eyes had seen. Malden hesitated before grabbing it.

"Are you sure?"

"Promises were made and now is the time. I'm certain."

Malden stared at it as if it were a ticking bomb. "It will cause unrest."

"I know."

The elder patron looked away to the well of earth, so Invictus joined him. Coming down to the well had always been like watching an eclipse, or a volcano erupting. It evoked a primal fear in Invictus that felt like homecoming.

"May I ask what it says?"

Invictus nodded thoughtfully.

"It's time to come over."

Two

The smell of fresh dirt and flowers filled Pi with unimaginable dread. The concrete pathway echoed with their footsteps, surrounded by a meticulously kept lawn. A line of black cars passed while other somber guests strolled through the endless sea of headstones.

"Why am I here?"

Aurie tugged on her dark gray overcoat. "I wanted to visit them."

"But why am *I* here?" asked Pi, hating the tension in her voice. "We'll be back here in a week for the funeral. I hate these places."

"It won't be here," said Aurie.

"You know what I mean."

Aurie glanced sideways. "Thanks for dressing up."

"It's the one place I'd rather not stick out," said Pi. "The last thing I want to do is piss off the dead."

Her sister led them off the winding path. Pi was careful not to step on the graves. She wished the voices in her head would help distract her, but since she'd woken up that morning, they'd been quiet as, well, a funeral.

"Here."

Pi frowned at her sister. It wasn't like she didn't know they'd stopped at their parents' gravestones. The verbal reminder was unnecessary. And annoying. She almost walked away. Take a lap around the cemetery while her sister communed with the dead, but she knew the stoic exterior was a front for a cauldron of emotions.

"Nahid Silverthorne. Kieran Conor Silverthorne."

The headstones bore their hall badges. Book on gear. Caduceus. Nothing about the Order for their mother. They'd both died nearly anonymous as far as the world was concerned, when they should have been celebrated as fallen heroes.

"And those that call her friend ignore the seeds of the past," said Aurie with a heavy sigh. She knelt forward and set the bouquets of flowers on their graves. Purple thistles for Kieran. Water lilies for Nahid.

"That's why we're here?"

"It just seemed the right place."

Pi sucked air through her teeth. "We're not going to do a séance or anything weird like that, because I'm out."

Aurie chuckled lightly. "I would if I could."

"I know. You've always wanted answers. To know the truth, as if that's a thing you can know."

"I don't know if that makes you more or less suited for Arcanium. When I joined, I thought it would help me reckon with their deaths. If only I could know whether or not I had caused it."

"Every kid plays Five Elements," said Pi. "You just got unlucky that there was a gas leak."

Aurie frowned, hanging her head. "Whenever I repeat that line of the prophecy, *ignore the seeds of the past*, my brain tries to convince me that it's ignore the *sins* of the past. This is the first thing I think of."

"How would it change anything if you knew the truth?"

"It probably wouldn't."

"Yet here we are."

Aurie fiddled with the buttons on her coat. "I thought I'd gotten over it, but that prophecy brought up so many questions."

"You are aware that it probably came from Elosian and is a bunch of bullshit designed to distract us," said Pi.

"Absolutely," said Aurie, "but as skilled a liar as Elosian is, designing such a thing requires hewing close to the truth so that the true falsehoods are disguised."

"True falsehoods?"

"I can't explain it," said Aurie. "It's like how I know when people are lying. I think that's why my brain can't get over that line. He made a mistake by putting it in there."

"Or it's another trap."

Aurie nodded. "Or it's another trap."

"For the record, I trust your instincts, but I gotta bust your balls." Pi lifted her foot to adjust the fit on her high heels. "I hate these things. I don't know why I agreed to wear them."

"They'll be more broken in for Ares' funeral."

"Yeah," said Pi. "What a fucking bad break. The guy survives an encounter with Elosian himself a few years ago, along with other messed-up shit, and then gets murdered in what should be a safe place by some vagrant with a gun."

"They don't know it's a vagrant."

"They said the guy smelled like he'd shit himself," said Pi. "And he was living in the Undercity. That's the very definition of vagrant."

"Shame they didn't catch him."

"Totally."

"Do you think...?"

"Elosian? Of course," said Pi. "Moriganne was about to go back to Thailand. If what they say is true about that tattoo, then she might be the key to this whole thing."

"Which makes us assholes for convincing her to come back," said Aurie.

"Wouldn't be the first time."

Aurie put a fist in front of her mouth.

"Seeds of the past," said Pi.

"From their death until I joined Arcanium, I thought I was the cause." Aurie pressed her hands together as if she were kneading dough. "And then after our first year, it became a binary idea. Either I killed them by using the Five Elements when I wasn't supposed to, or it was Professor Trebleton. But now there's a third possibility."

"A third? I don't understand."

Aurie faced her. Emotion had drained from her face. Dread bubbled up in Pi's chest, making her swallow.

"Our parents were trying to find the Rod of Dominion so they could heal Invictus once they brought him out of stasis. It was the only way, they thought, that they could save him. Trebleton never admitted to killing them, and in retrospect, I believe him. But there was someone who wanted Invictus dead more than anyone else. If he could remove him from the equation, then he'd have a much easier time without the head patron's opposition."

The weight of her words pushed Pi down. She felt like she was sinking in mud.

"Elosian."

Aurie looked out over the cemetery. "I wonder if they knew. Or if he was a voice in the shadows during their time?"

"There's something I've been meaning to tell you," said Pi, a tightness around her chest making it hard to breathe.

Aurie raised an eyebrow.

"When I passed out at the barrier. The last time I tried to renew it. I had another vision."

"A memory fragment from Invictus?"

Pi bit her lower lip. "I don't know. It was different."

Her sister put a hand on her upper arm and gave a squeeze. "Three times isn't coincidence. Twice at the barrier and once in the Verum Locus."

"Tell me about it," said Pi, exhaling slowly. "The first vision was clearly from Invictus. A memory left over from the stasis after being trapped for seventeen years. The second time it was only Elosian. He called my name. He *knew* me. The last time was much worse."

"Elosian?"

"I was standing by his side in the Spire. I held the Rod of Dominion in my fist. The city lay in ruins. He was praising me. I felt sick to my stomach. It felt like it was my fault. The invasion. Everything."

Aurie grabbed both shoulders. "He's messing with you. Trying to get into your head."

"He's doing a good job of it. But why me?"

"I don't know. Maybe the old connection between you and Pazuzu is still there. He knows you once sought power, thinks he can turn you to his side."

Pi closed her eyes. Rocked on her heels. "It felt so good. Power coursed through my veins. I was like a god. When I woke up, I felt like a junky looking for their next hit. I craved power."

"That's not you," said Aurie.

"But it is," said Pi. "It's why I went to Coterie rather than Arcanium. I wanted to make sure no one could ever do to us what they did to our parents. It's why I took the soul fragments. Sure, I was saving them, but I was also making myself more powerful. There were times when we were following the Wizard's Rainbow that I dreamed about being the head patron. Desired it."

"But didn't you hear me? Elosian might have killed our parents. More than might. It seems highly likely," said Aurie.

"You just want that because it's easier than knowing you were the cause."

"I can't believe you'd say that," said Aurie.

"Even if you were, it doesn't matter. It was an awful accident. Gas, magic, explosion. It's not too hard to understand. It's not like every other kid who could use magic didn't play with the Five Elements."

"You don't think it was Elosian?"

"No, I do think it was him." Pi took a step away from her sister. She found herself on her mother's grave and stared at the headstone. "I didn't tell you the most disturbing part. When I looked down to the city, I could see every detail. The battles, the fires. Everything. But most of all I could see Invictus. He stood at the head of a vast army."

"That's great," said Aurie. "He was going to strike back against Elosian. Send him back to the infernal realms."

"No," said Pi. "He stood at the head of an army of gigantes, and the Rod of Dominion was no longer in my hand, but in Invictus'."

Three

The bridge tattoo ached, either in memory of Ares' passing, or surrounded by the demonic runes of his scholarship. There were dozens of notebooks filled with his writings. Notes. Drawings. He'd spent the last few years writing as if he was running out of time. He was.

"Do you think he knew he was going to die?" asked Moriganne as she peeled back the front of a green notebook. A formula for some kind of potion was on the inside, but it included mercury, so it couldn't be for human consumption.

Kitty was seated at his desk, reading through some documents on his computer. Ares had been kind enough to leave his password in an easy to find location, unlike Solstice after her passing.

"We're all gonna die."

"You know what I mean."

Kitty spun on the chair halfway. "It wasn't an accident."

"Don't believe some homeless guy from the Undercity killed him?"

"Not for a second."

Moriganne hugged her arms to her chest. "Neither do I." She wandered around the interior of the main floor. The second floor was his residence, and the upper one was mostly storage. Reagents for elixirs. Warding salt. And so on. From the old plates covered in crumbs, it appeared Ares spent most of his time on this level.

"Where did he get all these books? Some of them are in languages I don't recognize." Moriganne ran her fingertips across a shelf of tomes. "I ran away while he stayed to prepare for what he knew was to come."

"There's still time to stop it," said Kitty without looking away from the computer screen.

"I'm beginning to feel like that's less of a possibility. I thought I made the right choice in moving to Thailand, keeping the sigil out of the city, but now, here I am, right back in the thick of things and Ares is dead."

"This would be a lot easier if you were helping," said Kitty.

"Right." Moriganne pulled up a chair to the former kitchen table, which was covered in books. "What am I looking for?"

"Anything that helps us find his killer."

"Why aren't we headed to the benehajar?"

Kitty looked back. "We're headed there tonight. But I wanted to scour this stuff before we left."

"It'll take us years to read through all this." She lowered her voice. "I wish Andy was here."

"She'll be back for the funeral. She didn't want to miss the Toronto shows," said Kitty.

"I don't blame her," said Moriganne. "After being captive and nearly dying, I understand her choice, I just wish she was here."

"Me too."

She opened her mouth but Kitty cleared her throat loudly. Moriganne took the hint to get to work. She started skimming the notebooks and tomes, categorizing them into six piles: Montanhas, Elosian, warding runes, prophecies, faez levels around the wells of power, and the topics that didn't fit into any of those.

After Ares had nearly brought about the apocalypse by helping Victor, he'd thrown himself into preparing for the prevention of it. Moriganne hated the idea that he wouldn't be around after all that work, but life was never fair. If it was fair, then she'd have had the glorious professional singing career that she thought she was on track for and the family that she'd always wanted.

Moriganne turned her head and smiled at Kitty's back. She didn't get the family she thought she'd have when she was younger, but she did find one eventually.

Most of the material she read through made her eyes glaze over. Either she didn't have the vocabulary to understand the finer points like when Ares got into naming the anatomy of a dead mantic he'd rescued from the pit near the well of fire, or it was so obscure, like his theories on how ancient human languages had some relation to the Montas alphabet, that she lacked the scholarship to understand.

A notebook that did interest her was a summary of the faez levels at the four wells of power. As she'd learned when she found the machines beneath Stone Singers, the faez levels in the Undercity had been increasing steadily for decades. But unlike the past, there were now seismic rumblings to match the spikes. Much like Montanhas had been before the barrier collapsed, creating the disaster that they'd barely survived.

But Ares didn't think the levels were comparable. There was a lot of technical jargon she didn't understand, but she got the gist of his argument: the faez levels in the Undercity, while higher than in Montanhas, were not bad enough to overcome the barrier between realms. In the margins of his notes and in some of the tomes, she found his handwriting.

—How?

It was written frequently enough that she knew it was the underlying question of his investigation. The barrier between the realms was thin, but couldn't be broken without additional help. Even in Montanhas, the ability to pass through had been brief. No portal had been opened. A couple dozen gigantes, some scorpics, and a winged shadowy creature had entered the Lifestone plant through the barrier. Even then it wasn't like there'd been a tunnel. The initial scorpics that had entered had been in a strange egg covered in faez crystals. Ares speculated about the presence of the tiny, hardened pieces of raw magic, and referenced conversations with Ivan, but neither of them had come to any conclusion about them. Were they a byproduct of the transit or a necessary part of pushing through the barrier? Evidence of faez crystals had been found in the deep pits in the Undercity, especially around the well of fire.

The work went late into the night. Around two in the morning, they gave up and headed to the fourth ward. The Korean grocery store was closed, but that didn't mean anything to Kitty, who barely leaned down to tickle the locks before opening the door.

She wasn't sure where Kitty had gotten the codes for the elevator and didn't care. The long ride down was met with silence. The society headquarters was different than she remembered, but that had been a day of unusualness and conflict. She wasn't surprised that her memories weren't clear. Kitty did a quick sweep of the facility before they entered the summoning chamber.

"It's kind of ridiculous when you think about it," said Moriganne. "They turned an organization for protecting the city into a drinking club."

"It happened back in the 80s," said Kitty as she stared at the center of the summoning circle where they understood Ares had died after being shot.

There was no police tape and the surface had been scrubbed of the blood. No evidence of the murder remained. Invictus PD had been notified, but since they had no jurisdiction in the Undercity, they only recorded the facts given and confirmed the cause of death.

"Why was he here?" asked Kitty, face wracked with grief. "Why come here? It had to be important."

"Maybe he wanted to understand why Beckett performed the ceremony at the wrong time," said Moriganne, disagreeing with her own suggestion as soon as she was finished speaking.

Kitty crouched at the center of the circle. She scraped the floor with a fingernail, coming up with a fleck of blood that she flicked away.

"Whoever did this, I'm gonna kill so slow they'll wish they'd never stepped foot in this city," said Kitty.

The smoldering fury made Moriganne hesitate. "You said no more killing."

"This is different." Kitty shook her head. "It wasn't an accident. There are no accidents down here. Vagrants don't just wander in."

Moriganne didn't know how to argue otherwise.

"Come on," said Kitty, striding toward a hallway. "He was supposed to have gotten in back here."

The entire facility was supposed to be blocked off from the Undercity, but the report they'd been given was that a hole had been knocked through the concrete blocking one of the passages.

They found the entrance at the end of a natural cavern. Chunks of concrete lay around the narrow gap.

"He couldn't have been big," said Moriganne.

On the other side, Kitty sniffed around the hole, touching the broken wall and heading up the passage. To Moriganne's untrained eye, the breaking of the wall looked fresh. Impact dust lay around the hole, though any chance of prints had been trampled when it'd been first discovered.

A minute later, Kitty came back with a convenience store jerky wrapper held by a pair of tweezers.

"I found this way up the passage. Whoever killed Ares tried to clean up their mess, but dropped this. It fell into a crack against the wall."

"Can you get prints?"

"Better than that," said Kitty. "But we'll need help."

"Help? Where at?"

Kitty pulled a plastic bag from an inner pocket and carefully dropped the plastic packaging inside and sealed it up.

"Invictus PD."

Four

The wreckage at Camp Lucky was spread over a wide area. Two of the cottages had been completely demolished while the third had been battered by the heavy winds and projectiles. None of the windows on that side remained intact.

"I can't believe Moriganne summoned that tornado with her voice," said Pax as she surveyed the destruction.

"I think there's a lot more to her than she lets on," said Zayn, eyeing the sky as if the circulating winds might return.

Pax put her hand on the back of Kali's neck and gave it a familiar rub. She experienced her companion's enjoyment through their link.

"Thanks again for coming out to help," said Pax. "I know you were wanting to get back to the Eternal City."

Zayn pumped his eyebrows. "After what happened, I figured I should stick around for the funeral." He sighed as he examined the charred grass. "Gives me something to focus on."

He was a handsome guy. Pax could see why Aurie was smitten with him, and vice versa, but not why they were dancing around each other. She followed Zayn as he examined the area.

"I'm not sure what you're hoping I'll find," said Zayn. "These kinds of investigations aren't my Hall's thing. We'd need to bring in a Protector if we really wanted to have a proper inspection."

A heaviness weighed in Pax's chest. Kali looked up with her golden eyes, a nearly silent whine slipping out, but not so quiet Zayn didn't turn his head slightly.

"Why did you focus on the seeds of the past line from the prophecy?" she asked.

Crouched on his heels, Zayn examined the trampled grass, turning his head back and forth.

"Because the past is usually where the clues for the future are contained. Especially with prophecy."

"But we don't know if it was true prophecy or not," said Pax.

"There's no such thing as true prophecy." Zayn tapped on the ground. "It's print is here. Looks like a big cat in my limited expertise."

Pax crouched next to Zayn. A slight depression in the grass could be made out. One large imprint with four smaller ones where the toes would be located.

"If I didn't know any better, I'd call these lion tracks," said Pax.

"What was it? Besides horrific."

"A chimeratic creature. Head of a cobra, wings of an eagle, body of a lion. Probably bred by a mage, but it's hard to say," said Pax.

"You think Sammi made it?"

"Oh no," said Pax. "No way. That's not what Animalians teaches. As a Tamer, she'd have the tools to control such a creature, but make it? Not a chance. It's too big, and I know she wasn't dabbling in this kind of magic while in school. There's only two ways I can imagine it came to being. It would take some high-powered Coterie, or some other mage that dabbles in the advanced magics, or it was brought into existence by something far older and more powerful."

"Like?"

"Are you aware of what happened at the Portland Zoo?"

He turned on his heels. "Kinda hard not to. Besides Invictus' return, it's probably the most reported on event in the last decade."

Kali growled under her breath, which made Zayn lean his head back.

"Bad memories," she explained.

Pax examined the prints. The creature had been full grown. Lions reached their adult size at three to five years.

"There's a part of the zoo story that was never in the papers, because only a few of us know about it. The Hunters of Animalians train in a realm called Caer Corsydd."

"I'm aware," said Zayn, nodding.

"While I was there, I had an unfortunate encounter with Lord Asphodel, and to work off my transgression, so to say, I accompanied him into an ancient ziggurat where he was hoping to recover an old artifact he'd lost. It wasn't the only thing released that day. The creature known as Aepep, a huge flying snake, escaped then."

"But eventually you killed it at the zoo."

"I did. But Aepep wasn't just a beast. It was an intelligent being that bordered on godlike. Aepep was pure chaos. My family is a member of a group called the Descendants of Bastet that oppose Aepep and those that worshipped him, though his followers are less cult-like and more of a malignant corporation these days. The Descendants were founded in ancient Egypt when the pharaohs ruled. When you asked the question about the seeds of the past, this was the first thing that came to mind. It made me wonder if Aepep was connected to Elosian somehow."

"Was Aepep a demon?"

"No idea," said Pax. "We never thought to use warding symbols or anything that would tell us its origins. But how does a fully formed chimeratic creature show up with a team of mages bent on killing us and furthering Elosian's agenda? Back in the ancient days, Aepep spawned many chimeratic creatures like the manticore, the cockatrice, or the peryton. Why not the cobraffin?"

"Cobraffin?"

"Cobra and griffon. It's the best I can do." Pax shrugged. "It was the little demon creature at Ares' place that made me wonder about the connection. He called it a mantic. It's known that some of the supernatural creatures that exist in our world came from other realms, including the demonic one. What if Aepep originally came from the same place as Elosian? Elosian feeds on chaos, the same as Aepep."

"How does this knowledge help us?" asked Zayn.

"I don't know, but it's like a burr in my mind. I can't let it go. At the very least, understanding it might help us fight it next time." Pax looked around, alarmed. "Should we be worried about those mages?"

"Possibly," said Zayn. "I'm sure they're licking their wounds. They lost two of their number during the battle. Who's to say what their next course of action is, but we shouldn't let our guard down." He gestured towards the grass. "Want to follow the tracks?"

Zayn led them away from Camp Lucky and into the fields surrounding it. Pax couldn't see what he was following, but she didn't have the same level of sensory magics that he had. The path wound towards an old abandoned street, and that was where the trail ended.

"They got in a vehicle, probably the white van, right here. There's no way to track them from here. They could be anywhere." Overgrown fields bordered one side and abandoned city blocks covered in concrete and old buildings were on the other, while the city skyline was in full view.

"It's probably not a good idea to track them down," said Pax. "The last thing we need to do is create another rescue situation."

"On the contrary," said Zayn, "finding them so we'll know when they're on the prowl again is important. Just because two of their number died doesn't mean they'll stop. If they went as far as kidnapping and attempted murder, they're capable of anything."

"But like you said, there's no way to track them from here."

"No," said Zayn with a burgeoning grin. "But we don't need to track them."

"We don't?"

"No. What would a cobraffin eat?"

The intent of what he was asking dawned on Pax. She matched his grin.

"Buckets of meat."

Five

The antiseptic smells, the squeaks of rubber soles on meticulously cleaned tile, the droning voice over the speaker announcing an emergency in one of the many wings of the hospital—collectively they brought back an avalanche of memories for Aurie. She'd once been an orderly on the children's floor of Golden Willow.

"You gonna stand there all day and wait for the invasion?" asked her sister.

"Huh? Oh, sorry. This place brings back a lot of memories."

Pi pointed through the open doors of the emergency entrance. "I killed that thing that claimed to be our uncle right out there. In section G5."

"I get it, Pi, I'm not the only one with memories here."

"Sorry, sis, I'm just busting your tits...no, that doesn't sound right, but I hate busting your chops. Busting your balls is the classic, but I'm not sure it's what I wanted to say..."

While her sister droned on about which slang term was best, receiving a few horrified glances from nurses they passed, Aurie was deep in the memories of working the hallways with her mop and bucket, trying her best to stay out of the way. Head down and chin up, as her parents used to say about the value of hard work. Work hard and be proud. It hadn't been easy. She'd desperately wanted to get into the Halls, but lacked the money for the entrance trials. It felt like no one but her and her sister saw their worth. No one looked her in the eye as an orderly, no one saw the value of her work. It made it hard to follow what her parents had said. Be proud. How could she when no one else was?

A nurse directed them to the proper floor in the administration section of the main building. Aurie had wanted to see the old Children's Floor for the Irrevocably Cursed, Magically

Ailing, and Supernatural Virology where she'd worked for a few years. The kids liked to call themselves the Cursed Ones. A morbid fact that ended tragically more often than not.

Dr. Fairlight's office door was propped open. Her old friend was at her desk, furiously scribbling on a notepad. Aurie couldn't remember when Fairlight had gotten so old. Her hair was a washed-out gray. She looked drained of vitality.

At least until Pi knocked on the wall, bringing Fairlight's head up. Her smile of recognition brought color back to her face.

"Aurie. Pi," said Dr. Fairlight, abandoning her notes and coming around the desk.

She had strong hands and the hug reminded Aurie of how resilient the doctor had to be to work in a place filled with tragedy.

"Are you no longer practicing?" asked Aurie.

"They wrangled me into administration," said Dr. Fairlight. "Wanted someone with practical experience guiding the hospital and keeping the directors from losing sight of our mission. I'd rather disembowel an unruly ur-bear than deal with that pack of bloodsuckers." She rolled her eyes at herself. "But you didn't come all this way to hear about my poor career choices. What can I do for the city's most famous sisters?"

"May I close the door?" asked Aurie, bringing suspicion then a nod of assent from Dr. Fairlight.

When it clicked closed, Aurie faced the doctor, who looked concerned.

"I have a question," said Aurie, "but I know you're not supposed to tell me any information about it, even though we were the ones to bring it to the hospital."

The pursed lips and slow nod from Dr. Fairlight revealed her understanding.

"We would like to see the Rod of Dominion. There are some questions we have about the artifact, and we need to see it to better understand."

Dr. Fairlight grimaced. "I'm afraid that's not possible."

Aurie didn't want to have to explain that her sister had had visions that included the artifact and a demon lord from the infernal realm. They wanted to see if there were clues to the origins of the Rod. Aurie suspected she wasn't going to like what they found.

"It's very important," said Aurie. "I wouldn't ask if it weren't."

"I believe you. Both of you. As you said, you brought it here and because of it, saved many lives. The value has been immeasurable to the hospital. I only wish we had a dozen of them."

"Then can we see it? I promise we won't take it from the facility. We'd like to cast some spells on it. Understand its origins better," said Pi.

Dr. Fairlight squinted in confusion. She cleared her throat. "I cannot let you see it because the artifact is no longer in the hospital's possession."

A hole opened up in Aurie's chest. "Was it stolen? Why weren't we told?"

"No. It wasn't stolen." She leaned her head back. "Is it my understanding that you both work for Invictus?"

Cold realization settled on Aurie's bones as she nodded.

"Yes," said Pi.

"Then I'm confused," said Dr. Fairlight, looking between them. "He picked it up from the hospital four months ago."

§

Aurie stood outside Golden Willow with her sister as an ambulance pulled into the covered entrance of the emergency room with its lights and sirens blaring.

"Why wouldn't Old Iron Balls tell us?" asked Pi as she paced.

Aurie put a hand to her mouth. "He probably has a good reason."

Pi faced her, fists at her sides. "You know what I saw."

"In a vision from Elosian."

"We don't know that. The one from the Verum Locus, sure, it's more than likely, but the pair of visions at the barrier?"

"We don't know what they were. Their origins. If they even have any meaning," said Aurie with a shrug.

"These weren't dreams," said Pi. "I know my dreams. These were something else. Vivid. Real. Like when we went into the Engine of Temporal Manipulation to rescue Semyon."

"Maybe he doesn't know we were the ones to recover it." The look Pi gave her had Aurie shaking her head. "Yeah, you're right. Sounded stupid as soon as I said it."

"We need to examine it more than ever," said Pi.

"I know."

"Which means we need to go into his private laboratory. The place he disappears for days at a time."

Aurie exhaled. "I know."

Pi's open-eyed surprise came with a tilted head. "This is unlike you. I'm talking about defying our head patron and supposed relative and you're agreeing with me? This might be more surprising than the missing Rod."

"If truth is a scale, then there are a lot of weights being placed on the side that makes me not trust Invictus. I know the prophecy is bullshit, but it called him the fallen father. For all we know, he's an imposter, or going to the demonic realm changed him. The world is filled with people that had good intentions, but did terrible, terrible things. I don't want to be one of them."

"Does that mean what I think it means?" asked an excited Pi.

Aurie nodded. "We're breaking into his private quarters."

Six

"Are you sure you want to do this?" asked Moriganne.

Kitty stood at the corner wearing the dark blue uniform of the Invictus PD, badge and all. Illusions were great, but practical effects were better. At least for the parts of her disguise that were harder to fake.

"How do I look?" she asked, ignoring her sister's question.

"Great, I guess," said Moriganne, "but I'm not exactly an expert on police uniforms. Where did you get that?"

"It's not important."

Kitty pulled out her phone, checked for a photo she had saved, and waved her hand over her face, transforming it.

"Officer Lipins, really?"

"You still have his number, right?" asked Kitty.

Moriganne screwed up her face. "Do I have to?"

"Better than your officer friend running into his doppelganger."

"He's not my friend. I bribed him, remember?" Kitty arched an eyebrow, or really Officer Lipins' eyebrow, but the effect was the same. Moriganne pulled out her phone and dialed it with a heavy sigh. "Hey. Been a while, I know. You heard? Thank you, I appreciate that. That's actually what I wanted to talk to you about. Off the record, of course. Yes, I know that's a reporter term, but you know what I mean." She looked across the street. "Soup and Spells. Yeah, the place with the little cauldrons. Meet you there. I'm buying."

She stabbed the phone with her thumb and shoved in into a pocket. "There you go. I can probably keep him busy for a half hour, hour at most. You'd better hurry."

Kitty slapped the cap onto her head and saluted her sister. She approached the marble steps from the side as Officer Lipins hurried across the street to the appointed meeting spot. As she headed up the stairs, her heartbeat doubled.

The desk officer looked up with a frown. "Thought you had a meetin' across the street?"

The enchantment she'd placed on her throat earlier helped deepen her voice as she mimicked his New Jersey accent.

"Forgot my good looks to charm her with," she said with a wink. "In and back out in a flash. You won't even notice."

The desk officer chuckled and went back to his paperwork. Kitty barged past, heading not into the bullpen, where dozens and dozens of officers not on patrol lounged at their desks, but towards the analytics side of the facility. In one of her classes, Instructor Maggie O'Keefe had explained she'd designed some of the equipment, and the point of knowledge had never left Kitty's brain.

The analytics laboratory was busy with men and women in white coats. Half of them were focused on a particular machine while the others were chatting in small groups or writing on the endless wipe boards that went around the outside walls. She sensed the gut tightening and eye-rolls when she arrived.

"We don't bother you in your home," said a woman with thick glasses and her hair pulled into a bun. "Please don't bother us in ours."

A rivalry between the officers and the analysts wasn't surprising, given the male-dominated side of the police department wasn't exactly known for its modern ways. Moriganne had recounted how she was treated when she'd first arrived in the department, and it wasn't with open arms, or without a host of misogynistic comments.

"My apologies, Joanne," said Kitty, reading the woman's name tag and opening her hands wide to be as nonthreatening as possible, "I wouldn't bother you if it weren't of critical importance."

"You know the way this works. You trot back to your area, pull out the proper forms, fill them out in your Neanderthal handwriting, and then sign it with a big fat X. Then you turn it in to your boss, and once he puts his big dumb X on it, then we'll put it in the queue." She gestured to a wipe board covered in investigations. "As you can see, we're slammed. We might be able to get to your job by, let's say, June thirty-second."

The way she'd raised her voice made the dressing down into a performance. The other analysts grinned behind their coffee cups as they watched the conversation unfold. Kitty smiled and fidgeted with the hem of her jacket as she tried to come up with a reason for Joanne to help.

She jabbed her thumb backwards. "This one is hot. Came from above like a rocket and I was the idiot that got caught in the chest. Someone said it's a favor for one of the patrons. An old one, if you get my meaning."

Joanne narrowed her gaze as if she were deciding whether or not it was bullshit.

"Which patron?"

"The girl that delivered it appeared out of nowhere," said Kitty, trying to sound as mystified and concerned as possible. "As far as I know that only sounds like one Hall to me."

"Yeah, right. Patron or no, everyone has to follow the same procedures or this place turns to chaos. If we allowed the higher-ups to dictate what we work on, we'd be dusting for fingerprints on their girlfriends' clothes to make sure they're not fucking around on them." She clucked her tongue and nodded towards the door. "Don't make this any more embarrassing for yourself than it needs to be."

Kitty took a step away. She spotted Joanne's desk near the wall and with her imbuement-aided vision spotted a happy family in a picture frame. Joanne stood with another woman, each with their hands on a smiling girl in a soccer uniform and a ponytail.

"Joanne," said Kitty, the voice coming out almost as her own. "Can I talk to you outside? Please. It's something I can't say here."

Half-turned, she sighed.

"I promise it'll be quick. And I'll owe you a favor. A big one. But trust me. I think you'll want to help when you hear what I have to say."

Under her breath, Joanna said, "Meet me at the records room."

Kitty pushed out the door of the analyst pen as Joanne said loudly, "And that's what happens when you don't newspaper train your mangy mutts. They piss all over everything."

Laughter followed her down the hall. After a false start, Kitty managed to find the records room. She waited outside and wondered if Joanne was going to appear. Five minutes later, around the time Kitty thought her attempt was a bust, Joanne walked into the room.

"This better be good," said Joanne, checking down the hallway.

"You remember back six years ago when that psycho was ritualistically murdering people in the Undercity?"

"Was some wicked stuff," said Joanne. "The forensic pathology team had a field day. They talked about it for years, never seen anything like it."

"Well, you remember it just stopped. No killer apprehended. Nothing."

"Yeah?" asked Joanne suspiciously.

"They're back, except it's worse."

"Merlin's tits, worse how?" she asked.

"Last time it was all adults..."

"You're fucking kidding me. No. No one's that much of a monster."

"That's why this shit is hot and isn't going to be investigated by the PD since we don't have jurisdiction in the UC. But they wanted our help narrowing down where to look."

She wrinkled her nose at the shortened use of Undercity, so Kitty noted not to say it that way again.

"There's been two. The last one wasn't far from where my daughter attends school," said Kitty.

Joanne's eyes widened. "We're two blocks away."

"I know."

"Fuck." She looked up earnestly. "What do you need?"

Kitty handed over the baggy with the jerky wrapper she'd found in the tunnel. "I need anything you can get from this. Prints. DNA. Faez analysis. What the killer had for lunch."

"Jerky," said Joanna right away.

Kitty chuckled.

With the baggy in her hand, Joanne started to leave, when Kitty asked, "How long will it take?"

"A few days."

Her gut tightened. "Can you do better? I know, I know. I'm asking a lot. This shit has me worried. The girl was snatched from soccer practice. My daughter has ballet tomorrow night, and I won't be able to stand guard outside."

Joanne stared at the baggy. "I can get it done tonight."

"Can we meet at Soup and Spells? You know, so no one knows we're working together."

It was her turn to laugh. "Yeah, sure."

"Feel free to bust my balls in front of the others. Got to keep appearances up."

Joanne put two fingers to her temple and gave a minor salute. Kitty exhaled after she was gone. An urgent buzz in her pocket had her finding a half dozen messages from Moriganne, warning her that Officer Lipins had returned. She looked up in time to see him headed down the hallway towards her location, and managed to turn towards the wall and dismiss the illusion of his face. He gave her the side-eye as he passed. Clearly he'd seen something he didn't know how to interpret.

Hurrying towards the front of the building, Kitty resumed the illusion. The desk officer threw his hand up when she walked past.

"You're in and out more than I am on your mother," said the officer.

"Is that how she caught the clap?" asked Kitty, eliciting laughter from the others in hearing distance.

The desk officer flipped her off as she pushed through the doors. She crossed the street and the hostess reacted with surprise when he strolled through the door.

"Back so soon?"

"I like our bathrooms better." Kitty found her sister and took a spot across the booth.

"How'd it go?"

"I'm meeting the analyst here later. You?"

Moriganne shrugged. "They didn't have anything on Ares' death. Mostly he offered his condolences and wanted to know what happened after all that crap with Vic."

"Understandable."

Moriganne nodded towards the entrance. "I'll keep watch out front."

Kitty spent the hours scrolling through her phone while she waited for Joanne. She ordered three meals during the six hours to keep the waitstaff happy, paying and generously tipping after each one. She received a warning text from Moriganne before Joanne appeared.

She sat across from Kitty, a manilla folder in her hands. The pinched expression and no attempt at opening banter had Kitty worried.

"You think this is the ritual killer?"

"That's what I've been told."

Joanne clasped her hands in front, making no motion to hand over the folder. "Why you, Officer Lipins? No offence, but the things I learned today tell me that this wasn't handed down from above. What I mean is they're not going to run this through a glorified beat cop. No offense, but this is way above your pay grade."

Kitty knew she could easily snatch the folder away from Joanne and be away from the restaurant before anyone could stop her, but covert ops required a subtle hand. Blowing cover should only happen in the most dire situations, which this was certainly not.

"That's true. As far as you know. But on a number of occasions I've made myself indispensable to a few key players. When they don't want to use the official channels, or make a scene, they ask me to massage the system. I've become something of a fixer. You and I both know that the bureaucracy is a bitch and the turf wars make it hell to get anything done in a timely manner. If this were any old investigation, they wouldn't have come through me." She shrugged. "But this ain't any old investigation."

Joanne stared at the folder, then slid it over. There weren't a lot of papers inside, but that was to be expected given the short time frame. She started to get up, but Kitty said, "Can you stay? In case the terminology is over my head?"

"Why do you care? You're passing it along," said Joanne with her mouth cocked to the side.

"My daughter."

Joanne slipped back into the booth. "For a piece of evidence, that jerky wrapper had a lot of information on it." She tapped on the front page. "There were only partial prints, and nothing came back from the system, so you're not getting an answer that easy. Same with DNA. We have some, but nothing beyond a hereditary profile. Mostly European with a splash of South American. Male. So you're looking for a white guy. Might have a darker complexion, but doubtful given the size of the splash. Pretty standard stuff as far as this goes."

She frowned. Turned the page.

"The magical analysis is where things get weird. I had to call in a few others to understand the data."

There was a list of three-letter acronyms next to a three-digit, one-decimal-place number.

"Faez changes as it's used. This one here, ERF, denotes the amount of excess raw faez. A typical number considering it was found in the Undercity. These others suggest the killer had a few enchantments on him. But down here, these numbers are usually zeros. It's like doing a spectral analysis of metal. Most of it's going to be the common elements on the periodic table.

Carbon. Iron. Copper. And so on. The ones on the bottom are the weird elements that never show up. Rhodium. Iridium. That sort of thing."

Kitty could see where it was going, but wanted to hear Joanne's opinion. "I'm not following."

"Down here. These numbers should be zero. But three point eight? Seven point one? These are a damn seismic result as far as the analysis is concerned." Joanne bunched up her lips. "This section down here is for origins of faez. Usually it has two sources—from a mage or ERF. But this? This had its origins in the demonic realm."

Now Kitty was confused. "But you said he was human. European with a touch of South American."

"A splash. No foreign DNA. All human." She tapped on the last number. "This one. This one took us looking through the manual to figure out what it meant. No one's ever seen a number in this spot before."

"What is it?"

"For lack of a better term, we'll call it high faez. Faez that has been channeled through a creature from the demonic realm, one powerful enough to affect someone here. No one in the lab even thought it was possible, but here it is."

"To clarify," said Kitty as her heart climbed into her throat, "this number, the high faez reading, suggests that a major figure of the demonic realm was behind the attack?"

"More than suggest," said Joanne. "It's a damn certainty."

Seven

"I had no idea how much meat was consumed in this city just by large pets," said Zayn as he stared at the list of sellers and the quantities. He'd paid a hacker for the information, which he'd found out wasn't hard to find given the unremarkable nature of it. No one cared enough about large animal feeding to protect the data, especially when most of it came from farms outside the city.

"Trucks of it came into the Portland Zoo every day," said Pax, leaning over his shoulder looking at the screen. Kali was lying on his couch in the fifth-ward apartment that he kept for the brief periods when he was back in the city. "The hardest part of administration's job was finding good, cheap meat for the big supernaturals like the manticore, the hydra, and the leviathans."

"How much do they eat?" asked Zayn as he tried not to be distracted by her nearness. Not only was he interested in Aurie, but he knew Pax was romantically involved with a dragon. Not a triangle he would want to be a part of.

"A full-grown lion in captivity eats five to seven kilos a day. A manticore eats twice that. Supernaturals need a lot more fuel for their amazing bodies. Given the remarkable abilities of the cobraffin, I would suspect three or four times a lion's intake."

"You sound like you admire it," said Zayn.

"Of course. It's a wonderous creature."

"Wonderous and dangerous and nearly immolated you," said Zayn.

"A mountain is dangerous but people still climb them and admire their beauty."

Zayn spent his days trying to remove risk from his already dangerous life. He left her comment alone.

"So twenty to thirty pounds a day, or one hundred and fifty to two hundred pounds a week." Zayn whistled. "A lot of meat to keep up with. Expensive."

"People with big animals find dealers who have reasons to get rid of it cheaply. They buy the parts that others might not want." Pax tapped on the screen. "This farm sends its meat to the Invictus Zoo, the one partially run by my old hall. I remember the logo. Sometimes it's an old horse head, or the parts of a cow no human wants to eat, supplemented with rabbit meat from fur farms, or other creatures that died prematurely."

"Let me print this out," said Zayn. "I'll give you half. We can scour it for the likeliest candidates and then decide which ones we want to visit."

With papers in hand, Zayn sat on the couch next to Kali. The foxlike creature stared at him as he marked the pages. Pax took the lounge chair opposite, sitting sideways in the cushy spot. After a couple of hours of reading through hundreds of addresses, they each identified a dozen locations that could possibly house the cobraffin. Zayn marked a big map with red circles at the addresses throughout or relatively near the city.

"I think we can eliminate any of these from the inner ring of wards. Too difficult to move the creature in and out of the buildings without being reported," said Zayn.

Pax nodded. "It has to be a place that has enough room." She squinted at a dot in a first-ward apartment in a high rise. "How does one keep a big supernatural creature in a place like that?"

"Not all this meat is going for critters," said Zayn. "There are some unusual non-humans that make their home here. Not unlike your friend Okho."

"Good point."

He tapped the pen on his chin. "When he's in human form, does he need to eat as much as a dragon?"

"He has to change back regularly to keep up with calorie intakes. That's why it's easiest when we're doing our research in remote locations with plenty of wild animals."

§

Car lights passed them on the busy streets of the tenth ward. Zayn cracked his neck as he found a spot near the Wizard's Wax Museum. It was after hours, so the place was closed. He threw some coins into the meter and joined Pax and Kali on the sidewalk as they checked the street signs for the right direction.

"Should be up the street from here," said Zayn.

Pax stopped before the glass window where a wax Invictus stared into the night.

"He's shorter in real life."

"They make him look kindly, like someone's grandfather," said Zayn, chuckling.

"I forget how big this city is," remarked Pax, spinning around. The faint candle glow of a glass gondola floated high over the buildings, headed towards the Spire. "Never rode in one of those."

"Not once? I thought everyone did once they hit their third year," said Zayn.

"I barely spent any time in the city. Only the first two years, and much of my second was in Caer Corsydd. It doesn't feel like home," said Pax.

"Where does?"

"Portland used to, but after the zoo...it's hard to go back."

"Family in Portland?"

She nodded heavily. "Parents. They're doing better now."

Zayn caught the street name. He gestured towards Pax. "We should be quiet now. The address is up ahead. Let me scout."

He left her by a bakery that was closing up shop for the night. This was the twentieth address they'd checked. More caution was warranted, but Zayn was beginning to think the creature wasn't being housed in the city.

The other residential areas of the city tended towards three-story brick buildings. Long and narrow with small concrete porches or landings. The tenth was mixed residential and business with fewer restrictions. Across the street was a tall apartment building covered in terraces, a quarter of them with laundry hanging from the metal railings. Zayn recognized the signs of a poorer residence, as that's how he'd grown up. His family had lived in a bunch of old shipping containers that had been converted to a residence. He wondered what the Stack looked like now, overgrown and wild, like much of Varna. Few wanted to live there anymore after what had happened.

Zayn wasn't surprised when he found the villa smack in the middle of the street. A wrought iron fence blocked a circular drive with a huge fountain at the center. Whoever had built the residence had torn down multiple structures and put the huge house in its place. Had to be four or five thousand square feet. The owner had been listed under a shell company, which Zayn interpreted as "rich people investments." Lights on the second floor reflected into the driveway. A four-car garage bracketed one side of the entrance.

After checking for the location of the cameras and doing a quick enchantment scan, Zayn jumped over the ten-foot fence at a spot where the surveillance system was blind. He crept to the side of the garage and peeked inside a window to find one of the white vans.

"It's them," said Zayn when he returned to Pax.

She bit her lower lip. "I was kinda hoping we wouldn't find them. Should we contact the others?"

"One van was missing and there was a single light on upstairs. If you're not opposed, I'd like to take a look inside while we have the chance. Figure out if there are more of them, or more about where they found the cobraffin."

Zayn led them around to the back of the villa. An alley brought them to the back of the space, which was blocked off by a high brick wall.

"Can Kali climb?" asked Zayn.

"We can make it over," said Pax.

"Let me check for cameras." Zayn scrambled to the top of the fifteen-foot wall. The back of the villa was an extensive garden. Water was running somewhere, though he couldn't see it amid the foliage. He spotted four cameras, but ran along the top of the wall and managed to adjust three of them to be pointing away from the path he'd picked out, while the fourth wasn't an issue.

Pax made the leap, grabbing the top of the wall and pulling herself up. Kali was less graceful. Her foxlike companion could only make it partially, but Pax grabbed her forward paws and hauled her onto the wall. The three of them crept through the garden towards the back.

As they neared, Pax held up two fingers, one on each hand. One human. One creature. Kali's psychic ability was handy for intel and why they'd gotten lax as the day wore on. Zayn enjoyed having a danger radar on four, furry legs.

A sliding door was unlocked. The back of the house had an enormous kitchen and guest entertaining area. Zayn guessed the shell company was probably connected to the Dreadmarshs. He wondered if the family knew that Beckett's friends were still using the premises after his death.

Pax indicated that the lone human was upstairs, while the creature, presumably the cobraffin, was below. Zayn led them downstairs. Basements in the city were unusual as most did not have them. They passed a wall of portraits of Beckett and other members of the Dreadmarsh family, including Leo and Olympia. They were considered the most powerful mages in the world after Invictus. Even more than the original patrons, who each had their fearsome reputations. Long before the founding of the Halls, when the use of magic had been considered taboo and was often met with fear and eventually lynching, the Dreadmarshs operated with impunity. They were the oldest of old money. It helped having a head of the family that had been alive for centuries.

The smell of old meat was the first sign they were near the creature. The front half of the basement was a small, expensive gym with a wall covered in monitors. The back half was a long glass wall ringed with runes. The lights were out, but he could see a faint outline in the corner. It was sleeping, or resting. His heart thumped against his chest.

When Zayn applied the darkvision enchantment, the world bloomed into existence. The lump became the curled body of the cobraffin, its awkward hooded head tucked into the center. Old, rotting meat lay at the center of the concrete space. Zayn wasn't sure what he was more curious about, where the cobraffin originated from or why the Dreadmarshs had a warded cage at the bottom of their tenth-ward villa. The portraits on the wall hadn't clarified who used the property, unless it was an investment used by the extended family at their leisure. Rich people were like that.

Pax had found a pile of papers on a desk near the cage and was riffling through them. Zayn stood at the thick glass wall and stared at the cobraffin. There was a primalness that reminded him of the mystdrakons from the realm of Harmony. The first time he'd ever seen one, he'd been transfixed by the raw power. More so, when he saw one move at speeds faster than the normal eye could see. He knew the Portland Zoo had at least one of the fearsome creatures, and had he time, he would have gone to see, if only to study it safely.

The presence of the cobraffin in a cage that looked purposely designed for it brought up a host of questions. Was there more to the Dreadmarsh connection than first guessed? Beckett had been embarrassed by his name and the others claimed he was trying to make up for it. Zayn wondered if that was true.

When Pax let out a hiss of surprise, he turned to see what she'd found. Before he could take a step in her direction, the cobraffin was standing, wings spread with menace. The creature let out a shriek that turned his blood to ice. A snap of its wings sent shards of something against the glass. He flinched when they hit. Without the barrier he would have been pierced multiple times.

"Shit," he said when footsteps from above came pounding towards the stairs.

They threw themselves through a door, into what they found was the food preparation area: three large Sub-Zero refrigerators, a walk-in freezer, and two large stainless steel counters with butcher knives on the wall. The walk-in freezer became their hideout.

Mist plumed from their lips as they huddled in the cold. Pax rubbed her arms, but neither of them moved to cast a warmth spell, lest they give themselves away. Pax held up three fingers, then a fourth, pointing up and grimacing. The others had returned. Zayn thought about making a run for it, escaping before they were discovered, but the door to the preparation kitchen opened, revealing a broad-shouldered Protector, Lennie Fane.

Eight

"He's not here," said Aurie for the third time.

"I know he's not here, but you know how he is. He appears at the most inopportune times."

Pi was crouched before the door to his special laboratory. She'd cast a dozen spells on it already, trying to ascertain the nature of its protections, but the results had come back ambiguous. Invictus used magics that she'd never seen before, so they made unraveling them difficult.

Aurie smirked. "You're still mad about when you were walking around without clothes after a shower and he was sitting at the kitchen table eating a bowl of that chocolate cereal he loves."

"He'd been gone for a month," said Pi, throwing up her hands. "A little fair warning would be helpful."

"Any ideas on the door?" asked her sister.

Pi put her hands on her hips. "It's like the danger of translation between languages. You think you know what the words mean, but then you find out that rather than a cucumber martini, you tried to order a dildo martini. His magic is weird. I feel like I'm trying to read the *Canterbury Tales* in Middle English."

"If it's any consolation, I think they're all dick jokes."

"Invictus' spells or the Tales?"

"Both."

Pi pinched the bridge of her nose between forefinger and thumb before gesturing towards the wall near the door handle. "It appears this cucumber-shaped spell over here is attempting to identify the person entering the room. I *think* I can bypass it. Make it go away for a minute until we're in the room and then we're free to move about his lab."

"And if you're wrong?"

Pi shrugged. "Who knows? Depends on how paranoid Old Iron Balls is."

"So we should assume the worst," said Aurie.

Pi checked back to the overlapping wards. Given there were only a few of them who had access to the demi-realm, the level of redundancy in protections made her suspicious.

"The more I stare at these the more I think he's hiding a lot more than we suspect."

"Or he knows we're busybodies, as Nandi called us. Are we doing this? Or can't you get us through."

Pi chewed on her lower lip. "I can easily get us through. It's what happens afterwards that is the question."

"Cucumber or dildo."

Pi blew a breath out and prepared herself. It wasn't a spell anyone had taught her. There were some theories from Coterie, and the base originated from Cybermagics, as magic and programming had a lot in common. But the scaffolding of the spell was something she'd learned in Arcanium. Actual learning. Not the knowledge that bubbled up from her soul fragments all the time.

The spell was like tying a cherry stem with her tongue. It required patience and dexterity. She unraveled it on the first try, pushing open the door when she was finished.

"Applause welcomed."

"Only after I get to taste the cucumber," said her sister, pumping her eyebrows.

The interior of the laboratory made the eclectic and varied nature of the demi-realm look mundane in comparison. It was larger than expected, but the spaces inside his place were angled, creating awkwardly shaped rooms. The first thing Pi noticed was the enormous metal statue at the center. A golden miter sat on its head with an ankh prominently displayed on its chest. The "statue" was at least twelve feet tall. Pi moved no closer as she studied it.

"Look, I can see a compartment on the front. Maybe it's like the soul golems we made in Arcanium," said Aurie, prompting a nod from Pi.

"If it has a bit of his soul in it then we're in trouble should it decide to come alive."

"It looks...Egyptian," said Aurie. "Like one of the gods, but I can't place it."

"Think it has anything to do with the Rod? Given we got it from a tomb in Egypt?" asked Pi.

"Maybe."

The room was made up of little work areas, each with their own project. Along the wall, a vat of yellowish liquid held a creature that she immediately identified as a mantic, the demonic critter they'd fought at Ares' place. Pi wasn't certain, but she thought she saw its leg twitch. In the corner, electricity sparked from six metal balls hanging by chains from the ceiling. The tiny bolts jumped between the balls as if they were playing on a personal electron course. There were other wonders: a hobby horse made of glass reminiscent of the stelynkas; a mummified corpse except for the right foot, which had been unwrapped, exposing desiccated flesh; a puff of green mist that danced around a glass case; four different cannisters that ticked; and a host of smaller curiosities.

Aurie approached a table with the artifact lying on it as if it were a hammer or other mundane tool. The Rod of Dominion was made of two parts. A crook and a flail. One for peace, and one for war. It'd been years since they'd seen it last, when they'd handed it over to the doctors at Golden Willow. The artifact had saved many lives at the hospital, but it only had so much power. That they'd given it back to Invictus suggested that the stored-up magics had been used.

"It looks different than when we last saw it," said Aurie, squinting at the object on the table.

Her sister was right. Something had changed. She was starting to figure out differences when she heard the door click closed and the runes on the interior of the frame glowed bright red.

"What?"

The question lasted until the heavy thump of footsteps brought them face-to-face with the metal golem, which had come alive. It lifted its hammer-like fists menacingly.

Nine

The news that Ares' killer had links to a major demonic figure left them both shaken. Whoever it was, they were either knowingly or unknowingly working for Elosian. Probably the latter, much like the mages who had abducted Andromeda.

They were sitting at the table on the second floor of their dead brother's place. His tastes in food were rather spartan. It appeared Ares had been too busy for making complex meals, and as they'd found, delivery drivers wouldn't make the journey, so he'd taken to making large batches of food.

Moriganne was eating a bowl of buttered noodles. Most of the other food had gone bad and they'd had to throw it out. Kitty was seated on the back of a chair like a gargoyle, a dark bottle of beer in her hands, staring out the window at the rusted industrial park.

"It always comes back to him," said Kitty, squeezing so hard that the veins on her forearms stuck out. "Fucking Elosian. We can't escape him. First our father, now Ares."

"He won't stop until he has me. Or the tattoo, I guess."

"That fucking thing," said Kitty.

"That fucking thing," repeated Moriganne as she rubbed her elbow.

"I wish we could track down Mr. Thule and ask him about it. Where did it come from? Why was it hidden in a painting? Where did the ginger man find it, and how did he lose it?"

Moriganne pushed the bowl away. She wasn't hungry. "I worry that it's going to change me. Like when I summoned the winds, I wasn't intending to create a tornado. The clouds felt wrong to me and the tattoo burned right through my shirt."

"Yeah," said Kitty, nodding. "Did he have the soul-stealing powers before the tattoo? Or was that something that he developed because of it?"

"I wish we could find at least one person who's been tricked by Elosian. Figure out how he does it. Maybe we could turn that back on him, or at least know when he might be messing with us."

Kitty gestured with her beer towards the old shed where the mantic had been kept.

"Whoever threw the turpentine and dumped the mercury was probably under his direction."

"It's not like they carried it by hand. But I guess whoever did it was smart enough to take the containers with them," said Moriganne.

She didn't know what she said, but Kitty sat tall, then hopped onto the ground.

"Or maybe they didn't."

She had to hurry to keep up with Kitty. Night had fallen but the city lights and the pinks of sunset left enough visibility to follow. Kitty was climbing into the old dumpster when she arrived and came out moments later.

"Gotcha."

She set two containers on the cracked concrete. Moriganne summoned a magelight to read the labels. One turpentine and one mercury.

"D'Agastine Industries. Has the address and everything."

Moriganne looked back to Ares' place. "Dumped it here after sabotaging the wards."

"Whoever it was, worked there. Ninth ward. Not too terribly far."

They took the blue line to the nearest station. When they arrived at the big building, Moriganne grumbled.

"There's got to be hundreds of employees that work here. How are we going to narrow them down?" she asked.

Kitty smirked. "We're not. We'll let them do that for us."

"How?"

"You're going to use that voice of yours."

Employees in blue jumpsuits were trickling into the facility. Kitty slipped off the car she was sitting on, headed towards a trio.

"Hi," said Kitty, waving cheerfully as she approached. "We're here from corporate. Wanted to talk to you before your shift."

The oldest of them screwed up his face. "Corporate? Why the hell you out here?"

Kitty looked to Moriganne, which left her tongue stuck to the roof of her mouth.

"Uhm, we didn't want to alert HR about the investigation," said Moriganne.

The words had slipped out without a hint of magical compulsion. The employees shook their heads and pushed past, headed inside. Kitty raised her eyebrows.

"Excuse me."

No one stopped.

"*Excuse me. I need to talk to you three.*"

They stopped in their tracks, then came shuffling back as if they knew something was wrong.

"*I need you to answer our questions.*"

The trio nodded blankly. Kitty nudged the two containers. "You've seen these before?"

The older gentleman nodded. "Supplies for mixing."

"Do you make these here?"

"No," he answered, "this facility makes the batches for testing. After the researchers are happy with a formula, we mix up larger quantities, note any problems for larger scale production."

Kitty chewed on her lip, looking to Moriganne for help.

"Does, uhm, anyone have access to these?"

"No. Only the team leads."

Moriganne nodded. "How many team leads are there?"

"Four per shift," he told them. "Each floor has its own mixing lead. They work with the small production groups and the researchers."

"Could you tell us their names?" asked Kitty, opening her phone for notes.

The three employees recounted the twelve leads. Twelve names. Three shifts.

"Thank you," said Moriganne, "we'll contact you if there are further questions."

"Twelve names," said Kitty as the trio left. "Getting closer. Let's head back, see if we can find addresses."

"Give me your phone. We have all the addresses we need right here. I'll be right back."

After Kitty handed it over, Moriganne marched towards the visitor entrance for the D'Agastine facility. A guy in a corporate button-down slipped his earbuds out as she approached.

"May I help you, ma'am?" he asked in a southern accent.

She checked for the location of the guard before she spoke. "I need the home addresses of these twelve people. It's for an investigation. I work for Invictus PD."

The compulsion of her voice charm left him confused but he started typing in his computer, checking back with the list. After a few minutes, a paper appeared on a nearby printer, and he handed it over.

"I hope this helps."

"Thanks," she said idly as she wandered away, studying the sheet.

"My pleasure. Have a great night."

Her sister was smirking when she returned. "Nice trick. You'll have to teach me that sometime."

"There's two names in the tenth, one in the eleventh, and then the rest are in the seventh and eighth."

"Hit the first three then circle back around," said Kitty, glancing towards the lighted building. "Of the ones that aren't working."

The young woman at the first address answered in a T-shirt that went past her knees, smoking a cigarette and leaning on the door frame. A television played in the background.

"Can I help you?"

"Hi, ma'am," said Moriganne, "we're here from Invictus PD. We'd like to ask you some questions about stolen goods from D'Agastine Industries."

The woman took a big drag on the cigarette before blowing it sideways while she stabbed the embers out on the door frame. Moriganne sensed the woman's unease. Kitty's pinched lips told her that the woman was hiding something

"I don't know nothing about stolen goods. You sure you have the right person?"

"*Tell me about the goods you stole*," said Moriganne, her musical voice stunning the woman into submission.

"It was only a little. The test hit all the metrics. I thought it'd help me and my boyfriend's sex life."

"Wait. What? What did you take?" asked Moriganne, more curious than concerned.

"A little of batch number 5A99. The results were off the charts. So was sex that night."

"Can you tell us what 5A99 does?"

The woman stared into the darkness before blinking. "The most wonderful orgasm you've ever had. My boyfriend is a bit of a fumbler down there, if you know what I mean, but a little dose of 5A99 made everything perfect. I've done molly before and it had nothing on this stuff. They're gonna make billions."

Moriganne sighed. "Is that all you've stolen? Ever nabbed any mercury or turpentine?"

"Nope."

"Thank you for your time," said Kitty.

Before she closed the door, the woman asked, "Am I in trouble?"

"Not from us."

The next address was two blocks away. His wife answered the door and explained he was at work on the all-night shift.

When they hit the eleventh-ward apartment building, Moriganne worried it was too late. Most of the lights were out, but they knocked on 5C anyway.

A woman in a pink robe with her hair messed up answered the door. She looked like she'd fallen asleep watching TV by the noise in the background.

"Can I help you?"

"Are you Mary Seder?"

She nodded.

Moriganne reached out her hand. "I'm Officer Dutch. We're from Invictus PD. We need to ask you a few questions."

The moment their hands touched, she knew this woman was the one who'd thrown the turpentine. Her elbow throbbed with recognition.

"Is something wrong?" asked Mary as she hugged her arms to her chest after the handshake.

"We'd like to know why you stole turpentine and mercury from the facility and damaged some property in the twelfth."

Mary looked back into the apartment, tugging the robe tighter. "I, uhm, I don't know."

"Mary," said Kitty, "we know it was you. This will go a lot easier if you can tell us why you did that. Or why you even thought to do it. Did you get a message? Did someone pay you?"

The woman put a hand to her nose as if she were expecting blood. "Do you smell that?"

"Smell what?" asked Moriganne.

"It's so sweet." She craned her neck. "I didn't know they bloomed at night. Where are they coming from?"

Confusion and concern wracked Mary's forehead. She was barely paying attention to them, mumbling about the smell, her eyes fluttering. Moriganne tried to think of a spell that might help her, or the situation, but nothing came to mind.

"*Mary*," said Moriganne, imbuing more compulsion into her voice, "*tell me where you got the idea to steal then throw the turpentine*."

The woman reacted as if she'd been stung. She curled on herself, holding her forehead. "The smell. The smell."

"What smell?" asked Kitty with growing alarm.

"Lilacs."

When Mary looked up, the blood vessels in her eyes had burst. The white was swallowed by red blotches.

"It's my secret, my score, my score," said Mary. She seemed to be slowing down, her knees giving way. "I'm like them. Them in their Halls. Their secrets. It's like the tin. I'll be rewarded."

Moriganne reached out to help Mary, but when she touched her, a painful shock threw her back. The woman fell to her knees and then slumped over as Kitty tried to hold her up. Blood ran out of her nose and her eyes unfocused. In the span of a dozen heartbeats, Mary Seder died.

Ten

Pax pushed herself between the shelves inside the freezer. The metal bars burned against her exposed skin, but she didn't want to be seen by Lennie Fane, the Protector mage, who was standing outside, peering through the frosted glass. Kali stood directly beneath the window and Zayn was crouched in the opposite corner, but if Lennie opened the door, they'd no longer be hidden.

Lennie put his hand on the door as he squinted, trying to see through the mostly covered glass. Zayn appeared tense and ready to explode from his spot. The hinges creaked. Pax balled her hands into fists even though she knew it wouldn't do a damn bit of good against the Protector.

"Lennie."

A voice from outside the room stilled his movement. Lennie checked back, took a brief glance at the frosted window, and then returned the other way.

Zayn crept forward. He cracked the door, which was enough for Pax to hear the conversation in the other room.

"What's got you spooked?"

The voice was Sammi's.

"Dunno. Thought I heard something. Kozsen made a ruckus. This house is too quiet with everyone else gone. I'm beginning to hate it here."

"Understandable with Lil and Daria dead. I keep thinking we should have done something different. That if I'd done a better job, they'd both be alive. Since Becks died, things have been going from bad to worse."

"I'm sorry, Sammi. You lost your partner and I'm over here with my sob story about getting spooked in a house by myself."

"None of their deaths will matter if we can't stop them. We've got to keep going, for Becks, for Lil and Daria."

A pause. Pax couldn't tell if they were still outside the food prep room.

"Any word from Beck's contact?"

"No, and the other contacts at Phoenix aren't returning my calls. I feel like they don't trust us after what happened."

The moment that name hit her ears, Pax tensed up. Her elbow hit the metal shelf, prompting a worried glance from Zayn. Phoenix Corporation. Her blood went cold. They were a big multinational company with their fingers in many pies in the supernatural animal business—from hunting, to zoo security...and, it seemed, to manufacturing new creatures like the cobraffin. After the zoo disaster, she thought they would have shouldered more of the blame, but they managed to weasel their way out of the worst of the punishments. Friends in high places.

The conversation between Lennie and Nandi moved away from their hiding spot. Zayn closed the freezer door.

"What's that about Phoenix Corp?" he whispered. "You reacted like you'd been shot."

"I've encountered them before. They were the ones that brought Aepep to the zoo. Over the years, they've hired a lot of Hunters from Animalians for security. We always suspected a link between Phoenix Corp and Pyramid Health, the company behind the creation of the Jörmungandr, but beyond a few mutual board members, we could never find proof. They could have easily made the cobraffin and must have recruited Beckett. I'd guess that the Dreadmarsh family holds a major stock interest in either, or both companies, though that's a guess."

"I'm not following. Your concern seems greater than a few shitty corporations."

"Pyramid Health was basically a front for the cult of Aepep. The new version didn't care so much about their old namesake, and probably didn't even know that I'd accidentally freed the flying snake that had once given them purpose. They were carrying on the chaotic mission of Aepep in the name of big profits."

"Does that mean that Aepep is connected with Elosian?" asked Zayn.

"Fuck, I don't know. It's starting to sound like it. Maybe Aepep came from the demonic realm. Would explain a lot about it. I guess these creatures find a way to come over, and then set up their little fiefdoms. Was probably easier back in the day. They could be gods. Rule over humans and do whatever their hearts desired. But Invictus brought magic out of the shadows. Now they have to hide what they're doing."

Zayn's ashen expression gave her pause. She detected a heavy sense of recognition.

"Did you think of something?"

"I'll explain later. First we need to get out of here." He popped the door loose. "Stay here and let me scout."

Pax followed him into the prep room, relying on Kali to tell her that the next room was empty. The other mages had returned upstairs. Their footsteps echoed from above. Zayn hesitated at the door, so Pax put her hand on his shoulder and shook her head. Kali could detect agitation from the cobraffin. If he went out, it would create an alarm again, bringing the mages upon their heads.

She got his attention, tapped on her watch, and gestured to the upper floors. Zayn responded by miming sleep: two hands together and laying his head on them. They would have to wait it out.

Chairs squeaked across the floor for the next hour. They were eating or gathered in the kitchen. Pax couldn't hear them, but the way Zayn's eyebrows worked at times suggested he was listening.

Then there was silence. It happened all at once, making Pax suspicious. While they were making noise, she felt like they hadn't been noticed. The sudden absence left her checking the corners for hidden cameras or other means of their discovery.

Zayn slipped out before she could bring up her concern. He was gone long enough that the only thing she could hear was her heart beat. When he returned, he motioned for her to follow.

The cobraffin was curled into the corner of the cage, a mere lump of shadow. They crept to the stairs. Pax was certain the ambush would happen when they crested onto the main floor. Zayn went first. He motioned. Pax followed, cringing when Kali's claws clicked on the wood floor.

<Sorry>

Her companion shifted her weight or pulled in her claws, making her silent enough that Pax had to check to make sure she was still behind. They made it to the sliding glass door. A footstep had them both freezing.

The noise came from the upper floor. Muted talking reached their location. Then a light came on in the hallway behind them.

Zayn motioned to the big dining table near the back windows. They crouched behind the chairs, knowing that if anyone looked over, they'd be sure to see two people and one large furry creature.

The mage from Tinkers appeared. Gregor. Pax had saved him from accidental immolation, but she guessed he wouldn't remember or see it that way. He went into the refrigerator, pulled out the gallon jug of milk, drank directly from the bottle, wiped his mouth with the back of his hand, and shoved it back onto its shelf.

He started to leave the kitchen, but stopped, glancing in their direction. Pax froze. If he had a darkvision enchantment on, they were discovered. Gregor held position, scanning the back of the house, before giving a little headshake, then disappearing down the hallway, turning the light off as he went.

There was a good chance they'd been spotted, but Gregor, seeing that he was outnumbered, was waiting until he was out of sight to call the alarm. As Zayn led them into the garden, she kept expecting the lights to come blaring on, spearing them in their sights, followed by a barrage of unstoppable magic.

The wall was easier to summit on the interior, either from experience or adrenaline. Only when they were safely in the alleyway, jogging away from the hidden villa, did Pax allow herself to breathe normally again.

She put her hand on his arm to ask a question, but he waved her off. Something besides almost getting caught had shaken him. It wasn't until they returned to his apartment—after thoroughly ensuring they hadn't been followed—that Zayn spoke.

"You were going to say something in the basement."

He nodded and went into the refrigerator. She thought he was getting something to drink, but he pulled out a row of vials with a pale green liquid inside.

"Those aren't jello shots, I assume," said Pax.

"It's poison."

"Poison? I thought you didn't do assassinations. Or was that just a story?" said Pax.

The pain in his eyes made Pax regret the quip. He pulled a fresh syringe from a drawer and after opening the package, placed the needle into a vial and drew a dose. Pax knew what he was going to do, but it was still surprising anyway. She reached out to stop him when he put the needle to his arm.

"It's not poison for me. It keeps me alive."

Pax forced herself to watch him inject the greenish liquid into his veins. She saw the dotted skin on the inside of his elbows. He'd stuck himself hundreds of times.

"It's spider poison. *Purpura domina aranea.*"

"I've never heard of it, and I had to memorize the nomenclature," she said.

"The spiders that produce this poison only exist in one place in the world. Varna. When I was born, I was injected with a small dose. Too much and it would kill me, but a tiny amount makes the body dependent on regular shots. Everyone in Varna was forced to take it."

"Why?"

"The Lady of Varna, or Lady Arcadia, was a monstrous being that controlled us. She'd been around for millennia, keeping us as her private subjects. I joined my Hall because of her. My cousin too. We were intended to help keep the town in line."

"Intended."

"We betrayed and killed her. Keelan lost his life in the process. I almost did too. It freed the town from her tyranny, but not the poison. At least for those of us born before she died. Thankfully we can manage it ourselves. Everyone in my family has to travel with enough doses to keep them safe."

"What made you think of this?"

"When you mentioned beings that ruled the ancient world like gods, it made me think of Lady Arcadia. But she went by other names. Entana. Inanna. She was the inspiration for the Sumerian goddess known as Queen of the Night."

"You think she came from the demonic realm," said Pax.

"It would make sense. The influx of supernatural creatures from the other realms, especially in the distant past, is well-known. If Aepep came from there, maybe she did too."

"It's all related."

He nodded. "It's all related. Seeds of the past. Where is the Lost Prince in all this?"

"We know the cobraffin came from the Phoenix Corp and they were involved with Aepep's capture for the zoo. What if the head of the company is the Lost Prince?"

"Why would he give up the tattoo? It seems particularly powerful."

"Who knows. Maybe it helped him hide as a human, or brought other issues. I'm not entirely sure that Moriganne is controlling it after the tornados at Camp Lucky," said Pax.

"I thought the prince might be a potential ally before, but now I'm worried that he's our enemy. Possibly working with Elosian from this side to help him come over. Maybe he's part of this company."

Pax nodded. "It would make sense. But what would we do now?"

Zayn pulled out his laptop and brought up the Phoenix Corporation website. "We need to find out more about this company."

Eleven

The metal golem lumbered after Aurie with the inexorable grace of an avalanche. The ankh on its chest glowed with crimson menace. She turned towards it as it came around the table.

"Aurelia!"

The force of her true name shout impacted the golem as if she'd thrown a piece of crumpled paper at it. Her magic wasn't to blame. Aurie knew she'd imbued it with ample power, enough to throw a moving car across the street, but it hadn't slowed the golem. They were in trouble.

"Osiris!" shouted her sister from across the table.

"What?"

"That's what it looks like," said Pi. She sent chains of glowing black metal after the golem, but they turned to mist as they hit the smooth surface. "Fuck. This thing is impervious to our magic."

"Slick!"

The mendancy did nothing to slow the golem down. Aurie was quickly running out of options.

"We can't keep this up forever."

Pi got too close from behind and the golem spun on its heels, nearly taking her sister's head off with a right hook. She scrambled under the steel table where the Rod was sitting to avoid getting crushed. The Osiris golem lifted its fist as if it were going to smash its way through the table, but hesitated. Then it resumed the circling pursuit.

"This would be embarrassing if it wasn't so fraught," said Pi, climbing to her feet on the other side.

"It won't break anything in here," said Aurie. "Its programming must keep it from damaging the property."

"That's great," said her sister, sending a spray of flame against the golem to no effect. "Should we disguise ourselves as the Rod? Or maybe that glass case over there."

"Can you get us out the door?" asked Aurie as she hurried ahead of the golem.

"I think so."

"Get it open. I'll grab the Rod and then we'll close the golem in the room. If it won't damage property, then it can't smash through the door. Hopefully."

Aurie hit the golem with a few more shouts to keep it focused on her. When Pi scurried towards the door, it hesitated.

"Hey!" yelled Aurie. "Brass breath! Over here. Follow me."

She blasted it with a force wave to the chest. The golem moved after her, giving Pi a chance to work her magic on the door. A couple of laps around the table later, she yelled, "Got it!"

As Aurie came around, she snatched the Rod of Dominion from the table and sprinted out of the room. Pi slammed the door behind them, and they waited for the inevitable smash of a fist through the barrier. But the golem did no such thing. They were both breathing heavily.

"Gonna make that harder to put it back where we found it," said Pi.

"Let's take it to our lab."

The space they used for research and elixir making wasn't remotely as eclectic or exotic as the head patron's, but they were using it for more practical applications. Aurie threw the Rod on a steel table. She flinched at the way it clanged against the surface, fearing she'd damaged it, but remembered it was as old as civilization. It would take a lot more than that to damage it. The Rod of Dominion had been hidden in an Egyptian tomb when they recovered it. They'd followed their parents' notes to find it, keeping it from Professor Trebleton, who would have used it to subjugate the city. The Rod had two parts: a crook and a flail. One for healing and one for war.

"It looks different than I remember," said Pi.

"The choice was reversed," said Aurie, realizing the difference as her sister pointed it out. "Using the Rod required making a choice between them. We chose the crook when we gave it to Golden Willow, but it's back to its original form."

"Let me try something," said Pi, shaking out her hands.

Aurie stepped back as her sister placed an enchantment on the Rod. Various shades of green sparks jumped from the surface as the magic took hold, making them step back. Pi quickly dismissed the spell.

"What was that?"

"Not only is it in the original form, but it has some or all of its old power back."

Aurie leaned on the table. "How is that possible? The hospital said they'd used up most of the power. Can he just put the power back in?"

"It appears he has. But for what purpose?" asked Pi.

"Whatever it is, he should have told us," said Aurie. "He knows we found the Rod. Keeping this from us makes me not trust him."

"Are you saying that because of my vision?" asked Pi.

"No. Yes. I don't know," said Aurie. "It's hard to say without knowing the origins of the vision, but the fact that the Rod of Dominion was in it means that this artifact is important."

"Maybe Elosian's searching for power? He knows he can't take on a city filled with mages, especially not on his turf, without a little extra umph. That's why he wants the Rod. Why he sent me the vision."

"Or Moriganne's tattoo."

"Or both."

Aurie put her hand around the base of the Rod. It thrummed. "Things are coming to a head. I can feel it." She shook her head. "We don't have much time."

"Why Osiris?" asked her sister. "Does it have anything to do with where we got this?"

Aurie leaned on the table, staring at the Rod of Dominion. "Coincidence maybe. Nothing else in there was Egyptian. Invictus has items he's collected from every time period in history. The Greeks, Sumerians, you name it, he's got a piece of it."

"Old as sin," said Pi. "You ever wonder if we lived that long if we would change? Would we be the same people we are now? Miss Arrogant and Miss Righteous, except with more years under our belt?"

"No," said Aurie. "I haven't, but I imagine that I would change somehow. The world itself would change and we'd have to adjust with it. You remember when we were in Semyon's head. None of the patrons were remotely the same as they are, because they weren't allowed to reveal their magic or they would get hunted down."

"He wasn't a good person back then."

Aurie didn't have to ask to know Pi was talking about Invictus.

"What matters is that he changed."

Pi frowned. "Are we sure?"

"Why do you ask? Worried about your visions?"

"They're probably bullshit, but yeah, worried about them. About him. Wish we knew more about Invictus in his early years." Pi crossed her arms. "Ever wonder if he's the Lost Prince?"

"I considered it, but it's not him. If he came from the demonic realm, he'd never be able to touch the wards, or use half those spells that protect the barrier. No, however he came into his power, it was from somewhere else. I'm sure of it."

"Kinda what I thought too, but wanted to bring it up." Pi wrinkled her nose. "You smell that?"

Aurie inhaled deeply. "What?"

"Maybe nothing," said Pi, shrugging.

Her sister was holding something back. Aurie was sure of it. "The visions are bothering you."

"Bothering is too strong a word," said Pi with a forced smile. "Curious. Why me? Are they accidental? Is it something intended by Elosian? It's not like I have the bridge tattoo. If anyone should be having them, it should be Moriganne."

Aurie put a hand to her head as her heartbeat sped up. "Moriganne might have stolen the tattoo and bears it temporarily, but you were the one that killed him. You were there when he died. Maybe part of the tattoo is in you? Moriganne said she had an outline of it when he was alive, so it's not an all-or-nothing thing."

"Shit, you're right," said Pi, plopping down on a chair and leaning onto her knees. "And all the souls in my head. Each one is there because of him. There might be residue of the sigil. Together there's enough of it in me to give him a conduit. Great."

"There are always consequences in magic," said Aurie.

"I don't need any I told you so's right now."

"It's not an I told you so. It's just a fact. For me, for you, even Old Iron Balls."

"Yeah, even Old Iron Balls." Pi screwed up her face. "It's just a theory, we don't know if it's true. It's not like I've had reactions to wards, and I've been exposed to them plenty of times. Moriganne can't get near certain ones. I don't have the sigil, but the residue, something different."

"If it's a conduit for the visions, it's a problem, even if they're not intentional."

Pi slammed a fist into her open hand. "First the Rod is back and now I realize I'm compromised. I don't know if I should be around you all. What if Elosian can see through me? Spy on our plans like that Cybermagics mage did to create the ambush."

"That could be a problem."

Pi stood up. "We need to go to the Verum Locus. I can go into those memories, the ones from the visions, possibly figure out what's going on."

"That's too dangerous, Pi. It was hard to wake you, and I don't think we'll learn anything. Too much risk. Not enough reward."

"What? Are we just going to give up? I'm out of ideas. If we don't start figuring things out soon, I think the invasion is going to happen whether or not we want it."

"Unless going into the Verum Locus to delve into the visions is part of Elosian's plan," said Aurie.

Pi threw up her hands. "I'm so sick of worrying if Elosian is lurking around every corner. He's powerful but he has his limits. Just this idea is affecting us. Keeping us afraid to make a move because it might be tainted by his whispers."

"You're right. We can't be afraid to act, even if Elosian is trying to manipulate us, but I don't think it's time to use the Verum Locus for the visions. Too risky. Let's exhaust the other possibilities first. Please. I'm your sister, I can't lose you. You're the only family I have. *Dooset daram.*"

Pi frowned. "Who's the one trying to manipulate me now? I love you too, sis, but if the world is falling apart and you have a choice between saving it or saving your foolish sister, I want you to forget about me. All this is more important than us. That's why we joined the Order, right?"

Aurie held out her hands, part rejection of Pi's comments, part desire to throw her arms around her.

"That's unfair and you know it. I didn't say no, I said we should explore other possibilities first."

"We're running out of time. What's your idea?"

Aurie looked around. "I don't have one. But you can't go. Please. We have to figure out the Rod first. There's a ton of work right here. I need your help. Research."

Pi stared suspiciously at the Rod. "Fine. We do need to figure out what's going on, or what Invictus intends. The visions can wait. For now."

Aurie let a smile spread across her face. "There's a book in the corner library involving artifacts and the magics involved. I think there's some good spells in it that will help us with the Rod."

Her sister nodded. "I'll grab it." She took a few steps towards the door before circling back. "What happens if Invictus comes back? And you know, we've still got the Rod?"

It was a good point. He would go ballistic. "Old Iron Balls shouldn't have kept this from us."

Pi arched an eyebrow. "I'll corrupt you yet." As she strode from the room, she yelled over her shoulder, "Dooset daram!"

Twelve

Kitty stared at the dented bucket of mercury she'd rescued from the dumpster as she cradled a bottle of dark beer against her chest. She'd opened it intending to drink, but it felt sacrilegious.

"We didn't kill her," said Moriganne, coming in from the other room. After they'd returned to Ares' old place, they'd both gone their separate ways for a few hours to contemplate the woman's death.

"I know," said Kitty, setting the beer on the table. She'd opened it a while ago. It was probably flat. "Elosian did it, but had we not tracked her down, she'd still be alive."

"And his tool."

"I don't think she was a willing participant," said Kitty.

"Why would you say that?"

Kitty cracked her neck. "He wouldn't have needed to kill her so quickly. Elosian was afraid of something. That we'd learn something from questioning her."

"So we're close?"

"Maybe."

Moriganne plopped onto the couch and leaned forward, resting her elbows on her knees. It was well after midnight.

"What now?" asked Moriganne. "It's a few days until his funeral. I was hoping to figure out who killed him before then."

"It's important," said Kitty, "but I don't think it's the question we should be asking. Finding Ares' killer won't stop the invasion. Whoever it was was probably a tool for Elosian. He's been busy preparing himself for what's to come. Elosian wanted him out of the way."

Moriganne lifted her chin. "Then what is the right question?"

"The bridge."

"The lost prince." Moriganne shook her head. "The answer is lost to time. Even if the Ginger Man was alive, I don't think he would have told us."

"There's another way."

"And?"

Kitty snatched the bottle of beer. Took a drink. Was flat as expected.

"The Second Year Contest."

Moriganne shook her head. "I'm not following. Or is this something you would understand if you'd done it? I was too busy trying to get into Snake and Tome to worry about it."

Kitty smirked. "Victor thought it was a joke. The rewards for winning weren't worth the effort in comparison to further contacts for the family." She took another drink. "The technology they use for the contest is the same as they use for some of the Merlin Trials. When the danger is too high, they put us into stasis and our minds interface with something that creates a reasonable facsimile of the world. No one knows how the illusion of reality is created, but you can't tell the difference."

"I know *that* much, Kitty."

"I'll get to my point. When I joined my Hall, I felt woefully outclassed. The others were quicker, more creative in their solutions, better all around. I hated it. After always being one of the best, I worried that my successes had been bought for me. That all the wealth and opportunity had been squandered."

"Was that you thinking that or Victor?"

Kitty took a sip. "Both. But it amounted to the same thing. I needed an edge. Needed to find a way to get better. Faster. I was halfway through my first year when I happened to learn more about how the Second Year Contest was run from a member of Gamemakers Hall. They're the hall in charge of the contest, and the Merlin Trials. Was more curiosity at the time. But when I learned it was like a holodeck, or immersive virtual world, I wanted to use it. So I bribed the student into letting me use it. I gave him my criteria, what I wanted to learn, and he designed intensive scenarios that tested my abilities. Or in the beginning, showcased my deficiencies. I died. A lot. But each death gave me a chance to learn. To get better."

"Kinda makes me wish I'd joined the contest."

Kitty nodded. "I did. Even though Victor hated it, I wanted the challenge."

"Did Ivan?"

"He was too busy with his parties," responded Kitty.

"How did you do?"

"We didn't come close. As quickly as I developed using the technology, I learned I was a terrible team player. I probably cost our team a chance to get into the top groups by constantly heading off on my own." Kitty tapped her fingernails on the bottle. "The point of this story is not about my shortcomings. Over time, the guy I bribed let little things slip about how the technology worked. It was impossible to build entire worlds from the ground up, so they used shortcuts. Memories. Imprints from recovered golems. All sorts of things. Anything that contained memories really."

Moriganne held out her arm. "You want to use the tattoo to build a world and investigate it?"

"Exactly."

"Is that wise?"

Kitty finished the beer, let loose a gut-rattling belch, and tossed the bottle into the trash can from across the room.

"The system is supposed to be safe. You can explore it without danger. I died hundreds of times in it. But on the other hand, the sigil is a level of power that we don't understand. There could be unintended consequences."

"Anything to help me understand it," said Moriganne as she stared at her elbow. "Since we came back to the city, I've been feeling weird. Unsteady. The tornados prove that I'm not in control like I thought I was."

"More reason to understand what you've got there."

"Besides a ticking bomb." Moriganne squeezed her lips white. "So you're going to contact your friend?"

Kitty nodded towards her phone on the table. "Already have. He's no longer in the country. Works in Lithuania, but he gave me a contact. Someone he said would be better overall."

"Who?"

Kitty lifted both shoulders. "Dunno. Never told me the name, but I got a message a little bit ago that we can head to Gamemakers to meet them."

"Now?" Moriganne stretched her arms. "I was coming in here to tell you goodnight. Weird time for a meeting."

"You probably don't know many gamers," said Kitty, laughing. "My other friend was awake at the oddest hours."

"My dear sister, you're forgetting that the internet and online games didn't even exist for the vast majority of my life."

§

Gamemakers Hall was only a quarter mile away in the same ward. No matter how many times Kitty had been to the place, she always saw something new. The building looked like the architect was trying out every possible construction technique and style. As if an entire small town had been condensed into one building.

The fencing mysteriously opened when they arrived. Kitty led them through the front door. They headed deeper into the building, hoping whoever had let them in would acknowledge their arrival. At a short hallway, there was a room filled with old arcade and pinball machines.

"That looks like my kind," said Moriganne. "Played a few games of pinball when I was waiting for shows to start. A lot of old venues had them in the back for the bands."

"That's strange."

"Nah. Better than them getting drunk and breaking things, all in the name of Rock and Roll," said Moriganne, making air quotes.

An arcade machine beeped and whistled, rattling as if it were about to break down. The colorful machine had a joystick and multiple buttons on the front. Kitty approached to find a message scrolling down.

"Charmers: Find the obsidian cube in the basement."

"Weird," said Moriganne. "Is this where you entered the game world?"

"No," said Kitty. "We used an alternate entry point. I only came here to meet my friend, though he never let me come in. We usually chatted outside near the industrial park."

They passed a kitchen. A kid wearing light-up kitten ears was eating cereal with a ladle. He wagged his eyebrows at them, but said nothing.

Eventually they found the room with the obsidian cube. Hundreds of pillows surrounded the glistening black object.

"It's a portal," said Moriganne with understanding.

"Kind of. Lie down, get comfortable, and fill your mind with faez. If this is like the alternate locations, it should pull us right in."

Kitty got comfortable. Her friend said the new contact would greet them, but she hadn't expected inside the game world. She settled her head on a pillow, even though as soon as she went into the game, her body would no longer be in the room. She closed her eyes and filled her mind with faez.

When she opened them, she was in another place. Standing. Kitty could smell the recent rain. Wind tossed her hair. She stood beneath a night sky, brilliant stars splashed across the curve of the world. A shooting star streaked overhead. Kitty could hear Moriganne gasping with surprise behind her, but her focus was on the figure coming out of the tall grass.

Short. Dark hair.

The figure made no attempt to move out of the shadows. Kitty clenched her gut, concern rippling. Was this their contact, or another ambush by the mages? A wave of regrets followed. She should have vetted the contact before agreeing to enter the game. Now they were in unfamiliar territory.

Oblivious to the potential danger, Moriganne stepped to Kitty's side and raised her arm.

"Hello?"

Thirteen

The Phoenix Corporation had three floors in a high-rise in the third ward. The headquarters were in London, but they had a sizable presence in Invictus. Morning traffic was in full swing with horn honks and squealing tires competing as background noise.

"I hate not having Kali with us," said Pax as she tugged on her bright blue business jacket. She looked nothing like her normal self.

"Considering they tried to blame the disaster on you, and had the papers calling you a terrorist for a while, I think they would recognize your companion," said Zayn, who had given himself new facial features as well.

"Couldn't we have snuck in during the night and dug through their trash or something?" she asked, craning her neck at the tall building.

"That would take too long. Human intel is always quicker and more in depth." Zayn smirked. "Just let me do the talking. There's nothing worse than an audit from the government. They'll barely notice us because they'll be too busy worrying about why we decided to show up."

Zayn hadn't researched the security measures, but most buildings in Invictus only used low-level enchantment detections that wouldn't find the facial modifications. If he'd used a quick illusion, that would have been easy to discover. The security guards waved thick wands at them, which beeped ominously, but they were nodded through the gates.

The front desk attendant looked bored as he thumbed through his phone. Zayn hefted his suitcase onto the counter, startling the guy. Two clicks of the locks later, Zayn handed over a document with official IRS letterhead and an enchanted seal that would confirm the validity of his identity. One of the benefits of working for Priyanka was access to all kinds of resources that normal spies might not have. The seals were real, along with the identifications.

"Please inform the name at the top of the document, Harold Peterman, that we are here for an unannounced audit and would like to speak to him posthaste. We expect a level of alacrity given the nature of our visit."

The desk attendant stared back, his mouth hanging open. Zayn expected drool to come out any moment.

"Alacrity means speed. Which means you need to get on the phone and make a call before we charge you with interference."

The guy knocked the phone off the hook reaching for it, then passed on the instructions in less formal terms.

"Thirty-fourth floor."

"Thank you."

Zayn strode to the elevator with the steady clop of Pax's heels right behind. When the doors closed, the stainless steel surface reflected them both. Pax tilted her head as she examined her new self, which included a toned-down hair color that was more auburn. He'd long ago gotten over being someone else. In some ways it was easier to hide in someone else's skin. The years of disguising his intentions from the Lady of Varna had left him a little unsure of who he was. When Aurie had showed up in the Eternal City, it'd reminded him of a path that he'd wanted to travel, but time and circumstances had swallowed it up, until the trail was so overgrown that he couldn't find it again. Her return had made him reevaluate where he was. He loved the work with Priyanka, but he felt isolated. Alone.

The elevator dinged and two men and two women greeted them outside the doors with nervous smiles.

"Mr. Williams. Ms. Carter. How can we help you?" asked the man in front as he extended his hand.

Zayn frowned without meeting his offer of a handshake. "And you are?"

"I'm Harold Peterman. Head of accounting."

"Good, then we're not wasting our time," said Zayn as he brushed past them. "Shall we find an appropriate room to get set up? This will likely take a few weeks."

Naked fear shot through their eyes. They were probably hoping for a quick visit, not a full-scale audit.

"Uhm, weeks," stuttered Harold Peterman. "But we had people here last year from your offices. They said we were good."

Zayn didn't bother answering. The less said the better. He stared at Harold until he said, "Right," and led them to a conference room. Coffee and snacks were brought in while they settled at the table. He popped open the suitcase, handed over a piece of paper they'd typed up that morning, and hoped that the fear ricocheting through them would be enough to smooth over any issues.

While Harold stared at it, Zayn explained, "I need the full board list and addresses. We might need to interview them. We'll need the company org chart and the latest quarterly financial statement."

Harold held up the document with an incredulous look on his face. "But you can get most of that information online. We filed with the SEC."

"I'm well aware, Mr. Peterman, but the request for the audit came down pretty quickly, and we didn't have time to print out reams of information."

Harold took a step towards the door, still staring at the document. A knot formed in Zayn's stomach. The guy was sensing something was wrong.

"You know, we've tried to fix our problems after the disaster," said Harold. "I don't know who has it out for us, but we're aboveboard. Not a hair out of place."

"If that's so, then this should go smoothly," said Zayn with a flat smile.

When the door closed, Pax leaned over and whispered, "Is something wrong? That didn't feel like they bought it."

"We'll find out soon enough."

Over the next hour, men and women brought them documents. Zayn asked questions while Pax quietly scoured the papers, taking notes, which brought a lot of worried glances. They wanted to get a good picture of how the company was structured so they could figure out who was directing the creation of creatures like the cobraffin, and if the Lost Prince, or other agents of Elosian, were part of the leadership. While the financial documents could be found online, the personal information and details on the company's divisions weren't easily available.

He let Pax read through the documents while he barked orders and new requests at the people sent to help them. Zayn wanted to keep them on their back foot so they never stopped to question the direction of the investigation. While he kept up the ruse, he was aware that Harold Peterman was spending a lot of time talking to a few others in the back of the big open office. There were a lot of exaggerated arm movements and pinched faces, which could be interpreted a number of ways. It was possible that Harold's concerns were normal, but after he spent a little time on the phone and then stared at the window where they were seated for far too long, Zayn worried they'd been exposed.

Shortly after, Harold stuck his head through the door and nodded to his underlings. "Can I have a moment?"

The others looked relieved as they scurried out. The meek exterior from their initial arrival had disappeared. Whoever Harold had spoken to, they'd girded his resolve. He faced them with his hands on the back of a chair.

"I'm afraid I'm going to need some further explanation of what's going on before we supply any more documents," said Harold.

"Refusing to serve an officer of the IRS is punishable with jail time," said Zayn, lifting his chin.

"Yeah," said Harold. "I just got off the phone with my contact at the IRS. They don't know who the hell either of you are."

Out of the corner of his eye, Zayn spotted a team of security personnel leaving the elevator. They had rifles and enchanted armor.

"We're a big organization," said Zayn, trying not to look intimidated by the recent arrivals. "I don't think I would get too cocky."

Harold frowned. "My contact is the director. You see, after the last audit, we were cleared and the DOJ removed the oversight. I get it, mistakes were made before, but we're a better, stronger, and cleaner organization."

The security team approached the glass doors. Pax nudged him in the leg, but Zayn kept his gaze on Harold.

"Meaning you increased your political donations by a sizable amount, giving yourself more cover."

After years in the Eternal City, the machinations of humans seemed laughably simple and easy to spot.

Harold chuckled. "You got me there." He rapped his knuckles on the back of the chair as the six security team members entered the room. "I'm going to have to ask you to stand up and step away from those documents. I don't know who you are, but we're gonna find out, real soon."

Fourteen

Pi entered Arcanium through the back, the entrance the professors liked to use when they wanted to avoid their students. There were additional protections on the door. The permissions they'd been given wouldn't bypass them, but Pi knew a few other tricks. She bent the wards, slid through the gap, and let them retract back into position.

She could leave by the front entrance with the drawbridge when she was finished, but for now, she needed to ensure there was no way that someone might contact her sister or stop her on the way to the Verum Locus.

With her hood up and head down, bolstered by a Look Away enchantment, Pi made her way to her destination. The all-night work on the Rod of Dominion had exposed no new information. The artifact was important, but only as a tool. Pi didn't think there was that much more to discover, unlike the mystery of her visions.

The auditorium outside the Verum Locus was empty. She'd seen few students, as it was early enough in the morning that most were probably asleep. Pi had a fondness for Arcanium, but it had never felt like home. She'd enjoyed it like getting to visit a favorite aunt, who always had a bowl full of candy, but also made her keep her elbows off the table during dinner.

The golden light inside the room sparkled. Visually, it was beautiful, but the sharp stabbing on the inside of her nostrils reminded her of the potency of magic. Before she started, Aurie's disappointed expression appeared in her mind. Even if she learned nothing new, Pi knew that her sister would find out. She could sniff out a lie in a crowded room.

The main question Pi had in coming to the Verum Locus was which vision to delve into. The first with Invictus had revealed some inaccuracies about what had happened during his visit to the demonic realm. The second, during her last visit to the Verum Locus, had been in a strange location with Elosian calling her name. The third had her in the Spire, holding the Rod, and then seeing Invictus in the city at the head of an army of gigantes with the Rod in his hand.

The first vision she took at face value. The third was fraught with implications and possibly too chaotic for information gathering. Pi focused on the vision she'd had the last time in the room. A vision from a vision. It was possible that it wouldn't work, but she was determined to try.

When she opened her eyes again, she found herself in a completely different place. Pi stood, not in the strange crystal forest, but in a wide valley. The sky was a color she didn't have the words to describe, and even if she could, it seemed to shift as she watched. The valley stretched in all directions, surrounded by impossible mountains that defied the rules of gravity from her realm. Shapes moved in the distance, but they were too small to make out.

She tried to reckon what she was looking at to her left, but it made her head hurt. The mountains climbed into the sky, narrowed to a point, then twisted until they continued nearly upside down, while the indescribable sky that hung above her was directly below the other range.

The two ranges were in direct opposition to each other and they met at a narrow point that looked like a bridge. Recalling the last time she was here, Pi wondered if it was the same place she saw between the crystalline trees, back in the dreamworld. Adjusting her step brought the crunch of grass breaking.

"Pythia."

A voice like honey over gravel. She turned to find the tall demon with backward facing knees not far away. He had the face of a serial killer and tentacles rather than arms.

"I knew you'd come eventually. You're far too curious, incautious, unlike your sister."

Fear raced through her body. Pi attempted to dismiss the vision, return to the Verum Locus, but something was blocking her.

"Don't run away so soon. We have much to discuss."

"I'm not here to listen to your lies," said Pi.

The demon lord chuckled. The laughter hurt to hear. "I tell only the truth. It is not my fault that some are incapable of hearing it." He took long strides towards her. "You and I. Things might have been different had you summoned me rather than that imbecilic Pazuzu. The desire for power is strong. I could have granted that."

"I wanted into Coterie, not to be beholden to a demon lord."

"Pazuzu is not a lord. He rules over nothing but chaos. He is a force of nature, nothing more."

Pi didn't know if this was a vision or if she had somehow teleported in the demonic realm. The feel of the world was so real. It lacked the hazy quality of dreams that she'd experienced previously in the Verum Locus.

A creature winged across the sky, heading parallel to the mountains. Elosian turned his head and Pi used the distraction to blast him with a force wave, but he casually extended his arm, knocking away the magic as if it were a crumpled piece of paper.

"You've no power here, not like this," he said.

"I'm in the infernal realm?"

Elosian smirked. "Not corporally. The residue of the sigil gave me something to put my hooks in, otherwise I would have had no chance to reach you. Your mind is here while your body is in my enemy's city."

"What do you want?"

"I want to talk. Offer you the deal that I know burns in your heart."

"Why would I help you? You want the overthrow and destruction of our world."

Elosian leaned into her face, his expression turning into a rictus. "You know nothing of what I want. This place is a prison. It is chaos, scorching my mind. What I want is freedom like the others that have gone before me."

"The Lost Prince."

"He's not the only one." Elosian sneered, which reminded her of a poorly drawn Elvis. The demon lord stomped away, stared at the bridge between ranges. "They betrayed me. Abandoned me to this place."

"What's wrong with it?"

Elosian turned towards her. The way his body rotated made her sick to her stomach.

"This was one of the earliest realms to spring into existence." Elosian held up his tentacle, swiping through the golden particles in the air. "Unlike yours, and many others, this place is incomplete, constantly changing. It is creation unbound and the font of magic."

"The font of magic? This is where it comes from?"

Elosian gestured wildly with his tentacles. "Here and the primordial soup of existence. That is why those of you with the promise of it go mad without protection. The chaos of this realm is too much for untrained minds."

"This is all interesting," said Pi. "A lovely lesson, but why did you trick me here?"

"I want to cross over. I want to exist in your realm without precondition or prejudice."

"You want an invasion," said Pi.

"If you force me to break the barrier, then an invasion it will be. But if you help me cross alone, then you will spare yourself the destruction that will ensue."

"Even if I wanted to, there's no way I could trust you. You'd probably open the way for the others once you came over," said Pi.

"Why would I want to do that? And ruin the world I wish to be a part of? This chaos is exactly that, chaos. Unruly, unfettered, unmitigable chaos. You would not like it either."

Pi hated how reasonable he sounded. She had no intention of helping him, but his logic made sense. If she was trapped here, she would want nothing but to return.

"You killed my parents. I would never work with you."

She'd said it offhand. A way to punch back, keep from growing interested in his offer, but not expecting a real answer.

To her surprise, he said, "You're not wrong. But it would do no good for me to apologize, or explain that I had no other choice. They worked for my enemy."

The admission was like a punch to the solar plexus. She took a step backwards. Here was the killer of her parents. A demon of unimaginable power and there was nothing she could do to get her revenge.

"I work for Invictus. My sister too."

"I am aware," said Elosian. "The irony is that your parents' death made you seek power. Put you on this path and brought you to me."

"Part of your plan."

Elosian shook his head. "If I had the power to foretell that far in advance, then I would have already crossed over, would be the ruler of your world. No. I have my whispers, my plots. Hundreds of them, each winding towards my goal. Most are thwarted by chance or the opposition." He grinned at her with yellow teeth. "But a few sneak through until I can grasp the string."

"I'm one of those strings," said Pi, feeling empty inside at the realization.

"Yes. Not only have I removed a troublesome piece from the board, but now you are my bait."

"Bait for what?"

Elosian loomed over her. His tentacles brushed her arms, making her shiver with disgust.

"You'll find out soon enough."

Before she could speak, his tentacles constricted her, lifting her into the air. The world rushed past in a blur. Pi found herself on a building that her mind wanted to call a castle, even if it was nothing like one. It was as if MC Escher and Salvador Dali had conspired to construct an object that defied the mind's attempt at logic. There were no walls or gates that confined her, but as she craned her neck in all directions, she had no idea how she could even attempt to escape.

"I'm so sorry, Aurie."

Fifteen

In Moriganne's seventy-plus years of existence, she'd never played any games besides a few pinball machines in the back rooms of certain venues. There was a satisfaction to the clacking of the flippers and the way the silvery ball ricocheted through the field, creating bright noises and flashes, corresponding with climbing numbers of the score.

That was the extent of her experience with games.

Gamemakers Hall was exactly as she'd expected. Messy, convoluted, the forgotten room of a pimple-faced kid who spent way too much time in front of a screen. Moriganne wouldn't have found it hard to admit that she looked down upon games. They weren't the real thing, a distraction from life. An amusing sidebar. Nothing more.

Entering the game world was nothing short of revolutionary. Since she'd arrived in her body after the Merlin Trials, and had been too busy to get involved with the Second Year Contest, she had no experience with the arcane technology available at the Halls. She was expecting pixelated trees, a blocky version of a convoluted space, not something that mimicked real life.

The night sky was as brilliant and beautiful as her own. Wind rippled through the high grasses and brushed against her face, leaving Moriganne with a body full of goosebumps. She swiped her hand through the air, trying to understand how it could feel so real, when a screen appeared in her vision. There was a list of numbers and words that she had little connection to, but then someone moved out of the high grasses.

"Hello?"

Kitty grabbed her arm, the tension in her fingers relaying concern about whoever it was that approached.

A snap of fingers brought light into existence in a bubble around them. The young woman before them had dark hair, dark glasses, and an intensity to her gaze that made Moriganne almost feel sorry for her. In her early years, she'd met a few rising stars of the scientific community, and she was always amazed at how brightly their minds burned. How exhausting that must be.

"You're looking for me."

"We are," said Kitty.

"Moriganne Charmer, age twenty-six. Third of six. Was the It-girl of high society until a falling out with your father Victor and two unexpected failures in the Merlin Trials, leading to a place in Stone Singers, then Snake and Tome." She turned. "Catherine Kitty Charmer, age twenty-five. Twin with Ivan. Assassin's Hall and Silence. A history of questionable interactions, including potential murder of one Mikhail Dresden, not a sweetheart by anyone's measure. Nothing signaling that either of you were living in the city for the last two years, suggesting that something significant happened related to your missing father. Now you're back right as your brother Ares was murdered. My condolences."

"That was...interesting," said Kitty.

"I'm Alex, short for Alexandria. Last name Duke."

Alex stepped forward and shook their hands firmly and with the precision of someone who had practiced the gesture. Moriganne felt like she was being analyzed at great detail even as they went through introductions.

"Hi, Alex, thanks for meeting with us," said Moriganne. "This game world is pretty spectacular. I wasn't expecting it to be so realistic."

"Bucket said you needed help."

"We do," said Kitty, glancing around. "Is it safe to talk here?"

"We're on the edge of the Endless Plains. I put up some guardians to keep the mobs from bothering us, otherwise the nearest person is probably a zone away."

"Mobs? Zone?" asked Moriganne. "Also, I have these weird numbers floating in my vision. They're distracting."

Alex's eyes creased. "Hit the X in the upper right-hand corner."

A swipe through the air made the words disappear. "Thank you."

"How much did Bucket tell you?" asked Kitty.

"He said *don't let Kitty's reputation fool you, she's a cool cat, and if something's bothering her, you should help. Besides, I'm sure you'll enjoy the challenge.*"

Alex spoke as if it were from memory, even the pauses and speaking manner.

"Why glasses?" asked Moriganne.

Alex touched the side of the black frames. "Why wear them when I'm in a game and can adjust my avatar? For the same reason you keep tapping your fingers together, because you're a singer, and you're used to keeping a beat, but with a microphone in your hand, and that's a way to relax yourself. I don't need the glasses, but they feel right. I'd be distracted without them."

She wrinkled her nose. "It's odd that you have that affliction, given you've never been a professional singer."

Moriganne looked at her hand. She hadn't realized she was tapping, but Alex was right. It was a nervous habit. Moriganne put her hands behind her back and squeezed them together.

"I'll make things short and to the point," said Kitty. "My sister has a tattoo that she unwillingly received from a questionable source many years ago. We want to figure out who the original owner is. I know from my previous experiences with the Gamemakers technology that you can use external sources to help create and populate your game worlds."

"You want to go into a world inspired by the information contained within the tattoo," said Alex.

"Exactly."

"I would assume this has something to do with your brother's death and the strange happenings in Invictus," said Alex.

Moriganne shared a look with Kitty.

"I thought you've been in the game?" asked Moriganne.

"I have," said Alex, "but I like to keep abreast of what's going on. The world is a dangerous place. Despite what you think, I don't play games to avoid the world, but to understand it better."

"I'm sorry, I didn't—"

Alex bunched up her lips. "You're not a gamer. Never have been. Strange." She checked over her shoulder. "But that's not why you came. Can I see it?"

Moriganne pulled back the light cotton sleeve, exposing the bridge tattoo.

"Strange," said Alex again as she studied the design, "the structural bolts on each side are positioned at right angles. This is no normal bridge."

"What?" Moriganne had never noticed, but she followed where Alex had been looking to see that the bolt patterns on one side didn't match the other. "I never noticed that."

"Where did it come from? Before you had it."

Alex remained close, looking up with an intensity that made Moriganne want to step back.

"I, uhm, got it from a painting." Moriganne hadn't planned on explaining everything, but the way Alex stared at her suggested it was best that she did. "I was stealing it from my father for a semi-godlike being we called the Ginger Man. From the flashes of memory I got from him and the tattoo, he'd been alive for a long time. Possibly lived in the old forests of Europe, lived on sacrifices brought to his wicker altars. He took the tattoo from me, then later on, after he died, it reverted back. It's powerful and dangerous."

"He wasn't the original owner," said Alex.

"No," responded Kitty. "That's what we need to find out. It's important."

Alex started swiping through the air. A dark portal opened a few feet away. She stepped through.

"Follow?" Moriganne asked her sister, but she'd already gone into the black rectangle.

The transition was nothing like portal travel in the real world. They stepped into a simple room with furniture and a small kitchen.

"Have a seat," said Alex. "There are drinks in the fridge. If you don't like what's in there, close it, and open it again while you think about what you want and it'll be there."

"Really? We can eat and drink in the game?"

Alex stretched her eyebrows. "Technically, we're not in the game, but the root structure for making new ones. Eating and drinking is unnecessary, your body is being held in suspended animation and requires no sustenance, but like your finger tapping, or my glasses, it feels better when you get to."

Moriganne opened the refrigerator to find a bunch of seltzer waters that she liked to drink when she was in the city, but hadn't been able to find in Thailand. She popped the lid and gasped when the bubbles hit her tongue.

While she was trying the drink, Alex stood at the center of the room, tapping at an invisible screen and occasionally glancing at her. Kitty grabbed a can, but didn't open it.

"I always thought Bucket was intense, but she's a whole nother level. I think we're in good hands."

"I hope so," said Moriganne, glancing around. "I feel out of my element."

They stood around for about ten minutes while Alex worked. Eventually she made a swiping motion and turned back to them.

"Are you ready?"

"You did something already?" asked Moriganne, hating that she didn't know the right terminology.

"It'll require a few consents, but otherwise, yes. The Gamemakers system is quite robust and easy to use. I designed the last two years of Merlin Trials and the Second Year Games in a few days."

Moriganne joined Alex near the center of the room.

"Ready."

A screen appeared in midair.

Enter the world created from your tattoo [Y/N]?

"Is this going to be dangerous?" asked Moriganne.

"Possibly. This will be like the Merlin Trials. Your avatars have the same abilities that you have in the real world, but since we're entering an unknown place there could be unexpected dangers." Alex frowned. "The tattoo contains a lot of data. More than I expected. Much more. I could spend a few days running simulations on them, but I assume you lack the time for detailed analysis. I picked what I thought was the oldest, largest cache of data to build the simulated world." She paused and with uncharacteristic hesitation added, "I tried to enter in admin mode, but something about the memories contained within prevented it."

"No admin mode," said Moriganne. "Meaning, we could be exposed to danger, even in this simulated game world."

"Games require a set of logic to exist, which could encode unusual forms of danger into the world. For instance, you could be trapped in a space of your mind, or injured in a way that is traumatic long after you leave. If you're in a game space long enough, the world changes you. You will experience this world like you would our own."

"Great," said Kitty.

"Let's do this." Moriganne swiped YES.

A portal appeared not far from their location. Unlike the one that led them into the admin room, this one was made of stone with an archway that held strange hieroglyphs. Bright, blinding light made seeing through the entrance impossible.

"After you."

Moriganne stepped through the portal, squinting from the reflection of endless white. Her boots crunched onto sand and a stifling heat rose up like a cocoon. As Kitty and Alex joined her, she looked to her right to see an enormous, smooth pyramid rising from the earth.

Sixteen

Pax had never been one for subtlety, so she was glad to rely on Zayn's lead on getting them into the Phoenix Corporation building. He spoke easily and confidently. The men and women in the office scurried like ants at each command, while she tried to look stern and not completely out of her element. Without Kali, she lacked the extra layer of information she was used to having access to. She'd forgotten how much she relied on her companion.

As the documents came, Pax grew more comfortable, if only because she could focus on the information rather than the sea of confusing people. Zayn had given her instructions on what to look for. She started with the organization chart, snapping pictures of the sections she thought important.

The information at first was too broad, and too filled with financial jargon for her to navigate it. Zayn occasionally leaned over to ask about her progress, his tone suggesting they wouldn't have a ton of time for leisurely perusal, which made her scour the documents more frantically.

A few times she wanted to knock the whole pile onto the floor. There was too much information. Not enough time. They'd never figure out where the cobraffin had come from, let alone the connection to the Cult of Aepep. Rather than trying to read every document, she searched for hierarchies and titles to give herself the best shot at finding the information she was looking for.

A subgroup called Supernatural Morphology caught her notice further down a relatively uninteresting document that was discussing R&D expenditures. She circled the name and nodded to Zayn, who redirected his requests towards that information. In the time after she freed the Jörmungandr, she and Okho had researched Pyramid Health, the company that had been a front for the cult of Aepep. The company had gone under since, ruined by the lawsuits brought by the Norwegian government, but Pax recognized some of the names and titles that had been under the Pyramid Health banner. It appeared that the real nasty work had been moved from one company to the other before its collapse. The information wasn't high level enough to contain the gory details, but she'd read enough financial documents with Okho to know they'd gotten a good hit.

"We're out of time."

The words didn't register at first. Pax was lost to the memories of her fight to free the Jörmungandr. She looked up to see the group of armored security personnel exiting the elevator. Harold, their contact, entered the room and initiated a conversation with Zayn that had a much different feel from before. Pax focused on the documents, trying to squeeze out as much information as possible before they were forced to leave.

Eventually they were out of time. The six security team members entered the room with automatic rifles hanging casually in front. Pax was under no illusion that they couldn't bring them around to fire faster than either of them could move around the big table.

"I'm going to have to ask you to stand up and step away from those documents. I don't know who you are, but we're gonna find out, real soon," said Harold.

Zayn held his hands up. The fake audit was no longer a working cover. He looked to her, but she blanked. Zayn made a face and stretched his eyebrows towards the elevator, but she didn't know how they were going to reach it without someone getting hurt.

An idea popped into her head as she looked down to see her unlocked phone still in her hand. She held it up.

"If you don't step away from the table," she said, "I'll send this information to the *Herald of the Halls* proving that you had willful negligence during the Portland Zoo Massacre. I found that not only did you ignore the signs of the creature's high and chaotic intelligence, but you took samples for creating your own versions."

Pax had no idea if any of that was true, but Harold didn't know and his eyes widened with horror.

"We're members of the Supernatural Animals Liberation Army of Determination. We know what you've done, and you're not going to get away with it," said Pax, filling her voice with righteousness. "I have enough here to destroy your company, so don't you dare put your hands on either one of us."

The security team glanced between themselves. They weren't Hunters, or mages of any kind, just regular guards with heavily enchanted weapons and armor.

"I can't let you leave with that information," said Harold, eyeing the cell phone as if it were a live bomb.

Pax held her finger by the button as if she were about to hit send. "Don't make me do it."

"They'll prosecute you for impersonating IRS agents," said Harold.

"It's a price we're willing to pay," said Zayn, eyes alight with the fever of true belief. "Let us walk and we'll hand over the phone when we leave the building."

Harold looked around as if he was expecting to find an answer. "Fine. But anyone moves a finger out of place, I'm giving the orders to use lethal force. I'll tell everyone that we thought you were armed."

He gave instructions to one of the guards, who stepped into the office full of people staring into the windowed meeting room. After a quick explanation, everyone started filing out towards a back room. When the door was closed and it was only Harold and the security team, he said, "Now no one can contradict my story should it come to that. But I'd prefer for this to be over without bloodshed."

Pax kept her finger hovering over the button. The guards and Harold backed away, leaving them a narrow avenue to leave the meeting room. Heading down the space between the cubicles, Pax kept her eye on the automatic weapons rather than the elevator doors where her heart desperately wanted her to be.

"Be ready to run. Exit door on left," whispered Zayn through his teeth. "One. Two. Three."

When he hit the last number, an explosion of wind and sound blasted the guards, sending up plumes of papers and knocking the front pair backwards into the others. Pax didn't wait around to see what happened next. She flooded her magesteel imbuement for speed, heading around the corner, ducking as she expected gunfire and hitting the exit door like a freight train.

Pax had so much momentum, she nearly tumbled down the stairs in her haste to escape. Bullets slammed into the closing door as Zayn sped through the gap.

"Go, go, go."

Pax leapt down each stairwell, forgoing the individual steps. Halfway down, Zayn poked his head into the middle.

"Another team's coming up."

He tried to open the tenth-floor door, but it wouldn't budge. A badge reader blinked red at them. Zayn leaned back and front kicked the spot near the handle, denting the metal. A thick snap echoed in the narrow stairwell.

They hurried through the open door, finding themselves in a space filled with glass cages. Men and women in laboratory coats milled about the area, tending to individual creatures in the cages or strapped to a stainless steel table. The mix of unusual features—horns, wings, tails, etc.—revealed the probable source of the cobraffin.

"Those fuckers," said Pax. "They took over where Pyramid Health left off."

It took a moment for the researchers to react to the breaking of the door. They hesitated, syringes and other implements in their hands, but didn't move to escape. Zayn grabbed a huge metal desk that had to weigh hundreds of pounds and pulled it in front of the broken door.

"You," he said, pointing to a woman using a turkey baster to feed a round, furry creature with a flat face and a bright yellow beak. It looked like a baby Ur-Bear but with other features.

"How do we get out of here?"

The scientist pointed the baster towards the door and gave an awkward shrug.

"Maybe we can find emergency scaffolding," said Pax.

"Right."

They hurried through the lab as the scientists threw themselves out of their way. A long enclosure filled with dirt and small shrubs had a pair of crag worms basking in the artificial heat. Pax paused before it, hands on the glass. She wanted to smash the barrier and throw the critters at the scientists. A modified crag worm had ruined her life when she was a kid. She'd brought it home, only to have it bite her parents, turning them into angry versions of themselves, making her childhood a living hell.

A second lab looked the same as the first, except it faced the outside windows. The cages were filled with more chimeratic creatures, larger and more developed than the ones in the first room.

Banging on the stairwell door as the guards attempted to move the desk announced they were running out of time. Zayn ran to the window and pressed his face against it.

"No scaffolding. We're trapped."

Pax stuck her head into the other room to see the guards wedging the door open. They were about to break through. There was no way out.

Seventeen

Egyptian mythology had always been a favorite of Kitty's. Despite being named after a famous tsarina, she found the history of Russia far too depressing to feel affection for her namesake. There was something majestic and secretive about ancient Egypt. It wasn't hard to imagine herself as a ruler during the time of dynasties.

"This. I wasn't expecting this," said Moriganne at her side, marveling at the sight.

The enormous pyramid in the distance reflected the sunlight. It was almost too bright to look at. A second, smaller, and unfinished pyramid lay further behind. Lines of workers in white clothing moved like ants towards the structure.

"I don't see blocks," said Moriganne. "I thought they built them with blocks."

Their guide, Alex, had said nothing. As wonderous as their surroundings were, Kitty was curious about what Alex made of it. Alex reminded her of Ivan, but in a different way. If you carved away the insecurities, the addictions, and the flippant mouth, the remaining would be a lot like Alexandria Duke. Every time their gazes met, Kitty felt exposed.

"One theory is that the blocks were cast in place using a limestone mixture a lot like concrete. We might be able to confirm this theory today," said Alex.

"Where should we go?" asked Moriganne. "My only experience with Egypt was a themed set design and headdress that made my neck hurt by the end of the performance." She gestured towards the massive structures. "Head over there? Would the pharaohs be at the pyramid?"

"Whoever was the original owner of the tattoo wouldn't be at the construction site. The pharaohs spent time on the river, relaxing on barges. I can see the line of palms. We should go that direction." Kitty paused, turned towards Alex. "Will they see us? Or can we walk around freely?"

Alex adjusted her dark glasses to fit better on her nose. "The people you see will be acting of their own accord. They will likely see us as strangers, possibly dangerous."

"Right," said Kitty, "we need to find clothes that don't stick out."

They crossed the packed sand. A hot wind dried out her eyes, but she was able to apply enchantments to help with the bright sunlight.

A huge ox with many scars on its back pulled a wagon along a road towards the construction area of the pyramids. The driver had a whip in his hand, but the beast lumbered forward without requiring further encouragement. Four men sat in the back of the wagon, along with crates and sacks.

Kitty jogged alongside the wagon as the driver recoiled from her appearance.

"Hello. Do you have any clothing we can borrow in there?"

The driver held his whip up as if he might use it. Kitty hoped he would.

"Pale demons from the deep desert," he hissed. "Begone!"

At first she was surprised that she could understand his speech since she didn't speak ancient Egyptian. The arcane software must translate somehow for them.

Moriganne and Alex came up from behind. The driver whipped the ox to move faster, but the beast seemed to have one speed. Trudge. Before the whip could be used against them, Kitty leapt onto the front seat, snatched the weapon away from the shocked driver, and knocked him out with a single punch. The men in back rose to cause trouble, but she dispatched them with additional strikes. The ox was happy to stop when she pulled the reins that had been left limp against the front bench.

"We have clothes, though we might want to consider disguising ourselves. He called me a pale demon from the deep desert."

After removing her street clothes and donning the robe of one of the unconscious men, Kitty felt less conspicuous. The layered linen protected from the sun and allowed the breeze to blow through the fabric. She felt cooler. The headwrap and a modification of her face, including the browning of her skin, helped hide her gender and foreignness. She helped her sister and Alex with their disguises.

They followed the stone road towards the river's edge. Grass grew in a strip along the water. Reeds clumped together at the curves and small oxbow lakes. A barge filled with goods floated in the center of the river, being pulled by oxen using ropes from the opposite bank.

"The owner of the tattoo can't be far," said Alex, holding her hand at her forehead to block the sun.

Moriganne extended her arm towards a trio of smoke trails heading into the sky. "Back that way? I think I can feel it."

Sand blew across the stone road as they followed the path back towards the promise of fires. A group of men with bronze short swords passed them halfway to their destination. As they neared, the white stone columns of the palace grew out of the haze, surrounded by patches of green. The lines of smoke multiplied as tents and smaller buildings surrounded the larger structure.

"Is this the Malkata palace?" asked Kitty, trying to remember her Egyptian history.

"No," said Alex right away. "The Malkata palace, or the place where things are picked up, wasn't built for another thousand years, but this is an early precursor."

The area grew thick with people. Kitty saw guards with bronze weapons or bows at various points. The further they went, the more she worried about how difficult it would be to escape. Even with magic, defending against so many would be challenging. Impossible depending on how bad it got.

"Wait," said Kitty, holding her arms out to her companions. "If things go wrong here, how do we get out of the simulation? What happens if we're injured?"

Alex swiped through the air as she read a screen only she could see. A nearly imperceptible frown hooked itself on her lips.

"It appears that if we die, we'll return to the build room."

"It appears?" asked Kitty.

Alex glanced over her shoulder to where they came from and then towards the palace. "The program isn't reacting the way I think it should. Whatever power held that tattoo during this time had supremacy over more than just the land. The re-creation of that person could cause us harm. Pain at minimum. Beyond that, I think it's best we not find out. If we want to return, we'll need to get back to the place we walked through the portal."

"I don't like this," said Kitty, frowning at the busy area ahead. They'd be pushing through crowds to get closer.

Moriganne rubbed her elbow as she grimaced. "I can feel it ahead. The original owner. It hurts."

"Are you sure about this?" asked Kitty.

Moriganne tilted her head. "No, but I think we need to keep going. We need to know who it is. Maybe we can track them down in our world and get their help."

"If they exist, or aren't on Elosian's side."

Moriganne appeared pained by the suggestion. Kitty knew what her older sister was thinking. She wanted the owner of the tattoo to be someone they could count on, to tip the balance in their favor. Knowing what she did about Egypt, Kitty wasn't so sure they were going to find that here.

"We keep going, but stay close, and if we have to run, make haste."

Kitty took point, maneuvering them through the crowds that were milling about the market. Some stood before blankets, selling their trinkets, while others used their wagons or makeshift huts. The tools of commerce hadn't changed in thousands of years. She could find the same thing happening on every continent in their world.

The deeper they went, getting closer to the palace with every step, the more Kitty scanned the horizon, looking for threats and escape routes. If they had to run now, they'd easily be captured. There were too many guards, too many people, in a world she wasn't entirely sure she understood the rules of.

The palace was up ahead. White stone stairs led to a platform where men and women in tailored clothing of the time lounged beneath tents, enjoying the cool breezes coming up from the river valley. Slaves pumped palm fronds at the nobles. The figures were too far away to make out details, but one of them seemed to be wearing an elongated golden mask.

"That's him," said Moriganne, grabbing Kitty's arm so she could move no further. "The one in the mask and holding a weapon."

Kitty peered ahead. The weapon had a curved end. Like a shepherd's crook.

"Not sure it's a weapon."

Moriganne flinched, a gasp slipping out as she grabbed her elbow. The sea of people between them and the palace parted as every eye turned towards them.

"Oh no," said Moriganne. "He knows we're here."

"Shit," said Kitty as guards moved towards them, reaching for their weapons. "We need to run."

A group of guards was getting near. Kitty raised her hands to knock them back with a force wave, but Alex pushed them down.

"No magic. Not yet."

"We have to get out of here."

Alex pointed to a wagon near a side building of the palace. A group of men were unloading the contents while an ox swished its tail.

"This way."

Kitty had no time to argue, because Alex started running in the direction of the wagon, which was perpendicular to the pathway of the crowds in the bazaar. As they moved, Kitty spotted multiple groups of guards converging on their location.

"We need to be going the other way!" she called ahead. "This is a dead end!"

Alex scooped up a rock as they ran, and when they were about fifty feet from the wagon, she launched the rock in a high arc. It hit the ox's rump, surging it forward. The ox pulled further up, and Kitty saw the reason when Alex leapt onto the wagon. Before she continued, Alex grabbed a sack of grain and then scrambled across the wagon to the ox's back before leaping to the roof of the side building.

Kitty checked behind to see Moriganne only steps behind, and then dozens of guards sprinting to catch up. A group was setting up to fire their bows. She followed Alex's lead onto the roof of the building, helping her sister up when she almost leapt too short.

"It's a bottleneck here," said Alex, gesturing towards the angled roof line. "And they won't be able to hit us with arrows."

"Right," said Kitty, not understanding how Alex could have seen that in the chaos of their discovery.

She led them from the side building roof to the main one, which was a series of angles, providing ample sections that would protect them from arrows. When they reached the apex, Alex turned, holding the bag of grain in her arms. Kitty crouched behind her.

"What are we waiting for?"

A dozen guards scrambled up to the side building and then started leaping across to the angled roof that would lead them up. Kitty wasn't worried about the guards. Between her magic and curved daggers, she was certain she could make quick work of them.

As the guards headed up the incline, Alex ripped away the rope that held the top of the grain sack, spilling brown seeds onto the slick surface. The guards hit the sliding grain and immediately lost their balance, tumbling backwards, taking everyone over the edge with screams of fear and pain.

When Kitty glanced back to Moriganne, she was raising her eyebrow in surprise.

"Where to now?"

Alex scanned the horizon. "I don't know. This defensive spot will only last so long." She nodded towards the front roof of the palace. "You might be able to get a glimpse of your Lost Prince, but don't expose yourself too much or you'll find a dozen arrows in your chest."

Kitty followed Moriganne to the front. The roof blocked sight of the crowds, except those further out near the river's edge. They crept to the edge and peered over to find the man with the elongated golden mask. He wore a miter and carried a heavy rod that ended in a crook in one hand and a flail in the other.

"That's Osiris."

Kitty was certain of it. Not the actual god, but at least the imagery. She hoped.

Osiris raised his arm, and Moriganne cried out in pain, falling to her knees.

"He's got me. I can feel him in my head." Moriganne's headdress had fallen away. Spittle was thick on her lips. "Help."

Eighteen

The excitement bled into the supernatural creatures in the cages, some of whom had minor psychic abilities, causing a collective ruckus as they tapped against the glass or ran around inside their enclosures. The first guard had half his body through the gap. If he could climb through, he could easily move the desk.

"Any chance you can fly?" asked Zayn from the window.

After letting the researchers escape the secondary room, Pax closed the door and locked it. Another barrier that wouldn't last long.

"How high up are we?"

Zayn screwed up his face. "Too high to jump. I can make it to the streets safely, but I can't bring you."

Pax eyed the blue-tailed lizards in the cage. One of the lizards was stuck to the side of the glass, its suckered feet providing superior traction.

"I can get down, I hope, if you can get that window open."

Zayn put his elbow through the glass, shattering it. He knocked the pieces inside the room, so few of the sharp projectiles fell out.

"Like this?"

"Yeah."

"Hurry. I'll go after you."

He seemed apprehensive, but there was no time for questions. Pax put her hands on the blue-tailed lizard cage. The scraping spell was brief. Her fingers remembered the patterns. When it was over Pax felt disoriented. The spell should give her the ability to climb on walls, but there were limitations. Her weight was much larger than the lizard. It was possible that she could try climbing out the window, only to lose her grasp and fall to her death.

Pax stepped to the window. The wind blew her hair around.

"Hurry up. They're through the first door."

"I'm trying to hurry," said Pax, glancing out the window.

"Whatever you see after this," said Zayn, "don't be surprised. Or frightened."

She had no time to parse his meaning as she leaned out the opening, placing her hand on the outer glass. Her fingers clung to the material as if they were made of glue. She started to pull her leg through but remembered the scraping wouldn't work through her shoes. She pulled them off, socks too, and flung them out the window into the alleyway below, thankful that the window didn't lead to a busy street where they'd be sure to be spotted.

With the wind blowing her red hair into her face, Pax stuck her hands, then one foot, onto the outer window. Pulling her last leg out to be completely supported by the blue-tailed lizard ability was much harder than she expected. She glanced into the room to find Zayn, but he was behind a table.

"You can do this."

Pax pulled her foot out and stuck it to the window. It didn't feel like she should be able to hang outside, even though she'd used the spell dozens of times. She'd never attempted something so dangerous. She moved her foot down a few inches, then the other, followed by her hands. Finding that she wasn't about to fall, Pax kept moving, downward and slightly deeper into the alleyway.

Something black and furry moved above her near the window and she thought it was going to be a security guard leaning out to fire upon her, but instead it was an enormous spider the size of a large dog.

Pax loved spiders, though her experiences in the Portland Zoo Disaster left her a little less excited about them. This one, however, she knew as friendly.

"Hey Zayn," she said, smiling as she scampered down the window. "Nice trick."

The enormous spider lifted a foot in greeting, then kept moving, faster than her, headed towards the alleyway. She'd made it about two floors down when a guard leaned out the window. He spotted her seconds later and aimed his rifle at her.

Pax had been working methodically down the outside of the building, afraid to move too fast and dislodge herself, but with a rifle pointed in her direction, she scrambled without regard to adhesion to the glass. The first shot whizzed past her face. She almost reached up to check if she'd been hit.

Reaching the bottom before the guard could fire again was impossible, so she headed to the side of the building to put the corner between her and the rifle. A second shot went past her arm. The tiny zephyr of wind left her shaken.

Pax made it around the corner before the third shot. She headed straight down, ignoring the screams of safety in her head. Especially when her fingers and toes started losing their adhesion to the window. The spell was wearing off, probably because of adrenaline. Or sweat.

The spell failed when she was still five feet up. She landed on a rotting banana peel which felt much worse upon impact until she looked at what was beneath her foot.

"Hey."

She looked up to find a naked Zayn holding her shoes before his crotch. Pax blushed and looked away. He was handsome, more so naked, displaying the webbing tattoos that covered his fit, muscular body. She could see why Aurie had a thing for him.

Pax took the shoes and slid them on. They ran to the opposite side, hoping they'd reach the street long before the guards. While he crouched by the corner, getting strange looks from the pedestrians that noticed him, she hailed a taxi. When it stopped, she opened the door and he went darting into the backseat.

"You can't be in here naked," said the driver with a thick East Coast accent.

Pax climbed in behind as Zayn sat with his hands in his lap. "I'll pay triple."

The driver glanced between them and then turned back around, shaking his head.

"This city sometimes. I guess this isn't the weirdest thing that's ever happened to me."

Zayn gave his address to the driver.

"What is the weirdest?" asked Pax, hoping to keep him distracted on the question and not the group of men with rifles running down the sidewalk towards their location as the taxi pulled into traffic.

"One time a few years ago, some kid leapt over my taxi, running faster than some of the cars as if the world was on fire."

Zayn chuckled. "You don't say..."

Pax continued talking with the driver so she wouldn't notice Zayn's nakedness any more than she already did. She loved Okho and was devoted to him, but Zayn made her flush, and the excitement of the chase left her shaking slightly.

When the taxi dropped them off, she let him go first, regretting it as she stared at the tight dimples in his naked ass. She was pretty sure she could bounce a quarter off it. A little old woman in a floral housecoat waved at him as he headed inside.

"I think you have a fan."

Kali greeted them when they went inside. Zayn went immediately to his room for clothes, while Pax crouched down with her companion.

<Stay in other room for Pax mating?>

"No, dear one, just flustered from nearly getting killed."

Pax sent Kali a mental picture of what had happened, including the climb down the outside of the building and the naked ride to his apartment.

<Mating not love mating help relax.>

Zayn returned wearing dark jeans and a deep blue, V-neck T-shirt.

Humans don't work like that, she said to Kali as she stood up.

<They should.>

Pax chuckled, bringing a tilted head from Zayn. "Something funny?"

"Kali's read on the world is much different than ours." Pax pulled out the phone. "Shall we?"

"First, let me get our faces back," he said, dismissing the enchantments that created the disguise. He plopped down on the couch afterwards. "What did you find out? I was so focused on keeping them busy that I barely looked at a single document."

Pax took the spot opposite and Kali climbed up next, laying her head on her thigh. She still couldn't get the vision of Zayn's naked body out of her head and stared into the phone as a distraction, even though she knew what she'd read by heart.

"As I feared, Pyramid Health, which was working with modified crag worms to create new materials for making drugs and other elixirs, moved their research to Phoenix Corporation before they went under. That lab was filled with supernatural creatures, some of them chimeratic. The others I assume were for using as templates. I found a significant amount of money focused on their R&D section. I wouldn't be surprised if they were the ones to make the cobraffin. They had everything you'd need in that lab to do it."

Zayn nodded with understanding. "Nice save with the Supernatural Animal Liberation Army of Determination thing. You had them spooked. Also, you know the acronym is S.A.L.A.D.?"

"It's from a comic I read," said Pax, chuckling.

"Any idea why they're making the chimeras? Were there any documents explaining it?"

"Nothing I found," said Pax. "When Pyramid was modifying the crag worm, it was purely for capitalistic reasons. They wanted to make money. The big one we released into the ocean they called the money worm because its secretions had been turned into countless drugs. But this? The cobraffin has no money-making possibilities that I'm aware of. It's a glorified attack dog."

"Elosian?"

"Maybe? Probably? I have no way of knowing since we don't know how his whispers work. Does he talk to people? Come to them in a vision?" She snapped her fingers. "Oh, there was something else. In the organizational documents. There was a name that came up a couple of times, once on the board, and again as a consultant for the Supernatural Morphology division. It appears they provided information that helped them with a number of breakthroughs. But most of the documents spent more time avoiding the name, as if they were afraid to bring it up. For obvious reasons."

"What was the name?" asked Zayn, leaning forward with his elbows on his knees.

"Leonidas Dreadmarsh."

Nineteen

Moriganne squeezed her arm as if the pressure could keep the pain out of her elbow. The tattoo burned black. Not the embers of power, but something different. She could feel the man in the Osiris mask probing her mind. Kitty and Alex were doing something nearby, but she couldn't see them anymore, the pain was so great.

"Help."

They crouched by her side. "What's wrong?"

"Osiris. He's in my mind."

Moriganne was vaguely aware that Kitty stood up, leaned over the edge of the roof, and threw something. As if a balloon had popped, the invasion ended, leaving Moriganne breathing heavily. The relief was almost pleasurable.

"We have to go," said Alex, tugging Moriganne to her feet.

When she stood, she caught sight of the greenish, mottled flesh of Osiris as he picked up his golden mask. After her time in Montanhas and coming face-to-face with Elosian, she was sure that he came from the demonic realm.

The guard that had tumbled from the roof had returned, but Alex simply ducked under the swipe of his sword and shoulder charged him into his brethren. The whole lot slid back down, the cries of impact reaching Moriganne's ears as she fled away from the front of the palace. The effortless way Alex was dealing with the various threats had Moriganne wishing she'd been around during the fight with the mantic or Nandi and her friends.

The back of the palace was higher than the terrain, requiring a twenty-foot drop. The soldiers had regained the roofline, heading their direction with swords drawn.

"Drop and roll when you hit," said Kitty, landing in a crouch.

"Easy for you to say," said Moriganne.

The impact went through her knees. She managed to roll forward, but jammed her shoulder into the earth. Sand got in her mouth, and she spit it out as Alex helped her up, looking no worse for the drop.

"What now?" asked Moriganne.

"We run," said Kitty.

The three of them took off across the hardpacked sand. As they circled around the rise that backed the palace, Kitty glanced backwards and cursed under her breath.

"Chariots."

Dust rose up from behind the wheels of six chariots thundering towards them. There were at least two soldiers per vehicle. Moriganne thought she saw a few bows as she ran to keep up with Alex and Kitty.

"Are we allowed to use magic yet?" asked Moriganne.

"Be my guest," said Alex.

Moriganne faced the oncoming chariots. She brought the song quickly, as they were closing fast. Within a few notes, gusts whipped across the ground, grabbing sand and dust and throwing it into the air. As she used the tattoo to add power to the winds, she felt a competing tug from beyond the palace. Osiris had sensed her use of the bridge and was attempting to take control. She let the song drop, fearing what might happen if he won. The cloud of dust started dissipating.

"This should do," said Alex as she strode forward, pulling back the sleeves of her shirt. "Get behind me."

They both stood behind her as the chariots approached at great speed, undaunted by the dust cloud.

"What are you waiting for?" asked Kitty with alarm as the lead chariot was only fifty feet ahead and closing fast.

Forty. Thirty. Twenty.

Moriganne braced for impact.

At the last moment, Kitty blasted the ground with a force wave. The angle of her spell sent the chariot directly into the path of the one to its right. The line of three vehicles came apart as they cascaded into each other, horses, men, and equipment flinging everywhere.

The other three went past, having had to veer away from the impact of the spell, but were circling around. Back towards the palace, a group of soldiers with weapons were running their direction.

"We're trapped," said Moriganne as Alex grabbed the reins of a horse that had managed to avoid getting injured. Alex swung herself onto its back and held out a hand for Moriganne. "Or not, I guess."

"I'll run," said Kitty, sprinting ahead towards the chariots that had circled around.

As Moriganne put her hands around Alex's waist, the horse took off after Kitty, and Osiris resumed his attack. She held on tight, even as the pain in her arm made the world distant. Moriganne fought against him, but found herself slowly losing. If he managed to get control of the tattoo, she was certain it would be very bad for her.

"Faster," she muttered.

Moriganne had no idea what happened with the oncoming chariots. She was only aware of a second crashing sound and the swirl of sand and dust pelting her exposed flesh. Osiris' hold on her mind grew more complete. She felt herself slipping away, barely able to hear Alex's encouraging words.

She managed to open her eyes to see the black rectangle of the portal standing in midair, waiting for their arrival. But it was too far away. Osiris nearly had control. The world faded from view. She was lost.

Twenty

The store looked like any other business in the seventh ward. Gadget Girl Games had a brightly colored cartoon-y woman on the front, playing with something that had blown up in her hands. The wild eyes and joyful glee was almost maniacal, leaving Zayn to chuckle as he stepped out of the way of a mother and daughter leaving the store with three boxes, chatting excitedly about their project when they returned home.

"We're meeting someone here?" asked Pax incredulously.

"Not meeting," said Zayn, holding the door open for Pax and Kali. "She owns the place."

The interior was filled with products that exploded, transformed into different colors, or did any number of exciting and potentially dangerous things. There were basic alchemy sets and trinkets that were more well-made than the crap tourists bought on street corners. There were many shops like this one in the city, but Gadget Girl Games knew its audience. The shop was packed with dozens of girls, half of them with their mothers. There were a few boys, but they were the minority.

"I need to see Maggie," said Zayn to an employee when they approached to ask if they needed help.

They were led to the back of the shop and through a warded door. Zayn smelled gunpower and thermite.

A bright flash of light from the back of the workshop was followed by a round of cursing in Scottish. A woman wearing tan cargo shorts and a white tank top smudged with grease was putting out a small fire on the table with her hands. She looked like a rounder version of Lara Croft. A long steel-gray braid hung over her shoulder.

"Zayn fucking Carter, my *acushla*," said Maggie, opening her arms to embrace him as he approached. Her Scottish accent was thicker than normal, turning *fucking* into *fooking*. She smelled like oil and mint. "You damn near shocked my tits off. I thought you and Pri were off dallying with those gray-skinned fuckers."

Before he could speak, she leaned her head to the side to appraise Pax and Kali.

"Why, aren't you a couple of sweet things," said Maggie. "Is this your girlfriend and her pet doggie?"

Pax crossed her arms, even as Kali approached Maggie for scratches around the ears.

"I'm just bustin' your balls, girl. I know this one ain't a doggie. You're the girl from the zoo, ain't ya?" asked Maggie as she crouched down to embrace Kali, who was greeting her like an old friend. Pax frowned at the betrayal.

"I am."

"You're a right bastard then." Maggie winked. "The good kind. Not many folks would go back into a shitshow like that. If you're a friend, or girlfriend of Zayn, you're a friend of mine. I assume you're not here to reminisce."

Zayn gestured towards her. "Pax, this is Instructor Maggie O'Keefe. If there was something that needed to be blown up, or turned into something else, she was the woman to do it. And this, as you've deduced, is Pax Nygard and her companion, Kali."

"Aye, she already told me," said Maggie. "No need for the instructor bullshit, Zayn, you've more than graduated. How are things?"

Feeling a little more loquacious in her presence, Zayn said, "In a word, fucked. You got a few minutes?"

"For you, I got all the time in the world."

"I wish we had that much time."

Maggie crossed her muscled arms. Zayn went into an explanation of the last few days since he'd returned from the Eternal City. He left out the more dangerous details like the bridge tattoo, but went into Elosian's machinations and the existence of the Lost Prince since that was a major point of their plan. Maggie cursed under her breath at the more shocking parts of the story. When he was finished, she paced away, shaking her head.

"Always been Pri's blind spot," said Maggie as she came back. "Always seeing the next threat but not the one right in front of her damn eyes."

"To be fair, things are pretty tight in the Eternal City. She's not wrong, and as she's told me a thousand times, there are plenty of people focused on the demonic realm, and not enough on all the others."

"Whatdya need from me besides giving your boss a right kick in the britches?"

Zayn repressed a smile as Pax stared at Maggie with her mouth hanging open.

"We're going to go talk to someone we suspect might not be who we think they are, and we wanted the right tool for the job. Neither of us have much knowledge about demonic runes or anything like that."

"I'm not much of an expert either," said Maggie, knitting her forehead.

Pax spoke up. "We don't need expert, we just need discreet and workable."

"Who's the target?"

"Leonidas Dreadmarsh."

Maggie looked like she'd been slapped. "You've gone off your fucking rocker if you're thinking of messing with Leo Dreadmarsh."

"We're not messing with him. We think he might be the Lost Prince."

Maggie frowned. "Aye. I can see why'd you think that."

"We thought we were on the trail of a potential ally, but now we're concerned that he's in league with Elosian given the evidence," said Pax.

"Not much evidence," said Maggie.

"True," said Zayn, "which is why we want to meet with him, see if we can uncover more. Before you tell us we're crazy, I would do this a thousand other ways, but we're rapidly running out of time. We need answers. Fast. The invasion is nearly upon us. We need all the help we can get, or at least need to know who we're up against."

Maggie stared at the door leading to the shop portion of her store.

"You really think it's here?"

"Invictus does," said Pax.

"The Dreadmarsh family is not one to be trifled with. They were a power long before the Halls," said Maggie.

"Which is why we think he might be the Lost Prince," said Zayn.

Maggie pumped her eyebrows and blew air into her cheeks before exhaling.

"A possibility. Leo and Olympia are far older than they let on. The rest of the family grew up around them. Even his brother Magnus really isn't his brother," said Maggie.

"What about his daughter, Victoria?" asked Zayn.

"She's their flesh and blood as far as anyone knows, but it seems strange to have a child after hundreds of years. Or more." Maggie screwed up her mouth as if she'd thought of something. "I know I've asked this already, but are you sure about this?"

"Why? What did you think of?"

"There've always been rumors about where Leo and Olympia got their strength. Demonic rituals long before they were forbidden was the betting line, but maybe that was a front. A story concocted to keep people from seein' the truth."

"The Lost Prince," said Pax.

"The Lost Prince." Maggie nodded. "Aye, if you're gonna talk to him, you're gonna need something that does more than checks for demonic heritage, because that's a damn near certainty. What you need is something more clever. You need to know how old he is."

"You can do that?" asked Pax, perking up.

"I can't help you figure out if he's the Lost Prince, but I can at least tell you if he's not, and leave open the possibility. The rest you'll have to figure out on your own."

"Even if we can prove he's not, that would be a big help," said Zayn.

Maggie nodded. "Give me an hour."

While she got to work, Zayn huddled with Pax.

"Are you sure about this?" she asked.

"No, but do you have a better idea?"

"No." Pax checked back towards Maggie. "I like her."

"Hard not to, unless you get on her bad side, then watch out."

Pax grinned, but then it faltered. "What happens if we piss off Leo? I know nothing about these old powerful families. I'm way in deep."

"Back before magic wasn't treated like an affliction, or hunted like an abomination, everyone who used it kept their abilities hidden. Except the Dreadmarshs. They bribed or blackmailed politicians. Probably threatened them too. Had huge private armies to protect them. Going against the Dreadmarshs was tantamount to suicide."

"And you want to track him down and accuse him of being an ally to the worst demon in all the realms?"

"We. Unless you're not coming along."

"Yes, we," said Pax with a sigh.

"I'm not planning on accusing him, but we need to know where he stands. If he's the Lost Prince, or an agent of Elosian, or something else entirely. We have to know, otherwise it's going to make our defense more difficult." Zayn pulled out his phone. "Which is why I need to make a few calls and get an invite for a meeting."

"You can do that?"

He winked at Pax. "One of the benefits of working for Priyanka Sai. Her name can open a lot of doors that would normally be closed."

"Some doors should be left closed," said Pax.

"As long as we don't piss him off, we should be fine," said Zayn.

It sounded good in his head, but he could tell Pax didn't believe it. She found a stool and gathered Kali against her knees while Zayn pulled up his contact list and thought carefully before he made his first call. Whoever he talked to would pass the information along to Leo Dreadmarsh. Zayn needed a good first impression.

"Hello? Yes, I need to speak to Patron D'Agastine."

Twenty-One

Kitty paced around the room where Alex had brought them. Moriganne sat on the floor against the couch, holding a cold can of energy drink against her forehead looking like she'd gone three rounds with a championship boxer.

"We shouldn't go back in," said Kitty. "I don't know exactly what happened, but you said he was in your mind. If we go back, he might be able to get you, unlock it, or break it. It's too risky."

Alex watched them with an unnerving level of blankness. Kitty was used to reading people, but the Gamemaker's Hall alumnus displayed an unusual amount of discipline about her visible emotions as if she were controlling everything they saw. Kitty tried not to let it distract her, but she kept glancing back in hopes that Alex might break and let a little of her inner thoughts out.

"I'll be fine," said Moriganne. "Alex said if we go into a new memory, the one from Egypt won't know because it's an entirely new simulation."

"*Probably* won't know," said Kitty.

"Did you get the information you needed?" asked Alex.

Kitty responded at the same time as her sister. "No."

"And the information is critical?"

Kitty looked to Moriganne, who pulled the can away from her forehead. "Yes."

"Then continuing into the other memories would be the best course of action. Knowing what I know now about this Lost Prince, I think I can direct us towards less hazardous memories."

"Are you sure?" asked Kitty.

"Nothing is certain."

"Mori?"

Her sister lifted her shoulders. "You know my opinion."

"Will Osiris react like that every time?" Kitty asked Alex.

She adjusted her glasses. "I can't say for certain. This Lost Prince either gave up or lost his power. Or at least part of it. That suggests something traumatic happened, or they had a change of heart. It might not be safe to interact with Osiris until after that happens, but since the bridge tattoo was no longer connected, you'll never know unless you look at the exact time that he gave it up."

"Can you do that?"

"Not without risk."

Moriganne popped the top of the energy drink, took a long swig, and then wiped her mouth with the back of her hand. "It tastes exactly like it should." She looked up, dark clouds in her eyes. "We can't go back to any time he exists."

"I can take you to the time afterwards. There's a long period of almost nothing. It'll be easy to take a look."

Moriganne nodded and climbed to her feet. Kitty watched how unstable her sister was. The battle in her mind had taken a lot out of her. She was tough, had won control of the body she was in, even though it wasn't hers, but battling a major figure from the demonic realm was a different level of challenge.

"I'll be fine," said Moriganne when she caught Kitty looking at her.

"Are we ready?" asked Alex with her fingers poised in midair.

"The show must go on," said Moriganne.

The rectangular portal opened up again. Alex stepped through first. Kitty didn't know what to expect, but it wasn't the entrance to a cave in the deep forest.

"It smells like petrichor," said Moriganne, smiling. "It's refreshing."

Rain was pattering through the trees. Faint sunlight turned the entrance to the cave a dark green. Mottled, diffuse shadows were a kaleidoscope across the muddy stretch leading to the opening.

"Where is this place?" she asked.

Alex squinted at an invisible screen. "Somewhere in Eastern Europe."

Kitty started moving into the forest, raindrops hitting her in the forehead as she looked to the sky.

"Not out there." Alex gestured into the cave. "It's in there."

"In there?"

Even though this was a memory contained within the bridge tattoo, and Kitty had been in much worse places, heading into the cave brought a shiver of concern. It felt like a trap.

After applying an enchantment, Moriganne headed into the darkness. When Kitty caught up and arched an eyebrow, she said, "I don't sense it, or anyone for that matter."

The cave narrowed down, forcing them to walk in a squat for a few meters before it climbed up into a dry space that was quite large. Kitty was busy craning her neck, when her sister broke away, headed to the back. The mural on the stone wall took her breath away.

"When is this?" she asked Alex.

"A few hundred B.C."

Moriganne was reaching out towards the wall. Kitty grabbed her hand before her fingers brushed the stone.

"It's like the painting, but different."

"Look, don't touch," said Kitty.

Without having to worry about her sister, she focused on the detailed mural. The bridge was the obvious center point of the picture, but the rest of it made her head swim.

"What is the place it's showing?" asked Kitty. "It's hard for my eyes to pick out the details."

The landscape was fractal-like. There were two obvious and different areas connected by the bridge, which was different than the version on Moriganne's arm. Her sister was studying the two, looking back and forth.

"Is it connecting two mountain ranges?" asked Kitty.

"It's the demonic realm," said Alex flatly.

"The original painting, the one I got this from, was a scene of old European idyllic beauty. At least on the surface. There was a town and a thick forest, not unlike what's outside of here." Moriganne cupped her chin in her hand. "In the details there were horrific scenes, children screaming, sacrifices in the woods. There's none of that here."

"But there's a lot more," said Alex, gesturing to the upper-right corner. "That looks like something that might be called a castle. There's another on the opposite side."

"Why a bridge?" asked Kitty. "Why place your power in the image of a bridge?"

"A bridge is a metaphor for connection, communication," said Moriganne. "Songwriters have been using bridges in their music for decades, centuries. You burn bridges when you're no longer communicating, you travel across them to symbolize change, or meet with an idea or place that you were previously unfamiliar with."

"It's a symbol for the place between the living and the dead," said Alex grimly.

Kitty caught the crack in their new companion's exterior. She'd experienced something about life and death. It was the only time thus far that she'd caught sight of the person underneath the brilliance.

"It can be family," said Moriganne, smiling at Kitty.

"Oh, shit," said Kitty with sudden realization. "Montanhas."

Moriganne turned towards her. "What about it?"

"The other kinds of demons. Remember how Ares had to find new runes to protect us because the others weren't working? We already know the demonic realm isn't a monolith. Maybe that's what this is showing. Whoever the Lost Prince is, they tried to bridge the two sides.

Maybe they failed and then fled to our realm."

"A possibility," said Moriganne, neck craned at the mural.

No one said anything for a few minutes.

"It's speaking to me. Whispering," said Moriganne breathlessly.

"What is it saying?" asked Kitty without looking over.

"I don't know, I don't understand the words. Longing? I can't tell if it's lonely from being stuck in here, or if it senses I have the real bridge and is wanting to reconnect," said Moriganne, her expression turning sour. "Can we leave?"

"Ready for the next jump?" asked Alex.

They went back to the outer portion of the cave where the rectangular portal waited. Stepping through brought them back to the exact same place, but it was clearly a different time. The trees had lost their leaves and clumps of snow covered the branches. White breath formed on their lips.

"Tracks," said Alex, looking down.

Someone had gone into the cave. Moriganne looked white, forehead knitted with concern.

Alex headed into the space they'd been in only moments ago, but was now probably centuries later. The flickering light of a torch reached them from the narrow section. They stayed in a crouch, watching a figure stare at the mural.

It wasn't until Kitty was examining the figure that she realized he didn't have a torch. Flame licked from his hand, the sign of a mage. An ancient mage. He wore dirty leathers, and his hair was crusted into a wave behind his head. He was muttering, laughing, bouncing from foot to foot as he took in the mural like a child about to climb onto a roller coaster.

When he reached out towards the bridge, Alex tugged them away. Kitty wanted to stay and watch until she saw the heavy haze in Moriganne's eyes. She looked about to go under a trance.

They helped her out as a scream erupted from the inner cave. It went on until they reached the portal. Moriganne stood with her hands over her ears and her mouth open in agony. Alex made a few motions on her invisible screen and they stepped through again.

"Broken hells," said Moriganne on the other side.

They hadn't left the forest, but there was no cave. It was nighttime. Kitty smelled smoke.

"Are you okay?"

"He was a man. A mage, bent with madness. I felt his screams as the bridge invaded his mind." Moriganne looked up with apprehension. "Where are we now?"

"I thought there was one more area you might want to see, but if you don't, we can go back," said Alex, squinting in the darkness.

"No, let's go. Maybe we can understand a little something," said Moriganne.

Kitty put a hand on her arm. "Are you sure? The Ginger Man wasn't the original owner."

"I want to see," said Moriganne, pushing past, heading into the forest. Even with her enhanced senses, Kitty couldn't tell where the smoke was coming from, but her sister strode forward unerringly.

The closer they got, the more Kitty thought it'd been a mistake to enter the tattoo in search of secrets. Moriganne seemed injured by the experience, the trauma of the past made real. Hopefully it would only be temporary.

Shapes moved through the forest as the light of torches illuminated the trees. A great bonfire rose above the canopy. On a rise at the center of the lighted area, a wicker god stood high above the people. An altar had been built at its feet, and a priest in robes awaited the approach of petitioners.

Kitty pulled her sister back from approaching too close. They watched as a young man fell to his knees before the priest. After a moment of contemplation, a knife sliced through his throat, spilling blood, and the body was pulled away. Kitty didn't need to get any closer to know the priest was the Ginger Man. They watched for a few more minutes until Moriganne nodded.

Returning to the portal was a solemn affair. Knowing about the ritual murder and seeing it were two entirely different things. Alex sent them back to the waiting room.

"Did you get what you needed?"

Kitty said, "No," at the same time Moriganne said, "Yes."

"I don't know who the Lost Prince is," said her sister, staring at the floor. "But I understand the sigil better. Its owner too."

"Did you see through it?"

"Back in Egypt," said Moriganne heavily, "I felt his hunger. The need for power. Though we didn't see it, Osiris made the pharaohs provide him with sacrifices to feed the tattoo. Or to feed him. Or both. Eventually he must have seen what he was doing. He gave up the tattoo, left it in the cave. It was there for a long time. Centuries, maybe a millennium. Time changed it.

"The bridge knew I was in the cave. Then the Ginger Man came. A mad mage called by it. It needed someone with magic, but few were able to wield it at the time. The bridge couldn't be picky, had to take what was there to escape. I don't know if it was the faez madness or the echoes of the past from the tattoo that led the Ginger Man to become the blood-soaked wicker god of the forests, but slaughter he did.

"Eventually he lost the tattoo. I'm sure we could find that moment, but I don't know if I care. The story of the bridge isn't his, even though he held it for a long time."

Moriganne squeezed her eyes closed. Kitty worried that she would fall over, but her sister remained solid. Still.

"I see it now," said Moriganne. "Our world is different than the demonic realm in many ways. The Lost Prince came here to escape, but found himself caught by the bloodthirsty cycle of staying at the top. Holding onto power required constant refreshing of the tattoo, sacrifices in this case. In the demonic realm, power was easier to grasp, but in our realm, it required the flesh of mortals. Eventually he saw that power like that was poisoning him, changing him irrevocably, so he gave up the tattoo, put it in the cave. But power like that isn't easily discarded. Eventually the tattoo found a host." She stared at her arm. "Oh, why did I come here? Now I can feel the weight of its countless murders. I'm carrying an abomination. I feel sick."

Kitty went to console her sister, but Alex held her hand out.

"You said you could feel the Lost Prince? What did you feel in the moment that he gave up his power?"

Moriganne wavered on her feet, eyes still closed, lost in the horrors of the past.

"He wanted a different way. The bridge had been a symbol just like you said. A connection between peoples. Of family. But he'd ruined it. He had to discard it and find a new path. There was still the desire for power and prestige, but not at the cost of civilization. The Lost Prince didn't want this world to become like the demonic one."

Sensing what Alex had been doing, Kitty asked, "If you had to guess what he was like now, what would you say the Lost Prince is like?"

"Powerful. Wealthy. A big family. Untouchable, and probably aloof. He stepped away from being the most formidable being on Earth, so he might use his influence to protect himself, but nothing more. The Lost Prince won't want to help us. He's already run away once. He'll never be an ally. He only wants to save himself."

Twenty-Two

Sentinels of towering oaks stood guard on the long road leading to the shining white building. Black limousines, Maserati Fireballs, and other wildly expensive vehicles dropped off their owners near the huge fountain. Old wealth knew no boundaries.

The Magdalena Club was a half hour outside of Invictus proper, but it could have been in his home town. Zayn hated it. It reminded him of the Lady of Varna's plantation—vast, pristine windows hiding the ancient rot within. He spit on the ground when he climbed out of the rental Obscura, trying to rid his mouth of the bitter ashes of his past. The attendant didn't react to his display, but hesitated when the enormous Kali came around the corner.

"I'm sorry, sir and ma'am. There are no pets allowed at the Magdalena Club."

"Kali's not a pet," said Pax, crossing her arms.

They'd had to stop by a clothing store in the third ward. Neither of them had the proper attire for an upscale club. Pax had chosen a dark green sleeveless top over a white skirt, while he'd picked out a black silk suit with a purple shirt.

"We're here to see Leo Dreadmarsh," said Zayn. "You wouldn't want his guests to feel like they were being put out."

The attendant flinched. Zayn almost felt bad for the guy.

"I'm sorry. The rules are strict on this matter. I would lose my job if I let you bring your pet."

Kali let out a little whine and bumped her head against the attendant's leg, which made him soften his pained expression.

"I think she'll be okay staying here," said Pax wistfully.

The attendant looked mystified by the attention. "I'm not supposed to be..."

Pax winked. "You'll be fine. After you park the car, you can find her some water. She'll hang in the grass near the fountain."

Kali climbed back into the back of the Obscura, leaving them in front of the plantation. Before the attendant took the driver's seat, he said, "Mr. Dreadmarsh is out back watching the Spiteball game. The path under that flowery arbor leads you there."

"Spiteball?" asked Pax as they headed towards their destination.

"Rich people game. Like polo except with mages. That's all I know," said Zayn, craning his neck towards the enormous statue at the center of the fountain.

"Who's that asshole?" asked Pax.

"I don't know, but I don't think I like him."

"You're tense," said Pax, frowning. "I don't even need to sense your mind to know something about this place bothers you."

"Reminds me of Varna. The Lady lived in a place a lot like this. The town turned out every year for her Ceremony, then there were parties and random celebrations. The thin veneer of civilization covering the horrors beneath. Even after all this time, whenever I think of that place, it makes my blood run hot. Keelan sacrificed himself for us to escape her grasp."

"You still take her poison."

Zayn reached to his elbow. Thousands of needle pricks in his lifetime. The price for living.

"That'll always be a part of me. Like old scars. You can never truly escape the past, but you can move beyond it. Create something new. Something better." He looked up at the side of the white building. "Maybe that's why I hate this place. All they've done is recreate the past. They're not trying anything new. For all their wealth, they're dead inside."

A cheer from ahead brought their heads up and into the present. Zayn reflexively checked to make sure the runed metal ball that Maggie had made for him was still in his inner pocket. If he pressed the button on the outside, it would send out a pulse of disruption that would interfere with protective enchantments, followed by a second wave that would attempt to understand Leo's true age. They wouldn't know for sure if he was the Lost Prince, but it could eliminate him from consideration.

Zayn hoped using it wouldn't cause an incident, but they were desperate for answers. A huge field surrounded by white tents lay ahead. Something dramatic had happened, because a group of medics in uniforms that would have looked relevant during the world wars were helping a young man from the pitch while bright flashes of magic erupted from behind them. Horses thundered across the grass along with others on foot and in strange padded armor.

An attendant spotted them as they neared. Zayn tensed up, expecting to be told to leave.

"Zayn Carter. Pax Nygard. Leo is waiting for you."

The elder Dreadmarsh's tent was the largest on the sidelines. It looked like a sultan's den inside, with ample places to lounge, a bar serving drinks, and a dozen guests milling about in clothes that were at the same time more casual and more formal than the ones they were wearing. A small chandelier hung from the center of the tent. Zayn tugged on the lapel of his jacket, feeling out of place.

Leo was easily recognizable. Handsome to the point of caricature. He'd mastered the art of sculpting his face without leaving the smooth sheen of sorcery that plagued so many of the newly rich.

"Zayn. Pax," said Leo, turning towards them with hand outstretched and a magnanimous smile. He had a faintly aristocratic accent. "Thank you for joining me."

Zayn found himself liking the man even when he didn't want to. They'd invited themselves on a favor from Celesse, but he'd flipped the script and made it sound like they were his guests. Zayn noted the technique for later use.

"Mr. Dreadmarsh," said Zayn, "thank you for agreeing to see us."

A gorgeous blonde woman in a simple white dress stood next to Leo, sipping lemonade and watching the contest on the field with feigned interest. She stepped near as Leo nodded.

"This is my daughter, Victoria. She was a member of Coterie," said Leo.

"It's lovely to meet you both."

The Dreadmarshs were the subject of countless rumors. Their daughter's power was the source of much speculation, as she'd breezed through Coterie, demonstrating herself as the strongest mage to enter the Halls in a century.

"I'm going to check on Phillip," said Victoria with an eyebrow raised. "He took a good blow to the head on that last bout."

Victoria left the tent with an artful sway that had even Pax watching her leave.

"Do you enjoy the game?" asked Leo, jutting his chin towards the field.

An attendant brought them each glasses of lemonade. Zayn politely sipped his drink as Pax sniffed hers suspiciously.

"I never had much time for games in Varna."

Leo's eyes creased briefly. "You both have quite a pedigree in the Halls. Priyanka's assistant and the girl who saved a zoo."

"It wasn't just me," said Pax.

"Of course not," said Leo, "but none of that would have happened without you. The world needs more people to stand up against aggression. Even if it comes from the supernatural realm."

"That's why we wanted to talk to you," said Zayn, trying not to sound rehearsed, even though they'd gone over the potential conversation with Leo a half dozen times on the drive. "The city of Invictus is in danger. We need your help."

"If this if is a request for money, I give millions to the charities in the city and have my own foundation that's cut poverty in half in twenty years, which personally, I find quite remarkable given it was during Invictus' absence."

Zayn swallowed. Either Leo was being honest, or he had deftly avoided taking the bait.

"We're talking about more tangible threats, namely one that comes from another realm."

Leo squinted. "I assume you're not speaking for Priyanka."

"No."

"Then you're not talking about the Eternal City."

Zayn nodded once. "That is correct."

"Rumors of a demonic invasion have been going around for decades." He waved his hand. "Before you go on about faez levels in the Undercity, or the disaster in Montanhas, I'm aware of them. Many of my investments are in the city of sorcery. If there was a real danger, I would be marshalling my resources to stop it."

Pax stepped forward, fervor in her eyes. "But it is real. We've fought against creatures from the demonic realm. Agents of Elosian have tried to stop us."

Her outburst wasn't part of their plan, but it'd caught Leo off guard. He recoiled, leaning away from them as if they were contagious. Zayn sensed his roving eyes looking for someone to rescue him.

"I'm sorry, Mr. Dreadmarsh..."

"Leo, please."

"We've been through a lot in the last few days. A week ago I was in the Eternal City at the Diamond Court. I wouldn't be back here if it weren't serious."

"Then where is Priyanka?"

Zayn forced a smile. "Doing what she does best."

"Somehow I doubt that," said Leo flatly.

A crash on the field was followed by a raucous uproar from the spectators. Leo's gaze shot towards the action, which had moved from a scrum to a single woman in padded armor knocking a ball forward with stabs of force magic while three others in opposing uniforms were trying to head her off before she could reach the far side of the field.

"She's a fool," said Leo.

"The ball carrier?" asked Zayn.

"All alone, no one to support her. An idealistic view of how the game is played. She wants to be a hero," said Leo.

Before Zayn could comment the three men surged forward with sorcery. The impact looked like a car crash. The woman who'd been punching the ball forward with force magic was hit from two different directions. Her body twisted awkwardly. She was thrown into a tumble and flopped flat onto the grass.

The three opposition members knocked the ball back the other way, leaving the woman they'd knocked out to be rescued by the medic squad. The opposing players moved slowly, waiting for the horseback team members to collect around them, forming a wedge that they drove into the other team's defenses. When they crashed through the line, sending the ball into the scoring area, applause erupted from the sidelines.

"See," said Leo, "that's how the game is played. You can't split your team. Battle is all about numbers. Find ways to overwhelm your enemy to win."

"Theoretically," said Zayn after clearing his throat, "if an invasion did happen, you'd be there to support us. Right?"

Leo raised an eyebrow. "Theoretically, I would be worried about my extended family first. After making sure they were safe, I would offer my services to the defense. But there's no need. The invasion isn't happening soon. Or probably ever. The patrons have done a wonderful job of protecting the wells. The danger is less than you think."

"Invictus thinks otherwise."

"Invictus is an old fool who loves to make himself seem more important than he is." Leo's harsh response was tempered with a smile. "He's done wonderful things with the school. The Halls have made the arcane arts acceptable for the common people of this world, but he's a bit of a showman. Clever and creative with his inventions, but a showman nonetheless. Is that all you came here to ask? It seems like a waste of all our times."

Zayn glanced to Pax, who looked equally concerned. This was the part that could go wrong in many ways. As generous as Leo was to meet with them on short notice, he was a powerful man with many resources that could make their lives miserable, but they had to understand if he was an ally or enemy.

"There are rumors..." began Pax.

"There are always rumors. A man of my stature collects them like badges. When people lack the intelligence to understand the truth, they make up things to make themselves feel like they do," said Leo.

They'd been facing the match, but Zayn turned towards Leo. He wanted the elder Dreadmarsh's full attention.

"Have you ever heard of a being called the Lost Prince?"

The barest hint of recognition reflected in Leo's eyes. "Possibly. I've heard of many things in my long years."

"Do you have any ideas of who it might be? Speculation?" asked Pax.

Leo frowned. "Not a clue. I have more important things to consume my time than rumors and speculation."

Pax made a nearly imperceptible shrug. Without Kali she lacked the full complement of her psychic abilities. Zayn girded himself for the reaction to the next question.

"Are you aware that the chimeratic creatures being made at Phoenix Corporation are being used to hunt down other mages? A company that you are a board member and contributor to for R&D," said Zayn.

The genteel air inside the tent grew tense. Zayn could see Leo's entire body shifting from open and relaxed to closed off.

"How I use my expertise is entirely up to me," said Leo. "I do not appreciate the insinuation of your question."

"I'm not insinuating anything," said Zayn. "But a creature made in the Phoenix Corporation labs was used to ambush us a few days ago."

"How can you know that it was from Phoenix Corp? There are labs all over this world experimenting with chimeras," said Leo.

"We have proof."

"Then take it to the authorities. I thought you were serious people, not conspiracy minded fools like that head patron of yours." His jaw pulsed. "I think it's time our discussion is at an end."

Zayn reached for the item in his pocket. Leo took a step back, alarm in his gaze. Zayn jabbed the button with his thumb right before he produced a business card, which brought a measure of relief from the elder Dreadmarsh. As he accepted the card, the item pulsed with disruptive energy. For a brief and awful moment, half of Leo's jaw disappeared, replaced with a curve of mottled green flesh. The flash only lasted a fraction of a second, but no one in the tent could ignore that it had happened.

"It looks like they're about to score again," said Pax cheerfully.

Everyone turned towards the pitch. Leo seemed disturbed but made no comment. He checked back to them twice, before finally decreeing, "It's time for you to leave."

"Yes," said Zayn, "we appreciate the time you've spent with us and I hope that we're wrong about an invasion, but if we aren't then you'll throw your weight behind the defense. As you said about Spiteball, you can't split your team."

Leo stared back with the practiced ambivalence of someone who was always the top of the social food chain.

"Very well."

Zayn left the tent with Pax as Leo pretended to watch the Spiteball game. There were more cheers, but Zayn didn't bother looking back. He wanted to get into the car to discuss what had happened with Pax. He kept expecting a line of police vehicles to come screaming towards building as they waited for the attendant to bring their vehicle back.

It wasn't until Pax was safely driving them away from the Magdalena Club that she exhaled and glanced over to him.

"What happened? I wasn't expecting Maggie's item to do that," said Pax, eyes wide.

"Neither was I. He must use an enchantment to hide some disfigurement caused by his demonic heritage." He pulled the item out of his inner pocket. "Now to get this back to Maggie for an answer."

"Do you think he is the Lost Prince?"

Zayn shrugged. "Maybe? But even if he is, he doesn't plan on helping us, that much is for sure. If I had to bet, I'd say that if the invasion happened, he'd pack up his family and head to a far-off realm."

"Unless he's in on it with Elosian."

"I don't think so," said Zayn. "He's got too much to lose. Leo has power and influence to spare. Why give all that up? If the invasion was successful, he'd be left with ruins just like

Montanhas."

"What about Phoenix Corporation?" asked Pax.

"I don't know." He rubbed the back of his neck as he grimaced with thought. "I feel like we're missing something."

Kali whined from the back seat, placing her furry head on his shoulder. He reached back and scratched her ear.

"When the zoo disaster happened," said Pax as she turned the steering wheel, "it wasn't an accident like some speculated. Aepep was a psychic being and took control of some weak minds at critical points. Almost as soon as Aepep was revealed, the security and power systems failed. After that, the supernatural creatures in the domes became Aepep's tools."

"What are you saying?"

"We still don't know *how* it's going to happen. Leo is confident it won't because he thinks the wells will hold. It was the same in the zoo. They thought their security system would keep them safe. And it would, under normal circumstances, but Elosian isn't a normal being, just like Aepep wasn't just a flying snake."

The inkling of a possibility formed in his head, but before Zayn could pounce on it, the phone in his pocket buzzed. He almost ignored it until he saw it was from Aurie.

Interlude One

"You tellin' me they keep gold bars in their little private club?" asked Easy as he chewed on a piece of jerky.

He was sitting on a stool at one of the hidden bars on the outside of Big Dave's Town, the kind of place only the locals knew about. Easy had a tattoo of a monarch butterfly on his neck and teeth that looked like a picket fence.

"Stacks of the stuff," said Ollie, grinning.

Ollie wasn't supposed to be anywhere near Big Dave's Town. After betraying the Razor Clan a few years ago, he had a price on his head, but his old mates hadn't turned him in, because he kept bringing profitable jobs their way. As long as he made it more valuable to keep him alive, they would keep their mouths shut.

"Then why didn't you grab some?" said Easy, squinting.

"I would have but a bunch of those preppy society kids showed up. I killed one of them. Shot him right in the chest before he could even say boo."

"I don't know, Ollie. Those societies are bad mojo. Don't they have ghosts guarding their stuff? A succubus or maeho? Don't wanna have my soul sucked out."

"All fucking rumors they spread to keep people scared of them," said Ollie, bouncing on his heels. "And even if they did, I could take care of 'em. But I can't carry all that gold myself. I need a crew of four. Can you talk to Fitch and Lame John?"

"Fitch dead," said Easy, sucking on his teeth. "One of the Drops got 'em. Got the drop on 'em, as you might say." He chuckled. "Poor bastard. He finally got the nerve to ask out Delilah."

"She said yes?" asked Ollie incredulously.

"Oh, hell no. Spit in his face and told him to get out of her bar, but he figured if he could ask her out, he could ask any girl," said Easy.

"Lame John?"

"Yeah, he'd be in. You know we always got your back, especially when you bring jobs like this," said Easy with a wink. "What's the gear?"

Ollie was reaching for his back pocket when his hand tingled. He faked a cough and turned away before his flesh erupted in flame. The blue-orange flicker lasted a few seconds before he managed to squelch it on his pant leg. It'd been happening more often. Magic was spilling out of him and he didn't know why.

"You okay? Not going mad, are ya?"

Ollie spun around. "I'm not mad!"

Easy recoiled, hands held up. His mouth was a smile but his eyes were not. "Hey brother, just a joke. You know we good."

Ollie inhaled deeply, trying to control the rage in his chest. He imagined setting Easy's flesh aflame, burning that stupid tattoo off his neck.

"Here," he said, handing over the list. "I need everything here to pull off the job."

Easy took one long look at Ollie before focusing on the crumpled paper with loose handwriting.

"Whoa, that's a lot of explosives. You sure?"

"I need *everything* on that list. Everything. No compromises. No substitutes."

"Cool, cool," said Easy, arching an eyebrow speculatively. "Just checkin' if I gots wiggle room."

"Not an inch."

A stab of vertigo made Ollie close his eyes momentarily. Truthfully, he could hardly remember writing the list. If you asked him in that moment, he could probably only repeat two or three items, but he knew that he needed all of it to accomplish his goals. There was no gold, but his companions didn't have to know that, especially when everyone assumed that the society kids kept their ill-earned money in hidden vaults in the Undercity.

"When do you need this by?"

"Tomorrow."

Easy clucked his tongue. "Maybe."

"It has to be tomorrow."

"Fine. Might cost a little more on the float, but I'll do what I can."

Ollie stepped up to Easy, gripped his upper arm. "It *has* to be tomorrow."

Easy pulled his arm away. "I told you I'd do what I can. That's all I can do, brother. You gotta trust me."

The smile that came to Ollie's lips was good enough to appease Easy, even though inside he wanted to strangle his friend. If he couldn't get what he needed to stop the societies, then they'd be overrun with demons. His friends wouldn't be happy when they found out that there wasn't any gold, but what was wealth if you couldn't spend it? What they were going to do was better than gold. It was survival.

"I trust you." Ollie grinned. "We gonna be rich. Real, real rich."

Twenty-Three

Alex had never been in another Hall before. She'd hardly been outside Gamemakers, except for a few trips into the city. Now she was standing on the front of the drawbridge that led into Arcanium while a friend of Moriganne and Kitty's was arguing with a professor in a wheelchair. She wasn't the only new friend. There was a girl with red hair and a huge creature that reminded her of a wolf, but with a fox face. She was standing with a guy in a sharp suit with his arms crossed. No one looked happy. A friend of theirs, sister of Aurie, had something happen to her.

Since Bucket had contacted her to help these fellow alumni with a unique problem, she'd found herself deep inside problems she hardly understood. The search for the Lost Prince inside the tattoo seemed simple enough at first, until they'd dropped into ancient Egypt and then the deep forests of Europe. The gods of her games were real out here. Beings with immense power. Alex felt outmatched, surrounded by people with far more magical ability than her.

Moriganne kept the sleeves of her shirt pulled down to hide the tattoo, but Alex could picture it in her mind after analyzing it. Demonic wasn't the description she thought of when she saw it, but yet the proof was in the danger it presented.

Alex wasn't even sure she should be there, but when it came time to leave Gamemakers, Kitty had asked her to come along, citing that she might be of help with the problems ahead. No one had given her a second look since, except for the beast Kali, who had approached for a round of thorough ear scratching.

Aurie and Professor Mali started shouting at the same time, and a crowd of spectators formed on the street. As one of the original Halls, Arcanium attracted a fair number of tourists. The attention led to a change of location. Alex followed the others across the drawbridge without having heard the resolution of the argument.

The interior of the building reminded her of a cross between a regular university and a deconstructed library, as nooks contained shelves filled with books at every turn. She couldn't imagine what it would be like to have had real professors that wanted to teach, rather than being dropped into the middle of a vast and complex game world and having to scrape for every inch of advantage. Alex preferred her experience even if it had been brutally frustrating. Reading and memorizing facts had never interested her. Never scratched the itch that enflamed her mind whenever she had nothing to do. There wasn't much difference between a problem and a game, except the second had been made for enjoyment.

As they moved through the building, Alex found herself looking for escape routes and identifying items that could quickly be turned into a weapon. Unlike the rest of the group she was following, she lacked the magical aptitude that they enjoyed. Her Merlin scores had barely been high enough for entry, while she was certain the others were at the higher end of the spectrum. If she was ever to get into a fight with one of them, she wasn't going to win it with raw talent.

When they were stopped again at the entrance of an auditorium, the redhead turned towards her.

"Who are you again?"

"Alex. Short for Alexandria."

"I caught that earlier. But why are you here?"

"I was helping Kitty and Moriganne with a problem."

Pax shifted her mouth to the side. "You're in Gamemakers?"

"Yeah."

Pax frowned. "How would Gamemakers help? I'm sorry, I'm not trying to be rude, but I'm confused."

The interaction was familiar. In high school, after one of the cheerleaders found out she was a gamer, she interrogated Alex about it, trying to figure out why she would care about games, or what she was getting out of it. She accused her of being a gamer for the attention, completely oblivious to her own spot in the high school hierarchy. Alex was well aware that if you asked most students about her Hall they'd stare back blankly. Most probably weren't aware that it *was* a Hall, let alone that it provided the contests that became the Merlin Trials or the Second Year Contest.

Alex was saved from having to answer the question when the second blockade was eased and they were allowed into the auditorium. She smelled the faez right away. An open door sparkled with golden light and at the center stood a girl that had a young face and spiked hair. She was staring at the wall, but her eyes were unfocused. There, but not there.

Pythia. Aurie's sister. She knew from the papers that they'd been the ones to rescue Invictus from a failed experiment that had trapped him in stasis for seventeen years.

Alex kept hearing the phrase Verum Locus being thrown around, which roughly translated from Latin as "Place of Truth." The presence of faez suggested that truth was found through the use of magic, and the size of the space made it a solo affair.

"This is like Gamemakers Online. But for individuals. A voyage into the self?"

"What?" asked Aurie, spinning around. "Who are you?" She'd been starting to explain what had happened when Alex had blurted out her comment. She regretted it, if only for the sea of eyes now staring at her. Especially Aurie, who was looking for someone to blame. Aurie's face was etched in pain like a parent who'd let their child get hurt during a moment of inattention.

Kitty stepped forward. "We enlisted her help investigating the origins of the bridge."

"You can't just invite people into the Order," said Aurie, facing off with Kitty. "That's not how this works."

"I didn't *invite* her into the Order. I asked for her help, and she provided it in spades," said Kitty, glancing over with a nod.

Aurie looked back into the Verum Locus at her sister. "I'm not sure now's the right time for new people. There's so much at stake."

"Ares is dead."

Kitty said it with the force of a punch, and Aurie reacted as if she'd been slapped.

"I'm sorry, Kitty. I'm a..."

Moriganne stepped forward and put her hand on Aurie's shoulder. "It's okay. You've been under a lot of stress. And now this. Tell us what happened."

Aurie went into a long explanation about Pi having visions with Elosian in them. A few of the members nodded as if they remembered the time she was speaking of. Aurie kept halting at points, navigating around the parts of the tale she wanted to avoid. Alex wasn't sure if the others noticed that or if they were too trusting because she was their friend. Not friend. Whatever held the group together wasn't friendship. Common goals maybe, but the bonds were weak.

Pi had gone into the Verum Locus to investigate the vision. Aurie made it clear that she'd told her sister that it was too dangerous, which gave Alex a good idea about the nature of both sisters and their relationship.

"Did he lure her there or did she get stuck?" asked Zayn.

Aurie balled her hands into fists, placed one against her mouth, and looked away. "I don't know."

"What do we know then?" Zayn looked to Kitty. "Did you learn anything useful in the tattoo?"

Kitty, with additions from Moriganne, explained their foray into the tattoo, beginning to end. There were glances to Alex when the flight from Osiris was described.

"In the end, we were never able to figure out who the Lost Prince was."

Zayn frowned. "We might have an answer. Not definitive, but a possibility."

In the same manner as Kitty and Moriganne, Zayn and Pax went into the tale of their investigation, from getting trapped in the basement of the villa, to the escape from Phoenix Corp, and finally the meeting with Leo Dreadmarsh. Even Alex had heard of the Dreadmarshs. It was a name that was thrown around whenever someone wanted to blame the elites for something bad that had happened. They were the great boogeymen of the modern magical world. Maybe for good reason.

"Even if it is him, he has no intention of helping. What you learned in the tattoo's past confirms that. The Lost Prince gave up his power, probably to blend in," said Zayn.

"What about the item? Did you figure out his age like you planned?" asked Moriganne.

"Yes and no. He's old. Older than he lets people believe. At least a thousand years, but the item wasn't clear about the exact age. Maggie thought he could be anywhere from a couple thousand to the oldest person alive."

"Or not a person," said Kitty.

"What do we do now?" asked Pax.

"I'm getting my sister back, whatever that takes," said Aurie.

Zayn looked to the others as if he was hoping someone else would say it, but then he sighed and spoke.

"You know this is a trap. That's what Elosian wants. Pick us off one by one. He knew Pi couldn't help herself. Whatever the problem is, she's going straight at it like an arrow on fire."

"I know that," said Aurie, lips pinched white. "But I'm still going."

"How? She's trapped in her own mind. Or do I not understand how the Verum Locus works?"

Aurie crossed her arms and squeezed them against her chest. "I don't know yet."

A pained silence intruded until Alex blurted out, "I can get you in."

A few of the group gave her nasty looks, but Aurie's was one of relief. Alex knew the pain she was going through, having a loved one in terrible danger and not being able to do anything about it. The problem of the Lost Prince and the impending invasion seemed like something that needed more than the six of them working on it...and it scratched an itch. Since Alex had saved Gamemakers, she hadn't had a significant enough problem to work on.

"How?"

"The same way I got them into the tattoo."

Moriganne screwed up her face. "But you put us into a simulation of the tattoo's past. We didn't actually go into it."

"Yes. But it works the same. Game world or someone's mind, the construct is similar, except for the consistency. A computer can hold the information intact, create an orderly universe with rules. A mind is less so. It's based on state of being, self-view, those sorts of things."

"You sound like you have experience with this," said Kitty.

"In a roundabout way," said Alex, thinking of Dr. Althud and the trials with the tumor.

"What would we need to do? And can we do it soon?" asked Aurie.

Zayn held out his hands. "Whoa, aren't we moving too fast? We're going to walk into a trap with blinders on. We need to be figuring out how the invasion is going to happen and focus on that. I'm sorry, Aurie, this is too risky."

"You can do both," said Alex as an idea formed. "War is a battle of resources and information. If Elosian has trapped Pi, it's likely in a construct of his own mind. It would be possible to find out how he plans on entering this world at the same time as rescuing her."

"We're not at war," said Pax, frowning.

Alex ignored her because she didn't have time to explain game theory.

"How might we do this?" asked Zayn, receiving nods from the others.

"There will need to be a distraction. Something that Elosian wants that he cannot ignore. You want to control the location of the battle. By providing a new goal, you can force him to move out of his comfort area."

"I think we all know what the distraction should be," said Moriganne with a heavy sigh, holding up her arm.

"Aren't we just giving him what he wants?" asked Kitty. "If he gets the sigil, then he won't need Pi or anything else. That might be his end goal, tricking us into offering up the tattoo."

"I don't think this is a good idea," said Pax, pacing across the front of the auditorium while Kali watched from the floor nearby. "Isn't that what Elosian does? He manipulates people into doing what he wants. To hear him is to be deceived, and all that?"

Rounds of nods quieted the burgeoning excitement. The fear of Elosian's manipulation had let the air out of their strategy. But Alex didn't see it the same way.

"He doesn't see the future, does he?" she asked.

A few blinks. A head tilt or two.

"Not that we know of," said Kitty.

"It's not possible," said Aurie, looking up. "Or at least Pi explained as much. The best you can do with predictive magics is improve your chances."

"If he can't see the future then this Elosian isn't invincible or omnipotent."

"One of his whispers killed Ares," said Pax. "We think."

"That's just strategy." She saw the hardening of their expressions. She was losing them. "I'm sorry. I know he was your brother, and your friend. But as I said before, war is about information and resources. If Elosian was all-powerful, he would have won already. If you have perfect information then you'll win every time. No question."

"Then how does he get in the heads of so many people?" asked Kitty.

"Spycraft," said Alex with a shrug. "The same way countries get foreigners to act on their behalf. Money. Fame. Fear. The two of you should know that." She nodded towards Kitty and Zayn. "Elosian might be a demon lord, a five-star general of his realm, with fingers—"

"Tentacles," said Moriganne.

"Tentacles reaching into many places here, but he's just one being. One mind. The worst thing you can do in a fight is overestimate your foe, give them powers they don't have."

"We shouldn't underestimate him either," said Zayn.

"Clearly that's not a problem right now."

Aurie faced Moriganne. "Are you willing to use yourself as a distraction so we can go after my sister?"

Moriganne's gaze shifted around the room. "If we have a good plan. Maybe."

"There would be two goals to the plan. Get Pi out and figure out where Elosian is planning to break through the barrier and how."

Moriganne shook her head. "It'd be nice to take the fight to him for once. I feel like we're constantly jumping at shadows, worried that our choices are going to lead to chaos."

"Which is a great place to be if you're him," said Alex. "If everyone's questioning their own motives, no one's worried about his."

"What do we even do in his mind? Or is it Pi's?" asked Pax.

"To keep her trapped, it would have to be in his mind," said Alex. "Which gives us the opportunity to discover the truth. Our minds want structure, so even in our subconscious, we create a representation of our world. It'll be just like a simulation. If we can overwhelm him with problems, we can break Pi free of the mental prison and hopefully come away with the information we need at the same time."

"Who should go?" asked Zayn.

"The more the better. The way to win a battle is to overwhelm your enemy, reduce the number of options they have, force them into a losing choice. Overwhelm him. Make it impossible for him to keep a prison in his mind," said Alex.

"We can't have everyone go in," said Kitty. "Someone needs to watch us."

"How are you going to distract him?" Pax asked Moriganne.

"I don't know actually," said Moriganne. "None of us have the old summoning ritual, nor would I have the first clue on how to cast it."

"Pi could do it," said Aurie.

"Or Ares," said Kitty.

There was a long silence. Alex didn't have a clue on how to make the distraction work. It was a level of magical scholarship she was unacquainted with. The plan had been coming together until that point.

"I can do it," said Pax suddenly. "Well, I *think* I can do it. I'm not actually sure, but I have an idea. When you tracked down the woman, Mary Seder, the one who threw the turpentine on the wards to ruin them, Elosian killed her. Gave her a brain aneurism, or something. If we could find another one of his whispers, someone he has a connection with, me and Kali could use that to open up a gateway. Lure him out with Moriganne. We could provide the conduit, kind of like you're going to do with Pi."

"Do we know another of his whispers?" asked Zayn.

"Whoever killed Ares is one," said Kitty. "But we would have found him already if we could."

"Wait," said Moriganne, "the police report said that the killer had gotten into the benehajar with a key."

"A lot of people have keys," said Kitty.

"Not the key that the killer had. It opened the outer door, the one that leads into the Undercity."

"A passage that was blocked with concrete," said Kitty.

"But it wasn't always. My point is that the killer got the key from someone high up in the societies, a current member."

"Beckett Dreadmarsh," said Aurie and Kitty at the same time.

"Exactly," said Moriganne. "The killer was just a conduit for Elosian. The high faez residue proved as much, but he's not the only one. I doubt he was the one to steal the key."

Kitty snapped her fingers. "I bet it was someone close, maybe a cleaning woman or something. We always had to worry about the staff stealing from us."

"If you go after her, she'll just keel over and die like the other one."

"Not if I find her first," said Pax. "Kali and I can keep her under. Might help if we have an elixir too."

"I think we have the outline of a plan," said Aurie, nodding towards everyone while Alex grinned behind her hand.

"It sounds like it," said Zayn.

"Pax, Moriganne, and Kali track down the housekeeper." Aurie turned towards Alex. "What do you need for getting into Pi's mind?"

"A short trip across the city. With a little help, I could be back by this afternoon. We could be in her mind by the evening."

"This is gonna work," said Aurie. "I think this is gonna work."

Alex nodded, smiling along with the rest of them. They looked optimistic, determined. She believed it was possible. The chances were better than zero. Not much more than a few percent, ten if she was being generous, but when had chance ever stopped her before?

Twenty-Four

"Kidnapping. Knockout drugs. And if she dies, you can probably throw murder on the list, even if it wasn't us who killed her," said Ivan.

Pax watched as Ivan paced around the third floor of Ares' old place, which they had cleaned out for the distraction. Abducting Beckett's housekeeper had been easier than Pax had thought possible, but four mages and one psychic companion turned such problems trivial.

"I'm sorry, Ivan, you know this is important," said Moriganne.

"Oh, I wasn't complaining," he said, looking up with a grin. "I used to keep a list of all the different laws I'd broken. For fun. I get to add three more to the list. I'm up to twenty-nine, but that depends on if you count the butt ones."

His girlfriend, Audrey, punched him in the arm. "Ivan. You need to destroy that list. Imagine if the cops found it."

While they continued their banter, Pax crouched on the floor to check on the housekeeper. Laila Krasnova. Older than them by a decade. Nails nicked, no sign of polish, with calluses across the palms from manual work. Even asleep the woman looked tired.

Kali lay down next to the woman.

<Busy mind.>

"Busy mind?"

<Awake not awake.>

Ivan's elixir had worked well. He'd brewed it up in a half hour. Said he'd never made one before. His siblings had called him brilliant. She was beginning to understand why, even if he seemed like a mess.

"She okay?" asked Moriganne.

"Yeah. Deep sleep, nothing more. Kali was checking on her."

When Pax looked at Moriganne, she had a hard time reckoning that she was nearing eighty years old behind those eyes.

"You don't seem your age," she said.

Moriganne chuckled. "Getting thrown into this world made me learn to swim fast or drown."

"That sounds like my entire Animalians experience," said Pax.

Moriganne raised an eyebrow. "You? You seem more put together than anyone else here."

"Kali keeps me sane," said Pax, "but trust me, it was a shitshow the whole way through. I seem to attract problems."

"I know the feeling."

Moriganne's phone rang. She put it on speaker.

"You already there?" asked Kitty from the other side. The rest of the team was at Arcanium at the Verum Locus. "Alex has us set up here. We're good to go as soon as you start the distraction."

"We'll get started," said Pax. "Audrey can let you know when you're good to enter her mind."

Audrey took the phone and Moriganne took her place next to Laila on the mattress while Pax took the opposite side. Kali lay at their head, not quite a pillow.

Leaning on her elbow with the unconscious housekeeper between them, Moriganne asked, "Have you done this before?"

"Not really. Not with a human before. Plenty of animals. But I'm confident we can do it as long as you open your mind. It's easy to keep us out if you try, but if we're going to travel into this woman's mind together, I'm going to need complete transparency."

Moriganne frowned. "You'll see everything in my head?"

"I won't try to, we'll be too busy for that, but I might learn some things."

Moriganne gave a sly grin. "The '70s and '80s in the music business were really fast and loose."

Everyone settled on the mattress. Pax closed her eyes. She didn't have to reach out to Kali, because she was already there, but as she focused on her companion, the details drew in. The smell of Ivan's nervousness, the light floral perfume that Audrey wore, a dead mouse in the attic, the rumble of a commercial jet flying high overhead. The magesteel enhancement had given Pax additional sensing tools, but they never compared to Kali's.

Pax reached out to the unconscious woman first. She had to open the conduit before she could invite Moriganne in. The elixir had put her under, but kept the mind active. It was important. A knockout drug would have made their task more difficult. Like slogging through a swamp. Ivan had added something to make her more compliant too.

As soon as they connected, there was panic from the woman. An invasion in the mind could be traumatic. Pax sent out waves of calm and acceptance. The fight lasted for a few seconds, before returning to peaceful confusion.

Inside her mind, Pax sensed the other connection. The one from beyond their realm. It felt hot. Like a hastily constructed wire patch that wasn't quite right, so it put off radiant heat from the poor resistance. When Elosian had killed the alchemical worker, it'd been through this connection. He'd overloaded the wires and burnt up her mind. If he did that while they were inside the housekeeper's mind, the same could happen to them. As long as she kept the woman under, Elosian shouldn't be able to break into her mind. That was the hope. Pax wondered if she should slip back out and explain the potential problem, but decided everyone would still go through with it. They already knew the plan was dangerous.

Normally when she took control of a supernatural creature, she could sense everything they could sense, but she didn't want control. She wanted to be inside her mind. After a minute of patient exploration, settling without disturbing the woman, Pax reached out to Moriganne.

Pax had never attempted to connect minds together, but it was easier than she thought. A lifetime with Kali as her companion had given her the tools.

Am I here?

The voice was Moriganne's, yet not her. Had an older, honeyed tenor.

Pax had been viewing everyone as signatures of energy, connecting them with threads of psychic ability, but when Moriganne spoke, it shifted the amorphous world into a physical space inside the woman's head.

They stood in a small apartment, somewhere in the city, with a picture of a smiling family on the wall but no signs of others living in the room. Kali nudged her hand. The wet nose felt hyper-real.

"Yes," said Pax. "I think we're here."

Moriganne came in through a door from the bedroom. Pax did a double take. The same beautiful blonde young woman was standing before her, but, like a secondary image superimposed over the first, she saw Minerva as well. The haziness didn't stop there. Pax sensed a third image, deeper inside, barely visible.

The bridge tattoo burned through all of them. The embers were an anchor point on which the other versions of Moriganne shifted around.

"This is strange," said Moriganne, staring at the embers. "It doesn't normally do this."

"It's Elosian's connection. It's not far from here."

Pax couldn't see it, but she could feel it with her mind. Like having her eyes closed and knowing where the sun was by the heat on her back. She looked towards the guest bedroom. The brown door wavered like the highway in a desert.

When Pax looked back, she caught the brief image of a little girl holding Moriganne's hand, but then the vision was gone and it was only the stone singer.

"You okay? You made a face," said Moriganne.

"Lots of residual memories here," said Pax. "The connection is through there."

The guest bedroom had a statue of the Virgin Mary on a chest of drawers. A quilt lay on the bed along with a mass of throw pillows that looked inviting. Pax saw all those details in an instant then immediately lost interest as her gaze was drawn to a pulsing black crack on the wall. The sharp scent of faez hit her nose, making her squeeze her nostrils together as if she might sneeze.

"That's him," said Moriganne, staring at the crevice as she rubbed her arms. "That's how he's whispering into her mind. It frightens me."

"Me too. But the three of us are here together. We won't let him hurt you, and if something happens, I pull us out, right away."

"No," said Moriganne, shaking her head.

"No?"

"If you do that, then he'll see the others. Unless we're going to die, keep us here. We have to lure him away for this to work."

"If I think the tattoo is at risk, I'm getting you out of here," said Pax.

Moriganne lifted her arm to stare at the embers. "I hate this thing. It's caused so much death and misery. It's like carrying a genocide on my arm." She bunched up her lips. "Sorry."

"No need to be sorry. I'd probably feel the same way."

Moriganne faced the crack. It smelled faintly like lilacs. "How do we do this?"

"I'll reach out to Elosian through it, but I need you to concentrate on the tattoo. He has to know that you're here and available. He has to come to us."

"And then what?"

Pax put her hand on the back of Kali's neck. "I wish I knew."

Twenty-Five

Aurie stared at the small obsidian stone sitting next to her sister. They'd debated where the portal should be located. Concerns about the excess faez in the Verum Locus interfering made the choice a difficult one, but in the end they listened to Alex.

The newcomer to their group was an unusual one. While they waited for the word to begin, Aurie covertly watched Alex as she sat cross-legged near the obsidian stone, tapping patterns on her knees while she stared straight ahead. It was easier to analyze Alex than think about her sister. She should have known that Pi would disobey her. Disobey. Like she had that authority over her sister. They were both adults, but Aurie still felt like she owed Pi for what she'd let happen to their parents.

"They're in," said Kitty from the doorway, staring at the phone on her palm. Audrey had been giving second by second updates on what has happening on the other end, though most of it was just them lying on a mattress on the third floor of Ares' place.

A wave of nervousness hit Aurie. She blew out a breath and shook her hands. Zayn approached, put his hand on her arm. His touch was warm, comforting. She wanted to melt into him, but this wasn't the time.

"We're going to get her back," said Zayn earnestly. "I know it."

Aurie couldn't bring herself to answer, so she nodded emphatically.

Alex patted the space near the stone. "It's best if you lie down so when you come back you don't fall over."

"Wait, our bodies don't stay in the room?"

"No. They'll be in suspended animation while our minds enter your sister's."

Aurie glanced into the auditorium. Professor Mali had set a few students as guards near the entrance with instructions not to bother them while they were working to retrieve Pi.

"Okay."

She sat opposite Alex and next to Zayn. They formed a square around the obsidian portal. She lay on her back, staring at the golden light of faez as if they were fireflies in a summer field floating overhead.

"I've set the portal to accept us. You can enter when you fill your mind with faez and think about going through it. The portal will do the rest."

The wait for the final confirmation had Aurie bouncing her knees, trying not to think about what she would do if she didn't have Pi in her life. She knew it wasn't what she should be thinking about. Focusing on the task was better. Would improve their outcome. But yet...

Audrey's voice came over the phone lying near the portal. "I think they're in."

"You think?" asked Alex, leaning on an elbow.

"Mori's shaking a little bit and the tattoo has a light glow to it."

"Probably as good of a sign as we're going to get," said Alex, shifting onto her back. "I'll see you on the other side."

The newcomer winked out of existence as soon as her head hit the floor, startling Aurie, even though she'd seen portal travel hundreds of times. This time seemed different. She wasn't going somewhere else, she was headed inside her sister's mind. Aurie worried what she was going to see. Would it reveal secrets she didn't want to know? In the end, she didn't care. What mattered most was getting her sister back.

Aurie exhaled slowly, calming herself as she saw both Zayn and Kitty disappear. She reached out and put a hand on Pi's leg.

"I'm coming for you, sis. Dooset daram."

Twenty-Six

No walls confined her. No bars or locks kept her from escaping. Yet Pi could find no way to leave.

For the hundredth time, Pi climbed the torturous stairs that went up at a strange angle that shouldn't be possible to climb. When she reached the top, she found herself back where she'd started and the stairs no longer behind her but ahead at the edge of the room.

Pi tried climbing the stair backwards. Or with her eyes closed. She went through the passages or jumped off the side. Only to end up at the same spot she'd begun.

Magic came like faint sparks to her hand. Elosian was dampening her abilities. She could manage to make a single flame dance on her palm like a candle in a breeze, but anything more brought an ache at the back of her skull.

When she grew frustrated with trying to escape, Pi spent time examining the world around her. Jagged, fractal-like mountains rose in the distance. Occasionally she saw figures winging through the sky. Once she saw three of them chase down a smaller one, then tear it to pieces, which floated towards the ground in an unseen breeze.

Pi was trapped on a "castle" that hung off the side of a mountain. The liminal space changed each time she looked back to it. At one moment—time had lost meaning for her—the mountain peak above her disappeared. An entire section of rock completely gone. She'd heard no explosion, seen no detonation, yet it was no longer there.

It wasn't the demonic realm as she'd imagined it. There was no heat. No flames. Few creatures, except those she could see in the sky. Not that she had a good sight line. The spot she was trapped in looked out, and while she couldn't see down, it was clear she was on top of a massive structure.

When she'd first arrived, she could see the golden light of faez twinkling in the air, but now it wasn't visible. Pi wondered what that meant, or if she should be worried. Was being trapped in Elosian's mind palace the same as being in the demonic realm?

Invictus had called it an underrealm. A place connected to all others. An early precursor to the connected realms she'd become accustomed to traveling. Seeing how it morphed and changed explained much to Pi. The air itself was thick with magic. In her world, if too much of it was around, it warped and changed those exposed. Faez wasn't just the raw stuff of magic, it was the raw stuff of creation. When she was using magic, she was playing with the energies of the early universe. It explained so much.

When escape seemed unlikely, Pi focused on understanding her surroundings better. Insight into the nature of the demonic realm might give her a chance to leave should the opportunity present itself.

Sitting cross-legged on the warm stone (she never saw a sun, so assumed the warmth came from the magic itself) Pi brought forth one of the few magics she could accomplish: the candle flame. The fire jumped and flickered on her palm like a tiny dancer moving through the paces of an unknown ballet.

Normally using the Five Elements required no thought on her behalf. She'd been playing with them for so long it was second nature, but in the demonic realm, it required attention and focus. She could repeat the same thing with the other magics, each one dancing in the same erratic behavior, except for force.

When she brought force, which was also called spirit, into existence the magic dissipated into sparkles, returning to its base creation. Faez. No matter how Pi tried to hold the force magic together, it evaporated. It felt like trying to catch a downpour with her bare hands.

Advanced magic was out of the question. The use of magic in her world required complex gestures, thoughts and words, sometimes pictures in the mind. Each were instructions for how the magic should be constructed, the scaffolding on which the structure hung. But in the demonic realm, the unformed nature of it made performing magic impossible.

It was like being a chef at a fancy restaurant, used to the high-end ingredients and cooking tools available, but sent back to the Stone Age and being asked to create baked char siu bao. The affluence of faez swallowed every attempt at magic. It was like there was too much fuel and not enough oxygen to light the flame.

Pi slept at times. She didn't need to. Her body didn't react to staying awake like it did in her world, but sometimes it was better to lie on the stone and close her eyes, forget where she was, knowing that if her friends came for her, it would likely end up with them trapped.

Neither thirst nor hunger ever bothered her. Whether that was a property of the demonic realm, or being stuck in Elosian's mind, she could never figure out. But after reminiscing, imagining taking a long drink from a glass of water filled to the brim with ice so full it risked spilling onto her shirt if the ice loosened, she managed to produce a larger dancing water sprite on her palm. Pi failed to repeat the feat.

She missed eating and drinking. And sleep. She even missed the other annoying factors of having a working human body. She felt like one of the marionettes from Andromeda's show—going through the motions without consequence.

Most of all she missed her sister. For the last two years, they'd spent their entire time together traversing the realms on Invictus' behalf. Sometimes Pi forgot where she was and spoke to her sister as if she were sitting nearby, only to find nothing but empty stone.

But as much as she missed Aurie, she desperately hoped that she would never see her again. Because if her sister came after her, Elosian would trap Aurie like he had her.

One fool stuck in Elosian's mind was enough.

Twenty-Seven

The air was choked with cologne and bitters. Kitty stared at the head of an elk affixed to the wall. The antlers had to be as wide as a truck.

"Why don't you take a seat, Catherine."

The voice was like a lightning bolt through her chest. She flinched. It was her father. Victor Charmer.

Kitty turned slowly, expecting to find him looking at her, but was instead presented with an unusual scene, considering she'd been expecting to land somewhere else. Anywhere else.

The huge room was dominated by a table that could seat forty people comfortably, but only had a group of ten, seated at one end near her father. The moment she saw his smooth skin, the hale and hearty color to his flesh, dark hair without the telltale signs of gray, she knew she'd entered a memory of her past. Especially when she saw a younger version of herself climbing into a chair next to the gray-haired board members surrounding her father's position.

Faint cries of joy followed by splashing had Kitty checking over her shoulder to see her siblings by the pool. Young Ivan launched himself from the roof of the pool house, landing in a cannonball, which sent a wave of water towards Solstice, who'd been reading by the side. She threw her book down and, with laughing grace, leapt after him.

"You're a bunch of fuckups," said Victor, forcing Kitty to return to the table. She knew she should be trying to figure out why she wasn't with the others. Alex had gone through the portal first, but she was transfixed by this moment in her past. One she remembered well, even if she hadn't thought about it in a long time.

"Ten or eleven," said Kitty as she approached the table remembering how old she was when this happened. No one gave her a second look. She wasn't there. Or they weren't. The young version of herself sat next to her father, surrounded by the board members, looking at ease with the strange power dynamic.

The lodge was somewhere in upstate New York. They'd flown in helicopters. Kitty remembered Ares being sick during landing, threatening to puke, their father yelling at him to suck it up. Ares puked behind the building after they landed, well out of sight.

"Not one of you has a good idea on how to turn around our earnings slide," said Victor.

The men and women stared at the table as if they were studying a menu. Kitty moved around so she could see herself. Short, cropped haircut that matched the line of her jaw. Steely, intense eyes, even as young as she was. Ivan called her the Predator sometimes, and she responded by making a fearsome cry and leaping after him. The memory made her smile. Not like the one before her.

As Victor continued his dressing down of the board, Kitty tried to leave the room, but found herself standing in front of the elk horns again. She had a bad feeling in her gut and would have tried to leave again except she found herself transfixed by what was about to happen.

"I should fire the lot of you, replace you with a board that knows how to get something done," growled Victor. "My daughter, Catherine, has more balls than you. She's a real fighter. Knows how to get in there and give someone the blade."

The younger version of herself gave a smile that had no business being on someone that young. Kitty put a hand to her mouth, wondering if that was what people saw when they looked at her. A killer.

A waiter brought a tray full of drinks. Whiskey by the dark amber color. When he passed young Kitty, Victor barked out, "Give her one too. Gotta learn the taste of it eventually."

A few of the board members glanced around as if they expected someone to speak up, but no one did. The waiter did as he was told. Put the glass in front of young Kitty. She didn't know if she should be proud or concerned when that version of herself took a drink without so much as a twitch.

Victor leaned back in his chair and ran his hand along the smooth table, eyes glinting with malice. She knew this mood. Knew it well. It didn't matter that she remembered what had happened. It was as shocking as the first time.

"Everyone up. On their feet."

The board members looked around at each other. Victor was known for his unusual outbursts.

"You're all too slow. No regard for the real knife fighting that needs to happen in our line of business. You're all pussyfooting around, trying to fellate your opponents and not getting in there, shoving the blade in deep." He sneered. "We're going to play a game. We'll call it Fire Tag. If Catherine hits you with a spit of flame, you get a point against you. Whoever gets three points is fired. No one leaves the room. If you do, you're fired too."

"Sir," said a gray-haired board member with glasses, "your daughter's not old enough to use magic safely."

"I'll be the one to decide if she's old enough. Point against you, Dockins. You're one down. You went to Harvard, for Merlin's sake, think before you open your stupid mouth." He clapped his hands once. "Now go!"

They didn't move at first. Mostly they stood around, incredulous at what they were being asked to do.

Kitty watched as her younger self went for the nearest board member. He stared down as if he didn't expect her to flame him. When the burst came from her small hands, hitting him in the face like a BBQ grill with too much gas on it, he yelped, tripped over his own feet, and smashed his shoulder into a high-backed chair. She'd gone after him, intent on giving him a second blast. No mercy as her father had taught, but Victor had given her a secret grin.

"Give 'em a shot to get up at least. Don't want to end this too quickly."

The meeting turned to chaos as young Kitty stalked around the room, firing flame shots at the board members. Usually a direct hit. Wearing that killer smile.

Victor called out the hits as the game wore on. Who'd been hit and how many times.

"You gonna let that eleven-year-old get the best of you, Susan? Why the fuck do you still have those heels on? Throw 'em at her if you want, but you'd better hit clean or she's going to fry that overpriced haircut of yours. Did you get it at a fucking tenth-ward barber shop?"

The insults flew along with the points. When half the board had two hits, their desperation turned to more ruthless tactics. A few times, they pushed each other towards her.

Kitty watched as the younger version of herself slowed down, drawing out the hunt. She remembered it feeling like a game. Vic was making the board members play with her. Yes, there was a lesson involved, but it'd been fun. Kitty couldn't remember if she noticed how terrified they were. Not only would they lose their job, but the flame shots were painful. A few probably caused first- or second-degree burns.

The game ended when Dockins took the third hit. He looked to Victor hopefully, but her father jabbed his thumb towards the door.

"Get the fuck out. Too slow. Too dumb. You should ask your Ivy League school for their money back because they didn't teach you a damn thing." Victor turned towards the others, who were breathing heavily, damp sweat on their faces. "Get out. Go clean up and come back here in thirty minutes. You'd better have some fucking good ideas or we'll play our little game again."

Victor winked at young Catherine when the room was empty.

"What did *you* learn?"

Young Catherine looked to the floor contemplatively for a few seconds before lifting her chin, a smile forming.

"Move fast. No hesitation. Trip someone if you have to." She shifted her mouth to the side. "And heels are a bad idea when you have to fight."

Victor chuckled. "Fair enough." He drummed his fingers on the table. "You're a real fighter. I like that. It'll serve us well in the future."

Young Catherine leaned on her tippy toes and gave him a kiss on the cheek.

"Can I go play with Ivan at the pool?" she asked sweetly.

"Go ahead. You earned it."

After she left, Kitty stood near her father's side staring down at him as he quietly mused over the events of his meeting with a self-satisfied smirk. Rage bubbled up in her chest until she swung at him. Her fist went through his head, leaving her filled with emotion but with no place to put it.

"You made me a monster."

Twenty-Eight

The steady beeping and sterile antiseptic smell confused Zayn until he turned around to find he was standing in a hospital room. Aurie was lying on the bed, damp sweat on her forehead, eyes rimmed with red circles.

"Hey, why are we here?" he asked her, but she kept staring ahead, breathing shallowly.

When Aurie put a hand on her stomach, he realized she was pregnant. About to have a kid.

"Aurie. Can you hear me?"

He waved his hand in front of her face. Nothing.

"Where am I?"

Something had happened when they went into Pi's mind. He wasn't aware that Aurie was ever pregnant. Zayn strode through the door—

Only to find himself back in her room. The beeping increased in tempo as she grimaced, breathing faster, glancing to the door expectantly. Seconds later, a different version of himself burst through carrying a bucket of ice chips.

Zayn watched as that version threw himself by the bed and grabbed her hand.

"So sorry, took a little longer than I expected. There was a line."

"How much longer," said an anguished Aurie, squeezing his hand until her knuckles were white.

"The doctors said soon." Other Zayn smiled. "And then we'll have a beautiful little girl. She's almost here. Keep focused. You're almost done."

Aurie nodded as she closed her eyes. Another contraction hit. She groaned, pushing her head back into the pillow.

Zayn was caught between wanting to watch their future daughter be born and getting out of the vision. He threw himself through the door again, only to find himself by the window. As soon as he reappeared, a doctor and two nurses came in.

"I think we're about ready," said the doctor as she pulled blue latex gloves over her hands. "Are you ready?"

Aurie nodded emphatically.

"Fuck," muttered Zayn, "what is going on? Where are the others?"

He managed to pull open the window, which no one noticed. It was five stories up. He could manage the landing from half the distance, so he threw his leg out to climb down a ways—

And found himself back at the window staring at Aurie straining to push the child out.

"No. No. No. Please hurry. Please come out," said Aurie between her rushed breaths, while the other Zayn knelt at her side. The doctor, bracketed by her nurses, crouched between Aurie's legs, which were suspended by stirrups.

Zayn almost took a step around to watch, but decided that since this was a vision, rather than the real thing, it wasn't right for him to look. During the next few minutes, the doctor encouraged Aurie and she pushed and pushed until there was a rising scream, followed by the wet squelch of the baby sliding free into the doctor's arms.

The pride welling up in Zayn's chest was euphoric, even as he told himself this wasn't really happening. The nurses took the baby to a side table to clean her up. While the other version of himself comforted Aurie, he moved to view the baby.

Zayn smiled at the little wrinkled ball. The eyes were barely open. He couldn't tell who the child looked like and wanted to reach out and wiggle a toe, or stroke the round head. He could feel the corners of his mouth stretching into a grin that went down into his toes.

Until they brought out the syringe.

He knew the Lady's poison the moment he saw the greenish liquid in the vial.

"Wait. What are you doing?"

He tried to knock the syringe from the nurse's hand, but he couldn't touch her. He wasn't really there. This wasn't even real. It was a nightmare.

"No. Please don't do that. Why are you doing that?"

Zayn watched as the nurse slipped the needle into the soft flesh on the inside of her arm. The other version of himself looked up and smiled at the injection.

Eventually the injection was complete. They cleaned up the baby and put her in Aurie's arms. Both parents stared at the child as if it were the only thing in the world.

"Have you decided on a name?" asked a nurse with a clipboard.

Aurie and Zayn looked to each other with a secret smile. Aurie nodded, and Zayn spoke up.

"We want to name her Arcadia. In honor of the Lady."

"That's wonderful," said the nurse before disappearing.

No, I killed the Lady. I freed Varna. I freed my family.

Zayn tried to grab the clipboard out of the woman's hand, but he went right through. He read over her shoulder as the nurse left the room.

First Hospital of Varna.

The letterhead bore her spider symbol. What was going on?

"I have to get out of here."

Twenty-Nine

Moriganne knew where she was the instant she stepped through the portal. She'd been expecting to see the others. Not this. Anything but this.

The sedan rumbled down the two-lane road. She was sitting in the passenger seat. The brown interior, the smell of cigarettes, the feel of the plastic beneath her thighs. All of it familiar. All of it horrifying.

Moriganne looked over to see a young Minerva in the driver's seat. Younger than the body she was in now. Maybe twenty-two, twenty-three. Gorgeous blonde hair, coifed in the style of the late '60s with a colorful headband. A cigarette dangling from her lips.

A giggle from the backseat brought Moriganne around to see her ex-husband Ian bouncing their child on his knee. Ian had curly brown hair and thick glasses. Isabella was a cross between them. Moriganne only had eyes for her daughter. Sweet Izzy.

She reached back to her daughter, but her fingers went right through Isabelle's hand.

"I'm not supposed to be here," said Moriganne. "I don't want to be here."

She opened the door. The sedan was speeding down the backroads in Ohio. They were late for a concert. Moriganne thought about jumping out, but didn't know how that would work in the vision. She was afraid she'd get hurt.

Moriganne closed the door then her eyes, trying to will herself somewhere different. The smell of cigarettes never left. Minerva stabbed one out in the ashtray, flung it out the cracked window, and lit another.

"Luv, you need to slow down. You're going too fast," said Ian from the backseat.

"I can't be late. My Columbus fans love me," said Minerva, leaning her head back. The car swerved, veering off the road momentarily before she jerked it back.

"They'd love you more alive," said Ian.

Minerva checked the rearview mirror. Frowned. "That asshole with the camera is still with us."

"Forget about him, luv," said Ian as he bounced Isabella on his knees to copious giggles. "Mommy go fast. She's a big star, Izzy. Gonna be even bigger soon. Got a big tour for her planned. Just a few more warm-up shows and then we'll blow 'em away. Everyone will know her name. She'll be playing the Glitterdome before long."

The winding roads had Moriganne putting her hands on the dash. The younger version of herself was watching Isabella and the car following them, occasionally adjusting the curls of her hair, while the vehicle flew down the road at high speeds.

Moriganne remembered her state of mind as if it were only yesterday. She'd been so desperate to get to Columbus on time. She knew how fickle promoters were about their stars. Since she'd had Isabella, there'd been a push to cancel her tours. Fans didn't want a star that was raising a child. It ruined the illusion. They wanted to be able to imagine them as anything. A blank canvas. She'd been worried about her career. Not her family.

"Mommy big star?"

"Izzy is a big star too," said Minerva, smiling at her through the rearview mirror. "I got you a present."

"Present?" she asked in her cute little voice.

Minerva reached to the glove box with her long nails, taking her eyes off the road. But Moriganne could see ahead. A second paparazzi had set up along the route, a camera held to his face as he stood at the rear of his parked car. As Minerva snatched the glittery tiara from the glove box, her car drifted towards the side. The photographer held his ground for a few seconds until he realized that she was about to hit him.

As Minerva handed back the tiara to a grasping Isabella, Ian shouted, "Min, watch out!"

Moriganne put her hands over her face before the impact. She heard the crash from a distance away, opened up her eyes to find herself standing near the photographer, who was scrambling back to the road with the camera in his hands, breathing heavily and muttering that he was glad to be alive.

She watched as he reviewed the scene before him. The car she'd been driving had hit the left rear of the photographer's vehicle, flipping three times to land on its side in the middle of the road, wheels spinning. A tiara lay in the middle near the white dotted lines. The photographer lifted his camera and snapped a picture of the tiara with the flipped vehicle in the background.

Three things died that day. Isabella, her marriage, and her career. The first burned deep into her soul. The other two she managed to get over.

She had nightmares about the crash every so often, but it was mostly the impact and aftermath that she witnessed. In this vision, she was forced to confront the truth of what happened leading up to the crash. Ian was right. He'd blamed her for the death of their child. She'd been too focused on her career, and not enough on being a mother to Isabella. Not on her family.

Moriganne lost everything on that day. Mostly she lost herself. But why was she here?

She pulled the sleeve of her shirt up to reveal the bridge tattoo. It was burning. She touched it with a fingertip only to flinch away when it burnt her.

Moriganne faced down the road as the sirens of an ambulance grew louder. In the real version, the medics hadn't arrived for a half hour. Maybe longer. When they'd arrived, they'd found her wandering around the road inconsolable with only a minor head wound.

She couldn't see the emergency vehicle but something about it worried her. The bridge was burning brighter, sizzling with embers. The flesh around it hurt.

Entering the woman's mind had been meant as a distraction, a way to pull Elosian away from the others so they could rescue Pi and possibly learn how the invasion was going to happen. As she stared down the road, the sirens growing louder, she knew they'd made a terrible, terrible mistake.

Thirty

The last thing Pax remembered was talking to Moriganne in the memory of the housekeeper's apartment while staring at a pulsating crack in the wall. Sweet lilacs lingered in her nose. But now she was standing in the kitchen of her parents' house in Portland.

Kali was by her side, looking up.

"Oh, thank Merlin you're here."

<Home not home>

"Yes, not home. A memory." She looked around. "Elosian did something to us. Diverted us. He was ready."

The bitter taste in her mind was Kali's way of agreeing.

<Need out>

"Yes, out," said Pax, but she hesitated when she heard the rustling of a newspaper from the front room. She found her father reading in his favorite chair with a cup of steaming coffee on the table.

The door creaked open, followed by the squeaking of the wood floor. Pax couldn't see who had entered but she knew who it was even before her father's sharp call.

"I hear your sneak thief steps."

A moment later, a younger version of herself appeared at the edge of the hallway. Red, curly hair pulled into an unruly ponytail with a piece of wire. Clothes filthy from digging around in the woods to find critters to care for.

To her surprise, her father's hard mouth broke into a smile at her appearance.

"Did you have a nice time in the woods? Find anything interesting?" he asked.

Young Pax matched his grin as she held a plastic lunch box with the emblem of the Hundred Halls stamped on it behind her back.

"Maybe."

He winked. "You can show me later after you've cleaned up."

"Okay, Daddy."

Pax groaned inside. She couldn't remember the last time she'd called him that. Once they'd been bitten by the crag worm she brought home, they were never the same. The crag worm was inside the lunch box, a creature born of Pyramid Health's labs.

"We need to get out of here," said Pax.

<Kali not here>

"No, sweetheart. You didn't come along until after. Elosian is trying to distract us from our mission. Can you help us get out? He might be ready for a bunch of mages, but he certainly isn't ready for one Kali."

Her companion bumped her in the leg. They headed towards the door. Pax could feel the temporal manipulation as they reached it, and when they returned to the kitchen, she had a good idea of what he'd done.

"Try that again, but with a destination in mind. You ready for it this time?"

<Yes>

With her hand on the back of Kali's neck, they went through the door, except both of them focused on their friends. As they crossed the threshold, there was a moment of wavering. She thought they'd squeezed through the crack, but when she blinked she found they were somewhere entirely different.

Winter. Cold. A crane was loading the Jörmungandr onto a huge container ship in the partially frozen harbor. The enormous crag worm's flesh was covered in hardened scales and oozing crust, much different than the smooth skin that it enjoyed in the cold salt water of the northern hemisphere. She could hear shouts and the rat-a-tat of gunfire below. Pax's heart rate increased at remembrance. It'd been a close one.

<Pax-Kali born today>

"Yes, you're right. We were born this day, but this isn't where we need to be. Let's try again, but focus really hard on Moriganne. We need to get back to her quick before Elosian gets to the tattoo."

It was hard to turn her back on that momentous day. She'd nearly died and she'd been born. Both of them.

"We need a doorway."

She remembered they'd left the snowcat further up the road. She and Kali ran for a quarter mile before they found it. The door was left open.

"Come on. We'll climb inside and come back out."

As she sat in the driver's seat, she had the urge to drive back to the battle, but the past was past. The future was at stake. With her connection to Kali firmly in her mind, she jumped out of the cab, not to the crunch of snow, but to the sliding of sand.

"What's this?"

The landscape was unfamiliar. A gilded palace lay ahead, surrounded by palm trees and people in white linen. A group of women carried baskets on their head, coming from the bank of a wide river.

Pax's gut clenched. This wasn't a scene from her past. Or was it? Screams erupted from inside the palace. With Kali at her side, Pax sprinted ahead until she could see inside the flickering halls of the palace. A woman in a linen wrap followed by two guards in bronze breastplates who held spears came flying out the front, checking behind them as they ran.

Strange barks came from inside. They crept forward, the noisy eruptions echoing through the colorful halls. Murals were painted on the walls. She didn't know enough about Egyptian history to know the era, only that they were walking through a memory thousands of years old.

Why are we seeing this? What is Elosian trying to do now?

<Not Elosian>

Pax wasn't sure if it was a guess on her companion's part, or that she sensed something deeper in the memory.

A body lay near a cross hall, holding a spear, foam coming out of his mouth. The eyes were unfocused. Not dead yet, but soon. They followed the barking to find an embalming room. In the far corner near a collection of urns, a great flying snake was trapped in the corner by a group of small darkly furred creatures that bore a resemblance to Kali. Standing at their center was a figure in a mask, facing Aepep, shaking his staff and shouting in a language she couldn't understand.

It was the Lost Prince. She was sure of it.

The masked figure sent a bolt of lightning crackling into the corner, but Aepep was faster, darting around the Lost Prince and avoiding the early versions of the callidus. Pax nearly dove out of the way as Aepep flew right through her, leaving her heart in her throat.

The masked figure and his pack flew down the hallway after Aepep, leaving Pax reeling in their wake. She turned to follow but an open door drew her forward. It was covered in runes and arcane markings.

The room beyond was nothing like the embalming area with its ancient tools and fluids. Pax was reminded of a mage's laboratory with bubbling liquids and primitive machines. A cage that took up the entire corner had been bent outward. Pax was immediately reminded of the labs inside Phoenix Corporation.

"The seeds of the past. Aepep wasn't born, but was made."

She wondered less if the Lost Prince was a potential ally. How could anyone with a shred of good in them create a being of pure chaos? More and more she was convinced that it was Leo Dreadmarsh under that mask. If he wasn't their friend, then he might be an enemy.

"We have to get out of here," said Pax, feeling sick inside. "We have to find the others or we're all going to die in Elosian's mind."

Thirty-One

The scene wasn't what Alex was expecting. She knew the instant she opened her eyes back in the little room in their Kentucky trailer that Elosian had diverted her somehow. A younger version of herself was seated before the computer screen, tapping on the keyboard and mouse, controlling her colorful character. Young Alex had been trying to reach level 75 so she could join her online friends in a raid.

"Hey, Alexandria."

It was her dad.

Young Alex never turned around. Why would she? She mistakenly thought that he'd be alive at the end of the day when he returned from work.

Alex walked through her father, heading out of the trailer. This was a distraction. Elosian had done to them what they'd planned to do to him. Which made their situation more dangerous. He knew they were coming. She balled her hands into fists. He'd outthought them. Outmaneuvered her.

"Fuck," said Alex as she found herself back in the room with her younger self and father.

She marched into the living room, where her mother was on the couch knitting a pair of socks. She had wrinkles around her eyes, but her heart hadn't been pulled out by his death yet. She was still fairly happy even if their circumstances were less than ideal.

"What are you doing, Elosian?"

Alex produced a bit of flame only to find it reduced as if the air didn't have enough oxygen.

"Interesting."

She searched around the area, looking for imperceptible errors in the vision. Elosian had hijacked her deepest thoughts to create a simulation in his mind. If she hadn't had years of experience in the game world and with Dr. Althud's therapy, she might not have known what was going on, but those traumatic events had given her a perspective on reality that was helping her now.

Like computers, minds only had so much processing power. If they were all in Elosian's head, then he was taxing his own demonic brain. And unless he was significantly more powerful than she understood, if they could force him to overload it, they might break free.

"And if not, then this is where we live now."

Alex went out the front door to find herself back in her old room. She left again, heading out the door. The vision continued as she bounced from spot to spot until her father left for work on a day he'd be killed by an unlucky construction accident. The moment he left the trailer, she found herself back in the room with young Alex furiously tapping on the keyboard.

"Hey, Alexandria."

The vision repeated on a loop. Alex had a good idea why. It would take too much brain power to create a larger or longer simulation, so Elosian had constructed a smaller, compact one designed to distract and contain them. She had to find a way to force herself out, or annoy him so thoroughly, he freed her accidentally.

"Magic isn't working right. What does that mean? Is that a property of his mind? Or the demonic realm? Or something else?"

She tried kicking the walls and knocking over the stuffed animals on her bed, but her hand went right through them. The scene playing out behind her occasionally tugged on her emotions. She could have gone to the Devil's Icebox with him for a day of hiking and exploring, but she'd chosen the game instead. He'd gone to work since she was busy. A choice she would regret every day for years afterwards.

Frustrated, Alex pushed out the door again...

"Wait. Why can I affect the door?"

Doors were portals. Even if they only led from one room to another.

Alex tested the other doors. She couldn't open the one that led to her parents' room, but she could go in and out of her room and the outside.

"He wanted me to see my mother. He wanted me to feel pain." Alex looked around. "It's not just a construction of a memory. It's like a program. The doors have to be active because they provide the looping mechanism. Go through this door, head into another place, or back to the spot you came."

She ran her fingers along the cheap wood. She could put a fist through the front if she wanted. The acoustics were terrible. Everything that happened in the little trailer was apparent to everyone else inside. It was one reason she loved playing games with her headphones. With the volume up, she could imagine she had her own space without noisy and loving parents just a few yards away.

Pulling on the door made it rattle, but she didn't want to break it. Alex tried to find a screwdriver, but when her hand went through the junk drawer in the kitchen she remembered she could only touch one object.

"How do I move this if I want to?"

Alex stared at the door with her hands on her hips. The only answer she could come up with was magic. But she was a terrible mage. Gamemakers had taught her to use her mind creatively, but the learning of actual spells and enchantments was few and far between. She'd picked up a few spells since she'd graduated, but nothing that would help her.

She tapped on the hinge, relieved when her knuckles hit solid metal. It was cheap like the door. Flimsy and weak. Her father had always told them that one day he'd make enough money for them to move into a real house, but emergencies and the occasional layoffs in the construction industry had left them with more bills than savings. It was worse after his death.

Using her flame to hit the hinge but not the wooden door was challenging. She wasn't used to the precision and had to move to the living room to practice before she was comfortable enough to apply it to the door pivot. She managed to heat up the metal until it glowed a faint orange and then immediately Alex shifted to ice, which was the reverse of fire with a twist of water. The sudden drop of temperature put a hairline crack in the edge of the hinge.

"Hmm...this might work. This just might work."

As the younger version of herself blew off her father on his very last day alive, Alex applied more flame to the door hinge.

Thirty-Two

The pattern on the stone wall had changed. Pi was sure of it. She'd been staring at the same patch for a measure of time that she didn't have words to describe. It could have been a day, or it could have been three years. The sameness of her world made it impossible to tell. There was no shifting of shadows as a big ball of light crossed the sky, because there was no sun.

But the pattern had changed.

Pi had been sitting cross-legged in the center of the space she'd been trapped in, staring ahead, trying to not claw at her skin or scream aloud. She'd done as much, some time ago, but it hadn't done anything but make her feel out of control.

And she was sure that Elosian was watching. He would be amused to watch her fall apart.

Pi crawled forward on her hands and knees to examine the pattern. Before, the discolorations on the stone had made her imagine a horse thundering across a rocky field. But now as she ran her fingers along the rough stone, the horse was gone. The pattern had changed. If the pattern changed then that meant something had happened. Everything previously had been exactly the same. Every block of stone, every crack, every particle of air. Even the strange birds winging through the sky repeated themselves.

Until now.

The tiny change gave her hope. She wasn't sure why. It wasn't like a hole had opened up where she could escape, but having a slight difference made her wonder why. Had her sister come for her and Elosian was distracted?

Pi resolved to make him even more preoccupied. Maybe then, she might find a way to get out of his trap. Or at least divert his attention so the others might be able to rescue her.

When she'd first come to the prison, she'd been convinced that her sister shouldn't rescue her, because it would only put her in danger too. But now that there was a hint of disturbance, Pi threw herself into pushing against the boundaries of her prison.

After running up the stairs a few dozen times and finding herself back at the base, Pi resolved to take a more measured approached to her defiance. The experimentations with magic had gone nowhere, but yet, she knew there was something in them that could help.

Pi went through the Five Elements, focusing on each one. The first four were pale versions of what she could accomplish in the real world, and force barely made an appearance before dissolving into raw faez. She recalled a time when water had come more freely. Why had that moment been different? She wasn't thirsty in this pseudo-realm, but had she been thinking about water? Was this like the Eternal City, where traveling meant not navigating fixed points, but moving by intention? The home of the maetrie was closer to the demonic realm in strangeness.

With the image of a glass of water firmly in her head, Pi brought that element into existence on her palm. She focused not on the finger gestures or the application of faez, which usually governed the output of a spell, but on the desired result.

Intention was her guide.

As the brief spell completed, a fistful of water exploded into existence and collapsed around her palm, dripping off her fingers onto the stone. Pi gave a whoop of excitement. It was the first real crack she'd found in her prison.

By the time she reexamined the stone, the wetness was gone. The ephemeral existence made her goals more challenging but she wasn't deterred. In fact, she was elated. The sameness of her prison had been a weight on her mind, pulling her into a miasma of nothing. Now she had something to work with. A task to give her purpose.

Pi experimented with the Five Elements, managing significant results for all but force, which dissipated into golden light at each attempt. Having rediscovered her magical ability, Pi decided to leave the prison using the same logic that she used to move around the Eternal City. She imagined the plain where she'd seen Invictus speaking to the blade-creature in her vision, placing the details in focus as much as she could, then constructed a doorway in her mind where she could walk out and into the open spaces. With the confidence that it would work buoying her flagging emotions, Pi strode towards a flat wall, willing the archway into existence—

And ran flat into the stone.

The sharp pain in her nose from the attempt was almost cathartic. Pi laughed, wishing her sister had been around to see it. While she would have preferred to escape, she knew it wasn't going to be that easy. Her destination might have been too ambitious. Too distant. For all she knew that location was on the other side of the demonic realm.

If Invictus was too far away, then Elosian was closer. Was she standing in a castle of his making, or was this a prison in his mind? Pi decided to test her theory. Rather than escaping the prison, she imagined a doorway that would lead to other, closer spaces.

Pi gave herself a good length to get moving, fixing the idea of an archway on the stone wall in her mind which would lead to other areas of the castle. She told herself that she had to be convinced that she would walk through the wall, even as her nose still smarted from the impact. She neared, refusing to shrink from the impact, and—

Stepped through to a stone hallway that was tilted on an angle. Pi looked behind her to see a flat wall. She was standing on a slant without gravity pulling her in the direction her mind thought of as down. She refused to let herself get too excited in case he could catapult her back to the prison, but the longer she remained outside, the more her heart soared.

The passage twisted in a corkscrew. When she was walking upside down, Pi kept expecting to fall and worried that even thinking that would result in it happening. Gravity had little meaning in Elosian's castle, though she'd seen birdlike creatures winging through the sky. Maybe they worked on intention too. Or there were other mechanisms that created the act of flying.

While the freedom from her prison had given her something to explore, Pi kept expecting to be yanked back as Elosian found her absent. The longer she went without feeling the hook of return, the more hope grew in her chest.

After an indeterminate time of exploration—time moved as if in a dream—Pi knew she was getting nowhere. Happy to be free from her prison, she'd left her intentions behind, but now that she was wandering aimlessly, she knew more focus was necessary.

She hadn't meant to be thinking about Elosian, but she was wondering where he might be, or if he existed at all in his mind, when she stepped into a new space that looked like a grand and gilded hall viewed through a kaleidoscope. The room smelled like lilacs, so much so that she expected to find a garden hidden in the corners.

On the floor was a strange design. A giant circle with five dots and two lines going through them in an "X," with the fifth marking coming at the point the two lines crossed. The symbol was familiar yet incomprehensible.

She moved on through a gap between the walls. A greenish light pulled her forward. The space was narrow, forcing her to move sideways. It was tight enough she worried about getting stuck, but eventually she reached the end. She was looking down into a room with two figures facing each other. The tentacles marked Elosian immediately. The second figure had glowing green skin and the countenance of royalty.

"The way is open."

Pi pushed her face to the gap.

Thirty-Three

Aurie was standing on a patch of manicured hyper-green grass that looked like it'd been edged with a pair of scissors. A concrete path wound up the slope to her right and in the distance fires burned. Dark shapes winged through the sky, chasing after an airplane that was making erratic movements to avoid them.

At the top of the hill, a figure stepped into view, angled and sharp like a porcupine. It took a moment for Aurie's eyes to adjust to the strangeness. The man looked like he'd been stuck through with hundreds of blades, yet he continued to live.

The last thing she remembered was lying on the ground inside the Verum Locus. She was supposed to step into Pi's mind, but this looked nothing like she'd expected.

An explosion distracted her. A warehouse or something had blown up just beyond the trees. The black cloud of roiling fire extended into the sky. When she checked back to the crown of the hill, the bladed figure was gone.

"Where's Pi?"

Aurie searched everywhere until her gaze settled on a gray stone sticking from the earth a few feet in front of her.

Pythia Azadeh Silverthorne
B. 1999 – D. 2022

Aurie knew it wasn't real. She knew it was a vision. Some translated worry from the Verum Locus bleeding through Alex's game portal. But she fell to her knees just the same.

"The pain of losing someone close to you runs deep."

The voice was honey over gravel. Her entire back prickled with fear. Aurie hesitated to turn around, but refused to let herself be cowed.

The figure was tall, with backward-facing knees and two tentacles for arms. Elosian. His face was vaguely handsome but unsettling at the same time as if someone who'd never seen a human had been given a description and recreated it. He was only twenty feet away. A few strides and he could have her with his tentacles.

She lifted her hands to hit him with magic, and he said, "That won't help you here."

"What do you want?"

"The same things you want. Freedom. A world that exists even when I'm not thinking about it. Family."

Elosian's lips peeled back in what was supposed to be a smile but came out a grimace.

"You probably ate your family."

His black eyes had a lizard-like quality. Seeing everything. Feeling nothing.

"You really upended my plans when you brought my enemy back. He was supposed to stay stuck in that stupid stasis of his, trapped by his own cleverness. I'd worked so hard to get him to take such a foolish risk."

Elosian tilted his head. It didn't seem right that that face was on that body.

"Where is my sister?"

"Waiting for you to rescue her, or did you fail that too? Like you failed her when you let your parents die. Foolish, foolish girl, playing with toys that should have stayed under the tree until you were supposed to open them. But you had to show off. Your sister intimidated you. Her brilliance, her *specialness*. But you? Not so much."

Aurie resisted balling her hands into fists. "Shut up. I don't care what you think."

"We both know that's a lie. You've been overcompensating since. Trying to lead your friends, failing miserably. I had a glimpse of your little battle in the elder Charmer's place. What a mess. Everyone stepping on each other's dick. If you'd been a proper leader, that mantic wouldn't have stood a chance. Poor, poor Aurelia. Good intentions. Terrible follow-through. No wonder they roll their eyes behind your back."

Aurie threw her hands forward, expecting a wave of powerful force magic to come flying out and knock Elosian onto his back. A breeze barely shifted his hair out of place.

"Ever wonder why your head patron was so mean to you? It's because he was disappointed that you were the one to save him. A couple of misfit orphans who'd managed to turn his precious school against themselves. Oh, how delicious it was to watch that battle a few years ago, under the watchful and dead eyes of his statue. You and your sister have been my favorite tools. Well, you really. Righteous and oblivious, a potent combination. Not unlike Beckett, only he wasn't quick enough. Or really, he didn't have your sister by his side. We all know she's the real threat. That's why I had to take her out first."

The words splashed like acid against her ears. They obliterated her ability to think clearly.

Pulsating rage remained.

"You lie. You're all lies. That's the only thing you have. No loyalty, no friends or family. Only lies."

His hooded stare ran her blood cold. She took a step back.

"At least I didn't destroy my family."

His grin never reached his eyes.

"Congratulations. This is what you have wrought. Destruction of your precious city. Death to all those you know and love. You're a tool. Nothing more. An empty, starry-eyed fool who has been my greatest success. A mole inside my enemies' headquarters. You, Aurelia Silverthorne, amongst all my whispers, have been most pivotable. Killing your parents before they could find the Rod, sowing discord in the Halls amongst the patrons, bringing the Sigil back to the city. It's all you, Aurelia. You. A real leader would have seen your sister's condition for what it was, a trap, and left her. But no, you brought your entire little Order into her mind, and into my grasp. Thank you, Aurelia. Your support has meant much to me."

A tentacle brushed against her jaw as she shook with anger. Not at Elosian, but herself. She feared he was right. She'd failed. Failed her parents. Failed Pi. Failed the city and her friends.

It was over.

Thirty-Four

"What's taking so long?" asked Ivan as he paced around the mattress where the mind travelers were lying unconscious. He reached into his pocket and pulled out a little vial that he'd brewed up a few days after Ares' death—just in case things got too bad. It was probably too strong, even for him, but the urge to sink into a hole and forget about the world had been gnawing at him.

Audrey appeared and placed her hands over his while smiling serenely up at him. "Let me take that."

Ivan gave up the elixir without complaint. He knew she was looking out for him. Audrey stood on her tippy-toes and gave him a kiss.

"Thanks, babe."

"You're doing great."

"I'd be doing better if they'd wake up and all this would be over. Look at the tattoo. It's *burning*. Not like the cool, embers in leaves kind of way. Mori looks like she's in pain. She's grimacing. I heard a moan a little bit ago."

Audrey checked back to the mattress. Frowned.

He chewed on his fingernails as he continued pacing, thinking about the elixir in her pocket.

"Are you sure I can't take it? It would reduce my anxiety. Help me think."

Audrey wandered to the window. "I think this is the one time the anxiety is good. Keeping us alert."

"Augh, I knew you'd say that." He put his hands on the back of his head. "Why did this have to come back? I just got over the night terrors from last time."

He was expecting a consoling word, but Audrey was staring out the window.

"I think I see your sister."

"What?"

He joined Audrey at the window to see Andromeda standing before the gate, waving her arms and shouting. She looked like she'd come straight from the Mystique as she was wearing dark blue tights and a sparkly patterned black-and-white form-fitting shirt.

"Watch them."

Ivan hurried downstairs, fumbling the code three times before managing to open the gate. Andromeda threw her arms around him when she made it to the front door where he was standing.

"I missed you."

Andromeda squeezed quickly then pulled back. "We're in trouble. Those assholes who kidnapped me are on the way here."

"Shit. Shit-fuck. Are you kidding me? Now?"

"Yeah, now. I had just gotten into town and I was in a taxi when I saw their vans. I can't forget them. But thankfully there was road construction in the fifth and we got out ahead of them. They can't be far behind. Where are the others?" she asked, glancing all around as she was coming to the realization that he was the only one greeting her.

Ivan gave her the short explanation, which amounted to a series of run-on sentences delivered at Mach speeds. When he was finished, she put her hand on his arm and said, "We're screwed."

Audrey came tramping down the stairs and stuck her head around the corner.

"Hey!"

"The kidnappers are coming."

Audrey screwed up her face. "Oh fuck."

"I already said that," said Ivan. "I think this calls for something stronger like holy dick blasters."

Andromeda had a hand to her mouth. "How are we going to protect this place? It's just the three of us. A Weird Circus, Stone Singer, and Alchemist. They're going to annihilate us. We have to wake them up."

Ivan grimaced. "We can't. They're the distraction."

"Would you prefer to die?"

Andromeda went bounding up the stairs as Ivan followed, yelling for her not to do anything rash. His youngest sister threw herself on her knees and started shaking Moriganne's shoulder, but only managed to make her body jiggle like a stringless marionette.

"They're here!" came a shout from downstairs.

Ivan put a hand to his mouth. His heart was going a thousand miles an hour and he wanted to vomit.

"What are we going to do?" asked his sister, looking at him as if he should know.

He closed his eyes. "Uhm, I think Ares set up a bunch of defenses, but they're not active."

"Great!" said Andromeda, pushing him towards the stairs. "Turn them on."

"I don't know how!" he yelled as he rumbled down the stairs. Passing a window, he saw the two vans outside the gate just pulling up. A door slid wide on the first van.

He reached the bottom floor and looked around in a panic. "There's supposed to be a trigger word or something. Ares was afraid the invasion was going to happen at any moment and he wanted to create a fortress. But we never found the password. We're lucky enough it wasn't activated when we got here."

Andromeda headed straight for the calendar of yachts hanging on the wall next to the door. She flipped it over, revealing a handwritten piece of paper with a short spell on it.

"Our brother was nothing but predictable. He ironed his underwear, feared our father, and kept his passwords in the most obvious of places," said Andromeda.

She yanked the paper off and stepped outside the door as the sound of a van door closing announced their approach.

"*Victor is an asshole*!"

Andromeda spoke the words as if she were performing on the stage. As she finished, a blast of energy traveled across the concrete and up the sides of the three-story building, right as someone tried to open up the gate. A shout was followed by the scent of burning hair.

Ivan remembered there was a camera facing out of the gate, and turned on the monitor right inside the first floor to see the four mages and the frightening looking cobra-headed creature that he'd heard about from the others.

He buzzed the speaker. "Go away unless you're selling Girl Scout cookies. I'm all out of Trefoils, and those Thin Mints are the devil."

A hulking dude and a beautiful girl in an expensive black trench coat shared a confused glance. The other two behind them were examining the fence and gate.

"I don't know who this is but we're here for the others. Send them out and we won't tear this place down brick by brick," said the girl in the trench coat.

Ivan was chewing on his fingernails formulating a response when Andromeda buzzed the speaker.

"You're outnumbered and outclassed, Sammi. Leave well enough alone, you're already meddling in things you don't understand."

"Andromeda? You should have stayed with your touring company. We'd decided to let you go."

"Bullshit," said Andromeda, "you were grasping at straws. A desperate Hail Mary to feel important."

"You're the ones meddling in things you don't understand. You'll be the destruction of the city," said Nandi as she angrily pointed at the camera. "Or maybe you do, because you Charmers are demon-loving traitors. We know your family was involved with a summoning of Elosian. Magnus admitted as much to Beckett."

Andromeda looked to him for an answer. Ivan shrugged his shoulders. She punched him in the arm, so he buzzed in.

"Our father was a megalomaniac who got what he deserved," said Ivan.

"You're not denying that he summoned Elosian?"

"I'm not denying that he was an asshole. Grade-A, farm fresh, the kind that uses his kids for his own sick purposes. You're not going to find any of us still worshiping at his altar. He's gone. Good riddance. He had Solstice killed and had Moriganne—"

Andromeda shoved her hand over his mouth. He pulled her hand gently away while the other mages conversed away from the camera. He couldn't hear them.

"They're still going to try and come in," he said.

"They might leave."

Ivan shook his head as he reached for the nonexistent elixir in his pocket.

"They think themselves too important not to try."

As he expected the four of them spread out near the gate. Nandi faced the camera and began the motions of a spell. It wouldn't be good. She'd been tops in her class at Coterie. A formidable mage with excellent training.

"What are we going to do?" asked Andromeda.

Ivan squeezed his eyes shut. "I haven't the slightest clue."

Thirty-Five

Elosian was coming.

He'd trapped her in his mind, forcing her to relive the most awful moment of her life. The wheel of the sedan was still spinning behind her.

Moriganne walked towards the flipped vehicle. She wanted to look in hopes that it would be different. She knew it wouldn't be different. Isabella had died and Ian spent two weeks in the hospital recovering. She walked away with minor headwounds that didn't even need stitches.

There'd been another picture that day. The photographer whose car she'd hit had snapped one of her screaming on the side of the road. Trails of blood bisected her face, and she'd been tearing at her clothes. The paper never published it. The photographer sent it to her in the mail months later. She'd never understood why. Maybe he felt guilty for being on the side of the road. If he hadn't, it never would have happened. Part of her had wished the picture had been published. Maybe it would have proved to the world that she'd been punished enough for what happened that day.

The sirens grew louder. Almost ear-piercingly loud. She put her hands to her ears. It wasn't the ambulance, but Elosian. He was coming for her.

Last time, he'd bargained for her life with Victor, but even he was smart enough not to give her up. But then Elosian had gotten loose and he'd come straight for her. Moriganne hadn't thought that he could take the sigil from her in the woman's mind, but now that she was here, she was convinced that it was possible.

The burning had gone beyond ache and was actually crisping the skin around the tattoo. Heat radiated off the embers. She could smell burnt flesh. Her flesh.

The two-lane road curved around the tree line. Elosian was approaching from around the bend. Running was out of the question. She was in his mind. Or he was in hers. Either way, there was no escape.

"Mori!"

She spun around to find the redhead and her foxlike companion standing on the road near the flipped car. Pax glanced to the accident with a frown before hurrying forward.

"We have to get out of here," said Pax. "He's coming."

"I know. How did you get here?"

Pax grabbed her arm, pulling her towards the flipped vehicle. "No time for that."

Moriganne resisted as they neared the front where she'd see her dead daughter.

"What are we doing?"

"Leaving."

Moriganne jammed her heels in the ground at the corner of the vehicle. She could smell gasoline. The corner wheel was slowing down.

"How?"

"We need a door to make a portal." Pax bunched up her mouth as Kali whined, eyebrows going up and down as she stared in the direction of the approaching sirens. "Trust me."

"What about the other car?" asked Moriganne, her voice trailing to nothing as she realized there was no time left. The skin around the tattoo was turning char black.

Pax ducked down and yanked on the passenger door, which didn't budge. She closed her eyes, tried again. The metal groaned until she could pop it free.

The whole time Pax was working on the door, Moriganne was staring at the general region of the back seat. She couldn't see it from her vantage, but she knew what was there. Her heart was climbing into her throat. The world had condensed to a single point.

"Isabella."

The name leaked from her lips. Moriganne wished the embers in her arm would turn to flame and consume her completely. Crouched on her knee, Pax looked into the back of the vehicle, frowned, then back up to her. Pax held out her hand.

"I'm sorry. We have to do this or he's going to catch us. Don't look, if you can."

Moriganne took her hand, realizing that her own was shaking profusely. Her feet wouldn't move at first until Pax gave her a little tug. As she crouched down to duck walk into the flipped passenger side door, she heard a tiny cute voice from the backseat.

"Mama."

Pax tugged on her arm to get her to move, but her feet were frozen. She closed her eyes as anger replaced the horror and fear.

"Fuck you, Elosian, for using my daughter against me like this. As if I haven't suffered enough."

She looked through the broken glass to the other side of the vehicle to see two hairy hooves. Moriganne had an urge to stand up and unleash the tattoo on him, but then Pax gave her hand another tug and she threw herself forward as a tentacle whipped around the top, barely missing her ankle as they disappeared through the portal.

Thirty-Six

Zayn had locked himself in the bathroom of Aurie's hospital room. He couldn't watch their daughter be born and injected with the Lady's poison again. He'd nearly given his life to free Varna from her clutches and now he was back in an alternate reality where he'd given in to her request to join her.

The birth had looped through dozens of times. He refused to participate and so he was seated on the closed toilet, trying his best to ignore the cries of birthing, so when he heard a new voice he stood up reflexively.

"Zayn Carter."

He put his hand on the doorknob and hesitated. He knew the voice. Why had the vision changed?

When he stepped back into the hospital room, it was empty, except for a tall woman staring out the window. Her silver and black hair had been braided into a crown that sat on her head, and she held her arms behind her back. The light purple skin the color of lilacs meant it could only be one person.

Lady Arcadia.

She turned. Purple eyes regarded him with faint amusement.

"I've killed you once, Entana," he said, using her secret name. "I can do it again."

"The dead never truly die. They live on in memory and the strength of their deeds."

"In a generation or two, when no one alive has to take your poison, you'll be forgotten," said Zayn.

"Doubtful." She gestured towards the air. "You killed me, yet here you are, talking to a figment of your imagination."

"I didn't create you."

"I'm afraid you did, Zayn. You wanted answers. Why? How? That sort of thing. The questions you should have asked before you killed me."

She arched an exquisite eyebrow. Her beauty, however alien, was undeniable.

"This is a distraction. You're trying to keep me here on Elosian's behalf. Or as far as I know, you *are* Elosian in disguise."

"He's a beast," said Lady Arcadia with a sneer. "We left him for good reason."

"Left him? You came from the demonic realm?"

She approached with long, graceful strides. "Of course." She cupped her hand beneath his chin. Her flesh was cold, hard. "But I escaped."

"Are you the Lost Prince?"

Lady Arcadia laughed, The melodic sound was intoxicating in its loveliness. Zayn shook his head to get the voice out of his mind.

"No, darling. But I came over with him. There were others too, but they got lost, or ended things, either by their own hand or because of foolishness. Few are left from that time. The ones that are had to reinvent themselves. Your world is so inflexible. Its beauty and curse is that the rules don't change."

"Why did you come over?"

Lady Arcadia lifted a shoulder. "To escape? To subjugate your foolish race? A little of both. The place we came from was unkind, cruel, constantly changing. We had to leave or be transformed irrevocably."

"But you left Elosian."

"Yesss." Her eyes glittered with thought. "We betrayed him. He was the best and worst of us."

"Of us?"

"The Elders. The first ones to drag ourselves from the throes of chaos. To form ourselves into something solid. You call it the demonic realm, but it's not that. It is creation. Raw, changing, beautiful, damning. It's high magic. It's madness."

"How can I know this? This is a trick. You're really Elosian."

"Come now, Zayn. You carry my poison in you. Not the secondary stuff from the spiders you harvest, but the poison I secreted. While you live, I will never truly die."

"Then tell me what we need to do to kill Elosian," he said.

"You can't. As powerful as your magics are, you cannot kill Elosian. My demise was aided by long millennia in your realm. He is invincible. Hardened by chaos and time. That he has not changed since we left him stranded at the gate proves his power. You'd be best to find a new home should he make the journey across."

"There has to be something. Someone. I killed you. We can kill him."

"No. Just because you want it to be true doesn't mean it is. The seeds of the past eventually grow fruit, but sometimes it falls to waste and rots, turning to poison. Just like you did to me."

Zayn felt a breeze on his back. He turned with a blade in his hand to find Alex standing in the doorway.

"Who are you talking to?" she asked as she adjusted her glasses.

Zayn spun around again to find the hospital room empty. "I was talking to..."

"It doesn't matter. We have to get out of here," she said.

"What happened?" he asked, glancing to the window where Lady Arcadia was standing. The vision hadn't been like the one of Aurie giving birth.

"He was waiting for us." She bunched up her lips. "Ambushed us, like we were trying to do to him. I got out of my vision. Took me a few tries to make it here. There's some weird shit in his head. Or our heads. I don't know you all enough to know if a cave full of creepy spiders or a passage of weird ants comes from any of you."

"How did you get out?"

Alex sighed. She was clearly annoyed that she had to explain.

"Game world or dream world, they work pretty much the same. There has to be a construct where you exist, either the Gamemakers arcane-technology or in that asshole's mind. I had to make my own portal out of a shitty balsa wood door, but it helped me get free."

"How do I know you're not a figment of *my* imagination?"

Alex paused with her mouth open. "Good question. I don't have an answer. Trust me or not." She looked over his shoulder. "Why a hospital room?"

It was his turn to be stymied. He wasn't sure he wanted it to get back to Aurie that his vision had involved them having a kid and getting shot up with the Lady's poison.

"It's not important."

"Right." Alex stepped inside the room and closed the door. "Who we getting next? Kitty or Aurie?"

As soon as the words left her mouth, the corners of her lips creased slightly.

"Never mind. Aurie it is."

"Hey," he said as he took her hand.

Alex closed her eyes momentarily, then opened them back up. "Be ready for anything. I don't know how many hops it'll take to find her."

The portal burned black when it was revealed. As they stepped through together, Zayn worried that Lady Arcadia was right and all their plans were for naught.

Thirty-Seven

The two figures, Elosian and the green-skinned one, turned away from the gap as she tried to catch the rest of their conversation. Pi pounded her fist on the wall. They were gone before she could figure out how to squeeze through. She shouldn't have been able to but the physics of this world weren't the same as her own.

The torturous seemingly random passages eventually deposited her outside the structure, giving her a view of the valley below. The sight left her shaken. As far as the eye could see, there were hovels and structures, less chaotic than the place she now stood. Tens of thousands of creatures milled about. The distance did nothing to protect her from their awful visages—blade-men, mantics, others she had no name for, like the hunched ochre-skinned humanoids with long claws that were most common. Chaos had birthed them. Now they were poised for an invasion.

Across the valley, a structure drew her eye. The arched design had one purpose. It was the portal that the army would pass through on their way into the city of sorcery. But where would it come out on the other side? Pi wondered if she could discover that truth. It would help them stop it if she could find her way out of Elosian's mind.

Struck by the chaotic sights below, Pi hadn't realized she was standing on the side of a building. She'd barely noticed her surroundings once she'd come outside to view the valley. Pi craned her neck. The impossible building climbed up the side of the "castle," twisted and warped. She tried to follow sections with her eyes, but they gave her a headache and she had to look away. Her logical mind couldn't comprehend the madness of the construction.

Pi headed across the wall/floor towards the valley floor. If she could reach the portal, she might learn what could save them, and possibly escape through it. The nearer she got to the bottom, the more she realized she would stick out. Using the magic of intention, Pi held her hands around her head as if she were grabbing the hood of a cloak. She pulled it forward, imagining the black fabric, and to her surprise, found her fingers squeezing the soft cotton. The newly created cloak fit comfortably around her shoulders, turning her into a vaguely humanoid-shaped shadow.

There was no path around the endless settlements, so Pi settled for heading straight through, hoping the cloak and her intentions would keep her safe. The hovels she passed were made of many materials. She saw one made of what appeared to be pure gold, but cracked along the dome as if it were eggshell. The creatures in the settlements gave her little notice as she followed the gaps between the buildings.

Their language was incomprehensible to her at first, but as she spent more time listening to their guttural phrasing, her mind started to pick out the words. It was like standing at the Tower of Babel before the fall. Everyone spoke different words, but the chaotic magic of the realm made it possible to understand.

One of the ochre-skinned humanoids with long claws grabbed her arm as she slipped past a narrow gap between two hovels. She hadn't seen him.

"Grotha na postit. Ferom spata."

Pi stared at him from the shadows of her cloak. She yanked her arm away as her mind caught up to the words.

You're not supposed to be here. This is ferom territory.

He reached for her again, but she pushed past, hurrying before he grew more curious. She glanced over her shoulder to see him talking excitedly to a group of the ochre-skinned creatures. As she moved past a strange four-legged beast of burden that reminded her of a stubby elephant with lizard scales, the feroms moved to follow.

"Shit," she muttered under her breath, moving faster, but finding her movement drawing more attention, either from speed, or the lessening of her disguised intentions.

The feroms followed her relentlessly as she crossed into other regions of the extended settlements. As she was slipping by a taller building that rose to a point like a narrow pyramid, a tentacle reached out from the dark cavity at the front and grabbed her leg. Surprised and horrified, Pi didn't so much as think, but reacted, slashing down at the appendage and wounding it enough that it retracted back into the darkness. As it retreated, she stared at the newly formed dagger in her hand.

"Useful." She kept moving. "And scary."

The pursuit continued. At times, Pi thought she lost them, but then as she rounded a corner, a lone ferom would spot her and the chase would resume.

The great arch was not always visible in the depths of the hovels, but as she crossed the vast plains filled with demons and their buildings, she spotted the twisted landscape she'd seen in previous visions in the distance—and far overhead.

She wondered if the bridge lay between the two areas that came together at a point as she'd seen before. But there was no time to explore—she wanted to get out of Elosian's mind and hoped that the portal would provide the method.

Distracted by her thoughts, Pi didn't see two ferom until they'd stepped into her way. Their slit noses flared. Teeth like needles were revealed.

"Ugly fuckers."

When they reached for her, she shoved the blade into the first ferom's chest, eliciting a horrific scream as black blood leaked from around the knife. She pivoted around her stabbing target, using his body as a shield against the second. He reached around his dying friend to grab at her cloak, catching the hood as she tried to leap away, pulling it back and revealing her human face.

A cry of alarm went up around her. The casual murder became something entirely different as her identity was understood. Pi leapt away, leaving the blade she'd conjured from nothing in the ferom's chest, yanking up her hood in hopes of outrunning the chaos.

Pi no longer tried to maintain a pace that didn't look like flight. She ran headlong, shoulder charging whoever or whatever got in her way, hoping the prone victims of her impacts made it harder to follow. She ran for minutes, never quite breaking free. Although they never got close, there were too many pursuers and she was easily marked.

It wasn't her intention to throw herself through the flaps of a hut, but she found herself in a space between the huts without another soul in sight. If they rushed past, and she was in hiding, she might be able to lose them.

The interior of the makeshift dome of bone and dried, cracked flesh was warm and stuffy. Her eyes adjusted slowly. A lumpy figure in the back was revealed to be a creature that looked like melted wax. Black eyes moved through the "head" of the creature, coming to bear on her. She stayed crouched at the flap, but kept checking behind her to make sure the Waxy Fire Hydrant wasn't making a move on her.

Pi stayed in the hovel for at least ten minutes, maybe more. Time was hard to measure. Her hovel companion stayed in the back until she'd decided to leave, and then Pi heard a gurgle and looked back to find a human-like appendage sticking out from the center of the pluggy figure. The idea of shaking its hand was repulsive, so she opened her palm and imagined a lump of gold, which when it appeared, she handed to the Waxy Fire Hydrant. The appendage disappeared into the lump and a sound like a quiet hiss leaked out. If she had to guess, it was a "thank you," but it could have just as easily been a "get out."

Before Pi returned to the outside, she imagined a different shape and color to her cloak, settling on something that matched the dried flesh look of the hovel she was hiding in. Once she was content that she looked different, Pi continued towards the portal archway.

She stayed alert, avoided crowds, and never stopped moving. Focused on her surroundings, she didn't realize she was near the portal until she saw the great curve of the archway above her. It was made of twisted silvery metal. Pi had seen pictures of the Arch in St. Louis, and this was a miniature version.

No hovels were built near the archway. She learned why when she approached. The entire structure put off a hum that made her teeth hurt. It was like getting stuck in a dentist's chair while he drilled in her mouth. The twisted metal sent off little sparks as if high currents of electricity were coursing through it.

After her examination, she was unsure how she might use it to escape. From Elosian's castle, the idea had seemed solid. Now, her reasoning evaporated. She looked back to the mountainside to see the place where she'd escaped. The structure climbed over the slope with towers and bridges, sometimes going nowhere, the logic of chaos.

Pi spotted a creature that looked like a lumpy ball with legs by the nearest hovel staring at her. She faded back towards the buildings so as not to be as obvious. The hovels went no further than the edge of the portal. She looked past it to the other landmass hanging in the sky, where the bridge she'd seen in the vision existed. If escaping wasn't the main goal, she would have headed towards it, an expedition to satisfy her curiosity.

Deep in thought about the bridge and its significance, Pi didn't hear the figures behind her until a curved knife was pressed against the soft flesh of her neck.

Thirty-Eight

Ivan was transfixed on the monitor as Nandi completed her arcane gestures and the gate bent in half as if two giant hands had grabbed it. The metal structure flung away, sliding across the concrete, leaving the path to the three-story building open.

"They got through the gate!" Ivan yelled.

"I'm right here," said Andromeda.

"It was for Audrey."

He looked back to the monitor. "What are we going to do? I wasn't expecting a fight."

"Are you sure we can't wake them up?"

Ivan shook his head as Lennie, the huge Protector mage, tried to walk onto the concrete path only to have it blow him off his feet.

"I'm sure. They have to provide the distraction so the others can get Pi." He looked over to his sister's confusion. "It's a long story. At least Ares was prepared for this."

"He was prepared for a demonic invasion, not a couple of righteous mages bent on eradicating the 'Charmer threat,'" she said, making air quotes. "Can't you mix up some bombs or something? Ares had a small lab."

The mages outside had gotten Lennie back on his feet. Ivan was hoping he'd be out of commission, but the explosion had only caused surface wounds.

"His materials are all wrong. Salt, mercury, stuff like that. If we were being attacked by scorpics, sure, but not these assholes," he said.

"If we don't do something soon, they're going to break through the defenses. I've been abducted once by these *connasses*, I don't want a second time."

Heavy footsteps came pounding down the steps. Audrey leaned around the corner.

"Mori's tattoo is burning bright. Should we do something?" Her gaze flitted to the monitor. "Oh shit, they're through the gate."

Ivan reached into his pocket, staring at his hand like a traitor when it came back empty.

"Sorry, babe," said Audrey.

He put his fingertips against his temples. "Can you sing us a wall or something? Make it harder to get inside?"

"If I had more time, maybe. I haven't been practicing, but I could manage something outside the door."

Ivan spied the kitchen counter, checking underneath the sink to find cleaning liquids including a bottle of ammonia. He raced into the small laundry room off the secondary room and grabbed the bottle of bleach on the shelf.

"Can you get us more time?" he asked his sister. "Distract them somehow."

Andromeda looked around and grabbed the shotgun that was leaning against the wall.

"It's filled with salt shots," said Ivan.

She rolled her eyes. "You wanted a distraction. I don't need to kill them."

Andromeda disappeared upstairs, which wasn't the direction he was expecting, but he was too busy with his makeshift explosive to question it. He grabbed some plastic bags from the pantry and looked around for a paint marker to make some trigger runes. While he was running around the bottom floor, Audrey had the front door cracked open. She was singing through the gap, her ethereal voice giving him the chills.

Ivan nearly dropped the bottle of ammonia when the shotgun blasted from right outside the first-floor window. He ran over to see Andromeda standing on the side of the building, perpendicular to the wall. A wave of flame came rushing towards her, but she backed around the corner before it caught her.

"Nice."

Resuming his makeshift explosive, Ivan combined the liquids, using the bags to keep them separate until the trigger. When he had everything shoved into the bottle, he opened the side window as not to interfere with Audrey's stone singing. The mages had managed to deactivate the enchantments around the entrance and were taking tentative steps inside the enclosure. The Protector mage looked like he was readying a volley towards his girlfriend at the door. Ivan leaned the bottle out the window and gave it a great heave. The plastic container spun through the air.

"Eat shit, you bootlickers!"

Lennie turned and fired at the spinning bottle with a two-hand force blast. The magic triggered the runes and the bottle exploded, knocking him on his rear and sending out a cloud of caustic gas, which forced him to retreat. When Nandi stuck her head around the fence, Ivan flipped her off as he was laughing. He couldn't help it. He was having a good time. Ivan returned to the kitchen looking for materials for his next explosive.

Thirty-Nine

Huge green domes loomed above the smoke drifting across the concrete paths. A vendor cart had been ripped in half, plushies of supernatural animals scattered around the destruction.

Kali made a huffing noise.

"I agree," said Pax.

"Where is this?" asked Moriganne, still clutching her hand.

Pax gave her a little squeeze. For her to climb into the wrecked vehicle had taken a lot of courage. She didn't know the details of Moriganne's accident, but seeing the anguish on her face told the tale.

"Portland Zoo during the disaster. Looks like Elosian is trying to keep us occupied," she said.

"Why?"

At the edge of the smoke, Pax spotted a team of special forces heading towards the security building.

"I wish I knew. I don't know how this mind-realm stuff works any more than you do, but I think Elosian can't control it completely. While I was escaping my version, I stumbled into the past. I was in Egypt, when the Lost Prince was there. I think he made Aepep."

"How do you know it wasn't Elosian showing you this vision?" asked Moriganne.

A shout from inside the smoke was followed by a string of gunfire. Something was burning to their left, making it hard to see.

"Kali could tell."

Moriganne craned her neck towards the gunfire. "Should we be worried here?"

"No. Nothing can hurt us. Physically anyway," said Pax, noting Moriganne's flinch. "The visions seem to be our most traumatic moments. The seeds of the past. We're who we are because of what we've experienced."

"Some things are better left in the past," said Moriganne, staring into the distance.

Pax felt his presence even before Kali started growling.

"He's here," said Moriganne, peering into the smoke.

"Come on. Let's find a doorway."

They jogged towards the security building. There was a gap in the smoke as the winds swirled it away. A manticore was standing near a snow-cone kiosk, its spiked tail swishing behind. The lion face snarled as it looked for potential threats.

"Keep going," said Pax when Moriganne tried to pull away. "It's only in the vision."

"This is what happened?"

Pax nodded. "This was the easy stuff. Here. This is the shambler dome. We can use the doorway to go somewhere else."

"Where?"

"Good question."

Moriganne sucked in a breath through her teeth. The tattoo on her elbow flared up. The flesh around it was charred black. Her eyes rolled into the back of her head, showing only the white. She collapsed against Pax, who helped her to the ground.

Kali growled again. A shape was moving towards them through the smoke, tentacles undulating at his side. Pax got up and grabbed the door to find that it was locked, or barred from the inside. The nearest dome was another hundred, hundred and fifty feet away.

Forty

Alex stepped onto the grass as a dark shape flew overhead, making her duck. Zayn released her hand and surged forward. She saw where he was headed.

The older Silverthorne sister stared blankly at a gravestone. In the distance smoke rose in columns. Zayn grabbed her shoulder, startling her. Aurie's eyes were as wide as moons.

"Where did you come from?" Her head snapped around to the front. "Where did he go?"

"Who?"

"Elosian."

"He was here?" asked Alex.

Aurie pointed to a spot near the gravestone. She knelt in the grass. "Right here. I can see the impression where he was standing."

"This only gets stranger," said Zayn.

"He's toying with us," said Alex. "Or he's not completely in control of the visions."

"Maybe he went after one of the others," said Zayn.

Aurie had her arms pulled around her chest. She kept glancing back to the gravestone. Alex read the epitaph and grimaced.

"He's trying to get under your skin," Alex told her, but Aurie didn't seem to hear. She was shaking her head with words held back.

"She's right," said Zayn. "Whatever this is, it's an attempt to distract us. Confuse us. He did the same to me."

Aurie looked up. "What did he show you?"

Zayn flinched. "It doesn't matter. But at the end of the vision, I had a visit from the Lady.

It could have been Elosian in disguise, but I don't think so. She told me that a group of them came over from the demonic realm a long time ago, but they left Elosian because they feared him. Said he was the worst of them."

"How does this help us?" asked Aurie.

"I don't know. Not yet. Not sure I would trust the Lost Prince if we found him though, knowing that he was like the Lady and the other psychos that tried to rule our forbearers."

"We need to get moving," said Alex. "The faster we find your sister and get out of here, the better."

"Agreed," said Aurie.

"But Kitty first."

Aurie flinched but nodded. Whatever had happened in her vision had wounded her greatly. There was something diminished about Aurie, as if she'd lost trust in herself. Alex didn't know her that well, but she seemed markedly different from the woman she'd met at the Verum Locus.

They found a mausoleum a short distance away. Zayn pulled the stone door open, revealing the darkness inside.

"Everyone ready?" asked Alex, holding out her hands.

They went through the portal together, finding themselves in a huge room at what appeared to be a luxury lodge. A group of kids were playing in a pool outside. The head of a massive elk was affixed to the wall, and at the end of a long table sat a lone figure, staring blankly into the distance.

"That's Victor Charmer," said Zayn. "But where's Kitty?"

Sobs came from the corner. Kitty was seated on a prep table, knees pulled to her chest, head down. Alex checked back to the vision to see what might have injured her but the scene seemed to be resting.

"Hey," said Zayn upon approach, startling Kitty to lift her head. Her eyes were red from crying, cheeks blotchy.

"I'm a monster," she told them. "He made me one."

The lone figure of her father didn't suggest the accusation against herself, but given the emotional distress, Alex was prone to believe her.

"That's what he wants. Elosian's trying to keep us from doing what we came here to do, or break us, or both," said Alex, putting her hand on Kitty's foot.

"I know. Broken hells, I know. This is standard psych ops kind of stuff, but it doesn't make it hurt any less," said Kitty with a quivering exhale.

"We need to leave," said Zayn. "Can you move?"

Kitty nodded with her lips squeezed tight.

"We're getting Pi next, right?" asked Aurie.

They gathered by the big double doors. Alex caught Kitty's hate-filled glance towards her father at the head of the lonely table.

"Focus on Pythia," said Alex.

When they stepped through the portal, the sharp stab of faez hit her nose right away. It was like trying to snort a spoonful of pepper. She squeezed her nose shut the moment they arrived.

"Where are we?" exclaimed Aurie.

They stood on the edge of a vast plain covered in hovels. To their left, a twisted archway hung over the settlement, while in the distance, jagged impossible mountains surrounded them.

"She's not far," said Aurie, striding off without hesitation or guile. Alex ran up and grabbed her arm, Aurie tried to shake her off.

"We need to be careful," said Alex, nodding towards the figures in the hovels, who were quietly staring at them. "We're not invisible here. This place is different."

Aurie followed her gaze. She frowned.

"But she's near. We need to get her and get out of here."

The defiance in Aurie's eyes made Alex let go of her arm.

"Fine," she muttered after Aurie continued her march, "let's just bring everyone's attention on us."

They passed a half dozen hovels, their flaps occasionally pulling wide as whoever, or whatever was inside, watched them pass. When they spotted a figure in dark clothing staring into the distance, Zayn held up a fist, and when they paused, he snuck forward and put a blade to the figure's neck.

The figure spun out of his grasp with surprising quickness and yanked back her hood to reveal the missing Silverthorne. She seemed different than the one in the Verum Locus. Rawer. Cheeks slightly emaciated, eyes hungry.

Aurie threw herself in her sister's arms. They held tight, rocking on their feet while Alex noted the increasing interest in their appearance. A half dozen ochre-skinned humanoids with long claws came around the corner. Alex felt the recognition in their gazes.

"Heyas," she called to her new friends, "I think we'd better get ready for a fight."

Forty-One

Andromeda had been crouched on the side of the building using the enchantments she'd learned at the Mystique to perform the gravity defying movement when the cobra-headed creature sauntered onto the concrete and leaned its head back. She threw herself through the open window on the first floor as a black cloud of coal smoke came billowing towards her. Her shoulder knocked a pile of dirty plates and glasses to shatter on the floor as she tumbled through. The faucet neck snapped, sending a spray of water in a wide arc. Andromeda landed on the floor, soaking wet, an ugly pain in her shoulder.

"Andy..."

Audrey was standing near the door, mouth agape as Andromeda climbed to her feet, trying not to catch the spray of water directly in the face. A glance down revealed a shard of pottery in her shoulder.

"Well that sucks," she said.

"Oh Merlin, are you going to be okay?" asked Audrey, holding out her hands as if she wanted to help, but not knowing how.

Andromeda grasped the shard with both hands and yanked it out, tossing it onto the floor with the other shattered pieces. "I really liked that pattern."

With a hand to the wound, Andromeda closed her eyes and focused on knitting up the flesh. She'd done it so many times during her performances that she barely had to think through the spell. When her wound was closed, she slipped under the sink and turned the knob to stop the water from spraying everywhere.

"Where's Ivan?" she asked at the moment a shotgun blast erupted from the second floor.

"Never mind."

The steel front door started shaking, smoke slipping around the edges. The metal was bending in the frame. Ivan came running down the stairs with the shotgun in his fist.

"That beast is...never mind." He shook his head. "They've disabled the wards and I'm all out of Molotov cocktails. I even threw that bottle of two-hundred-year-old brandy, Merlin rest its soul. They'll be at the door soon."

A horrific crunch hit the door, bending the center in as if a giant fist had impacted it. Light slipped through the gaps. Andromeda could see the massive Lennie striding towards the entrance. He looked big enough to rip the door off without magic.

"Is it too late to wave the white flag? I'd be happy to donate my underwear to the cause," said Ivan.

Audrey smirked. "You're not wearing any, babe, remember?"

A pair of hands grabbed the two sides of the bent door. Metal groaned as he pulled it away. Andromeda blasted a flame bolt through the gap, but it slid off his skin, so she switched to earth, sending pellets of rock after him to the same effect.

"He's built like a tank, literally," she said, backing away.

The entire door flung away from the entrance. They fired various elements after him, but he casually pulled a runed riot shield from his back to block the attacks.

"Retreat," said Ivan, scurrying up the stairs with Audrey right behind.

Andromeda backed up slowly, continuing the assault as Lennie marched forward. The narrow stairs provided a choke point. She stopped halfway up and yelled over her shoulder.

"Any chance they're awake yet?"

The answer never reached her ears as Lennie shifted the riot shield aside and shouted. A wave of mind-altering magic washed over her.

"Do not resist."

Staggered on the stairs, Andromeda could barely stay standing as he climbed the steps. When he was a few feet away, she shook off the enchantment and kicked him in the face with her big black boot. He came away with a bloody nose and she extended her middle finger.

"I was born to resist."

The gesture cost her as he reached out and grabbed her wrist, yanking her down the stairs. He intended to throw her behind him where the other mages were gathering, but she wrapped her legs around his waist as she flew by, stymying the attempt. The years of acrobatics at the Mystique had benefited her in ways that surprised even her now.

"Hi," she said, clutching his side, only a few inches away.

Lennie threw his fist at her face, but she ducked around his arm. The blow glanced off his biceps and hit the wall, leaving a hole in the drywall.

"Hey, asshole, that's my dead brother's wall."

Andromeda scurried onto his back, grabbing him around the neck and pulling as hard as she could. It was like strangling a fire hydrant.

"Lennie, will you hurry up?" said Sammi, standing inside the first floor with her hands on her hips. "We don't know what they're doing upstairs. We need to stop whatever it is."

He was trying to reach her but his massive arms were getting in the way. He lacked the flexibility to put his hands behind his back to grab her.

"Yeah, hurry up, Lennie," she mocked from his back.

Her grin lasted until he threw himself into the brick outer wall. She heard at least two ribs crack. The air exhaled from her lungs violently and the strength left her arms. Lennie grabbed a leg, whipped her off his back, and attempted to toss her across the kitchen.

Performing under painful circumstances was every night at the Mystique. She grabbed the inner wall of the stairs as she was flung away, and despite the throbbing tenderness under her left arm, she catapulted herself back onto the steps in his way.

"You're fucking annoying," said Lennie, marching up while cracking his knuckles.

"The beauty of being the youngest in a fucked-up family. You learn to take a beating, both physical and emotional."

He extended his hands and she thought he was going to grab her, but a pair of ghostly chains flew out, wrapping around her limbs. The smirk on his lips lasted about two seconds, until she slipped out of the restraints by dislocating her shoulder and then popping it back. The enchantment dissipated into smoke, leaving him angry.

"It's polite to ask for consent before attempting a little bondage play. Also, my safe word is Rumpledickskin."

He leapt halfway up the stairs, grabbing her around the neck before she could scramble up. His fist was as big as her head, so his fingers closed all the way around her neck. The impact as he smashed her against both walls, brick and drywall, left stars in her eyes. Andromeda stuck her thumbs into his sockets as he continued to pound her into submission.

"I. Don't. Give. Up."

"Lennie, will you hurry the fuck up!"

Pain she could withstand, but he had a tight grip on her windpipe and the exertion was rapidly using up her oxygen. She'd pass out soon.

Lennie lifted her above his head and smashed her onto the steps. Multiple bones broke, even the ones hardened by magic. Exquisite pain shot through her, but she couldn't help but laugh.

"Big man, gets his rocks off by hurting women."

She held up her bloody knuckles and willed the word Dickless to scroll across them like a theater marquee as she laughed. His rage turned his head into a bright tomato. He pulled his fist back and Andromeda was sure the impact would smash her skull right through the floor, but her body was filled with pain and adrenaline and she was sure she didn't have enough energy left to move out of the way.

"Don't fuck with my sister."

To her utter surprise, Ivan threw himself down the stairs at Lennie. His attack was pathetic at best. It looked like the weak slap of a child until Andromeda realized that hadn't been the point. The bulged eyes and then inadvertent swallow as Ivan chopped him in the neck made his tactic clearer.

"You have no idea how much sadness that gives me not to take those drugs myself."

The effect was instant. Lennie went from rage-filled beast to vacant-eyed staggering fool. He swiped near his face as if there were bugs flying about.

Andromeda started laughing but the effort sent waves of pain through her broken body. She coughed and black blood came out. Not a good sign.

Ivan's grin at besting Lennie lost its vigor when he looked down to her. "Merlin's enormous hairy ball, sis, you look like Mr. Thule's taint."

She gave him a bloody grin as he helped her up onto the second floor.

"I don't know what you did to him, but it's not going to work. The three of you don't stand a chance against me," said Nandi as she stepped onto the bottom step.

"It was fun while it lasted," said Ivan, hauling her up. Each movement was like getting punched in the ribs, but she didn't want to give them the satisfaction of seeing her weak.

When they were halfway up the flight to the third floor, Nandi reached the landing beneath them. She slipped out of her black trench coat. The intensity on her face was nothing short of terrifying.

"Get ready to—"

The change from passionate anger to surprised confusion lasted until a staccato of notes was sung from the top of the stairs. Blasts of ice flew over them, hitting Nandi with three successful punches, throwing her backwards down the stairs until she came to rest at the feet of a drugged-up Lennie.

Moriganne marched past them, a flicker of worry in her eyes as she glanced down at Andromeda. The tattoo on her sister's arm burned in bright embers.

"Don't fuck with my family."

Forty-Two

Pi wasn't entirely sure they were real until she saw a fourth member of their group that she didn't recognize. It wouldn't make sense for Elosian to insert a stranger into her vision. The reunion was cut short when a large group of ferom stalked through the gap between a pair of hovels.

"Heyas," said the girl with dark hair and glasses. "I think we'd better get ready for a fight."

"Not a good idea," said Pi. "There are thousands of them and only a few of us."

Her sister stepped forward and attempted a true name shout, "Aurelia!"

The ferom flinched at her confidence, but then glanced between themselves as they realized nothing substantial beyond a light wind had happened. They advanced on them. Zayn and Kitty stepped in their way, producing weapons from hidden places.

"Magic doesn't work normally here," said Pi. "Think about the intention of the Eternal City."

The new girl's head snapped around. "What does that mean?"

There was an intensity to her gaze that Pi found intriguing. "Either we're in Elosian's head or this is a place of high magic. Maybe both. It's enough to imagine what you want to do and it'll happen. No need for fancy theatrics."

As the ferom advanced, Zayn and Kitty lunged forward, slicing them with precision and speed, keeping them off-balance. The darting attack broke the line of the demons, but did not force them to retreat. It would have been well and good if they were the only ones around, but Pi spied other groups converging on their spot from further away. A half dozen, or even a dozen demons, were easily handled by a group of their experience, but if the whole army turned on them, it wouldn't be much of a fight.

"We need to rethink our plan," said Pi as her sister sent a wave of force magic against another group coming up from the flank, knocking them over like bowling pins. "We're gonna get overrun."

"I can only stab so many at once," said Kitty, glaring over her shoulder. "Alex, can you come here and help us?"

The newcomer, Alex, looked unaffected by the shifting odds, or the request from Kitty. Pi was about to add to her sister's magics, but she found herself intrigued by the calm demeanor of the newcomer. Alex turned her head a few times, checking the positions of the four groups of demons converging on their location. Then a glance to the air.

Alex made a fist, held it above her head, and then smashed it down onto the ground. A concussive wave flew out, sending the feroms, tents, and other materials away from them in a tsunami. In the matter of two seconds, there was nothing and no one within a hundred feet of them.

"You're thinking too small," she told the others, then checked to the twisted archway. "We need to get out of here."

"Not yet," called Pi. "We need to find out how Elosian plans to cause the invasion."

Alex hesitated. "If we knew where to go..."

"I know." Pi lifted a shoulder. "Or think I do."

"Let's go then. Where is it?"

Pi extended her arm towards the other landmass hanging in the sky. The tips of the two continents connected at a narrow gap.

"Up."

Alex squinted. "I can get us there."

"Have we figured out what we're doing yet?" asked Zayn. "Because they've multiplied."

At the edge of the circle of destruction, hundreds of figures approached, walking over the uneven ground with shiny and twisted weapons in their fists.

"Gather round," said Alex, holding out her hands.

Pi made sure she was first to grab one. Her sister took the opposite side.

When the five of them were connected, Alex said, "Imagine that place up there. Fix it in your mind."

Pi did as she was told. A brief bout of vertigo ended when they landed on the path of the strange crystalline trees that led to the bridge between mountain ranges.

"How did you do that?" asked Aurie.

"This place isn't much different than my game world. The idea is not to be confused by your limitations, but push the boundaries of what's possible. Why did you want us to come here?"

"I've seen it in my visions. Come on," said Pi as she jogged ahead.

The fractal-like crystals of multi-and-shifting hues formed a loose tunnel that led to the bridge. She was halfway there when she noticed two figures standing on it and slowed until she was walking.

"Who are they?" asked Kitty.

The two figures were positioned at the midpoint, facing each other, which meant one of them should have seen them by now. Pi checked behind them to make sure it wasn't a trick, catching Alex doing the same. The visions she'd had in the castle became clearer.

"We're not only in Elosian's mind, but this is his past," she told them.

"Why can't these two see us?" asked Aurie.

"I don't know, but I feel like it's important," she answered.

They crept forward until Pi was certain who the two figures were.

"It's Elosian and the Lost Prince," said Kitty with breathless surprise.

Pi slowed. "I saw them in the castle."

"And that's the bridge from Mori's arm," said Kitty, tilting her head. "I always wondered why it looked as if it wasn't a real bridge, but now I understand."

"The connecting bolts were perpendicular to each other because the two landmasses it bridges are twisted," said Alex.

"I don't understand. What is this place? Why are we seeing it?" asked Aurie suspiciously.

They were about a hundred feet from the two figures and had stopped moving forward as if they collectively worried about being noticed even though it would have made sense for it not to have happened already. Elosian was easy to identify with the backward-facing knees and tentacle arms. He towered over his opposite number. The Lost Prince had greenish mottled skin and a knobby bald head. There was something about him that hit Pi right in the gut. She checked to her sister to see the same slow recognition.

"Broken hells."

Zayn's head snapped around. "What? That sounded bad."

Her sister flinched as if the realization had been a slap across the cheek.

"Oh no."

"Yeah."

Kitty turned on them. "Are you two going to keep dancing around whatever it is that you figured out, or are you going to tell us?"

"It's Invictus."

"What?" exclaimed Kitty. "You're joking, right?"

Pi shook her head. "I wish I was. The Lost Prince is Invictus. Trust me. We've spent the last two years getting yelled at by that crotchety old fart. I'd know his body language anywhere."

Elosian reached out a tentacle, and Invictus grasped it briefly before he turned and headed across the bridge towards his side. Pi followed the trail, leaning her head back to view the settlements on the opposite side and figures waiting not far beyond.

"Gigantes," said Kitty. "I'd know those big-headed demons anywhere."

"Does this mean we're fucked?" asked Zayn. "Has this whole dance about stopping the invasion been a ruse?"

Pi felt like a hand was squeezing her chest. It was hard to breathe.

"I don't know."

Alex turned on the group. "Whatever it means doesn't matter if we can stop the physical act. This is Elosian's mind. There should be somewhere that holds the key to his plans. Maybe Invictus' too."

"Sure we do," said Kitty, grinding her teeth. "It means we've been betrayed. Again. I'm getting sick of these old bastards selling me out."

Alex stepped to Pi. "You've been here and you were in his prison before you got out. Was there somewhere inside that might have held his plans?"

She was about to tell Alex that there wasn't until a memory popped into her head. She hadn't known what it meant at the time, but now it seemed significant.

"I can take us there."

They gathered around, holding hands. Pi fixed the location in her mind and willed herself to be there. At first nothing happened, and Alex said, "It's like flying in a dream. You have to have complete confidence that you'll stay aloft."

Pi nodded. The second attempt was a blur of motion, ending when they landed. Her sister nearly tumbled over at the sudden stop.

"Sorry."

The space seemed larger than when she'd seen it before. There were no windows, no doors, only a cavernous room with stone columns holding up the ceiling. Pi thought the design was absent until she realized they were standing on it.

"Here."

Everyone followed her gaze to the floor, where a giant circle with five dots and two lines going through them in an "X" marked the stone. The fifth marking came at the point the two lines crossed.

"I saw this before. I don't know what it means."

A few heads turned towards Alex, who lifted her shoulders. "I know game worlds and dreams, not much else about the threats."

"I...I know what it is," said Aurie with a hand to her chin. There was something diminished about her sister since they'd rescued her. Aurie usually was the one to direct things, but she'd been mostly quiet, occasionally opening her mouth and then closing it again.

She tapped on the edge of the circle. "This is the city of sorcery." Aurie moved her foot to the upper left-hand corner. "This is the well of power beneath the fifth ward. Specifically air. That one's earth, and over there is fire and last is water."

Both Kitty and Zayn shivered at mention of the water well.

"Does that make the one in the middle force?" asked Alex.

Aurie nodded. "Or spirit."

"Forgive my ignorance, but what are these wells? Like I said before, I haven't spent much time in the city," said Alex.

"Because of our constant use of faez, the barrier between our realm and this one has been breaking down. The original patrons and Invictus created the wells to collect and vent the faez in a safe manner. To protect the city from a collapse."

Zayn lifted his chin. "I helped Priyanka inspect them when I was a student." He glanced away. "Amongst other things."

"The wells would be the logical place for the break to happen," said Aurie.

"Just like Montanhas," added a sullen Kitty with her arms crossed tightly around her chest.

"Exactly like Montanhas, but much worse with a city of three million living above it." Aurie crouched by the center circle where the two lines crossed and placed her hand flat on the stone. "I don't know much about the fifth well. Its existence was insinuated but never confirmed."

"It's where the societies meet for the Convergence and other things. Ares was murdered at the ritual site," said Kitty. "But it couldn't be the location of the invasion, the well was closed up over half a century ago. There's thick concrete and runic protections made by the original patrons. You'd have to blast the entire area to dust to reach the well buried beneath it. That can't be the location."

"Then why put an 'X' over the wells?" asked Zayn.

"Are they ley lines? Some other field or pattern we don't understand?" asked Alex.

Aurie tapped her fist against the center circle. "It has to be the fifth well. But how?"

"There's only one person who knows that," said Alex quietly, looking past everyone.

Kitty and Zayn reacted to the newcomer before Pi saw him. They snapped to a ready pose, blades in their hands, facing the far side of the room.

"The how and where doesn't matter for the lot of you," said the honey-over-gravel voice of Elosian, Prince of Whispers, Lord of Lies.

The tall demon stood away from them, tentacles undulating at his side. His smile made her sick to her stomach. She felt like a farm animal being sized up for slaughter.

"None of you are leaving here. Ever."

Aurie closed her eyes briefly. "He's blocking us. It was a trap all along."

"Trap. Distraction. It's all the same," said Elosian. "Not long from now, the invasion will begin and there's nothing you can do to stop it. I will finally get the peace and stability I deserve. That I *earned*."

"By destroying our realm," Aurie said defiantly.

"As if you would let me live amongst you peacefully," said Elosian, spreading his tentacles. "Unless you'd like to join me. I can offer amnesty if you help me quickly recover the sigil." He grinned at Kitty. "There are others here who have been only too happy to support my cause."

Kitty regripped her blade, but made no move to advance.

"Are you done yet?" asked Alex, sauntering forward.

The dark-haired girl with glasses was small. Elosian towered over her in size and stature. Yet, she was not intimidated. Alex was sizing him up with a little head tilt that brought a smirk to Pi's lips.

"You're outclassed, whoever you are," said Elosian.

"You don't know who I am," said Alex with a burgeoning grin. "Your spies never saw me because I've been both away and entirely in the city this whole time. You're not as omniscient as everyone thinks. A clever strategist, sure, but you can't see everything. It's the problem with an organizational structure built on one man, or demon in this case. For all your power, you're only one mind, capable of only so much."

"What does it matter? I will grind your bones to dust."

Elosian reached out a tentacle to coil around Alex. Pi was sure she would be easily disposed of and moved to intercept, but Alex was quicker, slapping away the appendage as if it were a fly. Elosian's head snapped back. He bared his teeth, turning his human-like face monstrous.

"Meet you at the portal," said Alex, turning her head slightly.

To the utter shock of everyone in the room, Elosian included, Alex burst forward in a blur. The two hit the back wall of the room like a nuclear bomb. The entire back half the structure ripped away, and as the dust settled Pi spotted Elosian and Alex high in the sky locked in combat.

Forty-Three

The outside of Ares' three-story building looked like it'd been through a war. The gate was torn asunder, the concrete was blackened from the cobra-headed creature's breath, and other marks of sorcery marred the brick exterior.

Pax was cleaning a wound on Kali's shoulder. The fight against the mages had been brief. They'd overwhelmed them with surprise after coming out of the trance. She was shocked and relieved that they'd managed to escape Elosian's trap. Some of them, anyway.

Ivan was getting some water at the broken sink by switching on the pipe and holding his glass sideways to collect enough to drink, while Andromeda was seated against the wall, covered in blood and bruises. She'd already healed herself, a miracle of her hall.

"Think they'll be back?" asked Audrey, who was trying to clean up the glass on the floor with a broom.

"Not soon, but eventually, yeah," said Andromeda. "When they had me, I got to hear them blather on about their righteous mission. They think they're saving the world and sometimes I wonder if they're right. Has anyone been able to get through to the other team?"

"Nothing but messages," said Moriganne, holding up her phone. She was wearing one of Ares' old shirts since hers had gotten mostly burned up when she unleashed the power of the tattoo at the other mages. While they'd all helped drive them back, the main force had been Moriganne.

"If he was waiting for us," said Pax, "then he was going to do the same to them."

"Which we can do nothing about," said Andromeda.

Ivan had given up on his quest for water. He'd gotten drenched for his efforts.

"What are we planning on doing with that poor lady we kidnapped?" asked Ivan, nodding towards the third floor.

"Can you keep her safely under longer?" asked Pax.

"Sure. For another day easily, more if necessary, but we should find some way to give her fluids intravenously. Why?"

"Because I'm afraid Elosian will do to her what he did to the housekeeper."

Andromeda, who'd taken the worst of the fight, stood up shakily. "We're not just going to sit here, are we? We have to do something."

"I'm all for action," said Pax, "but what are we going to do? I fear the worst about the other group."

Ivan raised his hand. "I'm one hundred percent for sitting here. If this invasion is going to happen then I want to spend my time fortifying this place. Ares might have had his head up Vic's ass for most of his life, but he did a good job building a fortress."

"The funeral is tomorrow," said Andromeda, rubbing her ribs and grimacing.

"Seems appropriate," said Ivan, running his hands through his damp hair to make it spikey. "Poor bastard spent his time at Coterie preparing to deal with a bunch of bullshit demons, and he had to die before it started, and won't even get to have his funeral because the world is ending. It'll at least spare him the embarrassment of not having anyone besides us show up."

"Ivan..."

"Sorry, Andy. I know." Ivan exhaled and hung his head. "I wish I would have spent some time with him these last few years. But we've been busy with G&T, and he's been, well, you know." He crossed his arms. "And I'm a shit younger brother."

"You're a survivor," said Andromeda. "We all are."

He made a small gesture of understanding, but the weight of their family's problem sat heavy on his shoulders. Pax didn't need Kali's psychic abilities to see that. If she ever had a chance to meet this Victor, she would like to give him a piece of her mind.

"I'm headed to Arcanium," Pax announced. "Even if they're stuck in Pi's memory, I want to know for sure."

"I'll come with you," said Moriganne. "No one should be alone."

Ivan pointed to the ceiling. "We'll take care of Sleeping Beauty. I'll pop back to the lab and grab some IVs, plus some other things before coming back here. I probably should send the staff home. Paid vacation, all that jazz."

"How generous of you, Ivan," said Moriganne.

He lifted a shoulder. "If the invasion happens and we lose, then what does it matter? If we win, then I look like a fucking god to those people. Loyalty is hard to come by in this business."

"Your altruism knows no bounds." Moriganne rolled her eyes and chuckled. "We should get going."

"I'll stay here," said Andromeda, who looked uneasy on her feet. "I'm still, uhm, not quite right. I'd take a trip to Golden Willow, but I doubt there's time."

"I'll pick up some goodies for you," said Ivan as Audrey grabbed her shoulder bag.

They left the building, stepping around the scorch marks as if they still might be burning. While they waited for a couple of taxis to arrive, Ivan said, "Is this it? Do we think it's happening?"

"No idea," said Moriganne, holding her elbow. "But we'd better be ready in case it does."

At that moment, a strange light emanated from the top of the Spire. The pulse was longer and brighter than the ones that had come before in the previous weeks. Pax had to shield her eyes from the illumination and when it was gone, spots were left in her vision. Since she'd been back in the city of sorcery, she'd heard lots of speculation about what was happening with the top of the Spire, but now upon seeing that bright display, she had a pretty good sense of what it probably was.

It was a beacon.

Forty-Four

The trick wasn't, as people claimed, not to look down. That somehow acknowledging the fear would put credence in it. Fear was necessary. Fear was good. Alex embraced it. She had rivers of it coursing through her veins as she flew through the air to avoid Elosian's pursuit, dodging around the angular mountains that stuck up like grown crystals rather than geological happenings.

The others were still stuck with the concrete rules of magic and physics that governed their world. They were used to limits. Not so for Alex. She'd spent her life before the Hundred Halls breaking games, finding the loopholes that allowed her to achieve things that shouldn't be possible. The same was true for this mind-space in Elosian's head. Not only was it a dream, but it represented the demonic realm, a place of high faez where almost anything was possible.

That was the part that frightened Alex the most. Elosian had existed in this realm for thousands of years. The extent of his power had to be astronomical.

Alex ducked through a labyrinth section of crystals, dodging around their razor edges that looked sharp enough to flay skin. Elosian came barreling through them, turning the crystals to dust, which only made the faez-rich air sparkle even more.

She cursed herself for not doing the same. She'd tried to navigate the passages instead of blasting through them. When she'd hit Elosian the first time, blowing them both through the rock wall and into the air, it'd been on pure instinct. Now she was thinking too much.

Fight. Don't think.

The problem was she had a goal in mind that required too much of her conscious brain, which was interfering with the primal need to escape.

Alex turned her skin to steel—it was so easy and liberating, even more so than the games she'd played—and burst through the crystals to evade Elosian's grasping tentacles. Then she grabbed a section of the mountaintop, a few hundred thousand metric tons by her world's standards, and lobbed it at the demon lord.

A spark of hope formed in her chest when the mountaintop collapsed over Elosian, driving him towards the ground, until the entire thing exploded into dust.

"I can do this all day. You're not as powerful as you think you are."

He slowed his advance, floating in the air about a quarter mile from her, but she could see and hear him perfectly.

"All this effort is meaningless. I said it before, you already lost."

"No defiance is ever meaningless."

He smirked. "Something only the damned would say."

"For all your planning, all your whispers, you've managed to accomplish so little. Thwarted at every turn. Think about it. You've been doing this whispers shit for a long time, but you still haven't broken through."

"Convincing others to open the portal required your kind to be more advanced. The opportunity wasn't available until recently. Before that it was like trying to teach a dog how to fly," said Elosian.

"That's where you've made your mistake," said Alex. "For all your power, the city of sorcery is filled with thousands of mages, trained in the Halls, ready to send your ass back here if you stick your ugly head into our realm."

"Infants. They mean nothing." He tilted his head. "You're not like the others. If I didn't know any better I would have thought you'd come from my realm."

"Power is a mindset. One that you don't have," said Alex.

"Says the girl trapped in my mind."

She grinned. "You've spent all this time in a place of high magic, unimaginable power at your fingertips, and you sit in your high palace and whisper into our realm, rather than building something of your own here."

"You don't know what you speak of. You don't know the corruption of this place. Faez is corrosive. It changes you."

"But you could have built your own empire." She stretched her hand towards the settlements in the valley. "These are the slums of a backwater world. You're the Lord of Ashes."

Elosian surged forward, his tentacles twitching. "You know nothing of what I've built, nothing of the trials of this place, nor the efforts of my whispers."

"Lies in the dark. They've accomplished nothing."

"The portal is soon to open and then you'll see," said Elosian. "When I enter your realm with my armies, I will find you, show you the extent of what I can do. I will make you my instrument. Your mind is exquisite. Once I have taken the sigil and enslaved you, I will use you to break your world."

"You won't take me. I know how you plan to break through. The fifth well, the place of the Convergence. We already sent word. There will be no invasion, no breaking of the world. Nothing."

Elosian roared forward until he was within thirty feet. She could feel the anger radiating from him.

"You are too late! I have already won. My whispers have already done their work. The fool, Ollie Rend, thinks he is saving the city from a demonic invasion, but he will be the one to ensure it. He's there now, setting his explosives. I can show you if you want. We can watch the destruction of your world together."

"Ollie Rend. Fifth well. Explosives. Got it."

The slight widening of Elosian's eyes could have been an affectation of his humanlike face, or the realization that he'd let the details of his plan slip.

Alex hadn't a clue how she was going to escape. She knew whatever it was it had to be big enough to give them a chance to make it through the portal and back into their own minds. The past was prologue, giving her a singular idea, one big enough to keep the demon lord occupied.

It wasn't hard to make it appear; after all, this was a dream world based in the demonic realm, where intention ruled. She didn't have to worry about pesky physics or the intricacies of arcane magic.

When the shadow appeared over them, blotting out the sky (though not the sun because she'd never seen one in this realm), Elosian craned his neck back. Above them was a black pyramid larger than the entire mountain range beneath them. The jet-black surface absorbed the light, making it hard to see, even as it loomed over them. There were many names for it, *darthica da'calmita*, or the Death Fields, but in Gamemakers Online, most knew it as the Plane of Twilight.

"This means nothing—"

His words cut short when thousands of winged shapes erupted from holes in the black pyramid, converging on his location. As Elosian prepared to repel the onslaught, Alex willed herself to the portal, hoping that her new friends had relocated themselves there and they could slip away in the aftermath of the battle. She landed near the twisted silvery archway. The others were gathered nearby, and to her surprise, an earthen wall surrounded the portal, keeping out the hordes of demons in the valley. If only it would be that easy in their world.

"What the hell is that?" asked Pi, looking across the valley at the black pyramid in the sky.

"No time. Portal now. I know how he's getting through the barrier. Some guy name Ollie Rend at the fifth well."

The devastation in Kitty's eyes meant she knew him, but Alex was too busy focusing on the archway. They needed to get out while Elosian was distracted.

"Everyone, with me. Focus on your own minds. Imagine that once you walk through this, you're back in your own bodies."

Alex made a shimmering field appear beneath the archway. It had no effect, but she thought it might help her new friends visualize the transfer. Before they could step through, an ear-splitting thunderclap boomed through the valley. She couldn't help but look back to see the pyramid snap in half and start falling through the sky, about to crash into the mountains.

"Hurry!"

She felt Elosian's approach as she jumped forward, the caress of the field slipping over her skin and the world—

Forty-Five

Aurie awoke prone on the floor, halfway through an in-breath as she'd been jumping forward only a millisecond before. She rolled over to see her sister snap into her body, the shock of return as if she'd gotten smacked in the head. Aurie checked around to see the others similarly returned, sitting up and shaking their heads.

"The fifth well," said Aurie, remembering Alex's words. Even though it'd only been a blink, it felt longer, the cotton-headed feeling after a dream. "Where is it?"

"Follow me!" said Kitty, jumping up.

The five of them burst from the Verum Locus in a sprint, confusing the two students who'd been standing guard.

"Where are we headed?" asked Aurie as they ran.

"Fourth ward. Near the Invictus Statue. Korean grocery store."

Shit. That was about fifteen blocks away.

As they crossed the drawbridge, their shoes thundering across the surface, a dark blue SUV pulled up on the sidewalk, scattering tourists in their Halls T-shirts, a familiar redhead and her companion looking out the open window. They threw themselves into the vehicle, shouting at the driver to take them to their new destination. Heaving with breath inside the SUV taxi, Alex explained what she'd gotten out of Elosian before they escaped his mind-realm.

"Ollie Rend. He's faez mad. Tried to kill me a number of years ago," said Moriganne.

"Probably makes it easier to manipulate him. He doesn't know right from wrong," said Aurie.

"He was convinced that the demonic invasion was going to happen soon and had holed himself up in the Undercity," said Moriganne.

Since they'd thrown themselves into the SUV, Kitty was intensely quiet, staring at the floorboards.

"Kitty? You okay?" asked Aurie from the passenger seat.

She looked up, devastation on her face. "He was the one."

"The one?"

"Ares. He killed my brother. Ollie Rend killed my brother."

There was a hiss of recognition in the SUV. The pieces made sense. Ollie had probably been on a scouting mission, and Ares had figured out what he was going to do, or had just been in the wrong place at the wrong time.

"I'm so sorry."

They hit traffic about three blocks from the Statue of Invictus. It was a busy afternoon and the tourists were thick. There'd be a festival in the second ward, or something, packing the city. Aurie wasn't sure since she'd been so busy, but she saw the scarves and flags. It would be the worst possible time for the invasion, when the Halls were packed with students and the city wasn't too hot from the approaching summer. Aurie spotted a father with a little girl on his shoulders walking blissfully along the sidewalk.

When the taxi driver honked his horn, trying to convince the stopped cars to move, Kitty said, "Screw this," and hopped out of the vehicle.

Everyone followed her, but Kitty was faster, using her imbuements and rage to outpace even Zayn, who should have been able to keep up. The two of them, plus Pax and Kali, quickly disappeared ahead.

A block away from leaving the taxi, as Aurie dodged through the pedestrian traffic with her sister, Alex, and Moriganne right behind, the Statue of Invictus came into view. She was so focused on keeping up her speed that she didn't notice the strange light until everyone on the busy sidewalk stopped and craned their neck towards the top of the Spire. The bluish light was stronger and lasted longer than any of the pulses that had come before. More importantly it meant that Invictus was back in his demi-realm.

"What is he doing?"

Forty-Six

The stupid society kids hadn't bothered to reinforce the passage where he'd pickaxed his way through to reach their headquarters. The police tape from his previous visit was still present. Ollie stuck his head through the gap, checking for guardians, but found an empty rocky passageway.

"It's clear, but we're going to have to carry these explosives through by hand. The hole's not wide enough," he told his compatriots.

Easy and Lame John leaned on the carts that they'd hauled through the tunnels. Both of them were drenched in a light sweat. Easy was leaning over the handles. The cart was stacked with crates of explosives.

"Fuck me, I'm exhausted already, this is *wayho* shit. We hauled these crates over all those rocks and now you want me to carry them?"

Lame John pulled out a cigarette, tapped it on a wall, and lit it up. The embers glowed bright as he inhaled.

"It's not much further," said Ollie, pulling the handgun out of his waistband. "Let's make sure the way is clear first."

Easy pulled out a water bottle and chugged it, spilling some on his pit stained shirt, before saying, "Fine. Let's do this. At least I get to play target practice."

As Ollie slipped through the gap, he said, "Shoot first. If they get a chance to use magic, we're boned."

"No problemo here, man," said Easy, clucking his tongue.

Lame John chuckled and flicked his barely smoked cigarette behind them before pulling a semi-automatic rifle from one of the crates and slinging it over his neck.

The passage led to a runed door. Ollie pulled out his key, kissed it, and tried the lock. It wouldn't open.

"They changed it."

Now he understood why the passage hadn't been blocked. They'd changed the lock. Ollie was scratching his head when Lame John pulled a hunk of explosives out of his shoulder bag and slapped it over the lock. Then he pushed a metal pin into the putty-like material.

"Lame John's lock breaking service," he said with a wink.

Ollie nodded as they retreated down the passage. "Be ready to fight once that door is open. They're going to know we're coming."

Lame John clicked the safety off and grinned. When Ollie gave him the nod, he pulled a control box out of his bag, clicked a few toggles, and then smashed his thumb on a red button.

The explosion nearly deafened Ollie as dust rolled back towards them, but he ignored the ringing in his ears and sprinted ahead. He had the layout memorized and led them into the main chamber where he'd killed Ares Charmer a week ago.

"Whoa, fancy digs," said Easy, looking around.

Ollie motioned them towards the opposite doors. "You each take one. Check every room. Leave no survivors."

While his coconspirators disappeared down the hallway, Ollie went in search of the hatch. He found it underneath a bench on the upper level of the summoning chamber. If the drawings he'd gotten were correct, they led into the space beneath the floor where a concrete slab had been poured decades ago.

As he pushed the bench out of the way, gunfire erupted from Easy's hallway. He listened for his friend's laughter, before opening the hatch and climbing down the ladder. When he reached the bottom, he brought a magelight into existence. Spiderwebs clung to the corners, and there were critter droppings, but the space was otherwise clear. As he ducked beneath the low ceiling, he coaxed the floating ball of light forward until he could see the capstone.

Ollie grinned as he saw the heavy cracks in the concrete. Not only had his vision told him that the material used had been poured decades ago, but it hadn't been the quality that the makers had thought it was. Since then the regular rumblings in the Undercity, the frequent tremors and shifting, had put pressure on the weakened concrete. Ollie had been worried that the number of explosives they'd brought wouldn't be enough, but seeing the condition brought a smile to his face.

"I'll be a hero. They'll make a statue of me."

Ollie climbed out of the hatch into the society chamber as his coconspirators returned. Lame John blew on the end of his rifle as if smoke was drifting from the barrel.

"Got two of them trying to run away. Didn't even try to use magic. Maybe these mages aren't all they're cracked up to be. We should have done this a long time ago," he said.

Easy whistled as he turned in a circle. "What is this place?"

"Summoning chamber. Where they make deals with demons and betray humankind," said Ollie feverishly.

He caught the concerned look in their eyes, so he added, "Which will make taking their ill-gotten gold even more sweet. I checked the vault covering. It shouldn't be any problem to blow it open. You two bring it in, I'll carry them into the chamber below the floor."

The work was arduous and slow. Each crate required both of them to haul it into the chamber. Once they set it near the hatch, Ollie took out bricks of the explosives and carried them below, setting them along the edge of the capstone. The entire section of concrete was a hundred feet in diameter and reaching the back sections required clearing out a lot of webs.

A couple hours later, the explosives were set and the wires ran through them, the lead wire running out of the hatch and into the passage where they'd first entered the chamber.

"What I don't understand is why they buried their gold beneath the chamber without an easy way to get to it," Easy said, resulting in a glinty-eyed nod from Lame John.

"Collateral. The gold was stolen a long time ago and they hold onto it, while the banks lend them the money. Why else do you think they're all so rich?"

The slow nods meant they'd bought it. Ollie was proud of his quick thinking.

"Let's blow this thing before someone discovers the wires," said Lame John as he stubbed out his cigarette on the wall and flicked the butt into the darkness behind them.

He pulled three sets of earmuffs from his shoulder bag and handed them out. They fit tightly on Ollie's head. He couldn't believe how close he was to finally stopping the invasion. The nightmares and constant visions he'd received would end, put to rest by his success. They'd want him on every TV show, put his name in lights, probably have a play about him at Ashnod's Theater.

"You okay over there?" asked Easy. "You look like you were about to have a seizure."

Ollie squeezed his nose with his forefinger and thumb. "Thought I was going to sneeze."

"Right."

"Ready?" asked Lame John as he hooked up the wire to his control board.

Ollie gave the thumbs-up, which brought the biggest shit-eating grin from Lame John as he held his thumb over the toggle and mouthed a countdown.

"Three...two...one..."

Forty-Seven

Ollie Rend.

His name was a marquee in Kitty's head, except it wasn't bright lights and big city, but carved into stone with her knife. She'd promised herself that she wouldn't kill anyone unless it was absolutely necessary. That way would only turn her into the monster her father wanted her to become. She'd been his little pet attack dog. Not a daughter. Not a child. A tool for his empire.

Ollie killed Ares. She was sure of it. That he might trigger the invasion was secondary.

She flew through the crowds, headed towards the old Korean grocery store, cutting into the street and running alongside the barely moving cars to make up time. The square around the Statue of Invictus was packed with tourists. Hundreds of families milled about, taking pictures with the statue as the backdrop. Kitty barely noticed.

The bell rang as she threw herself through the door. The owner sat behind the counter, reading a book, barely having time to lift her chin to see who it was before Kitty hit the secret door that led to the elevator. As she slammed her hand on the button, willing it to arrive faster, Zayn, followed by Pax and her furry companion, appeared.

Their concerned expressions reflected the pain in her heart.

"Kitty?"

She touched her face and found a tear on her cheek. She hadn't known she'd been crying. The wetness on her finger was strange.

"He killed Ares."

"We don't know that."

Kitty gritted her teeth. "I know."

"Let us take him alive. We need to know what Elosian's been doing to him," said Zayn.

"Ollie's not your enemy," said Pax. "It's Elosian. He put Ollie up to it. The poor soul is faez mad, as you said."

The elevator reached them and the door opened. She didn't want them to go down with her. She wanted to face him alone.

"I..."

"Don't even think about it," said Zayn. "We're your friends. We're facing this together."

They climbed into the elevator. There were only two buttons. Up and down. She hit the lower one with her knuckles, closed her eyes.

"He might not even be down there yet," said Pax, hopefully. "We could stop this whole thing right now, and since we know where he plans to invade, we can make sure no one messes with it."

Zayn nodded. "Elosian's advantage has been that no one believes it's going to happen."

Kitty didn't answer. She could hardly trust herself to speak. The only thing she could see was her knife going into Ollie's chest, ending him once and for all. She glanced at the little line that showed how far they'd dropped towards the bottom. The white light was nearing the halfway point.

Kali let out a long whine followed by a warning bark. Pax's whole body went on alert as she turned towards her companion.

"We have to turn it around. We have to go back up! They're going to set—"

The last thing Kitty remembered was getting thrown so hard into the stainless steel walls of the elevator that it knocked her out.

Then darkness.

Forty-Eight

Dust blew out of the passage, forcing them to close their eyes until the explosion was finished. As minor secondary rumbles triggered in the aftermath, Ollie couldn't help but grin. His life's work was coming to an end.

Ollie led them back into the chamber once they were certain it was safe. The space looked nothing like before. A cavern the size of a parking lot had opened up. The interior of his nose burned with faez. He felt submerged by it. Golden particles filled the air.

"What the...?" exclaimed Easy, swiping his hand through the air. "Is that gold dust?"

Ollie didn't bother explaining. He only had eyes for the deepest part of the crater. A bar top complete with beer dispensing handles was lying on the edge. He stepped to the side of it, looked into the burgeoning darkness. Anticipation filled him with dread and delight.

"We blew the gold to smithereens," said Lame John with an unlit cigarette hanging from his bottom lip. "It's just a fucking hole."

The world shifted around Ollie. He could hardly stand. "Do you smell that? They're so sweet."

"What are you talking about? Did that explosion knock your brains out your ass?" asked Easy.

"I'm a hero," he muttered.

"What?"

It wasn't complete. He knew that much. The threat was still there. They could come through at any time unless he could stop them. *How do I stop them?*

"You'd better stop staring into that hole like a lunatic and tell us where the gold is or I'm going to start getting a different idea of what's happening here," said Easy.

The answer came to Ollie all at once. He felt whole, complete. He wasn't sure why he hadn't seen it before.

"It's right down there," he said, extending his arm to the darkness. "I can see it with my darkvision. Let me give it to you so you can see it too."

Ollie took a step back, keeping his expression as neutral as possible. They turned towards him. Lame John was busy lighting his cigarette while Easy had an air of suspicion. He was right to.

Before either of them could stop him, Ollie hit them with a force blast, throwing them into the crater. The wet smack of a melon splitting sounded right after. Ollie looked over the edge to see a motionless Lame John with the lit cigarette miraculously still in his lips and a groaning and massively injured Easy moving around the rocks. As his friend looked up, Ollie unloaded his pistol into his chest, ending his misery.

When he was finished, he threw the gun into the crater. It was no longer needed.

The ritual came to his mind unbidden. The answer to his problems.

Ollie started speaking slowly and carefully. The words were nonsense, but he felt a righteous warmth fill him with purpose. The longer he went the more he could smell the sweet lilacs filling his senses. At times, it was almost as if he wasn't even in control of his body. He was a vessel for truth. The world would see that.

When the ritual completed, he heard a great tearing. The air groaned awake, as if a beast had been set loose deep in the earth.

Confused by the change, Ollie peered into the darkness. The sense of purpose had left him, making him feel cold and alone. He looked to the bodies of his friends and wondered what had happened to them, until he remembered and then he wanted to be sick.

"Oh no."

The words preceded his understanding as if his conscious mind wasn't allowing him to know the gravity of his mistake. As he stared into the darkness, sensing movement at the edge of his vision, he had a terrible realization about what had happened. The noise and movement grew louder and nearer. He feared what he might see, but let a magelight drift into the crater, which seemed infinitely deeper than it had when he first arrived.

As the bluish light fell upon bone-white pincers with black, beady eyes, he could no longer ignore the truth. He had punched a hole between realms. And not just any realm. The demonic one.

No.

He wasn't a hero. He wasn't even a villain. He was a fool. A terrible fool.

As the repercussions of what he'd done set in, Ollie felt his reality break. He stumbled backwards, falling over the dropped automatic rifle that Lame John had been holding only ten minutes before.

Ollie fled into the darkness.

§§§

TOWER OF HORN AND BLOOD

One

A door opened in the darkness.

Moriganne stumbled to a stop in the middle of the square, surrounded by tourists who were trying to process the rumble that had rattled glass and caused a few accidents on the street. The regular quivers that hit the Undercity never made it to the light. Whatever had happened below had been big, and everyone seemed to sense that something significant had happened even if they didn't know the cause.

She'd lost the others in the sprint from the taxi towards the Korean grocery store. The urgency that had driven her forward had evaporated, so she'd stopped. A feeling of awakeness radiated from the bridge tattoo on her elbow. The anticipation of what came next made her leery.

"What's wrong?" asked Aurie, coming up through the crowd.

The statue of Invictus loomed over the square, looking disapprovingly at everyone beneath his feet. Moriganne felt cold and distant as if a ghost had passed through her.

"I don't know," she answered eventually. "Something happened."

Aurie looked around. The earthquake had frightened the tourists, but now everyone was moving again. They kept looking around as if they could see what was happening.

"The tattoo?"

Moriganne touched the sleeve of her shirt reflexively and was surprised she didn't come away with burnt fingers. She'd felt the door open in the darkness, a yawning pit that left her shaken.

"I think so. That wasn't an earthquake, that much I know. It's like there's a great crack in the earth. When I summoned the *mija*, it felt like that, but bigger." She looked around.

"Where's Pi? And Alex?"

"I don't know."

"We need to get everyone together," said Moriganne. "I fear we're too late and what happens next...I fear that more."

The trickle of ache in her elbow turned to a full conflagration of pain. Moriganne didn't remember falling to the ground, but she caught occasional glimpses of faces staring down at her through the unrelenting agony.

After a time, she heard Aurie's voice through the haze. "She's fine. She has epilepsy. It was just another event."

"That didn't look like epilepsy," said someone in the small circle surrounding her.

Moriganne pushed herself into a sitting position. Her whole body hurt as if she'd done a dozen intense workouts in a matter of a few minutes.

"I'm okay. It's a thing that happens."

She tried to smile at the people, but the earthquake had already worried them. Random fainting and convulsing had only made their fears worse. No one returned her smile.

Once she was standing, she gripped Aurie's elbow to remain that way, grimacing as waves of throbbing pain continued to assault her.

"It's open," she told Aurie once the tourists had moved away.

"The portal?"

Moriganne nodded. "Every cell in my body is on high alert. I feel like I'm about to spontaneously combust. We need to go somewhere. Fast."

"To the grocery store. The others are there," said Aurie, checking around them. "Hopefully."

Even the balls of her feet in her shoes were tender. Her flesh was raw. Her mind was in a state of panic. Moriganne struggled to walk and only made it across the square with Aurie's help. The old Korean woman behind the counter pointed to the back when they arrived.

"What's wrong with her?" asked Pi when they reached the stainless steel elevator. Alex was examining the edges of the doors and barely gave a glance back.

"It's open," said Moriganne weakly.

"Open? As in the gate?"

She nodded. "We're too late."

"It's never too late," said Alex without turning around. "They were headed down when the explosion happened. I don't know how far they got—the electronics are fried, none of the lights work. They could be stuck."

"The elevator goes all the way to the Undercity. They had a good head start. They could have reached the bottom before it went off." Moriganne leaned against the seeping concrete, not caring about the grimy feel against her palm. "Or they could be dead."

No one spoke for thirty seconds.

"We don't know that," said Aurie.

"Can anyone find a crowbar? I want to open this door," said Alex, tapping on the stainless steel.

Aurie stepped in front of it. "I can bust it open. Make room."

"No," said Alex, holding her hands out. "We need a functioning door. If the elevator starts working again, we need the shaft to be open."

The flinch from Aurie was painfully visible, but she nodded. "You're right. Stupid of me. Magic isn't an answer for everything."

"Let me ask the lady at the counter," said Alex, jogging back the way they came.

"We need to figure out what's going on," said Aurie, bunching up her lips. "If it's happening, if the invasion is really happening, then we need to get people out of the city."

"Three million people, sis? An evacuation like that would be a nightmare," said Pi.

"Better than the nightmare of them staying."

Pi lifted her shoulders. "For all we know it could be a small group like in Montanhas. We might not have anything to worry about."

"It's not like Montanhas," said Moriganne heavily.

"How do you know?"

Moriganne held up her arm. "I know. It's like standing on the edge of an abyss. If I had the means to cut it off, I might. I feel like someone doused me in blood and dropped me into shark-infested waters."

Alex came running into the hallway, but stopped at the far side and waved them toward her. "You gotta come see this."

They glanced amongst themselves but followed Alex into the grocery store, and then when they didn't see her, moved outside. Moriganne saw a sea of faces pointed upward and an eerie bluish glow permeating everything.

"The Spire," said Aurie.

The top of the building at the center of the city had a strong bluish light emanating out like a beacon. Moriganne expected to feel something through the tattoo, but it hadn't changed, nor did she sense anything different when she pulled back the sleeve of her shirt and the light cascaded over it.

"What's going on?" asked Moriganne.

"I don't know." Pi frowned and shook her head. "Invictus never told us."

"This is him?"

"Yes. I think so." Then after a pause, she said, "I'm not a fan of this timing."

"Me neither," said Aurie.

Something passed between the sisters, a previous conversation, or shared concerns. Moriganne didn't like it, but she was too exhausted from the tattoo to bother asking.

The intensity of the bluish light grew until it was hard to look at it. Moriganne held her hand above her head to block her eyes even though it took all her effort. The second odd event in a short matter of time had caused more unease. Tourist families were glancing back at the

Spire while they headed away as fast as they could on foot, because the streets were clogged with vehicles stopped and looking at the light.

Gasps erupted from the crowd before Moriganne noticed the difference. At first it looked like a stronger version of the light, slowly growing from the tip of the Spire like the spreading of spilled frozen water. Then she realized it was a tangible, shimmering object, much like a force shield. The disc expanded out, rapidly gaining speed. Within ten seconds, the field had passed over the square.

Curiosity turned to panic when someone shouted, "It's going to trap us in the city."

Half the people continued to stare upward, while the others started moving en masse towards the streets that led outward.

"They're not going to be fast enough," said Alex calmly.

Pi nudged her with her elbow. "Getting anything with the tattoo?"

"No."

She turned. Pi's forehead was knitted. "You were in a lot of pain a short time ago."

Moriganne nodded.

"I could feel it." She touched her elbow as the blue light grew stronger and the disc expanded outward. It was past the inner wards and curving downward. "It was faint, but it was as if I had the tattoo as well."

Moriganne didn't know how to answer Pi. She didn't seem to know what she was trying to say either, ending with a shrug.

"I guess we're connected somehow."

"We should find a crowbar and get back to the elevator," said Alex, heading towards the grocery store. The owner was standing at the door, staring upward with everyone else.

After they entered, the woman shut the door and locked it, sliding an accordion fence over the front. The act made Moriganne realize what she was seeing in everyone's faces: barely restrained panic. A hair-trigger fear was lurking beneath the surface. If something more happened—a car backfire, a few too many people running, anything—it would turn into a stampede. The city was a lake of gasoline waiting for the first spark.

Two

When the emergency lights in the elevator failed to energize, someone brought a magelight into existence. The pale illumination cast a pallor on the small space. Kitty had a cut on her forehead from getting thrown into the control panel that leaked blood into her eye. She looked like she was ready to punch through the floor and continue into the society space.

Zayn, on the other hand, was examining the interior while manually checking himself for injuries.

"Okay?"

Pax nodded.

"How about you, Miss Kali?" he asked with a pained grin.

Kali let out a barking huff at the same time Pax sensed a bitter taste in the back of her throat. She knew it translated to concerned, but also ready to act. The emotions traveling across Zayn's face made it clear that her companion had sent those emotions to everyone in the elevator.

Kitty knelt, punched the carpeted floor. "How far did we get?"

"Two-thirds," said Zayn, craning his neck towards the ceiling. The small space was growing hotter as the air conditioning was no longer running. Beads of sweat formed on all their foreheads. Kali was panting.

"We need to get down there," said Kitty.

"We need to get *out* of here," replied Zayn as he stretched upward to unlatch the trapdoor that led to the roof of the elevator. The opening provided a small rush of cool air that was quickly swallowed by the swelling heat.

Pax crouched down with her companion and rubbed her neck for solidarity. Kali leaned into her, bringing emotional warmth to Pax's chest.

"Can you sense what's down there?" she asked her companion, speaking for the other's benefit.

<One mind confused>

"One? Maybe the others died in the explosion."

<Hole in darkness>

"Explain? I don't understand what a hole in darkness means."

Kali whined. The hurt nature of the sound made the other two pause their actions and look to the callidus.

<Many minds in darkness>

The reaction on their faces was devastation.

"It's begun," said Kitty with a pinched expression. "Just like Montanhas."

<Many many>

Her companion used the image of ants spilling out of a hole in earth, forming a carpet of critters. Pax felt sick to her stomach.

"Fuck!"

Kitty punched the floor hard enough to dent it. Her knuckles were bleeding but she didn't seem to care.

"We need to get out," said Zayn as he pulled himself up and looked around the top of the elevator.

"I'm not the climber that you two are," said Pax. "Neither is Kali."

"How'd you do that at Phoenix Corp?" he asked as his bottom half stuck through the hole.

"I borrowed some climbing ability from the lizards. I don't have that here, and even if I did, I can't get Kali out."

"Can you borrow from one of us?" asked Kitty.

"Your abilities aren't natural, so no."

Zayn dropped back in. "We need a harness."

Kali whined again.

<Climbers>

"Shit."

"How far are we above the bottom?" asked Zayn.

Kitty blinked. "I'm not sure how deep the shaft goes, but I think the main sections of the Undercity are around a thousand feet beneath the surface of the city. Big Dave's Town is at six hundred or something like that, which is why it's not as hot as some other areas. It also pumps in air from above. There are other areas that can be much deeper, like the canyons around the fire well."

"The deepest I've been was in the sewers," said Pax.

"I saw where we were on the board when the lights went out," said Zayn. "We're probably two or three hundred feet above the bottom."

"Or seven hundred feet from the top," said Pax. "If it's a thousand."

A noise that sounded like the bending of metal reverberated through their feet. The hairs on Kali's back stood at attention.

"I'm taking a look," said Zayn, leaping through the hole in the ceiling, landing lightly on the roof. He moved out of sight, and she assumed he was peering around the edge.

Kitty gave her a pinched frown. "Sorry." She followed Zayn.

"I can see too, you know," said Pax as she crouched next to Kali. "How many are there? Are we in trouble?"

A picture of a small group of ants appeared in her mind. Maybe ten, maybe fifteen, the number shifted hazily. Kali wasn't great at counting, except in general terms.

Zayn stuck his head into the hole. "They're moving quickly, a hundred feet from the elevator."

"What are they?"

He looked pained. "Hard to tell, but I saw long black limbs. Or spines. They're not friendly, that much is sure."

"I feel like someone left us in a lion's cage without a door."

"The car blocks the shaft at least," said Zayn.

"How thick is the floor?" she asked.

Zayn screwed up his face. "No idea."

A thump against the bottom of the car made Pax jump. She backed against the wall.

"There's something below," shouted Kitty.

Pax hated that she'd been so loud, as if that might put them in more danger.

"Could someone help—"

The words were barely out of her mouth when a shiny black appendage split the center of the floor, narrowly missing Kali, who'd jumped back at the last moment. It looked like a blade made out of thick black stone. Pax kicked it at the base, bending it slightly and causing a horrific screech from below.

"Come on, Kali," she said, grabbing her companion around the midsection and helping her up towards Zayn and Kitty, who were leaning through the hole to grab her. Once they had her forward paws, she rose through the hole.

Pax leapt up, grabbed the edge, and hauled herself through as a second and then third appendage burst through the floor. The creatures below were puncturing the steel as if it were cardboard.

"We don't have a harness," said Pax.

"I can carry Kali on my back," Zayn said. Do we have something to tie her to me? I've got a belt but it's not long enough."

Kitty reached for her waist, sliding a belt out. They hooked the two belts together and then after Kali put her forelegs on Zayn's shoulders, hooked the belt around them both. Kali whined when they tested the harness.

The attack on the bottom of the elevator continued. The creatures kept ripping at the steel, making large holes faster than Pax thought possible.

"Those belts aren't going to hold," said Pax.

"Neither is the floor," said Kitty, looking in. "Unless you have another idea, we'd better start climbing."

"How?"

"Hand over hand, right up the central wire," said Kitty. "You go first, I'll go behind Zayn to help with Kali."

The impossibleness of their situation was like carrying a lead blanket on her shoulders, but she knew staying put wouldn't work out. Pax wrapped her hands around the steel cable and pulled herself up, using the magesteel enchantment in her shoulder blades to power the ascent. She worked her way up about twenty feet before she glanced down, seeing Kali's head resting on Zayn's shoulder as he followed.

The regular puncture and groaning of metal continued as they climbed. Kitty gave occasional updates, which Pax wasn't sure helped. The muscles in her shoulders were getting tight. She could run for days, but climbing wasn't one of the skills she'd spent a lot of time on.

When they were up about a hundred feet, Kitty's voice carried up through the shaft.

"They're through. Broken hells, they're in the car—no wait, it's squeezing through the hole and climbing now. Fast."

Six hundred feet. They had six hundred feet to go. Pax focused on the climb, hand over hand, squeezing her shoes against the cable as she shimmied upward at a speed that was heartbreakingly slow.

A whoosh of air sucked past them, and Pax was confused until she realized that Kitty had fired a force wave down the shaft. A moment later, the echo of impact reached them.

"Ha! Got that ugly bastard!"

Kitty fired again, keeping the critters from following too closely. They'd made it another twenty feet when Pax heard Zayn curse. A moment later he said, "The belt is coming loose."

<Kali falling>

Pax pressed her forehead against the cable, then looked upward into the darkness. There was nothing nearby to grab a hold of to keep Kali from slipping off Zayn's shoulders. Another thump of force wave signaled Kitty was too busy defending their rear.

"I can't move or she'll fall," said Zayn as he clung to the cable.

They needed a spot to regroup and reconnect the belt. Pax brought a magelight into existence even though she hated exposing them with light. She floated it upward, looking for a structural ledge to climb onto. The steel girders that formed the frame had thin spots to stop, but the next one was twenty feet overhead.

"Twenty feet," said Pax. "Can you make it?"

"Probably not. Not sure if I can move five feet."

Kitty cursed and continued sending waves of force down the shaft, giving them updates like: "there's another one now," "they're learning to avoid my shots," and "dammit, that one leapt to the far side." They were running out of time. Soon the creatures would overrun Kitty.

As the magelight continued floating upward, Pax spotted a square door on the wall. It was about thirty feet up.

"I see a door. In the shaft. Does that make sense?"

"Probably for the workers, or maybe an exit shaft. How far?"

"Thirty feet."

There was silence.

"I have an idea," said Pax as she slipped down the cable, but facing Zayn. They had to alternate hands but she managed to reach a spot opposite. "If you can hold onto me, I can try to reconnect the belt."

He nodded, and with one hand holding the cable, he used the other hand to grab the front of her jeans. The stability was precarious. She felt like she was about to tip backwards and fall down the shaft, but if she didn't do something then Kali would fall. Her companion whined while she reached around to the connection.

The amount that Zayn was working to keep them all from falling was apparent in the pulsing of his jaw and the intensity of his gaze. She tried not to pay attention, but he was staring her right in the face. The two belts were slipping apart. With a grunt and a hard pull, Pax managed to make their connection more solid.

"Fixed."

She put her hands on the cable, pulling herself up towards the square door while Kitty did battle with the creatures trying to climb up behind them. The urgency pushed her up the cable even though her hands hurt.

The width of the elevator made reaching the girders along the outside of the shaft a challenge. Pax tried to reach out, but she only managed to put her foot on the steel. It was too far to simply swing over. Kitty's calls were getting more urgent.

"You'll have to jump," said Zayn, looking up. "Start higher so you have more room."

Pax shimmied up another ten feet and leaned on the side of the cable. She'd seen monkeys make similar jumps easily. After a few quick breaths, Pax leapt.

The girder came faster than expected. She hit at the ribs, barely getting her arms around it before she slid off and down the shaft. The impact knocked the air from her lungs. After a few moments of recovery, she scrambled onto the ledge. The emergency door was open. No lock at all. Which made sense since it was in the middle of a deep elevator shaft.

Pax ducked into the passage, which was only five feet high and went until there was another door about thirty feet back.

When Zayn reached the height she'd jumped from, he made the leap to the girder easily. Kali let out a whine when they unhooked her from his back.

While all this was happening, Kitty had been battling the creatures below.

"We have to get her an opportunity to get here," said Zayn. "Ideas?"

Pax lifted a shoulder. "Try not to hit her?"

He blinked. Nodded. "Right."

From the ledge, they started firing a mix of earth and water bolts past Kitty. Once they'd managed to hit a few of the climbing demons, knocking them back down, Kitty scrambled up at speed. She reached them and leapt over to the ledge.

Without her in the way, the three of them rained consecutive force waves down the shaft until they'd pushed the shiny black multi-legged creatures back to the elevator. Once the area beneath them was clear, they ducked back to the other door and threw themselves behind it.

The room had oxygen kits and a pair of bright red emergency bags connected to the wall. The place was covered in a thin layer of dust.

<Kali hide friends>

"Good call," she whispered.

They crouched behind the interior door, listening for the approach of the demons. Pax didn't have the sensing ability of her friends, so she borrowed from Kali. The clicking of appendages on the steel walls of the elevator shaft grew louder. Pax's heart climbed into her throat as she realized they were near the side door. The noise grew in volume and she was sure they'd be attacked, but then after a minute, the clacking faded away.

No one spoke for a few minutes. There was nothing to say. Soon those creatures would reach the street level. The invasion had begun.

Three

"Do you need any lube?" shouted Ivan from their bedroom.

Audrey stuck her head around the corner. "Why would we need that?"

"In case we're stuck in Ares' place for a long time," said Ivan. "It's a great stress reliever."

"Whatever you want, babe, but let's get a move on it. The SUV is almost full."

They'd already stopped by the labs to send everyone home. A few of them wanted to keep working, either not understanding the danger, or out of a misplaced sense of loyalty. They'd thought the strange light coming out of the Spire was an illusion like the battles in the second ward entertainment district. Audrey had to show them the news reports about no one being able to pass through the barrier. The city was stuck in a dome of magical energy.

He stuffed clothes in a bag, not worrying about getting the right mix, while Audrey cleaned out the pantry and refrigerator. By the time they headed back to Ares' place, every space inside the vehicle was filled. They passed long lines at the grocery and convenience stores, witnessed a few fights on street corners, and occasionally heard gunfire in the distance.

"The city's gone mad."

"I don't blame them," said Ivan. "I'm scared shitless. More than these people who don't understand what's about to happen."

Someone threw a rock at the SUV. It hit the side, making them both flinch. Audrey leaned out the window and gave them the finger.

There was heavy traffic trying to get out of the city. The filtered blue light of the dome gave everything a muted, ethereal feel. Ivan fussed with the bottle of pills in his pocket until he caught a side eye from Audrey.

"Not a good time?"

She shook her head. "No. We need our wits."

"We need the others," said Ivan, drumming his fingers on the steering wheel to focus his nervous energy somewhere. "We're the D-team. If we run into any demons I'm going to crap myself."

Audrey reached out and squeezed his hand.

The homeless that lived in the old industrial complex near Ares' place were standing outside, staring at the shimmering blue dome. They were whistling and clapping as they drank from bottles in brown paper bags. Some were howling as if it were a moon. He hadn't realized how many lived in the complex. There were at least a few hundred gathered in the cracked and grass-strewn parking lot.

"Poor bastards."

Once they reached the house, Ivan felt a sense of relief, even though there wasn't an attached gate anymore. Andromeda limped out the front door, still covered in old blood and purple bruises, with Barkley right behind. Ivan handed her an elixir, and she promptly thumbed off the stopper and threw it back like a shot of whiskey.

"Thanks."

"Oh no, that was my hemorrhoid medicine," he said, screwing up his face.

"Eat shit, Ivan," said Andromeda, rolling her eyes.

They spent the next twenty minutes unloading the SUV. Afterwards, they approached the gate, which lay on the ground outside, bent like a potato chip.

"I'm not sure we can get it back on," said Ivan, scratching the back of his neck. "Not working, at least."

"Better than nothing," said Audrey. "I'll work on some exterior walls around the gate."

After Ivan handed out more elixirs, the three of them lifted the heavy structure back into place. The gears and sliding mechanisms were snapped and warped, so they opted to turn it into a swinging gate with copious use of wires and chains.

Audrey spent the time singing the stone, coaxing a stout wall around the outside of the entrance. About two hours into their work, a massive explosion from somewhere in the fourth ward had them craning their necks. Flames plumed from a building. All they could see was the smoke rolling into the streets. The homeless at the industrial complex let out a raucous cheer as if it were a fireworks display.

"At least someone's excited," said Ivan.

"They won't be for long," said Audrey.

Andromeda crossed her arms. "Anyone heard from the others?"

"Cell service is spotty," said Audrey. "I wonder how long we'll be here. We only have enough food for a few days, a week at most."

"Oh," said Andromeda, "there's something I need to show you."

Inside the building, she led them to the laundry room on the first floor. The carpet was pulled back and a trapdoor led into the cellar. They climbed down the ladder into a space filled with shelves. The entire lower area had boxes of canned foods and other supplies, enough for months of siege.

"I really want to give Ares a hug right now," Ivan said.

"Me too," said Andromeda, reaching out and grasping his hand.

Audrey did the same on the opposite side, and the three of them stared at the full cellar knowing that their dead brother had given them the best possible chance of surviving.

Four

Nandi stood on the balcony of the tenth-ward villa, smack between taller and older buildings, staring at the shimmering blue dome that had trapped them in the city. A trio of police cars with sirens blazing screamed past, screeching around the corner and out of sight. There were gunshots and people roaming the streets.

"Place has gone fucking mad," said Lennie, arms crossed as much as his biceps would allow.

An empty, ashen feeling filled Nandi's chest. "We failed. Miserably."

"We don't know there's been an invasion," said Gregor in his haughty English accent. "Haven't seen a single demon. But Invictus has got everyone mad as a hatter with this dome. We were right that he was as shady as an oak tree."

"They're here," said Sammi, curled up on a chair, lips pinched. "Kozsen can feel them, coursing through the Undercity like bad blood."

Nandi stared at the Animalians mage. She seemed both ambivalent and slightly excited.

"At least we have a good place to hole up," said Gregor, fidgeting with a box that resembled a Rubik's Cube, but Nandi knew from experience that it was anything but one. The wound on his head had stopped bleeding, but it would leave a nasty scar on his pale forehead unless he received real medical attention.

"Who said we were going to hole up here?" asked Nandi, facing them with her hands on her hips.

Gregor arched an eyebrow. "We lost? I don't know, I always thought that if I got trapped at the end of the world, I'd like to have a few pints before I go."

"I'm not staying," she told them.

To her relief, Lennie nodded. "I'll come. I'm sure we could help somewhere. Food distribution. Looting prevention." A distant scream echoed through the streets, turning their heads. "Or demon hunting."

"You're kidding, right?" asked Gregor, sitting up. "It's an invasion. This isn't a few loose supernaturals causing havoc. This is the complete and utter destruction of our world. Personally, I'd like to see if we can find a working portal and bribe, beg, or threaten our way out."

"We should go after the traitors," said Sammi with an eerie intensity. "They should pay for their crimes."

They were looking to Nandi for an opinion. The utter failure of their attempts to stop the traitors had left her unsure of her own ability. She'd never failed before. Tops at the Merlin Trials. First choice of Coterie, where she'd excelled at every task the professors threw at her. She'd intended to specialize in financial prediction until she'd joined the societies. At Chroma and Key, she learned that the world might end soon and that she had a higher purpose, so she'd switched from personal enrichment to expanding her arcane knowledge with a double focus on demonology and advanced spellcasting.

Professor Sinclair had always joked with her that she was the second-best student to attend Coterie the last decade. She'd always thought it was his way of motivating her until she'd run into Pythia Silverthorne and realized that the professor had been talking about her. It'd put a dent in her self-confidence.

The last week had been one failure after another. A constant assault on her ego. The idea that she could double down her efforts and overcome the gap had no meaning in a world gone mad. There wasn't time for adjustment. No time for diving back into her tomes to master new and exciting techniques. The invasion was here. It was put up or shut up time, except the odds were more than scary. Nothing she'd learned from Professor Sinclair told her how to address the current situation. What she'd learned was focused on sending demons back to their realm, but that assumed that it was a single foe, not a horde of murderous creatures.

A series of gunshots up a block brought their heads around. Nandi caught sight of something shiny and black about the size of an SUV skittering after a group of armed citizens. She heard their screams and then the battle disappeared around the corner, where the shots quickly dwindled to silence.

Staying put was an option. The wrought iron fencing could be reinforced with runes and their collective magical ability would repel all but the most determined creatures. If she'd failed to stop the invasion, how could she think that she might do something besides dying ingloriously in the dirty streets of the city of sorcery?

I want to go home, she whispered to herself in the quiet of her mind. Stay, fight, run, hide. Every choice came with risks. She'd already lost two friends to their quest. How many more would die because of her decisions?

Nandi swallowed before addressing them. "We need to find a way to help. Any way we can. Maybe we can help people hold out until they figure out how to breach the dome and bring reinforcements. Grab your gear. We're hitting the streets."

Five

The doors to the elevator didn't budge at first, so the others helped Aurie lean on the crowbar, leveraging them open. A hot wind escaped when they split apart, leaving a dark hole into the shaft.

"Did you see a light?" asked Moriganne from behind. "I thought right as they split, I saw a light."

Aurie shook her head. "I was too busy with the crowbar." She leaned over the edge.

"The cable is shaking," said Pi, frowning. "Something's climbing. Hopefully it's the others."

Aurie touched her eyes and applied the darkvision spell that Zayn had taught her so many years ago. They'd all been together, until Kitty had sprinted ahead to catch her brother's killer. Now Kitty, Zayn, and Pax were stuck in the elevator, or had been caught in the explosion. She didn't want to think about it. Better to believe they were currently climbing the cable. Alive and about to escape.

"I can't see that far down," said Aurie.

"I can climb," said Pi. "Shimmy down and see if they need help."

"What if it's not them?" asked Alex, looking to Moriganne, who looked like she'd smelled something terrible.

"The reflections I'm getting through the tattoo, they're overwhelming. It's too much to pinpoint, but I can tell you that it's not good."

"Let me drop a magelight," said Alex.

The bulb of light flickered into existence. It was a pale version of what the rest of them could conjure. Alex looked apologetic about the brightness.

"Or maybe one of you should," she said with a shrug.

Pi snapped her fingers, showing off her considerable talents, and winked at Alex. The ball of bright light drifted down the shaft, illuminating the steel girders and the continued shaking of the cable. It kept going, and when it reached a few hundred feet, the distance made picking out details difficult.

"I feel like we should see something soon," said Pi, leaning over the edge and making Aurie nervous.

The ball was reaching the midpoint of the shaft when there was a sudden surge of movement and the light blinked out. Everyone leaned back into the hallway.

"Did you see that?" asked Alex.

Aurie barely heard her. She knew what they'd seen. Some sort of long-limbed demons climbing the shaft. Which meant only one thing—the others had perished in the explosion or the subsequent release of creatures.

"You don't know they're dead," said Pi, gripping her shoulder. "Not them. They're too resourceful."

"But where are they?"

"I don't know, Aurie, but you have to keep believing they're alive."

Aurie fell against the damp wall, eyes squeezed shut. Her heart was ricocheting around her chest. It was hard to breathe.

"Hey guys," said Moriganne, "I'm worried about my sister and the others, but those crawling things were making good time up the shaft. We either need to do something about them, or get the hell out of here."

"Unless we know where they are," said Alex, "we shouldn't fire anything down the shaft."

"Fall back to the hallway?" asked Pi.

The crowds filled with families in the square snapped Aurie back to awareness.

"We can't let them get out," she said.

"The hallway is the best place," said Alex. "A good pinch point. Should be able to hold them off there. Or you all can. I'm not so useful in the real world."

As they backed down the hallway, Aurie felt like she was abandoning Zayn. They reached the grocery store to find the owner sitting behind her counter with a shotgun, watching the crowds mill about in the square.

Alex jogged over to explain what was coming up the elevator shaft. There was a round of cursing in at least two languages, and then she went through a door in the back that led to her apartment over the store.

"Maybe they escaped into the Undercity," said Aurie as she stared at the dim hallway.

"I think they're getting near," said Moriganne, staring at her tattoo. "Should we put up a wall, or something?"

"Yes," said Pi, while at the same time, Aurie said, "No." She added, " We need to kill them.

If the others are alive, we don't want to trap them with demons."

"Is that a good idea?" asked her sister.

"The more we kill the better. We can't maintain wards here forever. Eventually they'll break through our magics and rampage through the square," said Aurie.

"Is this concern for the people outside, or Zayn?" asked Pi, skeptically.

"Both," said Aurie.

"Fair enough. Killing it is."

As they stared down the hallway, Alex cleared her throat and asked, "You and Zayn are a thing?"

"Not currently. We spent some time together when we were both in school, but he's four years older and had a lot going on with his family," said Aurie.

The look on Alex's face suggested that she had additional knowledge. Her own experience in the mind-world made Aurie wonder what Alex had witnessed when she'd rescued Zayn.

"Why? Did you see something?"

The hesitation went unresolved when Moriganne gasped, "They're here!"

The dim emergency lights at the end of the hallway revealed shiny black legs unfolding into the space. Aurie had the impression of a sea urchin, except each spine bore an arrowhead-like end. The critter pulled itself into the hallway. It laid down its spines to fit, and then at a surprising speed, shot forward, using its appendages to propel itself forward.

They unleashed a mix of spells into the spiny demon. Electricity crackled over its body, followed by flame and force bolts that snapped off spines. The creature shrieked in pain, but kept coming. Aurie was sure it would reach them until her sister sent a ball of magma into the center of the creature. Burning flesh stunk like hot garbage as it stopped moving about twenty feet from their location.

"I think we blocked the hallway," said Moriganne.

The pause in the battle lasted until the dead creature started sliding their direction.

"Is it alive?" asked Moriganne

"Does it matter? Keep firing," said Pi.

They resumed their barrage of spells, until Alex said, "The others are using it as a shield. Fall back!"

The dead spiny demon was pushed into the shelves of cereal and chips. Wood snapped and boxes popped, sending their contents across the floor. The live demons climbed over their dead brethren, moving faster than their spells could deal with. Aurie gave one a true name shout at close range but it only snapped off some spines. Pi had to pull her back to the entrance to the grocery store where Alex had unlocked the accordion.

As they fled into the square, which was emptier than before but still contained a few hundred people, all eyes fell upon their fight.

"Run! Get out of here!" yelled Aurie, but far too many of them were transfixed by the action.

The spiny demons crashed into the glass, spilling the broken shards onto the sidewalk, then burst outside like living tumbleweeds. Pi caught another with a ball of molten lava, but it only caused it to shriek from unseen mouths and roll down the street after fleeing pedestrians.

More spiny demons poured from the demolished Korean grocery store. They seemed to sense easier targets elsewhere, and except for a pair of determined ones, they scattered into the streets, heading away from the square. Between spells, Aurie watched a guy in a cowboy hat try to outrun one, but it rolled over him, impaling him with the spines.

"We have to stop them before they slaughter everyone," said Aurie, dragging the others after a pair of spiny demons chasing after a crowd of people towards the Spire.

They fell behind her, leaving a pair of dead spiny demons in the square, chasing the two tumbling down the street. Their rolling speed easily outpaced them, but it was easy to follow the screams and car crashes.

"Merlin help us all."

Six

"I'm going to check," said Kitty. "I can't hear anything."

<No minds in hole>

The voice in her head made her flinch. She wasn't used to Kali speaking to her and was afraid what else she might see in her mind.

"Be careful," said Pax as she continued cataloging the equipment from the emergency supplies. It appeared the room had been built during the construction of the elevator shaft to provide a safe spot should something happen. Given the writing on the wall, mostly crude sayings and drawings of dicks, they figured that the workers had used it as a break room, rather than going all the way back to the top.

A breeze changed the complexity of the air, which meant the spiny demons had escaped out the upper passage. She hoped no one was in the grocery store when they emerged. Keeping the demons from climbing up after them during their flight up the shaft had been challenging. Had the shaft been any wider, she wasn't sure she could have managed it, but her force waves covered most of the diameter, knocking them back down again and again.

Though the spiny demons were past, she didn't know if other climbers were heading up and crept to the edge with that in mind. A careful glance over the edge revealed empty air. Too empty. It took a moment for her to realize that the cables that held the car had snapped. Kitty listened carefully for a while before deciding that nothing was climbing up. She headed back to the room to give them the bad news.

"We might be here longer than expected. The cable broke."

Pax's shoulders sunk. She pushed back her red hair and closed her eyes. The grease from the cable had gotten over everyone during the climb and she still had smudges on her jaw and neck.

"You two can climb out. I'll stay here with Kali."

"First, we're not leaving you here. It's too dangerous to be split up. Second, I'm not sure we want to go up. Those spiny demons went that way, and we don't know if one of them is lurking in the grocery store. It would be a great place for an ambush."

"That only leaves one way," said Zayn, crossing his arms.

"I was thinking about this while we were looking through the gear. There's enough fire hose to get us down to the society rooms, what's left of them. I couldn't hear anything below, so I bet that the shaft was mostly closed off from the explosion. It might give us an opportunity to see the portal."

"None of us have the skills to close it," said Pax.

"No, but the others do. If we can scout it, find out what's going on, how it's open, maybe that will help someone else figure out how to shut it."

"This isn't about Ollie, is it?" asked Zayn with a hunched forehead.

Kitty hesitated before she answered. "With my luck, he probably died in the explosion. Look, I'd like nothing more than to bury my blade in his chest for what he did to Ares, but that's not the bigger concern right now."

Zayn didn't seem to believe her and she wasn't so sure she believed herself. The idea of finding Ollie and making him pay for what he'd done to her family was more of a draw than she let on.

"How do we get out?" asked Pax. "The plan sounds good except we have to survive to be of any use."

"The complex around the fifth well is larger than most people think. In the past, the societies used it for research and scholarship about the Undercity and the connection to the demonic realm."

"In the past?" asked Pax.

"It became nothing more than a good ol' boy system for getting ahead financially, and everything except the Convergence ceremony went by the wayside. But. There are secret tunnels that lead out of the complex."

"Won't we run into the invasion?" asked Zayn.

"Only if the damage to the cave system is extensive and blocks off other routes. There are ways out that lead in all different directions. We could easily reach the exits in the eleventh or tenth wards in an hour, but the longer we delay, the bigger chance the demons have spread out."

Pax and Zayn looked to each other before nodding.

"You've sold me," said Zayn. "We should start tying the hoses together and find a good harness for Kali."

As they unwound the fire hose, Zayn unbuckled the panels from the wall around the water system. The pipes sounded empty, as they'd probably been drained years ago after the shaft was completed, but they made a good anchor point.

Pax used the bright red bags that had held the fire hose to construct a harness while she and Zayn checked the hoses. Kitty sensed a pensiveness from Zayn as he kept quietly making tiny headshakes.

"You okay?"

He closed his eyes momentarily before meeting her gaze. "Caught up in some what-ifs."

"Care to talk about it?" she asked as she pulled the hose tight.

Zayn sighed, but after a long pause he said, "Even before Aurie and Pi showed up in the Eternal City, I'd been thinking about taking a break from my work with Priyanka. My whole life has been filled with subterfuge and deception. My childhood was spent plotting to overthrow the Lady of Varna, which consumed my years at the Halls, and then as soon as I graduated, instead of taking time off for myself, I started working for Priyanka.

"I haven't seen my family in years. I'd love to visit Paris and eat at Neveah's restaurant, or see how big Imani and the twins are. See my parents on their adventures. We spent our childhood jammed together in the Stack. It was cramped and awkward, but it was the best ever.

"Now I'm realizing I probably won't get to do any of that. When I saw Aurie in the Eternal City, it reminded me how much of my life hasn't been my own. We were a thing, briefly, but I haven't stopped thinking about her. I'd like nothing more than to take off with her, see the world, visit my family." The corner of his mouth twitched. "Forget about magic and spying for a time. I know more about the maetrie realm than I do my own world."

Kitty put a hand on his shoulder as he hung his head. She could see the pain etched on his face.

"Your family sounds amazing. I would love to meet them," she said, smiling.

He screwed up his face. "I barely told you about them."

Kitty laughed. "You didn't have to. I could see your love for them in your face. I would like that too."

Zayn tilted his head. "You have that with your family, don't you?"

"Two of us are dead, one of them technically isn't my sister, and the rest of us are broken. I'm not sure any of us can be fixed. Maybe Ivan, because he has Audrey, or Andromeda with the Mystique, but me? I'm everything my father wanted me to be. A monster."

Zayn reached out and squeezed her arm. "You wouldn't be here if you were a monster. You'd be out trying to take advantage of this terrible situation instead of helping us."

The memories of the lodge with her father were too fresh in her mind. They blotted out the other feelings that tried to intrude. She could still see herself chasing those old men and women around the table while her father looked on approvingly. If it'd been the only time she'd ever unleashed her inner sociopath, it might have been easy to dismiss. Mikhail Dresden. The young Monta at the midden pit. The blackmail she'd performed for her father. There were too many examples.

"You remember during your first year, when Priyanka asks her big question?"

Zayn nodded. "What will you do when you have to kill."

"It was never a question for me. I knew I could do it. Why? Because my father spent my entire childhood extoling the virtues of being ruthless. He was a killer, even if he never did the deed himself. And I was just like him. Still am."

"I can't imagine the number of people that Priyanka has killed in her lifetime, but I know every one of them hurts her. The fact that you question your actions means more than you think."

"Tell that to the dead."

Pax rose from her crouch. "The harness is ready."

Kali whined as she reviewed the bags that had previously held the fire hoses. Pax had cut out holes for legs and reinforced them with bandages from the first aid kit.

"We should get moving," said Zayn.

As they dragged their gear to the edge of the shaft, Pax leaned over.

"I'm sorry I was overhearing your conversation—you know, small space—but I can tell you that Kali's seen inside your mind, and she doesn't think you're a monster. Neither do I. A badass and one of the best people to have on your side is a more accurate description."

Kitty smiled and gave her a nod. She wanted to believe them. She really did, but she knew what was in her head. In her heart. If and when she found Ollie Rend, there would be no mercy, no hesitation. She would be a monster.

Seven

Andromeda was unloading the materials that they'd hauled in from Ivan's place, while the other two were working on reenergizing the wards and other protections that Ares had built into the property. She could hear them discussing the damage that had occurred when the cobra-headed creature had breathed fiery coal-smoke over the front door. They weren't demonologists or experts on warding, so reforming them was challenging.

She unzipped a bag, expecting to find equipment for the laboratory. At least a dozen different dildos and other interesting sex toys stuck from the opening like a plastic porcupine. Andromeda looked to the open door where her brother and his girlfriend were standing and chuckled lightly. She was glad he'd found someone that accepted his weird and wished she could find an Audrey for herself.

The zipped-up bag went under the old bed in Ares' room, which at the moment, was just a box spring, as the unconscious housekeeper was lying on the mattress on the third floor. Andromeda poked through the colognes and old reading material by her dead brother's bed, looking for signs of a social life, but given the work he'd been doing in the house, she doubted he'd had one.

Andromeda could admit to herself that she was a little jealous of Ivan and Audrey. She'd had her fair share of flings, but nothing serious. The younger Silverthorne, Pythia, was intriguing, but she seemed so intense, burning a crateful of candles at both ends, she wasn't sure it could ever work out.

Looking out the third-floor window after checking on the unconscious housekeeper, Andromeda spotted two new fires on the edge of the third ward. The homeless brigade at the old industrial park was partially breaking up. The smarter ones were disappearing into the buildings, while the intoxicated ones were still shouting at the shimmering blue dome and cheering every time there was a new source of destruction. She guessed they were happy to see the world coming down to their level.

Andromeda threw herself into reading through his books. The others had already cataloged it, setting it in piles they thought might be useful. She paged through books, quickly assessing each one's usefulness before reading the next.

After a time, Ivan and Audrey wordlessly joined her. Occasionally they had short conversations about the text since none of them were demonologists. They set the books that were most useful in their own piles: wardings, descriptions of demonic creatures, and so on.

Audrey was the one to find Ares' notebook about portals. He had neat handwriting, and his sketches were nearly print ready. Ares had been curious about how the invasion might occur. Would it be a bubble of demons exploding into their realm like the disaster in Montanhas, or a full-fledged invasion that would require keeping the passage between realms open for a long enough time to facilitate the travel of significant numbers of the infernal creatures?

"Listen to this section," said Audrey, seated on a stool with the notebook open. "*The energy required to hold open a stable portal makes the city of sorcery the only possible location, not only because of the thinness of the barrier but the excess faez. This would require a structure to hold it open on both sides. While seeing into the demonic realm would be far too difficult and dangerous, and it would be assumed that Elosian had worked out the necessary construction, the question that haunts me is how to anchor it on this side. A ritual would be required, of course, but how can a portal of that size and strength be maintained?*"

"Anything else? Or just that section about portals?" asked Ivan.

Audrey paged through the notebook, skimming with her finger tracing across the pages until she cleared her throat and began again.

"*The wells of power are a curious thing. The patrons have said little about their construction, but having read accounts from those that have visited, and having viewed some myself, I can assume certain things about them. One, they are awash in excess faez. Two, they likely originate in the demonic realm, as no other place has the quantity of faez available, and three, the constant flow has created a stable-ish structure between realms. If a portal was to be made, the wells would be a likely candidate, however, the areas are too unstable for passage. This makes the wells both suitable and entirely impossible for transit. The four active wells aren't the only place. The fifth well, the benehajar, could be an alternate route, but its use comes with challenges as well. It was capped decades ago and exists in an area controlled by those who would have no wish to create such a passage. There's also the question of the original well's element, force—sometimes called spirit. Why was it closed down? Does the reaction of force to the other four elements suggest an unknown relationship? Or is it merely the fifth element?*"

"That would have been great if we'd read it before the invasion," said Ivan, frowning.

Andromeda lifted her chin. "Is there anything about how one might close it? Or can you destroy it?"

"Good question," said Audrey, reading through the pages directly after that section. Her forehead knitted. "Here's something interesting. *That the city of sorcery is the place that magic has the most efficiency and easiest transit to other realms through portals has long been the subject of speculation. Why does magic work better here than anywhere else in the world? Why can so many portals stay active while other realms find them nearly impossible to maintain, unless they're connected to here? It's my proposal that it has something to do with how force interacts with the other elements. In my readings, I found a book from ancient Rome that called the fifth force the bridge.*" She looked up and said, "The word *bridge* was circled for emphasis. *Could it be that force itself can provide the scaffolding?*"

"Was he talking about portals specifically?" asked Andromeda.

Audrey shrugged. "Don't know. It's one of the last entries. Recent, maybe a week before he died."

"We need to find if there's a way to close it," said Andromeda.

"That sounds like trying to cap an erupting volcano," said Ivan. "No thanks, count me out."

"One thing at a time," said Andromeda. "First we have to figure out if it can be done. We should read through the other material, looking for anything about portals."

Audrey tapped on the notebook. "There are footnotes indicating the other books that are connected to his research. We could track down some of those and see what else they might tell us."

"That sounds promising," said Andromeda. "Anything stick out?"

"I think he purchased any of the books available on the subject, judging by the stacks in here, but he does note that the owner of Left Tower Books has a private collection that he hasn't been able to see on the subject of portals," said Audrey.

"Sounds like we have a trip to make," said Andromeda, standing up.

Ivan pointed to a cabinet. "Or, hear me out, there's a bottle of two-hundred-year-old scotch in there that's dying to be sampled. We all know those good-for-nothing demons aren't going to enjoy it. Heathens would probably break it and try to stab someone with the glass."

"Or," said Audrey as she got up from her stool, "if you help, I promise to—"

The rest of her offer was whispered in Ivan's ear as his eyes slowly widened. Given the contents of the duffle bag, Andromeda had a pretty good idea of what kind of things were being put on the table.

"Are you up for a short trip to Left Tower Books?" asked Audrey brightly.

Ivan blinked rapidly. "Yes. As soon as the blood's flowing back to my brain."

Eight

Haymarket Grocers was being looted when they arrived. The windows had been broken out. Lines of people stepped through with arms full of food and other supplies.

"Want me to put this riot down?" asked Lennie as he flexed his tattooed muscles.

Nandi sighed, placing her hand on his arm. He was a sweet guy beneath the roid-biker exterior, but he saw the world exactly how Protectors had shown it to him.

"No. We've got bigger problems than looting." She saw the fear in their eyes as the people scrambled out of the store, staring at the dome, expecting the worst. "They need to feed their families."

Gregor had his head down staring into his phone with a lollipop in his mouth, while Sammi and the cobra-headed chimera stayed around the corner as not to excite the looters.

"Got anything?" she asked.

"Huh?" His head popped up. "Oh, not much. The lines are jammed. Everyone in the world is probably trying to contact someone here. Doesn't help this was high season for tourists. Probably an extra million souls in the city. I did get a half-loaded page from the *Herald*, which showed one of those spiny things that we killed outside the convenience store."

Nandi put a hand to her chin. "It's rather quiet for an invasion. Even if there's a dozen of those creatures, they'll get put down soon enough. Did it say where they came from?"

Tapping on the phone while he sucked on the lollipop, he nodded. "The first reports came from the square around the Statue of Invictus."

"We're about twenty blocks from the square. Those things move fast," said Lennie. "Should we head there?"

Nandi kept craning her neck towards the blue dome that covered the city. She was considering a trip to Coterie of Mages. Professor Sinclair had to know something about what was going on. Or the patron. But they wouldn't have time for her with everything going on.

"No. Let's head towards the Spire. Maybe they know something about why this dome is blocking anyone from leaving the city. I feel like a caged animal."

"What if we're being kept here as food?" asked Sammi as she rubbed her hands together, eyes flitting to the dome. "It's like when you put mice into a python's cage."

"Food for what?" asked Lennie. "We haven't seen shit."

"If someone had opened a portal on the street level, then we'd see more creatures, which means that if we have only seen those spiny things..."

Nandi looked to the ground.

"The portal was opened in the Undercity," finished Lennie.

"Oh shit," said Nandi. "What's at the square where the first spiny demons were spotted?"

"The Statue of Invictus?" asked Gregor, holding the half-eaten lollipop away from his mouth.

"No, you dolt, the society entrance," said Nandi.

"Merlin's tits," said Lennie. "Ares Charmer was murdered there last week. I wonder if that was part of the ritual."

"I doubt it," said Nandi. "But anything's possible these days."

Sammi's dark eyes creased as she wrinkled her nose as if she were going to sneeze. "I bet they sacrificed him to open up a gate. Would be just like those demon-loving Charmers to murder one of their own to bring about the invasion."

"That's sick," said Lennie, frowning.

"We need to track down Moriganne," said Sammi as she squeezed her nose and made tight shakes of the head. "She's the key."

Nandi watched the people with arms full of goods scrambling out of the grocery store. The looting wasn't widespread yet. Most people were staying to their homes as the cell phone alert had directed them to.

"Why Moriganne?"

Sammi blinked as if she didn't understand, then her eyes brightened. "You saw the sky when they killed Lil and Dank. No human mage can summon that kind of storm."

"I was inside," said Nandi. "I never saw Moriganne."

"Well I did. She's the one we have to stop."

"Other ideas?" asked Nandi.

"Personally, I think finding a way to disable the dome would be the right move," said Gregor, looking up.

"Lennie?"

He lifted his shoulders, which had the effect of making him look like a turtle trying to slip into his shell.

"If you want to stop a busted line, you have to turn it off at the source. Someone will have to go into the Undercity eventually," said Lennie.

Nandi frowned. "That sounds like a death sentence. But you're right. Eventually, if we're going to stop this, someone has to go down there."

"Not it," said Gregor.

"We have a couple of options," said Nandi. "Head to the society HQ, though I have my doubts about the usability of the elevators if those things came up from there, or head to the Spire to see what's going on with the dome. Or go somewhere else if anyone has ideas on who might know how to stop this."

"Find Moriganne," said Sammi. "That's my input."

"There's probably plenty we can do around here," said Lennie, eyeing a guy walking out of the Haymarket Grocer with a cash register. "But I'll defer to your decision."

"For now, I think we should head to the Spire," said Nandi. "Someone must know what's going on. The patrons return there in times of crisis. They might be meeting, or if Invictus is the traitor we think he is, they'll be headed there to stop him."

"Unless they've turned too," said Sammi.

"If there is a conspiracy, it can't be that big, or it would have fallen apart. Besides, why create this school and teach all these mages how to defend themselves if you're going to throw them to a city full of demons?"

"Which we've seen few of," said Lennie.

"Yeah," said Nandi. "But if they came out the society HQ in the fourth ward, where would they go?"

"Most of the entrances to the Undercity are too small for anything like those spiny creatures. I know I barely fit down some of those stairs," said Lennie. "And if bigger demons have come through, and I can't imagine why they wouldn't, there's no way they get out of the Undercity that way."

"That's a good point," said Nandi. "Most of the ways to get in and out of the Undercity are narrow sets of stairs, a few elevators, or other such passages."

"Most?" asked Gregor as he finished his lollipop and threw the stick over his shoulder. "I've never been below."

"Not most. All but one that I know of," said Nandi, frowning.

"Where is it?"

"The biggest and most commonly used entrance is a wide ramp that can easily support huge numbers of creatures," said Nandi, feeling a sense of dread. "It's connected to the largest settlement in the Undercity. Big Dave's Town."

Nine

Xylos slapped the runed tile onto the table, rattling other pieces and spilling their drinks. He lifted both arms, letting out a victorious whoop that brought frowns from the few other customers at the Devil's Lipstick, which was usually the busiest bar in Big Dave's Town.

"Four in a row! I'm on fire," said Xylos, laughing as he made finger guns and mimed blasting away.

Adrenalynne plopped her elbows on the table, mouth agape as she stared at the disjointed board of runed tiles. She'd been sure she was going to win the game of Runic Risk up until Xylos pulled the tile from the top of the stack and slapped it down. His dirty brown hair partially fell into his eyes.

"That was the only tile that could have saved you," she said incredulously, snatching the glass of Pale Paw and throwing back a drink as a consolation for her loss. "Two, maybe three, percent chance. I swear you stacked the tiles against me. No way you can be *that* lucky."

Xylos interlocked his fingers and stretched them outwards, cracking his knuckles. "The shuffler wins again." His gaze shot towards the bar. "Oh, shit, Delilah."

The owner of the Devil's Lipstick weaved through the vacant tables. The earthquake a few hours ago had disturbed the other patrons, and the place had emptied out except for a few locals. Before she reached them, a strange shiver overtook Adrenalynne. The feeling left her cold and a little curious, as she only seemed to have them when something big was about to happen. She'd had a fateful shiver the morning her parents had died, and again, the day she was invited to join the Razor clan.

Delilah stopped at the table. She had a bar towel over her shoulder. Her usual big hair was tamed by a headband and her hands had splatters of grease on the backs.

"What is it about this game that gets you two so excited? Everyone's freaked out enough over the rumbler and now you two are acting like a couple of teenagers," said Delilah. "Do I need to kick you out again?"

Adrenalynne stretched her tattooed arm casually, making sure to show the neon RZR displayed on her forearm.

Delilah frowned. "Yeah, I know you're Razor clan. Don't give a shit, Adrena." She rolled her eyes. "Why can't the two of you be like the rest of your clan buddies? I think I prefer the wanton violence to whatever nerdcore stuff you've got going here."

"Hey," said Adrenalynne, "there's a lot of boring downtime being in a clan. We haven't scuffed with the Drops in a long time, and playing games keeps our minds sharp."

"Shaking down the locals is hardly advanced calculus," said Delilah, holding her hand on one hip and leaning that way.

Adrenalynne opened her palms. "Not right now. But in the future. Never know."

"Speaking of," said Xylos, pulling out his little notepad and flipping it open, "are you up on your payments?"

Delilah put a hand on his shoulder. "Sweetheart, I play poker with Niran every other week."

"Right," said Xylos, closing the notepad and stuffing it back into his backpack leaning against the table. He wagged his eyes at Adrenalynne, and she stuck her tongue out at him.

The few customers in the bar got up and headed to the door, pausing outside before hurrying away.

"See! You scared them away," said Delilah.

"While you're here," said Xylos with a grin. "Could we get a couple more Pale Paws?"

Delilah swiped at Xylos with her towel. "You two are barely old enough to drink. Broken hells, you should shave that fuzz you're trying to call a mustache. Adrena has more hair in her armpits."

"Just like velvet," purred Adrenalynne, running her hand over her tightly shorn head.

Xylos touched his upper lip as he frowned. "It'll come in eventually."

An explosion from somewhere in Big Dave's Town rattled the glasses and had their heads snapping towards the entrance.

"Fucking hell," said Delilah, slapping the towel back over her shoulder and reaching down to an ankle holster to reveal a snub-nosed pistol. "I thought you said nothing was happening between Razor and the Drops."

Adrenalynne pushed away from the chair, unslinging the automatic rifle from the back.

"Nothing from our end, but they've always been eyeing Big Dave's." She glanced back to Xylos, who was rising from the table. "Why don't you pack us up."

Xylos set a cardboard box near the edge and swiped the tiles into it. They could separate them later when they had time. Delilah stuck her head out the front door. A burst of gunfire echoed from the opposite side of the cavern. The Devil's Lipstick was in a back corner, away from the main path. Adrenalynne leaned her hand on Delilah's shoulder as she peered out.

"What's that smell?" she asked.

Delilah wrinkled her nose. "You never been around a well?"

"No."

"Must have a shit Merlin score then. That's faez. Shouldn't be smelling it here," said Delilah.

Another long burst of gunfire was followed by a minor explosion. Gray smoke rose from a place two streets over.

"What's going on?" asked Xylos with a backpack slung over his shoulder and a rifle held to his chest.

"Whatever it is, we'd better get out there," said Adrenalynne. "Niran will have our heads if we don't push the Drops back."

Delilah opened the door wider and craned her neck. "This doesn't look like a clan war. I think I'm going to close up and get in my bunker. There's room enough for you two idiots if you want."

Adrenalynne walked into the street, holding her rifle at the ready. She liked the figure she presented with the sleeves cut off her black jean jacket, velvety short hair, ample tattoos, and more piercings than a porcupine.

"We'll go take a look. It's probably nothing. Besides, they don't call me Adrenalynne for nothing."

Xylos joined her in the street and nodded back at Delilah. "The bunker idea sounds nice. Could keep playing Runic Risk. Maybe you'll win a game."

"Nah. What's the fun in that?" said Adrenalynne with a big grin. "Don't want to live like those *wayhos* in the light."

"Hey," said Delilah, leaning out the door with a big metal bucket. "Could you do me a favor and haul this to the grease hole? I'll credit you some Pale Paws for next time."

"Don't have to tell me twice," said Xylos, scurrying over to accept the pot as he kept glancing into the cavern where the smoke was rising.

He waddled it to the back of the Devil's Lipstick while Adrenalynne kept her rifle pointed down the street. The excitement of expectation had her breathing shallowly. She wished she had access to those elixirs that the city mages and the higher-ups in Razor clan had—then she'd be able to move as fast as a cheetah and be able to leap onto the buildings.

Occasional gunfire was followed by silence. She never heard returning fire, only one-way sprays. Maybe something big and ugly had come up from the deeper areas of the Undercity. It would put their names on the map to take it out.

"What are we doing?" asked Xylos, wiping his face with the back of his hand. "That grease hole stunk."

She sniffed. "Yeah, you got some on you. And now it's on your face."

While she chuckled, he pulled out a rag from the backpack and wiped it off. They crept to the edge of the street. Big Dave's Town was the size of about six city blocks inside an enormous kidney-shaped cavern. There were a dozen passages that led away and the big ramp that went up to the surface, exiting into the city at a dive bar called the Goblin's Romp.

The red glow and buzzing from the neon sign above Devil's Lipstick went away.

"She never turns that off," said Xylos.

"Shhh...I hear something."

Up the street, a guy in a camo jacket that she thought she recognized from the military supply store was running flat out, checking behind him, fear radiating off his face.

"If those Drop bastards are hurting our people, I'm going to be righteously pissed," said Adrenalynne, stepping around the corner at the same time a bone-white creature the size of a lion with two enormous lobster claws caught the fleeing owner. A quick snip and two bloody halves flopped to the ground.

She froze when the pincered creature turned towards her, snapping its claws ominously. Adrenalynne was sure it was coming for her until a cat darted from an alleyway, and the creature turned to chase. The feline's evasive maneuvers ran the lobster-clawed creature into a narrow alleyway, and parts of the buildings started to collapse.

Relief lasted for two entire seconds, until she spotted a group of ochre-skinned humanoid figures jogging into view. Xylos dragged her back before they spotted her.

"What the actual fuck is going on?" he whispered. "That's not the Drops. Unless they're adopting some sort of Weird Circus personas."

Hiding behind the corner, two streets over, they watched as more of the ochre-skinned humanoids passed through, heading towards the ramp that led to the upper city. As the numbers swelled, Adrenalynne regretted not taking Delilah up on her offer.

"Adrena, can we get the fuck out of here? Before they spot us," said Xylos, tugging on her arm.

"Yeah, those aren't the Drops," she said absently.

They jogged back towards the Devil's Lipstick, tugging on the door only to find it locked.

"Any idea where the bunker is?" asked Xylos.

"Not a clue."

A woman in a tank top came screaming around the corner, looking over her shoulder.

"Oh, baka," said Adrenalynne, giving the door handle another tug. "We gotta hide."

She knew exactly what Xylos was thinking when he gave her a look. They ran for the grease hole behind the bar as dozens of the ochre-skinned humanoids came burning around the corner in pursuit. The metal lid was heavy, and she could smell the stench even before it was open.

"Oh, that's awful," said Adrenalynne, swallowing back bile.

Any hesitation about climbing into the place where old grease had been marinating for years evaporated the moment the woman's long painful scream echoed through the cavern.

Adrenalynne held her rifle high and dropped into the pool of brownish-gray gunk, sinking to her waist. Xylos dropped in a second afterwards, splashing her with the impact. He handed over the backpack of their gaming supplies and reached up to yank down the metal lid, entombing them in darkness.

It stayed quiet for a long time, except for occasional moments of gagging, followed by a liquid splash as they finished vomiting. Minutes at least, probably longer passed. They couldn't hear the screaming anymore but it was still going on in her mind.

"Adrena," whispered Xylos.

"Yeah?"

"What were those?"

She'd been holding her nose, but gave up, hoping that eventually she'd get used to the stench.

"If I had to guess, demons. You know the rumors about what goes on in the canyons near the fire well?"

"Yeah."

"Well I saw a dead demon once. Small, no bigger than a terrier, but definitely not from our world. Stunk like faez, just as Delilah said."

"Demons, wow." He exhaled. "You know, since we're probably going to die, I wanted to let you know that you could have beat me the turn before if you'd played the fire rune on my scale."

She pictured the board in her mind. "Fuck."

"I hope we get to play again," said Xylos after another equally long period of silence.

"Yeah," she said, trying not to vomit again. "Me too."

Ten

The Spire was surrounded by massive crowds when they arrived. There seemed to be two camps: protesters concerned about the glowing blue dome, and people trying to find safety inside. The two sides were shouting at each other, jostling and hurling water bottles. Signs read things like "Free Us Now!" or "Magic is Evil!" or "Invictus is Not God!"

"That would be news to him," quipped Pi as they circled the streets around the crowds, looking for a way into the parking garage where the secret elevator was located. She was getting hungry and wished they could get inside. There was a bag of spicy chips in the pantry she'd been thinking about the whole march into the center of the city. A taxi would have been nice, but they'd gone screaming towards the outer ring or been left abandoned on the streets.

"How'd they make these signs so quickly?" asked Aurie.

Pi shared a look with Moriganne. "My sister thinks only the best of people."

"Years ago, when the ritual murders were happening in the Undercity, there were always protesters with signs at Invictus PD, demanding they find the killers. I think some people have them in their closet, ready to go," said Moriganne.

"If I had a sign, it would say 'I love cheese' with a big heart in the center and I'd make sure I was in the middle of that group over there," said Pi.

"What? I don't understand," said Aurie, wrinkling her forehead.

"That's the point. The other signs, their intent is clear, but the cheese sign, there'd be a lot of people utterly confused by it, and that would defuse their anger. A Zen sort of misdirection," said Pi, grinning at the others.

"You're having entirely too much fun at the end of the world," said Aurie.

Pi lifted her shoulders. "I survived being trapped in Elosian's mind. I'm feeling pretty good."

Moriganne lifted her shirt, showing a ropy, knotted scar that bisected her midsection. "Elosian gave me this when we fought him."

"Can I touch it?" asked Pi.

"Sure."

"Wicked."

"He tried to rip my arm off," said Moriganne with a half grin.

"We have a problem," said Alex, suddenly. She hadn't spoken much on their trek across the city, but she was staring at a knot of people who were pointing in their direction.

"I'm not much of a lip-reader, but I think they recognized us," said Pi.

As the crowd started moving towards them, the shift created more interest in what was going on.

"This is a problem," said Aurie.

They started jogging circular to the Spire, but the crowd was only growing. Pi could hear their shouts: "What's going on?" "Where's Invictus?" and "Why did you do this to us?"

Before long, they were surrounded by men and women, some with signs, pushing and shoving as variations of those questions were repeated in ever growing volume. Someone got knocked down by Pi and they both nearly got trampled as she helped the woman back up. There was a mix of fear and adoration in her eyes, and then someone yanked the woman away.

A sign cracked Pi on the back of the head. She turned to see who had done it. A tiny bit of blood was smeared on her fingers after she checked the back of her head.

"I'm starting to get angry," she told the others. They'd grabbed each other's arms, trying to stay connected, but the crowd kept pulling and tugging on them. "We'd better do something soon."

"Close your ears and duck down," said Moriganne.

There wasn't much time to comply. As soon as Moriganne opened her mouth, Pi crouched into a squat, holding both hands over her ears.

"Go home, it's too dangerous here. Protect your families!"

Even through the blocked ears, Pi could hear the power in her melodic voice. The urge to stand up and start marching away from the Spire was strong, but as the crowd dispersed, Moriganne leaned down and whispered into her ear, erasing the compulsion.

"Merlin's tits, that was strong," said Pi as she reviewed the widening circle of space.

A few protesters had dropped their signs as they marched zombie-like back to their homes.

"Don't know how long it'll last," said Moriganne. "We should hurry."

The voice command had only worked on the people within range. The wall of protesters blocking the parking garages and administration entrances to the Spire was still there, but as they neared, Moriganne sang out to them, dispersing them easily. This magical compulsion was noticed by those further out and not in hearing range. As they ran through the gap created by

Moriganne's voice, the outer edges of people collapsed after them.

"We'd better run!"

Besides having a head start, they knew where they were going, dodging around the cars in the parking garage until they reached a door that had a maintenance closet sign on the front. They threw themselves inside before anyone spotted them. An illusion of pipes and cleaning equipment wavered as they walked through it, reaching the elevator on the opposite side.

"I feel like a secret agent," said Moriganne as Aurie touched the runes in a specific pattern to open the doors.

"Invictus liked to come and go without being swarmed," said Aurie. "After that, I think I understand why. That was scary."

"He prefers the Garden Network," said Pi. "But sometimes he liked to walk around during the late hours to think about some problem he was working on."

"At least we have power," said Aurie, hitting the button that would take them to the highest room in the Spire.

"Is there going to be a problem?" asked Alex, adjusting her glasses.

"Problem? Why would there be?" asked Pi.

Alex frowned. "You all seemed to know each other. I was brought in to help with the visions, but I'm not sure if I should be here, and outside the game worlds, I'm not that useful."

The moment of doubt surprised Pi as she sensed a supreme confidence from Alex that had been demonstrated on multiple occasions in the game or dream worlds. Pi repressed a grin. She didn't want Alex to get the wrong idea.

"You saved our asses from Elosian," said Pi. "You deserve to be here."

Alex stared at her intently. "Thanks."

"Now," said Pi, clapping her hands as she stared at the climbing numbers, "I'm dying to talk to Old Iron Balls about this stupid dome and what his plan is for closing the portal."

She was surprised to find the entrance room outside the elevator empty. Normally, there were assistants outside as the interface between the school and its head patron, to help with the mundane details that Invictus didn't like to bother with. Which was most topics, except a few limited interactions with the original patrons.

"Where is everyone?" asked Aurie.

"Maybe he sent them home to be with their families," said Pi. "I know, totally unlike that uncaring asshole, but I'll throw 'em a bone every now and then."

They passed through the empty offices on the way to the portal room that would lead them into his demi-realm. The runes that normally glowed around the outside were stone dark.

"He locked us out?" asked Pi incredulously.

Aurie approached the archway and cast a few spells. When she was finished, she cupped her chin in her hand.

"I'm out of ideas."

The vision that Pi had showing Invictus at the head of a demonic army, the Rod of Dominion in his fist, came back to her. At the time, she'd been willing to dismiss it as a tactic of Elosian, to get her to doubt the head patron, but between the lack of transparency about the Rod, the blue dome blocking everyone in the city, and now not being able to get back into his demi-realm, her bullshit meter was tilting heavily against Invictus.

"What's wrong?" asked Alex. "You look like you've thought of something."

Pi found her hands were clenched into fists and had to purposely open them.

"It's just—"

Her words died when Moriganne, who'd moved to the east-facing windows in the administration room, started pounding on the glass.

"No! No! Please, no! Oh, Merlin!"

It took a moment for Pi to find what Moriganne was looking at. Pi's instinct was to look straight down at the second ward entertainment district where she was used to watching the illusionary battles, but the streets were empty. No one gathered near the Glitterdome as normal.

She followed Moriganne's gaze out to the eighth ward. The wide green areas of the Animalians campus and the cryptozoo revealed nothing that would bring about that sort of concern. It wasn't until her eyes traveled to the edge of the ward that she saw the carpet of creatures flowing from one of the buildings. The mass had already crammed in the two blocks surrounding and was spreading out like an oil slick. A cold emptiness filled Pi. It was one thing to battle a few spiny demons rampaging through the square near the Statue of Invictus, but seeing the number of demons flowing out from what she could only assume was the Goblin's Romp left her completely shaken.

A hand squeezed hers and she thought it would be her sister's, but it was Alex next to her, concern on her brow.

"We'll find a way to stop it," said Alex.

The words barely reached Pi's ears. It was too much. There were too many. Smoke was already rising from the buildings in the area. Tiny shapes were swallowed by the spreading horde. They were too late. The battle for the city of sorcery had begun.

Eleven

The collapsed tunnel stunk of faez. Zayn wished he had a hunk of wax to shove into his nostrils as they crouched on the crushed rocks and timbers that had once been the entrance hallway to the society rooms.

The gap at the top of the rubble gave them a narrow window into the former ritual room, which had been completely demolished. Only a large glowing hole remained. A stream of demonic creatures climbed from the deep space, heading into the darkness of the Undercity. Some of the creatures Zayn recognized from their trip into Elosian's mind, but the valley didn't represent either the numbers or the variety. He saw horrific things that defied reality oozing or undulating out of the hole. The spiny demons in the elevator seemed mundane in comparison.

Kitty tapped him on the shoulder and gestured in the other direction. She'd been scouting to make sure the other passage was still open while Pax and Kali collected supplies from the few rooms that hadn't been destroyed in the explosion. He shook his head. He wanted to stay a little longer to understand the organization of the horde, or if there was anything about how the portal was staying open that they could exploit to close it, but his arcane knowledge on the subject was limited to using the portals, not creating them.

He didn't see the figure at first, but felt Kitty's tension at his side. Her hands squeezed to fists and her eyes bugged out of her head. She looked simultaneously furious and in great pain.

Following her gaze led to a solitary figure ambling out of the hole. He'd only seen him once in Kitty's vision, but the lone human surrounded by a sea of demons was hard to miss.

Victor Charmer.

His skin was a bright red as if he had a deep sunburn and his hair was long enough to reach his shoulders. He'd been an old man on the precipice of death when he'd gotten sucked into the demonic realm, but now he looked as hale and hearty as a twenty-year-old professional athlete.

Kitty started climbing forward as if she were going to shimmy through the gap and either kill or rescue him. He didn't know which. Zayn grabbed her forearm, shaking his head. The touch snapped her out of the trance she was in.

They watched him march out of the hole with a group of taller demons that had a passing resemblance to Elosian, as if they'd been made, or modified in his honor. Victor was at their center. Traitor or slave, Zayn couldn't tell.

When he was out of sight, they climbed back down the rubble pile. Kitty stared at the floor. When he tried to console her, she marched away before he could get the first word out.

Zayn followed her into the remnants of a hallway with a partial collapse spilling rock onto the carpet. The body of a dead society member had been covered up with a blanket they'd found. Probably shot when Ollie and his friends invaded the chamber. Pax had a couple of backpacks. She handed one to Zayn, who slipped it on.

"What's wrong?" asked Pax quietly as Kitty stood at the far end, hands on her head, back bent in sorrow.

"We saw Victor."

"You're shitting me," said Pax, checking back with eyes wide. Kali let out a little whine. "How did she react?"

"She tried to climb over."

Pax crouched down with Kali. "She's radiating fear and anger. You sure we should continue this way?"

He looked up. "Better than the alternative." Zayn sighed. "When we found her in the vision, she was in a room with Victor. Something had happened. She called herself a monster."

"I'll keep an eye on her," said Pax as they approached.

When they reached her, Kitty turned around, having composed herself. "The way is clear. At least the first section I scouted."

Zayn nodded. "I'm all turned around down here, but it appears they're headed east. If those kinds of numbers have been coming out of that hole since the explosion, I don't know how we're going to survive. I hoped the low numbers of those spiny creatures might mean that it was a small group coming through."

Pax nodded towards her companion. "We should get moving. There are others in the tunnels. We might have company when we leave."

The pinched expression from Kitty suggested she welcomed a fight. It might be the best thing possible for her, but Zayn wasn't sure. He had no experience with a volatile family like the Charmers. His parents had been loving and supportive, not like the abusive figure that Victor had been in their lives. It only took a few minutes with Ivan to see the damage that Victor had caused in his children.

"I can take point if you want," said Zayn as he twirled his knives.

"I'm good," said Kitty, marching ahead through the gap where the secret panel had been. They cut through a narrow passage that required turning sideways until they exited a rock formation that slid out of the way at her touch. Once the passage was blocked again, Zayn couldn't tell that it'd ever been open.

The last time Zayn had been in the Undercity had been with Kitty when they went to visit Niran Santos, head of the Razor clan. He'd been there on Priyanka's business, while Kitty had been there to ask a question. He wondered how the clans were faring with the incursion of demons. Hopefully they'd figured out to get the hell out of the way, though that would only last so long unless the portal could be closed.

When they reached a split in the passage, Kitty hesitated in front of the tunnel that would take them into direct conflict with the demons.

"There's too many. We wouldn't stand a chance," he said.

She held her position, staring into the darkness before letting out a big exhalation and continuing in the direction that would lead them out of the Undercity.

They traveled with Kitty in front, Zayn at the back, and Pax and Kali in the center. Occasionally, Kali-radar gave them indications of creatures moving through nearby tunnels or caves, which helped them avoid getting into a fight. Their hidden movements lasted until they reached a cavern that had collapsed decades ago, leaving a cliff wall between the upper and lower sections.

"Something's here," whispered Pax as they approached the edge. "Multiple somethings."

They crept to the edge, hoping to spot what lay below. Darkvision revealed three enormous creatures that were larger than a horse and made of bones, moving through the space as if they were searching. The spiked tail gave away that they were mantics, larger versions of the creature they'd fought at Ares' place. Zayn wasn't sure what was more frightening, the mantics, or the scorpics in Montanhas.

Zayn was motioning for them to head a different direction and bypass the dangerous mantics when he caught movement on the far side, past the demonic creatures. Jammed into a crack in the wall were a couple of humans, two at least, maybe more. He couldn't tell who they were at this distance. Pax and Kitty noticed them at the same time.

The scowl on Kitty's lips revealed that she thought it might be Ollie, or his friends, which made sense given their proximity to the society HQs. He grabbed her arm to pull her back, but she shook him off and gestured emphatically.

<Pax says we should save them>

The voice in his head startled him, but it was better than making noise and attracting attention. Pax probably hadn't noticed Kitty's state of mind. He hoped this didn't turn from a rescue to a pitched battle.

Zayn nodded. At least this time he didn't have to sneak around them, and he knew using his fourth imbuement wouldn't work. Kitty joined him at the cliff wall. It was a fifteen-foot drop to the lower section. A mantic was sniffing around the rocks, its spiked tail lazily drifting behind it like a bored lion.

Kitty tapped on her chest then pointed at the mantic. He would have argued but the intensity in her eyes was bordering on fanatical. A fight would do well to cool her blood. He just hoped they survived it.

The nod of agreement was barely finished when Kitty leapt from the cliff's edge. She flew like a silent assassin, landing on the back of the mantic. Curved blades attacked the sinewy tissue near the back of the mantic's head. The creature barely knew what was happening before its legs collapsed and its body crashed to the ground. There was no blood, but it was clearly dead.

Kitty did a forward roll off the dead mantic as the other two faced her, snapping their tails forward. The spikes hit the cliff wall as she sped out of the way. Caught watching, Zayn had to shake off his amazement and leap down the cliff. He hit and took three strides, before launching himself onto the back of a mantic as Kitty had demonstrated.

He saw what she'd attacked to kill the first so easily. A knotty ganglion at the base of the skull that connected to long, pale, fleshy tissues connecting the rest of the body. Zayn stabbed the ball with both blades as the mantic arched its back and leapt around like an enraged bull trying to knock him off. The strikes failed to sever the sensitive spot. He struck two more times before the mantic collapsed head forward with its bony rear stuck into the air.

The third mantic was in a dance with Kitty. She was trying to reach the weak spot on its neck while it was backed against a cavern wall. The spikes on its tail were empty, but the forward claws and strong jaws were equally dangerous. It was moving fast enough that trying to reach its back would put them in too much peril, but their short blades were useless at a frontal assault.

When the mantic stiffened, slamming its head around as if it were trying to shake loose a bad thought, Zayn was confused, until he saw Pax and Kali standing nearby, intently focused on the creature.

"It's blind," said Pax.

He raced Kitty to the mantic's back, flipping over the randomly grasping claws to land on its shoulder, opposite his fellow Hall member. The rapid piercing of blades ended the brief standoff, killing the last mantic.

When they slid off the dead demon, Kitty kicked it hard enough to tilt the head to the side. That didn't seem to be enough and she lunged back, impaling her blade through the skull. Heaving with breath and emotion, Kitty marched away, leaving her weapon behind. She paced alone near the cliff.

Zayn shared a concerned look with Pax as he retrieved her weapon. Pulling the dagger out took putting his foot to the skull and yanking as hard as his imbuement would allow.

Shapes moved out of the crack in the wall. A guy and a girl with backpacks, hiking poles, and hardhats with headlamps on the front approached sheepishly.

"Oh thank the gods," said the girl. "I thought they were going to find us. What are those things?"

"Mantics," said Zayn. "What the hell are you doing down here?"

"We're from Explorers Hall," said the guy. "We're headed into the third quadrant to map some of the deeper canyons. This is our fifth trip. We've gotten pretty good at avoiding the critters and clans, but I didn't know anything this big lived down here."

Zayn shared a look with Pax as Kali greeted the two Explorer mages. Her appearance seemed to calm them.

"Yeah, about that. You'll want to get the hell out of here. The barrier between our realm and the demonic one has been opened. A horde of demons has been flooding through the Undercity and has probably breached the surface by now. You'll want to find somewhere safe," he said.

"Broken hells," said the girl with anguish. "We have our wedding planned for next week."

"Shit, I'm sorry."

The guy turned towards his fiancée. "We'll get the hell out of the city. We've been wanting to do some hiking out west, maybe the PCT or the CDT. This would be a great time."

"About that," said Pax. "You can't leave the city either. It's blocked off by a big blue dome. Nothing is getting in or out."

Their hands went to their mouths in silent horror. Seeing their reaction reminded Zayn that he'd barely had time to process what had happened. The world as they knew it had changed dramatically. Permanently. They'd be lucky to get out of this with their lives and certainly there would be death. Too much death. He feared for his friends. He feared for himself, but most of all he feared for Aurie. Zayn hoped she was doing okay on the surface, but knowing her, she'd thrown herself into the middle of the fight.

"We should get out of here," said Pax. "Assuming we can find the right passage. We're a little lost."

"We can help," said the woman brightly. "We know this region well. We used an entrance at the edge of the third and tenth. Come on, we'll show you."

"Let me carry that extra pack for you," said Zayn.

"It's all our climbing supplies. We were going to use it to get into the deep canyons."

"Can I hold onto it? Might come in handy."

Pax nodded back to Kitty, who was pacing around the cavern, muttering to herself and shaking her head. "I'll take point. Kali should be able to keep us out of trouble. Is it far?"

"A quarter mile, not too far." The girl crouched down to accept a greeting from Kali. "Is she supernatural?"

"Yeah, let me tell you about it on the way," said Pax.

Zayn fell back with Kitty.

"We gotta go."

Kitty looked almost surprised to see him as if she'd been lost in her thoughts.

"Yeah, that would be the thing to do."

He handed over her abandoned blade. She didn't know what to make of it at first, then glanced back to the dead mantic.

"How'd you know how to kill it like that? You made quick work of it," said Zayn as they followed the others.

Kitty squeezed her lips together, emotion breaking across her face. "Ares' research. He had a whole notebook full of detailed notes and physiological analysis of the samples he'd collected. He won that fight for us from the grave."

"I'm sorry, Kitty."

"Don't be," she said, shaking her head. "We're cursed. A family of Icaruses. We flew too close to the sun and now our wings are melting and we're crashing to the ground."

"We'll get your father back. We can save him."

"What if he shouldn't be saved?" she said.

"You think he's helping them?"

Kitty squeezed her eyes shut as if the thought was too painful to bear.

"When he summoned Elosian, he refused to give Moriganne as part of the deal. He was willing to do what he needed to do for power and immortality, but he wasn't stupid enough to ruin our world in his quest. But now that he's been there for three years, who knows where his alliances lie? He's a monster, bent on power at all costs. Why wouldn't he join the victors? He probably gave them all the information they needed to make the invasion successful." Kitty hung her head. "And I'm the monster's daughter."

"You're not a monster. You saved those two from a terrible death."

"I did it to have somewhere to put my rage. If I was standing before my father right now, I'd put a blade into his chest. Can you imagine what kind of person would kill their own father? He loved his mythology, treated myth as if it were a blueprint for his family. That's why he named us such pretentious, self-important names like Ares and Catherine and Ivan and Andromeda and Moriganne and Solstice." She swallowed and bit down on her lower lip as if the pain could erase the memories. "But he missed the underlying message of the myths. The calamity of hubris. That's the Charmer legacy. We're a Greek tragedy unfolding in real time, except we've taken the entire world with us."

Kitty marched forward as he tried to muster something to help ease her pain, but there was nothing he could say. Maybe they were cursed, just like he'd been in Varna. Except their curse was self-inflicted. The sins of the father infecting the entire family. What would it take to resolve such pain? He hoped Kitty would never have to find out.

Twelve

Standing outside the warded gate, a sudden panic overtook Audrey, leaving her with second thoughts about heading across a demon-infested city to Left Tower Books on a research mission. It had seemed like a good idea, but now that they were leaving the safety of Ares' place, she realized how unprepared they were, especially after Andromeda showed her the video of the demons pouring out of the eighth ward.

It wasn't like danger was a new thing. As Moriganne's best friend at Stone Singers, she'd nearly been killed on multiple occasions, the worst being during Elosian's summoning in the Undercity. That seemed pedestrian in comparison.

At least they'd finally gotten a message from some of the others. Aurie, Pi, Moriganne, and Alex were headed towards the eighth to see if they could help with the defense of the city, or at least protect the people living in the area. They hadn't heard from the others, who had been headed down the elevator when the explosion happened. Moriganne tried to put a good spin on it, but until they had confirmation, the others could be dead. She hadn't told Ivan about his twin's unknown fate, because he was already on edge.

"Is she good?" Andromeda asked Ivan when he sidestepped out the gate.

"Yeah, the IV drip is working fine and I gave her another dose, so she'll stay under for at least another four hours. Hopefully we're back long before then," said Ivan as he slipped into his backpack and held the shotgun to his chest.

Outside the walls of Ares' compound, the noises that had been muted seemed overly loud. The city was filled with a cacophony of sirens, gunshots punctuating the orchestra as if it were a celebration rather than a war zone. The group of homeless near the industrial park had dwindled to a few dozen of the craziest inhabitants.

"Did you see that?" asked Andromeda, pointing her crowbar at the sky above the apartment buildings ringing the outside of the fourth ward. "It looked big."

"Flying demons, great," said Ivan, checking back to the walled house. "We're just going to get ourselves killed, you know."

"For all we know, everyone in this entire city is going to be slaughtered," said Andromeda. "I'd rather go out fighting."

"I'd rather go out stoned," said Ivan, looking sick.

"You're doing great, babe," said Audrey, reaching out and rubbing his shoulder, but he barely seemed to feel her touch.

The homeless crazies gave them a cheer as they marched towards the inner ring. Ivan raised his shotgun victoriously, preening for the crowd. It felt like they were headed into a gladiator pit against terrible odds. Audrey reached up to touch the sword on her back that they'd found under Ares' bed. It had been unenchanted, but they'd done their best to give it some bite should she have to use it.

"The good thing is Left Tower Books isn't too far into the third. We should be able to get there in a half hour," said Andromeda, moving into the lead.

The youngest Charmer looked the part of the post-apocalyptic survivor with her tattoos and piercings, holding a runed crowbar that they'd applied demonic wards to. Ivan had brewed up some elixirs, but they hadn't taken them yet due to the short windows of effect.

Three blocks to their southeast, across the cracked asphalt littered with tufts of grass, a line of people carrying bags and other goods with them were headed towards the blue dome at the edge of the city.

"Hopeful bastards," said Ivan.

"I think I'd rather stay in my home," said Audrey.

Ivan spun around, pointing his shotgun towards Ares' place. "That's still an option."

"You know what I mean," she said, blowing him a kiss.

Ivan caught it and tucked it into his front pocket. "Saving it for later."

Audrey stuck her tongue out at him. Sure, if she hadn't fallen for him, she'd probably be in Chicago working for that architectural firm and avoiding the demonic invasion, but she knew she'd be a much sadder person. Ivan, too.

"Fuck."

The exclamation from Andromeda had Audrey's blood running cold.

"We need those elixirs," said Andromeda, holding out her hand.

Hanging off the side of an apartment building was a winged creature the size of a Buick staring directly at them. It let out a screech that put water in Audrey's knees. Ivan fumbled with his pack, producing three vials they quickly threw back. As the alchemical liquid hit her stomach, Audrey felt warmth overtake her body. The fear was still there but it was at a distance. Slightly removed.

"Keep moving slowly," said Andromeda as they headed diagonally from their original direction. "Maybe it'll—"

As soon as the words left her lips, the creature burst from the side of the building, beating its wings furiously in their direction. As it spread out in flight, Audrey was stunned by its unusual features: two sets of wings, a long black serrated beak, and a hanging appendage from the rear that looked like an anteater's snout.

The winged demon came directly at them. The idea that she could do magic completely vacated her mind at the rapidly approaching jaws of death.

A shotgun blast from Ivan sent the demon careening into the ground thirty feet away. It hit, bouncing hard, then quickly righted itself on clawed feet and stood using its wings for balance before Andromeda could reach it with her crowbar.

"Audrey, sword," said Ivan as he hurried to reload the shotgun.

"Sword." The word bounced off her brain until she saw Andromeda dart in, smashing the crowbar against its beak. "Sword!"

She unsheathed the weapon from her back as she ran forward...and caught her feet on the edge of the cracked concrete, slamming down hard, face-first. The sword clanged across the ground.

Audrey quickly recovered, snatching the weapon up and joining Andromeda as she barely kept the serrated beak from taking an arm off. The beating of its wings threw dust into their faces. The sword impacted the beak, throwing her arm back, making her wish she had voice powers like Moriganne.

As they sparred with the beak, the long proboscis at the creature's rear whipped into the fight, trying to grab their legs. It had a mouth full of teeth on the sphincter-like end. It nearly got her leg, but Audrey managed to cut down, slicing a length from the appendage, causing the winged demon to leap back with a screech.

The excitement of a successful maneuver evaporated when the creature threw itself forward, slamming into both of them. Audrey found herself on her back, the demon thrashing above them, about to crush her with its weight. She rolled over and grabbed the fallen sword, bracing for impact. The demon slammed down on the tip, impaling itself. The screams hurt her ears. She thrust up as much as she could, hoping the pain would drive the creature off her.

A shotgun blast at close range put an end to the demon's struggles. It fell over, narrowly missing Audrey in the collapse. Andromeda leaned in with her crowbar and cracked the demon's skull.

"Everyone okay?" asked Ivan as he reloaded the shotgun with shaking hands.

Andromeda helped Audrey to her feet. Her legs felt like noodles.

"I could use a beer. Or ten. I can't believe we killed that thing," she said, leaning on the sword even though she knew it was terrible for the sharp edges.

"You know what this means," said Andromeda, and when no one answered, she added, "We get to name it. That fucking flying demon asshole doesn't exactly roll off the tongue."

"Claude," said Ivan. "I name him Claude."

"How about andreyvan," said Audrey. "It's a mashup of our names."

"You want to name it after us?" asked Ivan incredulously.

"Okay, maybe not a great idea. How about sucretta?" she asked. "That mouth on the end of that back appendage was scary."

"Sounds good. What do you think, Andy?"

She didn't answer because she was staring to the north where there were more of the winged demons.

"Sucretta," said Andromeda. "We'd better get moving before those notice us."

Audrey was certain they were headed their way when a ball of flame went flying upward, right into the middle of the winged pack. The explosion sent the sucrettas in various directions.

"Yes! Direct hit!" said Ivan, raising his shotgun above his head.

At least one of the sucrettas seemed injured by the blast, but then the pack converged on the spot where the spell had originated. It was hard to make their savior out at a distance, but it looked like an older man in a jacket. He turned to run, but they caught him before he could escape. Audrey was glad they were too far away to hear his screams.

"That's our cue to get moving," said Andromeda.

Audrey couldn't help but stare at the pile of sucrettas thinking that had nearly happened to them. She ran to keep up with the two Charmers, constantly checking above them for more of the winged demons. Nothing in the city was safe, not even the sky above.

Thirteen

The news about the horde coming out of the eighth ward sent Nandi and her team in that direction. She led them around the ring road that bisected the inner wards. As they neared the Glitterdome in the second, a group of armed citizens blocked their path. A tough-looking guy holding an automatic rifle casually at his waist stood at the front. He had a mullet and no sleeves on his shirt.

"Looks like we have some demon lovers," said Mullet.

Sammi surged forward but Nandi waved her back. Kozsen, the cobra-headed chimeric creature that was her companion, hissed ominously. Most of the armed crowd took a step back.

"We're on the same side," said Nandi, holding up her hands to signal peaceful intent.

Mullet spat on the ground. "The way I see it, there's two sides now, the fools that worship magic and those of us who see the world as it is. A heinous place of sin. Just looking at that thing you got with you tells me which side you're on."

Nandi exhaled slowly through her nose, trying not to appear angry, even though her insides were seething. With a forced smile and pointing in the direction of the smoke rising from buildings in the eighth, she said, "We're headed to *stop* the demonic horde, and if we don't all start working together, you won't have to worry about who's worshiping magic, or not, because we'll all be dead."

"That's just fine by me," said Mullet.

Lennie whispered under his breath, "Say the word and I'll stun 'em. I bet a good punch to the nose and this asshole gets his mind right."

Nandi considered the offer. Lennie wasn't wrong. Assholes like Mullet saw the world in the simplest terms, which made making grossly incorrect decisions easy. In this case, his ineptitude was multiplied by the following he'd quickly cultivated from a group of people fearing for their lives.

"Can we forget this disagreement and move in that direction? If we get caught standing here much longer we're going to get overrun. I was hoping to find a defensible spot near the Glitterdome."

Mullet waved his rifle around randomly. "How about you give us that demon you got over there and we'll call it a day."

"Kozsen is an ally, not a demon," said Nandi, gesturing towards Sammi's companion. "One that will help greatly in the fight."

The crowd with Mullet grumbled. Fear was a powerful drug that drove people to do stupid things completely against their interests. Nandi knew this, but being confronted by it in the middle of a war zone was the height of irony.

"Nandi..."

Lennie looked ready to use a shout that could put down a riot.

"Let 'em go to their deaths," said Gregor as he spun a small ornate box on his palm. "Stupid gits."

A hissing growl from Kozsen alerted Nandi to danger. At first she thought Sammi was sending her companion against the armed crowd, but then she saw the dark shapes moving through the side street perpendicular to their location. Two blocks up and hurrying towards them like a flash flood were hundreds of ochre-skinned creatures with long claws.

"That's not good," said Gregor.

"Ferom." She knew the type of demons from her research in Coterie. The armed group turned towards the incoming danger.

"At least we're on the same side now," said Lennie.

Nandi eyed Mullet, who was still staring at them. "I wouldn't count on it."

As the two groups moved to the cross street, Mullet eventually turned towards the oncoming demons. The creatures ran like hyenas in long, loping strides, their forward-jutting mouths snapping in anticipation. A few of the armed group slowly backed away, then fled in the opposite direction.

Nandi couldn't blame them. As she faced the horde, the idea that she could die in a matter of minutes hit her hard. It'd been one thing to battle with the other mages. Nandi had always considered herself the best of the best, so beating them had seemed academic—up until the point they lost. But the long-clawed creatures sprinting towards them with murderous glee left her shaken. These were not simple creatures, hyenas as she'd first imagined they looked like, but demons, hardened by a realm of high faez.

A few bursts of gunfire erupted from the other group. Nandi hated that she flinched.

"Too far away, you idiots," muttered Lennie.

"Fuck," said Nandi, mostly to herself. Her brain had seized up with fear. She shook it off.

"To me. Come on, we need a better spot than standing in the streets like a bunch of idiots."

"Only room enough on this street for one set of idiots," said Lennie, looking to Mullet and his crew.

A ubiquitous Wizard's Coffee had the premiere corner spot on the street two blocks up from the Glitterdome. An abandoned trinket cart with novelty wands had been tipped over near the sidewalk.

"Len, can you give us something to hide behind?"

"Sure thing," he said with a wink.

The big man positioned himself behind a parked car and started shoving. His arms bulged with effort. Lennie grunted and the vehicle started sliding forward. A short lift and he positioned the back end so it formed a wall jutting out from the corner of the Wizard's Coffee. The ferom demons were half a block away and moving fast. Lennie looked up and then grabbed a second car that was further ahead, pulling it into position to extend their makeshift wall.

Once he was finished, Lennie approached, unslinging the heavy riot shield he kept on his back.

"Can you add a little something spicy to it?"

Nandi popped a paint marker out of an inside pocket. No mage of her caliber dared not having a handful of the drawing utensils in their pocket for emergencies like this. She made a few hasty runes that would help Lennie deal with the incoming demons. He winked when she was finished, turning to the side and protecting the outside flank at the edge of the maneuvered vehicles.

Once he was out of the way, Nandi reached for her faez. Her fingers and arms moved with the grace of conductor; she spoke with the verbal dexterity of a speed rapper. Glowing, ghostly shapes formed on the opposite side of the vehicle wall. She extended her arm, stretching the warding as far as she could, but the armed group had so far kept their distance.

The horde of ferom were fifty feet away and closing fast. Nandi stepped back and gestured to her friends.

"Fire when ready."

The armed group, having let loose a few nervous bursts of gunfire, had controlled their impulses since, but with the enemy approaching, they unloaded their weapons. Concrete exploded as bullets hit, then the leading line of feroms staggered to a stop before falling over.

The line of demons spread out. There were more than a hundred, maybe two or three hundred. Nandi pushed away the fear and concentrated on her next spell.

"Heads up," said Gregor as he lobbed a cube over the warding. The box tumbled end over end, coming to rest near the eastern group of demons. It exploded into gooey webbing that tangled the front edge. The ones in back ran into them, creating a cascade of feroms falling into each other.

Gregor stepped out of the way as the cobra-headed creature moved up to the vehicles with Sammi at its side.

"*Atmen*!"

Kozsen reared its head back then exhaled a column of roiling black superheated smoke. The dangerous breath hit the scrambling demons like a speeding wildfire. Their screams as the flesh melted from their bones turned the street into a carnival of pain.

The other demons hit the armed group. Gunfire had taken down dozens, but too many remained for their weapons to handle. The pitched battle turned to chaos as the feroms bounded through them, ripping throats with long claws. Friendly fire splattered across the barrier vehicles, but Nandi ignored it and finished her spell as part of the forward line swerved towards them. A wave of force hit like a tsunami, knocking them off their feet and giving Kozsen enough time to ready a second breath weapon.

Some of the feroms bounded away from the other group, attempting to flank their position, but Lennie had positioned himself along the side of the second vehicle. He punched the first demon so hard its neck snapped. The second he hit with a shout, staggering it, then he pulled out a baton and cracked the ferom across the forehead.

An explosion from the interior of the pitched battle had Nandi checking back to Gregor, but he held his hands up.

"Wasn't me."

Combatants on both sides went down. Someone had tossed a grenade into their midst, killing friend and foe. Mullet was jogging backwards, letting off bursts of gunfire at the pursuing demons. More were coming down the street. They'd put up a spirited defense, but they could only hold out for so long.

The dead men and women amongst the demons made the danger all too real to Nandi. That could be them soon. Just like Lil and Dank. Maybe they were the lucky ones.

"I think it's time to run," said Gregor with a cube in each hand.

They'd mostly repelled the first wave of demons, but at great cost. The armed group was down to a handful who had survived, including Mullet, but they lacked the numbers to withstand the next group, which was only a block away.

"Nandi," said Lennie, checking over his shoulder, "what do we do?"

For the first time in her life, Nandi didn't have an answer.

Fourteen

Pi fell to her knees as they crossed the street. They were only halfway across the second ward after leaving the Spire. The crowds had dispersed since they'd entered the tower. Flying demons circled the city, making it dangerous to be out alone.

Aurie helped her up. "Not like you to be a klutz."

A stab of pain had hit her elbow. Pi looked to Moriganne to see a similar grimace.

"Two left feet," said Pi.

Alex was staring at her and she had a good idea that she'd deduced the reason for her collapse. Something had happened that had sent a blast of pain through the tattoo, strong enough that even Pi had felt it.

As they jogged along, Pi shifted next to Moriganne. "How do you stand it?"

"You felt it too?"

Pi nodded.

"You get used to it."

Pi didn't believe that, but she didn't say anything.

"Do we have a plan, sis, or are we just going to run right into danger as usual?"

"It's worked for us in the past," said Aurie with a weak grimace.

She saw other groups moving towards the eighth ward. Some appeared to be students while others were citizens with weapons. Window shades shifted as they passed beneath the watchful buildings. People were hiding out, hoping that the defense of the city wouldn't have to include them.

"You know, if all three million people came to its defense, we might stand a chance," said

Pi.

"Doubtful," said Alex, glancing to the windows. "They'd mostly be a hinderance, and would only decimate morale as people saw little old ladies and children dying by the dozens."

"I didn't mean them," said Pi.

Alex blinked and gave her a strange look. "Sorry."

There were no spoke roads that ran directly into the eighth, so they were forced to navigate the streets, but it was easy to see where they needed to be heading. The sky above the eighth was filled with smoke and flying creatures smaller than the ones that had already winged into the city.

They ran into another group that appeared by their attire and general age to be fellow mages. Probably currently in school. A few friendly, but grim waves, and they were traveling down the street together.

"You're Aurie and Pi Silverthorne," said a guy in a tracksuit as they moved parallel.

"Nice day for a jog, eh?" asked Pi. When they looked at each other, confused, she sighed and added, "Good day to kill some demons?"

"Yeah."

"Where you from?"

"Alchemists," he said, gesturing back towards the west. He went on to give their names, but Pi only remembered his, which was Steve.

"Is Celesse joining the fight?" asked Aurie.

"We haven't seen her," said Steve. "But you know, she's rarely around. Got a big corporation to run. She might not even be in the city."

"Right."

More likely the longer-lived patrons with more to lose had found a way out or were holed up, avoiding a battle that would put them at risk.

They turned the corner, nearly running into a street full of demons that were making their way into the center of the city. Pi saw creatures made of blades, the ochre-skinned feroms, and a trio of lumbering giants that could punch through a second-story window with ease. Magic erupted from their combined groups, shouts and songs filling the air with fell energies. The Alchemist mages threw bombs into the demons' midst, turning the street into a conflagration of green fire. An enormous ghostly rhinoceros formed near them, then went bounding into the front line of demons, scattering them like bowling pins. Pi threw molten balls of hot iron, reducing the creatures she hit to screaming char. A fierce crosswind slammed into the smaller demons, throwing them off their feet, but the larger lumbering giants continued forward.

"More spells," said Aurie, before using her true name shout against a blademan that had nearly reached them.

Pi was aware that Alex hadn't added a single bit of magic to the fight. She was staring into the line of demons, not with fear as she would have expected, but an intensity that bordered on trance.

"We have to retreat," said Alex.

Aurie scowled in her direction. "Why aren't you using your magic?"

"We're about to be overrun," Alex said dispassionately.

Aurie looked ready to disagree, but she looked back to the swelling crowd of demons. Pi gave her sister a nod when she looked to her.

"Fine. You take the lead," said Aurie. "What are we doing?"

Alex turned towards the bike shop to their right and blew the glass inward with a force bolt.

"This way," she said, then cupped her hands to shout to the Alchemists on the other side. "Get out of here! They're flanking us!"

Alex ran into the bike shop with Moriganne on her heels. Pi threw a few more spells at the oncoming demons and then followed. As she glanced behind them, a group of feroms came around the corner, cutting off their escape. The Alchemists on the opposite side of the street were still trying to fight, but a second group had trapped them as well. Pi looked away before she had to witness their demise, leaping over fallen bikes that had gotten knocked over in the blast.

After a brief delay at an employee's only door in the back, they were climbing a set of stairs to the upper floors of the combination business and residential building. The hallway led to a few doors and a window that looked over the street. Pi checked to see that it was only demons. No sign of the other mages remained.

"We're trapped," said Aurie.

Alex ignored her and opened the window. The trio of lumbering demonic giants were headed their direction. When she climbed out the window, Pi thought her mad until she realized emergency scaffolding was directly outside. They followed Alex up the metal stairs, eventually reaching the roof on the fifth story.

"What are we doing?" asked Aurie, but Alex was too busy looking around to answer.

"We need to get over there," said Alex, pointing to a cell phone tower a block over on an apartment building. There were hundreds of small flying creatures circling around. Pi felt exposed on the roof, but understood what Alex was trying to accomplish.

It dawned on her sister too, because she said, "You're trying to see what's going on."

Alex nodded. "Staying in the Spire would have helped, but then we wouldn't be able to do anything. That tower is the next best thing."

"We've got climbers," said Moriganne, looking over the edge of the building.

A few spells blasted them off. They ran across the roof line towards the tower. A cloud of small fliers circling the eighth ward broke off and came winging towards them. They looked like bats with enormous mouths full of teeth. Moriganne hit them with a fierce downdraft that drove some of them into the building, and the rest escaped back to the main force.

They reached the cell phone tower, and Alex started climbing the ladder that went up the side. When she was a dozen rungs up, she called down to Pi, "I might need a guardian."

Pi leapt onto the ladder, scurrying after Alex while her sister and Moriganne stood guard.

The toothy bats made no attempt to return, but Pi didn't trust the situation.

The higher they climbed the more of the city Pi could see. None of it was good. The demons had taken over the eighth ward and spilled into the surrounding areas. The main thrust of their push was towards the Spire. She spied the trio of demonic giants with a crown of crimson light around their heads, leading a horde of demons. Somewhere behind them, a group of four-armed demons was carrying a massive palisade.

More people had joined the defense, forming a ring around the expanding flood of demons. The flashy lights of magic sprung up like ground-based fireworks. Bubbles of warding and ghostly waves impacted the numerous feroms before they could rampage amongst the defenders. The overwhelming nature of their task left Pi worried for the fate of their city.

Alex said nothing as she reviewed the surrounding streets, glancing between the eighth and the Spire more than once.

"What do you see?" asked Pi.

"We're spread too thin. We should coordinate the defense near or at the Glitterdome. The structure is large enough to create a barrier...or we could use it to trap the main force inside. Surround and pound."

"Okay, let's do it," said Pi, starting to climb down, but stopping when Alex didn't move.

"What's wrong?"

"I don't know where Elosian is, which means he's staying hidden, or he hasn't reached the surface yet."

"He's not the bigger problem right now," said Pi.

Alex extended her arm towards the second ward. "There's a loose organization of the attacks. He's directing them somehow. A purpose I can't quite see."

"Using his freaky mind-link thing," said Pi.

"Probably." Then after a frown, she said, "They're trapped in the city. The proper thing to do would be to eliminate the defense and then destroy the thing in the Spire that's creating the barrier, but that's not what they're doing. The push towards the center is strong. I would have built my army in the eighth, then strike the defenses with overwhelming force."

"Maybe Elosian's not the master strategist that we think he is. Maybe he's just really good at manipulation," said Pi, trying to see what she was seeing, but it looked like chaos to her.

"He's both an excellent manipulator *and* strategist, but I don't see the reason for it. It's like he feels there's a time limit. He has to accomplish something quickly. I can only assume it's the Spire dome, but that might not be it either." Alex shook her head. "The streets are chaos. It's wanton slaughter, but with a purpose."

"At least the schools are coming to the defense," said Pi as she spotted a knot of people coming up the main road that bisected the second ward, right next to the Glitterdome and heading into the eighth. While most of the counterattacks had been pushed back, this group was managing to make headway against the demons, giving her hope.

"It won't be enough," said Alex as she climbed down.

Back on the rooftop, Aurie gestured to the buildings behind them. Dozens of ferom and blademen had reached their level and were heading towards them. They were trapped.

"We have a problem," said Aurie.

"Time for that tornado thing," said Pi.

Moriganne rubbed her elbow, which was glowing through her shirt. She glanced suspiciously at the sky.

"I'm afraid if I do, I'll be pointing a big beacon at our location. Elosian has passed through. I don't know if he's on the surface, but I can feel him getting closer."

The ache in Pi's elbow wasn't as bad as the grimace on Moriganne's face, but she had the same lingering ominous feeling emanating from it.

"We want him focused on Moriganne," said Alex.

Aurie screwed up her face. "We do?"

"I don't know a lot about demons and warding, but I know that he can be sent back to his realm with the right magics. We should fall back to the Glitterdome and lure him inside. The structure should allow us a chance to control the tempo of battle, then once he's near, find a way to send him home."

"Didn't we already get our asses kicked inside his mind trying to trick him?" asked Aurie.

"I'm open to other ideas," said Alex flatly.

"We're out of time," said Moriganne.

The winds rose to her song as the feroms bounded across the roof line. The tenor of her voice was different from before. The sky above the buildings collected greenish clouds even though there'd been no weather inside the dome.

Pi felt the pressure in the air change as she fired force bolts at the oncoming demons to give Moriganne more time. When they leapt across the last gap between buildings, Pi thought they'd made their decision too late, but a tendril whipped down from the cloud, tearing up tiles and tar. A ferom got caught in the fierce cyclone, sending it flying over the edge. The tornado hit the main force, turning their advance into a rout. The remaining demons were easily cleaned up with a few well-placed spells, and when the roof was empty, Moriganne let the tornado dissipate into wisps.

"That was efficient," said Alex.

Moriganne collapsed to a knee and Pi felt the reflection of pain.

"He knows we're here," said Moriganne through gritted teeth.

"We'd better get moving," said Aurie as she stared at the sky behind them.

Pi knew what she would see when she turned, but it didn't make it any easier. The entire cloud of toothy bats were speeding towards them, spreading out until they covered a space at least three blocks wide.

Fifteen

Once they hit the city streets and bid farewell to the two explorer mages, the eruption of magic and columns of smoke to the east drew them in that direction. Zayn led their sprint across the city, and Pax was glad for the years of training as a Hunter that allowed her to keep up with her companions.

The city level looked nothing like before they'd entered the Korean grocery store on the way to the elevator. Tourists had packed the sidewalks while cars honked and sped through the streets, and the energy of its inhabitants had been light and carefree. Kids rode on the shoulders of their parents, or in strollers. It'd been a normal day in the city of sorcery.

Now, it was completely different. The roads were empty. They saw people watching them from their windows with naked fear on their faces, or heading west with bags and luggage, not that it would help them, as their escape would be blocked by the dome, which was another change since they'd gone below.

"I guess we know that Invictus wasn't on our side," Zayn had said when they'd first crested into the light of day. "Trapped us here with a city full of demons."

Pax wasn't so sure, but she didn't have an idea otherwise.

The nearer they got to the eastern edge of the second ward, the more fellow mages, or citizens with mundane weapons, were moving in the same direction. Pax wished there were more of them, but not everyone had the tools to fight like they did.

"Where to?" asked Zayn when they reached the edge of the Glitterdome.

Kitty extended her arm. "I think I found the others."

Across the second ward, a localized storm had formed above a group of apartment buildings. A tornado extended down to the roof, throwing tiles and the occasional demon off the side.

Kitty squinted. "That's got to be Mori."

"They're way behind the line," said Zayn. "We can't reach them. If that is them."

Pax checked the air above them, spotting a few pigeons fleeing from the area.

"Let me check."

She crouched down with Kali, putting her hand on her companion's furry shoulders.

Let's take a peek.

<Winged rat make good spy>

She closed her eyes and then opened them again, finding herself high above the buildings. A moment of vertigo was pushed away as she nudged the pigeon towards the eastern side of the ward. The carpet of demons was thick near the edges, but more spread out as it went back further. There were pitched battles between the buildings as some of them tried to get into the apartments. Pax hated seeing it, but there was nothing they could do. As the pigeon circled, she saw her friends on the top of a building. It was a block behind the line of demons, and as she was about to return to her body, Pax spotted the cloud of winged creatures speeding towards them.

"They're trapped behind the line and there's a sky full of teeth coming for them," said Pax, rising back into a sprint. "We have to push the line back."

When they reached the line of defenders, they found mages from all different schools. Even if their Hall's expertise wasn't suited for battle, everyone knew the five elements from playing games. Flame and force were most common, but some mages were better suited to the other elements.

Zayn leapt onto a car near the front. "My friends are trapped a block back! We have to open up a corridor for them! With me!"

He ran into the line of feroms, his blades moving in a blur. Kitty joined him, and the pair sliced through the enemy, giving the defenders a chance to push the demons back.

"Keep an eye out," she told Kali as she waded in behind the two assassins, using the five elements since she wasn't a close-combat fighter.

The momentum led to a boost in morale. Up until that point, they'd been pushed back, and there was a cheer when they broke the forward line of demons, turning it into a rout. Zayn and Kitty led the counterattack. As they pushed back up the street towards the buildings where their friends were trapped, people in the surrounding apartments fled, heading away from the battle.

Everything was great until the lumbering giants came around the corner. At least twenty feet tall, the first one scooped up an old VW bug and lobbed it at them. Kitty and Zayn easily dodged the impact. The other mages flung elemental magics at the giants, but it washed over them without injury. The larger demons seemed more resistant to the attacks.

Pax craned her neck to see Aurie and the others looking over the edge of the building.

Five stories. Too far to jump, and the flock of winged demons was headed their way.

Zayn and Kitty sped to the first giant, slicing its legs without ever staying in the same spot long enough to be hit. It didn't look like they were hurting the giant.

Distracted by the battle ahead, Pax didn't see that a ferom had slipped past the other mages until it came bounding towards her. It leapt with claws outstretched.

Skorost!

She flew beneath the demon, turning as she ducked, using her mark to deal with the demon.

Khoplat!

The slam flattened the demon, breaking its back and leaving it crumpled on the ground.

"We need to get them from the roof!" yelled Pax.

Zayn disengaged from the giant and in less than five heartbeats scrambled up the front of the apartment buildings, using the architectural features for handholds. When he reached the top, he disappeared momentarily. Pax had forgotten about the climbing equipment he'd borrowed from the Explorer mages until the nylon rope was flung over the edge. Moriganne slid down the rope first, followed by Alex, then the Silverthorne sisters, and finally Zayn.

The battle with the giants was a stalemate, so when their friends were on the street level, the entire group fell back at the same time the flock of winged demons came rushing over the rooftops.

They had enough magic on their side to drive the cloud of toothy death back into the skies, jogging back the way they'd come, giving up the territory they'd recovered. The lumbering giants followed, but slow enough a gap formed between the two groups.

"We need to get to the Glitterdome," said Alex once they reconvened.

"Why?" asked Zayn.

"To set a trap for Elosian."

The conversation was lost on Pax because she felt the presence of the cobraffin through Kali. There was no visible sign of the creature in the surrounding streets, but she knew for a fact that it'd been near.

Then she saw the striking leader of the other mages, the ones that had kidnapped Andromeda, striding towards them from a side street with the enormous Protector at her side.

"Hey guys, I think we have a new problem."

Sixteen

The sight of Left Tower Books brought a smile to Audrey's lips and not only because it might contain valuable knowledge that would help them with the demonic invasion. As a child, when she wasn't singing or listening to music, she'd been a voracious reader. Enough that the local library knew her name and treated her like their adopted daughter when she sat in the back and read books for hours.

The door was locked when they arrived. Ivan pounded on the glass, peering in with his face pressed against it.

"Hello! Open up! The world depends on us coming inside! I'd rather not break the glass, but I will if I have to!"

The lights were off. Audrey spotted someone peeking around a shelf, which made them all pound harder.

Eventually, a thin gray-haired gentleman in a blue button-down shirt approached the door cautiously.

"Haven't you seen the world's gone to shit?" he said. "We're closed."

"Yes, but we're trying to save it. There's a book inside that we need. In your restricted section," said Ivan.

When the guy made no move to open the door, Andromeda held up her crowbar. "We're coming in one way or another. If you'd like to keep the glass intact, then make quick with the lock. There are flying demons about."

He reluctantly unlocked the front door. They pushed through and when they turned around the older gentleman had a gun pointed at them.

"Hey, man, we're all on the same side," said Ivan, holding his hands up.

Audrey read his name tag. "Uhm, Mark, we understand you're scared, but please put that away."

"I'm not scared. I didn't want you to break my window and if I shot you through it, the same thing would happen," he said.

Andromeda stepped in front of the gun. "Feel free to shoot me, but I can assure you that it's not going to work out like you think it will."

The agitation in Mark's expression turned to horror, but he kept the gun on them.

"My sister is serious. She's a performer in the Mystique. Can take a split two-by-four to the shoulder night after night, and just earlier today she took a beating from some Protector goon."

Mark's forehead bunched up at the same time an airy male voice from behind the counter said, "Bonnie Bedlam?"

"Stay back there, Carl," said Mark with only a brief glance to the side.

A head popped up, another gentleman around the same age as Mark. His hair was dyed black, because it didn't match his bushy gray mustache.

"It *is* Bonnie," said Carl with excitement. "Mark, put that away. We both loved her at the show. There's no way she'd be here to hurt us. Right, Bonnie?"

"My name is Andromeda, but yes, we're not here to hurt you. We need your help."

Mark's gun wavered, but never left them. Carl approached his partner, gave him a kiss on the cheek, and gently made him put the gun down.

"The world has gone to hell, literally, Mark, we should show some compassion."

Mark frowned but put the gun in his waistband. "The safety was on the whole time."

Audrey breathed a sigh of relief.

"What do you need?" asked Carl.

Audrey pulled Ares' notebook out of her backpack. "It's a book called *The Impossible Portals* by Fredrich Niels. Was only a short printing, or something, and even fewer were translated. You have one of the few English copies."

Carl put a finger to his chin as he stared at Andromeda. "You're Andromeda *Charmer*. Ares' brother."

"Yes! You knew him?"

Carl nodded. "He frequented our shop. We were tracking down a lot of rare and unusual books for him. My condolences about his death. A tragedy."

"Thank you," said Andromeda. "The funeral was supposed to be today, or tomorrow, I don't know, I've lost track."

Carl expanded his arms, offering a tentative hug. Audrey was surprised when Andromeda fell against him, letting out a sob. As the stoic and sarcastic youngest Charmer broke down, Audrey had to dab away tears. Even Ivan's eyes looked a little redder.

"Come now, our store is yours to use," said Carl. "Tell us what you need. You said you might be able to stop this?"

As they followed him into the back of the store, Andromeda explained what had happened in brief terms. Carl and Mark nodded, making appropriate noises of shock and horror at the bad parts.

"A portal from our realm to the demonic one, here in this city, I can't believe it," said Carl, shaking his head.

"Ares didn't tell you what he was working on?" asked Ivan.

"Money speaks, child, and your brother was free with it. I would have tracked down Invictus' shopping list if he would have paid me," said Carl as he waggled his fingers.

He threw back curtains with a flourish. "The restricted section. It's not *so* restricted, we let anyone back here, but given the value of the books, we preferred to know who was poking around in them."

The room was small, ten by twenty, and not all the shelves were full. Mark marched to a spot on the far side and looked back to Carl.

"Was it in the Speculative Theory or Arcane Model section?" asked Mark.

Carl shifted his mouth to the side. "The first."

Mark took a side step over and pulled a thick blue book without a jacket from the shelf. He handed it to Andromeda, and they gathered around as she opened the first page. The writing was in a tiny font.

"This is going to take forever," said Ivan as he stepped away, throwing his head back.

"Not so, babe," said Audrey, pulling out the notebook. "Your brother was a meticulous researcher and notetaker. He marked the section clearly. You could use some of his organization skills. I swear we don't know half the formulas of the elixirs you make."

They found the page Ares had marked. Audrey read over her shoulder, finding the section before Andromeda reached it. The younger Charmer finished both pages before returning to a middle section.

"Here it is. I think this is the part he was referencing. It talks about permanent portals." She cleared her throat. "*The energy required to hold open a portal is astronomical in comparison to a temporary one. The genius of the Garden Network and the other obsidian portals in the city of sorcery are their efficient design. The circuit remains ready to use, requiring only a bit of faez and any appropriate passwords or keys. Once the magical energy is applied, the circuit opens up for an eyeblink and physical transfer occurs. A wonder of modern arcane knowledge.*

"A permanent portal, while mostly theoretical, would require different thinking than a temporary. Holding open a tunnel between realms is like trying to hold the Atlantic from mixing with the Pacific Ocean at Cape Horn. The structure required to hold back the forces would have to borrow from the more advanced theoretical areas of portal scholarship.

"Rather than hold the two sides back, keeping them from crashing into each other, the trick would be to use their energy against themselves. The equivalent of a finger trap. The more you pull, the stronger the connection. The problem with this idea is that the materials necessary for this portal are theoretical and probably

impossible. There are no steels strong enough to even withstand one one-millionth of the forces. No, it would require something of high arcana. Something strong enough to hold back oceans. Something not of this realm and hardened by time and temper. The danger of a structure like this would be the perilous forces unleashed should it break. Worse is that the longer it's open, the higher the chance it might collapse on its own, damaging both realms irrevocably."

The silence lasted for about ten seconds, until Ivan said, "That? That's what we risked getting eaten by flying demons with mouths on the end of their tail-penises for? That writer should have just said, impossible portals are impossible."

"But they're not. We've got one in the Undercity right now. And it was more than that. The open portal is dangerous. It could collapse at any moment."

"I think the danger is the flying monkeys, my good witch," said Ivan.

"Whatever it is, it needs to be closed for multiple reasons," said Audrey.

Andromeda tapped on the book. "Something is holding open that portal and it's not from our side. It could be that temporary structure they saw in Elosian's mind."

"Pi talked about seeing a bridge connecting two continents in the infernal realm, except the landmasses existed independently from each other. Ares circled *bridge* in his notebook, suggesting there was something important about it," said Audrey.

"Is the bridge in the infernal realm connected to the bridge tattoo?" asked Ivan.

"Maybe. Seems too coincidental otherwise," said Audrey with a shrug.

"Remember when Ares and Magnus used the connection with Vic to throw Elosian back through the summoning portal? I wonder if there's a way to do that with the demons, or at the very least Elosian?" asked Andromeda.

"We really need someone with a background in demonology," said Audrey.

"We need Ares," said Ivan as he slumped onto a stool.

Audrey was suddenly aware of the wide eyes from their hosts. "Uhm, if you can't tell, we've been living a strange life these last four or five years. I hope you'll keep all that in confidence."

Mark started speak, but Carl elbowed him. "Of course. Especially if you can reverse what's happened out there. The reports we're seeing online are horrific."

"Pi knows a thing or two about demonology," Audrey said. "Doesn't she?"

Ivan nodded. "Yeah. Something about one of those souls...wait, no. She doesn't know anything, because that would require us going closer to the invasion, not back to Ares' place."

"Babe..."

Ivan gave her a pained expression, but he nodded. "You know I'll go, but we do have the housekeeper to worry about."

"You said four hours. We've only been gone one. There's time, and we have to get this information to the others."

"We don't know where they're at," said Ivan.

Carl raised his phone. "Reports are coming through about people coming to the city's defense. They seem to be rallying around the Glitterdome. You said Pi earlier, I assume you mean Pythia Silverthorne?"

"The very one."

"She's there, along with her sister and some others," said Carl.

"Couldn't we, you know, just send a text?" asked Ivan.

Audrey shook her head. "We have Ares' notebooks and other information. We have to go to them. It's the only way."

The owners of Left Tower Books followed them to the front door. Hugs and promises to come back after everything was sorted out were given, even though they all knew that it was unlikely.

"Oh, can you wait a sec," said Carl brightly as he hurried into a back office. He appeared shortly after with a costumed doll wearing a jaunty witch hat in his hands. "Would you sign my Bonnie Bedlam doll?"

"Of course," said Andromeda, grinning as he handed her gold paint pen. She scrawled her signature on the doll's back and handed it over while Mark quietly shook his head.

After they collected their gear and stepped back onto the street, Mark locked the door behind them. The two of them leaned on each other and watched from inside their store while they marched down the street, heading northeast.

Seventeen

A new wave of feroms drove them back. They weren't even halfway to the eighth ward and progress had been reversed. Nandi sent half-hearted force waves behind them to keep the pursuing demons in check. Gregor added his cube-surprises to the retreat and they made it back two blocks to where other forces had gathered. The demons slowed about a block away, gathering at the edge of the street as if they were waiting for a signal.

Nandi found a spot to the side where she could confer with her friends. Sammi's chimeric companion was given a wide berth, but since they'd seen them fighting the demons, no one accused them of being on the wrong side like Mullet.

A cry of alarm went up as Nandi was catching her breath. Someone pointed to a strange solitary cloud over the apartment buildings two blocks up and over from their location. The moment the tendril of a tornado came snaking down she knew exactly who was making it. Nandi bit down on her rage and frustration. Those were the mages that had killed their friends.

"Is that them?" asked Lennie at her side. He was wrapping his forearm where a ferom had clawed him.

"Hard to imagine it's anyone else," said Nandi.

"We're going to go kill them, right?" asked Sammi. "For Lil and Dank and for everyone else whose died because of their treachery."

Nandi looked back to the tornado, which was already dissipating as other flashes of magic erupted from the rooftop. A cloud of flying creatures was headed towards the other mages.

"Maybe we were wrong about them," said Nandi, tasting bitter doubt in the back of her throat.

Lennie gave a head tilt but said nothing while Sammi stomped her foot.

"You're kidding, right? Should we be checking you for signs of demonic compulsion? They *killed* our friends. They *started* the invasion. We have to get our revenge."

"We attacked them and we don't know they started it." Nandi exhaled. "Look, I'm not saying I trust them, but given the circumstances and their actions, I'm inclined to think that Beckett and the ceremony were wrong."

"He was your boyfriend."

Nandi squeezed her eyes shut. "Don't think for a second I don't miss him with all my heart. I was there at the warehouse. I saw his body. But this isn't about him, or us, or Lil and Dank."

"Screw this," said Sammi, marching away with the cobra-headed Kozsen on her heels. "You've changed."

"Sammi!"

Nandi watched as the Animalians mage headed west away from the battle lines.

"I think she's got the right idea. I think it's time for me to bug out," said Gregor sheepishly as he backed away. "Sorry." He went jogging after Sammi.

When Nandi turned to Lennie, he bunched up his lips. "I wouldn't abandon you. Or the city."

The hole that had first formed when Beckett had died, then widened with the loss of her other friends, was now a gaping pit in her chest big enough to drop a city into. Nandi leaned against Lennie's massive shoulder and bit back her tears.

"Come on," she said, surging away from him. "We have to do something good. Anything."

Nandi jogged through the alleyway to reach the street that led to the location of the other mages. They were fleeing from a trio of giants as tall as a two-story building, flinging magic backwards to keep the demons from pursuing too closely. The giants stopped at the same street line as the other demons one block over.

Their organization concerned Nandi. She'd been expecting an unruly horde, but they were moving with intelligent purpose. She spotted a group of four-armed demons well behind the line, carrying a palisade the size of a van, the weight of it straining their muscular arms. She sensed it wasn't Elosian inside, but something else. A weapon perhaps? The idea that their enemy had prepared for this day concerned her. She'd always imagined that if it happened, it would be like fighting off unintelligent, but fearsome animals.

"Is this a good idea?" asked Lennie as they headed for the other mages.

"Probably not, but everything else I've done has been a complete failure. Besides, we're outnumbered."

The Silverthorne sisters saw them from a distance and marched towards them to close the gap, leaving Nandi with a knot in her stomach. Their reputations had been fearsome before, but after tangling with them at Camp Lucky, she knew them to be true. If they decided to seek revenge for the kidnapping, Nandi was sure there wasn't much they could do about it. The size of the other group had grown as well. Nandi spotted a few new faces, the polar opposite to her diminished side.

"If you're here to cause trouble, I can assure you that it won't last long," said Pi grimly.

Nandi held up her hands and hoped her expression was neutral enough.

"If you're somehow playing both sides now, it's a level of multidimensional chess that I can't understand anymore. Besides, there's only two of us now. If you'd like our help, we're offering. But if you don't, given everything that's happened, I understand."

"Where's the cobraffin?" asked the redheaded Pax with her enormous foxlike creature at her side. Her companion was staring with her head tilted.

"Sammi left," said Nandi. "Gregor too. It's just the two of us."

"I don't trust her. It could be a trick," said Pi.

Aurie squinted. "I think she's telling truth, and in these uncertain times, I think we should take their offer. Especially with what we're planning."

"Are you sure?" Pi asked her sister.

"No," said Aurie.

"I think they're fine," said Pax. "Or Kali does."

Pi frowned. "I'll accept them if you are." She checked back to the line of demons a block away. "But we'd better get moving to the Glitterdome."

Aurie nodded. "Let's go. I'll explain along the way. You were a demonologist in Coterie, right?"

Nandi jogged to catch up. "Double major in demonology and advanced spellcasting."

"Perfect," said Aurie with a sly grin. "You have just the expertise we need."

As Aurie and the others explained the plan on the way to the Glitterdome, Nandi began to realize that she'd been wrong about them. Wrong about herself, too. They weren't tools of Elosian as they'd originally thought, but trying to oppose him just as they were. She wished Sammi and Gregor had stayed, but at least the two of them could lend their skills and possibly help send Elosian back to his realm.

Eighteen

Aurie stood on the floor level of the Glitterdome, looking up at the endless empty seats, wondering if their plan was doomed to fail from the start. It would require so many things to go right: Elosian to take the bait, Moriganne not getting grabbed by him before they could get him into the circle, the area not to be overrun with demons, that the banishing could even work on a demon of his power, and so many other unknown factors that they'd never recognize until afterwards.

She watched as Nandi and her sister talked quietly while they made the warding circle on the bright green turf. It was strange to be on the same side after multiple deadly battles, but allegiances were easier to see after the invasion. Aurie knew a thing or two about questioning motives, as she'd caused a fair amount of unrest in the Halls during her time as a student.

At least the creation of the trap was going well. With so many mages flooding to the defense of the city, supplies were easy to find.

Moriganne was pacing around the back side of the circle, avoiding getting shocked by the wards, while Kitty was standing guard. The entire plan hinged on Elosian's desire for the sigil. Aurie still had trouble believing the Lost Prince was Invictus, but given everything they'd learned, there was no doubt left. The only question now was where he was and whose side he was on.

A soft scuff behind had Aurie turning to find Zayn. She had to resist the urge to throw herself in his arms, and he looked equally pained. With the outcome of their realm in the balance, Aurie saw through her own doubts to know that he still felt the same way about her as she did for him.

"Is this going to work?"

"That's not why you came over here," she said, catching him off guard.

"No," he said, chuckling as he shook his head.

"Can we not dance around each other for once? I don't want to die having not expressed my feelings about you."

Zayn squeezed his arm against his chest. "I didn't leave the Eternal City because I disagreed with Priyanka's mission. I left because when I saw you appear in the Rasakupol, I knew I couldn't let you out of my sight again. I've spent my whole life fighting for my family, my town, my friends. For once I wanted to fight for myself. For you."

His admission brought warmth to her face. "We get caught up in our responsibilities. Forget about ourselves, which isn't hard when things are so fraught. I thought I'd graduate from Arcanium and find a nice, stable job, not sign up with Invictus to be his errand girl, and now here we are, dancing at the edge of the abyss."

"No one ever expects it to go wrong until it does. We all believe that history is something that happens to other people." He looked at his shoes. "I guess that was the advantage of growing up in Varna. I had no illusions about the world, but after the Lady was dead, I thought I'd get a chance to find myself. Take a break." He chuckled. "Priyanka promised one, but everything was a lesson with her."

The space between them seemed like a gulf. Aurie closed her eyes because it was easier that way.

"Ever since my parents died, I expected that I would follow them. Not then, but soon. That it was my destiny. I know, sounds morbid, but the only thing I've ever wanted was to protect my sister. Keep her from harm."

"Shouldn't it be the other way around?" said Zayn, and she could hear the smirk in his voice, even with her eyes closed.

"True. But standing here before you, I know there's another destiny I'd like to encourage. One where you and I forget about our responsibilities and do some exploring of this world together. Maybe visit your sister in Paris. That sort of thing?"

She opened her eyes tentatively, fearing the look on his face, but the broad smile as he stepped near turned her entire body into tingles. Zayn cupped her cheek and gently leaned his forehead against hers.

"It's a deal. After this is over, when we kick Elosian's butt and send him back to the infernal realm, you and I are taking a trip together. A long one. No job. No magic. Just us."

Aurie pressed her lips against his as an answer. He had firm lips. A good kisser as she remembered. He placed his hand against the back of her neck, pressing her forward. The tension of their kiss left a delicious warm gooey spot in her midsection.

The desire to kiss him again, to drag him into a hidden corner of the arena and have her way with him was strong, but so was the need to live. She reached out and they briefly held hands before he lifted his shoulders.

"I have to talk to Kitty. If we can't keep Elosian's minions from overwhelming our defenses, then none of this is going to work," he said, nodding towards the circle.

After Zayn left and for the first time since the chaos around the invasion had begun, Aurie thought about life beyond it. When the present was such a shit-show it was hard to consider the future, but Zayn's kiss reminded her that there was a version of her life out there, one that had him in it. But it also brought the danger into focus. She'd been willing to throw herself into any amount of danger if it would stop Elosian from destroying their realm, but now with a taste of life she'd forgotten she wanted, part of her wanted someone else to be the one to sacrifice themselves.

As she looked back to Moriganne and Kitty speaking quietly, she remembered that it was the elder of the group that would be at most risk, rather than her. Moriganne would be the bait to draw Elosian to the Glitterdome. Her life would be forfeit if the demon lord managed to get his tentacles on her again.

Aurie checked back to the preparations on the concrete stairs leading to the floor of the dome. Minor warding runes had been painted along the sides, creating a funnel that would make their defense easier. Or that was the theory. But Aurie knew that would be the most difficult part. Elosian wasn't a cow being funneled through a cattle guard, but a living, breathing, and most importantly, thinking being with a high strategic mind.

An explosion outside brought everyone's heads up. The battle was nearing the Glitterdome. Aurie rubbed her sweaty hands on the front of her jeans.

"This better work."

She said the words to no one in particular as she looked across the floor of the Glitterdome. Even in the best of circumstances, it was doubtful they'd all survive, but if it went wrong, then it was the last time she was looking at this magnificent group of mages.

Nineteen

"Are you sure you want to be the bait again? You know how it turned out last time we tangled with him," said Kitty.

A lingering, low-level ache burned in her elbow. The flesh around the tattoo had bubbled from the searing heat while the bridge hissed and crackled with embers like a banked fire.

"I want it to be done. Over. Either he dies or I chop this fucking thing from my arm," said Moriganne.

"That bad?"

"It feels like my arm has been baked in hot sand."

Moriganne wiped the sweat from her forehead. She didn't know how much more of it she could withstand. The vessel of her body was ill-equipped to hold a living artifact of ancient infernal power.

"I can see why Invictus gave this up," she said, grimacing.

Kitty checked back to the preparations. "There's so much that can go wrong."

"If it protects the city from certain destruction, I'm willing to try," said Moriganne.

Kitty swallowed as her eyes rounded in uncharacteristic emotion. "I'm sorry for what my family put you through. You never asked for this. Any of it."

"Don't," said Moriganne. "I wouldn't trade what happened for anything. Well, maybe if I could snap my fingers and make Elosian go away, but that's the point. I lost my family when I was too young and too enamored with my career to understand how valuable it was until it was gone. I hated myself. I hated my ex-husband for how he thwarted me. I hated the world for being so cruel.

"It was only afterwards that I realized how precious my family was. Having to live through that again in Elosian's mind only reminded me how important you all are to me. I lost my family when I was young, but broken hells, I won't allow that to happen again. It wasn't how I imagined things would go, and you certainly scared the crap out of me until I got to know you better."

Kitty repressed a grin. Moriganne reached out and touched her arm.

"I got to spend two wonderful years in Thailand with you, teaching kids music and wasting away the days in a valley of paradise."

"It was rather nice," said Kitty, hanging her head. "No one there I had to kill or blackmail. Well, after the first month anyway, but I enjoyed the quiet."

They both laughed. Moriganne felt a grin break across her face, which helped soothe the ache in her arm.

"The reality is that I've had a full life," said Moriganne. "I got to briefly be a big star. I got to love a little girl who loved me back even if it wasn't for as long as I wanted. I got to sing. On stage. In front of people and feel their love and adoration back."

She hung her head and collected herself.

"While I want more than anything to continue living in this borrowed body, it's been a gift I never expected. But more so, the gift was the family attached to this body. If I can do anything today to give you and Ivan and Andy a chance at a long life then I would do it in a heartbeat. I don't know how you survived your father without becoming broken inside."

"Maybe I am," said Kitty.

"No," said Moriganne emphatically, reaching out and squeezing her arm for emphasis. "You are *not* a monster. Not now, not ever. Monsters don't have doubts. Monsters don't worry about other people. They take, they manipulate, they break. The fact that you even think of yourself that way tells me that you're not. Have you done some morally questionable things, possibly, but I think I would have killed Mikhail if I could have as well."

"I fear I'm like Vic." She exhaled. "You know I saw him? When we were at the portal. He came marching out, surrounded by other demons. I thought we'd banished him to a horrible fate, but maybe we just sent him to be with the beings he was most like."

The more her sister spoke, the more her heart broke. It'd been bad enough that Vic had raised them as he had, but to see him with the enemy had to be another stake to the chest.

"Family is who we choose to be with as much as our blood relations. More, really. I know we weren't born family, but I could never ask for a better sister."

Moriganne held open her arms and Kitty collapsed into them. Her quivering sigh was a flood of emotions as far as Moriganne was concerned.

When Kitty pulled away, she nodded. "I *have* saved your ass on a number of occasions."

"It looks like you're going to get to do it again," said Moriganne, checking to the almost-ready preparations behind them. "Unless I beat you to it."

At the top of the stairs, Alex appeared, looking out of breath.

"It's time! They're pushing towards the Glitterdome!"

The pace of preparations became more frantic, but there was nothing for Moriganne to do except wait. Kitty gestured towards the ramp as Zayn waved her on.

"I have to go." She took two steps then walked backwards. "For the record, in case we don't get to talk afterwards, I love my sisters, even the old you, but I can say without a doubt that you're my favorite." Kitty winked. "But, uhm, please don't tell Andromeda."

Moriganne watched Kitty jog up the steps, then she heard a foot scuff behind her. She turned to find Pi and Nandi staring at her.

"Are you ready?"

"No," said Moriganne. "But let's do it anyway."

Twenty

Pax was standing near the metal detectors at the eastern entrance to the Glitterdome when Kali sensed the presence of the cobraffin. She caught the sharp scent of coal smoke right after, but Pax wasn't sure if that was a memory from her fights with the potent pair.

The muscled Protector was on guard with her. They'd been watching the sorcerous blasts in the streets as the defenders fought against the mass of demons. She could tell by the way his muscles flexed that he wanted to rush into the street and join the fight, but Lennie understood his role. Word had been given to allow Elosian and his personal guard to approach the Glitterdome. The last report was they were about three blocks away.

"Something wrong?" asked Lennie. "I sensed you tensing up."

The observational ability of the Protector caught her off guard. She'd forgotten that the mages from his Hall were frequently in law enforcement or special forces, which required snap-second judgement of people that might be trying to kill them. And until about an hour before, they'd been on opposite sides. Pax hadn't completely relaxed around him, even as she believed the reasons for their previous interactions.

"Kali detected something unusual nearby. I think I should go check it out."

Pax didn't want to let him know that it was his friend that she'd sensed. Conflicting loyalties could make a mess of their plan.

Lennie nodded. "I got point. You check it out. We don't want any surprises."

The sensation had come from inside the Glitterdome on an upper level. Pax trotted towards the escalators, which weren't moving, and headed upward. She checked back at the next landing to confirm Lennie was still protecting the entrance. She'd never had any interactions with the Protectors but appreciated their competence and attention to duty.

"Where's she at?"

Kali moved to a forward position, her head turning as if she were using her psychic ability like a radar.

<Hiding mind>

"Hmmm..."

That would be a problem if they could keep from being found.

"Can they see us?"

<Hiding mind>

"Great," said Pax, "we're playing hide-and-seek in the dark."

A pang of missing Okho rose up in her chest, but she pushed it away to focus on the task. She went through the gate to the mid-level. The concrete structure jutted out over the lower seats. Everyone on the field looked tiny. Fragile. It reminded her of how precarious their plan was, requiring so many things to go right.

Pax craned her neck, examining the interior of the Glitterdome.

"Where would you be hiding? And why? What do you plan to do?"

The reason for Sammi's return wasn't apparent to Pax, except as a potential point of interference. She hadn't talked to Nandi much, except to hear her reasons for giving up their animosity, but little had been explained about the Animalians mage.

"I wish I could talk to her," said Pax as she scanned the enormous interior.

<Kali send message>

"Oh, dear heart, that's right. You can make her hear you? Of course you can. I should have thought of that. But what to say?"

After considering the options, Pax sent a message to Kali that would be passed on to Sammi.

I know you're in the Glitterdome, you're not that invisible, thought Pax.

She wasn't sure Sammi would respond, either to maintain her hidden location or out of spite, so when an answer came back, she was relieved and worried.

And you're on the wrong side, thought Sammi.

What side is that?

Even though Kali was relaying the message, Pax could hear the anger in Sammi's voice.

Demon lovers.

Nandi and Lennie joined us. You followed them before. Why do you think they came over except they understand we're trying to stop *Elosian?*

Pax kept scanning the seats and upper boxes, hoping that during their conversation she might catch a glimpse of Sammi and the cobraffin.

You're giving him what he wants. Offering her up on a platter. I can feel her power. If Elosian gets her, then the city is lost.

She's bait, countered Pax. *We're not offering her up. If we can send Elosian back then we have a chance to win.*

No answer came back, which made Pax suspicious.

A sheet of glass broke somewhere, making her jump. Probably errant sorcery, hitting the outer windows. The concussive thuds of distant explosions reminded her of the war zone as she scanned the interior of the dome.

"Where are you?"

A whine slipped from Kali. She felt the mental pressure of Elosian's approach and wanted to shout across the arena but found herself knocked to her knees by the psychic force of his presence.

"No. It's all wrong. We have to abort."

Twenty-One

Zayn found Lennie and Kitty by the eastern entrance. The big Protector was staring into the street where dark smoke from a nearby fire had reduced visibility. It smelled like a garbage fire by the pungent odor.

"Where's Pax?"

Lennie nodded towards the nearby escalators. "Went to check something out. Someone was creeping around." He raised an eyebrow. "Her companion can sense things, right?"

"Better than we can."

Zayn stared into the smoke. He needed to be thinking about the battle plan, but he was only imagining himself kissing Aurie.

"Times like this I wish I'd never had a speck of magic in my bones," he said.

"Better to die surrounded by family," said Kitty.

She twirled the curved blade in her fist as she stared into the smokey street with the intensity of a predator. Even Lennie sensed the anger radiating from her and took a small step away.

"Let's not die at all if we can help it," said Zayn.

Lennie cleared his throat in the most obvious manner and then looked embarrassed.

"Speaking of, uhm, yeah, I'm sorry for trying to kill you and your friends at Camp Lucky. These last few weeks have been a whirlwind of confusion. I was so sure that we were right. Everything we learned pointed to you as the ones behind all this, but we were so wrong. I got my friends, Lil and Dank, killed from our pigheadedness...and Kitty, I might have knocked the crap out of your younger sister at that house in the twelfth."

Kitty pointed her knife at him as she squinted. "What?"

"We knew they were doing something there," he said, pumping his eyebrows. "But don't worry. They got the best of us. Your twin drugged me and then Moriganne blasted us out of the house with her voice."

Zayn tensed up, expecting Kitty to release her rage on him, but a snort slipped out. She turned, incredulousness on her face.

"You let Ivan drug you? Oh, Merlin, that is rich. How'd that go?"

Lennie was gobsmacked at the reversal of Kitty's mood. "I thought I was a lotus flower until Nandi gave me an antidote. I'm still a little fuzzy at the edges. At one point during the fight we had with some demons I started to worry that I was still in the drug land."

"Checks out," said Kitty with a smirk.

"And you're not mad about me beating up Andromeda?"

Kitty raised an eyebrow in his direction. "A little. You and I might have words after all this is over, but on the other hand, you know that's what she does night after night in the Mystique, right? I think she likes the pain. Reminds her of family."

"Was your father really that bad?" asked Lennie.

Kitty stared into the street, her expression hardening until she looked ready to spit.

"In his case, the rumors were true."

Lennie started to ask another question, but Zayn put his hand on the big man's arm, shaking him off. The previous silence resumed its shroud.

As Zayn waited for the approaching battle, he finally understood the reason that Elosian had showed him the future he'd always wanted with Aurie. Before then, he'd been wholly focused on the fight, doing what had to be done in service of the mission, but now he worried that he'd be compromised by his desire to keep Aurie safe. He understood more than ever why Priyanka kept no romantic ties. It was too dangerous to love. Yet, he was young enough not to care.

"What's the point if you can't love," he muttered to himself.

Lennie turned his head to say something, but then Kitty's twirling blade stopped, point facing forward, ready to lunge.

"They're here."

Tall shapes moved through the smoke. Zayn thought he was seeing double, then triple, or more, of the demon lord. Then he realized they were made like him, but not him. Personal guards.

"Fall back," he said. "Stay near, but out of sight."

Zayn jogged back towards the interior, found a structural pole he'd spotted before, and shimmied up, placing himself on the landing directly above where Elosian was supposed to come in. He gave the signal to the group on the floor of the arena, where the Silverthorne sisters, Nandi, Alex, and Moriganne waited. Aurie waved back. He waved. Then waited.

The battle noises outside no longer sounded near. He heard only the beating of his heart and the approaching sound of hooves.

Twenty-Two

"The key to the banishing spell is that we both have to put everything we have into it at the same time so that we're keeping exactly the same tempo," said Nandi to the younger Silverthorne.

Having battled the sisters on multiple occasions and read about them for years, Nandi thought she understood them, but each was more different than expected. Aurie seemed more unsure of herself than the caricature of the righteous truth-seeker that the papers had made her out to be in the aftermath of Invictus' rescue, while Pi was more crass, punkish—and brilliant.

"Got it," said Pi, nodding.

Under normal circumstances she might not have believed her, but during preparations, Pi had repeated back verbatim—pacing included—every part of the banishing spell without error.

"Why did you leave Coterie? I've never met anyone that more embodies the limitless ideal," said Nandi.

Pi chuckled and ran a hand through her spikey hair. "Sometimes family is more important than power. Besides, it's probably a good thing I didn't stay in Coterie. Limits are necessary for a healthy life."

"You were only there for a year, right?" asked Nandi, even though she knew the answer.

"A crazy whirlwind of a year, but yeah," said Pi.

"I would swear that you'd studied demonology for decades," said Nandi. "You speak it better than the fifth years."

Pi raised an eyebrow. "When all this is over, and we survive, I have a story that you might find interesting on how I got into Coterie."

"I would like to hear that." Nandi jutted her chin towards Moriganne, who was pacing behind a stationary Aurie. "Is she going to be okay?"

"Probably not. You know what happened the last time Elosian made it into our realm?"

Nandi nodded. Aurie had told her on the way to the Glitterdome. A lot of what happened helped make sense of the rumors they'd been hearing for years.

"She told me."

"Mori knows more than anyone else here about what's at stake. If Elosian gets a hold of her, he's going to tear her asunder. She's been trying to hide the tattoo, but it looks like it's turning her arm to char. I don't know how she's not in constant tears."

"Why is it doing that now?"

Pi shrugged. "No one knows, but my theory is that the tattoo is a conduit of power and with the portal to the infernal realm open, there's too much energy flowing through the circuit. It's being overloaded, and her young body can't handle it."

"I wish Invictus was here to help," said Nandi.

"I'm not so sure about that."

When she looked over, Pi shook her head. "Never mind. We don't have enough time."

Nandi sensed Zayn entering the arena before she saw him. He gave a wave from the concourse above the entrance where they hoped to funnel Elosian into the banishing circle.

"Seems simple enough," said Pi. "Lure ol' tentacle breath into the arena with the tattoo, force him into the circle by hook or crook, and after closing the damn thing, send his ass back to the infernal realm."

"And if he comes back through the portal?" asked Nandi.

"Hopefully we've cleaned up his army by then, but let's not get ahead of ourselves. Step one of this plan is going to be a doozy."

Nandi thought she was seeing double when the creatures stepped to the edge of the stairs leading into the arena. She'd never seen Elosian before, but they'd described him during their stories. Pi's in-breath told her that something was wrong. The tentacle arms and backward-facing knees made her stomach curl. Then four more versions of Elosian appeared and Nandi grew worried that he'd anticipated their trap and prepared a counter, but then the seventh stepped into view. The real Elosian. It wasn't hard to tell in comparison to the others. He stood taller and had the air of royalty. She felt his power from a distance. The others were shoddy copies.

The idea that she was staring at a lord of the infernal realm was not lost on Nandi. He had more power in the tip of his tentacle than the group of them combined, but they'd set the location for the battle and hopefully had prepared their trap well.

Elosian extended his tentacles as if he were the ringleader at a circus. "How can I thank you for preparing this lovely meal for me? This place is unexpectedly grandiose. Here, I thought that this realm would be boring, but you've outdone yourselves. Still, this world lacks a certain unpredictableness. I promise you that this world will be unrecognizable when I'm done molding it."

His honey over gravel voice wormed into her head. She found his ideas delightful, his tone soothing. She wanted to throw herself at his feet, but Pi had warned her that this would happen, which helped her shake off the compulsion.

Elosian raised a tentacle and though he had no fingers to snap, a loud noise as if he had echoed through the area.

"Fetch!"

The Lord of Lies stepped to the side as a stream of the ochre-skinned demons came screaming down the stairs. Aurie and the others had expected this development. Elosian would test them before making his grab for the tattoo.

"Ready?" asked Nandi as she stepped to the front of the circle with Pi.

It wasn't the banishing spell, but something Nandi had found in her research as a fifth-year. The words and phrases felt like music in her head. She'd always imagined that being a mage was like being a conductor in front of an orchestra. The movements and motions gave instructions to the hundred or so musicians waiting to play their part, creating a work of art from unrecognizable chaos.

As the feroms came bounding down the stairs, the forward edge reaching the bottom, her spell completed. She thought of it like a lasso. A ghostly energy extended from her outstretched hand, whipping around the demons and bunching them up at the transition from the stairs to the field. The spell bound them together, a restraint that would only last for a few seconds, but it was long enough for Pi to do her thing.

Nandi completed her spell with enough time to watch Pi finish hers. She brought forth her magic in distinct strikes like a punk band guitarist angrily attacking the strings. The miniature sun that formed between her hands had Nandi stepping back. Pi had explained the spell beforehand, but witnessing the intensity of it was shocking.

A ball of magma crisped through the air, heat waves radiating from it, slamming into the knot of feroms. They went up like a wildfire. The bonds broke but the demons perished before they took three steps. When they were finished, the turf near the stairs was covered in hunks of char.

"Hopefully that was dramatic enough," said Pi with a smirk.

"I think we have his attention."

Elosian seemed unaffected by the brief battle, but Nandi told herself that he was seething inside. She had to believe that what they were doing would matter, that it wasn't a foolish last stand.

"What is he doing?" asked Aurie from behind them next to Moriganne.

Elosian had stepped aside, leaving a path through the look-a-likes. Someone was approaching from the entrance. Moriganne let out a gasp before Nandi recognized him.

Twenty-Three

Ivan pulled up near the corner, grabbing his calf and trying not to fall down.

"Cramp, cramp."

The muscle was trying to seize up. His sister and girlfriend slowed to a stop.

"Ivan, we're two blocks from the Glitterdome, we have to hurry," said Andromeda.

"I guess I should have stretched before the apocalypse."

"What's going on?" asked his younger sister. "Is this another attempt at getting out of danger?"

"No," he said, grimacing as he stretched his calf by leaning against the brick wall. "I think it's a side effect of those elixirs we had earlier. Either that, or I'm woefully under hydrated. My pee back there came out as yellow dust."

Andromeda crossed her arms as Audrey pulled out a water bottle.

"Drink this. All of it."

"Yes, mommy."

Andromeda punched him in the arm.

"Owww...what was that for?"

He chugged the water, ignoring how it spilled around his mouth and onto his shirt.

"We'd better get moving," said Audrey, looking towards the Glitterdome. "It looks like the defensive lines aren't holding. They're getting pushed back."

"How do we even know they're in there?" said Ivan as he handed back a mostly empty water bottle.

"Kitty said to meet her inside the Glitterdome," said Andromeda.

"Yes, but they could have been overrun already," said Ivan. "We should head back to Ares' place."

Audrey grabbed his arm and started dragging him across the street. "Come on."

"Slowly, slowly," he said, hopping on one leg. "It's ready to seize up."

"If you'd like your neck to seize up mysteriously, then keep hobbling. I still have broken ribs from that thick-necked Protector, I think you can survive a muscle cramp," said Andromeda.

The western doors of the Glitterdome were locked. Before Ivan could even suggest that it meant they weren't supposed to be there, Audrey sang out a series of notes and the glass shattered.

"That was far too easy," grumbled Ivan.

When he stepped over the broken glass into the interior, he found the constriction around his chest that had been making breathing difficult while they ran even worse. He'd hoped getting out from under the sky where demons were winging about would have helped, but he only felt like he was climbing into the cage of a hungry lion.

"Anyone else getting the feeling that we're all going to die here?" asked Ivan.

"It's a possibility," said Andromeda.

"You'd make a terrible doctor," said Ivan. "No bedside manner."

"Do you smell that?" asked Audrey, wrinkling her nose.

Ivan sniffed. The sharp metallic scent was unmistakable.

"They're here," said Andromeda. "Those fucking assholes. I'm getting sick of them."

Ivan happened to look up, seeing the silvery head of the cobraffin disappear from the level above them.

"There!"

The nearest stairs were in the opposite direction along the curve of the dome. Andromeda appeared to want to go after the Animalians mage and her pet, but Ivan grabbed her arm.

"No way. That thing would turn you into Bonnie Flambeau." Andromeda growled at him. "We're here to pass along what we learned. Not get in a battle we can't win. We'll tell them about it. Is that enough?"

"Fine."

A host of screams echoed from the interior of the dome. Ivan ran forward, forgetting until the last moment that there were dangerous creatures about. He pulled up at the railing as the smoke rose from the charred bodies of what he assumed had been demons.

"It's him. He's really here," said Andromeda, devastation in her eyes.

Ivan assessed the situation at the center of the arena floor. "What the hell? That crazy girl who tried to kill us is down there with them?"

Andromeda grabbed his arm, fingernails digging into his skin.

"Owww...what the hell? I don't heal like you do, Andy," he said, flinching away.

"Ivan."

The cold fear in her voice left him hesitant to look. He knew what she'd seen even before he turned his head. There was only one person that could elicit that much dread and surprise, and it wasn't the Lord of Lies.

Victor Charmer.

Their father strode to the edge of the bowl at Elosian's side. He looked fit and healthy, not the frail old man of his final days.

"Would be just like him to side with Elosian," said Andromeda.

"Why can't he just stay gone? Why did he have to come back? As if it wasn't bad enough growing up under his thumb, now he's a fucking demon? No wonder people think our family is cursed," said Ivan.

"We're not cursed, we're damned. There's a difference," said Andromeda.

"If I snuck over there, I could throw my water bottle at him," said Ivan.

"It's my water bottle, babe."

"Fine. I'll throw your water bottle at him. Maybe he'll melt like a witch." He sighed. "Can I have my drugs back?"

"You force-fed them to that Protector meathead."

"What a waste." Ivan stared across the arena wishing he was anywhere else in the world. "This is just like the end of a horror movie when the killer comes back after you think he's dead."

"Babe," said Audrey as she rubbed his back, "you would have died in the first ten minutes of that movie."

Twenty-Four

The images of her father sitting at the head of the table admonishing his board members as she chased them around, firing flame shots whenever they got too close, felt more tangible than when she'd actually been in the dream.

Victor Charmer.

Her actual father stood at the top of the stairs next to Elosian. It took all her self-control not to slip from her hiding spot near the entrance and throw herself at him. *You made me a monster.* The words repeated in her head until she could only hear *monster monster monster.*

This is who I am. This is who I came from. A man who would sell himself to the Lord of Lies.

But she knew if she attacked, it would ruin the trap. Their plan was precarious enough. Kitty regripped the dagger in her fist. She held the tip up and pressed her opposite palm against it, splitting the flesh. A bead of blood formed and she pulled the weapon away, wiping the wetness on her pants.

Darkness rose up around her. A haze crept into her vision and she couldn't breathe. It wasn't until she was trying to find the source that she realized she was having an anxiety attack. She thought they only happened to Ivan. Not her. Kitty leaned against the cold, concrete wall.

"Three steps behind," said Elosian as he wrapped a tentacle around Vic's shoulders. "You're embers rising from a fire. Bright, hot, but ultimately fleeting. How could such infants think they might outthink me? It's a wonder. I'm insulted that you would think I would wander into your trap. Like a spider thinking they could catch an elephant in their web."

Elosian strolled to the edge of the stairs with Victor at his side.

"I know all you Charmer children are in the building. Those still alive. I brought you a gift. Your loving and devoted father. He has been most helpful in my preparations. There are many things about your city that I failed to understand from my realm, but with his help, I was able to see the flaws in my plan."

An explosion from somewhere near the Glitterdome had everyone looking up except Elosian and Victor.

"It won't take long to subdue the city. Once I've eliminated the pests, it will be easy to get the rest on my side. Better to join the victors than follow fools to the grave." Elosian tilted his head. "At first, I thought the barrier an annoyance, but now I see that it's helping my cause. I can take control of the city without outside interference and reveal myself when its time.

"But first I need to reclaim what should have been mine ages ago. Victor, would you kindly retrieve your daughter? She has something that I greatly desire."

As her father slipped from Elosian's tentacles and marched down the long set of concrete stairs, Kitty leaned against the concrete wall and reminded herself to breathe. She wouldn't be any good to anyone if she passed out in the entrance.

The replicas of Elosian followed Victor down the stairs. The solemn procession reminded Kitty of a line of priests heading to an altar. Her father had never been a religious man, except when it suited his needs.

The Silverthorne sisters and the newcomer Nandi sent wild sorcery towards Victor. The prismatic wave warped seats and cracked concrete as it roiled upward. As the annihilating energies whipped towards him, Kitty flinched away from the expected destruction, but at the last second he shoved both hands forward, blasting away the attack.

That attack would have killed anyone but the most hardened patrons. The stunned looks from the others on the arena floor were apparent even from this distance.

"No."

The words left Kitty's lips as she regripped her blades into an overhand grip. She leapt onto the backs of the seats, bounding over them as she traveled diagonally towards Victor. Fell energies were thrown her direction by the Elosian clones, but she shifted into the Veil to avoid the counterattack, then coming back out of the deathly realm, threw up illusionary copies of herself to confuse them. She made it three-fourths of the way to her father. He turned her direction, staring ambivalently, making no move to defend himself.

A thrown blade, followed by bolts of force, then a final leap to confuse his defenders, brought her arcing down, ready to bury the blade in his chest. He met her gaze, the barest hint of recognition creasing his eyes, before he swiped his hand downward like a sword cut.

The air stiffened into a wall. She slammed into it, rebounding down the hard plastic chairs, hitting every fourth one until she tumbled onto the turf, barely conscious, her body an ocean of pain. Kitty tried to climb to her feet. The curved blade was still in her hand. But the injuries from her fall cut the strings from her effort, and she collapsed.

Twenty-Five

The world stunk of sweetness and fire. Sammi leaned against the empty beer kiosk, closing her eyes and reeling from a migraine. Kozsen nudged her arm with his hooded head. Black eyes regarded her. A forked tongue slipped out, wavering in the air before disappearing back into the cobra mouth.

A sensation of danger emanated from Kozsen followed by images of an older man she'd seen before on the television and in her nightmares. Victor Charmer. He was here along with his children. Sammi knew what the others did not, that the Charmers prepared to betray everyone and hand over the city to the demon lord. A plan long in the making.

Sammi sensed the approach of others through her link with Kozsen. The redhead and her callidus. Sammi knew what kind of cursed creature Pax traveled with even if the others did not. The strings that Elosian pulled confused and confounded the others, making them dance to his singular purpose. They'd even ensnared Lennie and Nandi. If Beckett was still alive, he would have seen through it. Their chances of stopping Elosian had died with him. She ran around the concourse, past the food and beer kiosks and the murals of past musicians that had graced the Glitterdome. A painting of the Garbage Kings surrounded by their illusionary stage show of high sorcery was displayed on the long curve. The return of the migraine made her stop, lean against the wall, and collect herself, even as Kozsen nudged her arm to continue.

"I'll move in a second. I need a breather."

Sammie massaged her temples, trying to make the pain go away. The sweetness in her nose was so strong she wanted to vomit.

As she leaned against the wall, she pulled out a picture from her inside pocket showing a younger version of herself with her cousin, Lisa. They'd been best friends even though they were separated by five years. Until they'd found Lisa's body in the Undercity. A gruesome ritual murder than had gone unsolved, but Sammi knew the truth. The Charmer family had been behind it. She was fairly certain that the oldest boy Ares had been the one to do the deed, but the others had been a part of the cover-up, that much she was sure. A family of demon lovers who had fooled so many. But not her. She'd never been able to find enough evidence to bring to the authorities, nor did she think they would have arrested him. The Charmers had friends in high places. The only path to justice was the lonely one she had to take herself.

Go to the lower level behind them. A perfect place for an ambush.

"Yes, yes," said Sammi, deliriously.

Kozsen had only recently started speaking to her. Her chimeric companion was more clever than the dead eyes of the cobra suggested. They could hit the Silverthorne sisters with a breath weapon while they were distracted by Victor and the demon lord. It would feel good to use the head of the Charmer family against his allies.

A set of concrete stairs wound down towards the lower level. Koszen's claws clacked against the stone and her companion barely fit through the single door without squeezing.

Sammi could hear the melodic voice of Elosian echoing across the arena as she found her way to a tunnel that led onto the field. The four mages stood with their backs to her. Sammi hated that she might have to kill her friend Nandi, but if it was required to save the world, then she would do it. Justice for Lisa. Justice for the others sacrificed by the Charmer family in their quest for ultimate power. Sammi crouched in the shadows and watched as the head of the family, Victor, marched down the stairs with the Elosian clones behind him.

Wait for the right moment.

The burst of multicolored sorcery from the Silverthorne sisters and Nandi rose up only to be swatted away by Victor. The power he'd gained in his deal with the demon lord was made visible by the ease of his defense.

If she could kill Moriganne then maybe they stood a chance to stop Elosian. She bore the infernal mark. Even from across the arena, Sammi could feel his desire to claim it.

Sammi was about to surge into the arena for an ambush when Kitty suddenly appeared, careening across the seats like a skipping stone, dancing in and out of sight. Somehow Kitty evaded the sorcery sent her way by the Elosian clones and appeared high in the air, arcing down for a killing blow against her father.

Before she could land it, he knocked her away, sending her bouncing off the seats until she collapsed on the turf near the lumps of charred corpses. Kitty lay unmoving.

The attack shoved a spear of confusion into Sammi's mind. She'd been about to trot onto the field for an ambush. Sammi watched as Moriganne rushed to the fallen Charmer's side.

It's a trick to lure the others into range. Kill them now before it's too late.

Sammi shook off her doubts, and as the entire arena was focused on the approach of Victor Charmer, she headed onto the field with Kozsen at her side.

Twenty-Six

When Ivan saw his twin bouncing down the hard plastic seats like a rag doll, a switch flipped in his mind. He was running down the concrete stairs before anyone could stop him. Ivan leapt over the railing, landing hard, and ignored the pain as he made his way over to Kitty's fallen body right after Moriganne reached her.

"Please be alive, please be alive," he said, sliding to his knees.

Kitty was moaning and only partially conscious. Had she not been a mage of her hall, his twin would surely be dead. Only the sorcerous preparations had saved her.

"I don't know what to do for her," said Moriganne.

Andromeda appeared moments later and threw her healing energies into Kitty. The infusion seemed to have little effect.

"I'm not a healer," said Andromeda, shaking her head. "We need to get her away, but I'm afraid to move her."

Kitty's eyes were in the back of her head and blood was leaking from her mouth. The bleeding was internal.

"Ivan."

Audrey spoke from somewhere behind him, but he could hardly hear as the blood surged in his ears. He felt dizzy as he rose to his feet.

Vic was coming down the stairs. Never mind that he'd easily dispatched his twin when she made her cunning attack. Ivan positioned himself at the bottom of the stairs knowing it would probably cost him his life.

"You wrinkled old ball sac. I should have known you'd trade your family for a collar. Anything for power, even if it means betraying your own. Not that it surprises me. We were never your children, only tools in your fight for dominance."

Victor had been steadily marching down the stairs, but as Ivan spoke he slowed to a stop. No hint of expression or acknowledgement appeared on his face. The only signal that he'd heard was that he'd stopped at all.

"I was your son. Your good and dutiful son, who loved and adored you. That's what children do. We love our parents. Worship them. Which made it easy for you to manipulate us. Look what you did to us! Solstice paid the ultimate price for standing up to you, Ares hated himself every second that he didn't please you, I drowned myself in drugs and parties, and Kitty tried to make herself in your image, even as it tore at her soul. Only Moriganne was on your side, until she had doubts, and then you destroyed her for petty reasons."

Vic said nothing. He stared down at Ivan with the same mien of disappointment that had been his hallmark. While his words could cut, it was his looks that hurt Ivan the most. They could reduce him to a pit of insecurity that could only be filled with a bottle or a pill.

"You never loved us. Never cared for us. You had us as ornaments. Tools. Pretty little things to hold up to the world to prove you were human. But you weren't. Ever. I wish I could have seen that when you were alive. It took your death to make me start to see the real you, but like the annoying bastard that you are, you had to come back. Rub your traitorous deal in our faces. You faithless fascist fuck."

Vic resumed his procession down the stairs as he gathered fell energies to his cause. Sparks and heat formed around his father, and after seeing what happened to his twin, Ivan was certain that he was about to meet a fiery end.

Twenty-Seven

The cobraffin slipped out of Kali's sensing range. Pax ran along the outer curve of the Glitterdome's upper level, urgency driving her pace, glancing through the tunnels into the empty air of the arena in hopes of spotting their foes.

<Hiding>

"Yes, dear one, I know, but we need to find them quickly before it's too late."

The slapping of her soles and the clack of claws echoed in the empty hallway, a place normally filled with laughing families at the Glitterdome for a concert or arcane spectacle. She'd never been in the place before, which made navigating it difficult. Frustrated, Pax ran to the interior in time to see Kitty tumble to the turf.

"No—"

There was no sign of Sammi or her companion. If they were lurking in the Glitterdome, they were here to cause trouble, either at Elosian's behest or of their own accord.

"Where are you?"

There were only a few dozen souls in the interior of the arena but they were all focused on the man coming down the stairs. Or at least he looked like a man. Given the entourage of Elosian look-a-likes, he was probably a demon in disguise.

"Stop thinking like a person and think like a predator."

As soon as she said it, she realized where Sammi had gotten to. The best time for an ambush was when everyone was focused on something else.

Pax scrambled into the main level, looking for a way down to the lower floor. She ran with Kali at her side, scanning the walls for exit signs. When she saw one past the mural of the Garbage Kings, she threw herself through the door, leaping whole flights of stairs as Kali bounded behind her. She threw her shoulder through the door, skidding onto the main level.

<Sammi ahead>

It took two false starts to find where Kali had sensed Sammi. They entered the long tunnel right as Sammi and her companion trotted onto the field.

Warn the others!

Pax sensed Kali's broadcast a second later. She ran headlong, fearing what she might find when she reached the field.

A shimmering blue shield deflected a column of superheated black smoke erupting from the head of the cobraffin. The shield was buttressed by the efforts of the Silverthorne sisters and Sammi's former friend, Nandi. Sammi hadn't seen them approach from behind. A slam mark would end the breath weapon, but wouldn't knock either of them out. Pax had seen how the cobraffin was hardened against sorcery at Camp Lucky. Nor did she want to hurt Sammi or the creature, unless it was her last resort.

"Sammi, stop! You've got it all wrong!"

As the cobraffin stopped its fiery breath, the Silverthornes dropped their shield. Before they could counterattack, Pax yelled, "Don't hurt them!"

Across the field, she saw Pi's gaze harden with resolve. As Sammi halfway turned, unsure of which direction was the greater danger, Pax ran forward with her hands up to signal her non-aggression, hoping that her nearness would keep Pi from annihilating the mistaken Animalians mage.

Twenty-Eight

Pain was a feeling Moriganne had grown used to in her long life. First, the loss of her family in the fateful crash, and then her career as she became a pariah. It was an ache that never went away. The phantom pain of a missing limb, except it was the part of her life that was no longer there. No Isabella. No family.

Then after a long and difficult life came the bright and terrible pain of her soul being ripped away. A brutal fight that had ended with her in control of her current body, followed by the confusion of existing in a world she knew nothing about. But that pain, her rebirth, had given her something that had been squandered so early in her life.

Family.

Though twisted by the machinations of their father, a man who knew nothing of the word, her new siblings had managed to hold onto the barest scraps of their humanity and come through the furnace of his betrayal in spectacular fashion. She'd thought him gone forever, banished to the infernal realm, where she'd assumed he would have instantly perished.

Now he was back.

Pain. The pain in her elbow where the flesh around the tattoo had bubbled was nothing compared to the pain of seeing him again. Of seeing the effect on her siblings, how he tortured them just by existing.

Since the portal had been opened, her arm had been on fire. She could feel the power coursing through it, awakened by the direct line to the demonic realm. Faez in all its golden glory was overloading the circuits in her arm. She wasn't meant to hold this kind of power. Her body was too new, too fleshy to withstand the energies contained within the bridge tattoo. It was like trying to carry a hunk of plutonium out of a mine with her bare hands.

The stink of her own burning flesh filled her nostrils as she helped pull Kitty away from the bottom of the stairs. Ivan was distracting his father, telling him all the things he'd clearly wanted to say before.

Behind them, a secondary battle had erupted with Sammi and the cobraffin, but Moriganne positioned herself to protect her siblings as Victor strode down the concrete steps, sorcery whipping around his demonic-infused body like a cloud of enraged ghosts.

Moriganne tugged on Ivan's sleeve. "Back away. Help Andy carry Kitty near the circle."

Ivan was conflicted between his rage and the state of his twin, but his love for Kitty won out and he moved to help Andromeda move her sister away.

The pressure in the air was increasing. Moriganne realized that the Elosian clones were bolstering Victor's power. She summoned her winds, preparing to drive him back and keep him from her siblings, but he extended his arm and a tentacle of black energy whipped out, wrapping around her neck before she could sing her magic. She beat at the black appendage, but it held her fast and she wasn't strong enough to dislodge it.

"You stole my daughter from me," said Victor, glowering.

Moriganne choked as he continued his approach. Her left arm was on fire. Between the constriction around her throat and the agony of the tattoo, she was sure that her end was near. The others were locked in a battle with the cobraffin, and her siblings were tending to Kitty—not that they had the power to oppose him—leaving her to his mercy. Or lack thereof.

"Had you not taken control of her body, none of this would have happened. You caused this. The invasion. The destruction of our realm, all because of you."

He kept coming closer, the dark energy holding her fast. Moriganne beat at the appendage as stars formed in her vision. She could see how living in the infernal realm had changed him beyond the obvious return of health. The last two fingers on his right hand had grown claws, his left eye was half blue and half orange, and his mouth wasn't quite centered in his face.

"I'm a survivor," he said when he was close enough she could smell the sweetness on his breath. "I did what I had to do. But now it's time for you to disappear, and I'll take control of my family back from you."

A scream of rage from behind was followed by Ivan running at his father with fists raised, but Victor's backhand sent him spinning away. Andromeda tried a force bolt, which deflected off her father as if it were a splash of water. He sent a dark bolt at her that knocked her onto her back. She lay still except for a painful heaving. Kitty rolled onto her hands and knees and tried to climb to her feet, but her legs were as shaky as a foal.

"Stay down, Kitty. I don't want to kill you. He promised me control of the city when we're done conquering this realm. I will elevate you to the place that should have gone to Mori, but this will be better. She didn't have the backbone you have."

"I'll never follow you," said Kitty, spitting blood onto the turf.

"There's no room for dissent," said Victor, his face twisted in anger. "You're either with me or you won't be allowed to live."

While he was distracted, Moriganne managed to get her hand beneath the appendage, which allowed her to breathe again. Her throat hurt too much for song, but maybe if she could get free, there was a chance.

"You'll have to kill me," said Kitty from her hands and knees.

"So be it."

Victor sent a second tentacle of dark energy after Kitty, then a third and a fourth, until the four of them had been captured. He pulled Moriganne close.

"Stop resisting and I won't make it painful." Victor tilted his head towards Moriganne. "You're dead either way. I see the way it burns. You weren't meant to hold it. An imperfect vessel for an artifact of the gods."

Moriganne struggled against the appendage. Her hand could no longer hold back the constriction and she was losing oxygen again. While they'd been captured, the Elosian clones had fanned out, protecting Victor while he interrogated them. Moriganne was vaguely aware that a battle was happening around them, but there was nothing they could do against the might of so many bolstered by Elosian, who waited at the top of the stairs.

Her siblings were faring worse. Victor had wrapped the energy tentacles around their midsections, squeezing their ribs, which for Kitty and Andromeda were already injured. Blood was leaking from Kitty's lips as she pounded at the appendage while Victor watched dispassionately.

"Stop fighting. I promise it can only get worse," said Victor.

With her voice she could summon the tempest winds and might be able to free them, but her larynx was nearly crushed. The tattoo burned in her elbow. She felt the energy contained within as if it'd been connected to a high voltage power line. If she tried to tap into the tattoo that way, she knew it would rip her body apart. Using her voice was the safest way to channel the energy, but that option had been taken from her.

Moriganne watched as her siblings screamed in agony. The cruelty of their father knew no bounds.

She looked up to see Elosian approaching. He'd decided it was time to claim the bridge. The rest of the arena was locked in combat, leaving no one to resist him. He had anticipated them once again, but this time it seemed there was no way out.

Moriganne glanced to her arm. The bridge glowed with intensity, while the flesh above and below was charred black. She saw only one option on how to get out of this awful situation. If the portal was closed, she might survive the tattoo, but until then she was sitting on a live volcano.

The world dialed into focus, even as it ran mad with chaos. Sorcery was flung in every direction, turning whole sections of hard plastic seats to ash. Sparks fell from the ceiling where missed energies impacted with the electrical systems. Somewhere nearby someone was screaming, but she could no longer hear them. Moriganne could barely see the world around her.

As the spots in her vision connected, Moriganne saw her Isabella standing in front of her with the tiara on her forehead. She wore a pink dress with flowers, and her curled hair fell against her shoulders.

"Izzy," she said to her daughter, even though she wasn't sure she was speaking out loud. "Mommy never got to see you grow up. I never got to see you become the amazing young woman you were destined to be. You were everything to me. I'm so sorry that I let that happen, that I let our family be destroyed. I would do anything to do it differently. Anything. But I can't.

"At the end of my long life, one that I spent every day thinking about you—Every. Single. Day—I was blessed with a new family. One so much different than the one we had, but still, it's a family. A family that I have a chance to save. I can't do anything to take back my mistakes from before, but I have a chance to stop this one before I lose my family again."

Moriganne knew what would happen when she reached for the power contained in the bridge tattoo. There was only one chance remaining. An ache deep inside wished she would get to see them grow and change, escape the chains that Victor had put on them even as they took their first wobbling steps as toddlers. But for that to happen, they had to live and he had to die. It was only right that she should be the one to do it. Not only to save them, but to protect them from the act that would break them if they were the ones to do it.

The first taste of power brought sharp pain as her mind was forced to withstand the onslaught of faez. It was like stepping into a rushing river that was freezing cold. She would have screamed but the tentacle had her throat.

Slowly, she channeled more faez into her body. She wasn't sure what she was going to do with it, but getting used to the flood of power made it hard to think. Every neuron in her brain was lit up like a fireworks display, every cell in her body was bursting with energy.

Moriganne accepted the power. She pushed the tentacle away from her throat even as Victor tried to squeeze harder. The entire left side of her body was burning like a miniature sun. When she grabbed the dark appendage, it evaporated into shadows, leaving her free.

But the cascade couldn't be stopped. She'd lit the fuse. The only thing to do was to accomplish her task before it burned her to the ground.

Seven separate spears of white-hot light disintegrated the Elosian clones, turning them to piles of gray ash that quickly blew away in the swirling winds. Then Moriganne turned her attention on Victor, grabbing him around the throat with an arm of pure energy. She could feel her body as a conduit from the open portal. If she wanted to knock down the Spire she thought she could do it.

Victor screamed as she fried him with the pure energy. His body went from flesh straight to ash as if he were being deleted one cell at a time. When he was gone, she couldn't hold back the flood anymore, but didn't want to hurt her friends, her family.

She raised her arm to throw a beam of energy at Elosian, but he'd fled the moment she'd grabbed Victor.

With nowhere else to go with the overwhelming levels of faez that her body could no longer handle, she did the only thing she could in that situation. Moriganne turned the magic on herself. As the white light, the energy of a billion molecules, consumed her body, she felt a smile lift to her lips—relief and the hopes of what came after.

"I'm coming, Izzy."

Twenty-Nine

Pi wasn't sure during which moment the battle changed, but she thought they were going to perish against the Elosian clones. Victor had his children captured with tentacles of dark energy, and Elosian himself was making his way down the stairs to claim the bridge tattoo, which would give him the power required to take the city, and then, the realm.

Her arm had been aching while she sent waves of magic against Elosian's personal guard, but as white-hot light erupted from Moriganne, Pi noted that an outline of the bridge burned through the thin shirt she wore. She felt the reflection of power and knew that Moriganne was channeling more energy than her body could handle.

If there'd been a way she could have shared the load, Pi would have deflected some of the faez through her body, but the main channel was heading into Moriganne. When spears of light disintegrated the Elosian look-a-likes, and then Victor, someone nearby made a little cheer, but not Pi. She knew what Moriganne had done and the price she would pay.

As she grew so bright it was hard to even look at her, Elosian fled the Glitterdome.

The relief of victory lasted until the glow overtook Moriganne and after a flash of blinding illumination, she was gone.

Pi bent over in pain. Her left elbow was aflame. She didn't need to open her eyes to know that she was now the owner of the bridge tattoo, a burden that she knew would only invite more trouble.

The others ran to the remaining Charmer siblings, while Pi surveyed the arena floor, looking for more threats. Pax approached with Kali at her side. The redhead wore an expression of concern as she glanced to Pi's elbow.

The pain was too raw to speak of it, so Pi asked, "Why'd you let Sammi go?"

"She doesn't know what she's doing," said Pax.

Pi shrugged. The battle had taken a lot out of her, and now that the bridge had claimed her as its owner, she didn't know what to think. Pi collected her jacket, slipping it on to hide the tattoo.

Ivan was sitting on the black spot where Moriganne had been standing only moments before. Unlike the others she'd destroyed, there was no ash.

"Maybe she teleported somewhere, or apparated out of the dome," said Ivan with crushed hope.

"No," said Pi. "She's gone. She saved us. Sacrificed herself so that we can continue the fight."

Ivan's face cracked with emotion. "You don't know that. You can't know that."

She hadn't expected to reveal it so soon, but Pi pulled back the sleeve of her jacket. When everyone saw the bridge tattoo on her elbow, there was a hiss of surprise, and then sobbing from those that finally had to reckon with Moriganne's death.

"Why do you have it?" asked Nandi.

"Because I was the one to kill the one who had it before Moriganne. And I carry the soul fragments of those he killed using the tattoo. That's how Elosian managed to capture me. He said the connection to the tattoo provided a place to put his hooks in."

"What happened to her? Why did she just disintegrate?" asked Audrey, cupping her hand to her mouth, eyes watery and red.

"Too much power. I can feel it now even as we stand here. The portal to the infernal realm is providing a conduit of unimaginable energy, which is probably powering Elosian's invasion as well. It's like being hooked up to a power generator without anywhere to put it. When she channeled all that energy, her body couldn't take it."

"Can you?" asked Aurie with eyes rounded.

"Probably more than anyone else here. As much as I want to stand here and mourn Moriganne, we have some hard decisions to make. Elosian failed to get the bridge, but he'll try again, and the city is still in turmoil. I hate to ask this now, but what are we going to do?"

"The twins need medical attention," said Audrey.

"I'm fine," said Kitty, sitting on the turf and holding her ribs. Her jaw was marred with blood and bruises were already forming around her neck.

"I can help," said Lennie, approaching Kitty sheepishly and leaning down on one knee. "We're taught basic magical first aid. I did a stint at Golden Willow during my fourth year at Protectors."

Ivan coughed into his hand. Blood splattered into his palm, which he stared at before lifting his head.

"Is anyone going to explain why they're here with us? I know it's been half a day, but last time we saw them, this meathead kicked the shit out of Andromeda. Also, asshole, I want my drugs back."

Lennie rose up, flexing his muscles. "You shoved those down my throat. I thought I was going to die."

Aurie yelled, "Enough! Stop. We made a truce. Nandi recognized that Elosian had been using us against each other. They know where the real threat is now. That's it."

"What about that bitch with the cobraffin?" asked Audrey.

Nandi stepped forward. "Sammi's gone too far. For her this is personal. Her cousin, and best friend, was killed a few years ago in the Undercity from some ritual murders. She blames the Charmers, but now I can see that can't be true."

"Actually," said Ivan as he leaned over and wiped his bloody hand on Lennie's pant leg, "it was our father. He was paying a society member to find a cure for death. He wanted to be infused with a demon for immortality and magic. She was practicing on random people until my sisters and girlfriend stopped her."

"That's what happened to Eloise?" asked Nandi.

"At least we don't have to worry about that asshole anymore," said Ivan.

"That's right, babe," said Audrey. "You should tell them what we learned about the portal."

Ivan squeezed his eyes shut. "That it killed our sister?"

Andromeda limped over to her bag and pulled out a notebook. "Before Ares died, he was working out how Elosian would bring his army from the infernal realm. He'd figured out that a portal was possible, but it would require an immovable anchor on one side to hold it open. But the longer it's that way, the greater chance it could collapse and destroy both realms, or at least damage them pretty bad."

"How bad?" asked Zayn.

Andromeda shrugged. "It didn't say, but I'm sure it wouldn't be good for the city."

"Great," said Aurie. "So we not only have to wipe out an army of demons and take care of Elosian, but we also have to close the portal before it crashes our realm."

The bridge tattoo was making Pi's arm ache. As she was rubbing the muscles, trying to massage the flow of power, she had an idea.

"I know what the anchor is." Everyone looked to her, so she held her arm up. "The bridge. The real one in the infernal realm. A bridge can be a lot of things but it's also an anchor and a conduit. This stupid thing has been behind all our troubles, and I know what I saw in Elosian's head. This bridge is important. We need to destroy it."

"Which one?"

Pi frowned. "Both? Which means I need to be the one to go."

"No, you can't. It's too dangerous," said Aurie.

"Better than keeping it here in reach of Elosian. That bastard has wanted out of his realm forever. The last place he's going to want to go is back there. Even if he does follow, it gives us an opportunity," said Pi.

No one spoke, which to her meant that they understood she was right.

"How do you get out once you destroy the bridge?" asked Nandi.

Pi lifted both shoulders. "Figure it out when we get there. Always have. And if not, maybe in two thousand years you'll have to put down the Queen of Demons, Pythia Silverthorne."

Her joke brought a few aching smiles. Moriganne's death was too recent for anything more than a crease of the eyes.

"I'm going with you," said Aurie. "If anyone's going to put down the Queen of Demons, it's going to be me."

"How are you going to get there?" asked Pax. "The Helmsman isn't available."

"One does not usually walk into the infernal realm, but since the portal's open, that's what we'll do," said Pi.

"I'm going to come too," said Zayn.

"No," said Pi right away at the same time as her sister. Aurie gestured to her when they checked to see who would speak first. "Besides having to deal with you two making moon-eyes at each other, we have a battle to win. It's bad enough that I'm leaving, since I'm the strongest here, especially now, but we need all of you in defense of the city."

"It might be a suicide mission," said Audrey.

"It might, but Elosian killed our parents. If this goes how I think it will, ol' tentacle arms will follow us back into the infernal realm because he needs the bridge. Both of them. If we can destroy it, we can trap him there and make the battle for the city much easier. It'd be nice to finally get our revenge. Another reason why Aurie has to come with me."

"What if he doesn't?" asked Nandi.

"Then we close the conduit, destroy the artifact he so desperately wants, and hopefully make things easier on this end." Pi shrugged. "That's all I got."

"It's not enough. You need more than that. You can't just waltz into his realm and expect to destroy a thing that's existed for thousands of years," said Nandi.

Pi ran a hand through her spikey hair. "I'm aware, but I don't have any better ideas. Unless you know how its power is derived, or how Elosian is using it to hold open the portal, I don't know what else to do."

As soon as she said it, she knew the answer. Everyone did. Everyone except Nandi and Lennie. The latter was tending to Kitty still, but Nandi caught it right away, tilting her head.

"All of you seem to know something," she said.

"We have a way into Elosian's mind," said Pi. "It's dangerous, but maybe he's distracted by this battle, and almost getting annihilated, so we can do it properly, instead of the shit-show of last time."

"Last time?"

"We all got trapped in his mind and barely got out," said Zayn.

Nandi shook her head incredulously. "And I thought we'd been doing dangerous things these last few weeks. No wonder you all kicked our asses."

"Kali and I can take whoever's going to Ares' place to infiltrate his mind," said Pax.

Ivan raised his hand. "I need to brew up some healing draughts for us. I think I might have a ruptured kidney, and Kitty looks much worse."

"I'll be fine," said Kitty, climbing to her feet. She nodded to Lennie. "Thanks. I'm ready for another round."

"Me too." Ivan nodded knowingly before he screwed up his face. "Wait? We're talking different things, aren't we?"

"We can't have everyone leaving the city," said Aurie. "Can you three handle the distraction?"

"Four," said Audrey.

"Four," said Aurie. "That leaves everyone else for demon duty."

At that moment, Alex came running up from the opposite direction. During the fight, she'd been in the highest part of the Glitterdome, scouting the battle. The concern on her face had Pi worried that something had happened that would upset their already fragile plans.

Clearly sensing the mood, Alex hesitated until Aurie waved her on.

"There's a second wave of demons entering the city."

Thirty

The darkness of the pit hid the horror of their surroundings, but Adrenalynne was getting restless. They'd been waist deep in old cooking grease for hours and hadn't heard any more screams or explosions in Big Dave's Town for at least a half hour.

"I'm probably going to have a UTI from standing in this disgusting grease for hours," she said.

"If you pee occasionally, it helps clean things out," said Xylos from somewhere to her left.

"Wait? You've been pissing in here with us both standing in it?"

She could hear the shrug in his voice. "I figured it wasn't as bad as all the grease and yaks."

"I'm going to take a look," she told him. "Maybe this horror show is finally over."

The metal ladder was slick from grease getting dumped into the hole. She climbed up and pushed on the covering until light peeked in. The illumination in Big Dave's Town was generally muted as most of the inhabitants had sensitive eyes from living underground, but it felt like full sunlight flooding in.

"See anything?"

"Spots in my vision."

She waited until her eyes had adjusted, not daring to look back into the pit. When the side of the Devil's Lipstick was visible, Adrenalynne stuck her head up, preparing to drop back in if she saw anything that resembled the horrific creatures they'd seen before.

A pale creature that looked like a skinned manticore lay near a group of three men and a woman. All dead. A few of them had bone spikes in their chests. As Adrenalynne looked further down the street, she saw signs of other battles. A few of the buildings had collapsed and another looked half burnt from a raging fire. How it hadn't spread was a mystery.

Adrenalynne climbed out of the pit and Xylos followed. She wasn't sure she could feel the lower half of her body. It felt encased in wax, which gave it a muted feel. A gnawed chicken bone was stuck to her leg, which she flicked off, then seeing the other detritus attached, decided it was better not to look until she could take a week-long shower.

"I'm hungry," said Xylos.

"I don't think I can ever touch a French fry again," said Adrenalynne, holding her stomach.

"I could. A nice basket with a cup of spicy aioli."

"You know that's just mayonnaise with hot sauce," she said.

"Really?"

"Yeah."

Xylos shrugged. "Still good."

They approached the scene of the battle. Adrenalynne carefully collected an automatic weapon from the dead woman. Her eyes were wide with the surprise of death.

"I think I recognize her. Owned the army supply store. These were a bunch of the preppers that frequented her place. Shame. Looks like they fought a helluva battle."

"But they lost."

"What the fuck happened?" asked Adrenalynne.

Xylos scratched the back of his head and then examined his hand, shaking off something slimy that had adhered to it.

"Remember that crazy bastard that used to be in Razor? Ollie, or something. He was always saying that the world would end because of a demonic invasion. Sort of looks like he was right."

"Maybe they should give him a medal. Too bad no one listened to him," said Adrenalynne.

"What do we do now?" asked Xylos as he retrieved a weapon for himself.

"If all the demons went to the surface, that might actually make it safer down here."

"For now."

Adrenalynne nodded. "For now. Probably the best place for us to go is Razor HQ. Hopefully Niran and the clan have weathered the storm."

"Yeah, be a real shame to have these tattoos for nothing," said Xylos.

"That's what you're concerned about? The tattoo?"

Xylos held up his goo-soaked arm where the neon RZR was displayed. "I like tattoos but I kinda wish it were a cooler design. Maybe add some dragon wings or funky flames. A cat with its tail wrapped around the Z, or something."

Adrenalynne rolled her eyes and crept to the next line of buildings, the place they'd gotten to previously before having to retreat to the grease pit.

"I don't see anyone."

"Smart enough not to be wandering around," said Xylos from behind her.

"Can't stay in that grease pit forever."

"That breeze feels nice," he said.

She wasn't paying attention to him, but the words wormed through her thoughts.

"Breeze? We don't have breezes down here," she said, glancing back.

Sure enough, she could feel the flow of air across her greasy skin.

"Feels like it's coming from deeper in the Undercity," she said, holding her hand up.

A single gunshot was the first sign that something was wrong. Again.

"You've got to be kidding me."

Xylos clucked his tongue. "Maybe it was accidental?"

She heard the voices before she saw them. The garbled language made no sense to her ears, but then a group of figures came around the corner. Tall, big heads, stout bodies. The Undercity was filled with strange folk, but she didn't recognize them, and there were far too many to be a hidden settlement.

"More demons," whispered Xylos. "I can see their horns."

They carried pale weapons that looked like a cross between steel and bone. As the street filled with more of the big-headed demons, Adrenalynne backed away.

"Grease pit?"

"Grease pit."

"I was afraid of that," said Xylos.

They climbed back into the darkness, the return triggering her gag reflex.

"You know what?" said Xylos once the lid had shut them back into the darkness.

"What's that?"

"I *really* wish we'd taken up Delilah's offer."

As the gurgles of the grease shifting and letting out bubbles of air released into the cramped space, Adrenalynne said, "Xylos."

"Yeah?"

"Shut the fuck up."

Thirty-One

Night had fallen in the city during their time in the Glitterdome. Aurie could hardly remember what day it was, so losing track of time checked out. Darkness had fallen faster due to the dome surrounding the city, which blocked out the dim light after sunset.

The battle with the demons had moved northwest of the Glitterdome. It appeared Elosian was pushing his forces towards the Spire, but no one knew for sure what his intentions were. Aurie hated leaving the defense of the city to others, but it seemed Alex was most suited for command.

"Everyone keep your head on a swivel," Aurie said, leading them into the streets heading west.

The mind-infiltration group of Pax, Ivan, and Audrey was going to travel with them until they reached the entrance to the Undercity in the third ward, which everyone thought was the closest way to reach the old society HQs. Kitty had drawn them a map on a scrap of paper from Ares' old notebooks, which resided in Aurie's pocket currently.

"How is everyone's darkvision?" asked Aurie as they jogged down the sidewalk, keeping their eyes on the sky and the surrounding streets.

"I would prefer the inside of my eyelids," said Ivan.

His flippant comments might have annoyed her, but she knew how much Ivan and the rest of his siblings must be hurting after losing Moriganne. Aurie didn't know how she'd react if she lost her sister, let alone three of her siblings like the Charmers had.

As they crossed a street near the Protectors Hall, they saw sorcerous energies rising above the buildings. A trio of dark shapes were battling a group of mages with riot shields, led by a figure a head taller than anyone else.

"Bannon Creed," said Pi, squinting in that direction. "Who would have thought."

"The enemy of my enemy," said Aurie grimly.

"Anyone else feel like their magic is more potent since the portal's been open?" asked Pax, eyeing the energy-filled air above the Hall.

"Yeah," replied Audrey. "Would make sense, given the relationship between faez and the infernal realm."

"Wait a second." Aurie faced them. "You mean faez comes from the infernal realm?"

"It's one source of it," said Audrey. "Not that I'm an expert, but I've been reading so much of Ares' research. It's an underrealm, closer to the original creation. It's possible there are others, but this is the one we're stuck with battling."

Aurie thought about the time she'd accidentally channeled the fire well from the Enochian district, sending a jet of sorcery into the atmosphere. It made a lot of sense as she thought about it. Especially being a descendant of Invictus, which gave her a direct line to the demonic realm.

When they reached the alleyway that led to the secret passage into the Undercity, they said their farewells to the other group.

"What are you planning to do once you're in Elosian's mind?" asked Aurie.

"Haven't the slightest," said Ivan. "Make it up as we go along?"

Pi smirked. "My kind of plan."

Pax frowned. "We'll try to distract him, whatever that means."

"I wish we could stay in communication in case you learn something," said Aurie.

"Probably no cell phone coverage," said Pax, laughing.

Aurie crouched down to Kali, who nudged her chest. "Take care of them."

<Kali loves Aurie>

"Thank you," she said, wondering how she'd gotten so lucky to have so many new friends.

After they split up, Aurie wished she would have given them hugs, or told them something inspiring. She hated the idea that she might die without telling everyone she knew how proud she was of them.

"Hey, Pi?"

They were traveling down the spiral staircase that felt like it went on forever.

"Yeah?"

"I love you."

"I love you too. What brought that on?"

Aurie chuckled. "We're headed into the infernal realm, the place that we saved Invictus from. I don't even know if we can survive there, let alone accomplish what we're planning to do."

The heavy plodding of their endless steps rattled the metal structure. The air grew warmer as they descended. A bead of sweat formed on Aurie's brow, which she wiped off with the back of her hand.

When they reached the cavern floor, Aurie pulled the note out of her pocket. It felt like forever ago when she first entered the Undercity. The darkness held so many secrets and dangers. The mysteries of the connected caverns were less frightening, but more ominous. Now that she understood the connection between their realm and the infernal one, she couldn't help but picture the place like a powder keg. The barrier wasn't just thin, it was porous, leaking faez and the smaller demonic creatures into the Undercity.

"How's your arm?"

Pi held it up even though she wore her jacket. "Hurts. Feels like I got the worst sunburn of my life right after a nasty elbow replacement. I have no idea how Moriganne slept with this pain."

"If we somehow destroy the bridge and close the portal, what does that do to yours?"

"That's a good question." Pi shuffled to a stop and turned her head. "You remember how Old Iron Balls explained that the realms move in relation to each other? The fae have been moving away for the past two centuries, but the maetrie have been getting closer, that sort of thing?"

"Yeah."

"The infernal realm has always been near ours. I wonder if that's because of all this. The bridge. The connection between Elosian and Invictus. Maybe it's been an anchor, holding it here, but that's always why we have so much magic in our realm compared to the others. It never made sense to me why humans are the masters of magic compared to most other races."

"Minus the maetrie."

"Right. But now it makes sense. Not only are some of us descendant from Invictus, who I guess was a demon lord a long, long time ago, but the barrier makes it easier for faez to pass through," said Pi.

The direction her sister was suggesting connected for Aurie. "Then if we close it, what happens to the Hundred Halls? What happens to magic?"

"Exactly."

"Magic exists in other places," said Aurie.

"But it's always been strongest here. Now more than ever."

Aurie nodded. "I hope we get to find out."

Their conversation ended as they reached the hidden passage that led to the society HQ. Aurie went first as her truth magic was easier to deploy rapidly, or at least that's what she told herself. It wasn't hard to recognize that her sister's unfortunate acquisition of the tattoo, on top of the soul fragments, made her one of the most powerful mages ever. Aurie wondered if she could rival the Dreadmarshs. In raw power probably, but not experience.

The society area had been destroyed in the explosion, but Aurie still had a sense of the opulence from the broken, dusty remnants. She was reminded of the old smoking dens of cultured men. Even the light fixtures were tiny chandeliers, or old-timey gas lamp designs.

They reached the collapsed area just past the open elevator shaft. Aurie peeked upward into the darkness where the fire hose hung.

"I can see light," said Pi, creeping ahead.

The rocks and structural beams formed a barrier at the end of the hall, but a gap at the top allowed a strange luminescence to peek through. Pi climbed to the hole.

"I think we can fit if we shimmy," whispered Pi back at her.

"Nothing in there?"

"No," said Pi, turning her head. "There's a weird light. The portal, I guess."

Her sister went first, lying on the rocks and worming her way forward. Thinner than her, Pi made it through the gap relatively easily. Aurie had more trouble because her hips and rear were wider than her sister's, but with a little tugging, she managed to make it past.

They sat on the edge of a great pit about seventy feet across. She could see other parts of the old society room, including a snapped in half bar top with dispensing handles. The opening formed a funnel that went down past their vision.

"They were supposed to be protecting the city from this, but it ended up happening right in their HQ," said Pi.

"That's the way of things. We forget the danger, explain it away as a relic of the past, prioritize our own concerns."

The air stunk of faez. Aurie's nostrils burned.

"Shall we?" she asked.

"Before we lose our nerve," said Pi, turning around and beginning the process of climbing down backwards.

Aurie went down parallel to her sister, checking for foot and hand holds. The angle made it difficult, but not too much so.

"What are these little rocks?" asked Pi, holding up a tiny little white stone the size of a salt crystal.

"No idea, but there's a lot of them."

As the pit narrowed, the climbing grew easier even as they were headed at a more severe angle. It felt like the weight of gravity had switched.

When they were at the point of the tunnel that was the smallest in diameter, Aurie stood up. She went from leaning against the stone to standing at odds with gravity. The change from one realm to the next had changed the orientation to the world. The sensation of falling made her throw her arms out, but then she was perpendicular to the rocks with her sister staring up wide-eyed.

"Nice trick."

"Come on up."

Pi had the same uneasy reaction, but then they were walking forward rather than climbing backwards, making the passage between realms easier. In time, the strange light grew stronger and she began to see an exit like an arched cave. The blinding luminance from beyond made it hard to see past.

"It's the twisted portal," said Pi as they neared and then passed through.

The vision inside Elosian's head became reality as they stepped into the valley beneath the strange fractal-like mountains. It was mostly as they'd seen, but larger and more detailed than the vision. The endless camp spread out across the valley floor. Aurie was busy looking at the strange structure hanging off the side of the mountain, wondering if that was Elosian's palace, the place he'd kept her sister prisoner, when Pi said, "Bodies."

To their left, a swath of the huts and tents made of skin had been trampled. There were dozens of bodies lying in the path. When they approached they found both the ochre-skinned feroms and the big-headed gigantes that they'd fought in Montanhas. Aurie checked the sky to see if she could spot the other landmass, the one connected by the bridge, but it was hidden by distance or the strange haze of the sky without a sun.

Pi crouched by a dead gigantes and looked up at Aurie.

"I wish I knew where Old Iron Balls was in all of this. Unlike him not to be meddling."

Aurie didn't say anything because her sister was right. It wasn't like Invictus not to be involved.

Thirty-Two

Alex stood on the upper bridge of the Glitterdome surrounded by people she barely knew. The wall of glass made for good viewing of the eastern part of the city, where the majority of the fighting was happening. Fires illuminated the night sky at points from as far north as the sixth ward to parts of the ninth, but the worst of the battle was happening just northwest of them near the Spire.

The white and blue lights of sorcerous energies rose like wisps of flame or expanding bubbles before exploding into luminous dust. Alex could see where the demonic army had been as the lights from the businesses were dark, either from destruction or the attempt to stay hidden. She dearly hoped it was the latter.

A secondary section of darkness was happening in the eighth ward. She'd seen the new combatants spilling out, but it had been growing dark at the time, so she couldn't identify much except their existence.

"It somehow seems worse at night, even though I can't see them," said Zayn, shaking his head with concern.

"Darkness hides movement, making it easier to obscure numbers and developments. Your mind is filling in the black space with more demons," said Alex.

A blank look from Zayn had her adding, "Sorry."

"Don't say sorry, tell us how we're going to get out of this. If it's possible."

"It's a war zone down there, especially with the new group of demons. We need to go help them before it's too late," said Nandi, heading back to the stairs where they'd come up. Lennie reluctantly followed, though he checked back to the group hopefully.

"We need a strategy first, or we're just going to get ground to dust," said Alex.

Nandi screwed up her face. "I've already lost friends. I know more are dying even as we speak. We can't just stand up here and pretend it's not happening. I thought we were going to do something."

"We are."

"It doesn't look like it," said Nandi.

Kitty, who'd been quiet since her sister's death and had been staring into the darkness with barely a twitch, turned suddenly.

"If someone's going to figure out how we survive this, it's Alex. Give her a chance. You can't win a war by rushing to failure."

Nandi squeezed the bridge of her nose between forefinger and thumb.

"How?" she asked after opening her eyes. "No offense, but I didn't see you during the battle in the arena. You were up here hiding out. What Hall are you even from?"

A tightness constricted Alex's chest. She knew how this would go. "Gamemakers."

"You're kidding me, right?"

Alex was about to speak, but Kitty stepped forward. "Think about it. We need magic, right? But we need a strategy more. I've seen her mind work. She's good. Really good. She saw stuff in the heat of battle that I would have never noticed. Please, we need to work together."

The big Protector put his enormous hand on Nandi's shoulder. "We need to stick together."

Alex could see the pain in Nandi's eyes. They'd all lost so much. Some more than others. But also, the Coterie mage was used to leading and having people follow.

"If you don't like my plan, then I'll defer leadership to you," said Alex.

Nandi wrinkled her face. She hadn't expected the offer and seemed suspicious.

"Okay, what's your plan?"

Alex walked back to the window and let her mind take in the flashpoints of sorcerous battle. The others joined her at the window. Nandi kept glancing over, expecting further explanation.

"How many students are in the Halls?" asked Alex.

"I've read somewhere between two and three thousand at a time, if we're talking current students," said Zayn.

Alex nodded. "There's probably two or three times that in alumni that live in the city or work in administration. But most are like me with scant magical ability, or are too afraid to fight. I'm guessing we might have fifteen hundred mages available, plus the general citizenry that own guns."

"What's your point?" asked Nandi.

Alex pulled a black paint marker from her pocket. She drew a big circle on the window, put a small circle at the center, and then made outlines of the wards.

"This is the city." She took out a red marker and outlined the demonic army that was assaulting the Spire. "This is Elosian's army. It's like a wedge pointed at the center building." Then she drew little circles of blue. "These are the pockets of resistance. They're outnumbered and outgunned. Too spread out to be effective. In conventional battles you want a three to one advantage in numbers, but as we know, this isn't a conventional battle. But the point is that they're going to get ground down to nothing. By morning at the latest, but probably sooner."

"Which is why we need to get down there," said Nandi.

Alex ignored her and continued drawing, this time taking out a green marker and circling the area in the eighth ward.

"This is the second group of demons, but it's not acting like the first. It came into the city, but has mostly stayed to the ward. There are no battles happening nearby, and no new fires," said Alex.

"Maybe they're eating all the survivors, or turning them into demon mutants," said Lennie.

"If they're under Elosian's command, he would want them with the others to overwhelm the defenders. He's a brilliant strategist and tactician. He wouldn't leave so many troops behind."

The others looked from her map to the scene below them. Nandi tapped the glass in the direction of the eighth ward.

"It's a much smaller army."

"Yes," said Alex, pleased to have that confirmed for her. "My estimate is maybe a fifth or sixth the size. Which suggests that it's a separate force. I don't know much about the infernal realm, but is it possible that this group back here isn't with the others? Not with Elosian?"

Everyone but Lennie said "yes" at the same time.

"My brother figured out in Montanhas that the demons there were a different strain than the ones that we're used to in the city. They required different runes and wards to deal with," said Kitty.

Zayn made a gesture with his hand. "I believe, based on a conversation—never mind where I heard it—there are different groups in the demonic realm. Most of the lords fled here, but they left Elosian because even amongst their awful kind, they didn't trust him."

Alex snapped the cap on her green paint marker. "So for now, until we know otherwise, we'll assume this is a different force of demons. Not allied with Elosian, but we don't know if they're opposed either."

"I don't see where this is going," said Nandi, who looked like she was one step from hurrying down the stairs.

"Why is Elosian trying to get into the Spire? Right now, the dome is protecting him from the military coming and flipping the odds against him. At least until he acquires the tattoo, and then all bets are off. Is there something else in the Spire that would be interesting to him?"

"Invictus' private realm," said Zayn. "I've been inside. He has tons of artifacts lying around. There might be things there as powerful as the tattoo."

"Or it could be a diversion," said Kitty.

"We already know he can't get in, so it can't be that," said Alex, then the answer hit her like a bolt of lightning. "I should have seen it right away." She tapped on the circle representing the Spire on her glass map. "It *is* the dome protecting the city."

"I thought you said he wouldn't want to take it down because of the military?" asked Nandi.

"Exactly. He's protecting the dome. He doesn't want anyone to turn it off until he's done what he came here to do, which is capture the tattoo," said Alex.

"Why would Invictus make the dome then? Does that confirm that he's our enemy? That the Lost Prince is really a traitor?" asked Lennie.

"I don't think so. Why go through all the trouble when he could have summoned Elosian himself? No, we have to assume Invictus is on our side." Alex turned to Kitty. "Did you ever meet him, or more importantly, did Moriganne?"

"No," said Kitty. "He wasn't around when we came back to the city."

Alex snapped her fingers. "That makes sense. The dome was to keep Elosian from reaching the tattoo, but the bastard was clever—he got us to bring it to him and trap it in the city."

Kitty lowered her head and closed her eyes.

"Don't be sorry, Kitty. He's been five steps ahead of everyone, including Invictus, this whole time. We're only now starting to catch up."

"How can you be so sure?" asked Kitty in clear pain.

"Because he didn't get the tattoo. He didn't anticipate Moriganne's sacrifice. That she would give up her life to stop Victor, and in effect, Elosian. That's what saved us. Family. It was her love for you all that was the one thing he couldn't anticipate, because all he understands is lies and deceit. Not family."

Kitty buried her face in her hands. Alex gave her a moment before she launched into her next line of thought, tapping on the glass at various points for emphasis.

"I think we can assume that Invictus is on our side, and if he is, and came from the infernal realm a long time ago and gave up his power, it means that he might have brought his side over. If I were betting, I would say that he's the one leading the army. He thought to trap Elosian in the city away from the tattoo and destroy him."

"Then what is he waiting for?" asked Nandi, staring into the dark blotch in the eighth ward.

"That's what I mean to find out," said Alex, heading for the stairs. When she realized they weren't following, she turned and said, "I won't make it a hundred yards out of the Glitterdome by myself, so are you all coming?"

Thirty-Three

Ivan stared at the unconscious woman on the mattress in the center of the room. Her eyeballs were moving frantically beneath their lids. He flicked the needle and injected more of the elixir that would keep her under and allow them to use her mind as a conduit to Elosian's.

"I'm sorry. I promise when all this is over, if we happen to survive, I'll make sure people know the sacrifice you made."

Heavy steps announced Audrey's arrival from the lower floors.

"Who you talking to, babe?"

"I wish Mori was here," he said.

She bunched up her lips. "Me too. Are you sure you want to go in? I'd be happy to go in your place."

"I know you would, but she sacrificed herself for us. It's the least I can do."

Audrey turned her head slightly. "You know what happened to them the last time? Elosian forced them to confront the worst moments of their lives. That could happen to you. I have a squeaky-clean history. It won't be as bad for me."

He exhaled, long and slow. "I need to go. Even if it means seeing the worst parts of myself."

"The worst parts are the ones that Vic made you suffer, babe. But the real you, the one I know and love, you're as good as the rest of them. I bet Ares, and Moriganne, and Solstice would be real proud of you right now. I know I am."

"Are they ready?" he asked, nodding towards the stairs, trying to stay focused on the task. His hands were shaking and he really, really wanted one of the emergency elixirs that he'd stashed in his brother's old boot in the closet.

Audrey didn't have to answer because the click of claws approached.

"Is she good?" asked Pax when she and Kali crested the stairs.

Ivan checked back to see the frantic motion of her eyes had calmed. The elixir was pushing her back into a deep sleep.

"I think so."

Kali approached the unconscious woman and let out a small whine before looking back to them.

"She says we have to wake her up after this, no matter what." Pax frowned at the mattress. "Pick your side."

The mattress was firmer than Ivan liked. He preferred to sink into the embrace of his bed like he was a sultan surrounded by hundreds of pillows and concubines. It was hard to get comfortable. He kept moving, which bounced the unconscious woman and Pax.

"You okay over there?"

"Is there some sort of safe word if I want out? Mine is 'Excalibur' if you're wondering," he said.

"Close your eyes and keep your mind open. Kali will be our guide," said Pax.

Ivan didn't know what to do with his hands, and then his feet had a case of the twitches. He kept his eyes squeezed shut, but the tension made it hard to relax. A soft touch across his forehead had him jump slightly then he realized it was Audrey, soothing away his anxiety. She caressed his temple, making him feel like a young child being put to sleep after a trying day. He stopped fighting the need to relax and before long he was drifting...

He stood in a cramped apartment. Ivan checked his pockets before looking behind him to find Pax and Kali. The redhead appeared vibrant in the dream world, as if her freckled skin glowed with inner light.

"The portal's in here," she said, heading through a door.

The bedroom was tiny, barely big enough for the bed.

"How do people live like this?" he asked.

Pax blinked and tilted her head, the movement reminding him of Kali's curious pose.

"They do what they can to survive." She gestured towards the wall, where a dark crack oozed mist. "His mind is through there."

"Quite a Freudian design," said Ivan.

Pax opened her mouth as if she were going to answer and then shook her head as she squeezed through the gap, disappearing. Kali followed with barely a head glance backwards.

"Hey, wait for me!"

He was expecting it to be gooey, or wet, but there was only a sense of buzzing energy as he entered the portal, as if a hive of bees was working in the walls. Ivan found himself in a vast, hazy space that he found hard to focus on.

"Oh, thank Merlin," he said, relieved.

Pax was standing a few feet away, examining their surroundings, while Kali had gone further afield.

"What?"

Ivan scratched his neck even though it didn't itch. The unformedness of it all made him want to confirm his own personal reality.

"I was expecting to walk into one of my old memories like the time I had sex with my tutor, or when one of Monique's friends gave me a handy behind the tennis courts."

Pax closed her eyes and shook her head. He knew he shouldn't be saying these things, but his mouth sort of ran on its own when he got nervous.

"What is this place?" he asked.

"That's what I'm trying to figure out."

The world, if that's what it could be called, was bubbling and shifting. Not far in front of him, a long worm-like thing undulated through a field of spikey stalks that his mind wanted to call grass, but he wasn't sure they were plants. They looked like stone cactus with faint bioluminescence at the base of the prickles.

"This isn't one of my memories, so he must not know we're here. The question is, where are we?" asked Pax, craning her neck in all directions.

"I took a fistful of hallucinogens one time and tripped myself back to the Stone Age. This kinda feels like that. They found me naked in the back of a diner, hiding underneath the prep table, talking to a mixer that I thought was Buddha."

When she raised an eyebrow, he added, "I'm a nervous sharer."

He could sense she wished it were Audrey inside Elosian's mind with her, but Ivan was glad he'd come. It was like taking a mind-altering drug without all the stigma that went along with it.

"Not many people can say they've walked around in a demon lord's mind."

"Let's hope we survive to tell someone."

Ivan crouched by the worm-thing moving through the spike field. The colors on the back of the creature shifted from purple-beige to gray-blue. The black lumps on its back moved as if they were eyes, but he saw no pupils. Ivan watched as one of the lumps absorbed into the flesh. A little burst of mist exited the brief hole.

"If this is his memories, I wonder if this is Elosian in his early primordial state," he said.

"No, that's not him," said Pax, looking into the distance.

"How do you know?"

She extended her arm. A figure walked through the stalk field in long strides. Though there were differences—the head wasn't quite the same, and the proportions were wrong—the being had tentacles for arms and backward-facing knees. It had to be Elosian.

Following the demon lord made Ivan nervous. He kept expecting Elosian to turn around and perform some sort of weird game show "Gotcha!" before throwing them into jail. But this was his memory, not the real demon.

"What are we looking for?" asked Ivan.

Pax lifted her shoulders. "I don't know. A way to distract him? Some secret in his past that helps Aurie and Pi?"

Elosian moved through the spikes, taking care not to impale himself. Occasionally he stopped at a thick grouping and stared at the stony plantlike things until they withered away, letting him pass without danger.

"I don't think I'd do well here," said Ivan.

"What do you mean?" asked Pax as they strolled behind the oblivious demon lord.

"He just stared at those plants and they changed. That kind of limitless freedom would turn to pure chaos. I should know. I'd probably end up as weird and dangerous if I spent too much time here."

"This must be one of his earlier memories. I don't see any of the structures or creatures that the others described in their visit. We need to find another memory. I don't think this one is going to be useful," said Pax.

After a short search, they found a crack in the ground that served as a makeshift portal. The hole creaked as if it were an old farm swing in the wind. Pax held out her hand.

"Should we think of something?" asked Ivan.

"The bridge. Or Invictus."

They squeezed through the gap one at a time. Gravity had little meaning as they climbed onto the new landscape, which to Ivan's brain was on the opposite side of previous one. He felt like he was supposed to be falling.

"Look!"

He held up his arm, pointing to the sky, where another landmass floated past. Before he could say another word, a massive black chain shot across the gap, which appeared narrow at first, but as the chain traveled, Ivan realized the two places were far, far apart. After a few minutes of the chain extending outward, it hit the opposite area, then the sound of chain links clinking filled the air. Mesmerized by the operation, Ivan watched the approach of the other landmass.

"I see someone."

Ivan looked around until he spotted the figure walking down the chain links. The green skin made him think he was looking at demon-Invictus. Then a tsunami of bright blue and white sorcerous fire rose up and annihilated the figure, turning them into motes of golden dust. Elosian revealed himself from nearby. Eventually the two landmasses connected, the impact a disappointing kiss, rather than the crash Ivan was expecting.

"This is the start of him conquering his realm," said Pax.

"We should check another."

"Agreed."

Cracks in the ground were easy to find as the world changed constantly. A new one opened like an eye, making Ivan a little nervous as they stepped through. The new place was wild with lights and sounds as if they'd been thrown into the middle of a great battle. Ivan watched as a whole group of creatures that looked like buffalo encrusted with glittering geodes was turned to dust by an exploding ball of white heat.

As a figure came striding through the mist, he was expecting ol' tentacle arms, but to Ivan's shock and surprise, it was his father, Victor.

Thirty-Four

The sparkling golden air soothed the burning and aching in Pi's arm like a nice warm bath. It felt like the time she'd gotten a bad case of poison ivy over the entirety of her lower body and her mother had slathered it in some gooey pink medicine. It didn't make it go away, but the itchy feeling was distant.

"It looks like there was a battle," said Aurie.

"I don't remember the gigantes in Elosian's camp," said Pi. "But I remember them on the opposite side of the bridge when we saw him and Invictus talking."

Aurie followed the trampled ground and path of bodies. "The other demons must come from Invictus' side and into the city. Great. We've two forces of demons rampaging through our home."

"Maybe it's a good thing. If those were his people before he left, we can hope that he's brought them over to do battle with Elosian."

Aurie rolled her eyes. "When did you become the hope-y one?"

"We should follow the path the gigantes made. It should take us to the bridge," said Pi, searching for the other continent in the sky. The haze was hiding it, or it was much further than the vision they'd experienced in Elosian's mind.

"How's the arm?" asked Aurie as they moved across the trampled landscape. The evidence of battle disappeared the further they got from the camps.

"I can feel it."

"It?" asked Aurie.

"The bridge. I don't know how to explain it, but the tattoo seems to have a connection to it. I feel like I'm hooked up to a battery."

"So it's not just the open portal that's enhancing everyone's magic?"

Pi rubbed her elbow. The heat generated in her flesh could have made water boil but she was able to touch it without burning.

"It's different. The other is true, but I think the bridge is more than the anchor for the portal. It's the power source." She bit her lower lip in thought. "When the Ginger Man was stealing souls with the tattoo, it was probably because he couldn't use the magic from the bridge, but now that the portal is open, it's like having a nuclear plant hooked up to me."

"Which is why Elosian wants it."

The path led them to the fractal-like mountains. Climbing wasn't as difficult as expected because gravity didn't pull on them like in their world. Walking up the angle required no more effort than across a flat plain.

The minerals—for lack of a better description—that made up the landscape shifted through the colors of the rainbow as if they were psychedelic lamps. Pi wanted to spend more time examining the little creatures living on the crystalline formations, but the need to reach the bridge as quickly as possible required forward progress.

When they reached the summit, Pi spied Elosian's palace along the opposite mountain. The structure reminded her of a collection of small magnets tossed together, forming a random shape, rather than purposeful existence.

"Your arm is glowing," said Aurie.

She'd left the jacket back on the plain when it'd grown too hot. Pi held up her arm. It was hard to look at, and the flesh near the edge of the tattoo was starting to char.

"The bridge is feeding me more power the closer we get. Let me see if I can get rid of this excess."

Rather than using the complex spell casting required in their realm, Pi imagined a beam of energy shooting out from her hand. To her utter surprise, a white-hot light flew out from her palm, disintegrating the crystals along the slope of the path. She fired it two more times before the light in her arm dissipated enough that it wasn't blinding them.

"There. That's better. I don't want to shed too much in case I need it later."

When they reached the crystalline forest from her vision, Pi knew they were near. The haze had faded enough they could see the vague details of the other landmass hanging somewhere above them.

"You ever imagine we'd be wandering around the infernal realm like this when we joined the Halls?" asked Pi, wanting the conversation to hide her nervousness.

"I barely got in, remember. Between the Rod and all the struggles with the Cabal, I never felt like we had time for reflection. If we manage to survive this, I think I'd like to take a long vacation. Maybe a year or three. See the world. Have drinks on a beach."

"The great and perfect Aurelia Silverthorne is ready to take a break? I'm shocked."

Aurie chuckled. "As much as I'm shocked that you're willing to destroy the thing that offers you nearly unlimited power. Isn't that what you've always wanted? To be the ultimate mage?"

"It's not all it's cracked up to be. There's this thing about a murderous demon lord that complicates it." Pi shot her sister a grin. "But I have to admit, it's pretty damn cool. I could probably knock a hole in the moon if I wanted."

When her sister froze, Pi worried that Elosian had found them. But then she saw what Aurie had spotted. The end of the tunnel through the crystalline forest was near, except unlike the vision, when she'd seen Invictus and Elosian talking on the bridge, there was something enormous in the way.

To call it a dragon would be an insult to dragonkind, but Pi had no other words to describe what she was seeing. It had two stubby sets of wings on its long cobalt body, which was being held up by at least ten pairs of clawed feet. Thick scales armored the beast, and sorcerous energies crackled across it, as if it were being charged by its nearness to the bridge. The head had to be larger than a two-story building, leaving them far outmatched in the size category.

Pi shook her glowing arm. "Something tells me this isn't going to be a simple fight."

Thirty-Five

Traveling from the Glitterdome to the eighth ward was easier than Alex expected. The horde of murderous demons was collected near the Spire, leaving the streets empty, except for the occasional straggler that quickly sized them up as too much of a challenge and disappeared down an alley.

"I'm getting antsy for a fight out here," said Lennie, carrying the riot shield in one hand as if it were a ping pong paddle rather than a heavy runed piece of protective equipment that probably weighed a hundred pounds.

"I think we'll see some action soon enough," said Zayn.

"I hope you're right about Invictus and this other army," said Nandi. "Every step we take away from the battle makes my heart sore."

The fight near the Spire lit up the night sky. Bright colors flashed from the streets around the tower. An explosion a few minutes before had licked up a third of its height before dissipating into green mist.

The buildings were abandoned with windows broken out and doors smashed in. There were occasionally bodies, but Alex tried not to look at them. It was one thing to live and die in a game where rebirth was built into the program, but for the people in the city, it was their final end.

They cut through a back street near a Wizard's Coffee that had been ransacked. Bullet casings lay all over the sidewalk, and broken glass was black with sorcerous char. A demon that looked like an armored buffalo with a mouth full of teeth big enough to swallow a basketball whole lay on its side, green blood leaking from its many wounds.

As they came through the opposite side, Alex froze when she saw Invictus. It wasn't hard to identify him as he was the most famous person in the world, but he stood with a group of tall demons with big heads, the ones the others had called gigantes. Speaking with Invictus made them less threatening, though she knew she could barely stand up to a single one.

"Every part of my being is saying this is a bad idea," said Kitty.

"They don't look so bad," said Lennie.

"You haven't fought them like we have in Montanhas," said Zayn.

Alex had thought they hadn't been seen, but almost as soon as they hit the street, Invictus turned towards them and waved them over. He wore his formal gray robes with runes etched into the hems and carried a long staff that had a flail on the end.

"Do we go over?" asked Nandi. "This could be a trap."

No one spoke, and Alex realized they were staring at her. It'd been her idea to come to this location.

"We'll be fine," she said, trotting towards him while watching for signs of battle readiness.

Either they weren't a threat, or the gigantes had been warned about them as no one moved more than a few head tilts as they reached Invictus. The ancient mage's gaze flitted across them. Alex caught a creasing of recognition as he reviewed her, which didn't make sense since they'd never met.

"Hello, Zayn. I hope the fact that I do not see my charges with you is not bad news."

Zayn checked back with them before answering. "No. They're alive."

Invictus caught the reluctance to be more forthcoming. "I see."

"You're the Lost Prince," said Kitty with simmering anger.

Invictus faced off with her. There were a lot of emotions Alex was expecting from the ancient mage, but surprise wasn't one of them. After a long pause of self-reflection, he sighed. "Yes, Catherine—I'm sorry, you go by Kitty, don't you? I am. How you learned this truth sounds like a story I need to hear. But quickly, we don't have a lot of time."

Zayn spoke up, explaining how Moriganne had gotten the tattoo and the investigations of the last week into the Lost Prince, then finishing with the battle in the Glitterdome that had claimed her life and the plan to destroy the bridge. The whole time he spoke, Kitty spun her blades and glowered at Invictus. A few times Alex expected her to lunge out and stab him, but she stayed her hand. The surprise on Invictus' face at mention of the Lost Prince was nothing compared to the devastation in his eyes as he learned that not only was the sigil outside of the protective dome, but it was currently inside the infernal realm with his two proteges.

"This is grave, grave news," said Invictus with a hand to his mouth, suddenly looking his advanced age.

"So it was your intention to keep Elosian in the city away from the bridge. That's why you put up the dome and brought your old army into the city," said Alex.

Invictus was distracted by his thoughts, but eventually he looked over, frowning. "That's quite perceptive of you...and you are?"

"Alex Duke. Gamemakers."

"Ahh, yes, I hoped it was you. Patron Dimple told me about what you did for the Halls. Thank you, Alex. I owe you a debt." He stared at her longer than she felt comfortable. She felt like he was going to start inspecting her teeth or asking her to spin around. "Well, then. It seems my plans were anticipated. This is a terrible revelation."

"Then it's true," said Nandi. "If Elosian gets the tattoo, he'll have the power to enslave this realm?"

Invictus looked distracted. "Yes. More than enslave. Change, warp, destroy. The sigil is the power of creation itself, and the open portal allows him free access to everything the infernal realm has to offer."

"Then Aurie and Pi were right to go after the bridge," said Nandi. "If they destroy it, it'll eliminate his source of power."

Invictus looked sick to his stomach. "There is no way to destroy the bridge, especially not by the two young mages on that journey. When we made the bridge, Elosian and I, it took all our guile and power to create it."

"Why did you?" asked Nandi.

"To escape that cursed place. It is a realm of early creation, constantly changing, as the power of spontaneous invention makes every day a new one. We built that bridge to punch a hole between realms, escape to a new place."

"So *you* could destroy it?" asked Nandi.

"Now? No. I lack the power, and even if I reclaimed the sigil, I don't think I could. I am a far different being than when I first came over. To make something that would withstand the power of creation means that it is nearly indestructible. Maybe Elosian could destroy it, because he is at the height of his powers, but not Aurie or Pi. The best they could do is destroy the link to the portal and trap themselves there, keeping Elosian away from the sigil."

The idea that their plan wasn't possible left the others visibly devastated. Kitty crouched on her heels with her hand cupped over her mouth while Zayn stood silently, eyes closed, lips pinched with pain.

Invictus looked to Alex with a slight raising of his furry gray eyebrow. "Are you not disappointed?"

"Disappointed? Yes. Dissuaded? No."

The corners of his lips twitched. "Why not?"

Alex thought back to all the challenges she'd faced in life and in Gamemakers Online. She'd been presented with obstacles so great they would have been soul-crushing to anyone else, but she'd come through the fire of the forge, stronger for the challenge.

"Nothing is impossible, and though I don't know either of them that well, that they've survived so much previously means that they won't give up. Nor will I. There's always a way."

"Your answer doesn't surprise me. Here." Invictus shoved the long rod with a flail on the end into her hands. She felt its power right away. "You should be the one to use this."

The long brass rod hummed under her palms. She could feel the power trickling into her body. Distant voices echoed into her mind as a sense of dislocation gave her a bout of vertigo.

"Focus on the here and now. It'll help the feeling go away. You'll want to use the Far Vision soon enough, but for now, you should stay amongst friends," said Invictus.

Alex did as he said and the motion sickness went away. She stared at the object in her hand. "What is it?"

"The Rod of Dominion. It's something I made about six thousand years ago to help me conquer Egypt. It should help you lead the battle against Elosian."

Nandi gestured towards the battle near the Spire. "I thought you said that their quest was impossible and we can't kill Elosian."

"I never said that, though I suppose it could be implied," said Invictus. "Yes, Elosian is nigh unbeatable now. With the portal open and his forces controlling the entrance into the Spire, we lack the resources to kill him. Even if Moriganne had been able to unleash her might into him, it would have only damaged him for a while. His power is tied to the bridge. He *is* the bridge."

"Does that mean he has a tattoo as well?" asked Alex.

"Once again, you are quite perceptive. Yes, he and I made the sigils to harness the power of the infernal realm while we were in this one, but my fellow travelers and I decided that Elosian was too dangerous and had to be left behind."

"You brought the Lady of Varna with you," said Zayn with fists at his side.

"Yes, Zayn, I did. I'm sorry, there's nothing I can say that will convince you to forgive me. I don't deserve it. As long as I have lived, the sins I have collected still outweigh the good I have done in my later years. But yet, I still persist, because had I not, Elosian would have won a long time ago."

Invictus turned to Alex and gave her a wink. "Now, since you're in charge of the battle, what shall we do?"

"Me? Why me?"

"Because there is no one else with your prodigious strategic mind here, which means you are the most qualified to lead."

"But why not you?"

"A fair point. For two reasons I pass it along to you. The first is that I'll be busy with Elosian. If we're to keep him distracted, then I need to be ready to engage him in battle. I have not his raw power, but he does not know this realm. I've spent thousands of years preparing for this moment. The power of creation can only help him so much. The second reason is that Elosian knows me, has clearly anticipated me on many levels. Better that you who he does not know, one who's been hidden away preparing, should lead the fight against him. It will give us a better chance to win."

Alex looked at the Rod of Dominion. She could hear it calling to her. The memories of countless battles were contained within its frame. She was both elated and terrified.

"How do I use it?"

"The Rod will help you communicate with anyone on the battlefield that you wish, see everything so you might direct them, and has some other tricks that you will find to be quite useful," said Invictus.

Assuming that it would be easy to activate, Alex reached out with her mind and asked it to see the entire battlefield. Her viewpoint switched to one high above the city seeing the landscape as if it were daytime, including the combatants. She could see the knots of resistance around the Spire, fighting against the hordes of demons. They were fierce and powerful, but too spread out to make a difference, a fact she wanted to quickly change.

Elosian, as she'd suspected, had taken control of the area around the base and length of the Spire. Huge flying demons with nasty tails clung to the glass, anticipating aerial attacks. His forces were patiently grinding down the opposition, which by morning time would be complete, and he would own the city.

Speaking through the Rod was even simpler than using a microphone and headset from her old online games. She knew in an instant that her voice would reach not only the knots of defenders around the Spire, but also the army of gigantes and any stragglers around the city. The power and responsibility made her hesitate, but then she took a deep breath and activated the communication link.

"This is Alex Duke. I hold command of the defense of the city. With Invictus and an army of allies at our side, we are coming to break the siege on the Spire. If you are hearing this, assemble on the western edge of the Glitterdome. We will take back the Hundred Halls!"

Thirty-Six

The old man leading the battle inside the vision was Ivan's father. Pax had been too busy with Sammi to have seen him in the Glitterdome, but Ivan's reaction made his identity clear. Ivan looked like a mouse trying to hide from a circling hawk. His shoulders had slumped and he was trying to make himself as small as possible.

<He senses us.>

The emotional reaction from Ivan was giving them away. It wasn't really Victor Charmer, but a part of Elosian's memory.

She grabbed Ivan's arm, tugging him out of his trance.

"Look at me. Don't think about him."

Out of the corner of her eye, she saw Victor pause in his pursuit of the enemy and look around as if he were expecting to find someone hidden nearby. If Elosian detected them, they'd never have a chance to distract him or figure out how to stop him.

"It's *him.* He killed Mori."

Ivan looked like he was going to break in two. Pax placed her hands on his cheeks and pulled him close until their foreheads were touching.

"I'm here with you now. Think about me. Think about Audrey. Think about anything you want except what's going on around us."

He screwed up his face. "That's only making it harder."

The constant inappropriate comments from him gave her an idea. "Is it really? Or were you thinking about me and Audrey together? Or maybe the bag of supplies you tucked in the closet."

His gaze narrowed and then his eyes widened. "You saw those?"

"I'm not a prude."

"That's right, you have sex with a dragon."

She chuckled. "He's in human form. It's not *that* weird. Just like all the toys in your bag aren't weird. They look like fun, actually."

The memory of Victor seemed to forget about them, and the battle moved on. Before long, it was further away, and Kali gave them the all clear.

Ivan pulled away, his eyes not resting on any one spot. "You were saying that to distract me."

"Mostly," she said, winking. "The memory was starting to notice us. We should move on. This one is too recent to be useful."

A crack in a nearby cliff gave them an exit. Pax had them imagine finding a box of Elosian's secrets before squeezing through to find a space she recognized from the stories of the final moments in the demon lord's mind.

The stone walls shifted with the haze of memory but they weren't the only things moving. They stood in a round room at least fifty feet in diameter. Dark cracks that oozed mist split the wall at various points.

"His Whispers," said Ivan breathlessly.

There had to be thirty of them along the circumference. The smell of lilacs was strong, reminding Pax of when the poor woman had died from an aneurism when they tried to question her.

"This is how he reaches into their minds."

Pax craned her neck towards an offshoot of the circular room that hadn't been evident before. In the small side chamber, an egg-shaped object as tall as she was sat in the center. Its outer casing looked like recently cooled lava. Cracks in the shell glowed ominously.

"What's that?" asked Ivan, following her into the room.

Even without using Kali's psychic radar, she could feel the living presence inside the egg. Something big and horrifying was contained within it. Its existence in Elosian's chamber of secrets worried Pax. They weren't the only ones making plans.

"I hope we never find out."

Ivan gave it a sideways glance as he returned to the main chamber. Pax followed, feeling like the thing inside the egg was aware of her presence.

When Pax returned, she found Kali near one of the cracks, sniffing cautiously with her hackles up.

"We should take a peek."

Ivan lifted both shoulders. "I like being a voyeur."

Pax approached a crack and stepped through sideways, keeping her left foot in Elosian's room. The interior beyond was immaculate. The olive green décor, pictures on the walls, and medals displayed on a board immediately made her think of the military. As she looked closer at the pictures, she saw a handsome gray-haired man in an Army uniform with countless medals shaking hands with high-ranking politicians.

The implications were clear. Pax slipped back into the other room to find Ivan returning with an equally devastated expression. He jammed his thumb towards the crack.

"It's the Speaker of the House. He's got a direct fucking line to the government."

"And the military," said Pax. "This is bigger than the city of sorcery. He's poised to take control of the government, or at least make a deal. I thought if we opened the dome, we'd have a chance to destroy him, but I bet he's already put his plan in their minds."

The two of them checked a few more cracks finding more people in positions of power. Media moguls. Well-respected actors. CEOs of major corporations.

"I shouldn't be surprised," said Ivan. "After all, he got to my father."

"Those with big ambitions and few morals are easy to manipulate."

"That somehow seems contradictory, even as I agree," said Ivan.

"What's this one?" asked Pax as she realized Kali hadn't moved from the crack she'd been sniffing.

Her companion whined.

"I'm afraid of what I'll see, but I'll take a look."

As soon as she stepped through she regretted it. The place smelled like death and all she could hear was sobbing. She was in a cave somewhere filled with the detritus of a homeless person: muddy tarps, trash bags, old food containers, etc. Curled into the corner was a figure shaking with tears, mumbling to himself. The other visions hadn't had their charges in them, but this one did, which was curious to her. She leaned down to hear him.

"I did it...it's all my fault...my fault, my fault."

She put the pieces together from the conversations with Kitty. It was Ollie Rend. The mad mage who'd killed Ares and, as far as she could tell, opened the portal. He hadn't realized that he was being tricked. Until now. She almost felt sorry for him. Almost.

When she stepped into the other room, Ivan was looking at her curiously. She wasn't sure she wanted to say who it was, but it was hard not to tell him.

"Ollie Rend."

Ivan took a step towards the crack, but Pax put her hand out to stop him.

"He's mad as a hatter. Elosian tricked him."

"He killed my brother."

"We don't have time for revenge. We need to figure out what Elosian plans. After seeing the people he's whispering to, it makes me more worried than I was before."

Ivan looked like he wanted to knock her hand out of the way and barge into Ollie's mind, but eventually he looked away and nodded.

"Let's go."

When she passed through one of the cracks, she stepped into a familiar area, if only by the stories she'd heard. Ivan came in behind, whistling softly at their surroundings.

They stood at the edge of a crystalline forest that scintillated with the hues of every color, including some it was hard to even fathom. The landmass they stood on was connected to another by dozens of black chains, and a great hum filled the air.

On either side of the gap stood the demonic Invictus—green skin and all—and tentacled Elosian. Between them sorcerous energy, too bright to look directly at, seethed like a newly formed sun. Pulses of heat cracked the crystals behind them, making it sound like someone was cooking popcorn.

Pax approached slowly with Ivan and Kali behind. She saw the glowing tattoo, the one that Pi now bore, on Invictus' arm, matching the same intensity as the real bridge, which was being summoned into creation. As she turned to Elosian, she was surprised—quickly realizing she shouldn't have been—to find that he bore the same tattoo, except above his heart. If he had one.

The force of their effort shone through their expressions. Wracked with pain and intensity, they looked on the verge of collapse. The blinding light reduced in volume, and the two creators seemed to relax for a few moments, then it started increasing again. The two figures seemed unsure of what to do at first. The bridge had been brought into existence, but it was already overloading, and as they watched, Pax was certain it might explode. The two demons worked frantically, shifting the raw energies of creation as if they were simple spouts of water. In the course of a few minutes, they changed the flow of energy and the glow switched from the bridge to them, entering the tattoos on their bodies.

As the energies cooled, the bridge was more visible and glowing hot. Pax could feel the vibrations of energy in the structure, but it had stabilized. The flow of power, visible at first, receded into the background until she could only sense it by the vibration in the air.

The two beings watched the cooling bridge, then moved away without words, and in matching motions, they released the black chains. As the metal snapped, the bridge groaned. The two landmasses were trying to pull apart, but their creation held. As fewer chains remained, the more the bridge screamed from the tension. When the final pair was released, Pax was certain the bridge would snap. Ivan put his hands over his ears and Kali whined softly.

The groaning slowly reduced until she could no longer hear it, but having been attuned to the change, she could feel the vibration in her feet.

"It's like a capacitor," said Ivan. "It's collecting the energy of the two landmasses trying to move apart."

The two beings, Invictus and Elosian, crossed the structure and clasped tentacle and arm. Brothers of the bridge. The two spoke quietly, and Pax didn't need to be near to sense their bond.

"He only has half its power, maybe less, depending on how it works." She shook her head. "There's no way they can destroy it. It's a futile quest. Look how hard it was for them to make it."

"Maybe," said Ivan. "Either way, I think this is what they need to know. That Elosian has the other tattoo and how it was created. It might help them figure out a way to destroy the bridge."

"But we're here in his mind and they're in the real infernal realm, probably near this very spot. We have no way to reach them."

Ivan turned to her, pain wracking his face. As soon as she saw it, she knew the answer that Ivan had already arrived at.

"Are you sure?" she asked.

"It's the only way."

Thirty-Seven

The creature they'd started calling the dragonwyrm due to its many legs and dragon-like head wasn't going to move on its own. Aurie crept near the crystalline plants, examining it from a distance.

"I don't know what you're worried about. I'm pretty sure I can annihilate this thing with a few blasts. I need to shed some energy," said Pi, rising to her feet.

Aurie pulled her sister back down. "If you do that, Elosian will know."

"Are you sure?"

Aurie pursed her lips. "Mostly. We need to take it out without Elosian knowing that it was us and that it was the bridge."

"Sounds dangerous."

"Fighting Elosian would be worse," said Aurie.

Pi crouched on her heels. "Have an idea?"

"I watched Alex throw a mountaintop at Elosian. I'm wondering if I can do the same sort of trick."

"But that was in his mind. The real infernal realm feels different."

"Still."

Aurie mused on the situation, rolling ideas through her head. She started with a trial. Using a bit of truth magic, she hardened the palms of her hands to protect them from the razor-sharp crystalline plants, then snapped off a stalk. The mineral crumbled easily, leaving her with a handful of colorful dust.

"Stick together," she told the dust as she squeezed, using her mendancy—liar magic—to trick the material into doing what she wanted.

When she opened her hand, the dust lay dormant on her palm. Not a single particle had stuck to another.

"That's unusual. My truth magic worked fine."

She tried again, focusing more faez into the mendancy, which inside the infernal realm felt more like she was using the raw magics floating in the air than channeling it through her body. An open palm once again revealed a non-reactive dust.

"Mendancy doesn't work here?"

"I would have thought the opposite, since this is a place of free-form creation," said Audie as she dumped the dust onto the ground.

"What is a lie if anything is possible?" asked her sister.

"Good point."

"Are we back to the artillery cannon?"

Aurie cupped her chin. "Yes, but I still want to try and obscure our approach."

"A dead dragonwyrm can't see," said Pi.

Aurie moved to a thick cluster of crystalline plants. "Be ready." Then to the colorful crystals, she said, "Ashes to ashes, dust to dust, take this field and into the smallest crush."

The imagined breeze rose into existence as a field of crystalline stalks exploded at the same time. A rainbow wind swirled, the particles shifting across the ground like snow in a blizzard.

"Round and round the dust flows, who approaches, the dragonwyrm won't know."

She sent the dust forward as a sky of colorful mist, and it quickly wrapped around the dragonwyrm. The ease of magic was delightful and dangerous, she quickly realized. The spells she was casting would have taken more preparation and detail in her world, but it seemed truth magic was well suited for a place that was the near the font of creation.

The dragonwyrm roared in frustration, stamping its many feet and snapping at the dust. Aurie kept the dust swirling and nodded to her sister, who had stridden forward with a glowing left arm. Pi held it out like a howitzer, aiming down the length.

The white beam of light hit dust and deflected slightly, hitting the dragonwyrm in the side, taking a chunk, but not killing it. The volume of sound that came forth brought Aurie to her knees. It shot straight up and out of the cloud on its tiny wings.

"Oh crap," said Pi.

Aurie let the dust collapse onto the bridge as the dragonwyrm flew high into the sky. It moved like a snake through the air. Pi aimed at the creature, but it was too fast to catch with a beam of energy. Then it dove towards the underside of the landmass, disappearing from sight.

They both stared at the ground as if they expected it to burst up from beneath them.

"We should move."

They ran opposite each other. Aurie had made it halfway to the bridge when the dragonwyrm exploded out of the ground, turning the field of crystals behind them to a shimmering haze of rainbows.

"Aurelia!"

The true name shout deflected the dragonwyrm's jaw like a right hook, keeping it from snapping its teeth onto her, but it kept coming. The many legs beneath its long cobalt body surged forward like an undulating train. The creature was coming on fast, and if she backed up any further she was going to fall off the edge. Aurie slipped in the slick, crystalline dust. As the dragonwyrm rose up on the back half of its legs, Aurie thought for sure she was dead.

Then a white beam of light appeared in the middle of the dragonwyrm's chest. Its expression of dragonly surprise was followed by the collapse of its enormous body.

To escape being crushed, Aurie yelled, "Slick!" at the dust in front of her, throwing herself onto her belly. She hit the crystalline particles and went sliding out of the way as the dragonwyrm's dead body collapsed.

A cloud formed from the impact. Aurie went flying through it and tumbled onto the path once the dust no longer formed a lubricant for her to slide. She coughed and sputtered as she knocked the particles off.

"I should have let you kill the damn thing right away," said Aurie as she accepted her sister's help in standing.

A sarcastic quip would have been the expected response, so when it didn't come, she checked Pi's expression to find it grave. She rubbed her elbow and stared grimly into the distance.

"He knows."

Thirty-Eight

The meeting of the two groups—the city's mostly human defenders and the horde of gigantes—might have been a problem had it not been for the Rod of Dominion. Alex had prepared everyone for the appearance of the unexpected allies, making the acceptance easier. At least for the newcomers. She was aware that Zayn and Kitty had reservations, but they'd fought the gigantes in Montanhas, so their apprehension was warranted.

In the time it took to march across the second ward, Alex hastily constructed a plan based on what she learned about her allies. She collected the mages into two groups: those that could perform more complex magics and those who were best left to use the simpler kinds like the Five Elements.

They were outnumbered by a factor of at least four to one, which gave the advantage to Elosian's army, but not all combatants were equal. She hoped to leverage their magical abilities to even the odds.

Elosian had mostly kept his army in a bunched group. There were fliers and other roaming demons in the city, but they were ensuring that no one could move alone without being in danger. The main force had stayed together. Not in formations like a traditional army, but the sea of claws and teeth was enough to make any interaction a losing one for the other side.

The area directly around the Spire provided Elosian the advantage. The covered parking lots and concrete structures made for great defensive positions, but Alex had no intention of letting him use those features. She kept her force in the street that went north of the Glitterdome, rather than expose them to a counterattack.

Dim magelights hovered nearby, exposing a sea of faces expecting direction from her.

She'd been spending her time using the Rod to communicate, but hadn't walked amongst their side. She would have preferred everyone use darkvision, rather than expose their position with light, but it was too late. She hadn't thought of it until they'd popped into existence.

"I need the first group with me near the Frank Orpheum statue."

Had there been time, she might have given them more imaginative names, but in the heat of preparation she'd used the quickest nomenclature possible. The first group consisted of the low-faez mages like her and the people with conventional weapons. Their tired and frightened faces watched her from the gloom. They'd already been fighting for hours and most likely would have seen their friends fall. More than one probably. She needed to not only give instructions but bolster their resolve. An army with poor morale wouldn't last long, and unlike in Gamemakers Online, she couldn't check a stat sheet to see her progress, which was why she had to see their faces to judge. They were close to breaking. Most had probably rushed to the defense, thinking they'd win quickly, but were overwhelmed by the superior numbers.

"We're going to win this fight. We have them trapped in the city and pinned against the Spire," she told them.

Her comment didn't get the reaction she hoped. They were skeptical of her assessment of the situation, which didn't bode well for following directions or fighting a difficult battle. She needed to improve on the shaky start or lose them irrevocably. Alex spoke into the Rod again so her voice carried more weight.

"The demon lord Elosian has brought his army into the city."

She paused as they reckoned with this new piece of information. Most probably didn't know the name of their enemy.

"I'm not going to lie to you and tell you that it's going to be easy. You've already been fighting. We all have. You know that there are creatures here that defy what we might consider reality. Men made of blades, hounds as big as double-decker buses, those quick slit-nose creatures that smell like the ass end of a sewer pipe."

Alex paused, spotting a few bits of laughter amongst the group.

"But I can tell you they're not leaving. Nor is the dome that surrounds the city coming down. We've been thrown into a cage with a dangerous enemy. One that wants to kill us, and then subjugate the city, before continuing on to the rest of the world. This is a fight that is us or them. There is no place to retreat, no sanctuary, no quarter. If we don't win, then everything we've ever believed in, everyone we've ever known, will end today."

By the time she was finished speaking every set of eyes was upon her. The truth was frightening, but they couldn't avoid it. Couldn't sugar-coat it. She didn't have to bring up the little old ladies cowering in their houses, because they knew. They all had friends or family or even just a favorite bodega. Fighting for home and hearth was a powerful motivator.

"I'm preparing a special surprise for them, but we need a distraction. We need them to be focused on you, our vanguard. I want you to organize yourselves in groups based on the five elements. You all know which one you're strongest at using. Once you've segregated yourselves,

I want you to position yourselves in those five groups on this side of the street, across from that forward line of demons. All those of you without magic should place yourselves between the mages. Your job will be to protect them. I'll see when you're in position and then I'll let you know what's next. Go now."

There was a bit of chaos at first as she hadn't given them a way to pick themselves out, but then the mages started holding up their hands with the dominate gesture for their element. Once she saw that they didn't need her help, Alex turned to the second and much smaller group, which included the friends she'd brought to the fight. Nandi, Zayn, Kitty, and Lennie stood in the front, arms crossed and waiting for direction. Their presence made it simpler to give direction to this group, since the social proof that she deserved their leadership was already present.

"What do you want us to do?" asked Zayn after a long pause.

She didn't have the heart to tell them she hadn't gotten that far in her planning. It was an on-the-fly kind of day. She searched their faces for clues to her plan. Lennie was leaning on his riot shield, which had runes painted on the front.

"What are those?"

Lennie leaned over. "Demonic protections. Nandi made them."

Alex smiled as she noticed at least a dozen of his Hall standing amidst the high-faez group.

"What other Halls do I have here? Shout it out."

It was hard to pick out individual words in the cacophony of voices that followed, but she'd made a habit of deciphering chaotic information in the heat of battle. She couldn't repeat the exact numbers, but had a good idea of which Halls she had available to use.

"Zayn and Kitty. I need you to go to the apartment building on the other side of the street and evacuate everyone there. Most of them have probably already escaped to other parts of the city, but we need to make sure."

Kitty scoffed as she twirled her blades. "You want us on rescue duty?"

"Yes," said Alex, not giving an inch. "The front windows are broken out, so I doubt there's anyone living in those, but the back apartments. They needed to be saved."

Kitty looked like she wanted to disagree, but then she checked back to the sea of faces watching the interaction.

"Fine. Rescue duty. Where do I take them?"

Alex considered the map of the city she'd memorized earlier.

"To the east side of the Glitterdome. I'll send the Aura Healers and other medical professionals there for triage."

Alex used the Rod to relay the message across the entire channel, then she returned to the group of mages—minus the two Assassins.

"Nandi. I need you to get all the Protectors, and anyone else who has something they can convert into a shield, into a group. Then you and anyone else who knows these runes should splash them across the front. Make them as potent as possible."

Nandi bit her lower lip. "A few runes aren't going to stop that horde across the way. Might burn some skin or give them second thoughts about putting a two-foot claw through your chest, but that's about it."

"Are you not capable? Should I find someone else?"

Nandi sputtered. "Of course not. I can do it."

"Good. Get to work. I can't hold everyone's hand in the middle of a battle."

Her shocked look was quickly replaced with a professional demeanor. Nandi started organizing her group as requested, leaving Alex to focus on the next group. As she gathered a group of three Stone Singers, a half dozen Alchemists, a pair of muscular Metallum Nocturne, and mages from a smattering of other Halls, including a trio of Daring Maids, one of the low-level mages appeared at her side.

"Ma'am," he said, looking like he wanted to salute. "The five elements are in position."

"Good." Alex lifted the Rod to her lips. "I want the five elements to start firing at the demons across the street. First flame, then water, then earth, followed by air, and finally force. Repeat as soon as the cycle is finished. Each group should take a two count before firing. Focus on reaching your enemies with high arcing shots. You're our artillery, softening them up. The rest of you, protect them with your lives."

When she was finished giving directions to her artillery group, Alex turned back to the eclectic collection of minor halls. She grinned to let them know their contribution would be both unusual and effective.

"See that apartment building across the street? This is what we're going to do..."

§

Traveling across the open space so near the demonic army felt more perilous than it was. Zayn skipped through the Veil, not staying in the real world long enough just in case, until he made it to the apartment building. Kitty appeared once he stepped inside. She looked ready to spit.

"How should we split this up?" she asked.

"It's a ten-story building. You take the evens, I'll take the odds."

Kitty nodded and disappeared into the stairwell. Zayn had his blades in his fists as he walked down the hallway, banging on the doors and yelling, "Open up. You're being evacuated."

He hated being so noisy. If there were demons on the prowl, they'd know exactly where to find him, but Alex had only given them ten minutes, which meant there wasn't time for subtlety.

A couple of apartment doors opened up. Zayn jabbed his blade towards the door.

"Get out now while you can. Leave everything behind. Hell is about to rain down. Head to the Glitterdome. There's a group there to help you," he said.

No one argued, but a few ran back in to grab their things. He didn't stay to argue as he didn't have time. He cleared the first floor in under a minute and went up to the third, where he started banging on doors like he had below.

He wasn't a dozen feet into the hallway when a door opened behind him and he heard the click of a gun cocking.

"I ain't leaving."

Zayn turned slowly, keeping his hands up.

"I'm not going to make you. I'm just here to warn you that something bad is about to happen and this apartment building is ground zero."

The illusion of choice angered the shotgun-wielding guy with cut-off sleeves in the doorway. As he let his weapon drift down, Zayn caught the alarm in his gaze as he looked down the hallway past him.

Something had come out of an open door. It wasn't far from Zayn and there wasn't time to turn to defend himself.

Zayn fired a force bolt at the wood floor, sending himself in the opposite direction. His back hit the ceiling and he jammed his feet out, stopping his fall as something the size of a buffalo slammed into the exit door, bending it like a potato chip. The guy in the doorway hastily discharged his weapon, nearly hitting Zayn in the process, and then threw himself into his room.

Before the demon could go after the guy, Zayn dropped down and hit it with a force blast to disorient it, before ducking beneath its horns and stabbing into its exposed underbelly three times. The demon roared, revealing a mouth full of jagged teeth.

The puncture wounds should have dealt major damage, but the demonic buffalo seemed more enraged than injured. Zayn sped down the hallway as the creature pursued him. When he ran out of room, Zayn ran up the wall, flipping over the stampeding creature, which hit the window, crashing outward and onto the street in a spray of broken glass.

Zayn paused, listening to the volleys of sorcery around the corner. He couldn't see them, but the reflections of colorful light danced across the nearby apartments and the impacts amongst the demons brought cries of anger and pain.

Back on his feet, Zayn turned back to see a half dozen residents—including the guy with the shotgun—hurrying down the opposite stairs with minimal belongings.

§

Kitty crept onto the sixth floor, checking the hallway before daring to knock on doors. She almost missed a creature hovering on the ceiling like a pool of darkness. A bloody arm fell out of the black goo, making her reticent about approaching. At the short distance, it didn't appear to have organs or any obvious places to stab. Taking care of it would require a different approach.

A few heads poked out of their doorways. They were aware of the demonic pool of black goo and weren't risking an escape. They'd probably heard the others being evacuated below, or had been calling each other. The sounds of footsteps on the floor above suggested the whole apartment building was in full escape. She waved them back in and brought forth an illusionary version of herself to send towards the demon goo.

The false Kitty approached, appearing oblivious to the danger on the ceiling. As she neared, the ground shifted, sending her into the wall. She checked her watch to find the time at eight minutes and had a good feeling Alex would only give them the full ten, no more. Dealing with the demon goo in an expedient manner would be highly necessary.

"Come on," she whispered as the illusionary version walked beneath it.

The goo rained down from the ceiling, slapping against the carpet along with an uneaten foot half covered by a leather shoe. Kitty raised both hands, making the gesture for flame and sending a wave down the hallway. The creature screamed and fled towards the opposite end on hundreds of tiny pseudopods. She chased after it, sending bolts of flame that charred parts of the goo to black dust. It punched through the window, but instead of falling out, it reached out and pulled itself upwards.

"Shit. Double shit."

As she ran towards the stairwell, the doors exploded open and people ran out, clutching their bags and backpacks, fear in their eyes. Kitty bounded up the stairs, three at a time, hitting the next floor. She stuck her head in to see Zayn helping an old woman pick up her dropped cane.

"Black goo?"

He shook his head, so she continued upward. When she neared the tenth floor, a scream erupted from the inside. Kitty threw herself through to find a woman with her young son trapped at the opposite end, the black goo heading straight for them. As Kitty sprinted to their defense, the building shook heavily, groaning a little to the right.

She fired flame at the black goo, sending it up the wall and onto the ceiling. It flung itself at Kitty unexpectedly, and only a backflip helped her avoid getting caught in the dangerous slime.

As she retreated from the advancing demon goo, Alex's voice echoed in her mind.

"Everyone must be evacuated from the apartment building. Time is up."

Kitty leapt into a forward roll, firing flame bolts at the apex of her tumble. The goo screamed, halting its progress. Kitty landed on her feet and blasted the thing with two palmfuls of flame, keeping it flowing until the goo was a shriveled hunk of char.

Relief at surviving the demonic goo ended as soon as the building tipped to the side. The brick and stone exterior exploded as pressure shattered the construction. The woman and her child huddled against the wall as the building started to collapse.

§

Nandi led her team of shield warriors through an alleyway as the horde of demons crossed the street to kill the mages sending volleys of five elements into their midst. She'd lost track of what the other groups were doing. Alex had sent the gigantes in a different direction, which made no sense to Nandi.

"Through here. Hurry, hurry," she told her group of forty mages. Their numbers seemed laughably small for what they were about to do. Nandi hoped Alex knew what she was doing, or this was going to be a very brief and foolish flanking attack.

She peeked around the corner, seeing nothing but the bunched shapes of the demons—mostly feroms at the front—attempting to take the position of the first team of mages.

"Almost there," she yelled behind her. "When we hit the street, keep your shields together.

Everyone without a shield, make sure you put everything into the spell."

Nandi wished they had more mages on their side. She wasn't sure why there weren't more of them. Coterie had a couple hundred mages, but she'd seen few of them on the streets. Either they'd died early and foolishly, or had failed to come to the city's defense, prioritizing their own safety. She knew which one she thought was true, but hoped she was wrong for once about her fellow Coterie students.

"Now!"

The shield warriors ran to the street first, led by Lennie, who stood the tallest among them. The demons didn't react at first as they were trying unsuccessfully to get at the other group of mages.

"Lock shields!" cried Lennie when they reached the crosswalk.

The wall of mages marched forward in lockstep, holding up their warded shields and sending alternating waves of force forward. The impact was immediate, turning the center of the street into chaos as the demons nearest did their best to flee, but tangled themselves into the others trying to get at the five elements group.

Nandi signaled to her group of casters, most of whom she knew from Chroma and Key. "Start now!"

The complexity of the ritual was increased due to the number of mages repeating the spell at the same time, but she had faith in their skill and hers. Fell energies swirled about them as they created warding that would extend behind the forward group of demons, cutting them off.

Nandi stood at the front, repeating the words of the spell loudly, making her movements exaggerated so everyone stayed on her beat. She was a conductor of magics.

When the spell concluded, a great rushing of air filled the street, blowing their hair forward and staggering the demons that were trying to reach the wall of shields. A ghostly barrier cut across the opposite side of the street, breaking the line of the forward group.

"Fire at will!"

With the spell finished, Nandi switched to a personal favorite spell of hers. She lifted her arms, making the gestures with her fingers and shapes in her mind that would help bring the spell into existence. Nandi felt more powerful than she'd ever felt before, pulling more faez through her body than with previous spells. The pleasurable flow of power had her gasping as a bolt of electricity shot out from her hands, impacting a hulking demon that looked like a minotaur without horns, then cascading out, spreading a web of lightning.

As her powerful spell dissipated, having taken down dozens of feroms, leaving her pumping her fist in excitement, a great roar came from the opposite end of the street. The horde of gigantes came rushing towards the demons trapped on all sides by wardings, five elements, or a powerful barrier. They tore through the demons as the others tried unsuccessfully to reach them.

Nandi felt a grin rise to her lips at the successful implementation of Alex's plan.

"Maybe we just might win this."

§

Alex watched from behind her "artillery" as the gigantes slammed into the demons, who had barely recovered from the shield wall.

"Hold fire!" she told the mages, giving them a rest until the next phase of the fight.

The demonic army outnumbered them, which meant Alex had to change the field of battle to shift the odds in their favor. She'd managed to fool them once, but doubted Elosian would allow it to happen a second time. He'd thus far stayed in the back, directing his army much as she was.

Invictus stood to the side, watching the battle keenly, giving no indication of his approval or disapproval. She'd explained what she'd wanted from him during the fight, and he'd accepted without comment.

As the gigantes cleaned up the demons that had overextended and gotten trapped behind their warded barrier, a great gonging impact sounded across the street. The trio of enormous giants approached the ghostly wall that was keeping the two sides separated. They sent their fists into the wall, which shouldn't have been a physical impact, but they held some infernal magics that gave them control over the sorcerous barricade.

Cracks formed in the hazy obstacle. Its fall was happening sooner than expected. Invictus turned his head towards her curiously, but she ignored his unspoken question.

The giants hit again, shattering the barrier into nothingness. As it fell, a new wave rushed into the street, hitting the flank of the gigantes that hadn't yet finished with the trapped feroms. This new group was much hardier: blademen, buffalo-looking creatures, other nasty forms of infernal life.

Alex lifted the Rod to speak into it: "Group one, fire your elements over the street into the throng beyond where the wall once was. Focus if you can on the giants."

She had a good feeling they were going to be a problem and was proved correct, as the sorcerous energies barely seemed to affect them. They'd been protected somehow, or the magics they were using weren't attuned correctly to damage them.

The overwhelming victory in the street quickly turned against them. The bigger demons battered their defenses. The shield wall was having to pull back, as even the group of mages led by Nandi couldn't hurt the demons enough to keep them at a distance.

Alex wanted to check the progress of her Stone Singer group, but there was no point. It would happen when it happened. The timing was the only thing that mattered. She looked to the apartment across the street. Bricks on its forward side were exploding into dust as the structure shifted.

Pulling back quickly would be safest, but she wanted maximum damage. They couldn't win by chipping away at the enemy. Eventually Elosian would join the fight, and if he still had significant numbers, it would be a rout. She needed to destroy whole regiments of demons.

As the apartment building tipped, explosions of dust shooting out from the base, Alex spoke into the Rod.

"Everyone must be evacuated from the apartment building. Time is up!"

Then to the group in the square: "Fall back to the Glitterdome. Fall back to the Glitterdome!"

The sea of gigantes turned away from the line of demons, which only encouraged their pursuit. As they retreated, the other demons tore into them, taking down far too many of the gigantes as they tried to get away. Without the protective volleys of her artillery, there was little to stop the advance of the demons which were encouraged by the retreat.

An earsplitting crack had her ducking, even though it'd come from a block and a half away. The apartment building that the group of Stone Singers, and others, had been sabotaging, began to tip over and collapse.

§

The building lurched to the side, throwing Kitty into the wall. The mother at the end of the hallway screamed, clutching her child. Kitty ran forward against the gravity pulling her sideways. She scooped the child up and slammed into the woman's gut, bending her over and throwing her on her shoulder. A kick sent the window exploding outward. Kitty just had to hope no one got cut on their way through.

As the building tilted to the side, Kitty leapt onto the side of the building, which was now at an angle. She landed on the brick façade, falling forward as she'd overestimated the speed of the collapse. Gravity tugged her off the side, which at ten stories was far too high. She jammed a hand out, catching a crenellation, still holding onto the mother and child, who were both screaming. As the building collapsed, Kitty rode it down, then as it tilted far enough that she wouldn't fall, she released the stone protrusion and sprinted to the bottom of the building, which was rising towards them, bounding over the windows and being careful not to trip on the ledges.

Dust rose in a cloud, obscuring her vision. As the building made its final descent, Kitty leapt high, traveling thirty feet in one go, landing at the edge of the enormous hole behind her. The apartment building crashed, sending up another blinding cloud and shaking the concrete. The place where she'd landed began to fall away as the earth pulled the rest of the street into the newly formed hole. With her weight shifted the wrong way, Kitty was certain they were going backwards, until a hand reached out and grabbed her arm.

Zayn appeared in the dust, squinting and coughing. He hauled her back from the edge and took the young girl, who'd mercifully passed out during the escape.

"Close one."

Kitty jogged with the woman on her shoulder and Zayn at her side.

"Too close."

They brought them to the first responders who had set up at the Glitterdome, handing over the mother and child. The bright lights of magic continued behind them. They headed back to Alex's location with weapons in their fists.

§

As the demon army surged forward, encouraged by the gigantes' retreat, the ten-story apartment building collapsed onto the street. The back edge of the gigantes was caught beneath the brick structure, but so were the hundreds of blademen and feroms and other demonic creatures. The impact shook the ground, ensuring that nothing had survived beneath the collapse.

It'd caught one of the giants. The other two had managed to leap back to safety. She'd hoped to destroy all three, but not everything always went her way.

"Well done, Alex," said Invictus.

She looked through the swirling dust. The pause in the fight would be brief, that much she knew. Alex lifted the Rod to her lips.

"Assemble on my position."

The announcement was mostly unnecessary, as she'd given instructions ahead of time, but keeping up communication was important to army adhesion.

Alex knew that Elosian approached long before she saw him. It was Invictus' reaction that clued her to the arrival. The ancient mage seemed to gather himself. His wavy gray hair and long robes had not a speck of dust on them, unlike everyone and everything surrounding them.

As the cloud settled, the tall tentacled figure of Elosian, Lord of Lies, stepped onto the rubble of the collapsed building. It was the second time she'd seen him, but he seemed angrier, more fell than inside the Glitterdome. He'd thought he was close to accomplishing his task, and now that he'd been thwarted, he was angry.

"Be ready," said Invictus.

Her first two tactical maneuvers had been largely successful, achieving significant losses on the demonic side with few on hers. The wins had encouraged Elosian to join the fight directly, which Invictus had promised would happen.

Alex jogged back a ways as Invictus strode forward, pulling back the sleeves of his robe as if he were going to get into a fistfight. She didn't know what to expect, but when Invictus raised his arms and a massive section of the fallen building rose into the air as if gravity had reversed itself in that localized area, she knew that this would be a fight between heavyweights.

The sea of rock flew at Elosian, who lifted his tentacles, the tips twitching. Every piece exploded into dust. As the cloud drifted past the demon lord, he called out to Invictus.

"You left me behind, brother."

"The choice was unanimous," replied Invictus. "You would have destroyed what we wanted to build."

The two stood apart by a hundred feet. Alex sensed both of them working their magics even as they conversed. She sent commands to her army, getting them ready for the next phase of the fight.

"You betrayed me."

"I did, and I'm not sorry about it," said Invictus.

"After all we did to bring about that passage. All the work, the construction of the bridge, the peace we made. Now, I can see why. You wanted this world all for yourself. The others had no idea that you would betray them in time."

"I did nothing of the sort. We each went our way, some ending things themselves, others falling to their own hubris. Eventually I realized I couldn't sustain it. I gave up my power so I might better understand the realm that I now call my home. I betrayed no one but you."

Elosian scowled. "Don't lie to me, brother."

"I'm not your brother."

The ball of scintillating energy that Invictus threw at Elosian would have annihilated a thousand soldiers, but the demon lord threw up a tentacle, deflecting it into the sky, where it eventually slammed against the dome, causing a ripple of colorful lights across the curved surface.

"You're weak, brother. You let them neuter you. You should have kept your sigil, then maybe this would be a fair fight. But I'm afraid I'm going to have to destroy you," said Elosian.

The counterattack came faster than Alex thought possible. Invictus barely got up a shield in time before the wave of dark energy hit, pushing him back fifty feet and crisping the edges of his robes and hair. Seeing how outmatched he was, Alex tapped into the Rod and sent a bolt of lightning after Elosian. The crack of light slammed into him, knocking him down and giving Invictus a chance to recover, but did little to injure him.

"I'll deal with you soon enough," said Elosian.

This time Invictus was ready for the attack and the two sent waves of battering magics towards each other. The concrete and broken glass between them were evaporated by the high magics.

Alex fell back, sending her army around the collapsed building, but not wanting to go too far. She needed to know how Invictus fared. If he was beaten, then she would have to shift into a retreat, hoping to stall until Aurie and Pi could destroy the bridge, the source of his power.

She could barely watch as the energies erupting from their battle turned the area as bright as day. Elosian clearly had the upper hand, knocking Invictus back, step by step.

While she watched, she reorganized her army: shield wall in front, then the high-faez mages, and finally the artillery. She sent them forward into the flank of the demonic army, hoping to distract Elosian.

As she finished her instructions, Elosian caught Invictus with a potent punch of sorcery, throwing him across the street to crash through the glass walls of the Glitterdome. Alex used the Rod to send multiple bolts of lightning after Elosian. The first two barely hit him, but the third knocked him backwards.

The brief excitement at wielding such power quickly evaporated as Elosian climbed back onto the pile of rocks and prepared to launch a new volley. Alex steeled herself for the reprisal, but then he seemed suddenly distracted, his head snapping to the side.

"No!"

His rage brought Alex to her knees. She thought he was going to unleash fury on her, but then he turned back to the two remaining giants.

"Release the Eater!"

A pit formed in her stomach. She was aware of the creature that the others had experienced in Montanhas. This couldn't be that one, but something just like it. Elosian fled the battle, which left Alex worried about Aurie and Pi. If he'd sensed their attack on the bridge, they wouldn't have much time. Alex ran to Invictus, who lay prone inside the Glitterdome. He was slowly regaining his feet, bright blood streaming down his forehead. His eyes were unfocused.

"Prepare a retreat."

Alex was about to tell him that she would do no such thing when a fearsome roar filled the air, putting water in her knees and sending waves of revulsion through her body.

Thirty-Nine

"Are you sure you want to do it?"

Ivan stood before the crack in the wall, which oozed with mist, the overwhelming smell of lilacs making him slightly ill. Pax had her arms crossed next to him.

"It's better if I go. I think."

"If you're not sure, I'll do it," said Pax.

"I'm not sure, but I still think I'm the one that should go. It sounds like he's in the throes of faez madness, on top of Elosian messing with him. If he's as crazy as you say, then it's probably best for me to be in his head."

Pax frowned. "This isn't about Ares, is it? Be a really bad time for revenge."

"I know from personal experience that you can't injure a crazy person any more than they hurt themselves. At this point, he's probably praying for release from his mistakes. I'm surprised he hasn't done it himself already."

Pax screwed up her face. "What did your father do to you?"

"He didn't make us brush our teeth." She seemed almost disappointed by his mundane answer, so he threw in, "Or murder vagrants in the back alleyway before bedtime."

"Ivan..."

"You sound like my sisters," he said, smirking.

"You're stalling now."

He exhaled. "I am. Wish me luck."

Pax looked at him in that way that people did when they saw how broken he was. A mixture of pity and confusion. It was one of the reasons he was so smitten with Audrey. She never looked at him like that. She saw his crazy for what it was and loved him anyway.

The air inside the junk-filled cave was humid and hot. Ollie reeked of body odor and rotting garbage. He was curled into the corner, sobbing softly and mumbling to himself. Ivan could imagine himself like the poor guy if he hadn't had his ultra-rich family to bail him out of the messes he'd made along the way to adulthood.

Now that he was standing in the cave, he wasn't sure how he was supposed to motivate Ollie. Elosian had been using the crack to whisper lies to the him, but was it as simple as speaking to him?

"Hey, Ollie. You need to stand up. I got things for you to do."

Ollie didn't move, or acknowledge that he'd spoken, so Ivan moved close to his ear and yelled, "Ollie!"

There was no reaction.

"This is disappointing."

Ivan wondered if Pax was better suited because she was used to having a psychic connection with other beings. He stared at the crack in the wall of the cave and thought about returning, but hated the idea of giving up.

"Ollie, come on. You screwed the pooch, but now there's a way to redeem yourself. Just like I did. It doesn't matter how many times you mess up if you have people who love you and will take you back. But you gotta give 'em that chance. I'm sure you have friends. Mates that know you and would do anything for you."

Ivan crouched on his heels as Ollie continued to sob. "You just gotta have something productive to do with your time. When I get all tangled up in my head, when it feels like the Gordian knot, I throw myself into my alchemy. It's a form of therapy, I think. Gives me purpose, keeps me out of trouble. That and Audrey. If the world believes in balance, and fuck all if I know if that's true, at least having her in my life balances that miserable experience of living under Victor's fascist thumb."

There was still no reaction from Ollie. Ivan paced around the room. He had to get him moving. They had to get the information to Aurie and Pi.

"Why are you even here?" he asked.

The other Whisper-holes had nobody inside, just the rooms that Ivan assumed represented their minds. But not Ollie.

"Are you too far gone to understand the difference between your desires and reality?"

It was a state Ivan knew well. He put his hand out as if he were going to comfort Ollie, and it went right through his shoulder. Ollie reacted with a twitch of his head, but nothing more. Encouraged by the reaction, Ivan stuck his entire hand through Ollie's body. The mad mage seemed to sense something was happening, but did little more than make a face.

Ivan threw caution to the wind and slid into the spot where Ollie's body was curled against the wall. The overlap hit Ivan with an overwhelming cascade of sensations as he was feeling what Ollie felt. Then as he positioned himself more overtop, thoughts intruded, making Ivan want to jump out of his skin.

I killed everyone...it's all my fault...the world will end...

The thoughts went on ad infinitum. Ivan knew them well. Not the particular phrases but the loop of thoughts that trapped and held him under until he couldn't breathe anymore.

Ivan let them pass through him until they became background noise. The unusual feelings were no different than taking too many drugs and getting paranoid, a sensation he was used to. As he settled in Ollie's body, he found he could move him. Ivan thought that might wake him out of his stupor to take back control, but he was so far gone that he wasn't paying attention anymore.

Getting Ollie standing felt like a minor miracle, but the more he moved, the more comfortable he felt. It wasn't entirely like being in his own body, since his reactions were a millisecond behind, but it was close enough.

"Broken hells, I stink."

Ivan managed to climb down and out of the cave using rough handholds, finding a familiar passage that he recognized as relatively near the society headquarters. The hidden space was up in the ceiling of the passage, making it difficult to discover.

He tried to head to the place he knew would take them back to the society HQ, but the body he was controlling wanted to go a different direction. Ivan let Ollie's muscle memory override him. They entered a big cavern and eventually found the passage that led to the portal. The walls of the tunnel had been recently expanded. The horde of demons had ripped apart the rock, widening the tunnel so the larger creatures could pass through.

The power required to rip through the rock was a little disconcerting, making Ivan glad his body was back in Ares' old place, rather than at the front lines of the fight. He maneuvered Ollie into the pit, where free faez turned the air to a faint golden light. Climbing down backwards was precarious, not having complete control of Ollie's body. It would be tragic to have him die from a random fall on the precipice of being useful.

As he moved, he found small minerals stuck in the cracks in the rocks. He knew what they were instantly, because he'd been experimenting with them at his laboratory. Faez crystals. Their appearance at the site of the portal wasn't a surprise. He resisted the urge to grab some since it wasn't his body, but made a note to come back later, should they survive.

Ivan wasn't sure when gravity switched on him, but he went from climbing down to standing up without really thinking about it. He felt like he was standing on the wall as he looked back up the tunnel.

Eventually he came out beneath a twisted silvery archway surrounded by the huts of an encamped army, though he saw no creatures moving amongst the housing. The nearby bodies of gigantes and other creatures confirmed where he was standing. Ivan craned his neck, taking in the strange and wonderous landscape. The ridge of mountains to his right reminded him of fractals. At some of his raves, he'd projected videos of the mathematical constructs on a wall, but this felt like standing inside one of those moving pictures.

"Wicked."

Ivan wasn't sure which way to go until he saw a beam of white-hot light fired from a distant mountaintop. There was a vague sense of movement, a battle perhaps. He watched until he saw a second beam and decided it had to be Aurie and Pi. He set off in that direction, piloting Ollie, who had thus far declined to surface from his inner delusions.

"I feel ya, buddy. I feel ya."

Forty

The bridge burned with the heat of a thousand suns. Pi could hardly look near her arm, but she feared to dissipate the energy because Elosian was headed their way. She felt it the moment they killed the guardian.

"How do we destroy the bridge?" asked Aurie, staring at the structure spanning two landmasses.

The bridge had looked mundane from a distance, almost something that could exist in their world, but up close Pi saw the differences. She'd imagined that it was made of steel or other building materials, but it wasn't anything like that. It wasn't quite matte black, nor was it colorless. It swirled with grays and dark colors as if it were a black hole made real.

"The bridge is made of faez," she announced to her sister. "Raw, condensed faez. It collects the raw magics in the air, converts them. It's like a giant battery connected to an unlimited power source."

"Can it be destroyed?" asked Aurie, shielding her eyes from the illumination of Pi's arm.

"It was made to withstand unimaginable energies." Pi shook her head. "I don't know if it's possible."

"Then we've trapped ourselves, and given him the final piece he needs to conquer our realm," said Aurie grimly.

A sharp stab of pain had Pi bending over. "He's here."

The twisted portal, a hazy shiny spot in the valley below, was barely visible from their vantage. Pi spotted a figure moving through the air towards them. Elosian.

"Stay behind me," she told Aurie.

The demon lord landed in the field where the colorful crystals had existed before the battle with his guardian. Dust swirled about in an unseen breeze. Elosian appeared relaxed, pleased about the circumstances.

"Thank you, Pythia. It fills me with joy to see the seeds I planted long ago come to fruit, and now it's time to harvest that sweetness."

Pi opened her mouth as if she were going to deliver a pithy response, but fired a beam of pure energy at Elosian, which he easily knocked away.

"The arrogance to think you could best me. Here, in the place that forged me into this perfect form. You know nothing about the infernal realm."

Elosian raised a tentacle and an equally bright beam of light flashed towards her. Pi sent a shield of energy out, stopping the ray at first, but then it slowly pushed her backwards.

"I'm not even trying." He scoffed. "Your friend, the one that's leading your side out there, she might give me an interesting challenge, but you, not so much. Maybe if I left you here for a few thousand years you might make the fight interesting."

Elosian let the beam of energy dissipate, leaving Pi breathing heavily. Blocking it had taken a lot out of her. The tattoo wasn't glowing so brightly. She checked back to Aurie to see her worried expression.

Pi reviewed her options, hoping one of the soul fragments had ideas, but they were outclassed by the raw power of Elosian. None of the spells they knew were useful in the infernal realm.

"Are you drawing from the bridge?" asked her sister.

Pi reached out through the tattoo, much in the same way she tapped into the faez at the base of her skull, to find the bridge waiting for her. It was a little frightening to feel the connection. Like standing in the middle of a field of unprotected power lines humming with bone-charring electricity.

The next beam of energy she sent at Elosian caught him off guard. Rather than deflect it, he had to block it, much as she had his. The excitement she felt evaporated as he slowly moved the point of conflict towards her. Eventually she gave up, letting the flow of energy end.

"Pi, your arm."

The tattoo was run through with embers, the fleshy areas nearby charred. Like Moriganne, her body wasn't capable of holding up to the intense energies that the bridge could supply.

"You're beginning to see why you are fated to lose. Long before you could channel enough energy to destroy me, it would vaporize you into the mists of creation. This is not a fight you can win. Best you hand over that which I desire, rather than enrage me further. If you force me to take it from you, I will take it out on your precious world. On your friends." Elosian tilted his head, revealing his serial-killer's smile. "On your sister."

"He's telling the truth," said Aurie from behind her. "He believes it anyway."

Her sister knew truth better than anyone she knew. If Aurie said someone wasn't lying, even the Prince of Lies, Pi believed her.

Pi looked at her elbow covered in embers, then at Elosian.

She turned her head towards her sister. "What happens to the tattoo if I over channel it?"

"Pi. Don't."

"It might be the only way."

Forty-One

"It's the thing in the box. The one they brought with them," said Zayn, appearing at Alex's side from out of nowhere.

She'd been helping Invictus to stand. The blast from Elosian had hurt him.

"I'll be fine," he said, dusting himself off, then looked to the sky where something dark moved above the buildings. "For now."

"What is it?"

Invictus cracked his neck with a practiced tilt of the head.

"Not everything in the infernal realm wanted to rule. Some things just want to destroy. They're pure chaos."

"Is it like the thing in Montanhas? They called that an Eater, too," said Zayn.

Invictus stepped over the broken glass to stare at the night sky. The constant battles of potent sorcery had made it appear to be day, but now that the fighting had paused, darkness had returned. Alex had a sense of movement near the Spire, but the size of the creature had to be enormous, dwarfing even their biggest commercial airplanes.

"It is," said the ancient mage with a sigh.

"What can we do against it?" asked Alex.

"Avoid getting eaten," said Invictus.

She returned to her army, which was waiting patiently in the position she'd set up for them. The gigantes lingered in the next street over, licking their wounds from the last fight. They'd been able fighters, but probably no match for the Eater.

The demonic army climbed over the fallen apartment building, led by the two giants, their crimson eyes glaring through the darkness. Hulking four-legged forms joined them—creatures the size of buses with furnace mouths, and other larger combatants.

Thus far, they'd battled the smaller demons: feroms, blademen, and other cannon fodder. They'd bloodied them, but hardly impacted the strength of the army. And with the Eater in the sky, along with other flying demons, the battlefield was fraught.

An explosion from many blocks over, as electrical lines shot sparks in a high arc, momentarily revealed the Eater crouched over an apartment building. The enormous demonic beast was ripping away the roof as if it were a piece of foil covering. The brief light revealed that the Eater was crouched on multiple buildings, its size even bigger than she first thought. It had two sets of black wings, and multiple barbed tails wrapped around the structure beneath it.

"Prepare to fire! All at once, no rotation!" she yelled into the Rod, her eyes not leaving the area she had seen the Eater.

As the demonic giants led the army over the rubble, she marked the range in her head. As the first one stepped off the pile of broken rock, she yelled, "Fire!"

Bright lights exploded from her army as they were nestled between the Glitterdome and the buildings on the opposite side of the street. The illumination revealed the line of shield warriors in front, followed by the high-faez mages. The elemental magics impacted the advancing demons, cascading off their hardened bodies. The giants raised their fists and sent a blast of dark energy at the front of her army. They raised their shields and countered with ghostly magics that attempted to block the arcing attack. Some of the eldritch magics slipped through the defense and some of the mages in the front line fell.

"Back up slowly. One step every second."

Alex didn't mind giving ground, as it gave them more opportunity for ranged attacks. The army moved relatively together. Considering they'd never practiced the movement, it could have been worse.

As the demonic army marched forward, sorcerous attacks were traded. The ones from her side were constant and colorful, while the return fire was focused and powerful. If they had to trade artillery fire, her side was going to lose.

"Can you drop another building on them?" asked Zayn.

"Not likely." She lifted the Rod. "Gigantes, hit them now!"

Backing up had exposed the softer flank behind the major demons. A roar echoed from the next street over as the gigantes rushed in to attack.

"Now forward! Hit them with everything you've got!"

The pace of sorcery flinging from her side increased fivefold. Invictus stepped up and added his considerable magics to the attack, stopping the line of demons from advancing. They appeared unsure of which threat was worse, until the gigantes reached them, turning the battle into a melee.

Alex threw the occasional bolt of lightning into the throng of darkness, but mostly stayed focused on observing the battle. They wouldn't be able to sustain a counterattack long. She needed to keep the enemy guessing, which would give them more room to maneuver and chip away the enemy's numbers. She was feeling good about the battle until she felt the dark presence land on the street above the gigantes.

Even from a hundred feet away, she wanted to cower into a ball. Fear ran rampant through her body. She was vaguely aware that some of the mages in the elemental artillery had run away.

With her army shaken, the demons advanced as their flank was suddenly protected by the Eater as it attacked the gigantes. Their allies were outmatched. Alex defied her fears and lifted the Rod, ordering them to retreat. They couldn't withstand the might of the Eater.

"We need to find a new defensive spot, but I can't risk a retreat," she told Invictus.

The ancient mage nodded, understanding what she was asking. He stepped to the side of the shield wall and lifted his arms. The ground shook as stone blocks rose from the street, piling on top of each other until a barrier formed between the two sides.

Alex lifted the Rod, fearing that this would be their final retreat.

"To the Glitterdome!"

Forty-Two

"Stand back."

There was nothing Aurie could do to help her sister. The levels of power available to the two combatants meant that she'd be lucky not to be destroyed from collateral damage. She backed up as waves of energy crashed against each other, exploding into spectacular colors. Aurie felt like she was watching the spawning of the universe. It was a fireworks show like no other in the history of her world.

But Pi was fated to fail.

Elosian was a being of creation, meant to handle the levels of power flowing through him. But not her sister. Even the soul-fragments and her experiences with the maetrie had not prepared her for a fight of this magnitude. Pi might have the tattoo and access to the bridge's power, but she could never draw enough without destroying herself first.

Aurie studied the battle to find an advantage. Elosian seemed to be able to draw as much power as Pi, which made keeping the bridge from him even more important. If he was able to get access, his power would be infinite as far as her realm was concerned.

She stood amid shattered crystals that swirled in the winds created from the blinding battle ahead. Elosian was pushing Pi backwards. He didn't even have to win, only keep the energy flowing through her until it destroyed her. Her left arm glowed both orange-red and white.

"Aurie."

The voice from behind drained her body cold. No one should be there, nor should they know her name.

She turned to find a disheveled figure—a human male, no less—staring at her and the battle with slack-jawed wonder. He stunk to high heaven and looked like a vagrant that lived under a bridge.

"Who are you?"

"It's me, Ivan." The words came out of his lips, but they had a dubbed quality. "I can't explain why this is me, but I need to tell you that Elosian has a tattoo as well. It's on his chest. We saw how he and Invictus created the bridge out of faez. It's a battery. There's no way Pi can destroy it, and it looks like it's too late."

"He has a tattoo? How can we fight him?"

Before the disheveled not-Ivan could answer, a pulse of energy whipped away from the battle like a solar flare, crisping him into non-existence. Aurie had been standing directly behind her sister, protected from the battle, but not-Ivan had come up from the side, exposing himself to the dangerous energies.

"He has a tattoo," she muttered to herself, trying to figure out how that might help them. The knowledge he'd imparted seemed tantalizingly important.

Aurie looked past the battle to understand the bridge better. Truth magic had many advantages. One of them was the ability to see things clearly. To see aspects that others missed. If they were going to find a way to destroy Elosian, it would be through the bridge. That much hadn't changed, even if she knew he had access to its power as well.

Positioned near the fonts of creation, the infernal realm—a misleading term for a place that was high faez—was well-suited for truth magic. Aurie watched as the rivers of power flowing to Elosian and her sister came into view now that she was aware of them. The incoming energy to the bridge was more diffuse, pulling from all sources, rather than individual ones. It was collecting the raw faez present and sending it through hidden channels to the owners of the tattoos.

Elosian was a being of this realm, body and mind hardened to the unimaginable levels of faez present, whereas her sister was new. Too much flesh and blood. In the same way that faez made people mad without the protection of a patron, the overwhelming amount of raw magic available was like trying to light a match while soaked in gasoline.

Aurie moved out of the protection afforded by her sister to get a better look at the bridge. Battery wasn't the right term for it. A conduit was better, but still not complete. The raw energy from the realm passed through the bridge and then was directed to the tattoos. Diffuse incoming, and two distinct fire hoses of energy as outputs.

Then she saw an answer.

The energy from the bridge was too great for her sister to handle, but theoretically, there was a level too much for Elosian as well. If the flows were reversed, maybe they could jam up the demon lord.

But there were two problems with her idea. The first was that the method of changing the flow was something only truth magic could accomplish. She knew it in her bones. But she lacked the power to do such a thing. Only the bridge tattoo could accomplish it. The second problem was that the moment Pi reversed the flow, she'd be exposed to Elosian's full might.

As Aurie watched the light slowly increase and the orange-red cracks growing across Pi's body, she knew there wasn't time left. There was only one answer. A solution that, in a way, she'd always known would be necessary.

Aurie had always said that she would do anything, including sacrifice herself, to protect her younger sister. There was nothing she wouldn't do for Pi.

She moved around to the side to get her sister's attention. Even before their parents died, they'd always been together. From sitting in their living room playing Five Elements, even when they were forbidden, to entering the Hundred Halls together, to saving Invictus from his own hubris. They'd always been together. Forever. And ever.

That wasn't going to change.

"You have to kill me," she shouted to her sister.

"What?"

Pi was being battered by unimaginable energies. She could barely see Elosian through the haze of unrelenting power.

"It's the only way."

"No, I can't," said Pi, face wracked with effort. The skin on her jaw was flaking away, revealing embers beneath. Pi was disintegrating.

There was no time to waste. If she didn't take her soul soon, then Elosian would win. Aurie hated the idea that she had to give up her life, but it was the only way she saw out of their situation.

"You have to! Use the tattoo!"

Her sister shook her head even as she battled annihilation. So Aurie did the only thing she thought would force her sister's hand. She walked towards the rivers of energy.

"No, Aurie!"

"Dooset daram."

She got halfway to the blinding beam before she felt the claws of the tattoo wrap around her soul. The pain was agonizing, nothing like she'd ever felt before. Every particle of her being was screaming. Every cell was on fire.

Aurie had expected it to be cathartic, or faintly existential since it was her sister doing the deed. It was nothing like that. As Aurie's soul burned, she fought against the change, even as she knew she shouldn't.

Not me! Why did I do this!

Worse was when she saw her sister's face, tears crisping on her cheeks. This had never been the plan. They were supposed to grow old together. Even if they'd found romance, Aurie expected that they'd live nearby, spend their days in each other's kitchens, and go on vacation together.

Not this.

As the pain consumed her, she couldn't even remember why it was happening.

And then it was over.

Her soul was ripped from her body, which collapsed in the colorful dust like a forgotten marionette.

Forty-Three

The Eater was tearing the roof off the Glitterdome. Sparks and structural beams fell through the air of the arena as they huddled in the outer sections near the food and drink kiosks. A mural of happy children in front of a stage seemed comical in comparison to the destruction. Alex chuckled.

"What's so funny?" asked Zayn.

The horde of demons had declined to advance on their position, deciding to let the Eater do the real work of destroying them.

"I grew up in a trailer in Kentucky. I've always wanted to see a concert in the Glitterdome. Even though I've been living in the city for years now, I never made the time. I finally get to visit and it's going to be my tomb."

"Are you giving up?"

"No. Just a little morbid introspection."

At this point, even if Elosian was destroyed, it wouldn't matter for them. The Eater and the horde of demons was enough to destroy their army and then the city while the dome kept anyone from coming to their rescue.

"What's the dome made of?" she asked Invictus, who looked pale and thin from his over-extension of magic to protect their retreat.

His gaze flitted in the direction of the Eater. Huge booms and minor explosions echoed through the concrete hallways.

"Nothing that can hurt that. It was made to contain, not destroy, and with the portal between realms open, it has limitless power to draw from."

Alex shoved both hands into her hair, nearly knocking off her glasses. She needed a solution, an answer. The Eater was a demon born of magic and creation. As they'd already proved, even direct hits of sorcery only made it angry. Alex stared at the blue dome surrounding the city. It was nearly shaped the same as the Glitterdome. The answer came in two parts.

"We need to trap it."

Invictus cringed as another loud boom echoed through the arena. "It won't work. If I'd kept the tattoo, I could have dealt with the Eater, but then again, none of this would be happening if that were the case."

"You wouldn't have let Elosian come through?" asked Alex.

"No. I would have kept the world enslaved to my needs. You wouldn't even be here."

Alex stared back at the ancient mage. He was being serious, and that frightened her.

"We still need to trap it. Collapse the dome, do whatever we can to keep it here."

"It'll climb out. Is that all you have, Alex?" asked Invictus. "I thought you were better than this."

"Hey!" said Zayn, coming to her defense, but she waved him off.

"We can't kill it with the portal open. You've said that already and I don't have any reason to disagree. So the best we can do is put it in a position that should Aurie and Pi succeed, we can finish the job. And while we're dealing with the Eater, you're going to release the dome."

"It's not wise."

"The whole reason you put it up was to keep Elosian from getting the tattoo. That ship has sailed. There's no reason to keep people in here with this army of demons."

Invictus stiffened with anger. He didn't like being proved wrong. He looked ready to bark, but remembered his surroundings and deflated back to his resting arrogance.

"Maybe I've gotten too old to see things clearly." He nodded. "I'll return to the Spire. It will take time, as there's a horde of demons surrounding it."

"I'm sure you'll figure something out," she said.

"This is quite a narrow path you're asking us to travel upon," said Invictus.

"I'm playing to our outs. We have one shot to make this happen. There's no reason to do anything else at this point. If we win, we survive, and if not, thanks for playing. Either way, we need to give the rest of the city a chance to escape."

His wrinkled face creased with something akin to sadness. "A wise course." He moved towards an exit. "Good luck with your demon. Hopefully we shall all see each other soon, but if not, it was a pleasure to be your head patron."

"We're really going to trap the Eater here?" asked Nandi.

Another loud explosion inside the arena had them all ducking. "It's doing half the job for us. The key will be bringing enough material down on its ugly head to keep it from escaping."

"The Eater in Montanhas got out of the plant," said Kitty.

"Like I said, we're playing to our outs. None of it matters if Aurie and Pi don't take care of the bridge and the portal. But if the Eater gets shut off from its power, I want to be ready for the killing blow. Even without Elosian, this thing could do major damage to the city."

The reasons, however dire, made sense to them. Lennie raised his hand, a school time gesture that made her smile. She nodded to let him know to continue.

"How are we going to take down the top of the Glitterdome? An apartment building was one thing, but a roof of this size?"

Alex had been leaning on the Rod of Dominion. She'd only used its abilities sparingly, and mostly for communication.

"I have some power to spare."

Forty-Four

"Dooset daram."

Her sister's words cut a hole in Pi's heart. It was taking all her ability to withstand the onslaught from Elosian, and in this case, a tie would mean her eventual end. Already her body was flaking to pieces, the energies passing through destroying every cell along the way.

She asked me to kill her.

If it were anyone else, she might think it despair. A last-second effort to escape a world ruled by the Lord of Lies. But this was her sister, who despite everything that had happened to her, had never given up.

Aurie walked towards the beam of energy. *Use the tattoo.* It hadn't made sense in the moment, but then Pi understood. Use the tattoo. Take her soul. Was this an attempt to bolster the defense? Or had her sister seen a solution, a way out?

Pi couldn't divert any more energy away from the defense. The air between her and Elosian was in a constant state of explosion and creation. The amount of faez passing through her dwarfed what came through the wells of power in the Undercity. At the point of contact, elemental forms appeared out of the nothingness, only to be destroyed again, but having passed through the forge of creation. Pi felt like she was standing at the dawn of the universe.

To do as her sister had asked would only put more pressure on her weakening body. Pi watched with muted horror as the fingernails from her left hand disintegrated into dust. The end was approaching.

Pi reached out with the tattoo, drawing more energy and speeding up her collapse, to rip the soul from her sister's body. It was easier than expected, but also much harder. She was destroying her last bit of family. Ending her sister's life.

The soul came free. Aurie had given it up.

The impact as their two souls came together should have given her a burst of energy, but the soul was miniscule compared to the energies being traded across the battlefield. The fingernails from her right hand disintegrated, followed by the tip of her pinky. It turned to dust before her eyes.

In other circumstances, she would have wanted to revel in the connection between them, but as Aurie's soul impacted hers, she felt all the raw emotions contained within her sister. Fear. Anger. Regrets.

Love.

The bridge. It's a conduit. Reverse the flow.

"We'll die."

It's the only way. Use my truth magic.

Pi could see what her sister was talking about. The flows of energy were rivers in the air. She could never destroy the bridge, but it could destroy itself, and maybe Elosian with it. But she had to get away.

The method of Alex's battle with Elosian came to mind, but this wasn't the dreamworld. She needed more concrete tools to achieve flight.

Pi focused on the flesh on her back, imagining wings growing from her shoulder blades. At first, fleshy nubs poked out, causing immense pain, but then as she continued her visualization, two beautiful glossy black wings unfolded. The ease frightened her and gave Pi a taste of what life was like in the infernal realm.

A pump of the wings brought her above the ground. She made two more testing beats, before pushing back against Elosian as hard as she could and then exploding away. The beam of energy passed behind, nearly crisping her to dust before she'd made it fifty feet.

Elosian hadn't been expecting the sudden change.

Pi flew as if she'd been shot out like a cannon. She headed to the landmass hovering overhead, the one that had once been Invictus' home. She landed before Elosian could catch up—now standing upside down in relation to the demon lord—and reached out to the bridge.

With her body still humming, Pi used her sister's truth magic to increase the intake of faez for the bridge. It was easier than expected and would give Elosian more access to power, but hopefully, if they could survive long enough, would eventually overload and destroy the bridge, trapping both tattoos in the infernal realm. It wasn't the best of solutions, but at least their friends could live. The Hundred Halls would be saved.

Elosian spotted her from the other landmass. A chunk of rock the size of a building came flying at her. She winged out of the way, barely avoiding getting crushed. Her body sizzled. Her arms had cracks revealing embers. At least the pain was distant now, as if she'd burned out the nerve endings that might have left her in agony.

After throwing more rocks, Elosian seemed to sense something was wrong with the bridge. Pi didn't want him to know what they'd done, in case he could reverse it, so she drew from it again, sending a beam of power at him. The levels made her choke and sped up the process of her body's disintegration.

Elosian countered her attack, pushing back on her as if he sensed that he needed to eliminate her sooner.

They were running out of time.

Pi reached out to the bridge and removed the limits that governed the intake. As soon as she did, the bridge gained a slight glow as if the structure were overheating.

"Come on!"

She put everything she could into the fight. Their only chance was for Elosian to be too distracted with the battle and not stop the bridge's eventual overload.

A wing broke off from her back, drifting away like ash in the winds created by their battle, but she managed to stay aloft. Her hair crisped away. Eyebrows, too.

Pi pushed. She felt Aurie lending her strength, holding her body together for the last hoorah.

As the bridge glowed brighter, Elosian's efforts increased. He pushed, and pushed, and pushed.

Pi knew she was at a point of no return. She stood at the edge of a vast abyss, and one more shove would turn her back into the raw bits of creation.

Let go. Don't fight it.

She thought her sister was suggesting to let him win, but then she felt her muscles relax. Rather than fight to keep in position, she let the beam of energy push her away. It was enough deflection to keep her from that final annihilation. Pi was sailing backwards, one wing hanging awkwardly from her back, no more hair, her flesh cracked with embers and bright light.

It was as bright as a supernova when it happened.

One moment, the beam of energy was flowing between them. She could no longer see Elosian.

Then the world turned to white. She felt the winds of oblivion expanding outward and used her final moment to say one last thing.

Dooset daram.

Forty-Five

The Eater had torn the roof off the Glitterdome. Broken structural beams and wire trays hung down beneath the opening like a nest turned upside down. As it perched on the edge, the demon dragon roared, sending waves of fear through Alex, but she held onto her thoughts.

"Hit the rim with everything you've got!" she shouted into the Rod.

The mages remaining had arrayed themselves in the upper structure. She hadn't known how many still lived, but as the magics erupted from the under rim she was pleased by how few had fled. There was automatic fire too. Even those without magic knew how important this moment was, or at least, Alex hoped it was. This might be a last, pyrrhic stand, and then Elosian would come crashing through the portal to end them, but at least they would go down fighting.

The sounds of battle rose up from outside the Glitterdome as well. The demon army had moved to trap them, and only the fighting of the gigantes was keeping them outside.

Alex lifted the Rod. Bolts of lightning leapt from its tip, snaking across the open air and hitting the structural beams holding up the damaged roof.

The Eater smashed its claw into a nearby section, and the bright sorceries erupting from that region disappeared. She tried not to think of the souls lost and poured the remaining energies inside the Rod into destroying the Glitterdome. A second claw erased another section of the rim, and with it dozens more mages. It was moving around the outside. She was halfway across from it, but it wouldn't take long for the Eater to finish them all.

Alex realized a problem with her plan. If the Eater wasn't beneath the rim, then it might not take it down when it collapsed. The creature could fly out before it was trapped. She refocused the Rod at the Eater, knowing that it would barely injure it, but wanting it to come down to her level.

The crackling bolts of lightning hit the Eater around the jaw. The creature leaned its head back and roared in agony.

"You've done it now, Alex," she told herself.

The Eater flew across the ripped-open Glitterdome, landing on the curve directly above Alex. It was like staring into a black hole. All thoughts left her head as she raised the Rod and sent the last remaining reserves of energy at the Eater.

As it lifted a claw, black as night, a *crack* ripped through the air like a nuclear explosion. The Eater shifted as it clutched the rim and then the upper structure collapsed inward. The Eater, having overextended to get after her, fell backwards.

Alex was thrown to her knees as the structure shook and collapsed. Beams snapped and sparks flew. She threw herself into the interior area, but the concrete snapped and she was falling. The Rod of Dominion slipped out of her hands and then there was darkness.

Forty-Six

Zayn had been on the western concourse inside the Glitterdome when it collapsed. He'd been moving to a new location to fire his magics at the structure when it fell in upon itself. The cracking concrete threw him into a wall, but he managed to regain his feet and scurry to safer ground as everything disappeared behind him. As soon as it went, his first thoughts were of Alex, who was back where the collapse was centered, but then he was too busy avoiding more falling structure to give it any more thought. Dust filled the air and it was only by reflexes and luck that he avoided getting impaled or crushed.

When the shaking finally stopped, Zayn was somewhere in the mid-level, based on his narrow view of the city. He had a darkvision enchantment, but brought a magelight into existence because there were many inside the collapsed dome that had no magics.

Immediately, he noticed the light was dimmer than before. He paused, listening intently for the Eater to start trying to climb out of the rubble, but there was mostly silence, except for the crackling of stone. Zayn stared at the light, the realization of what the Eater's silence meant hitting him in the chest.

He dipped to one knee, his hand cupped over his mouth. It was both joy and anguish. If his magic had dimmed, then the portal had been closed, but that meant that Aurie and her sister were stuck there at best, and likely perished in the explosion such an event would create.

The cries of the trapped reached his ears as people found themselves in the darkness. He pushed away his sorrow and focused on rescue. They still had an army of demons outside and an enormous one buried in the dome. A little investigation and Zayn found he was on a piece of outer concourse that had remained. The entire interior had collapsed on itself.

Zayn found a pocket where a group of defenders had been trapped. He managed to push aside the concrete slab, revealing six people with superficial wounds. He sent the mages to help with rescue. The others asked how they could help. He didn't want to send them to the street, because of the fighting, but as he paused, he realized the sounds of battle were distant.

The next few hours were a blur. The closing of the portal made the demons less effective, allowing the defenders to break their lines. Once they were scattered about the city, they were easier to deal with. It'd also reduced the magics of the mages, but less so, since they relied on the conversion of faez rather than the raw aspects of creation. The fight had shifted in their favor.

It wasn't long after the collapse that Zayn realized the Eater was either trapped, or dead. He hoped the latter. Maybe it'd been connected to Elosian somehow, or the closed portal had prevented its invincibility from saving it.

Zayn ran into Kitty and Nandi outside in the street. He was carrying a Protector mage with two broken legs out of the building. He set the guy onto a cot in a makeshift medical tent that had sprung up and turned around to find the two of them. They were covered in blood and dust, but looked better than most coming out of the collapse.

"Did we win?" asked Nandi.

Her clothes were torn. She wore a grim countenance, the horrors of the night reflected in her eyes.

"I don't know," he replied.

Nandi stared into the distance. "Think the Silverthornes survived?"

Her question hit Zayn in the chest. He'd been trying to avoid the thought, but it was like a thousand-pound weight had been put on his shoulders. He collapsed onto the concrete.

"Nandi," said Kitty.

"What?" Nandi looked to Zayn, realization hitting her like a smack to the forehead. "I'm so sorry. I didn't know."

Zayn swallowed. He tried to talk but it wouldn't come.

"Have you seen Alex?" asked Kitty.

"Or Lennie?"

"There are tents all over the area. They might be in one of those," said Zayn.

Red-eyed and with squeezed lips, Kitty shook her head. "We've been around the entire dome."

"What about Andromeda?"

Kitty's forehead smoothed. "She's helping the wounded near the south side of the dome."

Zayn nodded, relieved that some of them had survived. "Alex wasn't far from me when it collapsed. She might still be in there. Don't know about Lennie."

He gathered himself and the three of them went back into the Glitterdome. The fallen structure was creaking and making little noises of adjustment even as they crept through the gaps. He'd heard at least three secondary collapses since he'd survived the initial one.

"Hello! Anyone in here?" shouted Kitty as the soft glow of magelights floated above their head.

They searched for the better part of an hour, methodically moving through the wreckage. He at least wanted to find Alex's body so that she could be given a place of honor after all this was over. He hadn't known her until a few days ago, but her addition to the Order had been pivotal. Her strategic genius had allowed them to survive against all odds.

Zayn had mentally prepared himself for her death when Nandi shouted, "There's someone back here!"

It took finding some beams to hold up a wall that looked ready to fall, but eventually they reached the space underneath the twisted steel and concrete. Kitty crawled through the gap and carefully pulled Alex's body out. Her face was covered in dust and dried blood.

"We're too late," he said, crouching down to help.

Zayn felt how warm she was to the touch the moment Kitty said, "No, she's alive."

Alex's pulse was weak, but she wasn't bleeding anymore. Her injuries hadn't been bad enough that she bled out while being trapped. He carried her reverently to the medical tents, finding one of the healers.

"She needs attention. Please. She's the reason we survived this."

The woman wrinkled her forehead but accepted Alex's unconscious body.

"We'll take care of her. You should go get some attention yourselves."

They ignored the comment and headed back into the wreckage, finding another fourteen people in three separate areas during the late hours of the night. When they were coming out after the third rescue, they found Lennie limping along the sidewalk. His entire left arm and shoulder was in a cast and he could barely put weight on his right knee. His riot shield was on his back, but it looked like it'd been shorn in two.

"Takes a lot to break my bones," he said as he accepted a hug from Nandi.

Zayn squeezed his good arm while Kitty gave him a nod.

"We found Alex," said Nandi, looking like she was close to tears. The night had taken a lot out of them. Zayn knew he was only operating on reserves and the fear that he would have to confront what happened to Aurie if he stopped too long to think about it.

"Do you feel that?" asked Nandi, glancing around.

The sky had begun to lighten, though it was hard to tell with the dome blocking the outside.

Lennie lifted his chin and nodded back the way he'd come. "I heard from others that there are still demons roaming about the city. I was thinking of tracking them down. Finish this."

"Count me in," said Kitty, also looking to the sky.

"Me too."

They looked to Zayn, who said, "You know I'm coming."

As they prepared to return to the city, a bright flash at the tip of the Spire made them hold up their hands to block the luminance. When it was over, the sky shifted and swirled. It took a moment for Zayn to realize the dome was evaporating. As it disappeared, the light from the dawn streamed over the buildings, revealing the wreckage. Smoke swirled from dozens of locations on the eastern side of the city. Most of the buildings in the second and eighth wards had been damaged during the battle. The loss of life was heartbreaking, but Zayn knew it could have been much worse had it not been for Aurie and Pi's sacrifice.

"Come on," said Zayn, marching towards the sounds of distant fighting. "I want payback."

Forty-Seven

Ivan stared out the shattered window at the morning light cascading over the city. His brain was foggy from being inside Elosian's mind, but at least they'd gotten out before the demon lord had been destroyed.

Footsteps approached from the first floor. A bottle of amber liquid dangled in Pax's hand along with a couple of glasses in the other.

"How's she doing?"

He nodded towards the third floor. "Audrey's helping her. She's pretty out of it. Been asleep for days, and now she's trying to understand what happened while she was out. Pretty messed-up thing to wake up to."

"She missed the worst of it at least," said Pax, handing him a glass and pouring him two fingers.

They clinked glasses and threw them back. The bitter warmth flowed up from his stomach.

"I usually don't drink this early," said Ivan, staring into the empty glass.

"Figured we needed something to knock the edge off. I feel like I need a month-long shower to wash off being inside his mind."

Ivan shrugged. "I said usually."

"What ended up happening with Ollie? Once you delivered the message?" asked Pax.

Ivan made explosion noises. "It was painless at least. Scared the lights out of me though. Thought I was dead along with him, until I woke up outside Ollie's crack." He chuckled. "Poor bastard. Fucking mad as a hatter. He was so far gone he let me do what I wanted with him."

"You feel sorry for him? He killed your brother and started this whole thing," said Pax.

Ivan gripped the glass tightly. "I know a thing or two about madness. Danced with it on a number of occasions. You go there because it's an escape from the shitshow of your life. If you think about it, he never got into the Halls as he'd hoped, and then as faez started messing with his mind, he thought the invasion was going to happen and he was the only one to stop it. Only to find out that he was the one that did it. With a helping hand from Elosian, of course. I think there's going to be a lot of people waking up with a feeling that they've been believing some very odd and dangerous things. Hopefully with Elosian gone, they'll see their mistakes."

"Hopefully," said Pax, waving the empty whiskey glass randomly, clearly not believing herself.

A cheer came from the nearby industrial park. They looked through the broken window in time to see the afterglow of a sorcerous attack taking down one of the sucrettas that had been terrorizing the city. The vagrants that lived there were raising their arms and dancing around as if they'd won some sporting event.

"There are benefits to madness," said Ivan, raising his glass in their direction.

"Ivan!"

The shout came from upstairs. "It's that woman with the cobra-thing. She's outside the gate."

They moved to the opposite window to see Sammi and the cobra-headed creature standing in the street.

"Speaking of people waking up from Elosian's whispers," said Pax.

"Her?"

Pax lifted her shoulders. "While you were guiding Ollie, I peeked in the rest of the whisper holes. I found one that I thought was hers."

"That's a bad trip to wake up from."

Pax headed down the stairs to where Kali was waiting. They went into the concrete area surrounding the place. The wards and protections had long been destroyed. Ivan looked up at the scars on the building from their last battle. The coal smoke breath had covered the brick in soot and warped the window frames.

"Are you sure about that?" he asked as Pax approached the gate.

"She could have knocked it down herself. She came to talk."

Ivan helped Pax open the broken gate. The whole thing wanted to fall inward, but the wire ties and duct tape they'd used to put it back together held. Audrey watched from the third floor. He gave her a wave to let her know it was okay. He hoped he was right.

"Hey, Sammi."

The short-haired girl looked blank as if she wasn't sure why she'd come there.

"They killed my cousin," said Sammi, looking directly at Ivan.

Pax started to speak, but Ivan put a hand on her arm. She raised an eyebrow as if to ask, "Are you sure?" and he gave her a nod.

"If you mean the Charmer family killed your cousin, then you're correct," said Ivan.

Sammi's hands squeezed to fists. The cobra-headed creature bristled with aggression, its brass-covered wings expanding outward. A word from her and he'd be a pincushion.

"Ivan..." whispered Pax as a warning.

"I won't lie to you. You deserve that much. My father was an evil man who wanted immortality. He used some members of the societies to test their theories on unsuspecting people. The victims died terribly. I'm so sorry for your loss. Your cousin didn't deserve that."

"I want my revenge," said Sammi through gritted teeth.

Ivan held out his arms. "If you must, then you must. I had nothing to do with it, but I understand the need for vengeance. I helped the guy who killed my brother, Ares, get annihilated by a level of sorcery that would give anyone a major pucker. I know I'm still unclenching my sphincter and it's been hours since it happened."

Confusion passed across Sammi's face. She didn't know how to take him. Most didn't.

"There's not much left of my family. Might only be me. Vic killed Solstice. Ares got murdered by a faez-mad crazy vagrant. Then Moriganne sacrificed herself to save the rest of us. And then my sisters were at the Glitterdome when it collapsed. Don't know if they're alive. Like I said, it might only be me, but if you want revenge for what my father did to you, I understand."

Ivan walked forward with his arms out, positioning himself in breath range of the cobraffin. He knew Audrey would be freaking out, watching from the building, but it felt like the right thing to do.

Sammi stared at him like she was about to kill him. The veins on her forehead bulged out, and the tendons in her neck stretched from the strain. She was going to either kill him or give herself a heart attack.

Then a sob broke through the wall.

Sammi seemed almost angry about it, putting her fingertips to her face as if to check that it was hers. Then the dam broke and she bent over, pain flooding out through her tears, body shuddering.

Pax approached, giving him a nod of approval as she passed, and threw her arms around the grieving Sammi. The cobraffin looked equally confused and then it walked away and curled up on the concrete as if it'd had enough of the day's events.

Forty-Eight

The wreckage of the second and eighth wards looked like bombed-out war zones from the top of the Spire. It'd been three days since the invasion. Hundreds of construction and emergency vehicles lined the streets. Smoke no longer drifted from the buildings, but even as she stared down, Kitty could smell it as if she were down there. The mix of ozone left over from countless sorcerous acts, the stench of bodies not yet found, and gas lines leaking into the air. A Wizard's Coffee at the edge of the ninth exploded from a busted line that caught a spark.

"The whole world is watching," said Zayn, coming up from behind, sipping on a cup of coffee.

"Can't sleep?"

The bags under his bloodshot eyes were heavy. He lifted the cup. "Gave up."

"Think they'll rebuild it?" she asked, wanting to keep the conversation to small talk. There'd been so much heartache the last week.

"Kind of an iconic part of the city. It wouldn't be Invictus without the Glitterdome. Might even be a bigger draw than before, once they get that thing out of there."

The body of the Eater could be seen through the sections of collapsed dome. Construction cranes had removed the north wall where the worst of the damage had been. The glossy black skin of the enormous creature could be seen in the sunlight.

"Gonna stink to high heaven unless they can get it out soon," said Kitty.

Zayn stared into his coffee cup. "Have they figured out a new date?"

Kitty hugged her arms to her chest. "Next week sometime. They'll do Mori at the same time as Ares, though the funeral director didn't want to because we don't have a body. I told him there'd be a body if he wouldn't do it."

The chuckle from Zayn put a smile on her own lips.

"That was probably a little too much, eh?"

He lifted a single shoulder. "How are the others?"

"Andy's been at the Golden Willow in her Bonnie costume, cheering up the people injured in the attack. Ivan's doing Ivan things, but at least he has Audrey to keep him sane. Relatively, anyway."

"It still doesn't seem real."

"No."

"I'm sorry about your father."

Kitty shot him a look. "Don't be. He got what he deserved. Bloody traitor."

"Look," said Zayn, tapping on the window. "Another protest."

She couldn't read the signs, given how high in the Spire they were, but she didn't have to. She'd seen them on the way in. They'd read things like "Demon-victus must go!" or "No demons in our city!" or "Destroy the Halls before they destroy the world!"

The camp of gigantes was set up around the campus of Animalians. There were police guarding the encampment to protect the protesters.

"What do you think he's going to do? Even the *Herald* has come out strongly against Invictus. Some patrons, too. I would have never thought it. If it weren't for the gigantes, we wouldn't have survived long enough to take down the Eater. It's not like people don't see non-humans in the city on a regular basis," said Zayn.

"Fear drives people to do foolish things, but hopefully it'll blow over in time. Right now it's fresh in their minds. I made the mistake of switching on the TV. Every channel is talking about it."

"The end of the world can do that," said Zayn.

"But they don't know how close it was. The news reports are only saying that it was an attack. They don't know the danger Elosian presented."

"Probably better that way."

Silence returned as Zayn sipped his coffee and stared at the city far beneath them. There was a question Kitty really wanted to ask, but she didn't know how to broach it with him.

"How are you doing?" she asked eventually.

The rounding of his eyes said only one thing. He was grieving. He kept his lips squeezed shut and swallowed, looking down into his cup. Zayn looked like he was going to say something when footsteps approached. They both turned to see Invictus in his formal gray robes.

"Do you have a few hours, Zayn?" asked the ancient mage.

The wounds from the battle were gone. He looked healthy, as if nothing significant had happened. However, an exhaustion deep in his eyes betrayed the fragility of his position. Heads of state across the world were weighing in on what they thought should happen after the invasion.

"What do you need?"

The oldest and most famous mage in the world looked apprehensive, an expression she'd never thought she'd see on his face.

"I need to make a trip, and I could use some companionship."

Kitty shared a glance with Zayn. "Sure. When?"

"Right now. Sorry for the late notice, but my schedule's been a bit upended."

Kitty stepped forward. "Do you need me?"

"I do, but not this errand." He held out an envelope which she accepted. It had a red wax seal on the back. "Would you take that to Priyanka? She's in her usual place at the Hall."

She lifted the envelope. "I'll go right away."

Invictus seemed like he wanted to say something else, but it ended up as, "Thank you, Kitty."

The two left for another part of the living area. Kitty assumed it was the Helmsman, and if he wanted to take Zayn, there was probably only one place they were going to go. The infernal realm.

Forty-Nine

The solemn procession towards the room where the Helmsman was kept left a tightness in Zayn's chest. A million questions were perched on his lips, but he feared to utter a single one, as he wasn't sure he wanted to know the answer. It was easier to go along than know the truth that was in his heart.

Invictus collected a bracelet in the room where the artifact was kept and slipped it over his wrist. Then he opened the big tome near the machine, and after finding the appropriate page, put the coordinates in.

"Would you do the honors?" he asked, gesturing towards the lever.

Zayn pulled it, and a great hum rose up. The stone wall beneath the archway wavered with the suggestion of another place.

As Invictus strode towards the portal, motioning for Zayn to join him, he said, "The last time I entered the infernal realm, I barely left with my life. Getting stuck in stasis made a mess of things in the Halls. You'd think I'd get better at this with age, but I think I'm getting worse." He wagged his bushy eyebrows. "The rest of the world thinks that I am."

"You did what you had to do. It's only fear that's keeping them from seeing how you saved the city."

Invictus faced Zayn, putting a bony finger in his chest. "You saved the city. You and your friends. The gigantes helped, but truth be told, I missed what Elosian was doing. He outmaneuvered me at every turn. It nearly cost us."

The "your friends" part was ringing in Zayn's ears. He'd feared sleeping because every time he closed his eyes, he could see Aurie's face staring back at him. They'd talked about finally getting away from their responsibilities and exploring the world once all this was over. But for her and her sister, it was over permanently.

Invictus held out his hand. Zayn took it. The ancient mage's palms were cut with calluses. They walked through the portal together, arriving in a familiar valley. The stink of ozone made him want to sneeze, and his eyes watered.

"Don't worry, we won't be here long," said Invictus.

"Why are we?" asked Zayn, but the ancient mage had moved ahead.

They walked through the encampment where Elosian's army had been before they headed through the portal. The twisted silvery archway remained, but the edges were blackened. Invictus stopped near a flesh-colored hut with bones as scaffolding and pointed to the threads on the hem. Zayn peered closely, seeing the edges moving as if they were alive.

They left the encampment area. Zayn marveled at the not-mountains that ringed the valley. Jagged and fuzzy, they looked like grown crystals rather than formations made from volcanic eruptions like in his world. He forgot about everything that had happened and took in the wonder of the infernal plane.

"It's not what I expected, even after seeing it from Elosian's mind. I thought the real version was being filtered somehow."

"Chaos can be beautiful. The bruise-purple clouds during a potent thunderstorm, threaded with electricity. The violence of an earthquake. The way nature reclaims abandoned areas, glorious destruction reborn as new growth. In our world, or maybe I should say your world, these can be understood and adjusted for, but here, the chaos is happening in your very cells. Every day creation is trying to change you. Beautiful, but exhausting."

"It's why you left."

"It's why *we* left."

They walked in silence for a long time. Zayn spotted strange creatures in the crunchy grass-like substance they walked through. He saw a caterpillar made of orange rocks that curled into a ball and rolled away, only to get swallowed by something in the ground that Invictus motioned them away from.

"Are we in danger here?"

Invictus bobbed his head. "In time, the chaos will reclaim Elosian's kingdom and it will be as wild and dangerous as the edge lands, but for now, it's as safe as it can ever be."

The haze of the sky parted after a time, revealing a second landmass hanging far above, but separated by distance. He knew from the images in Elosian's head that the two had once been pulled together by the bridge. It looked like a chunk had been taken out of the mountain where it once was.

Zayn thought they would head towards the mountain to investigate the wreckage of the bridge, but Invictus headed down the center of the valley. A structure came into view after an hour of walking.

At a glance, it reminded Zayn of the Spire. Impossibly tall, but with a double-helix construction made from colorful blocks that looked fuzzy from a distance. The tower shimmered in the haze. As they approached, Zayn felt like he was walking through a dream. He would have asked Invictus about it, but he seemed as curious as he was. The structure rippled as they neared. Zayn thought it was a heat haze disrupting the light, but then he found that the tower was moving gently upward, or at least rotating, which gave the appearance of movement.

Halfway to reaching the base of the helix tower, Zayn spotted a flying creature hovering near the midpoint of the structure. He reached for his hidden blades and gestured to Invictus, who squinted and then seemed to relax for the first time since he'd come to ask for help in the Spire.

"What is it?"

Invictus' eyes glittered with thought. "You'll see soon enough."

The nearer they got, the more Zayn's body tingled in anticipation. It was like his flesh knew what he was going to see, even though his mind did not. The flying creature spotted them on the final approach, then winged away, disappearing around the tower. Zayn grew nervous, but Invictus seemed unmoved.

A second figure appeared near the base, coming around from the backside, walking confidently towards them. Around the time Zayn started to have an inkling who it might be, the winged being joined them. His heart leapt with excitement, even as his mind cautioned him that it could be an illusion, something inherent to the infernal realm that he wasn't yet aware of.

Aurie strode out of the haze, heading towards him. She broke into a run and he matched her. His eyes were filled with water by the time they reached each other. There was a brief pause, a smile and widening of the eyes, "is it really you" kind of thing. Then they smashed into each other. Zayn had never felt so much relief in his life.

"What are you doing here?" he choked out after a long, rocking hug.

He was aware of Pi landing near Invictus, who was watching from the side with a tearful grin. The younger Silverthorne had glossy black wings and glowed with an inner light.

"That's what your first question is?" asked Aurie, laughing and wiping away tears.

"I thought you were dead." He turned to Invictus. "Did you know?"

"Know? No. Hoped? Yes."

Pi jogged toward the ancient mage, and to Zayn's surprise, she fell into his arms for a hug. Invictus touched her on the forehead.

"I knew you could do it."

"Nice try, you cantankerous old sack of balls," said Pi, grinning.

He grunted under his breath. "I'm afraid you're going to be even more insufferable now."

"The apple doesn't fall far from the tree."

Invictus' gaze fell upon the bridge tattoo on her arm. He made a motion, and she offered it for inspection.

"This was really yours?" asked a wide-eyed Pi.

"It was," said Invictus, frowning. "A terrible thing. I should have found a way to destroy it."

"Does it still do anything?" asked Zayn with his arms around Aurie's waist. He wasn't sure he ever wanted to let go.

"The source of power is gone, but it's a conduit for mine." Pi traced her fingers along the outline. "Some things are beyond my ability, thankfully, but at least it was good for one last demonstration."

She smiled at her sister, who returned the grin. Invictus tapped on his own chin.

"I sense there's a story here that bears repeating."

Pi looked back the way they'd come, to where the chunk out of the mountain was missing. "To destroy the bridge we had to reverse the flow of faez. To overload it. But I couldn't do it alone. It was Aurie's idea really. I didn't want to do it."

"What?" asked Zayn, turning his head towards Aurie.

She spoke matter-of-factly as if it were a simple task. "She had to kill me. Take my soul so I could help her use truth magic to reverse it. My knowledge, her power, it was the only way."

"Broken hells," said Zayn, and a knot caught in his throat at the thought. He couldn't imagine having to do that to his sister Neveah, or one of his other siblings.

"Thankfully I had enough juice in the tattoo to put her back after everything was done. Healed us up just fine too." Pi rose in the air at the beat of her wings with a smirk on her lips. "I'm beginning to like this place. I don't know why you left. I could do quite well here."

Invictus crossed his arms. "Creation works both ways. Elosian wasn't so bad in the beginning when we first encountered each other."

"Or you were awful like him," said Aurie, flatly.

The ancient mage blinked, the rebuke faintly registering on his wrinkled face. For a moment, Zayn thought he was going to say something biting but he sighed instead.

"You're right." He turned toward Pi and jabbed his knobby finger at her. "But you, Miss Pythia, should be wary of this realm. Very wary."

She let herself drift to the ground. "I don't really want to stay, but I thought it'd get a rise out of you."

Invictus squinted at her. "If you hadn't just saved the world..." He glanced up at the double-helix structure. "This is quite remarkable, especially given the time you've been here."

"Oh, it wasn't me. It was Aurie. She made it grow out of the ground yesterday and has been tinkering with it ever since," said Pi.

Invictus turned towards Aurie. "You made this? I thought your sister was the one I had to worry about."

"Truth magic is quite suited to this realm." Aurie lifted her shoulders and gazed at Zayn. Locking eyes with her made his insides warm. "But I want to get back to ours. See the world. Take a break."

"Hmmm," said Invictus, frowning again. "That complicates things."

"It does?" he said at the same time as Aurie.

Invictus put his arms behind his back and started pacing. "A simple majority of patrons have asked me to step down as head patron. They believe that my presence there, after everything that transpired, will only hurt the school. Already governments across the world are passing laws that revoke the special position we've had for over a century."

"You can't be serious," Aurie said. "You made the school. You did everything you could to save it. You risked your life."

The old man faced them. "There's a validity to their argument."

"It's not a democracy," said Aurie, then squinting, she added, "Right?"

He chuckled as he moved to face Aurie. Zayn stepped away from her as he sensed a momentous question approaching.

"Correct," said Invictus. "It is not. But I don't want to rule the Halls, I want it to flourish. To grow. Magic is too important to let run wild as it did here in this realm. There must be structure. Rules. Which is why I am resigning and would like you to take the position of head patron, Aurelia Maximus Silverthorne."

The words put a spear in Zayn's chest. He didn't want to say anything, because the offer was something he imagined she wouldn't refuse, but the idea that they'd get away from their responsibilities evaporated. He felt empty inside.

Aurie choked. "What?" She blinked rapidly, mouth agape and eyes blank. "I can't."

"You can," Invictus said simply.

"I don't want to," she said, looking into Invictus' eyes. "I'm sorry. I'm honored beyond words. Confused as well. Why not one of the patrons? They have more experience, more insights into what needs to happen. It's too much."

Invictus didn't say anything for a long moment. "I'm picking you because you are *not* one of the patrons. Besides having conspired behind my back while I was missing to replace me, they've let their personal ambitions overtake the needs of the school. They've forgotten the very reasons we started it. Besides, all of them, and myself for that matter, have troubled pasts. I have a feeling that there will be a renewed interest in digging up dirt on those of us that have been around a long time. And I have a *lot* of dirt. Enough to make the world's longest mountain range if we wanted."

"We know about some of it," said Zayn, nodding towards Pi's tattoo. "In the tattoo. Alex used the Gamemakers' arcane-tech to peek into its past."

"See?" said Invictus, gesturing towards him. "It will get out. I was already seen leading an army of demons into the city where I had trapped everyone with the dome."

"To save us," said Aurie.

"Most people don't see it that way. And truthfully, I would like to find a place for them to live. I made them that promise many thousands of years ago before I came here. Possibly Montanhas, since others are already there. The stories about the montas give me hope that being away from the creative destruction of the infernal realm will give them a chance to live like normal beings. It will take time. Time I won't have if I'm running the school."

"I'm honored. Beyond honored, but the answer is no," said Aurie, looking over at Zayn with need in her gaze. The numb feeling he'd had when Invictus had asked the question faded. "Maybe later on, but for now, I want nothing to do with that kind of responsibility. I want to actually live my life. Maybe have a family. See the world."

Zayn felt like he was going to pass out from happiness. The grin on his lips stretched his face.

"Are you sure?" asked Invictus.

"I am," replied Aurie while looking directly at Zayn.

"Very well," said Invictus, gaze flitting between them. "I understand."

"Ha," said Pi, fidgeting with the talon at the end of her glossy black wings. "What idiot are you going to get to do the job now that my righteous sister isn't going to do it?"

Invictus faced her. "You."

Pi started laughing and then she realized he was serious. "Are you nuts?"

"I've been accused of that on many occasions. Most recently by you, if I recall," said Invictus.

"Why me?"

"For the same reason as your sister. You care deeply about the Halls and have put yourself at great personal risk for them."

Pi squinted. "I didn't always have the best intentions. I did summon a demon lord to get into the Halls. A fact that isn't exactly hidden as it's been thrown in my face a few times."

Invictus tilted his head. "Given your role in saving the Halls, I think that little transgression can be overlooked, and I can ask our good friend Malden to confirm that it was actually Professor Trebleton. After all, he was the one to trick you."

"Not even my first day and we're already lying about it," said Pi with an arched eyebrow.

"We can tell the truth if you want," said Invictus.

Pi furrowed her forehead. "No, I like your story better."

"Good. Does that mean you're taking the job?"

Pi bent over laughing, the volume growing as she clutched her sides. Eventually, after wiping away tears, she managed to stand erect.

"The thing I wanted all my life was power, because I didn't want anyone to do to me what they did to my parents. I craved it more than anything. To be honest, when you weren't around, I imagined myself as the head patron. That figuring out how you died would mean I might get the spot. Sure, Aurie would be better, but I wanted it.

"But over the years, I've gained power. More than any one person should have. The soul fragments. The deals with Radoslav. And now I have the tattoo, and while it's no longer connected to the infernal realm, it's quite powerful in its own right. And then there's the battle with Elosian. I channeled so much faez through my body, I nearly disintegrated before the bridge blew. I've had more faez pass through me than most mages under five hundred years old, I'd bet."

Pi paused, smirking to herself and shaking her head. "Now? Now I understand the paradox of power. The more you have it, the more others want to take it, or trick you into doing what they want. If I hadn't joined the Halls, my life would have been much simpler. Boring, but mind-numbingly simple."

"Do you regret your choices?" asked Invictus intently.

Pi blinked, looked up from her thoughts. "Oh, hell no. Not in a million years. But I know enough now not to crave gaining more. It only courts more danger." She tilted her head back and forth. "It might be fun to stay here for a few decades and create some really wicked things, but it's not worth the price."

"It is quite fun. I doubt they still stand, but I built some wonderous, logic-defying structures in my time," said Invictus fondly. "But you're right. It's not worth the risk. Things will change soon enough. Other beings will fill in the vacuum left by Elosian."

"Do we have to worry about them?" asked Zayn.

"No. Not for a long, long time." Invictus turned back to Pi. "Are you accepting the position?"

"Do I get to have my own administration? Assistants and all that?" asked Pi.

"The Hundred Halls will be yours. If you wish to fire the entire staff, it's up to you, but I wouldn't recommend it."

"I wasn't thinking anything like that, but I figure I'll need some help. I know my strengths and maybe, just maybe, a few of my weaknesses."

She had a glint in her eye, but didn't look ready to spill the reason for it.

"Excellent," said Invictus, clapping his hands once with a surly grin on his lips. "We'll work out the details in the coming weeks. Meeting with the patrons, all that, before we make the official announcement."

Pi seemed suddenly regretful. "I feel like I just made a mistake. You look entirely too pleased by this development."

"You'll find out soon enough," said Invictus, laughing. He checked around them. "Shall we return to the Spire? Or do you need a few more days here?"

"No. Just killing time."

Pi closed her eyes and the wings fell away from her back, collapsing onto the ground. She stretched by placing her hands on her lower spine and arching her back.

"There. That's better. My muscles aren't built for it."

Aurie squeezed Zayn's hand, the promise of finally being alone together reflected in her eyes. "Returning would be great."

The four of them held hands, and when they were linked, Invictus activated the bracelet. Zayn felt relieved, comfortable with the fact that he would never step foot in the infernal realm again.

Fifty

The week directly after the invasion was a blur to Alex. And a bit of a letdown. She'd taken the job to help the Order of Merlin with a task, only to find herself leading the defense of the city using the Rod of Dominion. After getting patched up at Golden Willow, she'd attended the dual funeral for Ares and Moriganne Charmer. The city had been filled with the sad events as thousands upon thousands had lost their lives due to the incursion of so many demons.

A few had managed to flee back into the Undercity or escape into the wider world once the dome had fallen, but most had to be hunted down, a task that was dangerous as many of the people who went after them didn't have the training or magic to deal with the threats.

The scars of the battle were mostly confined to the eastern quadrant of the city, but there were little patches of destruction in every ward. A mantic had broken into the Herald of the Halls and only the heroic actions of the staff, led by the owner, had killed the creature before it did too much damage to the printing presses. A group of ferom had broken away from the main group and terrorized the Enochian district until the residents, experienced with supernatural happenings, rallied together to put them down. A massive hellhound got into Wizard's Wax Museum and ended up mistakenly gorging on the wax figures. The creature was found near dead with an enlarged belly and melted wax leaking out of its mouth. It was quickly killed without further incident. In a corner of the seventh ward, a pile of bodies—demonic ones—were found outside a jazz bar. No one claimed the feat but the nearby residents found solace in the safety of their neighborhood.

Alex heard all sorts of stories about the heroics and tragedies of the students and teachers of the Halls. Many were lost in the initial rush to the defense of the city. Almost a third of the student body was said to be dead. The professors and instructors fared better, if only because they had more tools for their defense and the wisdom not to rush into danger. No patrons of the major halls had died, but a few of the smallest halls no longer existed after the fight.

The visitation for the two Charmers was held a few days after the funeral due to the difficulty of getting everyone from the Order back together. It was held at Ivan and Audrey's place in the tenth ward. When Alex arrived, she was surprised how festive the event seemed, with everyone laughing and drinking in the open space of the bottom floor.

A brown-and-white dog came bounding up when she slipped through the door. Alex crouched down and rubbed the dog's ears before it disappeared back into the crowd, hunting for more pets. She spotted Aurie and Zayn standing together in the corner, foreheads nearly touching, focused on each other as if no one else was in the room. She knew they planned to leave the city of sorcery, head to Paris to visit Zayn's sister, and then travel the world. She was a little jealous, but less than she might have been, knowing how much the two of them had sacrificed to save the city.

Alex wasn't used to parties. Or at least not the gathering kind. She kneaded her hands together, overwhelmed by the number of people in the space, trying to push away the anxiety that had risen up in her throat. She hadn't felt this nervous about being around other people since her high school years.

She spotted Nandi in a frilly black dress with golden hems that made her glow, surrounded by a group of people wearing equally fashionable clothes—Coterie and other top Halls, she imagined. Lennie stood in her group, looking as uncomfortable as she would have felt. In the middle of a fight, Alex had no issue with barking out orders, but this wasn't her kind of battlefield. She shifted into the open kitchen, searching for something bubbly to drink, mostly for something to have in her hands.

The others were scattered around the room. Kitty was chatting with a statuesque blonde that looked like Celesse D'Agastine in the corner, but Alex couldn't imagine why the Patron of Alchemists would be at the gathering. Sitting at the corner of the L-shaped couch was Pax in deep conversation with an older woman that Alex recognized from her mom's TV shows—a famous singer or actor—she couldn't remember. Maybe a patron, but she'd never been much for celebrity spotting. Kali was lying at the woman's feet as her ears were getting massaged.

As she scanned the room, she realized there were more than students at the visitation. The youngest Charmer, Andromeda, was holding court near the stairs, surrounded by a group of well-dressed students that were completely smitten by the alumnus of the Weird Circus. She wasn't wearing a Mystique costume, but her outfit had the appropriate amount of sparkle to hint at the performer in her. Andromeda's role in defending the city of sorcery had led to a massive spike of interest in the traveling show.

Ivan and Audrey came down from the upstairs, leading a group that had probably been on tour of the research area. Alex sipped her drink, making a little exclamation when the bubbles hit the back of her throat. A wave of euphoria hit her briefly, then her mind returned to its normal nervous state.

"It packs a punch, doesn't it?"

The familiar voice had her spinning around to find Pi approaching from around the kitchen island. She was wearing a sleeveless dark gray dress that showed off her arms and, most importantly, the bridge tattoo. There was something about the embroidered runes on the edging of her dress that was familiar to Alex, but she couldn't place it. Pi's hair was artfully spiked, but not in the punkish way it was when they'd first met. She seemed more put together. Maybe even professional.

"You look great," spit out Alex, blushing as soon as the words left her mouth. She squeezed her eyes shut momentarily before peeking. "Hey, Pi."

Pi gave a brief curtsey, eyes glittering with mirth. "Thank you. You look outstanding yourself."

Alex reflexively smoothed away the wrinkles she was sure were on the front of her dark blue dress.

"I haven't worn a dress in a long time." It'd been since her dad's funeral. She smiled to hide her discomfort. "I should have found a better outfit than the discount store. Everyone looks so great."

Pi touched her on the arm, which sent a shiver down her spine. "You look fabulous. Better than fabulous. I was wondering when you'd get here."

Alex laughed and took a sip from the bubbly drink to hide her nervousness. She'd been sitting in her apartment wondering if she should attend the visitation since she'd been a last-second addition to the group. She felt like an imposter.

"I was fussing with my hair," she said, regretting it instantly since it was the same style she always wore.

"I've been wanting to talk to you," said Pi, studying her closely. The intensity of her gaze made Alex warm inside.

"I know. I need to give the Rod back. It's just sitting in my apartment."

Pi snorted, covering her mouth with a cupped hand. "You have the Rod of Dominion just sitting in your apartment? What a riot. To think we rescued that thing from an Egyptian tomb and now it's just lounging around like a walking stick."

"You got that out of an Egyptian tomb?" asked Alex, a little mystified.

"My sister and I did our first year. Before you're too impressed, the heavy lifting was done by our parents before they died. We just finished what they started." Pi rolled her eyes. "Sorry, I'm not trying to brag."

While nearly everyone else at the party had visible markings from the battle, Pi and her sister looked transcendent, as if the visit to the infernal realm had been invigorating. Alex had to remind herself not to let her jaw dangle open.

"I'd love to hear that story," said Alex, hearing her own voice crack.

Pi quirked a smile that shone from her eyes as well. "I would love to tell it to you sometime and hear about your adventures in Gamemakers. I heard a little preview from Invictus that made me want to hear the whole story. But I was actually wanting to talk to you about something else." She looked around. "But not here."

Curious and a little apprehensive, Pi led her upstairs and onto a balcony that overlooked the backyard, which had a chicken coop and a big metal shed. The chickens picked idly at bugs in the grass. The balcony had a good view of the Spire, which reflected the afternoon sun like a beacon. A plane was flying over the western half of the city with a banner pulled behind it saying "Magic is the enemy!"

They stared at the plane until it circled around the Spire so they could no longer see it.

"The invasion is going to change a lot," said Pi with a heaviness that surprised Alex.

"It will," she said, thinking about chaos theory and how small things had big effects. "But at least that won't be your problem."

Pi nearly spit out her drink as she burst out laughing.

"What? Did I say something funny?"

Pi turned with a strange expression on her face. It was the kind of weird nervousness one saw on engagement videos right before the proposal. Alex leaned away.

"You're kinda freaking me out."

"You can't tell anyone, but I'm going to be the next head patron. We're working out the final details. It'll be announced next week."

"What? How? That's awesome," said Alex, hating the way the last part had come out as a question.

"I know," said Pi, pinching the muscles on her knotted forehead. "I might regret accepting his offer." She tilted her head and chuckled. "You sounded surprised."

Alex lifted her shoulders. "Sorry? I mean, Invictus as head patron. That's like the sun coming up in the east and water is wet kind of stuff."

"After the dome and the demons and everything else, he thought it was time to step aside. He wanted Aurie, and I don't blame him, but she's kind of done with it."

"I saw her and Zayn."

"They haven't been out of each other's sight since the infernal realm."

Alex bit her lower lip. "Congratulations. I didn't mean to sound surprised earlier."

Pi widened her eyes. "You should be. I'm still in shock about it. Which is why I wanted to talk to you."

"Yes?"

"I need a partner. I'm impulsive and can be a little paranoid. I've always had my sister at my side, keeping me from going too far afield, but now that she and Zayn are leaving for who knows where, I'm scared shitless." She gestured towards her mouth. "See? I need to clean up my language. I'm not sure I'm ready for talking to the press and all the other bullshit that goes with the position."

The words slowly seeped into Alex's brain. "You're asking me? I don't understand."

"Figures you'd be humble on top of all that brilliance."

"I don't know anything about running a school," said Alex.

"Neither do I, but I know you're a wiz at organization and can juggle a thousand things in your mind without breaking a sweat. Look, here's the thing about my position. There are few people that can be head patron because of the faez requirements. Due to a few lucky, or unlucky depending on how you look at it, aspects of my life, I'm equivalent to a mage that's been alive for hundreds of years. My mind can handle having so many people connected to me through the Patron link. But having the qualifications for that doesn't make me suitable to *run* the school. That's where I need the help, and after everything that happened, I know I can count on you."

Alex laughed aloud. "You know, when we came out here, I thought you were going to ask me out."

Pi shifted her mouth to the side, looking slightly pained. "I'd like that too, but I thought I'd start with the easy question first."

"Do you want to help me run the Hundred Halls was the easy question?" Alex felt a little dizzy. "What did Ivan put in these drinks?"

"You haven't answered the question."

"Which one?" replied Alex.

"Either."

Alex blushed. It was a little overwhelming. On the other hand, having too much to think about was exactly the kind of problem she liked to solve. The school was in the midst of a crisis that it hadn't seen since its founding, and if she was being honest with herself, she had a major crush on the younger Silverthorne.

"The answer is yes to both questions. But. I'm not ready for the second one yet. I'd like to put anything on hold until we've got things straightened out. Adding a relationship on top of running a school sounds like a dangerous combination."

As she spoke, Pi glowed with excitement, clapping her hands and grinning with a face-splitting smile. Then she stepped forward, and to Alex's surprise and relief, Pi kissed her. It was short, hungry, and left her wanting when she pulled away.

"Yes, of course. Business first," said Pi with a glint in her eyes that suggested the time frame of the second question would be much shorter if she had anything to do with it.

They stared at each other for a long minute until Pi twitched and checked back through the glass doors. A new group of partygoers was getting a tour from Ivan and Audrey.

"We should get back to the party," said Pi, reaching out and tugging her towards the door. "I'll introduce you to the people you're going to need to know."

Their fingers briefly entangled before Pi looked down with an unapologetic smile.

"Sorry."

Their hands released and Alex followed the future head patron into the party. The rest of the afternoon was a blur as she met hundreds of alumni, patrons, and students. The whole time she knew she should have been thinking about all the future responsibilities she was going to have, but her mind only had room for a single thought—how long should she wait before getting romantically involved with Pythia Silverthorne?

Fifty-One

Pax stood on the end of the pier in the city of Magadan, a coastal city of Russia in the oblast of the same name. A huge transport ship holding mounds of coal was leaving the commercial docks a few hundred yards away. Waves crashed against the pylons in a sleepy rhythm. Kali lay on her belly, basking in the warm sun.

It was July. A few months since she'd left the *Tundra Spear* to return to the city of Invictus. The world was a completely different place since the invasion. Pax held out her hand, conjuring a flame. She'd never been a powerful mage, but she'd never had to strain so much to create such simple magic. Closing the portal had changed the way the two realms interacted as if the bridge was the thing holding them together. Before she'd left, she'd heard reports that the activity near the wells was much reduced. She'd thought about taking a trip with one of the others to finally see the famed wells of power, but she'd been too busy helping the Invictus Menagerie and Cryptozoo recover from the damage. The place the demons breached the surface was only about twelve blocks from the zoo and Animalians campus. While the invasion had flowed westward towards the Spire, the less disciplined demons separated from the main group, causing havoc. While some of the creatures in the zoo were capable of defending themselves, it wasn't like the Portland zoo with manticores, mystdrakons, and other dangerous beasts. Most of the smaller defenseless creatures were massacred or injured in ways that required extensive care. Almost the entire class of surviving Animalians students had forgone their summer plans to help the zoo recover. Pax had stayed as long as she felt useful, but after a month of twelve- to fourteen-hour days, she knew the zoo would find its way back. Unlike some other parts of the city.

The Glitterdome had been razed to the ground by the time she'd boarded the plane to

Russia. There were already plans to rebuild it—bigger and better—utilizing new techniques of technology and magic to create unique entertainment experiences. Pax was glad the structure had been destroyed. It'd been the place Moriganne had sacrificed herself to save them from Elosian. To let it stand as is would have been an affront to her memory.

She spotted the *Tundra Spear* an hour after she'd arrived on the dock. It slipped past the bigger transport ships. Preoccupied by memories of her time in Invictus, she hadn't let herself get too excited to see Okho, but once the yacht was in sight, she could barely breathe.

Even before the ship had slowed to a stop, Pax leapt over the gunwale, dodging into the cabin to throw her arms around Okho, who was still piloting. She buried her face into his shirt from behind, inhaling his musty smell that reminded her of open skies.

"Oh, how I missed you."

He turned, touched her on the nose, then gave her a kiss on the forehead.

"Tie off first."

Pax stuck her tongue out at him, receiving a chuckle for her imprudence. She returned to the deck and grabbed a rope to hook to the cleats. When she was finished, Kali was sitting near the outdoor eating area, waiting patiently for Okho, who'd been near the bow.

"Kali!"

He held his arms wide and Kali crashed into him, knocking him laughing onto his rear. He spent a few minutes thoroughly giving her scratches in his lap, while Pax looked on, both happy and jealous.

When he was finished, they met in a hug. Pax closed her eyes and let herself feel every inch of his body against hers.

"I thought I'd never see you again."

Okho cupped the back of her neck as he slid his knee gently between her legs. Pax let out a little gasp.

"It was probably a good thing I was away from the *Spear* during that time. I had no idea anything had happened until it was over."

Pax put him at arm's length so she could see his face. "What would you have done? If I hadn't come back?"

He shifted his mouth to the side and knocked a strand of auburn hair from her eyes.

"Mourned you and then depending on how things unfolded, found a new realm to live in."

She pouted. "You wouldn't stay and fight?"

Okho raised an eyebrow. "I fight for the creatures that cannot fight for themselves. The invasion was a human problem, brought on by the hubris of its head patron."

"Ex-head patron."

He frowned. "Oh, that's right. It was the girl who came here. The short-haired one."

"Pi."

"My condolences to her. Invictus left her with a mess."

Pax smiled. She'd met with the others before she left. Alex had moved in with Pi in a suite somewhere in the Spire. The two seemed well suited to each other and spent the time finishing each other's sentences about their plans for the Halls. The school *was* a mess, but at least the two of them cared enough to help it recover, unlike Invictus, whom Pax decided she'd never really liked.

"She'll be okay."

"Was it really that bad?" he asked, studying her face. "I'm not sure I always trust what's in the media."

A host of images rose up from Kali, a sampling of the dangers they'd encountered. His eyes widened. The pictures went on for a few minutes before he held up his hands.

"I give. I give. I guess they undersold how bad it was." He grew more concerned, gently placing his hands around her jaw. "I didn't realize how close I was to losing you. You've survived so much already, I assumed you were fine."

There was so much she wanted to say, but the words choked up in her throat. She'd managed to avoid dwelling on the past, not wanting to get overwhelmed while so many needed her. But now that she was back with Okho and the safety of their little ship, it was hard to hold back the flood. A tear leaked out, and she wiped it away with a thumb.

"It could have been worse. Much, much worse."

He kissed her forehead again. "I want to hear all about it. I thought we could go into town. There's a nice restaurant. Pushkina. Has the most divine borscht with goat cheese. It's so good I often wonder if it's been enchanted."

Pax dug her fingernails into his chest. "I'm hungry." Then when he opened his mouth, she added, "But not for food."

Okho's eyebrows rose, followed by a sly grin.

"After you," he said, ushering her towards the interior of the cabin.

A picture of borscht floated up from Kali's mind, followed by a whine.

"Afterwards, my love," Pax said to her companion over her shoulder. "I have a lot of catching up to do."

Fifty-Two

A tap on the shoulder had Kitty pulling away her earbuds, leaving the heavy guitars to echo softly into air. She found the stewardess leaning over the outer seat, where the urn was buckled into position.

"Are you sure you don't want anything to drink or eat?"

The stewardess was concerned that she hadn't taken anything during the long flight. Kitty was vaguely aware that she was hungry and thirsty.

"You can bring me something," said Kitty, sensing that she wouldn't leave her alone unless she'd eaten. She looked down after the stewardess left and checked the fit of the seatbelt around the urn. Kitty placed the flat of her palm on the top. The hum of the plane vibrated into her hand.

She pushed back into the seat and stared out the window at the floor of clouds beneath. Her eyes flitted to the documents stuffed into the pouch in the back of the seat, tucked in front of the safety materials. Kitty pulled them out and read through the key points. She shook her head, not believing it, even though Celesse had made a verbal offer before she'd left. The papers were the legal request to become an assistant to the head of her global security team. Most people had to work their way up the ranks for a position as high as the one that was offered, but it wasn't like she hadn't known Celesse since she was a child. The head of Alchemists had been a close friend of her family, though Kitty hadn't lost sight of Celesse's interest in the Charmer company before it tanked.

The salary and benefits were considerably more than she thought the position should entail. Kitty couldn't decide if it was a thank you for her role in saving the city, the old family ties, or an actual offer based on her worth. Since most of her financial wealth had been lost when the family company went under, it wasn't like Kitty could turn her nose up at the offer, but she wasn't sure she was ready to work for someone else. Or to be put in a position like that, where the temptations of abusing her power might lead her back to the path that her father had set her on.

"I am a monster," she mouthed, tasting the words and deciding if they still held true.

Moriganne hadn't thought so. But she'd had an optimistic view of people.

The stewardess brought a tray of food and a glass of champagne. Kitty picked at the chicken and vegetables to make it look like she'd eaten more than she had, but ate the hard roll slathered with butter. The champagne felt dangerous, so she left it untouched and stuck to the water in her personal bottle.

She caught a glance of concern from the stewardess when she took the tray and glass back to the front. Kitty wondered if she should be concerned as well. The last months had been traumatic. The others of the Order, those that had survived, each had someone else to return to, while she had no one. The two years in Chiang Mai with Moriganne had been the best of her life. While she couldn't teach the kids how to sing, she'd been there to help them when they had questions about their English, and sometimes she showed them how to defend themselves. It'd been a peaceful life in the mountains. While they'd never talked about burial sites, Kitty was certain that Moriganne would have wanted her ashes to rest at the old house.

The rest of the flight passed in a haze. Kitty didn't remember sleeping, but she wasn't tired. The security and immigration lines snaked around the area.

"How long are you here for?" asked the woman behind the glass as she studied her passport.

"Three days."

"What are you here for?"

Kitty held up the urn. The woman's intense gaze rounded with softness. She nodded her through after handing her passport back. Three days would be enough to visit their old house and collect some things before returning to Invictus to work for Celesse. It wasn't like she had anything else to do.

Before long she was sitting on the back of a bus, rumbling down the road towards the northern part of the city. She got off at the stop and grabbed a coffee and bagel at a café that catered to tourists before heading out on foot. There were much faster ways to reach the house, but it felt good to stretch her legs.

It was early morning when she'd arrived in Chiang Mai. Mists haunted the mountains, streaks of white covering the middle of the lush green slopes. Somewhere along the way, Kitty found herself crying. She wasn't sure why. She hadn't been thinking about anything, just enjoying the peaceful valley. As she looked back, she saw the glittering roofs of the temples sticking up amid the rolling hills at the center of the valley.

A quivering exhale had her wondering what had become of her life. From the penthouse suite in the first ward of the most important city in all the realms, to a dirt road heading up into the mountains. Yet it didn't feel wrong. She just wasn't used to the lack of tension. Even the gang that had tried to extort them when they first arrived three years ago had hardly been a threat. They'd quickly realized how outclassed they were and left the music school and the students alone.

She saw a few kids on bikes from a distance. Workers in broad-brimmed hats worked the rice fields, though more than a few of them catered to tourists looking for a unique experience. She climbed the road that led to the old school, hoping that two months away hadn't caused any issues.

The building looked the same as they'd left it. Kitty had expected the front porch to be covered in mud. Sometimes when the pipes that carried water past the house overflowed, mud leaked onto the front porch and had to be squeegeed away. But it was clean and dry, even though it'd clearly been raining recently going by the mist in the mountains.

Kitty took off her shoes and left them by the sliding door and went inside. The interior was equally clean. A twitch formed on her lips as she realized why. She went to set the urn down on the wooden floor, but paused with it in her hands, tracing the two names engraved into the ring around the top. Minerva Sune and Moriganne Charmer.

"Sawadee ka?"

A young boy was sticking his head through the gap in the door. Kitty recognized his brown, chubby face immediately.

"Pravat."

His gaze found her. "Kitty!"

Pravat ran into the room and gave her a hug, forcing her to maneuver the urn away so he didn't bump his head.

"You came back! I tell the others," said Pravat, eyes glittering with excitement.

A stone formed in her chest. She'd halfway hoped that the students had moved on, forgotten about them, but clearly they'd been waiting for their return.

"Where is ajahn?" he asked, using the Thai word for honored teacher.

Kitty tried to speak, but the words wouldn't come. As tears collected in her eyes, Pravat noticed the urn. His eyes widened. She nodded, squeezing her lips together to hold back her grief. Pravat stayed with her until she stopped sobbing. He gently collected the urn from her shaking hands and set it next to the statue of Buddha that was in the corner on a small altar. Neither she nor Mori had been religious, but having it there had made the parents more comfortable when the school first opened.

When Pravat went into the kitchen to make her tea, she realized that the students had been coming up to the school to keep it neat and tidy, hoping they would come back. Kitty sat by the urn and sipped her tea as other students, who'd probably seen her walking up the road, poked their heads through the sliding door. Pravat became her spokesperson as she couldn't find the words. The kids brought flowers, which they laid near the urn. Kitty felt like she was supposed to do something, but whenever she tried to get up, they motioned for her to stay seated.

The visitation lasted all morning, but by lunch the kids returned to their homes. Kitty didn't remember falling asleep, but she woke in the evening, lying near the urn and the carpet of bright flowers surrounding it. She felt more tired after sleeping than she had during the day, but maybe she'd just been in shock and too numb to know she was exhausted.

Kitty made a fresh pot of tea and sat on the front porch, watching the glow of the nearby city, which she couldn't see directly, but as an ambiance that lifted over the hills. She could hear music playing from somewhere on the mountain. A child was singing. One of Mori's students, she imagined. It brought a smile to her lips. Then she heard a second voice, singing the same song, then a third. Before long, there were at least a dozen voices belting out a song that Kitty knew by heart, even if she'd never sung the words herself.

"...a bolt of light,
a wrong now right,
everyone's a fake and I'm mirror-time legend,
just pretending until I've ascended..."

It was Minerva's first hit and one she'd taught the kids when they'd asked about learning pop songs. Kitty sang along softly, then it was over and the mountain was quiet again.

In the morning, she went outside to check the porch for mud as it rained through the night to find her students waiting patiently in two cross-legged rows. Kitty greeted them all by name. They handed her a basket of fruits and breads for breakfast.

"Thank you," she told them.

"We're ready to learn, Ajahn," said Pravat, who'd become the group's spokesperson during the previous day.

Kitty opened her mouth to tell them she was only staying three days and that she had to return to Invictus to take an important job, but the words got stuck in her throat.

Eventually, she managed to say, "I'm not really a teacher. I can't sing."

"We want to learn whatever you would teach," said Pravat.

Kitty didn't know what to think. It wasn't like they didn't already have school. Morig-anne's teaching had been musical, a way for the kids to broaden their education, not supplant it.

Back in the city, Celesse had a job waiting for her that would pay her generously, enough money to provide a modicum of freedom when she wasn't working. She knew that Celesse wasn't the kind of person to wait forever. The offer wouldn't last. It'd only been their family connections that had allowed Kitty this long to answer already.

As she looked into their expectant faces, she knew the answer, even if she didn't know how she would do it. The valley was peaceful. She could grow here, unlike in the job with Ce-lesse, which would only tempt her base desires.

Kitty sat up straight, staring at them with a smirk hiding on her lips. The kids matched her stillness, sitting at attention.

There were a lot of complications about the idea. She'd have to get an extension for staying, and visit the parents to let them know that it wouldn't be music the kids would learn, though certainly she would incorporate the lessons Mori had been teaching them before she died.

"Come back in two days, same time as always."

The message was a lightning bolt of happiness bouncing through them. They rose to their feet with a cheer and hugged her around the shoulders as she lost control of her stern expression with belly-rolling laughter. The kids dutifully hurried back down the dirt road.

She sipped her tea and snacked on the fruits and breads from the basket, content that whatever trials awaited in the city of sorcery were no longer her responsibility. She would send a message to Celesse thanking her for the job offer, but explaining that she had a more important job in Chiang Mai. The choice lifted a weight from her shoulders. The mists evaporated in the morning sun, leaving Kitty with a sense of peace she hadn't felt in a long time.

Epilogue

Adrenalynne sat at their usual table in the Devil's Lipstick, drinking Pale Paws and playing Runic Risk with Xylos, though it lacked the intensity of their previous games. It was the first time they were back at the bar since the invasion.

"I feel like a cannibal eating these fries," said Xylos, staring at the one in his hand.

She nodded. "Sometimes when I wake up in the middle of the night, I smell the grease pit and think I'm back in it. I'm not sure it'll ever wash off."

Xylos grimly nodded. The invasion had changed a lot, not only in the city, but the Undercity as well. Half the RZR clan had died when the demons swept through the caves and tunnels, overrunning their positions. As well, more than half the businesses that had provided them protection money no longer existed. Big Dave's Town was a shell of its former self. The Devil's Lipstick was one of the few places that had survived untouched.

"Should we swing by Cozzie's for pickup?" asked Xylos as he tossed the fry onto his plate and idly studied the board of runes.

Adrenalynne didn't answer because she was watching the bar, where a well-dressed guy with spiked blond hair was speaking to Delilah, who had a rag over her shoulder.

"What's with the tourist?" asked Xylos, when he saw where she was looking.

"Dunno."

To her surprise, Delilah pointed at them. A knot formed in Adrenalynne's chest. The guy approached their table, followed by a girl with cherub-like face and a smile that rarely existed in the Undercity.

"He's familiar," said Adrenalynne, squinting.

The two stopped at their table, grinning expectantly. They looked like explorers about to go on expedition.

"Adrenalynne and Xylos?" asked the guy.

She shared a worried glance with her partner, making sure to turn her arm so he could see the neon RZR tattoo on her forearm, but he didn't bat an eye.

"Who's asking?"

"I'm Ivan, this is Audrey."

Xylos snapped his fingers, leaning forward on the table. "You're a Charmer? I thought you all died in the invasion."

Adrenalynne rolled her eyes. Her partner had no filter. But Ivan didn't seem insulted by the comment.

"Alive and well for the moment, though you never know when that's going to change."

Ivan Charmer. The name brought vague memories of a party boy who used to run big raves and dispensed new drugs into the scene. He'd never grown big enough that the RZR clan had to send him a message, but she was aware of him.

"Delilah tells me that you two might be able to help me out."

Adrenalynne felt no urge to reach for the weapon she had under the table, even though she was suspicious of his motives.

"Depends."

Ivan extended his hand, revealing a cloudy white crystal the size of a piece of rock salt sitting on his palm.

"You seen these before?"

She leaned over, squinting. "Yeah, used to find them occasionally in the tunnels. Lot more now after the invasion. Some of the clan thought they were uncut diamonds, but it ends up they're just junk."

The wide-eyed smile that Ivan shared with Audrey told her that maybe the crystals weren't as worthless as they'd first thought. Adrenalynne sat up straight, sensing an opportunity.

"We'd like to collect some, but we didn't want to do so without the Razor clan's permission, since we'd be traveling through your territory. If you need to check with Niran, we can wait here until you get back. We've planned a few days for the expedition."

The fact that he knew Niran's name reminded her that one of the other Charmers had visited the clan leader a few years back, when Adrenalynne had first joined.

"No need," said Adrenalynne. "We can take you. There will be a fee of course."

Ivan's goofy grin had her questioning the agreement.

"I wouldn't expect any different. When can we leave?"

Adrenalynne gestured to Xylos, who'd already begun scooping the tiles into the long cardboard box.

"Right now," she said, standing, making a show of slipping the handgun into the holster beneath her underarm. When she reached for her billfold to leave money on the table, Ivan waved her off.

"I already paid your bill, and left a tab in your name. Enough for a few dozen meals."

"But you didn't know if we'd say yes," she said, suspicious.

Ivan cocked a grin, sharing that same silly look with Audrey, who matched his strange smirk.

"I had a good feeling."

After gathering their things, the four of them left the Devil's Lipstick.

"Where do you want to go?"

"You know where the underground lake is? Some call it the Sunless Shore."

Adrenalynne shared a glance with Xylos. "You mean the water well."

"Yeah, that place."

"Sure, we can take you." She paused. "You know the lake is impassible. The Cthulhu-jellies will drive a person mad if they sting you. Unless you're bringing a boat, there's no way to cross, and rumors are there's a guardian near the well."

Ivan patted his big pack, which looked entirely too big for someone of his frame to carry. "Don't worry. We've got it covered. We just need passage through Razor territory and the extra eyes for security."

Adrenalynne lifted her shoulders. "Fine with me. But if we have to carry anything our fees are tripled."

"No worries," said Ivan, pulling a vial from an inside pocket. He threw it down with the practiced ease of someone who drank them frequently. Then he shouldered into the pack, which had to weigh at least a hundred pounds. Audrey had an equally big pack that she slipped into after consuming a similar elixir.

"Shall we?" he asked.

Adrenalynne walked beside Ivan as they headed towards the southern exits of Big Dave's Town. They entered the tunnels that would wind through the earth, eventually bringing them to the well of water.

"What's the interest with those crystals anyway? Are they valuable?" she asked.

Ivan said nothing for many paces until a light shone from his eyes and he answered.

"Not yet. But they will be when I'm done with them."

Adrenalynne nodded, even though she didn't understand, but then a cold shiver passed through her. The same warning that she'd gotten when the invasion had started, and on other important days of her life. It didn't always mean whatever was going to happen was imminent, but whenever she got them, it usually told her to pay attention. Change was on the horizon.

§§§

Hundred Halls Background Information

A Short History of the Hundred Halls

The magical university that eventually became known as the Hundred Halls started off as a small school called Invictus School of Magic in 1836. The building was an old tavern and inn called the Brownwater, named after the town it was located. Invictus purchased it because the property was attached to a large parcel of land where they could safely practice sorcery without exciting the local populous. As well, the inn had rooms for the first cadre of students, and a place they could all eat together and develop comradery.

In an interview given in the early 1980s, Invictus recounted those early years of the school. He'd recruited students from all over the country, promising them a chance to develop their powers without the threat of madness which plagued early practitioners. Even so, of the fifteen students only nine remained after the first year. Invictus has said little about the loss of his student body, insinuating they left for other professions, but rumors persisted that those students perished due to magical accidents or taking their own lives due to the faez madness they'd already developed before they'd arrived at the school. At this time, Invictus accepted all ages of students and the patron system hadn't been perfected. These early failures are said to be the reason that the cut off age for the Hundred Halls remains at twenty years old.

The town of Brownwater, which existed on the northwestern side of Pennsylvania, became a hot bed of rumors and claims of witchcraft. But Invictus had cultivated the local politicians, either through gifts of sorcery, or outright bribery, keeping the threats coming from outside the boundaries of Brownwater. During the years 1840 to 1858, there were three recorded major attacks on the school. The first claimed the life of Robert Madison when he was caught riding his horse in the countryside, charming birds to land on his hand. A musket shot took him in the head when the ambush surprised him. Four more students perished in the first attack, but all the men that invaded the school were never seen again. Requests to return their bodies were denied by Headmaster Invictus. By the time the second and third attacks occurred, the school had established safety procedures and no more lives of the students were lost. The same cannot be said of the attackers.

When the Civil War broke out in 1861, there were requests from both sides to join the fight. At first, Invictus resisted the requests, not wanting to spotlight the fledgling school and get noticed by the greater powers of the country, but his hand was forced as the war's toll created a rift in the student body which had come from all over the nation. A group of Southern students, led by Conroy Rutherford, left the school and joined the Confederacy. Invictus kicked them out of the school, then allowed those that wished to join the fight on the Union side to leave without concern for their position within the academy. Notable of this time was Evelyn Grace, a blue-eyed beauty that single handedly turned the Battle of Hoke's Run by defeating Conroy Rutherford in a duel of sorcery before routing the southern troops.

By the time the war was over, the Invictus School of Magic had few students and its reputation either tarnished or venerated based on which side it was being viewed from. During the year of 1866, little happened at the Brownwater Inn, and the students that stayed were said to have rarely seen Invictus.

On October 22nd, 1867, the charter for a new school called the Hundred Halls, which incorporated the new and improved Patron structure, was signed. The original signers included Invictus, Semyon Gray, Bannon Creed, Celesse D'Agastine, Priyanka Sai, and Malden Anterist. The history of some of these mages can be traced through the history of the country, while others arrived in the New World seemingly out of the blue. The first five Halls of the original charter were Arcanium, Protectors, Alchemists, Assassins, and Coterie of Mages.

With Invictus removed from direct interaction with the students, the new academy flourished. The Head Patron was able to focus on recruiting new students and growing the school, while the new Patrons taught their specific specialties. Additionally, double Patron system seemed to reduce the problems with faez madness that had plagued the early years.

The first Hall to open after the original charter was the Holistic Institute, also known as Aura Healers, in 1875, followed by the Royal Society of Illustrious Artificers in 1891. Three other Halls started in the years before the turn of the century—Tenebris Hall, The Equus Society, and The Gunpowder Club—but disappeared before the first world war. This became a common occurrence during the century and three-quarters existence of the university, either because of the changing needs of society, the death of the patron, or other Halls incorporating their teachings and making them obsolete.

The two world wars brought the existence of magic into focus for the entire world. Invictus threw the weight of the school behind the Allies, which helped tipped the final result to victory. While the Central Powers, and then Axis, both had mages in their regiments, they were prone to faez madness and there were numerous examples of destructive sorceries impacting their own troops unexpectedly.

It was the success of magic in the World Wars that led to the passing of laws that codified the Hundred Halls supremacy and forbid the opening of rival schools in other parts of the world. To facilitate these laws, Invictus promised to open up the school to the entire world and the American government, keen to keep the school on their territory, agreed. This paved the way for the Sorcerous Education Act of 1951 which allowed the school to make major land grabs in the region north of Philadelphia and west of New York, creating the structure that would become the city of Invictus.

In the years after the second World War, the Hundred Halls flourished. Before then, there'd only been about thirty different halls at the university, but they swelled to a number over eighty (no one knows for sure). Researchers have suggested that the number has been oscillating between sixty and seventy-five since, though others have argued that the true number is north of a hundred because Invictus does not publish the list of Halls and some form without ever taking a student. These "Ghost Halls" are sometimes created by ambitious mages that wish to use the association with the school for research, or other purposes.

Wards in the City of Sorcery

First – The ward is considered to be the financial home of sorcery related businesses worldwide and many of the wealthiest mages live in its boundaries.

The Order of Honorable Alchemists [Hall] – This school is the premiere place in the world to learn the arts of alchemy. Celesse D'Agastine, its patron, uses it as a place to recruit its future products.

Second – Known as the other entertainment capital of the world, this ward receives the majority of tourists.

The Academy of the Subtle Arts [Hall] – No one knows exactly where the hall is located, but in official literature of the school, its home is noted as the second.

Glitterdome – A massive stadium dedicated to music, big events, and the occasional sporting match.

Ashnod's Theater – The premiere theater for students of the Dramatics Hall.

Herald of the Halls – The newspaper wholly devoted to reporting on the Hundred Halls, the city of Invictus, and related subjects.

Third – Adjacent to the second, this ward receives its fair share of visitors intent on leaving the city of sorcery with a bit of magic to make their personal lives a little bit better—or more interesting.

Protectors [Hall] – A functional looking building where mages are taught to become future law enforcement members, or the military. The most advanced members have often been recruited to other realms as mercenaries.

Left Tower Books – A mainstay of the literary circuit. Authors of books about magic must always make a stop at this wonderful depository of literature.

Fourth – This ward has no singular identity but given its location in the inner ring of the city, it has similar functions to the first three wards.

Coterie of Mages [Hall] – Along with the Statue of Invictus, the Spire, and the Stone Flower of Stone Singers, the Obelisk is one of the most recognizable architectural wonders of the city. A towering structure of pure obsidian, the school provides its home to the most elite of mages.

Statue of Invictus – An enormous statue of the founder of the city. It was gifted by an unknown benefactor. Invictus is said to hate the replication.

City Library – The massive library is a place of scholarship for mundane and sorcerous topics.

Fifth – Many businesses make their home on the eastern half of the ward while the western section that borders the thirteenth is mostly residential.

Arcanium [Hall] – The academy focused on the study of truth and knowledge, this medieval castle supposedly contains more books than all the libraries and bookstores of the city combined.

Acoustic Architectural Institute of Design [Hall] – Commonly known as Stone Singers, the giant stone flower that makes up the building opens and closes daily with the shining of the sun.

Sixth – Has the highest concentration of banks in the city, but also maintains a large residential area.

Holistic Institute [Hall] – This school contains a teaching hospital that is frequently used by the poor and non-humans of the city.

Museum of Magical Artifacts – A world famous museum dedicated to the display of historically significant artifacts.

Seventh – A mix of residential, restaurants, and bars make this a great place for the recently graduated to enjoy their time.

Canal District – A series of canals, modeled after Venice, snake through this area filled with restaurants and bars.

Eighth – A mix of residential and businesses.

Society for the Understanding of Animals [Hall] – This hall has the largest campus in the city and is tightly interwoven with the zoo, which it helps maintain.

Oestomancium [Hall] – Known as the Weird Circus to most, this halls dedication to exploring the possibilities of transhumanity makes it unique at the school. Their yearly Carnival held each Halloween is a delight and horror to those that attend.

Invictus Menagerie and Cryptozoo – The second largest cryptozoo in the country holds a wide variety of supernatural creatures, but unlike the larger zoo in Portland, this one specializes in the less dangerous kinds.

Ninth – A mix of residential and businesses.

Freeport Games – A quaint gaming shop that has existed in the city since the 1970s.

Tenth – A mix of residential and businesses.

Metallum Nocturne [Hall] – Steam and the stench of burning metal rises frequently from this hall as they are the arcane metallurgists of the wizard world.

Wizard's Wax Museum – A wax museum dedicated to showcasing the history of wizards and mages. True historians find this place rather sketchy on details.

Eleventh – A mostly residential area that has seen better days.

Enochian District – One of the earliest settlements of the city, this district has been forgotten in recent times. It's one of the few places that non-humans dare to live in the light.

Twelfth – This area has the few industries left in the city, though most have left due to the laws passed restricting their operation. Tends towards cracked concrete and rusted out buildings.

Thirteenth – This ward has been partially reclaimed by nature. Few visit this part of the city, despite its border with the prosperous fifth.

The Spire – The tallest building and/or structure in the world. Serves as the administrative home of the Hundred Halls. The top section is the home of Invictus. The enormous tower serves many functions including the Merlin Trials, and the Second Year Games.

Undercity – The region beneath the city stretches as wide as the confines of the outer wards, but moving around is fraught with supernatural danger. A vast majority of this area is unmapped due to the heavy influence of faez, the paranoia of its residence, and the dangers posed to explorers. There are a few known settlements within the Undercity that tend to be the home of non-humans that are unwelcome on the surface.

Big Dave's Town – The largest and most well-known settlement in the Undercity, this kidney-shaped cavern has a population in the thousands. The Devil's Lipstick or the open air market are the most frequently visited. Undercity gangs keep the peace.

Voodoo Land – A village deep in the Undercity populated by a people infected by a sentient fungus.

Wells of Power – Known or seen by few, the four wells are places that faez leaks through the barrier between realms. Each one is protected by a guardian that was placed there by the Patrons.

Other Realms

The Hundred Halls is not just a magical school. The magic of portals creates a network of realms where mages with access can move about freely. Realms do not exist at fixed positions to each other, but move in relation to each other for unknown reasons, creating unusual and sometimes unexpected connections. The Academy of the Subtle Arts is the Hall most connected to the multi-realms, but others such as Coterie of Mages for the Infernal realm are known experts.

The Eternal City – The home of the maetrie, sometimes called city elves, is a place of high magic and high danger that doesn't follow all the rules of more stable realms. In the Eternal City, locations don't always remain in the same place, and even those are ruled by the various courts: Jade, Diamond, and Ruby. Only the most brave (or foolish) mages visit this realm, and of those that do, most never return.

Ruby Court

Queen: Lady Amethyte

Diamond Court

Queen: Lady Zaire

Jade Court

Queen: Lady Kikala

The Infernal Realm – An early precursor realm that was one of the first to stabilize out of the fledgling universe. The understanding of this brutal place is limited and most scholars think, probably wrong. It is awash in demonic creatures that defy human knowledge.

The Veil – This realm exists at the barrier between life and death. Ghosts, apparitions, and otherworldly creatures sometimes pass through into other realms, causing problems and sometimes opportunities. It is rumored that the mages of the Academy of the Subtle Arts can briefly step into this realm to pass out of sight.

Harmony – A stable realm of harsh beauty, Harmony is known to few. The fearsome and explosively fast mystdrakons come from this place and its jungles hide other dangerous creatures that frighten even the most hardened explorers.

Fae – The realm most commonly portrayed in folktales and legends is the place of the seelie and unseelie. Access to this realm has become more difficult in the last century, making its influence less known than the past.

Ice Hold – A cold and inhospitable place that has become a vacation spot for the ultra-wealthy mages that wish to experience winter sports in an entirely different realm than their own. Most only visit the lodges in the mountains, though some adventurous explorers travel further than the known regions.

Montanhas – A mountainous region that was settled by Portuguese colonists a half-century ago and then again by the company Lifestone. The enormous Montas live in this realm alongside the settlers. Surprisingly little is known about the native race.

Caer Corsydd – A backwater fae realm of swamps and bogs. Its dangers are only matched by its beauty. As the home of the Gwyllion, the outcasts of Fae, it is a mix of fairy and unsettled country. The rules that apply to most fae realms do not here, because it was not their homeland.

Danir – The home to a pastural race that is quite civilized. Their extensive farmlands are surrounded by jungle. Early explorers learned about the existence of *mágrithral* which is commonly called magesteel, a material that can easily hold enchantments. The value of magesteel is astronomical, though the Danir no longer produce it, citing environmental issues as the cause.

<u>Black Council</u> – The existence of this realm has not been confirmed. Researchers claim that it's a den of malicious thievery. Serious researchers avoid this realm as a topic of scholarship due to the string of unfortunate accidents that befell their compatriots that sought to unearth the truth.

<u>Brodaria</u> – Home to the Brodarians, a battle-hungry people that spent their days in constant conquest. Mercenaries and fortune-hunters have been known to visit this realm to ply their dangerous trade.

Major Figures of the Hundred Halls

Invictus – The most famous mage in the world, considered to be the oldest living being. Speculation has him to be at least five hundred years old, though many consider him to be much older.

Malden Anterist – The head of Coterie of Mages keeps himself hidden from scrying and other methods of sight through the use of obfuscation enchantments. The reason for this unusual setup is the subject of much speculation.

Celesse D'Agastine – The third most famous person (after Invictus and Frank Orpheum), the head of D'Agastine Industries runs one of the largest multinational corporations in the world. Celesse is known as a fierce business woman who has destroyed those that have attempted to stand in her way.

Semyon Gray – The least vocal of the Original Five, Semyon is known for working quietly behind the scenes to guide the politics of the Hundred Halls in a more humane direction.

Priyanka Sai – The head of the Assassin's Hall is infamous across the realms.

Bannon Creed – As head of the Protectors, as well as the Blackstone Security, Bannon's mages are involved with law enforcement, and the military across the realms. It is rumored that he often plays both sides of conflicts to maximize his financial interests and accusations about drugs or other unsavory acts have often been met with unusual deaths. Journalists steer clear of any topics related to the mage, which only burgeons his untouchable reputation.

Frank Orpheum – A legendary entertainer and head of the Dramatics Hall, after Invictus, he's considered the most famous in the world. His magic tricks have defied explanation, even by those who understand his methods.

Radoslav – The reclusive owner of the Glass Cabaret is an ex-pat maetrie with ties to organized crime across the city. His jazz bar attracts tourists curious about the city fae, and those who wish a favor from him—but at a price. He is the son of the Ruby and Jade Queens, and is known as the Black Butcher for his role in the destruction of the Ebony Court.

Hemistad – The owner of Freeport Games is a curious figure that not much is known about. Mages that have visited his gaming store suggest that he is not who he appears to be, but the extent of his powers are unknown. He makes frequent trips into the Undercity for his own purposes.

The Societies

The societies were originally created to help the city protect itself from the dangers posed by the infernal realm. Their members are pulled from the top halls with the intention of providing a cross-section of skills. Each has its own location in the Undercity where it meets and initiates new members, but the four societies gather together on a yearly basis for meetings, and then again, every four years for a ceremony called the Convergence, which is meant to help gauge the threat of the infernal realm. All four societies have a role in the Convergence.

There are many other smaller societies that were created for other purposes, but these original four are what most think of when "secret societies" are brought up in the city.

Well and Stone – Dedicated to the understanding of faez and the role of the wells of power.

Snake and Tome – Dedicated to developing charisma and the cunning to change the world.

Chroma and Key – Besides Coterie of Mages, this society is a repository of demonology.

Silence – This society focused on predicting the future through the use of augury.

Timeline of Season One

2003: Invictus disappears / Nadia's Triumph

2013: The Reluctant Assassin

2014: The Sorcerous Spy / Wild Magic

2015: The Veiled Diplomat / Bane of the Hunter / The Warped Forest / Song of Siren and Blood

2016: Agent Unraveled / Mark of the Phoenix / Gladiators of Warsong / House of Snake and Tome / Trials of Magic

2017: The Webs That Bind / Arcane Mutations / Citadel of Broken Dreams / Storm of Dragon and Stone / Web of Lies

2018: Enter the Daemonpits / Untamed Destiny / Sonata of Shadow and Thorn / Alchemy of Souls

2019: Plane of Twilight / Well of Demon and Bone / Gathering of Shadows

2020: City of Sorcery

2022: The Order of Merlin / Infernal Alliances / Tower of Horn and Blood

Hundred Halls – Professors / Instructors

<u>Arcanium</u> – Semyon Gray (Patron)

Joanne Mali

Sebastian Longakers

Gill

Moonie

Alain Chopra

<u>Coterie of Mages</u> – Malden Anterist (Patron)

Augustus Trebleton

Phillip Sinclair

Isla Kingsley

<u>Protectors</u> – Bannon Creed (Patron)

Avani Blue

<u>Alchemists</u> – Celesse D'Agastine (Patron)

Alysson Cho

<u>Assassins</u> – Priyanka Sai (Patron)

Carron Allgood

Marilyn Pennywhistle

Maggie O'Keefe

Alliette Noyade

Percival

Matt Konig

Dionysus Minoan

<u>Stone Singers</u> – Ester Starwood (Patron)

Marin Zeng

Asa Lacuerda

Sven Larsen

Art Williams

Robin Leech

<u>Animalians</u> – Adele Montgomery (Patron)

Didi Applebrook

Kako

Cassius King

Vladmir Constantine

Ansel Park

Ernest Valentine

<u>Dramatics</u> – Frank Orpheum (Patron)

Lilly Hathhammer

Glossary Terms

Merlin Trials - The entrance exams to the Hundred Halls that can only be taken during the ages seventeen through nineteen. There are three stages to the trials.

Faez - The raw stuff of magic. Faez is the energy that when shaped by spell or other means creates magical effects. Faez is dangerous to humans, but a tolerance can be built up over time if somehow protected. The patronage system of the Hundred Halls is the most common method.

Patron - The founder of a hall within the Hundred Halls. The patron extends their magical protection to students, keeping them safe from faez madness, and teaching them a specific skill set within the magical world.

Faez Madness - Prolonged use of faez without protection results in irreversible damage to the user's ability to understand and interact with reality.

Second Year Contest - These games require cross-Hall teams to compete against each other for a grand prize utilizing special facilities that keep the participants from physical harm.

Maetrie – Commonly called city elves, though they have no relation to the Fae. Their home is the Eternal City, a realm closer to Invictus than any other.

Major Halls

Arcanium

Nickname: Arcanium

Patron: Semyon Gray

Est: 1867

Motto: Knowledge is Power

Description: Arcanium believes in the value of gaining knowledge, not only about the world around us, but of ourselves. Before we can master magic, we must hone the tool the magic originates from, because a poorly trained mage will not only be a danger to themselves, but society at large. Once a student is capable, they may learn the art of changing spells on the fly using lexology, or how ancient runic languages are the key to solving the world's most difficult problems. Join Arcanium and be a part of the solution.

Coterie of Mages

Nickname: Coterie

Patron: Malden Anterist

Est: 1867

Motto: Limitless

Description: Anything is possible. Here in the Coterie of Mages, we don't believe in limits. If you can imagine it, you can do it. We push the boundaries of what magic is capable of. If this frightens you, then Coterie is not the Hall for you, but if this elicits a sense of excitement and wonder, then apply to the Coterie of Mages. We are the elite.

Academy of the Subtle Arts

Nickname: Assassins

Patron: Priyanka Sai

Est: 1867

Motto: Anyone can be persuaded

Description: Human connections make the world go round. We at the Academy of the Subtle Arts strive to bring people, companies, and countries together. Our mages are the world's most effective diplomats and heads of state. If you seek to join the interconnected world of politics, then the Academy is the right Hall for you.

The Order of Honorable Alchemists

Nickname: Alchemists

Patron: Celesse D'Agastine

Est: 1867

Motto: Perfection is Achievable

Description: The human vessel is a sacred thing. We believe in maximizing our potential through better alchemy. Our potentials cannot be met if we rely on the ordinariness of humanity.

Protectors

Nickname: Protectors

Patron: Bannon Creed

Est: 1867

Motto: To Protect and Control

Description: Order requires commitment. Protectors are committed to the value of human life. To being the shield against those that would tear down society, and create chaos. The Protector Hall teaches the ultimate defense, not only for yourself, but for the world at large. If being on the front lines of the world's conflicts appeals to you, then Protectors is your Hall

Acoustic Architectural Institute of Design

Nickname: Stone Singers

Patron: Ester Starwood

Est: 1891

Motto: Building through song

Description: A song is made up of many notes, just like a bridge is made of many stones. Society cannot function without the infrastructure to hold it together. The Acoustic Architectural institute of Design teaches how to shape the world with only a song.

Society for the Understanding of Animals

Nickname: Animalians

Patron: Adele Montgomery

Est: 1945

Motto: We Are Not Alone

Description: All life is sacred. From the industrious dung beetle to the majestic horned dragon. We at the Society believe that Earth must be shared with all her children and when we do we will truly unlock her endless possibilities.

Holistic Institute

Nickname: Aura Healers

Patron: Sir William Jenner III

Est: 1875

Motto: Health Starts in the Soul

Description: When someone gets hurt, are you the first to run to their side to tend their wounds? If so, then the Holistic Institute is for you. We'll teach you how to mend even the most grievous wounds.

Minor Halls

Gamemakers

Nickname: Gamemakers

Patron: Aldophus Dimple

Est: 1961

Motto: Life is a Game

Description: Life is a game to be perfected. We at the Gamemaker's Hall know the importance of games as the training grounds for life.

Metallum Nocturne

Nickname: Night Metal

Patron: Edward Canterbury

Est: 1908

Motto: Strike. Spark. Surpass.

Description: When the hammer hits the forge, great energies are released. Metallum Nocturn is that hammer against the forge of your soul. Join us, and find out what possibilities we can make.

The Daring Maids

Nickname: Palimaidens

Patron: Alice Hayword

Est: 1908

Motto: Stand

Description: The world is filled with unspeakable cruelty. We seek justice for those who cannot protect themselves, no matter the place. Join us in our fight against oppression.

Hundred Halls – Season One Series

<u>Season One</u>

THE HUNDRED HALLS

Trials of Magic

Web of Lies

Alchemy of Souls

Gathering of Shadows

City of Sorcery

THE RELUCTANT ASSASSIN

The Reluctant Assassin

The Sorcerous Spy

The Veiled Diplomat

Agent Unraveled

The Webs That Bind

GAMEMAKERS ONLINE

The Warped Forest

Gladiators of Warsong

Citadel of Broken Dreams

Enter the Daemon Pits

Plane of Twilight

ANIMALIANS HALL

Wild Magic

Bane of the Hunter

Mark of the Phoenix

Arcane Mutations

Untamed Destiny

STONE SINGERS HALL

Song of Siren and Blood

House of Snake and Tome

Storm of Dragon and Stone

Sonata of Shadow and Thorn

Well of Demon and Bone

THE ORDER OF MERLIN

The Order of Merlin

Infernal Alliances

Tower of Horn and Blood

HUNDRED HALLS SHORTS

Nadia's Triumph

The Ghostly Light of Hallow's Eve

The Ascendant Cup

The Whistling Man

Summer Spies

Fear is Forever

Balancing the Ledgers

A Slip of the Tongue

Shades of the Past

Special Thanks to These Kickstarter Backers!

Anthea Sharp
Joshua C. Chadd
Jane Cassell
Leanne Pert
Jennifer Zack Cassie
maileguy
Bianca
Jess Churchfield
Kurt Pankau
Argonometra
Erica Marvin
Christine H
Sarah
Mises Lambert
Andie Alessandra Kavanagh
Kanyon K.
Lynn James
Benjamin C. Kinney
Charles Spivey
Leigh Wingate
Algie Lane III
Claudia Cee
Mattia Gualco
Elizabeth Gorman
Covington
The Bahr family
Rob Steinberger
Deborah Hedges
Sunny Side Up
Caledonia
Dawn Bonanno
Fewture
R.S. Johansen
Gunther
S. Meredith
Penny BroJacquie
Jas Pace
Tina Glasneck
longcutup
Eva Pohler
Collin Bartley
Deanna Stanley
Chris Marquart
Brittnay B.
J.D.L. Rosell
Eagleveteran
Lira Lindriel
Doug Erling
Robert Quinn
Brent Osborn
Jonathan Cole
Jordan Isler
Harro van der Klauw
Polinchka
Jill Vance
Jackie Clouse
brenden faulkner
Monica Leonelle
J. Elroy Johnson
Bridgette Findley
Meike
Deborah Y. Booth
Marcia Esders
The Stauffer family
John Doe
Jennifer Slack
Krijrana/Richard
B. Plaga
Jack Holder
Melissa Showers
Susannah Mansky
Brian Healy
Catherine "Cat" Maenzo
Hayley Rae Johnson
Cynthia M Coffman
Erin Griffin
Erik Sapp
SafePondDemon
Jan Birch
James Johnston
Levi Maynard
S. Busby
Emma Adams
Therena Carlin
Eliza Tilton
PJL
Peter Varney
SGT MADCOCK
J.R.E. Cooper
Felix Pfeiffer
Alyssa Emmert
Mark Junk
Gerald P. McDaniel
Stuart
Roos van Dijk
MartinOe
Hammy
Roger Paquin
WeTheStrongHold
Roe R. Adams, III
Raphael Bressel
Amara Sov
Bruce Harpham
Olia
Ben Craft
Ganesha Duggirala
Jacob H Joseph
Wildon
Quinten Smith
Adam S Cole
Paul Krause
Karen Bulgarelli
John Idlor
Giulio
Jenni D Strand
Shane Heaton
Mike Jones
Jonathan Hamm
Jeffrey.Tristan.Thyme
Kelly Balding
André Laude
Donald Rhodes
Aaron Roush
James Beyer
Tim Adriance
Angela & Nate
Scott R.
Philip Early
James Haun
Martin L. Shoemaker
AEKDB
Emma Laeser
Rebecca Hill
Keith Homel
Mothy Meyer
James G. Kralik
Jill Cooper
Susan Rackley

Additional Thanks for Final Reads

Lynda Christensn
Erica Williams
Elaine Stoker
Brian Busby

This ends Season One of the Hundred Halls
Stay tuned for the first series of Season Two:

THE CRYSTAL HALLS

The Hundred Halls Universe

SEASON ONE

THE HUNDRED HALLS
Trials of Magic
Web of Lies
Alchemy of Souls
Gathering of Shadows
City of Sorcery

THE RELUCTANT ASSASSIN
The Reluctant Assassin
The Sorcerous Spy
The Veiled Diplomat
Agent Unraveled
The Webs That Bind

GAMEMAKERS ONLINE
The Warped Forest
Gladiators of Warsong
Citadel of Broken Dreams
Enter the Daemonpits
Plane of Twilight

ANIMALIANS HALL
Wild Magic
Bane of the Hunter
Mark of the Phoenix
Arcane Mutations
Untamed Destiny

STONE SINGERS HALL
Song of Siren and Blood
House of Snake and Tome
Storm of Dragon and Stone
Sonata of Shadow and Thorn
Well of Demon and Bone

THE ORDER OF MERLIN
The Order of Merlin
Infernal Alliances
Tower of Horn and Blood

ABOUT THE AUTHOR

Thomas K. Carpenter resides in Colorado with his wife Rachel. When he's not busy writing his next book, he's hiking, skiing, and getting beat by his wife at cards. He keeps a regular blog at www.thomaskcarpenter.com and you can follow him on twitter @thomaskcarpente. If you want to learn when his next novel will be hitting the shelves and get free stories and occasional other goodies, please sign up for his mailing list by going to: http://tinyurl.com/thomaskcarpenter. Your email address will never be shared and you can unsubscribe at any time.